KU-826-343

The Dynasty

The Rochford Trilogy

Claire

LORRIMER

piatkus

PIATKUS

First published in Great Britain as
Fool's Curtain in 1984 by Bantam Press,
a division of Transworld Publishers Ltd.
This paperback edition published in 2011 by Piatkus

Copyright © 1984 by Claire Lorrimer

The moral right of the author has been asserted.

*All characters and events in this publication, other than
those clearly in the public domain, are fictitious
and any resemblance to real persons,
living or dead, is purely coincidental.*

All rights reserved.
No part of this publication may be reproduced, stored in a retrieval
system, or transmitted in any form or by any means, without the
prior permission in writing of the publisher, nor be otherwise
circulated in any form of binding or cover other than that in
which it is published and without a similar condition including
this condition being imposed on the subsequent purchaser.

A CIP catalogue record for this book
is available from the British Library.

ISBN 978-0-7499-5432-1

Typeset in Baskerville by Hewer Text UK Ltd, Edinburgh
Printed and bound in Great Britain by Clays Ltd, St Ives plc

Piatkus
An imprint of
Little, Brown Book Group
100 Victoria Embankment
London EC4Y 0DY

An Hachette UK Company
www.hachette.co.uk

www.piatkus.co.uk

Also by Claire Lorrimer:

The Chatelaine
The Wilderling

Claire Lorrimer wrote her first book at the age of ten. She was encouraged by her mother, Denise Robins, author and founder member of the Romantic Novelists' Association. Claire was further influenced by her job as a sub-editor on a women's magazine which gave her an insight into publishing. Having for many years written contemporary women's fiction, in the 1970s she was asked by her publisher to expand the depth of her story-telling potential and she began a successful new career writing meticulously researched historical novels. She now lives in rural Kent.

Please visit her website at www.clairelorrimer.co.uk

For my two sisters in particular and for those readers of *The Chatelaine* and *The Wilderling* who have pestered me for the past ten years to write another book about the fortunes – and misfortunes – of a later generation of the Rochford family.

Prologue

November 1929

"I have asked you all to be here today because, I'm afraid to say, the situation is a great deal worse than any of us expected! Knowing the dreadful effect on the Americans following the collapse of the New York Stock Exchange, you must all have realized that the Tetford Railroad and Transportation Corporation and its various ancillary companies could not go unscathed. What we had not anticipated was that it could be wiped out."

Toby Rochford adjusted the spectacles which had slipped to the end of his nose, and clearing his throat, he continued.

"I know that all of you invested heavily in TRTC and rely to one degree or another on the exceptionally good income it has always provided. I saw our accountant yesterday and he has asked me, as senior member of the family, to advise you that to all intents and purposes, TRTC no longer exists. That is to say, we, as a family, are virtually bankrupt and must now consider the future."

For the first time, Zandra paid attention to what her uncle was saying. Family conferences about money were of little interest to her and in the past she had been excused attention because of her youth. Today, only four months short of her coming of age, Uncle Toby had insisted she be present.

1

What exactly did it mean to be "bankrupt"? she wondered. Judging by the expressions on the faces of all her relations, it was something in the nature of a disaster. She recalled now the shocked voices of her uncle and aunt when they'd read in the newspapers of American businessmen jumping out of skyscraper windows because they were financially ruined. It had struck her as a stupid thing to do, and she had forgotten it until now. A dozen questions rose to her mind but, for once, she curbed her impulsiveness and was silenced by the look of distress on her aunt's face.

Aunt Willow and Uncle Toby had adopted her and her young brother Jamie after the death of their parents and she had grown up here at Rochford with Aunt Willow's son, Oliver, and his sister, Alice. Her other cousin, Lucy, had married Alexis when she was only eighteen so she, Zandra, had not seen so much of her in her childhood. Aunt Willow had always treated her as a daughter, and although there had been many times when she, Zandra, had resented her aunt's conventional upbringing, she sensed that she loved her even more than she loved her own daughters, Lucy and Alice.

Zandra turned to look at her younger cousin. Poor Alice! she thought. She so much wanted to be married, but although she'd been quite pretty as a child, she was now both plump and plain, and at the age of twenty-six, seemed resigned to the fact that she would be a spinster. Oliver had once said to Zandra that Alice would certainly find a husband sooner or later because she, together with Lucy and himself, had inherited TRTC on the death of their American grandfather. If it now no longer existed, so, too, were Alice's hopes of finding a husband! Alice was not very intelligent, Zandra thought, and as she was continuing in her usual placid manner with her embroidery, she assumed her cousin had not yet grasped the effects of Uncle Toby's announcement.

Despite Aunt Willow's determination to find her, Zandra, a husband, she had no intention of settling down to a life of domesticity for a long while yet. Oliver had promised to give her a job at Sky-Ways, the airline he and his friend Henry Barratt had started after the war. She was already an accomplished pilot and flying the Gipsy Moth was a lot more fun than being at the domestic science school Aunt Willow had chosen for her when she'd returned in disgrace from Paris! She had been staying with her Uncle Pelham and her French aunt, Tante Silvie, whose hairdresser, Léon, had fallen madly in love with her! When her secret meetings with Léon were discovered, Tante Silvie, understanding and sympathetic though she was, had packed her off home. Aunt Willow wanted her to have a Season like Alice, but she had balked at the idea; and in order to silence her guardian, she had persuaded Hugh Conway, the dull but worthy son of a neighbour, to pretend they were engaged. Since then, she had had a lot more freedom, and with Hugh to escort her – and keep her in order, presumably – she could come and go much as she pleased.

". . . sell my controlling shareholding in Sky-Ways. Jane and I are determined to keep to the plan to send Giles to Eton at all costs."

Zandra's eyes swung back to Oliver's tall, handsome figure. He was standing by the drawing-room windows, his arm around Jane's shoulders. The seven-year-old Giles was their only child, and Zandra understood her cousin's desire to send his son to his old school; but to think of selling his precious airline . . .

"Oh no, Ollie!" she cried aghast. "You can't sell Sky-Ways!"

Oliver crossed the room and ruffled her hair.

"Don't make a drama of it, Zee-Zee! I'll keep the Gipsy Moth so you can still have your joyrides! You may have to get a job and subscribe to its upkeep, though."

"I will, of course I will. I'll . . ."

"Zandra, this isn't the time to discuss your amusements," Willow broke in sharply. "Anyway, now that we are all going to have to make serious economies as your Uncle Toby has just explained, you will need to start saving for your trousseau before you indulge your whims. When your uncle and I gave our consent to your engagement to Hugh, we had supposed we would be giving you a sizeable allowance since Hugh is not exactly well off. That is no longer possible."

Zandra's mouth tightened and she jumped to her feet.

"As far as my flying is concerned, you've never approved of it just because I'm a girl. Well, Lady Heath and Lady Bailey fly so it's no good telling me flying is 'an unsuitable sport for young ladies' – and I don't care how hard I have to work, I'm going to go on with it. As for saving up for my trousseau – that won't be necessary!"

Zandra's voice was husky but rang out perfectly clearly as she announced: "I'm not going to marry Hugh. If you want to know the truth, I never intended to do so; so you and Uncle Toby can stop worrying about my bottom drawer! I'm sorry if I've upset you, Aunt Willow, and I'm sorry about everyone losing their money and TRTC collapsing and everything; but I might as well be honest and admit I'm glad for me. Now perhaps you'll stop trying to marry me off and let me live my life the way I want."

Her head high, her large blue-grey eyes flashing, she stormed out of the drawing-room before any of the astonished members of her family could protest.

Part 1

1929–1933

Chapter 1

November 1929

Zandra pulled the collar of her tweed coat more tightly around her neck and stamped her feet beneath the confines of the travelling rug. The atmosphere inside Hugh's parents' Lanchester was only a degree warmer than outside on this cold, damp November afternoon, and no place to linger. However, the car was the only venue she could think of where they could talk in complete privacy; and after making her announcement to the family, she was not prepared to face them again until the breaking of her engagement was a *fait accompli*.

"I really am dreadfully sorry, Hugh!" she said for the second time. "But honestly, you did know from the start that I never intended to marry you."

The hangdog expression on the face of the young man beside her momentarily exasperated her. Why couldn't he put up some sort of fight – at least accuse her of using him? Instead, he said miserably: "It was my own fault for not telling you right at the start that I was in love with you – I mean, you couldn't know, could you?" He cleared his throat and blinked nervously. "When you suggested we should get engaged to keep Mrs Rochford from going on about you having to do the Season, I knew you

7

didn't care about me – that way, I mean; but I suppose I started hoping that maybe you'd begin to feel differently – I mean, you said we'd stay engaged until you were twenty-one, and I hoped that I could somehow make you care a bit about me before then – not just as a friend, you see."

He broke off and began to fiddle nervously with the ends of his muffler. He looked so abject, Zandra's feelings of guilt intensified.

"I do care about you, Hugh, honestly I do. We'll always be friends, but I'm dreadfully sorry, I just don't love you the way you mean . . . that's to say, the way you think you love me. Don't you think you might be imagining it? We said we'd *pretend* we were in love to your parents and my family and you may have just got a bit confused acting the part of a doting fiancé. You were jolly good at it, too."

Hugh managed a wry smile.

"Well, it wasn't pretending for me. You were so good at it, I suppose even I began to believe you really did want to marry me when we were both a bit older! You'd have made a jolly good actress, Zandra!"

Zandra drew a deep sigh.

"Yes, I know, but Aunt Willow wouldn't even consider it and Uncle Toby goes along with everything she says. It's so old-fashioned! Nowadays girls can do all kinds of things they couldn't have done before the war; but Aunt Willow thinks everything has changed for the worse! At least Tante Silvie is a bit more modern. I can talk to her and she understands."

It had been Tante Silvie, she reflected, who had understood that she hadn't done anything wrong with Léon; that she had only agreed to the secret rendezvous with the Frenchman because it was fun, exciting to be treated like a grown-up instead of a schoolgirl. Her flirtation with him had been completely harmless – or anyway at the start. When she had agreed to meet Léon that first time at a discreet outdoor café for an aperitif after her hair appointment, it was like a "dare" at school, for she'd known perfectly well Tante Silvie would not approve. Léon, who was terribly good looking in a Latin kind of way, had paid her masses of compliments, and then told her he was mad about her before taking her hand and, in a wildly passionate manner, kissing the inside of her wrist.

In a way, the gesture had been almost funny; but even as she had suppressed a giggle, the feel of his lips, so hot against her soft skin, had aroused the strangest feelings somewhere deep inside her. She'd thought about it that night and wondered if it was the wine rather than Léon's kiss which had made her feel momentarily giddy. So she'd met him secretly a second time and a third, and discovered that despite her half-hearted protests, she sat longing for the moments when Léon would entwine his fingers with hers; murmur in that enchanting accent that he worshipped her; could not sleep at night for thinking about her; that she was "made by the angels to be loved by men!" His touches made her heart leap even though she was sure it was accidental when his arm brushed against her breast, or his knee pressed against hers beneath the table.

"But what on earth did you find to talk about to a man of his background?" Tante Silvie had moaned. "He is uneducated, a *gamin*, in the name of heaven! A hairdresser!"

Haltingly, Zandra had tried to explain that she and Léon did not converse in the way her aunt implied. Léon did all the talking – about her charm, her beauty, her Venus-like figure, her irresistible charm! That not only had it been very agreeable to listen to but exciting, disturbing, too.

"I shall have to tell your Aunt Willow," Tante Silvie had said, "much as I do not wish to do so! She placed you in my care, Zee-Zee, and I cannot lie to her. However, I will do what I can to mitigate her displeasure. You are twenty years old, *quand même*, and it is time you left the schoolroom and enjoyed the society of men. At your age, I . . . but we will not speak of that. Instead, I think it is time you learned a little about yourself so that you are not quite such a susceptible little innocent."

Although her aunt would not go so far as to reveal what transpired between a man and a woman when they fell in love and married, she had explained to Zandra that it was quite natural for her to feel a physical thrill when a good-looking young man like Léon kissed her. Had Zandra lived in an earlier era, Tante Silvie had said, she would have been married long since and be the mother of babies. Her body had become that of a woman several years previously and was ready and waiting for a lover, deceiving her into believing that someone like Léon was the one she desired. Zandra would doubtless be aroused by many more attractive young men before she met the right one to become a life partner – one who would ensure that it was a marriage of the minds and hearts as well as an attraction of the bodies.

Zandra's thoughts returned to the dejected young man beside her. Never once had she felt in the very least affected when poor Hugh had kissed her. Never once had she sat beside him hoping he would hold her hand. On the contrary, his hands were invariably hot and sweaty and it was always a relief when one or both of them were wearing gloves. Poor Hugh! He was little more than a boy, really, and only five years older than her tiresome young brother, Jamie. No wonder Hugh seemed gauche and childish after Léon!

"Look, Hugh, it isn't as if I am breaking off our engagement because there is someone else. I mean, maybe one day I'll grow up some more and feel differently . . . that is, if you haven't met another girl you like better than me. As a matter of fact, I'll let you into a secret. You know Katherine, Lawrence Rose's twin who comes to play tennis sometimes? She thinks you're terribly good looking. She saw you once without your glasses. I bet you don't know it was Kate who sent you that valentine last February! She's being presented next year when she leaves school and she's awfully nice!"

"Other girls just don't match up to you, Zandra. You're – well, different. I mean, you're not afraid of anything and you stand up for yourself. Gosh, you can even fly an aeroplane!"

Zandra's look of astonishment was genuine.

"So could you, if you wanted. It's easier than driving a car. I'm sure Ollie would teach you if you wanted to learn."

She broke off, remembering that poor Oliver was going to have to sell his partnership in his airline. Things must be pretty bad for such drastic steps to be necessary. As for Uncle Toby's announcement that they might have to sell Rochford – it was unthinkable! She had spent most of her life beneath its roof and it was home. She wondered whether to tell Hugh about the collapse of the American conglomerate that Aunt Willow's father had founded, but she decided against it. Money, after all, was something one did not talk about. As far as she was concerned, she had never thought about it. She had not the slightest idea how much money Aunt Willow spent on her and Jamie's clothes, or the cost of their school fees and seaside holidays; and since she, Zandra, never went anywhere unaccompanied, she had never needed money of her own. If she wanted cosmetics or sweets or to have her hair cut, she had only to charge the expense to the Rochford accounts.

Uncle Toby had looked very grave, she reflected, when he had made his announcement. He had been unusually forthright for he was a quiet, serious kind of person; gentle, kind, but vague. He absolutely adored Aunt Willow and when he wasn't poring over his precious medical journals in his study, his only concern was making sure she was happy! One day, Zandra hoped, she would find someone to love her as devotedly. What she would like most of all was a man with Uncle Toby's capacity for love and Uncle Pelham's jolly, adventurous zest for life. Tante Silvie never knew from one moment to the next what he was up to! According to her, he was quite capable at lunch-time of informing her she must pack their suitcases and be ready to go that afternoon to Venice, or Florence or the South of France for no better reason than he had happened to see an advertising poster in a travel agent's window and thought it might be an interesting place to visit.

Life had never been dull during her brief five months' visit to her much-loved French relations, and she was glad that the collapse of TRTC would not affect them too seriously. They were going to sell their beautiful château in Epernay and buy a smaller country house in the South of France; but Uncle Pelham had said that they were intending to do this in any event, and the sale of the château would compensate for their losses.

By the sound of it, her cousins Alexis and Lucy, too, were only mildly affected. Alexis had even spoken of raising the money to buy out Oliver's shareholding in Sky-Ways, but now it seemed as if his offer might not be necessary. Out of the blue, Henry Barratt, Oliver's partner, had had a telephone call from a man called Anthony Wisson who had somehow got word of the fact that it was Tetford money which had financed the airline, and of the collapse of the corporation. It seemed the financier was extremely anxious to buy Sky-Ways and wanted to meet Oliver to discuss the possible purchase. Zandra was far from sure what exactly a "financier" was, but she assumed he must be a wealthy old fuddy-duddy, and feared that he might well be as old-fashioned as her aunt and refuse to have a female pilot on his staff. Knowing he had arranged to meet Oliver at Sky-Ways the following morning, she was going to find out for herself what her own future prospects might be.

"I suppose I'll have to stop seeing you now our engagement has been broken off!"

Hugh's forlorn voice brought Zandra's thoughts back once more to the unhappy young man she had treated so cavalierly.

"We don't have to be so conventional about it, do we?" she said, more as a statement than a question. "There's no reason why we can't see each other just because we've decided not to get married after all. Why shouldn't we go on just as we have before?"

Hugh looked up eagerly.

"Gosh, Zandra, do you really think so? I shan't mind nearly so much if we can still see each other."

"Well, no one can stop us, can they?" Zandra said firmly. "Anyway, tomorrow is Sunday and you promised to drive me over to the airfield after church. There's bound to be lots of people flying with the weather so perfect. Aunt Willow said I could go to early service tomorrow instead of matins. It's such a dreadful waste of a whole morning sitting there listening to dull old Reverend Ellis' dreary sermons. You will take me, won't you, Hugh? I'd drive myself if only they'd let me. The chauffeur says I'm a really good driver and he isn't a bit frightened even when I go fast. He's teaching Jamie now and as soon as he's learned, because he's a boy, *he'll* be allowed to go out on his own. It's so unfair!"

Hugh felt obliged to protest.

"One would be frightfully worried about a girl going off on her own. Who would look after her if she broke down? Or was in a smash?"

Zandra's blue eyes flashed and her mouth tightened in a stubborn line.

"Girls did much more dangerous things than driving by themselves in the war," she said. "Lots of nurses were in the front lines! Lucy and Tante Silvie were!"

"Yes, and lots were killed!" Hugh said. "Anyway, we aren't in the middle of a war now, Zandra, and it's up to us chaps to look after you."

Zandra gave a deep sigh. There seemed little point in continuing the discussion for Hugh's parents were about as old-fashioned as her Aunt Willow. He'd never understood why she had been so against being presented and having a Season like all the other girls they knew. He'd agreed – albeit reluctantly – that she was right in a way when she said the débutantes' mothers were just trying to find eligible husbands for their daughters, and the Season was no different from a cattle market. But he'd been really shocked when she declared she didn't want to be married and obliged to lead her husband's life. "I want to be me before I am somebody's wife and mother!" she had said; and this he had

13

almost certainly not understood. What else could a pretty girl like her want, he had asked? It was not as if she was one of those dreadfully brainy girls pursuing a career at university just as if they were men!

"You *will* take me to the airfield tomorrow, won't you? I need you to look after me!" Zandra persisted in the soft appealing voice he was never able to resist. "Please, Hugh!"

It needed no further persuasion for Hugh to say yes.

Next morning, however, it seemed at first as if Hugh's services would not be required after all. At breakfast, Oliver, who had spent the previous evening on the telephone, informed his mother that he was going to the airfield to meet the potential buyer of his shares.

"I do so wish it wasn't necessary, my darling!" Willow said, her eyes distressed as she regarded her dearly loved son.

"He sounded a decent enough chap!" Oliver replied, putting his arm round her shoulders. "Of course, I've got to consider Henry. If I sell out, this Wisson fellow would be in control. If he looks as if he's going to interfere too much in the way we run Sky-Ways, I may well reconsider Alexis' offer."

"Quite right, too! Thoroughly decent chap, young Barratt! Couldn't have had a better partner," Toby grunted.

Oliver nodded.

"We make a good team – and we were lucky, too, to have Lord Sharples as our chairman. We'd never have got off the ground without his business know-how. It's a pity he died so soon afterwards! I must say, I'm very curious to know how Wisson got hold of his facts so quickly – quite a mystery. He's pretty keen to buy – didn't waste much time, and made an appointment to meet me – on a Sunday, too! He said he's too busy to make it on a weekday!"

"So you really do intend to sell out your stake, Oliver?" Toby asked.

"If I can do so without it causing problems for Henry. As you know, he does hold forty per cent of the shares. A lot will depend on what this Wisson chap is like, and if he wants to change our set-up. Henry has put as much time and effort into the business as I have – even if he wasn't able to ante the same amount of capital to start it up; so I owe it to him to consider his future as well as my own. We'll have to see what Wisson has in mind."

For once, Zandra curbed her tongue. If she were to remind Oliver that he had promised to give her an hour's spin in his newly acquired Gipsy Moth if the weather was good, he might tell her he did not want her at the airfield when so much of importance was happening. Far better, then, to just turn up with Hugh! There was always the chance that this Mr Anthony Wisson might be one of those old men who were susceptible to pretty girls, and she could charm him into employing her!

Having decided upon her tactics, she went upstairs and changed from the coat and skirt she had worn to church and donned a straight, camel-coloured wool dress with black jet buttons and two side pleats in the skirt. Tante Silvie had chosen it for her from Molyneux in Paris, and to Zandra's delight, it made her look older than her twenty years – and far more sophisticated.

Mollie, Zandra's personal maid, looked at her young mistress in astonishment as she brushed her page-boy bob and dabbed rouge on her cheeks before applying a cherry-red lipstick.

"You isn't going to the airfield like that, Miss Zandra, is you?" she asked. "Not in them high heels, any road!"

Zandra laughed.

"And why not, Mollie? You're as bad as Aunt Willow – telling me off for dressing like an aeroplane mechanic one minute and then complaining because I wear something decent for a change!"

Mollie handed Zandra her kid gloves, and gaped as she watched the girl pull on her fawn hat and fold back the brim at a jaunty angle.

"Why isn't you wearing your engagement ring, Miss Zandra?" she asked, and was surprised by Zandra's sudden grin.

"Because I'm not engaged any longer, Mollie. Mr Conway and I have decided we aren't suited, so we're just friends again. Now be a good girl and hand me my coat or Mr Conway will be here to collect me and I don't want to keep him waiting."

From her bedroom window, she had seen Oliver driving off in the Bentley and now she could see Hugh's small, bull-nosed Morris coming up the driveway. She had not yet had a chance to tell him that as far as the family were concerned, they were no longer going to the airfield; that she had told Aunt Willow Hugh was taking her to lunch with his family. As a consequence of this fib, she dared not keep Hugh waiting lest he became embroiled in polite conversation with her aunt and let the cat out of the bag.

Poor old Hugh! she thought. He simply didn't understand that it was sometimes necessary to tell white lies. He was probably relieved in some ways that they had broken off their engagement – the most momentous deceit in which she had so far involved him! She must remember to give him back his ring. It had belonged to Hugh's spinster aunt whose fiancé had been killed in the war, and she had given it to Hugh for his future wife. It was safely wrapped in a handkerchief in the bottom of her black clutch handbag.

An hour later, Hugh was parking his car at Sky-Ways alongside Oliver's Bentley and a large green Mercedes. It was an impressive vehicle and by the look of it, capable of considerable speed.

"Come on, Hugh!" Zandra urged her companion. "Let's go and take a peek at Mr Wisson!"

"I don't see how we can just barge in – I mean, it's all right for you, Zandra – Lord Rochford is used to you being here, but . . .

Zandra drew an impatient sigh.

"Ollie won't mind – and I do think it's silly the way you keep calling him 'Lord Rochford'; he's only nine years older than you. You make him sound so stuffy! Anyway, if you don't want to come in, you can stay here in the car."

The November morning was bitterly cold and despite his

warm overcoat, Hugh shivered. Knowing Zandra, she could start chattering if a subject interested her and go on for hours. Sometimes he wondered if she had forgotten he was present! Reluctantly, he followed her into the building.

The outer office was empty of its usual scurrying members of staff and pilots, and was occupied only by a tall, fair-haired young man in a well-cut, dark grey suit and maroon silk tie. He rose at once as Zandra entered the room.

"Hallo!" she said, pausing to smile at the stranger. "Is my cousin, Lord Rochford, here? I haven't met you before, have I? Are you Mr Wisson?"

A brief smile flitted across the young man's pleasantly featured face; but he spoke with formal politeness as he said: "I'm Mr Anthony Wisson's personal assistant – Guy Bristow. Lord Rochford is in conference with Mr Wisson in his inner sanctum!"

"I see! Actually, it isn't my cousin's 'inner sanctum' . . ." Her smile deepened as she echoed his words. "It's used by both the directors and the senior pilot. I'm Zandra McGill, by the way, and this is Hugh Conway!" She turned to Hugh. "You can stay here with Mr Bristow. I'm going in to see Ollie!"

Guy Bristow, who had been about to draw back a chair for Zandra to sit on, lifted a restraining hand.

"I don't think Mr Wisson wants to be . . . er, disturbed, Miss McGill," he said awkwardly. "That's to say, he told me to make sure he was not interrupted!"

Zandra's chin lifted and she looked directly into the hazel eyes fastened so anxiously upon her.

"I'm here to see my cousin, Lord Rochford, not Mr Wisson, and I really don't think I need anyone's permission to do so."

"I say, Zandra, if Mr Bristow has been instructed to keep every-one out, don't you think . . . I mean, if it's a private meeting—"

"Oh, stuff!" Zandra interrupted Hugh, her tone of voice giving no inkling of her inner misgivings. If this Mr Bristow had not virtually forbidden her to go in, she might well have waited for Oliver and his visitor to come out; but she saw his remark as a challenge and she was not going to climb down now. In any event, Mr Wisson's "watchdog" might be obliged to take orders from his master – but she was not!

Before her courage could fail, she swept past him and with her head high, sailed into Oliver's office.

Both men stopped talking as Zandra entered. Oliver looked up at her in surprise from his chair behind his desk.

"Why, hallo, Zee-Zee! What are you doing here? And in that get-up? I thought you were lunching with Hugh's parents!"

Zandra went over and laid her arm affectionately around her cousin's shoulders. Deliberately, she avoided looking at the other man.

"We're going there later!" she said vaguely. "I wanted Hugh to see your new Puss Moth so we dropped by here first, and then I saw your car. I hope I'm not interrupting something important."

Oliver gave her a friendly hug.

"Well, you are, as a matter of fact, Zee-Zee. Let me introduce Mr Anthony Wisson. Mr Wisson, my cousin, Miss Zandra McGill."

As the man rose quickly to his feet and extended his hand, Zandra was struck first of all by the directness of his glance. The expression in his grey eyes was indefinable, and as he continued to hold her gaze, she felt her cheeks beginning to flush beneath his scrutiny. A dozen different thoughts chased across her mind: the first, that he was very far from being the "fuddy-duddy" old man she had expected; the second, that he was quite remarkably handsome. He was tall with a sweep of dark brown hair, a long aquiline nose and a firm, square jaw. His skin did not have the customary Englishman's winter pallor, but was lightly tanned.

"It's my pleasure, Miss McGill." His voice was deep, resonant. "Your interruption is quite timely, as it happens, for I think your cousin and I have concluded our discussion, have we not, Lord Rochford? To our mutual satisfaction, I am glad to say."

Most definitely to his own satisfaction, Anthony Wisson thought wryly, since he'd bought a controlling share in the airline for a great deal less than he had been prepared to pay.

18

Young Rochford had proved to be as naïve in business dealing as most of his class. Titled, born to wealth and privilege, money was something not, preferably, to be discussed in polite society, and at best a somewhat embarrassing topic for discussion only when necessity required. Bargaining had not been on Rochford's agenda, and he had accepted the first figure he, Anthony, had proposed. With that easy, self-confident graciousness of his kind, Rochford had proffered his hand to shake on the deal, his brown eyes crinkling in a friendly smile.

Without warning, the face of Elerson Major flashed across Anthony Wisson's mind. It was all of twenty-three years ago that with the same casual smile, Elerson Major had selected him from among the group of new boys for his fag. He, Anthony, had been thirteen when his parents had plunged him into that unknown, unimaginable boarding-school life. Until then, his mother had tutored him, and because of the isolated life they led, he'd had no experience of the mores and hierarchy common to schoolboys. He had not even known what "fagging" entailed.

"What's your name, squirt?" Elerson asked.

"Antoni!" he answered in his ignorance.

"Not your Christian name, idiot. Don't you know we only use surnames?"

The other boys standing nearby sniggered.

"Antoni Wisniowiecki!"

Elerson grabbed his arm. He was no longer smiling.

"If that's supposed to be a joke, let me give you a word of warning, squirt. Cheeking us seniors will earn you a good thrashing. Now answer me properly. What's your name?"

"I just told you – Wisniowiecki! It's an ordinary Polish name!"

So at thirteen, he learned his first lesson – that he was never going to be accepted by his contemporaries as one of themselves because he was different. Because his parents were Polish, he was nicknamed "Poleski" although he had been born in England some years after his mother and father had immigrated and become British citizens. It took him only a few months to correct his Polish accent and copy that of his schoolfellows, but there was nothing he could do to change his parents. God, how he'd hated them – his round, fat, balding father and his tall, thin mother in their drab, shabby clothes driving to school in their rattling old Talbot, jabbering away to one another in Polish as they always did when they spoke to him or to each other! Their obvious poverty was almost as great an embarrassment as their appearance and their continental volubility. It might not have been so bad if they had been prepared to remain quietly in the background; or if they had been wealthy, like Elerson's parents who arrived in the immaculate new Rolls-Royce motor called the "Silver Ghost". Elerson was one of the only three boys in the minor public school whose father was titled and a personal friend of the Duke of York, which was enough to earn him a certain amount of respect.

It was the second lesson he, Anthony, had learned – that money and social position counted far more than brains, which he had in plenty; or even athletic ability, with which he had also been blessed.

The third lesson he learned in those first few weeks was never to believe another word his mother said. *"You are so clever, my precious Pumpkin . . . so handsome . . . so talented . . . you will be the most popular boy in the school. We are so proud of you, my darling!"*

Bitterly, he'd ripped the picture of himself standing between his two elderly parents from the silver frame his mother had saved so hard to buy. He tore it into tiny pieces and flushed it down the WC. A few weeks later, he sold the frame to another new boy who had an enlargement of his very English-looking father in shooting gear, a twelve-bore broken over one arm and four slavering black Labradors grouped at his feet beside a row of dead pheasants. The money augmented his meagre pocket-money which was proving totally inadequate for his needs at the tuck shop.

On his first night in the dormitory, he was fool enough to brag about the fact that his mother's family had been Polish aristocrats. (He'd not then been aware that she had been disowned by her family for marrying his father who had been the family bailiff!) In the mistaken belief that brains and hard work were laudable characteristics, as he'd always been taught, he further bragged that his father, although arriving penniless in England, had worked his way up from a junior clerk in a munitions factory to become a senior accountant, a junior partner and finally the owner. The fact that the ultimate purchase of the factory had rendered Wisniowiecki senior on the verge of financial ruin, he had carefully omitted. He had not been believed. The sons of the mill and mine owners of this northern area of England who made up the bulk of the pupils were perfectly well aware that the parents of boys on bursaries were unable to afford the school fees and it followed therefore that Wisniowiecki senior could not own a factory. Wisniowiecki junior was branded a braggart and a liar. His shabby suitcase and his parents' rusty old car proved his poverty.

It was his fourth lesson – that people were judged on appearances rather than brains, and therefore appearances as well as class mattered.

Certainly, if appearances were not in this instance misleading, Rochford's cousin was everything he found most desirable in a female, Wisson thought now as he concentrated his attention on the girl who had just come into the room. He met her gaze with a friendly smile.

"May I ask you a question, Miss McGill? I am curious, you see, to know more of your interest in aeroplanes. Is this interest common to all the members of your family?"

Oliver laughed.

"Great Scott, no! There's my brother-in-law; and my young son, Giles, spends half his holidays down here. He's almost as keen as Zandra, who I might say, is an accomplished pilot. After a few more lessons with our chief engineer, she will probably know more about the inner workings of the Gipsy Moth than most of the chaps who fly it."

21

"So – I have the pleasure of speaking to that most rare of species – a mechanically minded lady pilot!" Anthony Wisson's voice was genuinely admiring but none the less sounded patronizing to Zandra who was stung to reply: "Do you see any reason why women should not fly an aeroplane – or drive a car – every bit as well as men, Mr Wisson?"

She had expected he might argue the point about the suitability of such taxing occupations for "the weaker sex", but instead he merely smiled and said: "On the contrary, Miss McGill. I am a great admirer of the American lady, Miss Amelia Earhart, who I think has already proved the flying ability of the fair sex."

Zandra felt herself relaxing and she smiled warmly, unaware of the effect this change of expression had upon the man regarding her.

"Then if you really are going to take over Oliver's airline, will you fulfil his promise to me, Mr Wisson – to give me a job here at Sky-Ways? I promise you you wouldn't regret it. I'll—"

"Zee-Zee, you are a little minx!" Oliver broke in. "Mr Wisson and I have barely had the opportunity to discuss the future plans for Sky-Ways. We have yet to see what our respective accountants have to say, and I do assure you, Mr Wisson, that the future employment of my incorrigible young cousin is not a condition of sale!"

Anthony Wisson laughed.

"I did not suppose so, Lord Rochford. Nevertheless if our plans go ahead as I hope, I am quite prepared to find a place for so enterprising a young lady, if that is her wish. But don't you have more pressing social engagements that would preclude regular employment, Miss McGill? I imagine that with your charm and accomplishments, you must be very much in demand by Society's hostesses."

"Oh, Zee-Zee could have been Deb of the Year if she'd wanted!" Oliver broke in easily. "But she wouldn't allow my mother to launch her, would you, Zee-Zee? Mind you, I can't say I blame her entirely. I did the Season's débutante round one year and most of the girls have nothing to talk about except parties and fashions."

"Nevertheless, one can make some useful contacts on such occasions," the older man said more to himself than in direct reply to Oliver. "However, I don't doubt Miss McGill has enough admirers without having to be paraded before the eligible young men around town!"

"And she treats them shamelessly!" Oliver said with a grin. "What have you done with that unfortunate fiancé of yours, Zee-Zee?"

Zandra met Anthony Wisson's amused glance with a wicked smile.

"I've left Hugh with your bodyguard!" she replied. "Your Mr Bristow did his best to stop me coming in here, Mr Wisson, so please don't blame him for my barging in the way I did! And by the way, Ollie, Hugh isn't my fiancé any more. We've broken off our engagement by mutual consent."

"Have you now!" Oliver commented. "Well, I can't say I'm surprised. Poor old Hugh!"

"One must have sympathy for anyone who loses your regard, Miss McGill!"

The look in Anthony Wisson's eyes was unmistakable, for Zandra had seen it often enough in Léon's to know when a man found her attractive. She felt a sudden thrill of excitement. The fact that Mr Wisson was quite a lot older than most of the young men she knew need not prevent her from enjoying a flirtation with him. It might be dangerous – but it would certainly be exciting.

"What a pity I have another engagement in London this afternoon!" he was saying, his eyes holding her own. "Otherwise the three of us might have enjoyed a celebratory lunch together. However, there will be other opportunities. Now I really should be on my way, Lord Rochford."

As he bowed over Zandra's gloved hand, she was convinced that he had pressed her fingers more tightly than was customary. She was impatient now for him to be gone so that she could ask Oliver the multitude of questions that were milling in her mind. Who exactly *was* Mr Anthony Wisson? Was he married? Was he really going to buy a controlling interest in Oliver's airline? Had he meant it when he said he might give her a job? And most important of all, had he really found her attractive? That was something she could not ask Oliver, but it was a question to which she very badly wanted an answer – and for that answer to be yes.

Chapter 2

February 1930

"Anthony has asked me to marry him, and I've said yes."

Willow glanced quickly at her niece's flushed cheeks and away again. Zandra's declaration was not entirely unexpected, and when she had requested a private discussion after breakfast in the morning-room, she, Willow, had tried to prepare herself for this confrontation.

"My darling, you have only known Mr Wisson for three months. Aren't you both being a little premature?"

"We don't think so. We're desperately in love. We want to get married in June."

Willow, who had determined to remain calm, could not prevent her tiny gasp of protest.

"But that is only four months away. Quite apart from anything else, we could never have your trousseau ready in time."

Zandra, who had also determined to remain calm in the face of what she had anticipated would be her aunt's opposition, leant forward in her chair and said firmly: "Anthony says we can start our honeymoon in Paris and that I can buy anything I want whilst we're there. Don't you see, Aunt Willow, how absolutely angelic he is? He knows I've no money of my own and how badly

25

the family has been hit by this Wall Street business, and he's frightfully anxious that you don't have to go to any extra expense on our account. He says we can have a quiet wedding here in Havorhurst and then later, when we've bought our new house in London and I've furnished and decorated it the way I want, we'll have a huge party to celebrate – a sort of combined reception and house-warming 'do'. That way, you and Uncle Toby won't have to be responsible for any of the expense."

Realizing that some of her latent anxieties had been pre-empted by Zandra's ardent suitor, Willow returned to the issue which she considered far more important.

"It's only a few months since you thought you were in love with Hugh. I really don't believe you know your own mind, Zee-Zee. I don't deny that Anthony Wisson is a very attractive man – a charming man – and your Uncle Toby and I both like him. But he is a great deal older than you – thirty-seven, eight, perhaps even forty! And you have had very little experience of life. You've not even come of age yet!"

Zandra's mouth tightened.

"You were only seventeen when you married Uncle Rowell!"

"Yes, that's quite true – and it is possibly one of the reasons I am concerned for your future. Uncle Rowell and I were incompatible, and I have to say that our marriage was not a success. I want you to be as happy as I have been these past twenty years with your Uncle Toby."

"So why don't you think I'll be happy with Anthony?" Zandra's voice was defiant. Willow drew a deep sigh.

"I am not suggesting otherwise, Zee-Zee. It's just that we know so little about Anthony . . . his family—"

"Oh, that!" Zandra interrupted. "Anthony warned me you'd probably be prejudiced because he isn't 'one of us'. Well, his father was Polish and was forced to flee his country and make a new start here. As for his mother, she was the daughter of a Polish nobleman and there's nothing wrong with that even if his father wasn't blue-blooded. Anyway, Anthony's as English as

26

Ollie; he was born in England; and he went to a public school in the North of England. And as for the family relatives – they're all dead so you won't be bothered by them any more than I will. And I simply don't understand all this. I thought you *liked* Anthony, Aunt Willow!"

"Oh darling, I do!" Willow said with genuine warmth. How could she not do so, she asked herself, remembering Mr Wisson's perfect manners, the lovely bouquets of flowers he sent down from London after every visit; the mass of perfectly chosen Christmas presents with which he had showered her grandchildren. There had been a magnificent set of Meccano for Oliver's boy, Giles, and for Lucy's son, Robin; a hand-crafted doll's house for Lucy's Eve, quite apart from the elaborate Christmas food hamper from Fortnum's for the grown-ups. If Anthony Wisson's wealth had been self-made, there was no doubting his willingness to distribute it. According to Oliver, he had made a most generous offer for his shares in Sky-Ways and was paying Oliver a salary to continue managing the airline that was more than enough for him to keep Jane and Giles in comfort. Needless to say, Oliver was immensely impressed with the new chairman's grasp of the financial aspects of the business. "Frightfully quick on the uptake!" had been her son's comment, and "right up to date with developments in aviation".

For a moment, Willow forgot her niece as her thoughts turned to her beloved son. The collapse of the Rochfords' family fortunes was a disaster that was about to bring many distressing changes to all of them, but the effect it threatened to have upon Oliver's airline had upset her more even than the thought of leaving the beautiful home she had lived in for the past thirty-nine years. Oliver had tried to make light of his own dismay, but no one knew better than she, his mother, how much hard work and enthusiasm he and Henry Barratt had put into building the business up since the end of the war. It had seemed as if after eleven years of effort, with success now established, her son was going to be denied the rewards of its progress. Anthony Wisson's

27

take-over looked like turning a potential disaster into salvation. Not only had his offer for Oliver's shares been a very generous one, he had announced that his only interest in the running of the airline would be that it should maintain a private aeroplane with pilot instantly available should he wish to be transported somewhere in a hurry. Oliver's management would continue exactly as before. It was small wonder, therefore, that he regarded Mr Anthony Wisson so favourably!

"I shall have to discuss this further with your Uncle Toby!" she said now to Zandra. "I know he agrees with me that a longer engagement would be preferable. Of course, you will come of age next month and" – she continued with a wry smile – "be free at last to ignore our wishes."

"I know that, Aunt Willow, but I was hoping I would have your blessing, your approval. I love you both very much, and I'd be utterly miserable if I had to upset you. That's why I told Anthony I would speak to you before he makes a formal request for my hand."

She paused only to draw breath before saying: "I think you ought to know something else about Anthony. He asked me not to tell you until after you had given us your approval – in case you thought he was trying to bribe you into saying 'yes' – but he wants to make Oliver an offer for Havorhurst village and some of the land; and Aunt Willow, the wonderful thing about it is that he'd make over the deeds to me as a wedding present – so it could all remain in the family and we wouldn't have to sell the house."

Seeing the look of bewilderment on her aunt's face at her outburst, Zandra jumped out of her chair and went to kneel beside the woman who had always seemed like a mother to her. Catching Willow's hands in her own, she said in a quieter voice: "I know how much Rochford Manor has always meant to you and Uncle Toby. He was born here in this house, wasn't he? And Mummy, and all your children. Now we don't have to leave – any of us. Anthony says if you are all agreed, he and I could take over the Gatehouse after we're married to use as a weekend cottage.

Of course, we'll be spending most of the time in the house he's going to buy for us in London, because of Anthony's business affairs. Don't you see, Aunt Willow? Everything is going to be all right now!"

Willow withdrew her hands from Zandra's and cupped them about the pretty, heart-shaped face. How happy, eager, excited the child looked! And how young! She hated dampening such optimism but felt obliged to ask: "This isn't one of the reasons you want to marry Mr Wisson, darling? To save Rochford Manor for us, I mean? I understand from Oliver that he's an extremely wealthy man, and doubtless Mr Wisson can afford to do all the things he has talked to you about; but that would be quite the wrong reason for you to be marrying him. Mr Wisson may seem to you like a fairy godfather waving his magic wand to grant all your wishes and, indeed, solve our financial problems, but believe me, my darling, riches alone can never be enough to make a marriage a happy, fulfilling one – not unless you really love one another!"

Zandra met her aunt's gaze, her eyes unwavering as she said: "But that's just it, Aunt Willow – I do love him very, very much; and I know he adores me because he's always telling me so, as well as doing things to make me happy. That's all he cares about; and he's so wonderfully understanding. When he told me I would be much too busy as his wife to have a job in Ollie's airline – and it wouldn't be suitable anyway for me to be working! – he said I would be free to go to the airfield whenever I wanted; and that he'd buy me my very own aeroplane and Ollie could look after it for me. And he has promised to take me to New York when he goes there, which he often does on business, and you know how much I've always longed to go to America."

"Zandra, darling, I do understand that Mr Wisson is offering you a very pleasing future; and I do not doubt that he loves you very much, for who could not? I would have no objections to an engagement of perhaps a year – to give you time to meet other men more your own age – like that nice young man you introduced me to who works for Mr Wisson."

"Oh, you mean Guy Bristow! Well, you wouldn't think he was at all suitable, Aunt Willow, if I'd said I wanted to marry *him*. He couldn't be less eligible . . . no money and a widowed mother to support. His father was killed in the war and what money he left went on his son's education at Le Rosay – that's an international boarding school in Switzerland – so Mr Bristow is dependent upon the salary Anthony pays him to support himself and his mother. Actually, I quite like him. Anthony says he's very good at sports – plays tennis well, and golf and cricket, of course; and he's very far from stupid, or else Anthony wouldn't be employing him – or that's what he said. Aunt Willow, please don't let's change the subject. About Anthony and me—"

"Yes, my darling!" Willow said with a barely concealed sigh, for no one knew better than she how tenacious her niece could be once she had set her heart upon something.

"You really shouldn't look so worried!" Zandra said eagerly. "I have something else to tell you which I know will make you happy. Anthony agrees with you that I should be presented, even though he knows I think it's all rather silly. He says I'll make a lot of new friends and one can't have too many because you never know when you're going to need one! Anyway, he said I owed it to you as you wanted it so much; that it was the least I could do to thank you for looking after me all these years!"

"Oh, but darling, I wanted it for you, not for me," Willow protested, "besides which your dear mother had set her heart on it, and I promised her, you see, those last weeks when she knew she would not live to see you grow up."

Zandra's eyes clouded and her voice was subdued as she said softly: "You never told me that before, Aunt Willow. If I'd known—"

"I didn't think it was fair to put that kind of emotional pressure on you, darling. Dorothy – your mother – wouldn't have wanted it. I must say, I think it is very good of Mr Wisson to support my wishes, more especially as he must have considered them very much in opposition to those of the girl he has been seeking to impress!"

30

Perhaps, after all, an older man was exactly what Zandra needed, she thought. Poor young Hugh Conway was – and always would have been – quite incapable of influencing her for good or bad! This was certainly the first time she had ever known Zandra to give way on a matter where she had made up her mind. Well, she would speak to Toby – and Oliver who, these past months, had got to know Mr Wisson quite well, seemed to have a high opinion of him and even to be a little in awe of him! Oliver's partner, Henry Barratt, spoke well of him, too. Of course, a presentation in May with all the preparations that required – and then a wedding in June – would mean a dreadful rush. And a lot of extra expense, too, although perhaps that was no longer so fearful a sword of Damocles hanging over them all if Mr Wisson were to buy part of the Rochford estate.

Willow searched her mind, trying to recall the last conversation she had overheard between Toby and Oliver. Oliver had approached a big London estate agent and a brochure was to be prepared offering Rochford Manor for sale in the spring. There had been mention of a valuation, but, ostrich-like, she had not wanted to take in these unhappy facts. Now, if Zandra was right and Mr Wisson was happy to buy some of the land and farm cottages, maybe they would not have to sell the manor. Oliver and Toby must be told at once for they would be as relieved as she if their lovely home would not have to be handed over to strangers after all.

Would such a sale provide enough money for them to keep the Home Farm as well as the house? She knew so little about financial affairs, having always left such matters in Toby's and Oliver's capable hands. Meanwhile, she must consider more urgent questions. Would a June wedding and a court presentation be possible? Her elder daughter, Lucy, and her husband, Alexis, could provide a London base for Zandra in their big house in Cadogan Place. She herself had already decided to give Zandra a coming out ball at Rochford in May – one last splendid occasion before, as they had supposed, Rochford was sold.

31

Zandra's engagement to Mr Wisson could be announced at the dance. Possibly some of their friends and neighbours might, like herself, question the gap in the couple's ages; but from the little she had gleaned from Lucy, who had met Mr Wisson, he was much in demand by London hostesses. He was strikingly good-looking, always beautifully tailored and was an accomplished dancer – a most eligible bachelor, in fact! No one seemed very sure where his money came from, but he was known to be extremely wealthy and these days, it hardly seemed to matter any more if it was "new" money. That was no longer a social barrier. Unlike many of their friends, Mr Wisson appeared to be unaffected by the recent collapse of the stock markets. According to Toby, he must have foreseen the coming crash and "got out at the top" – whatever that might mean.

"Aunt Willow!"

Zandra's voice brought her thoughts back once more to the present.

"I know you think I'm headstrong and irresponsible and much too impulsive – and I admit I can be all those things; but this is different. I really do love Anthony. It isn't just because he's attractive, although you can't deny that he is! He's kind, thoughtful and enormously clever. Do you know he speaks six languages? And he has travelled all over the world and met hundreds and hundreds of women but never wanted to marry anyone until he met me. So you see, he really does love me and I'd never, ever be bored living with him because he's so interesting – and different from boys like Hugh, for instance. All they want to talk about is cricket or cars or their horses and the parties they go to! That's one of the reasons I never wanted to have a Season – being stuck with a lot of dull old dancing partners. Anthony's different!"

There was no doubting the sincerity in Zandra's voice, Willow thought. Like any girl in love for the first time, Zee-Zee could see no flaws in her chosen partner. But flaws there must be – however minor! Even her darling Oliver had them for, as Toby said, he utterly refused to take life seriously and was incurably optimistic, often without any justification. Toby himself – devoted as she was to her husband and he to her – could be so absent-minded as to border on the neglectful! He'd never yet remembered her birthday or their wedding anniversary!

"Which of the Services was Mr Wisson in during the war?" she asked, for if he was in his mid-thirties, he must have been old enough to have become involved.

"As a matter of fact, he wasn't in any of them," Zandra replied. "He was twenty-five when war broke out and he desperately wanted to join up, but he was in munitions. He did once disobey his father and volunteered for the Army under an assumed name; but the powers that be found out where he worked and because it was a reserved occupation he was obliged to go home. Poor Anthony! He was dreadfully cut up about it at the time; but when the war ended, he had a letter from the Minister of War, thanking him for his magnificent contribution. He has promised to show me Mr Churchill's letter."

"I'll talk to Uncle Toby this evening, Zee-Zee, and if he agrees, you can invite your precious Mr Wisson for the weekend and allow him to persuade us into giving our consent to this early wedding!" Willow said with a smile. "If he really wishes to purchase some of the Rochford estate, that, too, will need further discussion. It would indeed be a very, very generous wedding present if Mr Wisson were to have the deeds drawn up in your name."

"He's a very generous man, Aunt Willow!" Zandra declared as she flung her arms round her aunt and hugged her. "Oh, I'm so happy! Everything is working out quite perfectly, isn't it, for all of us, I mean. I think this is the happiest day of my life!"

"But you mustn't start celebrating yet, my precious. The decision is not yet made!" Willow cautioned when she could free her face from Zandra's kisses. "We must wait and see! Marriage is for life, you know, and should not be rushed into however much you may think you are in love. They don't always end as happily as those romantic novels you like to read."

"But some do!" Zandra argued as she picked up one of the silk cushions and tossed it into the air. "You and Uncle Toby still love each other even though you're both old!" She caught the cushion deftly and flung it up again. "And Ollie and Jane adore each other – and look at Uncle Pelham and Tante Silvie! As for Lucy – she positively dotes on Alexis, and although he doesn't say much, you can see he worships her."

Seeing her aunt's face, she dropped the cushion and ran to give her another hug.

"It's all right, dearest aunt – I know you haven't said 'yes' yet, but you will. You like Anthony already – I know you do! Everyone does! And I absolutely adore him and I can't wait to be Mrs Anthony Wisson. Zandra Wisson does sound a bit odd, but I suppose I'll get used to it. Do you know, I think I must be the happiest girl in the whole world!"

"I hope you will always feel that way, my darling!" Willow said huskily. Time seemed to pass so quickly as one grew older. Here was Zandra, almost twenty-one years old, yet it seemed only a year or two since, as a pig-tailed seven-year-old, she had danced and sung for the convalescent soldiers and declared that as soon as she was grown-up, she was going on the stage! How ecstatic they had all been when the horrible war had ended. Who had not then believed that the world would be a better place for everyone? But happiness was, as always, elusive. There had been too many dreadful casualties – men without arms or legs, men who had been blinded or gassed, and would never be fit enough even to join the terrible queues of unemployed waiting for their meagre dole money. Even the rich had not gone entirely unscathed, for there was not a household that did not mourn a husband, a son, a father. Too many girls of her daughter, Alice's, age were unlikely ever to find a husband because there were not enough young men of her generation left in the aftermath to marry them.

There had been other, less important problems such as the difficulty in obtaining good domestic servants. So many of them had discovered other occupations they preferred to do. The world had opened up new opportunities – for the women in particular, and Willow was far from certain that it was a better world. At least she had been able to keep Zandra away from the "fast" life which so many young women were living these days. She was a sweet, innocent child; virginally unaware as yet of what being a woman entailed. Hopefully if this marriage went ahead, her husband would be gentle, understanding, sensitive – and, above all, faithful. A man of Anthony Wisson's age must, she presumed, have had many liaisons with women, but preferably not one who would encroach on his life as her first husband's mistress had disrupted her marriage!

"Aunt Willow, may I telephone Anthony? I told him I would be speaking to you this morning and I know he'll be on tenterhooks to hear how you feel about it all. He respects you enormously and he said we mustn't do anything to upset you. Can I tell him that at least you don't *disapprove*?"

"Run along then, darling, although my failing to disapprove does not mean that you have my approval!"

"I'll tell him that!" Zandra said, smiling happily as she gave her aunt a last hug.

Her telephone call was not, to her dismay, to reach Anthony. She was put through by his office switchboard to Guy Bristow, who informed her that his boss had been called away unexpectedly on business and had left no forwarding telephone number.

"Is there anything I can do for you, Miss McGill?"

His quiet, pleasant voice momentarily soothed Zandra's immediate disappointment.

"Thank you, but there isn't really . . . I mean, I just wanted to chat. I suppose it was silly of me to telephone the office. I will ring him at his home tonight."

"I'm afraid Mr Wisson won't be back for two or three days, Miss McGill."

Zandra's frustration resurfaced, and she was unable to restrain the note of disappointment in her voice as she said: "How infuriating! I really did want to talk to him quickly. You see, I've got some good news for him."

There was a brief pause before she heard Guy say: "If Mr Wisson telephones me, I'll tell him you wish to speak to him urgently."

"Will you? Oh, thanks awfully, Mr Bristow. Maybe *he* will ring *me* anyway. I'm sorry if I've interrupted your work. I expect you're absurdly busy! Do forgive me!"

Zandra could not see the face of the young man on the other end of the telephone. His pleasingly shaped mouth had curved in a smile at her use of the popular adjective. She could not know it, of course, but nothing he ever did for Anthony Wisson was "absurd". Had it been, it would mean instant dismissal, and that was something he dreaded. He needed every penny he earned to keep up with the mortgage repayments for his mother's little bungalow in Eastbourne; and since the financial débâcle in the United States had begun to make itself felt in England, the bank had made it clear they would not increase his moderate overdraft.

The smile left Guy's face as he contemplated his future. It would be years and years before he could afford to marry at all, let alone a girl like Zandra McGill. It was really absurd of him to imagine that he had fallen in love with her the first time he'd set eyes on her. Yet he could not get her out of his mind. He had only to remember how she had looked when she'd walked into her cousin's office to feel the same jolt of excitement. She had virtually taken his breath away. She had not noticed him, of course – except in passing; but he had noticed everything about her, the large, blue-grey eyes, the thick, light brown hair and the tall, slim figure. Most of all, he remembered her lips – full, soft, a little moist and demanding to be kissed!

Now, the sound of her voice brought back that same hurried beating of his heart, and he fought against the longing to detain her in some meaningless conversation, just so that he could hear it a little longer. Perhaps if Anthony Wisson had not earmarked her for his own . . . but it seemed as if the girl had had the same effect upon his boss as upon him, for on the drive back to London, he'd said to Guy: "That's the girl I am going to marry, Bristow. She epitomizes everything I've been searching for!"

Knowing his employer so well, Guy had had little doubt that it would be only a matter of time before he acquired what he wanted. He always did! Wisson was a remarkable man in very many ways. His brain was sharp, clear, brilliant in its ability to judge people and circumstances. He would set about whatever business deal was pending with a clear-cut strategy which swept aside difficulties that might have unnerved a lesser man. If at times he seemed ruthless in his dealings with people, he never tired of telling Guy that "a good deal is one where both parties are satisfied with the bottom line". In the past few weeks, it seemed that his boss was going about his courtship of Miss McGill in much the same way as he might a business deal. There were the bouquets of flowers Guy had had to order to be sent to Mrs Toby Rochford; the presents he'd had to choose for the grandchildren; the enquiries about the Rochfords' finances and the discussions with the accountant about purchasing the family estate. No wonder if Miss McGill proved satisfied with her half of the deal – for she would be one of the wealthiest wives in the country if she married Anthony Wisson! Guy never doubted that if his boss was not already a millionaire, he soon would be.

Reluctantly, Guy assured Zandra that she had in no way inter-rupted his work, and replaced the receiver. He felt unutterably depressed. It was his bad luck to fall in love for the first time in his life with a girl so hopelessly unattainable. He really must try to forget her – although that was not going to be so easy if she did end up marrying his employer. There was nothing for it but to hope that Mr Wisson's interest was a passing one; or that Zandra McGill's parents thought the age gap too wide; or even that the girl lost interest. She was very young, after all, and there was that other chap who had brought her to see her cousin, Lord Rochford, that day at the airline – Hugh Someone-or-other. The poor fellow had been smitten, too, by the look of him, for his eyes had followed Miss McGill's every movement with a dog-like devotion. Maybe that was not what she needed – or wanted. If he, Guy, were to . . .

Guy stood up and, determined to distract his thoughts, went over to one of the filing cabinets. He would write that letter to the bank Mr Wisson had outlined. There was a new, pretty blond typist who would take his dictation. Miss Poppy Brown had arrived as a temporary replacement for Mr Wisson's regular secretary, Miss Bird. The middle-aged spinster had been employed by him for a good many years and, fanatically devoted to her employer, she was both maternal and possessive towards him. She was also extremely jealous of the position he, Guy, had been given as Mr Wisson's personal assistant and resisted any attempt he'd made to be friendly. Miss Poppy Brown was taking dictation and managing the typing while the woman was in hospital having an operation – the details of which were unknown until the youthful, outspoken Poppy announced with a grin that "the old trout had a hysterectomy but being the age she is, she can't have children anyway, even if she did find a husband, so it really doesn't matter!"

Poppy had made it abundantly clear that she would enjoy a flirtation with him. Her shoes had flatteringly high heels and she wore a bright scarlet lipstick which obviously she fancied, but which did not appeal to him despite the fact that she had a very pretty mouth!

At their very first encounter, the girl had suggested he call her by her Christian name, and he'd been obliged to explain that their employer preferred his staff to observe the formalities. He might have thought her both pretty and amusing had his thoughts not been so preoccupied with Miss Zandra McGill.

With a sigh, Guy tried once more to put Zandra out of his mind. The letter he must dictate concerned the purchase of Lord Oliver Rochford's airline. Mr Wisson had given no prior indication that he was about to become involved in this line of business until his announcement that he'd reached agreement with Lord Rochford to buy out his shares in the company – a controlling interest. But then, of course, Wisson would not have been interested in any project where he was not in some way or another in control. Guy had gathered that the unfortunate Rochford family were casualties of the recent financial collapse in the United States, and were in a bad way.

Guy's hazel eyes narrowed as an unpleasant thought struck him. Could Miss McGill be marrying his boss for his money? Whoever Anthony Wisson married they would be infinitely the richer. Was this why she had turned a blind eye to the big difference in their ages? And was he, Guy, being absurdly sentimental in believing that men and women should not get married unless they loved one another? His own parents had been devoted, and his mother had never really recovered from the shock of receiving that hateful yellow telegram in the first year of the war announcing his father's death. She had never been physically very strong, and in the past sixteen years, she'd been more or less an invalid, never leaving her bungalow, and seeing no one but her cook-housekeeper and charlady and, when he could get away, himself. There were times when he resented having to spend so many of his free weekends cooped up in those small rooms listening patiently to her reminiscences about his childhood and his father. Then he would feel guilty for wishing he were not so encumbered and could be elsewhere enjoying the company of some young, jolly girls on the tennis court or at a dance. The fact that he was financially handicapped by his mother had not bothered him too much until . . . he had fallen so hopelessly in love with the girl he would like to marry!

Everything I think about now comes full circle back to *her*, he told himself; and it is high time I took myself in hand and stopped behaving like a romantic fool!

Determinedly, he pressed the new electric bell on his desk top to summon Miss Poppy Brown to his office.

Chapter 3

June 1930

As the *femme de chambre* drew back the curtains and the room flooded with sunlight, Zandra's eyes opened. Slowly, like a cat, she stretched her limbs full length in the big double bed and yawned.

"Bonjour, madame! Monsieur m'a demandé de vous réveiller. Le petit déjeuner arrive tout de suite!"

Zandra nodded her thanks and still drowsy, watched as the girl picked up the heap of her discarded evening clothes and tidied them away before quietly leaving the room. She looked at the travelling clock on her bedside table. It was half-past eight – a half-hour earlier than was usual. For the past three mornings, Anthony had not ordered breakfast until they'd woken and then he had made love to her before he'd rung for the floor waiter. Why hadn't he woken her himself today instead of ordering the maid to do so? Perhaps, she thought, he had gone out for an early morning walk.

She glanced at the empty space beside her, and smiled as she yawned a second time. She was still sleepy, for it had been three in the morning before they'd returned from the Parisian night-club to which Anthony had taken her after the theatre;

and a further hour or more before, satiated with love, they had fallen asleep.

Slowly, she sat up and pulled the new delicate chiffon bedjacket around her shoulders. She was aware now that her body ached and her breasts and groin were hot and sore. Love-making, she thought with a contented sigh, was the most wonderful experience anyone could possibly enjoy – yet it was truly exhausting! It had come as a total surprise – not just because of the lovely things Anthony did to her, but because she'd never believed she could surrender herself so totally to another's domination. From the very first time when the loss of her virginity had proved painful, she had nevertheless wanted Anthony to go on invading her, taking possession of her, mastering her. If he had become her demanding teacher, she was no less his ardent pupil. She had never imagined on her wedding day that this was what being a wife meant! Now she was in no doubt whatever that she was really and truly in love and that Anthony loved her with the same passionate fervour. She had become his willing slave.

Her thoughts were interrupted by sounds from the adjoining room. They had a suite at the Hôtel Meurice, and as Anthony did not care to eat breakfast in bed, the floor waiters laid a table in the salon with a continental *café complet* for her and a full English breakfast for her husband.

Anthony put his head round the bedroom door.

"Don't bother to dress, Zandra!" he said, staring at her so intently that she blushed. "Wear the new négligé I bought for you yesterday. It's very becoming!"

As he closed the door, Zandra sprang out of bed and quickly ran a comb through her sleek, page-boy bob. Slipping her arms into the apricot satin Lanvin négligé Anthony favoured, she hurried into the salon. To her surprise, she saw that he was already sitting at the table fully dressed. So there was to be no love-making this morning, she thought, as she stooped to kiss the top of his head before taking her place opposite him.

"I left you to sleep as long as possible, my dear!" he said as he buttered a slice of toast and dipped it into his boiled egg. "I am afraid I shall not, after all, be able to take you to visit your aunt and uncle as we had planned. I had a telephone call from Bristow this morning and I must attend to some urgent business."

He was only half aware of the look of disappointment on Zandra's face as the thought of being able to pull off yet another highly profitable deal sent a shiver of excitement through him not unlike that of sexual anticipation. Unconsciously, he grasped his right wrist where his pulse throbbed beneath his watch strap. It was so easy to recall the first time he had felt this same sensation of violent elation. It was in Elerson's study that first term at boarding school.

"Lazy little squirt! How much longer am I going to have to wait for my toast? You're pathetic, Poleski – a useless little squirt! Now get a move on!"

At home, his mother waited on him hand and foot, called him her princeling . . . was his slave. Now he was Elerson's slave, constantly at his beck and call . . . make the toast, clean his shoes, wash his dirty teacups, fetch and carry . . . and worst of all, endure in silence his humiliating insults; but suddenly, without warning, he felt a swift surge of excitement. A way to get a little of his own back had occurred to him. On the floor beside him lay one of Elerson's exercise books – his Latin translation prep completed for next day's lesson. He waited until the toasting fork was white hot and then laid it down on the open pages. Seconds later, as he had known they would, they burst into flame.

"For God's sake, idiot! My book's alight . . . there, beside you. Don't just stand there. Get some water . . . stamp it out."

"I'm dreadfully sorry, Elerson! It was an accident . . . I didn't see it."

Elerson's face was distorted with anger.

"You blithering fool! It's ruined. I'll have to do the whole thing again. First you burn the toast and now . . . now this! I'm just about fed to the teeth with you. Accident my foot! Even you, stupid as you are, must have known that fork was red hot. Or perhaps you're too asinine to realize it! Well, it's time you learned a lesson, Poleski—"

With the charred remnants of the book scattered around his feet, Elerson knelt down, held the toasting fork in front of the gas fire for a few moments and then, his face flushed with temper, he thrust it against his, Antoni's, right wrist. As he screamed in pain, Elerson dropped the fork and regarded the two scarlet weals with alarm.

"I say, old chap, I didn't mean to hurt you . . . I mean, only a bit. Look, I'm sorry. You'd better go and see Matron and get her to put something on it – say the fork slipped or something. Come on now, get up and go to the San. And for goodness' sake, stop yelling like that. Someone might hear you!"

Elerson was frightened – more frightened than he was. He knew then that there was now yet another way of getting his own back. When he told Matron what Elerson had done to him she'd be bound to tell the housemaster and Elerson would be in trouble. He might even be expelled! The thrill of excitement that coursed through him far outweighed the pain of his seared wrist.

But it didn't work out the way he hoped. Matron did indeed tell the housemaster. He came up to the San to "talk it over, man to man". "It's up to you, Wisniowiecki. If I punish Elerson (and I don't for one moment deny that he certainly deserves it), then he'll know you reported him. As a new boy, perhaps you may not be aware of the attitude we have here to 'sneaks'. There isn't a boy in the school who'd speak to you; you'd be put in Coventry, ostracized. Think it over, Wisniowiecki. You can stay here in the San tonight and come and see me in my study after breakfast tomorrow morning. Right?"

It was very far from right, but he recognized the fact that this was not after all the best way to take revenge on Elerson. He'd think of another way . . . and sooner or later, when he was more familiar with this hateful school's practices, he would think of something. For the moment, Elerson would have to treat him more civilly for he owed him a favour – a big one – for not having sneaked. At long last, he had his first, small but satisfying, taste of power.

"Oh, Anthony, is your business that urgent? Does it *have* to be done today? Couldn't it wait?" Zandra's voice was husky with disappointment. His reply was emphatic.

"I'm afraid it's unavoidable, my dear!"

Zandra paused in the act of pouring coffee from the big, silver jug.

"Tante Silvie and Uncle Pelham are going to be dreadfully disappointed. And so am I. They barely had a chance to speak to you at the wedding and . . . well, I wanted them to get to know you better so they'd understand why I'm so madly in love with you!"

A brief smile crossed Anthony's handsome face as he looked at his wife's flushed cheeks.

"There will be other occasions, my dear!"

Zandra bit her lip.

"It's so late to cancel the luncheon, darling!" she said. "They've invited lots of their friends and—"

"I am sorry, but this is important," Anthony interrupted her protest. There was a slight edge to his voice. "I'll ask the hall porter to have a basket of flowers sent round to your aunt with my apologies, and I am sure you will make my excuses most charmingly. Now, drink your coffee like a good girl before it gets cold."

Zandra bit her lip. It was on the tip of her tongue to remind Anthony that this was her honeymoon and surely not the time to be bothering about his stupid business affairs; but he had been so sweet and adoring and attentive these past few days, it seemed churlish to complain if he wanted an hour or two for his own activities. Nevertheless, they *were* on their honeymoon!

"Couldn't you get away in time for lunch, darling? They never eat before two and—"

"I shall be away all day!" Anthony's voice was sharp – sharper than Zandra had ever heard it. It was bordering on a note of irritation – and she couldn't bear it if he was suddenly wondering whether he had acquired a nagging wife.

Impulsively, she left her seat and hurried round to his side of the table.

"Forgive me, darling! It's just that I hate the thought of us being apart – even for a few hours. I love you so much!"

To her relief, her husband's expression softened and he turned to put his arms around her waist. There was a look in his eyes which she was just beginning to recognize. Instinctively, she pressed herself closer to him and heard the intake of his breath as her breasts touched his cheek.

"I wish I *could* stay with you!" he said, his voice husky. He reached up and touched one of her nipples which hardened instantly. "You do have the most beautiful body!" he murmured, burying his face against her and enclosing her waist with his hands. "I shall take you to Schiaparelli tomorrow and you can buy some new dresses . . . something to show off your lovely figure . . . and some pearls, too, to match that perfect skin of yours."

Zandra felt herself expanding beneath his praise like the petals of a flower opening in the sunshine. How romantic Anthony was! Even more so than Léon had been – but then she had never enjoyed such intimacies with Léon. Thank heaven she had never allowed more than a kiss, for the mere thought of sharing such a personal and private experience as love-making with anyone but Anthony was totally abhorrent.

"I love you!" she whispered. "I love you so very much, my darling!"

"And I love you!" he replied; but he released his hold on her and directed her attention once more to her cooling coffee and crisp golden croissants.

"I must leave in five minutes!" he announced. "If I'm late, I shall miss my train!"

"Your train!" Zandra echoed. "But where are you going, Anthony? Isn't your business meeting in Paris?"

"Hardly, if I am taking a train!"

Anthony's voice had lost its gentleness and was now bordering on the sarcastic. Instantly, Zandra felt stupid – and, in an unexpected flash, resentful. He had no right to humiliate her. Surely he realized how hurtful it was to be verbally dismissed as if one was a silly schoolgirl? Well, she would ask no more questions. He could go off to his wretched meeting wherever it might be, and

45

she hoped it would be every bit as dull as she imagined. Not that she knew what her husband's business was exactly. Oliver had told her Anthony had fingers in "lots of different pies" but that in the main it had to do with munitions. Not even Oliver seemed quite sure what he did – only that he had become a very wealthy man doing it!

When Anthony kissed her goodbye, however, her mood changed once more. He looked so amazingly handsome, standing in the doorway in his well-cut, dark suit, holding his grey bowler hat and doeskin gloves, that her body, if not her heart, betrayed her. She could not stay indifferent to him.

"Come back as quickly as you can, won't you?" she pleaded. "I shall miss you!"

He detached himself gently, but firmly, from her embrace and with a last wave of his hand, was gone. Dejectedly, Zandra returned to the breakfast table and stared at Anthony's empty chair. She felt suddenly deeply depressed; but almost at once, chided herself for behaving so stupidly. Doubtless the tears which now threatened were due to tiredness, she told herself, for it was not even as if they'd had a quarrel. One thing she would not allow herself to be was possessive; yet somehow in the three short days of her marriage, that was exactly what she had become.

How had it happened? She, who had always been so independent, so totally in control of herself in the presence of one of her admirers, was now close to tears because momentarily Anthony had withdrawn his approval of her! It was quite ridiculous! She had thought herself in love before her wedding but now . . . now she was aware that loving a man as much as she did at this moment was a kind of bondage. She had become a slave to her husband's touch, the look in his eyes, his voice. Most of all she had become addicted to his love-making. However tired she was, however relaxed her body, he had but to take her in his arms and start to caress her for her whole being to ignite with a trembling longing – a desire which grew to fever pitch until the moment he chose to assuage it.

Lying on the verge of sleep, or in her bath – even seated in a taxi-cab beside him – she would remember those intimacies and her cheeks would flame. She remembered, too, how serious Aunt Willow had been when she cautioned her against marriage to the wrong man. It shocked her slightly to realize that her aunt had known very well what married life was like and it was disturbing to think that her aunt and Uncle Toby might have shared the same experiences as she now shared with Anthony. She supposed older people no longer did such things; but Robin, her cousin Lucy's youngest child, was only seven, and now that she knew this was the way babies were conceived, it meant that Lucy and Alexis were still making love! Lucy, at thirty-six, was about the same age as Anthony, but Alexis was nearly fifty!

With a sigh, Zandra returned to the breakfast table and poured herself a last cup of coffee. Recalling the revelations of her wedding night had reminded her that Anthony had said that he would ensure she did not have a child for some years to come. She must grow up first, he'd told her. Besides, he wanted her all to himself and free to travel with him when necessary without the worry of leaving a nanny and baby at home. Since there was nothing in the whole world Zandra herself wanted more now than to be with him, she was happy to set aside for the moment the thought of presenting him with a son or daughter. She could remember how unsightly poor Jane had become when she was carrying Giles. Until her marriage, she had never paid much attention to her figure but now, seeing the effect it had upon her husband when, as he insisted, she lay naked before his gaze, she wanted always to stay as desirable to him as he now found her.

Having thought herself into a happier frame of mind, Zandra rang for her maid, and after a leisurely bath in the luxurious bathroom, her body powdered and scented, she put on one of her new day dresses. It had white buttons decorating each shoulder and fastening the cuffs and pocket flaps. Pleased with her appearance, she perched a white pill-box hat on top of her head and went out into the June sunshine where the taxi she had ordered was waiting for her.

She wanted to do some shopping before going to her aunt's house in the Rue d'Artois, for it was her intention to buy a surprise present for Anthony. He had bought her so many beautiful things these past few days; more clothes than she could ever expect to wear, and the accessories to go with them; jewellery, flowers, even an oil painting she had admired. Since she had very little money of her own, she would not be able to buy anything of any value, so she planned to choose something for Anthony that would be special in other ways.

On the advice of her friendly taxi driver, she went to Cartier's where an admiring male assistant made numerous suggestions, among them one which seemed to Zandra to be exactly right. It was a Venetian glass paperweight coloured in red, white and turquoise. Not only was it very pretty but it would have a functional use in Anthony's office; and each time he saw it, he would think of her.

Happy with her purchase, Zandra decided to walk to the Rue d'Artois. As she strode down the Faubourg St Honoré and crossed into Rue La Boétie, she could not help but notice the admiring glances of the men seated at the pavement tables outside the cafés drinking their midmorning coffee. She was unaware that it was her glowing, happy face and the youthful joyous movements of her body which attracted their attention. Innocently, she supposed both they and the women whose glances lingered as she passed by, were admiring her new dress and hat – the very latest Verveine fashions. All her life, she thought, she had envied her brother, Jamie, for having been born a boy; but now she was relishing her femininity for without it Anthony might never have fallen in love with her!

Silvie and Pelham, two of Zandra's favourite relatives, welcomed her with amused smiles.

"I can see that married life suits you, *chérie*," Silvie said as she accompanied her niece upstairs to remove her hat and gloves.

"Your uncle and I are disappointed that Anthony could not come after all, but it is really you we wished to see. No need to ask if you are happy!"

"Wonderfully so!" Zandra replied with a smile as she straightened her skirt before following her aunt downstairs.

"So he is a good lover, your handsome husband!" Silvie remarked, noting the blush which spread over Zandra's cheeks. "You are fortunate in your choice. Your Aunt Willow was afraid your precious Anthony was too old for you; but it would seem you have chosen wisely."

"But I didn't 'choose' Anthony – he chose me!" Zandra protested with a smile. "The first time I saw him, I thought how attractive he was, but all I wanted then was a job of some kind at the airfield! It didn't occur to me he might be seriously interested in a girl like me. I still don't know why he chose me out of all the women he could have married."

Silvie Rochford remained silent and, as they walked towards the big salon, Zandra could not see the slight frown which creased her aunt's forehead. It was not for her, Silvie was thinking, to dim this radiance; nor, indeed, to add to Willow's and Toby's worries; yet Pelham had only this week discovered some disturbing information about Anthony Wisson. Had Zandra's wedding not already taken place, Pelham would certainly have told Toby; but there seemed little point in doing so now that the marriage was a *fait accompli*.

When Pelham had first learned of Zandra's engagement, he recalled meeting an Englishman in the war whose civilian occupation was that of housemaster at the minor public school Wisson had attended. The man was now in his eighties and retired, but being a bachelor with no family to interest him, he kept in touch with many of his former pupils. Pelham had thought, therefore, that it might amuse the old fellow to learn that his niece was about to marry one of them; so he had written to tell him. He had replied to Pelham saying that he had no recollection of a boy called Wisson. Could he have attended the school after his own retirement, he had enquired? Pelham had not thought the matter worth pursuing, and had given it no further thought until last week when a further, much longer letter from the old housemaster had arrived from England. He had immediately shown it to Silvie. He had written:

It is not very agreeable news, my dear chap, but I feel it my duty to pass it on to you in case you should decide that further enquiries into Mr Wisson's character are necessary. The facts are these: in 1906, a new boy arrived at the school by the name of Antoni Wisniowiecki, the son of a Polish émigré. He was a quiet, extremely intelligent boy with a particular bent for mathematics.

Unfortunately, because of his above average abilities and, I suppose, his unpronounceable surname, he came in for a great deal of ragging. The fact that his father dressed somewhat oddly, spoke in a very foreign accent and was "different" from the norm, could not have helped matters; nor, indeed, did the fact that he kept Wisniowiecki extremely short of funds despite the fact that he can't have been too badly off – always paid the school fees promptly! New money, of course. At the time, these facts were not known to the masters. A certain amount of bullying was in any case to be expected, as no doubt you yourself will recall!

However, by the time Wisniowiecki reached the senior school, he had acquired an extraordinary popularity – particularly strange in the light of the fact that he was a known "swot". That was when he was linked with an unfortunate tragedy involving a senior boy who took his own life. At the inquest it transpired that the boy had been seriously worried about his forthcoming exams. It was later discovered that he owed money to Wisniowiecki which he was unable to repay, and that this may have been a contributory factor.

Wisniowiecki had been playing the stock market – with considerable success. The boys were using their pocket-money

– often borrowing from Wisniowiecki himself – to provide the budding financier with the necessary capital. He had not only been taking a cut but had gained popularity of a sort.

In the light of what Wisniowiecki had endured at the hands of his fellows, one cannot altogether blame the boy, who had a very promising academic future. Of course his illicit activities were stopped immediately.

There was, of course, no proof that they had any bearing on the boy's suicide and the headmaster, believing that Wisniowiecki had learned a salutary lesson at an age when it must have come as a nasty shock to know that he might have been partially responsible for a schoolfellow's death, allowed him to remain at the school and decided not to take the matter further.

Apleton, the headmaster, remembered him well and recalled seeing in a newspaper some years afterwards that at the age of twenty-one, Wisniowiecki had changed his name by Deed Poll to Wisson. That was a good many years ago now, and you may well think that that youthful transgression is best forgotten. From what you told me, Wisson has done very well for himself since his schooldays and is a respected member of society.

The old housemaster's letter had worried Silvie far more than it did Pelham who'd spent the rest of the morning recalling some of his own schoolboy pranks, and considered it would be quite wrong for either of them to pass judgement on Wisson's past transgressions without knowing a great many more of the facts. The housemaster had not indicated that Wisson had put pressure on the boy who'd welshed on his debts. If that had happened, they would have expelled him! They should take the housemaster's advice and think no more about it.

Now that Silvie had seen for herself how aglow with happiness her niece was, she was inclined to agree with Pelham that the episode was no more than a youthful transgression. Doubtless there were skeletons in every family's cupboard and certainly there were several very dubious ones both past and present in the Rochford family.

She linked her arm now through Zandra's and said: "Anthony is a very fortunate man to have you for his wife, *chérie*. You come from a centuries-old family, and it will do Anthony no harm to be married to a Rochford. No doubt it will open many doors for him socially."

Zandra regarded her aunt with a look of surprise.

"But Anthony already knows all kinds of important people. You must have met some of them at my wedding!"

"Well, yes!" Silvie said awkwardly. "But they were moneyed people, Zee-Zee – politicians, industrialists, businessmen and their wives. There is still a level of Society who might not consider including him in their circle of friends."

Zandra frowned.

"Those sort of people are such snobs, Tante Silvie. Just because Anthony's father was Polish—"

"My dearest, that has nothing to do with it. It is a matter of breeding; and they are not all snobs, you know. There are many very charming people amongst the Rochford neighbours. Consider, for example, Sir John and Lady Barratt. You know how fond you children have always been of their youngest daughter, Eleanor. If I am not mistaken, they allowed her to marry a nondescript tea-planter who took her back with him to Ceylon. That does not sound very snobbish to me!"

Zandra smiled.

"You are quite right, of course! But as for it being advantageous for Anthony to marry a Rochford, as you put it, what about the enormous advantages he has provided for our family? You know, don't you, that Oliver won't have to sell the house, after all? Anthony has bought over one and a half thousand acres which include Havorhurst village, and the deeds have been drawn up in my name, so Oliver didn't mind a bit handing over part of his heritage since it was to me. He knows I shall leave it to Giles. Everything is to go on exactly as it was before we lost our money. And Oliver says Anthony hasn't once interfered with anything at Sky-Ways and they rarely see him except when he needs to be flown somewhere."

Silvie nodded.

"I had a letter from your Aunt Willow telling me all this. I am so happy for you all. There have been changes in our branch of the family, too. We have found a buyer for the Château d'Orbais, and at the same time, we have found a delightful house in the south-west, not very far from Biarritz. It is smaller than the Château d'Orbais but will make an ideal country retreat for us, and I think your uncle will go ahead with the purchase. We will be going down there next week but I hope before we leave we shall be able to arrange a lunch or dinner with you and Anthony in lieu of today."

"But of course!" Zandra said happily. "We are here for another two weeks, Tante Silvie. I'll telephone you this evening from the hotel to arrange a day, shall I?"

It was, however, quite late into the evening before Anthony returned to the hotel. Zandra, who had been awaiting him for the past four hours with increasing impatience mingled with anxiety, threw herself into his arms as he came into the bedroom.

"I've been so worried! I thought some dreadful accident must have befallen you!" she said. "It's nearly ten o'clock, darling, and—"

"My dear girl, there is really no need to make such a drama of this!" Anthony broke in, his face softening into a smile. "My business took a little longer than I had expected – that's all! So I was obliged to catch a later train."

"But you could have telephoned me, Anthony. Surely you realized I would be worried?" Zandra protested. "I'm hungry, too, but I didn't want to go down to dinner without you."

"It didn't occur to me to telephone you!" Anthony said, detaching himself from her embrace. "I knew you were perfectly safe here in the hotel – and since it's so late, I suggest you allow

53

me to get changed so that we can go down to dinner now as you're so hungry!"

He rang the bell for the manservant the hotel had allotted him and disappeared into his dressing-room. Zandra, who had been fully dressed for the past two hours, subsided into a chair. Two differing sets of emotions were at war within her: one, relief that Anthony was safely back with her; the other, that he seemed to have no idea how upsetting it was to be kept waiting in suspense for so long. It was not simply upsetting, she told herself, but irritating, when he could so easily have telephoned to tell her he had been delayed! Then she might have settled down to read a book, or make use of the time having her hair washed and dressed by the hotel *coiffeur,* or she might have telephoned one of the friends she'd made in Paris during her sojourn with Tante Silvie eighteen months ago.

Was she making an unnecessary "drama" of the incident? she asked herself as she listened to the sound of Anthony's voice next door. She could not accuse him of behaving inconsiderately towards her on any other occasion for, until today, he'd been the soul of attentiveness. A husband – even on his honeymoon – could not be expected to consider his wife's wishes every moment of the day – and night! The very last thing she desired was for Anthony to start thinking of her as a nuisance!

Tonight, at dinner, she wouldn't mention it again, she told herself firmly. She would regale him with pleasant anecdotes of her enjoyable lunch with her aunt and uncle and their friends; discuss with him when he would like to accompany her there for either lunch or dinner; plan what they would do the following day. Then, when they retired for the night, Anthony would congratulate himself for having married so understanding and sympathetic a wife, and make love to her as ardently as was his custom.

It seemed that the same intent was in Anthony's mind when later that night he dismissed his servant and joined her in the big double bed. Her heart beating fiercely, her body alight with anticipation, Zandra inclined her body towards him as he enfolded her in his arms. He looked down into her flushed face and gave a deep sigh.

"It has been a long and exacting day," he said, "and I had supposed that I would be too tired tonight to enjoy possessing you; but you bewitch me, Zandra, in a way I can't explain. I suppose some might say that you're not, strictly speaking, as beautiful as some of your débutante friends; and yet there is something about you which other women don't have and which I find irresistible. Moreover, I'm beginning to believe you married me for love rather than my money!"

"How can you say that!" Zandra cried. For a moment she'd thought he was serious rather than teasing her. "I've never loved anyone before you and I can't imagine ever loving anyone else. And I don't care if I'm not beautiful so long as you want me. We're going to be terribly happy together always, aren't we, Anthony?" She gave a soft laugh. "I think I bored everyone stupid at Tante Silvie's luncheon telling them how marvellous you are. They're all dying to meet you, darling; and that reminds me, I've forgotten to telephone Tante Silvie. I promised we'd make another date this week to go there."

"Not this week, Zandra. We're leaving Paris tomorrow."

Anthony's voice was husky and his hands were moving down her body, following the curve of her hips. With an effort, Zandra ignored the effect this was having on her and moved slightly away from him so that she could see his face.

"Leaving tomorrow? But I thought we were staying here for a fortnight. We were going to see Maurice Chevalier tomorrow at the Empire—"

Anthony's hands drew her back against him. She could feel the tenseness of his body.

"I'm taking you to Cannes!" he said quietly. "You'll like it better there, Zandra. I've booked a suite for us at the Carlton. In case you aren't aware of it, it's a very fashionable hotel and I think it will amuse you to see some of the people who go there."

Zandra bit her lip. Anthony had booked rooms for them and the decision to go was made – without his consulting her. He might at least have asked if she wished to go!

"I don't need other people to 'amuse' me, Anthony. This is our honeymoon and the only person I want to be with is you!"

"Well, I am not suggesting I go to Cannes without you!" Anthony's tone was vaguely patronizing, or so it seemed to Zandra.

"Of course not! I may be a lot younger than you and a lot less clever, but I'm not stupid!" she said sharply, easing herself purposefully away from Anthony's body. "It's just that you might have asked me if I wanted to go – so suddenly, I mean. I promised Tante Silvie that we—"

"Zandra, this is my honeymoon as well as yours, and I don't see any necessity for it to include your relations. And if we are to talk about consultation, you should have enquired what *I* wanted before you committed us."

"I haven't committed us!" Zandra cried. "But you have committed me!"

There was a brief moment of silence before Anthony spoke. Then he said quietly: "I had hoped to give you a pleasant surprise, Zandra – to make up for my neglect of you today, but I see my gesture has not been appreciated. I do, however, think we should clear up one small matter – namely that although I am your husband and may have vowed to 'cherish' you, that does not mean that I abdicated my right to be master in my own home. You, on the other hand, vowed to 'obey' me, yet it seems you are choosing to be contrary even on a matter that was supposed to have pleased you."

The coldness of his tone upset Zandra far more than his words, although they, too, distressed her. The very last thing in the world she wanted was to quarrel with the man she loved; and it was only a few hours since she had determined on no account to do so! She could see now that from Anthony's point of view, she must seem ungrateful, churlish, besides which, she did not really object in the least to going to Cannes. She had never been there, although she knew very well that it was a favourite playground for the world's wealthy and famous people. To go there with Anthony might be enormously exciting.

Almost as if he could read her mind, Anthony broke the silence.

"Must we quarrel, Zandra? And on so trivial a matter?"

He was quite right – it was trivial! Zandra told herself as she held out her arms to him. What did anything matter so long as they loved one another? And there was no doubt in her mind that she loved him; loved every part of his strong, male body and the miraculous if astonishing way in which it responded to her own needs. How magical his hands were, bringing every part of her to life; to a desperate yearning for fulfilment! Soon now he would possess her totally, merging his body with hers so that they became one person.

"I love you, Anthony!" she whispered, and then all thought ceased as he covered her body with his own and she waited breathlessly for the pleasure only he could bring.

Chapter 4

June 1930

"You are looking very well, Mrs Wisson. Are you enjoying Cannes?"

Zandra smiled at the young man seated opposite her on the crowded terrace of the Carlton Hotel.

"It is quite an experience, isn't it?" she replied. "So many famous people and the women have such gorgeous clothes! And please, won't you call me Zandra? Mrs Wisson sounds dreadfully formal!"

Guy Bristow looked down at his cocktail glass and pretended an interest in its contents. He was unsure how to react to her suggestion; how would his boss feel about him addressing his wife by her Christian name? He decided to be frank.

"If your husband has no objection, I'd be delighted. And please call me Guy!"

He felt his heart lurch as the girl opposite him gave the sudden little laugh which he had noticed before was peculiarly hers. It was almost a childish giggle and yet it was throaty and always accompanied a delightful sparkle in her eyes. Since his arrival at the hotel two hours earlier, he had found it practically impossible to keep his eyes away from her. Marriage obviously suited her, he told himself, for she was radiant and there was a glow emanating from her which he'd not seen before.

God, how he envied Wisson! This girl in her white silk, back-less evening dress was more than a match for any of the smart women milling around whom she seemed to admire. If *he* had been on his honeymoon with her, he would not have left her for a single moment – and certainly not to attend to business affairs. Clearly there was some big deal pending and knowing his employer, it would have priority. By the expression on Zandra's bright, happy face, she did not seem concerned.

His mind wandered back to the evening when Wisson had telephoned him from Paris. As usual, he had demanded a résumé, of the day's Information Sheet. Providing it was one of Guy's regular tasks, and it entailed gathering as much informa-tion as he could on the activities of fifty or so men whose names his employer had listed. On hearing that the elderly financier Sir Basil Zaharoff was enjoying a brief holiday in Cannes, Wisson had sounded – insofar as he ever raised his voice – unusually excited as he barked out his orders. He would leave first thing in the morning for Cannes, he said. Guy was to get there as soon as he could, taking with him the blue PENDING – SECRET file that was in the safe. He must get one of the Sky-Ways pilots to fly him down to Nice – it would be quicker than the train. The file was not to leave Guy's hands at any time. He was to pack suffi-cient clothes of an appropriate nature for wearing at the Carlton to last him at least three days. Whatever Guy was engaged on at the moment could wait.

To travel was one of the perks of working for Anthony Wisson which most appealed to Guy; and on any other occasion he would have jumped at such an opportunity. This time, he had uneasy reservations, for he did not see how he could avoid the company of Zandra Wisson. Yet at the same time, he longed to see Zandra again, however tormenting that might be. Now, he realized, he was not to be given the opportunity to avoid his boss' wife. On the contrary, it was Wisson's intention that he, Guy, should spend a great deal of time with her whilst he pursued his current business interests. If it was not to act as escort to Mrs

Wisson, apart from bringing out the file Wisson so urgently required, there was little purpose in him, Guy, remaining here.

"Give my wife cocktails on the terrace and keep her amused as best you can," Wisson had said when Guy had checked into the hotel and announced his arrival. "I'll try to be down in time for dinner – in which case you can make yourself scarce; but if I am not there by nine o'clock, you are to dine with my wife in the restaurant. Make any explanation you think fit but whatever happens, I don't wish to be interrupted. Is that understood?"

Zandra, Guy saw, was now gazing out to sea, watching the sailing boats and the smart white yachts as they made their way into the harbour.

"It's all so pretty, isn't it?" she said. "Anthony has promised to take me to Grasse tomorrow – it's a village in the hills about an hour's drive from here. The hall porter told me that the flowers there are quite beautiful. They grow them to make scent, but there are lots of wild flowers, too. I suppose I am really a country girl at heart, and trees and flowers are important to me. I spent nearly all my childhood in the country at Rochford."

"I saw something of the lovely gardens there at your wedding reception," Guy said simply. "You must have had an idyllic childhood."

Zandra smiled.

"I suppose it was – although Aunt Willow would probably tell you that I was more often in trouble than out of it. When I was quite small, my Uncle Toby described me as 'a disruptive influence', but would never explain what that meant! Mostly it was leading my young brother, Jamie, into mischief; so I was finally packed off to boarding school. I missed Rochford terribly. Of course, Anthony and I will be living in London because of his work, but I suppose I will get used to it eventually. I expect you know he has bought a house for us in Eaton Terrace? It'll be great fun doing it up. My cousin, Lucy, is going to help me – and she has perfect taste. Did you meet her at the reception?"

Guy nodded, grateful that Zandra felt sufficiently at ease with him to converse so naturally and thus free him from the effort of making conversation. The effect she had upon him was to make him ridiculously tongue-tied.

"I'm sure I must have met your cousin – but there were so many strange faces I can't be completely certain. Mrs Zemski, isn't it?"

Zandra gave another of her little laughs.

"Well, actually she is Countess Zemski. She became a countess when she married Alexis. You wouldn't forget Lucy if you'd been introduced to her. She's quite stunningly pretty. She has pale gold hair and her eyes are almost a violet blue. She's great fun, too. You'd never think she was practically middle-aged. She doesn't look anywhere near her mid-thirties."

Middle-aged! Guy thought. Was that how this girl thought of her husband? Anthony Wisson was two years short of forty! Did the big gap in their ages not concern her? She, herself, was so very young! Perhaps immature was a better description. Despite the new sophistication of her appearance, her naturalness seemed at times childlike.

As if to compound his opinion, Zandra now drew his attention to a group of people who had come out onto the terrace.

"That's Elsa Maxwell!" she whispered. "Anthony says she's the best-known gossip writer in America and Europe, and that she's known as 'The Queen of Pleasure' because of the divine parties she gives. He said if she spoke to me, I am not to make friends with her, but he wouldn't say why! And look, Guy, isn't that the playwright, Noel Coward? Anthony isn't really interested in literary people, though, but I suppose you know that." She paused as her eyes searched the terrace. "I wonder where Anthony is! Did he say how long he would be? I'm getting frightfully hungry!"

"Let's have another cocktail, shall we?" Guy prevaricated as he lifted a hand to beckon a passing waiter. "It's still quite early and Mr Wisson did intimate he could be detained for some time."

Zandra sighed.

"I can't think what he can be talking about to that old man!"

she said. "Or why he was so anxious to meet him. Perhaps you know why, Mr Bristow – Guy, I mean! We ran into him yesterday soon after we arrived. He's a foreigner, I think. Anthony said it was an amazing piece of luck running into him here."

Guy frowned thoughtfully. It was hardly a matter of luck, he thought, since it was the knowledge that Sir Basil Zaharoff was in Cannes that had prompted his employer's sudden departure from Paris.

"Actually, I knew his great-niece, Bunnie – we were at school together – and she's here on holiday with him," Zandra prattled on. "To be quite honest, we were never friends but Anthony insisted I invite her and her uncle for drinks, and so that's how Anthony got involved with him. I suppose it must be important – the business meeting this evening, I mean – if Anthony had to bring you all the way out here to the South of France, just to hand over some papers! Do you know what it's all about, Guy?"

Guy shook his head, glad that he could deny any knowledge of his employer's current interests. He had been expressly forbidden ever to open one of Mr Wisson's SECRET files which were always kept locked in the safe to which only he and his employer had keys. It was a matter of honour not to abuse his employer's trust, and although there had been opportunities, as on this occasion, when he could have read the files, Guy had never considered doing so.

"Only that Sir Basil is an immensely wealthy international financier and politician who is, I believe, involved in ship build-ing, oil and munition plants among other things." He gave a wry smile. "Your husband calls me his Personal Assistant," he added, "but if the truth were told, I'm really only a personal secretary. I arrange his journeys, appointments, business meetings – that kind of thing."

Zandra laughed.

"And make sure he is not bothered by unnecessary telephone calls!" she said, for there had been many occasions prior to her marriage when Guy had answered her calls to Anthony and told her his employer was too busy to speak to her. "There were moments when I began to think you were trying to come between Anthony and me, although I couldn't think why you should want to protect him from me!"

For a fraction of a second, Guy's hazel eyes narrowed uneasily. She was not, after all, so far from the truth. If wishes were horses, then he would have wanted to come between them – only it would have been Zandra whom he had longed to protect. It was not simply a question of desiring her for himself. If he had thought she might be happy with Anthony Wisson, he would not have felt so deeply averse to their marriage. But try as he had, he could not see how so intensely busy and ambitious a man as his employer could possibly find time to give a young, intelligent girl the kind of companionship she needed. Wisson spent at least three months in every year abroad – at meetings from which Guy himself was excluded. His personal diary was so filled with business lunches and dinners that Guy was sometimes unable to make appointments for him for weeks ahead.

There had, of course, been concessions made in this rigorous schedule when Zandra McGill had arrived on the scene. Time had been allotted for visits to Rochford; for attendances at the social functions appertaining to Zandra's Season. As her fiancé, Wisson had been obliged to escort her to Ascot, Covent Garden, the Derby, the Royal Military Tournament, as well as to numerous parties. For once, work had had to take second place.

How long would this last, Guy had asked himself as he'd watched, with an aching heart, Zandra in her bridal gown walking back down the aisle of Havorhurst church as Anthony Wisson's bride? Now she was already having to take second place to business – and on her honeymoon, too!

With an effort, Guy recovered his composure.

"Part of my job is to keep your husband as free from interruptions as I can!" he said. "He's a very busy man!"

"So I'm beginning to realize!" Zandra commented with a smile, although she added wistfully: "But I do wish he didn't have to be so busy whilst we're on holiday. How late is it? I'm absolutely famished!"

Despite himself, Guy laughed. He, too, was hungry.

"Why don't we go and start our meal?" he suggested. "Your husband said if he was delayed, we were to start without him. I am sure he wouldn't want you to starve on his account!"

"I suppose we could!" Zandra said reluctantly. For some reason, the happiness of her mood had given way to one of sadness. It was so very beautiful here on the terrace; so romantic! It would have been quite perfect to be sitting here alone with Anthony, perhaps feeling the pressure of his knee against hers beneath the table and to be sharing that special look of understanding between them. Although she knew she could never be really beautiful, by the time the hotel *coiffeur* had dressed her hair and she had adorned herself in her new Schiaparelli dress, she knew she had never looked prettier. She wanted Anthony to be here beside her telling her so, not this comparative stranger, however attentive and pleasant a person he happened to be. As a matter of fact, her maid of honour, Katherine, had drawn Zandra's attention to Guy Bristow's exceptional good looks and slim, athletic build. "If I wasn't crazy about your ex, Zee-Zee, I'd be trying to make a play for him!"

Zandra smiled at the memory for she knew very well that poor, plain Katherine had never had eyes for anyone but Hugh Conway, and now, at long last, he seemed to be taking notice of her. They were, in fact, very well suited and were likely to get engaged before the end of the Season. Her thoughts were diverted by the faint sounds of a dance band filtering on to the terrace from within the hotel.

"They're playing that new American song 'You're the Cream in my Coffee'!" she said. "Can you hear it, Guy? I really love dancing, don't you?" She gave another quick glance across the terrace and added with a sigh: "There's still no sign of Anthony, so I suppose we might as well go in to dinner. At least we'll hear the music better inside."

As Guy stood up at once and led her to the restaurant, it occurred to Zandra that he was perfectly at ease in these surroundings; and looking as he did in immaculate white tie and tails, there was nothing to indicate that he was merely her husband's employee and not one of the hotel's wealthy and illustrious guests. Was this innate good breeding one of the reasons Anthony had employed him? she wondered whilst Guy was explaining to the *maître d'* that they required a table for three as another gentleman would be joining them later.

They decided mutually to start their meal with crab soufflé – one of the many specialities on the elaborate menu. For a few moments they ate in silence and then the band struck up the opening bars of Cole Porter's "Let's Do It". Zandra put down her fork and turned to her companion.

"Hugh took me to see Jessie Matthews in 'Wake Up and Dream' and she sang this song frightfully well. Did you see it, Guy? It's wonderful to dance to. Come on, let's do it!" She gave her quick, husky laugh as she parodied the title of the song.

Obediently, Guy rose to his feet and led Zandra onto the dance floor. He was vaguely aware of the tune but it was not until the vocalist started the refrain that he remembered the last line – "Let's fall in love!" He was instantly conscious of the girl in his arms: the warmth of her skin where his hand rested against her bare back; the scooped back of her evening dress; the faint redolence of her perfume which he knew he would always associate with her; the occasional brushing of her thigh against his body.

Oh, dear God! he thought, there's no question of "Let's fall in love" – he was already head over heels in love with her. Mercifully she was totally unaware of it and was regarding him with eyes that were bright with happiness. She seemed to have forgotten the absence of her husband.

"This is great fun, isn't it?" she said. "You dance terribly well, Guy. Anthony's a good dancer, too, though he doesn't awfully care for it, but we did dance quite a lot last night. He said whilst you're here, we must ask Bunnie to have dinner with us one night. Her uncle goes to bed early so Anthony thinks it would be the charitable thing to do—"

She broke off as another couple accidentally bumped into them. As Guy steered her away, she forgot the subject and gave herself up to the enjoyment of the remainder of the dance. When it came to an end and they returned to the table, her face was glowing. It lit up still further when she saw Anthony approaching. She hurried to greet him.

"So you've arrived at last, darling!" she exclaimed, reaching up to kiss him. He ignored the gesture and his face was unsmiling as Guy drew back her chair. "I see you have already started your meal so I will forgo the entrée and join you with the main course, Zandra." He turned to Guy who was still standing. "I shan't need you again tonight, Bristow. I'm sure you're tired after your journey and would like to get an early night."

"But Anthony, Guy has only just started dinner," Zandra protested. "He's only had the entrée and—"

"Mr Bristow can order what more he requires from Room Service, as well he knows, my dear!" Anthony interrupted in a cold, meaningful tone.

"Of course! Good night, Mrs Wisson, sir!"

As Guy walked away, Zandra stared at her husband in disbelief. She was not only astonished but angry that he should have spoken to her as if she were a child to be reprimanded. Before she could find words to express herself, Anthony said: "Really, my dear, you must leave the handling of my staff to me. I asked Bristow to look after you until I arrived, for your convenience, not for his. Perhaps you have forgotten that he's merely an employee? Surely you are sufficiently *au fait* with the correct etiquette to know you should not have been dancing with him."

Zandra's face cleared and she laughed.

"Oh, that! You can't be serious, Anthony. I know Guy's your employee but he's a perfect gentleman – and anyway, you were the one who instructed him to dine with me and I *wanted* to dance, so in point of fact, *I* asked *him* – he didn't ask me."

66

There was no answering smile on Anthony's face.

"That is even less excusable! And whilst we are on the subject of etiquette, Zandra, I would prefer that you didn't address Bristow by his Christian name. Before you know where you are, he will be calling you Zandra."

Zandra's mouth, which had been open to protest, closed quickly. She felt quite unreasonably guilty knowing that it was she who had suggested they should use Christian names. It would be most unfair if Guy were to be blamed for it. Was it possible, she asked herself, that Anthony had seen what fun she and Guy had been having on the dance floor and was jealous? Surely that couldn't be the case, although Guy Bristow was a very good-looking, younger man. She was saved the necessity of deciding how to react to Anthony's dictatorial tone by the advent of the head waiter who was hovering nearby to take Anthony's order. By the time he departed, Anthony seemed to have regained his good humour, and in an affectionate voice, he complimented her upon her appearance.

"That dress is very becoming," he told her, "but diamonds would be preferable to pearls, I think. I'll buy you a necklace tomorrow. I intended to give you a small *cadeau* in any event. You see, my dear, your assistance in obtaining an introduction for me to Sir Basil has proved most efficacious. I shall be doing quite a large amount of business as a result of our meeting this evening."

"Oh, I *am* glad, Anthony!" Zandra said with genuine pleasure, the contretemps over Guy forgotten. "Tell me more about it, darling. In what way was Sir Basil helpful to you?"

Anthony stared at her with amusement.

"My dear girl, you wouldn't begin to understand the first thing about such matters – so there's really no point in my trying to explain. In any case, I prefer you not to become involved in my business affairs. If it's really your wish to be of assistance to me, then you can best do so by being your sweet, innocent self and by charming such guests as I invite to our house, as I have no doubt you will!"

With an effort, Zandra quashed the thought that Anthony was once again patronizing her.

"Well, of course I'll be as pleasant as I can to your friends, but wouldn't it be easier if I understood more about your business, Anthony? I know it has to do with munitions, but what exactly do you do? You don't make guns and things, do you?"

Anthony's look was now indulgent.

"Once, a long time ago, I managed my father's factory which made munitions. Now I negotiate deals between buyer and seller."

"But the war has been over for years and years – twelve, isn't it? Who could possibly want to buy armaments now?"

Anthony's expression became inscrutable as he said dismissively: "There are other countries in the world besides our own, Zandra. Now, my dear, here is our *escalope de veau*. Let's enjoy it whilst it's still hot; and afterwards, if you would like it, we shall dance."

"Yes, do let's!" Zandra agreed. "It's a wonderful band, and this is so much more fun than those dreadful deb parties where you had to wait for your programme to be filled in and ruin a perfectly divine tune dancing with a partner you simply couldn't stand. It's one of the nicest things about being married – being able to have all the dances with you!"

"I can think of even nicer things we might be doing!" Anthony said, reaching for her hand beneath the table. Zandra's heart leapt as she recognized the husky tone of her husband's voice. She had been afraid her remark might have reminded him that he had objected to her dancing with Guy. Now everything was all right again between them.

"I do love you, darling, and I'm so very happy!" she said softly. "Do you think we will always be as happy as we are now?"

"I see no reason why not – unless you ever get like that!"

Anthony pointed to an enormously fat dowager dressed in mauve satin seated at a nearby table. The white folds of her neck and arms were bedecked with jewels and an exquisite white sable wrap lay on an empty chair beside her.

Zandra giggled.

"She is a bit overweight, isn't she, poor thing! I saw that young man sitting next to her dancing with her a little while ago. It must be quite embarrassing for a son to have to do duty dances with such a colossal parent."

Anthony regarded the girl beside him with an indulgent smile.

"My dear, I doubt very much if the young man is the lady's son. I imagine he is her gigolo."

"Her what?"

"Gigolo, Zandra. That's to say, she pays him to cater to her needs."

"You mean he is paid to escort her?" Zandra enquired, screwing up her nose. "What a perfectly horrible job!"

"There are many penniless young men who make their living in such a fashion – and they are not simply escorts. They cater to *every* need."

It was a moment or two before Zandra appreciated the significance of his statement. When she did so, her cheeks flushed. Surely, she thought, Anthony must be mistaken? The mere idea of paying a man to perform such intimacies shocked her; still more so that a man would be willing to perform them with someone so hideous for *money!*

"That's horrible!" she whispered, trying to keep her glance from straying back to the couple.

"Perhaps! But such a gargantuan is hardly likely to attract a lover, however rich she may be. At least she has money to compensate her. Riches bring power, my dear, so she's far from helpless. Believe me, to be powerless is a great deal worse than being ugly!"

Anthony had spoken with such feeling that for a minute or two, Zandra forgot the couple who had evoked the discussion. Had *he* ever been "powerless"? she wondered. It was difficult to imagine Anthony without authority, without the means to acquire what he wanted; to protect or defend himself. Yet he had spoken as if he believed power to be all important. But power over whom? During the few serious conversations they had ever had in their short courtship, he had never shown the slightest interest in party politics or in religion – the two most emotive subjects in the world according to Uncle Toby. They had been the cause of most of the wars and disputes between people and nations since the world began! They were topics which, like money, must never be discussed in polite society. Was that why Anthony had avoided such subjects with her? Or was it because she was a female and therefore not supposed to have any interest in such things?

"Eat up, my dear. Your meal is getting cold!" Anthony said solicitously. "Tell me how you like this wine? I suppose Bristow ordered it. It's not dry enough for my liking!"

"He chose it because I said I liked it!" Zandra replied. She had forgotten Guy and wished Anthony had not reminded her of him. It made her uncomfortable to think of him having to dine alone in his hotel room; but instinctively, she knew it would not please Anthony if she expressed such feelings.

"I'll order a Chablis!" Anthony said, beckoning to the wine waiter. "That should suit us both, I think."

"That's Uncle Pelham's favourite, too!" Zandra said, happy to be on safe ground. "He always brings Uncle Toby a case when he and Tante Silvie visit us. I know you are going to like Uncle Pelham, Anthony. He's such fun – and terribly brave. Did I ever tell you that he was decorated in the Boer War? And in the Great War he helped some of the wounded French soldiers to escape through the German lines in his Sunbeam motor car! I always think Oliver takes after him. He escaped from a German prison camp in a home-made gas balloon!"

Anthony's eyes were thoughtful.

"As a matter of fact, I did notice a strong physical likeness between them!" he said. "There was another uncle, wasn't there? One who was also decorated?"

Zandra sighed.

"That was Uncle Rupert. He lived abroad so I never knew him.

70

He was shot by the Germans when they found him harbouring Allied soldiers. Aunt Willow was very fond of him. There was another uncle, too, called Francis. I think he was the black sheep of the family because no one ever talks about him. He died before I was born and there aren't any photographs of him so everyone sort of pretends he never existed! I wish some of your relations were still alive, Anthony. It must be so sad to have no family! But now you can share mine, can't you?"

"I would like to think so!" Anthony replied. "The younger generation certainly approve of me!"

"And so they should, mercenary little monsters!" Zandra said laughing. "You sent them such wonderful Christmas presents – just what they all wanted. You're a very generous man, darling. I just wish I could tell you how grateful everyone is for the way you've helped the family. Oliver says you allow him to continue running Sky-Ways exactly the way he wants and pay him for doing so! He and Henry are thrilled about the new de Havilland Tiger Moth. And of course, you've made it possible for us to keep Rochford Manor and I just don't know what Ollie and Uncle Toby and Aunt Willow would have felt like if they'd had to leave the house. I'm still finding it hard to believe I'm the owner of all that land – and Havorhurst village!"

"Yes, well, I don't want you worrying your head about the properties. I will see to whatever is necessary. Did the vicar tell you I had promised to restore the church roof? He was delighted!"

"Oh, Anthony, did you? What a wonderful gesture! Oliver had promised to make a sizeable donation, but of course, when great-grandfather's companies were ruined, he knew he wouldn't be able to raise the money. I know one isn't supposed to talk about such things, but I want to tell you how I feel. We used to be terribly rich, Aunt Willow said, and no one ever bothered much about money. When Rochford Manor was turned into a convalescent home in the war, she and Uncle Toby had to find a place for all the valuable paintings by artists like Rembrandt, Gainsborough, Van Dyck and so on; so they gave them to the nation. Oliver said they would have been worth a very great deal if we'd kept them, so I suppose it was rather a foolish if grandiose gesture! But no one ever imagined TRTC could simply vanish!"

"A great many businesses were destroyed by the Wall Street crash!" Anthony said. "I, however, have gained from it. Had I not learned that Sky-Ways was financed in the main by Tetford money, I wouldn't have thought to make an offer for Oliver's shares; and had I not done so, I would not have met you!"

Zandra's cheeks flushed and her eyes sparkled.

"Oh darling, what a lovely thing to say! I'm so very lucky that you found me! I will be a good wife to you, I promise. I want you to go on loving me for ever and ever."

"I shall keep you to your promise, Zandra!" Anthony said. "And now, if you have had enough to eat, shall we dance? I think I can prove that I am quite as adequate as Bristow on the floor!"

This time, Zandra would not allow the mention of the banished Guy Bristow to mar her happiness. She wanted nothing more than to be dancing in Anthony's arms to the haunting melody of "You Were Meant For Me", and to see the thrilling glow of desire in his eyes as he gazed down at her.

Far above them, Guy leant out of the window of his bedroom to stare across the sparkling lights of the harbour reflected in the water. He, too, heard and recognized the tune. With a barely audible cry of anguish, he pressed the back of his hand against his mouth and tried once more to tell himself that no matter how much he loved Zandra Wisson, she could never be his.

Chapter 5

June–July 1931

Alice Rochford handed the guest list back to her aunt and after a moment's hesitation, said shyly: "Please, Tante Silvie, could we invite Monsieur Calonne?"

The fiery red blush which followed this request spread across Alice's plump cheeks and down to her neck. With an effort, Silvie Rochford withheld a sigh. Sometimes this second daughter of Willow's drove her to distraction. They were about to celebrate the girl's twenty-eighth birthday and here she was blushing like an eighteen-year-old . . . only far less becomingly.

Alice had been staying with her for almost a year now – ever since Zandra's marriage; yet she, Silvie, had been able to achieve very little in the way of improving the girl's appearance. At five, Alice had been such a pretty little thing with silky brown hair and large, round blue eyes. Maturity had changed her almost beyond recognition. She had become big-busted – something very far from fashionable these days! – wide-hipped, and her once charming little face had lost its delicate contours. "*Mademoiselle est très bien développée,*" Silvie's dressmaker had remarked tactfully, but the truth was, the girl was unattractively plump! No wonder her poor sister-in-law had failed to find her a husband.

"Please do what you can to improve Alice's looks and figure!" Willow had begged when it was decided at Zandra's wedding to send the girl to France for a year. "Although she never speaks of it, I am sure she had hoped that the Guards Officer she met during her Season would propose to her and, even after all these years, she is still nursing a broken heart! I hate to have to say this, but I fear her suitor lost interest when Alice's inheritance went up in smoke with TRTC! The poor child would so like to be married, and you will have seen for yourself how wonderful she is with Oliver's and Lucy's little ones. Really, she has no talent for anything but motherhood although we all pretend that her water-colours are delightful. I feel so concerned for her and she is, as you know, such a sweet-natured, easygoing, adaptable girl – the very opposite of my volatile Zandra!"

Tactfully avoiding Alice's red cheeks, Silvie pretended to look again at the guest list. During the year in which she and Pelham had lived at their new home in south-west France, they had made many friends, most of whom were from a background similar to their own, some titled. She was not at all sure that they would be happy to welcome M. Claude Calonne as a fellow guest. Many of them patronized his *Galerie des Beaux-Arts*, and had even invited him to their homes to give expert advice when they were redecorating, for undoubtedly the Frenchman had artistic good taste; but he was not, to Silvie's knowledge, ever entertained by them as a guest. She herself had made use of his services when she and Pelham had first moved into the Casa Montijo. The old Basque farmhouse, four kilometres outside the town of Pau, had been expensively modernized by a Spanish aristocrat at the turn of the century. It had a magnificent view of the Pyrenees, and was near enough to the town for Pelham to frequent the golf course and for them both to enjoy the sophisticated lifestyle of the British colony who had settled there over a hundred years ago.

"I do not dispute the fact that Monsieur Calonne can be quite charming," she said now to Alice. "However, I am not certain that he would mix very well with our friends. They are his clients, *enfin*, and—" She broke off, aware of the look of acute disappointment on her niece's face. With a sudden sense of shock, it occurred to her for the first time that Alice might have "a crush" on the Frenchman. If so, Alice had hidden it well until now, implying that it was M. Calonne's interest in her water-colours that necessitated her going so frequently to his gallery whilst she, Silvie, was shopping! Now that she thought of it, the Frenchman could not have been seriously interested in Alice's little paintings which were singularly amateurish and at times lacking all sense of perspective!

With an effort, Silvie tried to envisage Claude Calonne in a romantic light. At forty or so, he was hardly a young girl's idol. Small, thin, with a pointed nose and weak chin, the best that could be said for him was that he looked like a starving poet! The fact that he wore his black hair far longer than was fashionable and wore flamboyantly coloured bow-ties added to this effect. He was undoubtedly very conscious of his appearance and frequently glanced at himself in one of the antique mirrors in his gallery or, if he were at the Casa Montijo, in the Louis XV giltwood mirror Silvie had brought down from the Château d'Orbais to adorn her salon.

Alice was now leaning towards her aunt, an uncustomary look of eagerness on her face.

"He is charming, isn't he, Tante Silvie? And he has given me so much encouragement with my paintings. I had always feared they were not very good but Monsieur Calonne has assured me they show great promise. I . . . I would be very happy if he could come to my birthday party. He would be someone I could talk to and you know how difficult I find it to converse with people. It's silly to be so shy but no matter how hard I try, I can never think of anything to say. I just feel stupid and clumsy, and although Mother is always saying that I am not, I know she is just being kind."

Which was undoubtedly true, Silvie thought as she put a reassuring arm round the girl's shoulders.

"But looks are not everything, *chérie*," she said quickly. "You have a sweet nature and an unselfish one, and we all love you dearly."

She felt Alice stiffen in her embrace.

"It's all very well for you to talk about my nature, Tante Silvie, but most men are only interested in a girl's looks and . . . and figure. And I am not even clever! I never learned to drive a car like Zee-Zee, and I'd rather die than try to fly an aeroplane! I'm quite hopeless on a horse and no good at tennis. About the only thing I am good at is dancing but because I'm so plain, I seldom get asked to dance." She paused briefly for breath. "I've never said all this to Mother because she gets upset if I run myself down, but you've been so kind and understanding and I can tell you. Everyone in the family thinks I'm perfectly happy living at home with Mother and being a good aunt to Lucy's and Oliver's children. They never think I might want children of my own . . . and a husband, too. There has only ever been one man who really liked me. I liked him, too, and I hoped and prayed George was going to propose to me; but in the end, he fell for another girl – she was very pretty and vivacious and I never blamed him for preferring her, but I am nearly twenty-eight years old now, and I don't want to grow into an elderly spinster, Tante Silvie. I want someone to love and to love me."

"Oh, *ma petite*, but of course you do!" Silvie said. "And I shall do my best to help you find someone. As to your age, I did not marry your uncle until I was thirty-five, although I had been married and widowed when I was in my teens. Believe me, *chérie*, one is often better equipped to make the right choice when one is older."

Alice's face was momentarily almost pretty as she regarded her aunt with glowing eyes.

"That's just how I feel, Tante Silvie, and I think I've met exactly the right person. Monsieur Calonne and I have such a great deal in common. He thinks so, too. Of course, he has never said that he cares for me – that would be much too premature when we've only known each other so short a while; but he seems to like me very much and yesterday when I was at the

Galerie, he asked me if I would allow him to take me for a drive to Biarritz as I've never been there. He really seems to like me, Tante Silvie, and I thought . . . I wondered . . . that lovely dress you chose for me for my birthday party . . . perhaps if he could see me in it . . . it's so beautiful and romantic looking . . . I thought perhaps—"

She broke off, her brown eyes soft and appealing.

Willow might not approve, but I cannot refuse her, Silvie thought, her heart full of pity for this plain, ungainly niece. Maybe M. Claude Calonne was not quite *comme il faut*; but he was well mannered and artistically well informed. Her own and Pelham's connections were such that the inclusion of a mere shopkeeper at one of their parties would do no more than raise a few eyebrows! As for Willow, would she mind too much if something came of this budding romance? Quite probably she would be relieved to have Alice happily settled. It was not, after all, as if Alice were really her own flesh and blood, although this was a family secret.

It was curious, none the less, how without ever knowing her own mother, Alice had inherited so much from her. Nellie Sinclair had been Willow's personal maid to whom she had been devoted. When Francis, the youngest of the five Rochford brothers, had raped the girl, and Alice, the resulting infant, had been born in Silvie's home in Paris, she and Willow had substituted the child for Willow's stillborn baby. It had seemed at the time the right thing to do for all concerned, for her father was, after all, a Rochford. Nellie had been able to marry the footman who was courting her and they had gone to live in San Francisco. No one had been any the wiser, and Willow had been a good mother to the child. Now, it seemed, Alice was leaning away from the aristocratic atmosphere in which she had been reared.

"Well, of course we shall invite your Monsieur Calonne, *chérie*," she said impulsively. "It is, *quand même*, your party. See, we shall put his name down on the list, and this afternoon you may take an invitation card to him."

Alice's usually placid face was wreathed in smiles.

"Oh, thank you, thank you, Tante Silvie!" she said. She looked suddenly almost pretty, and Silvie felt a moment of anxiety. Suppose Alice had read far more into the man's attentions to her than he intended? It was only natural that he should ingratiate himself with the niece of one of his most prestigious clients. She, Silvie, had spent a great deal of money furnishing and equipping her new home. Above all, Claude Calonne had proved himself an excellent salesman and if he had noted Alice's personal interest in him, he might well have decided to take full advantage of the connection. The fact that he had praised Alice's water-colours was sufficient to rouse her suspicions. She must make some enquiries about his background; find out where he lived and whether he could ever be considered a tolerable husband for her poor, plain niece! If her misgivings were to be proved well founded, Alice, fortuitously, was due to go back to England at the end of the month. She would have to be packed off home with yet another broken heart, poor child, but better that than to be married to a charlatan.

Early in July, Silvie wrote a long letter to her sister-in-law concerning Alice's future. Several days later, at Rochford Manor, having seen the cook to decide upon the day's menus, Willow took her sister-in-law's letter to the morning-room where she could read it undisturbed.

Alice has asked if she can stay on until the end of the summer when we return to Paris. You will know, from my previous letters, the reason she wishes to remain with us! *C'est l'amour, n'est-ce pas?* I feel very responsible for the present situation and am therefore putting you as fully in the picture as is possible, although both Pelham and I think you should come for a visit and see Alice's chosen one for yourselves.

What can I tell you that you do not already know? Yes, Claude does seem very genuinely interested – at least insofar as his attentions to Alice go. There are the customary flowers;

the invitations to little lunches, and expeditions in his elderly Darracq. He has even hung one of her paintings in his gallery! Alice is *bouleversée* – and I have to admit that love and happiness have had a remarkable effect upon her. She has lost a great deal of her shyness, smiles a lot, and has even started dieting to improve her *poitrine* – with some success, too. She is as eager as I am to take her shopping for clothes that are chic and becoming – and you know how in the past she has resisted such attempts by me to dress her well.

I, myself, do not dislike Claude. It is true, as Pelham says, that he is too suave, too anxious to please; at times, almost effeminate in his attentions to his appearance, but I find him quite amusing. Pelham insists that he is a pansy but you know your brother-in-law! He likes strong, virile, manly men who are *sportif* and prefer cars to *objets d'art*! Only yesterday, he complained to me: "But he is such a little man!" It is true Claude looks tiny beside my dear husband and his hands are small, too, like a child's. He is at least half a head shorter than Alice, though she does not seem to notice this when they dance together. His eyes are dark, very Spanish-looking; his hair slightly receding from the forehead with flecks of grey. Pelham insists that he would have grey sideburns were it not for the fact that he dyes them black. Really, *chérie*, your brother-in-law is impossible! Fortunately, for Alice's sake he is always pleasant to Claude when he calls to see us as he is very fond of her.

The Calonne family background does not seem so much of a problem as I feared. Most of the relatives (*très provincials!*) live in the north-east and I gather are either too poor, old or frail to travel. It is unlikely they would wish to attend a wedding in England if that were to be arranged. Alice has told me that if you will permit her to marry, she will, of course, live here in Pau with Claude, so it would seem that it might be best if she were married from here. She wants a quiet wedding without any fuss although I am not sure if this is what Claude would want. So far, the subject has not been discussed with him as Pelham and I have not openly given our approval to their betrothal since this must be for you and Toby to approve.

When I questioned Pelham for his opinion, his answer was – and I quote: *"Why not? I fear Alice is unlikely to find another husband at her age. Too many young men who would now be in their thirties and of an age to marry her were killed in the war and there are not sufficient left to go round for the less attractive girls."* I have to say I fear he is right. Alice has told me that she is anxious to have a family and I feel that given a few children, she will be perfectly content even if Claude does not prove to be as devoted a husband as he is a suitor.

Finally, *chérie*, I can imagine that Claude Calonne is not quite the son-in-law you would prefer, or indeed, of whom you would feel proud. You would not, however, have him underfoot! It is difficult to imagine that he would ever become part of the Rochford family in the way that the handsome Anthony Wisson has done.

I was so pleased to receive your last letter telling me how happy Zandra is! She looked so radiant when we saw her last year in Paris, and we were both disappointed that the happy couple could not visit us on their way back to England. Her new home sounds lovely – as I am sure it will be if you and Lucy have helped her to furnish and decorate it. Once we are back in Paris, we must find time to cross that horrible Channel and see it for ourselves. Perhaps we should ask Oliver to fly us in one of his aeroplanes! Pelham is most anxious to be up in the air again and loves to receive Oliver's letters telling him about the airline. My dear husband is still such a boy at heart, and I find it hard to believe when I look at him that he has just had his sixtieth birthday. Only one more year and I, too, shall be joining him. How quickly the years go by!

Willow laid down the pages and stared thoughtfully out of the window. She knew she should be concentrating her thoughts upon Alice, but instead she was pondering the conclusion of Silvie's letter. When she was a girl, old age had been something she would come to in some far-off distant future; yet that half-century had passed as if it were no more than a decade. Could it really be forty years ago that she had come from America to live in this house? Rochford Manor was now as much a part of her as her own skin and, although she had tried not to show it, she believed it would have destroyed her if Oliver had had to sell the house.

How immensely indebted they all were to Anthony Wisson! Fate was strange the way she handed out gifts and blows so unexpectedly. Maybe they evened out in the end, for although there had been blows Fate had made up for them with the blessings of her children, grandchildren and, of course, Toby – dear, kind, sensible Toby who was the quiet pivot around whom the family revolved.

With an effort, Willow turned her thoughts to her daughter, Alice. Most of all, she was concerned for the child's happiness. Such was the sweetness of Alice's nature that she had never resented Zandra's presence in the household, which well she might! Zandra had been a child who demanded attention; letting everyone know if she could not get her own way. As she had grown up, Zee-Zee had turned from a plain child into a very attractive young woman whilst the little girl, Alice, had turned from pretty to plain. It cannot have been easy for Alice seeing Zandra's popularity with her school-friends, and later with the young men who were attracted to her, whilst she herself continued to be the proverbial wallflower. But Alice had remained as loving and devoted to her young cousin as ever, and showed neither envy nor resentment at the unfairness of life. Nor had she shown any bitterness when her contemporary and friend Eleanor Barratt had, despite her plainness, found herself a husband.

With a familiar sense of guilt, Willow faced the fact that, provided Alice was happy in her choice of husband, it would be a relief to have her finally settled. This adopted daughter of hers had always been so self-effacing that she really would not greatly miss her, whereas when Zee-Zee had left home, she had been deeply conscious of the loss. At first, she had been uneasy about Zandra's choice of husband since her much-loved niece had, unlike Alice, such a passionate and mercurial nature. Fortunately Anthony Wisson had turned out to be just the right man for Zee-Zee, and if there was any fly in the ointment, it was that Anthony spent so much time abroad, quite often departing at a moment's notice and thereby disrupting the couple's social engagements.

This did have one advantage in that Zandra often came down to Rochford when Anthony was away, sometimes bringing that nice young man Guy Bristow with her so that there would be a fourth at tennis or to take Anthony's place at one of Oliver's jolly dinner parties. Somewhat to her surprise, Toby, who often as not had his head in the clouds and noticed little of the younger generation's relationships, had taken note of this and commented upon it.

"Seems a bit odd the way Wisson uses Bristow as a stand-in!" he'd said in bed one night as Willow had been on the verge of sleep. "Bristow's nearer Zandra's age than he is, and one would have thought he'd think twice about throwing the two together!"

Willow had reassured him.

"Anthony knows he has no reason to be jealous. Zee-Zee adores him and as for Guy – she treats him like a brother. Anyway, Toby, Anthony is not the man to act without thinking, and I am sure he has total confidence in his assistant else he wouldn't employ him. It's merely his way of making up for the fact that his business affairs oblige him to leave Zee-Zee alone so often."

Toby had not disputed the remark but, on the point of sleep, commented that he had never grasped what exactly Anthony's business entailed. Willow herself had no such curiosity since all that mattered to her was that Zandra had settled down so happily to married life with the added bonus that she still saw a great deal of her.

Once again, Willow forced her thoughts back to her sister-in-law's letter. If Silvie seemed to consider this Frenchman, Claude

Calonne, would make Alice a satisfactory husband, she herself would not raise any objections. She and Toby would have to travel to France for the wedding; but it was over a year now since they'd had a holiday and she was curious to see Silvie's new home. Perhaps Oliver and Jane would accompany them and if Anthony was too busy, Zandra could go with them, too. It would make a jolly family party. Nanny could take care of the children; and although not perhaps quite as efficiently as before the war, the house could run very well without her.

Pleased to have reached a decision about Alice, Willow decided to telephone first Lucy and then Zandra with the news before settling down to reply to Silvie's long letter.

Zandra herself answered the telephone although this was usually done by Anthony's butler.

"Aunt Willow! What a lovely surprise! I was off to Fortnum's and you've caught me just in time. You're not coming up to London, are you? We could go shopping together!"

Willow explained the reason for her call.

"Well, that's wonderful news, isn't it?" Zandra commented. "Although Alice never actually said so to me, I'm sure she was secretly dying to get married. A fine arts dealer, you said. I suppose there's nothing wrong with that if he's nice, but, oh dear, Claude! What a perfectly ghastly name!" She gave her quick, husky laugh. "Of course I'll go over with you for the wedding. I wouldn't miss it for the world – unless, of course, Anthony needs me here."

That, Zandra thought, was unlikely, unless she were needed to host one of her husband's many boring business dinner parties. How she hated them! The men and women she was obliged to entertain were rarely people she would have wanted for friends. Many of them were foreigners barely able to speak English or French, who monopolized the conversation with Anthony in their own languages. The Englishmen were little better, with only a veneer of social good manners. They brought with them either dull, colourless wives or far worse, overdressed bejewelled women she supposed were their mistresses. Only very occasionally was there a guest Aunt Willow would have had at her dinner table. From the very first, Anthony had swept aside her criticisms.

"I wouldn't have invited these people if they had not been important to me!" he had stated coldly. "You shouldn't consider entertaining them as a pleasure but as a duty. I don't think I am asking too much to expect your co-operation?"

There was a certain timbre to Anthony's voice at such moments which upset Zandra deeply. It was always accompanied by a narrowing of his eyes which seemed to turn a steely grey. They were so different when he was in a loving mood. When he made love to her, his voice was deep and caressing. Sometimes, if one of the servants had transgressed, he would use the same disparaging tone to them and she knew that most of them were in awe of him. After a year of marriage, she understood that her husband did not accept half-measures where discipline was concerned. He had already given notice to one butler and had threatened to sack the cook if she sent up overdone beef again. Zandra had argued in Cook's defence that Anthony had been half an hour late for dinner, but quite unreasonably, he'd insisted that a good cook would find some other way of keeping the food hot, and that if the woman was so incompetent, she could be replaced by someone else.

It was not that she herself was afraid of Anthony, Zandra reflected, but she had made a great effort not to become involved in arguments with him because his reaction opened up a chasm between them which did frighten her. It was as if he could, in a split second, turn off his love and treat her with a cold indifference which hurt her deeply. She loved him as passionately as ever and hated the nights when he was away from home and she must sleep alone. Even if they did not make love, she liked to have him there beside her where she could reach out and touch his sleeping body.

Now that the redecorating of the house in Eaton Terrace was

complete, and with a satisfactory household staff settled in, there was little for her to do during the day and she often found herself watching the clock when it neared the time Anthony had said he would be back from his office. All too often, he was late. Sometimes when he telephoned to say that he'd been unavoidably detained and if they were scheduled to go to the theatre or a concert, he would detail Guy to escort her.

Zandra drew a deep sigh as she bade her aunt goodbye and sat staring out into the street. Guy was as nice a person as she could wish for as a companion, but he was not Anthony! He was attentive, respectful, thoughtful for her well-being and, at times, great fun! But it was Anthony she loved and in whose company she wished to be.

What could have brought about this mood of introspection? she asked herself, her hands toying unknowingly with the glass paperweight she had given Anthony on their honeymoon. Was it thoughts of Alice's marriage which reminded her of those wonderful weeks in Cannes? Anthony had been all hers, his physical need of her paramount in his thoughts. Even in public he had touched her hand, her knee, or pressed his thigh against hers beneath a table. He had loved to dance the tango with her because he could hold her close against him; and with her newfound knowledge, she had been intensely aware of his body hardening against her and felt an answering desire.

Sadly, those precious moments of intimacy had become fewer since his return to work. Often, at night, he was preoccupied in his study until long after she had fallen asleep. In the mornings, he was in a hurry to get back to the office, or to catch a train or one of Oliver's aeroplanes to attend a business meeting in Scotland, Paris or Ireland!

Tonight, Zandra told herself, she would speak to Anthony again about his long-ago promise to find her a job at Sky-Ways. At least it would give her something more worthwhile to do in the daytime than lunching with Lucy or with one of her girlfriends, or going shopping. Anthony was adamant that he did not wish them to start a family as yet, although part of her, which she had not known existed, now longed for a child – a son perhaps who would resemble Anthony. She had noted how devoted a father Alexis was, spending time with little Eve and Robin whenever he could, and it was Zandra's hope that one day Anthony would be as loving and attentive a parent.

For once, Anthony arrived home early, and with two hours to spare before they need leave for the theatre, Zandra had the opportunity she wanted to speak to him about a job at the airfield. They were in the drawing-room – a lovely oblong room decorated and furnished in soft, pastel shades. The comfortable chairs and sofas were covered in the same pastel-coloured materials chosen from Lady Colefax's shop in Grosvenor Street. On the side tables stood several lamps whose soft glow lent an atmosphere of harmony and light. The new butler, Jamieson, had brought in a tray with decanters and glasses, and Anthony was stretched out comfortably in his favourite armchair, seemingly relaxed. Judging this to be a good moment to raise the subject of her job, Zandra went to stand behind him. She placed her hands on his shoulders and leant her cheek against the top of his head.

"Darling, there's something I want to talk to you about!" she said. "I've been meaning to do so for ages. I want to find some work to do. You are away so much and I really don't have enough to occupy my days now the house is finished. You know I've always wanted to work in Ollie's airline. Well, Sky-Ways is only an hour's drive from London so I could be back home long before you return from the office; and if you were away, why then I'd be close to Rochford and could spend the night there. What do you think, darling?"

Anthony sat up so suddenly that Zandra's hands fell to her sides. She could not see his face but his voice was icy cold as he said: "I'll tell you what I think, Zandra. I have never heard such an absurd idea in my whole life! You are never short of money for anything you need; and as for wanting to occupy yourself during the day, there must be plenty of charity work for women like you!"

Slowly, Zandra moved round the chair. Her cheeks were flushed and her voice was raised as she faced him.

"I am not quite sure what you mean when you say 'women like me'! With my background, I suppose. Well, there are plenty of *women like me* who work – they even have their own businesses – shops, for instance. And I didn't say I wanted to do it for money, although I *would* quite like to have some of my own. I hate having to ask you for money to buy you a Christmas or birthday present, for example. But that isn't the point. I want something worthwhile and interesting to do with my time. Yes, I could do charity work but it isn't what I *want* to do. I love flying. I love everything to do with aeroplanes and if I were a man, I would be working for Oliver. Before we lost all our money, *he* worked just for the fun of it."

Anthony's eyes were now the dark steel-grey she found so unnerving.

"I might remind you that Sky-Ways belongs to me, not your Cousin Oliver. Be that as it may, I will not have my wife taking employment, and I mean that, Zandra. I married you because I wanted you to run my home, grace my table, entertain my associates. I did not intend to marry an airline employee!"

Zandra's chin lifted defiantly.

"That's news to me, Anthony. I thought you married me because you loved me!"

Anthony's mouth tightened.

"Don't be silly, Zandra. That goes without saying, and—"

"Does it?" Zandra interrupted as she turned angrily away from him. "You may think it irrelevant, Anthony, but I don't. Loving someone means wanting them to be happy and to enjoy their life. You have your business, whatever it is you do, and I don't have any share in it. Well, I want something in my life, too. Lucy may find it enough to stay at home and look after Alexis and the children, but I haven't any children to look after and you're only ever here in the evenings – and not always then!"

"You're being ridiculous, Zandra!" Anthony's voice was sharper than she had ever heard it. "You are not housebound – as you seem anxious to make out. You are free to pursue whatever occupations you choose to amuse you. Anything you want, you have only to charge to my account. You may even fly that precious aeroplane of yours whenever you wish."

"No, I can't!" Zandra flared. "I'd fly every day if I could, but you know it's impossible in bad weather; and anyway, it's quite often booked when I want it; and Oliver says he must give priority to the pupils who are paying for their lessons, besides which, I know how to fly the Gipsy Moth and I need more time on the DH82 before I can go solo, and when the weather is good, the instructors are usually busy. Sometimes I spend a whole day there just waiting, when I could be doing something useful. Oliver still hasn't replaced John who does all the bookings, and he said I could do the job standing on my head!"

"I'm not in the least interested in what your cousin has to say. *I* am saying that I will not have my wife going out to work. I hope that is understood, Zandra!"

"And if I prefer to do as I please?" Zandra asked defiantly.

"Then you will regret it!" Anthony replied, and without a further word, he rose to his feet and strode out of the room.

The sound of the door closing behind him stayed with her long after he had left, as did the threat he had uttered with such cold indifference to her feelings. Such was Zandra's sense of dismay at the injustice of his attitude, she was unable to concentrate on the theatre performance. It was only when they returned once more to the house that she realized she was not only filled with indignation, but she had no intention of submitting to his threat.

Chapter 6

December 1931

It was five months before Zandra raised the subject of working for Sky-Ways again. Anthony had returned the previous day from a visit to the United States and, as always when he came back from a business trip, he had made passionate love to her on the night of his return. As was usual, Zandra had spent the time at Rochford whilst he was absent and, although he had never voiced any objection to such visits, she had once or twice asked herself if perhaps he resented her close links with her family. He had stated quite openly that they exerted too much influence upon her – a point she had argued fiercely was untrue. She had, she pointed out, been looked upon during her childhood as a rebel!

Now, reunited with Anthony, she wondered how it was possible for a married couple to be as physically close as they had been the previous night, and yet the following day, she could feel as if she was breakfasting with a stranger. He was immersed in his newspaper and seemed disinclined to talk. His early morning kiss had been perfunctory and when, still steeped in the aftermath of their love-making, she had reached up her arms to draw him closer, his eyes had seemed to lack all tenderness as he detached himself from her embrace.

Studying her husband's handsome profile, Zandra felt a ridiculous inclination to weep. Perhaps it was tiredness, she told herself, for she was certainly not given to tears – unlike Alice who could weep copiously over a dead bird or a mouse in a trap! In any event, what genuine reason had she for this strange feeling of melancholy? Anthony was home and had been even more impatient than herself to go to bed. He had possessed her with a wordless urgency and only afterwards, demanded in a fierce passionate voice that she should tell him how much she loved him; that she belonged to him body, heart and soul!

How could he doubt it? she had wondered, when at such moments she became a slave to his needs – and her own. He could rouse her to such heights of pleasure that she wanted nothing more but to surrender herself to him in an ecstasy of love. These heightened emotions remained with her the next day when inexplicably, Anthony seemed to have forgotten the wild kisses, the caresses, the intimate touches and the final, incredible moments when he thrust himself into her, merging his body with hers so that they became one. It was as if, having possessed her once more, he preferred to disclaim his need of her.

When at last Anthony laid down his newspaper in order that she could pour him a second cup of coffee, she requested his attention.

"Darling, I was talking to Oliver on Saturday. He said if I still wanted to work at Sky-Ways, there would be plenty for me to do, and if I couldn't manage a full week, it would be perfectly all right if I just went down on—"

"No! I thought I made it clear last time you raised this subject that I will not have my wife working. Kindly don't mention it again, Zandra!"

He was about to pick up his newspaper once more, but Zandra caught hold of his arm.

"Anthony, please! You don't understand how bored I get when you're away." Her voice was soft, pleading; but there was no answering softness in Anthony's voice as he said sharply: "No,

Zandra! Now please don't nag! I've had a tiring fortnight; the Atlantic was rough the whole way over and my cabin was uncomfortable and noisy. I have no wish to come home to this kind of nonsense."

Zandra withdrew her hand and her voice became firmer as her temper rose.

"You aren't even *trying* to understand!" she flared. "In a few weeks' time it will be Christmas; and I may go shopping today with Lucy and I shall have to ask you for money to buy *you* a present. At least when I was a child Aunt Willow gave me pocket-money – something of my own to spend as I wished. It's not even as if you give me a dress allowance or money for the housekeeping. I could save something then."

"Exactly! And that is why I prefer that I should pay the bills. You know perfectly well you can charge what you please to my accounts, and I am finding it extremely distasteful that you should be implying I am anything less than generous in that respect."

Zandra bit her lip. Her heart was beating furiously, and she was almost beginning to wish that she had never started this conversation. Nevertheless, she was not now going to retract or drop the subject.

"I have never said you were ungenerous!" she countered. "How could I possibly say such a thing when you've given me so much – and Rochford, all that land! And of course I'm grateful, and you *know* I am! But I'm not a child, Anthony, nor stupid, yet you scrutinize every bill that comes into the house as if you didn't trust me to manage. I hate it when you check each one as if expecting Cook is robbing you, or you're looking to see if I've spent too much on a coat or dress!"

Anthony's eyebrows rose and Zandra was shocked to see something approaching a sneer on his face.

"I happen to be aware that you and your family were born with silver spoons in your mouths and never paid the slightest regard to money. Good God! When I think that Mr and Mrs Rochford gave all those priceless paintings to the nation, I could vomit at such stupidity! Well, I suppose you've all had to learn the hard way what it means to be poor. I, on the other hand, had to work my own way to riches."

It had taken him a very long time, he thought, and thanks to the mathematical skill he had inherited from his father, he'd made an early start – in his third year at boarding school, to be precise. By then, he'd discovered the existence of the stock market. His mother's brother, Uncle Sigismund, whilst paying his once yearly visit to the family, had explained how the market worked. He, Anthony, had wanted his father to buy some shares in a company he felt was undervalued. His parsimonious parent denied he had money to spare for what he called "a gamble"; but the shares had soared in value. It was then he realized that his father was a fool, slaving all hours of the day to make money from his factory when he could have sat back and made twice as much with clever investments.

It was easy now to recall the exact date when he'd decided not to follow in his parent's unenterprising footsteps, for the advent of his fifteenth birthday had produced a welcome addition to his term's pocket-money.

He wrote to his uncle from school, enclosing nearly all the money he had. By the half-term holiday, the shares had doubled in value. Aware that as a minor, he could not deal on the stock market in his own right, and knowing that his uncle would not act for him again, he enlisted the help of the school caretaker. Open to bribery, the man was more than willing to allow his name and the address of the lodge cottage where he lived to be used as a *poste restante*. He proceeded to invest the profits he had accrued from his first venture and succeeded in increasing his capital.

Even the boys of the wealthiest families in the school were always short of pocket-money. On hearing of his success, they were only too willing to add their contributions to his next share purchase. Before long, he was running a moderately profitable syndicate, keeping a 10 per cent commission for himself. Some of the senior boys became interested – Bellamy amongst them.

Bellamy was captain of cricket. Despite the fact that he, Anthony, had scored two centuries last season for the Second XI and was top of the batting averages, Bellamy refused to give him a place in the First XI.

Even now, after all these years, he could recall the contemptuous tone of the older boy's voice when he'd denied him his rightful place in the team.

"You play for yourself, Wisniowiecki, and cricket's a team game. You're only interested in your score, and you take unfair risks with your fellow batsmen. Scoring runs isn't everything, you know. You may be a brilliant bat, Wisniowiecki, but you are a rotten sportsman! You'll never make the First XI until you learn not to be."

It was a moment of supreme elation when not long afterwards he saw Bellamy approaching him with a ten-pound note in his hand. It crossed his mind that he could, if he wanted, invest it in a dud share. The prospect of seeing Bellamy's face when he told him the gamble had not paid off was immensely satisfying; but he had other more grandiose plans. He invested the money wisely and, as he anticipated, with every successful deal he did for Bellamy, the senior boy increased his stake, borrowing from him to do so.

In Bellamy's last term at school Antoni decided he could delay his revenge no longer.

"My uncle sent me a foolproof tip this morning, Bellamy. It's a guaranteed cert! If you're hard up, I can lend you quite a bit, you simply can't lose on this one!"

He then purchased on Bellamy's behalf shares in a company which had been steadily going down hill. Before long, they were worthless, and Bellamy owed him money which he couldn't possibly repay.

"I've got to have it back, Bellamy, and that's all there is to it. If you won't write to your parents, I will. They're bound to fork up then."

The more abject Bellamy became, the more urgently he pressed his demand and renewed his threats. It was hugely gratifying to sit back and watch as worry inhibited Bellamy's concentration on his exams and his performance suffered. It was rewarding to observe the silly fool becoming more and more depressed, fearing not only his failure to get to university but his parents' wrath! Revenge was indeed sweet until, three days before the end of term, Bellamy decided to hang himself in the gymnasium.

It was an unexpected stroke of bad luck and when, as a consequence, his stockbroking activities came to light, he blamed himself for not anticipating the degree of Bellamy's panic. Fortunately, with so many boys involved in his syndicate, no one was prepared to point the finger of blame for Bellamy's suicide at him. He was severely reprimanded by the headmaster who, he sensed, was secretly interested in his remarkably successful financial acumen!

"You are a very able scholar, Wisniowiecki, and a promising athlete who has much to contribute to this school. I would not want to lose a pupil of your potential. However, whilst I am prepared to concede that Bellamy may have been motivated to . . . er, end his life . . . on account of his poor examination performance, I cannot entirely exclude the part you played in adding to the poor boy's depression. Mr Watson tells me that you are a quite outstanding mathematician, but in future, kindly confine your abilities to school lessons. You may go . . . and by the way, Wisniowiecki, there will be an inquest, of course, but I see no necessity to mention this . . . er, irregular activity of yours. And I shall take it for granted that you will not . . . er, add to the distress of Bellamy's parents by informing them of his . . . er, failure to meet his . . . er, debts."

The headmaster's insistence on his paying back any commission he'd made from the other boys' dealings and cancelling any other debts meant that he was obliged to part with a large amount of the capital he had accumulated. It was a relatively small price to pay, however. Now that he knew how to make money, he was confident that it was only a matter of time before he would build up his capital again. He wrote to tell his parents that he was going to Bellamy's funeral. Needless to say they were surprised since he'd always denied having any close friends at school.

Wearing his Sunday suit, bare-headed, he stood in the pouring rain watching with pleasure the dirt being shovelled onto Bellamy's coffin, his left hand gripping the twin white burn scars on the inside of his right wrist. Although it had made inroads into his funds, he'd had no compunction in contributing to the school wreath in the form of a cricket bat which the headmaster was now laying on the grave.

Inimicum ulcisci vitam accipere est alteram, *he thought as he followed Bellamy's mourners out of the graveyard. The phrase – part of last night's Latin prep – could not be more appropriate or timely: To be revenged on an enemy is to obtain a second life. It was one he was unlikely ever to forget.*

"No, I don't intend to squander my wealth, Zandra," he repeated, "or allow you to do so! And I shall continue to supervise the household bills."

Zandra was momentarily silenced. She'd had no idea that Anthony felt this way – or indeed, that he resented what was obviously an impoverished childhood. Nevertheless the unreasonableness of his argument had not escaped her.

"My wish to have some work to do is hardly that of someone who contemplates 'squandering' money," she said softly. "On the contrary, Anthony, I'm trying to find a way *not* to spend yours!"

Anthony's pale cheeks flushed an angry red. He banged his fist on the table so that the china and cutlery rattled alarmingly.

"You miss my point entirely, Zandra. I have worked my way into a certain position in life because that is where I wish to be. I command respect. How do you think others would judge my circumstances if I permitted my wife to go out to work like some common labourer? There are times when, despite your belief to the contrary, you are quite extraordinarily stupid, my dear!"

Angry tears welled into Zandra's eyes but she turned quickly away so that he should not see them. How could Anthony talk to her in such a manner? Or in such a disparaging tone? And so soon after they had been as close as any two people could be? The very last thing in the world she wanted was a quarrel, but short of accepting his point of view – however uncompromising she thought it – what possible way was there of making him see her own without this argument becoming a very real rift between them?

"I'm beginning to wonder why you married me, Anthony, if

you really do think I'm so stupid. I am also beginning to wonder what *you* mean by the word love. At least we should be able to talk things over without . . . without this unpleasantness between us. I love you very much and I don't want to do anything that upsets you, but—"

"There are no 'buts'!" Anthony broke in sharply. "This is not a matter where I am prepared to consider a compromise. If you want the truth, I do not believe in compromise. A man should be head of his house – and it's his wife's place to stay at home and look after him. That's all there is to it."

"You're being ridiculously old-fashioned!" Zandra retorted as he rose to leave the room. "Suppose Edith Cavell had had a husband who said she mustn't have a job; and what about Lady Colefax? Amy Johnson? Perhaps you wouldn't be objecting if I went into politics like Lady Astor! Think of all the useful contacts I could make for you! Anyway, why shouldn't I use my brain just because I'm married to you? If you'd wanted a wife who was like most of those feather-brained débutantes I came out with, you should have married one of them, not me."

Zandra expected that Anthony would now tell her that it was she with whom he'd happened to fall in love; her ability to think for herself which had attracted him. Instead, he regarded her coldly.

"I have more important things to do than to stay here arguing about so ridiculous a matter," he said, "and I suggest that you find something else to do with your time. I shall not be back to lunch as I have an early afternoon appointment. I'll see you this evening."

For a moment Zandra was tempted to run after him. She needed to know that their quarrel was not really important and that nothing had changed since last night – that he still loved her; wanted her. Pride, however, soon swept aside this moment of weakness, and resentment resurfaced. Even if Anthony believed he had good reason for not wishing her to undertake employment, he had no right to talk to her in the way that he had – admitting quite openly his indifference to her feelings; her needs. Had he put his arms around her and said: "Darling, please don't do this. I'd hate it if people thought you needed to work; that I couldn't support you; that it wasn't enough for you just to be my wife . . ." then she might easily have acquiesced because she loved him so much and all she really wanted was to make him happy.

He doesn't love me enough to want *me* to be happy! she thought miserably. It was all so different before they were married. When had it started to change? After their honeymoon when he'd handed her that guest list for their first dinner party? Not one of *her* friends or relations were on it, and she had been looking forward so much to entertaining them with Anthony in their new home. He'd taken it for granted that she would comply with his wishes – and she had done so. Then there had been the matter of hiring the servants. Anthony had insisted upon attending the interviews and making the final decisions – something she knew Uncle Toby or Alexis would not have dreamed of doing. Anthony had sacked their first cook without even warning her he was going to do so. She had told herself at the time that he must have thought her too inexperienced to deal with such matters and that he would delegate the household affairs to her once he realized she could manage very adequately without his help.

That time had not yet come and now, not a little frightened by the thought, Zandra wondered if it ever would. Could the reason be that her husband was so much older than herself? Was this the danger which Aunt Willow had foreseen?

Knowing that Anthony would be newly back from America, Zandra had failed to make any appointments for the day. Ordinarily, she would have met one of her friends for lunch; perhaps gone to see one of the new films; called round to see Lucy and, if they were not at school, taken the children to a museum or art gallery. Since there were but three weeks to Christmas, she might well have gone shopping with a friend.

With none of these occupations pending, the long day loomed ahead, and her resentment deepened when she recalled that before Anthony had gone to America, he had promised not to go in to the office on his first day home. Presumably he wished to make it clear that he did not want her company following their row.

After a moment's hesitation, Zandra went into the morning-room and searched her desk for her address book, which, when she found it, she took with her to the telephone in the hall. Not unexpectedly, most of her girlfriends were already committed to other engagements. After five such abortive calls, Zandra found herself welcomed eagerly by her former school friend, Monica Boswell. Like herself, Monica had only recently been married and was living in London. A bright, cheerful girl with a ready sense of humour, she greeted Zandra with a cry of pleasure.

"I'd simply love to join forces, sweetie-pie!" she said. "You couldn't have rung me at a better moment. I was feeling fearfully depressed. It's poor Charles, you see – he's just discovered we have lost all our money . . . you know, darling, in this stock market thingymebob that started in the States. I don't really understand it, but Charles says we're absolutely stony-broke. He's gone off to the office to see what he can do about it, so here I am, madly miz, just needing someone to cheer me up!"

Zandra laughed.

"I'm sure it won't be as bad as you think!" she said comfortingly. "You know how you always exaggerate, Monica. Anyway, I'll come round in half an hour if that's all right with you, and we'll plan what to do with ourselves."

Monica, Zandra thought as the taxi-cab took her through the busy Knightsbridge traffic to Rutland Gate, was one of the empty-headed débutantes she had in mind when she'd told Anthony he should have married one of them! Petite, blonde, entirely scatter-brained, Monica was nevertheless fun to be with, provided it was not for too long a stretch of time. Zandra was shown upstairs to Monica's bedroom by the parlour-maid. She stood in the doorway, her eyes widening at the heap of clothes piled high on the white lace counterpane covering the bed. Monica was in a white silk petticoat and her maid was reaching for yet another dress from the wardrobe.

"Darling, I'm so sorry not to be ready. I simply can't make up my mind what to wear! I love this blue-and-white check suit, but I've worn it so often everyone will think I've nothing else to put on." She gave a deep sigh as she took a straw-coloured draped dress from the pile on the bed. "I suppose if we really are stony, I'll have to get used to wearing the same clothes until I'm sick to death of them. Just look at this Lanvin two-piece – it's one of the most expensive outfits I bought for my trousseau and I've not had it on since my honeymoon. Charles hates me wearing something he recognizes. He says he likes surprises! I suppose I'd better bung the whole lot off to some charity or other."

With another sigh, bordering on the theatrical, she donned the suit and allowed the maid to dress her hair before dismissing her.

"You look divine as always, Zee-Zee!" she said, crossing the room to kiss Zandra. "A bit pale, though. You aren't getting this beastly influenza bug, are you? When are you coming to dinner? Charles is dying to meet your Anthony – he only spoke a few words to him at your housewarming. He's divinely handsome, isn't he? Are you as madly in love as ever? I am with Charles."

"Yes, of course!" Zandra said quickly, and because she was afraid Monica might question her further about Anthony, she turned to the heap of clothes on the bed. "Do you think you really should give all those to a charity?" she asked. "I mean, if you really are in financial trouble, you might need some of them!"

Monica shrugged.

"I hadn't thought of that! And yes, I think Charles really meant it when he said we hadn't a penny to our name. Honestly, darling, I can't for the life of me understand how this could happen. Charles says he's going to have to look for a job but that it won't be easy – because of the depression. I thought it was only poor people who were unemployed – you know, Zee-Zee, people like those workmen in the dole queues!"

"My family have suffered, too!" Zandra said gently. "Look, Monica, if you really are . . . well, up against it, couldn't I buy this red dress from you? It's frightfully pretty and I'm going to need something new for Christmas. I don't imagine anyone would recognize it as yours and I'd really love to have it if it fits me."

Monica's blue eyes widened.

"You mean you wouldn't mind wearing something of mine?" she asked.

Zandra laughed.

"Why on earth should I? I often wore my Cousin Alice's cast-offs when I was little, and believe me, they weren't half as pretty as this." She held the red gown against her, and surveyed herself in the mirror. "It's a little short but I could get my dressmaker to let down the hem. Do let me buy it from you, Monica! It's a Schiaparelli, isn't it?"

"I can't remember, darling. Anyway, you can have it if you really want it. As a gift, I mean. I couldn't take money for it. Charles would have a fit if he thought I was selling my clothes!"

"Then don't tell him!" Zandra said laughing. "You know, Monica, this has given me an idea. I've got a wardrobe full of dresses I never wear. Why don't we go into business together – very discreetly, of course. There must be hundreds of women who couldn't possibly afford to buy a Schiaparelli or a Chanel or Molyneux model who'd give their right arms to have one. And there must be dozens of women like us who only wear a dress a time or two and then give it away. If we could get the two together—"

Monica giggled.

"Yes, but how, Zee-Zee? And what on earth would our husbands say? I mean, second-hand clothes . . . !" She screwed up her nose and gave a little moue of disapproval.

Zandra sat down on the edge of the bed, moving a sable stole and an embroidered velvet evening cloak out of her way.

"People sell their cars and other people buy them," she said, "so I don't see why they can't do the same with clothes. They would all have to be sent to the cleaners first, of course – we'd insist on that! And I don't see why either of us should ever have to see any of the people ourselves. We could set aside an afternoon – ask your maid – Primrose, isn't it? – to answer the door and take any prospective customers to a room where all the clothes were laid out. They could have price tickets on them – half their original price, and we'd keep 10 per cent when we sell other people's clothes."

Once again, Monica screwed up her nose – this time in bewilderment.

"What is 10 per cent then, darling? You know how hopeless I always was at school when it came to arithmetic!"

"Well, if a dress sold for fifty pounds, we'd keep five; or if it sold for twenty, we'd keep two. Then you'd have something to spend on new clothes, Monica, even if Charles is broke!"

Monica's face cleared and she clapped her hands.

"I think it's a perfectly topping idea! Let's do it, Zee-Zee. Do you really think anyone will want to buy things? Suppose they did and wore them to a party or Ascot or something and the person who'd sold them recognized it?"

"Then they'd hardly be likely to admit to having owned it, would they? You know how snobbish people are! The last thing they would want would be for their friends to know they had been selling their clothes!"

"You are clever, Zee-Zee. I'd never have thought of that! But how do we start? I mean, once these are sold" – she pointed to the heap on the bed – "what then?"

"I'll tell Lucy, and Jane. They both buy lovely things . . . and I have quite a few garments I haven't worn since my honeymoon. I think people will pass it on to their friends who are hard up as a kindness. It's a sort of charity, in a way, isn't it?"

Certainly not the kind of charity work Anthony had in mind for her, Zandra thought as she and Monica spent the remainder of the morning elaborating their idea. But it would be quite fun! They would have to set aside time to assess the clothes which people wanted sold, put prices on them, display them attractively. Monica had a sewing room that was rarely used which, she said, would be an ideal place for their enterprise. It needed only a dressing-table and full-length mirror so that visitors could see how they looked; and two or three hanging rails such as they had in department stores on which to put the clothes. Payments would have to be made by cheque and a bank account opened in Monica's or Zandra's name; and Zandra would keep the accounts since Monica was so hopeless at figures!

Zandra took Monica out to lunch at Fortnum's to celebrate. Her earlier mood of depression disappeared completely as they sat at their table watching the women who came in and trying to guess which *couturier* had designed the expensive model suits and coats they were wearing. They giggled over the semi-serious idea that they might have visiting cards printed that they could pass on to these wealthy women informing them where they might dispose of their clothes when they were tired of them; or where they could purchase new ones at a fraction of the cost they normally paid.

"We will only handle really beautiful things!" Zandra said. "Not that dreary brown tweed, for example. And no furs – in case they've got moth in them!"

Monica was less practical. She was already exaggerating the enormous success of their exciting business enterprise.

"We'll make so much money, Charles won't need a job!" she enthused. "I'm going to tell him all about it, Zee-Zee. I expect he'll think we're quite mad, but he won't mind. He's used to me being utterly crazy and he says he never wants me to be any different. I do so adore him, Zee-Zee. Isn't it utterly wonderful being married?" She leant forward and whispered confidentially in Zandra's ear. "We do terribly wicked things, like making love on the drawing-room carpet. Just suppose one of the servants came in! Charles says they are so well trained, they'd just go out

102

again; and anyway, it's our house and we'll do what we like in it! And last Sunday, we didn't get up until lunch-time. Charles wanted to stay in bed all day. He said it was a waste of time getting dressed when it wouldn't be long before he'd have to undress me again. Anyway, Mummy and Daddy were coming for lunch, so we had to get up."

She leant back in her chair and drawing out a silver cigarette case, lit a black Turkish cigarette which she had put in an amber holder.

"What I can't understand, Zee-Zee, is why Mummy should have warned me before my wedding night that I'd probably hate . . . you know . . . doing it. I think it's quite divine fun and if I hadn't thought she'd be shocked, I would have told her so when Charles and I got back from our honeymoon."

"Maybe you wouldn't have liked it if you'd married someone you didn't really love. My cousin, Lucy, said that made all the difference."

Aware that Monica's attention had wandered and that her friend was not interested in the opinions of her Rochford relations, Zandra put down her empty coffee cup and took up her gloves.

"We shall be late for the matinée if we don't get a move on!" she said. "I've been longing to see *The Blue Angel* but Anthony doesn't like the cinema. Lucy said Marlene Dietrich is quite gorgeous!"

Three hours later, the two girls emerged happily from the cinema, humming the German film star's song, "Falling in Love Again"; but as they parted company, Zandra to drive home in a taxi-cab, she felt a sudden return of her earlier depression. After the angry exchange of words she and Anthony had had at breakfast she could hardly expect him to be in a loving mood this evening; besides which, she was not feeling particularly loving herself! There was no easy solution to their altercation, unless he changed his attitude towards her – and somehow she could not see that happening. Well, she was not going to be treated like a child. Just because neither Jane nor Aunt Willow ever disputed what Oliver or Uncle Toby said was no reason for her to be a slave to Anthony's dictates. Maybe his staff at the office had to jump to attention every time he barked out an order, but she was his wife – and entitled to think for herself.

One thing she would *not* do, Zandra told herself as she entered her house, was tell Anthony of the plan she and Monica had devised to earn themselves some pocketmoney. She was partly amused and partly frightened to think of his reaction if he knew of it, although there was no reason why he should. Although Monica was a known gossip, neither she nor Charles were very likely to advertise the fact that part of their home was a second-hand clothes shop!

Now that Oliver and Jane had had to tighten their purse-strings, she was sure Jane would jump at the chance to buy Monica's unwanted white ballgown and thus she, Zandra, would be doing each a good turn. There was no need for her to tell Jane where it had come from. Had she had more than her taxi-fare in her own purse – or a bank account of her own – she would have bought it for herself! She and Monica would have to open a bank account, she thought, as the parlour-maid brought tea to her in the drawingroom. Charles would tell them how to go about it. Lucky Monica to have such an easygoing husband!

I am being quite unfair to Anthony! she reproached herself. He can't help it if his business affairs take him away so often; or at such short notice. If he didn't work so hard, he wouldn't be so successful – and it was entirely due to his success that he'd been able to put her family back on its financial feet. Moreover, he had bought this lovely house for her and allowed her to furnish it as she pleased, regardless of cost. Nor was his generosity confined to her. Guy had told her that his father had died in the war; and that what money he'd left had gone on his education; so he was desperate to get a job when he left school. For one thing, he couldn't raise the money for the major repairs needed to his mother's bungalow in Eastbourne. Anthony had taken him on to his staff *and* offered to give him a mortgage with very easy repayment terms, without which Guy's mother could not have continued to live there. After a year working in the accounts department, he'd been promoted to his present position with a big rise in salary. It was no wonder, therefore, that Guy was such a loyal, conscientious employee.

"I'm really little more than a glorified organizer!" he'd told her on one of their drives down to Rochford. "But I do seem to be able to cope when things get hectic. Otherwise I've no real qualifications other than that I speak French! My father was a diplomat before the war and we lived abroad until war broke out. Father came home to join up and left me at my boarding school in Switzerland for the duration. After the war ended, I came home to spend my school holidays with my mother. She insisted I complete my education at the Sorbonne, but by the time that was over, jobs in those post-war years were hard to come by."

Guy's revelations, Zandra thought, explained what Anthony had meant when he'd told her that, because Guy had had such a cosmopolitan background, he was able to mix faultlessly in any company and be self-effacing when he wasn't needed.

As if her unbidden thoughts about Guy Bristow had projected it, the telephone rang in the hall and the maid came in to tell Zandra that he wished to speak to her. Zandra's heart sank as she went to answer it. This could only mean one thing – Anthony was going to be late home. He invariably got Guy to give her this message rather than ringing her himself.

"Mr Wisson has had to take a client out to dinner!" Guy said with the usual note of apology in his voice. "He expects to be home by eleven but he could be later, so—"

"So don't wait up for him!" Zandra broke in. "Oh well, it can't be helped. Thanks for letting me know, Guy!"

"I'm sorry . . . I mean, Mr Wisson is very sorry that he couldn't let you know sooner."

"Of course, I understand. Thanks again!" Zandra said before replacing the receiver. She stood for a moment in the deserted hall, lost in thought. Perhaps she wouldn't have minded quite so much if Anthony had taken just a few minutes to telephone her himself. She didn't want to hear that note of pity in Guy Bristow's voice. It was as if he knew exactly how miserable an evening she would now have to spend on her own. Resentment welled up inside her. This was only Anthony's second night back in England and yet he'd not wanted to spend it with her. Perhaps this was his way of punishing her because she had argued with him about the airline job! Or was it something more serious than that? Was it possible Anthony had a mistress – another woman in his life of whom she knew nothing?

No, not that! she told herself as she went slowly upstairs to her bedroom where she knew Mollie would be waiting to help her change for dinner. Anthony loved *her*, and last night he'd been as passionate in his love-making as she had ever known him. However indifferent he might sometimes appear to be in the daytime, at night he would claim her for his own with a passion that was at times almost violent.

In all probability he was quite genuinely busy, and she was being stupid and fanciful to imagine otherwise. On the other hand, if he *was* trying to show her that he intended to withdraw his love whenever she displeased him, then she could do the same. She would go to bed early, and even if she was awake when he came home, she would pretend to be asleep, for much as she loved and wanted him, she was not going to be any man's slave.

Chapter 7

December 1931 – January 1932

Willow's gaze travelled slowly round the drawing-room, her face bright with contentment as she surveyed her large family. In a few minutes' time – in accordance with Rochford tradition – the servants would carry in the steaming bowl of hot punch which would be placed on the floor between two lighted candelabra. The entire family would form a circle around it, the wireless would be turned on, and they would wait for the booming tones of Big Ben. At the last stroke, Alice would seat herself at the piano and as everyone linked hands, they would bring in the New Year with the familiar words of "Auld Lang Syne".

Next year, she thought with a sigh, someone would have to take Alice's place for it seemed unlikely that once she was married, Alice and her husband would travel all the way from Pau for this family gathering. Indeed, she was reluctant to return once more for her own wedding next summer, preferring to be married from the Casa Montijo. According to Silvie, the couple would not be very well off, and, moreover, Alice was hoping to start a family as soon as possible.

They would miss her, of course, Willow told herself as she glanced at her daughter who was chatting to Jane – eulogizing about her Claude, she thought with a wry smile, for Alice had talked of little else since her arrival with Silvie and Pelham for Christmas. It was good to see her so happy, and indeed, her happiness was reflected in her face which was almost pretty now that she was so animated. If this Claude Calonne could achieve such a transformation, it really didn't matter that Pelham could not stand the fellow whom he had unkindly described to her in private as being "a typical bourgeois Frog!"

"It is not that Pelham is being *très snob!*" Silvie had explained. "It is because Claude is artistic and at times, one has to admit, appears slightly effeminate in the way he gesticulates . . . and dresses. Nor does the poor fellow play tennis or golf, and I fear is somewhat lacking in a sense of humour. He is not Pelham's type but, as I have told my beloved husband, it is Alice and not he who will have to live with Claude!"

How fond she was of Silvie and Pelham! Willow thought. Their infrequent visits to Rochford Manor passed all too quickly. Ever since they had removed to the South of France, she had been promising to visit them to see their new home. Now there was an added incentive and this coming summer, she and Toby would be making the journey to Pau for Alice's wedding. Oliver, of course, was trying to persuade them to fly to Paris by aeroplane. There was a new Handley-Page model about to be introduced by Imperial Airways which had an enclosed cockpit and could travel at 110 miles an hour, he had explained; they would find it so much pleasanter than crossing the Channel on the ferry, and far, far quicker.

Oliver was currently deep in conversation with Pelham and Anthony – talking about aeroplanes, she surmised. According to him, Anthony's intervention in Sky-Ways had been a double blessing, for he had authorized the purchases of two new aeroplanes and a third, a biplane, was on order. It was equipped with a wireless so that the pilot could keep in contact with radio stations on the ground. New offices had been built and fully furnished; trained mechanical engineers employed to service the machines, and a third pilot engaged to cope with the growing demand for their services. Sky-Ways had become commercially viable and was making a lot of money. No wonder Oliver held his employer in such high regard! There seemed little doubt now that Oliver would, after all, be able to afford to send Giles to Eton and Oxford.

With a fond smile, Willow looked up surreptitiously at the gallery where her grandson, in dressing-gown and pyjamas, was sitting with Lucy's little ones, Robin and Eve. The three children had determined to see the New Year in, and imagined that their parents and grandparents were unaware of their presence. She was reminded suddenly of another child crouched in the gallery watching the grownups in their beautiful ballgowns down below. Could it be as much as forty years ago? She had been fifteen years old and, so she had imagined, was in love with Rowell, the eldest of the Rochford brothers. Toby – even then the kind, thoughtful person he was – had brought her some of the party fare to eat. She must ask him in a moment if he remembered that night.

Meanwhile, she would tell Lucy or Zandra to take the children a few pastries left over from the five-course dinner they had not long consumed; and then pack them off to bed! How lovely Lucy looked in her slim blue panne evening gown! No wonder Alexis had his arm around her shoulders and was gazing at her so adoringly.

Willow's thoughts were momentarily interrupted as Zandra came to stand by her chair.

"Shall I put the wireless on now, Aunt Willow? It's five minutes to midnight."

"Yes, darling, please do!" Willow answered, and watched as her niece crossed the room and began twisting the knobs on the wireless set. She felt a sudden twinge of anxiety. Zee-Zee had lost weight since her marriage – a lot of weight. How had she not noticed it before? Her face, too, was thin and drawn, and now Willow came to consider it, the child had not been her usual animated self.

Her anxiety increasing – for Willow loved this child almost as dearly as she loved Oliver – she searched her mind for possible reasons. Did Zandra's busy social life in London not suit her? Whenever Willow telephoned, Zandra seemed to be planning a big dinner party for Anthony's business associates which, strangely, she seemed to find a strain despite the fact that she had a retinue of servants to carry out her wishes. It was not like Zee-Zee to find such a task in the least nerve-racking, for she had frequently organized dinner parties at Rochford for Willow, and always done so most efficiently. Moreover, shyness was not a part of her nature as it had been Alice's; or, before her marriage, Jane's. Zandra enjoyed talking to people and could always converse easily and intelligently, and revelled in being the centre of attention! From what Zandra had told her, some of these guests were politicians, some prominent industrialists, some foreigners, all important in their own fields, so she was not having to converse with men she chose to call "chinless wonders" – her description for some of the titled but brainless young men she had met during her brief Season.

Willow rejected the idea that these parties might be the cause of Zandra's changed manner. It was more probable that she missed the countryside, for she had always been an outdoor person who loved riding, her dogs and pets, tennis, swimming and, to her own dismay, flying Oliver's dangerous little aeroplane! Zee-Zee had been a tomboy and indeed, Toby had often remarked that she should have been a boy! Nowadays, of course, it was difficult to remember the untidy ragamuffin she had once been. No one could look more feminine, more fashionable. Even Silvie had commented that these days Zee-Zee was as chic as any French woman – a high accolade indeed from her Parisian sister-in-law!

The door opened and two of the parlour-maids came into the room bearing the lighted candelabra, followed by a manservant with the punchbowl. Zandra turned towards her aunt and at that moment, it suddenly struck Willow that her niece might be

110

pregnant. Lucy had had exactly that same pinched, drawn look when she was first carrying her babies. If it were true, no wonder Zandra looked tired. How exciting for her and Anthony if her guess was correct! She rose quickly from her chair and, as her family began to form a circle, she took Zandra's hand in hers and said softly: "I hope this coming year will be the happiest of your life, my darling!" Then crossing her arms, she linked her hand with Toby's, for he was always the first to kiss her when Big Ben struck the final midnight hour.

As Alice played the opening bars of "Auld Lang Syne", Zandra turned to smile at Anthony, and for a moment, her voice faltered as she saw that he was not joining in the song although he was mouthing the words. He did not return her smile. His eyes were – as so often of late – that dark, unfathomable grey. Although he had been jovial enough during the New Year's Eve dinner and even joined in the charades that were part of the family seasonal ritual, he now seemed to Zandra to be detached; no longer part of the family group.

Ever since Anthony had entered her life, all her relations had put themselves out to welcome him into the fold. Everyone genuinely liked him and this Christmas he was being as generous as ever with flowers, fruit, Fortnum's hampers, the best wine and port, for all the adults; magnificent toys for the children; handsome tips for the servants. It was as if, having no family of his own, he was only too anxious to merge himself into that of the Rochfords. Why should he be so withdrawn now? she asked herself.

Perhaps at this special time when the old year had ended and the new was just beginning, he was remembering his own family, and that this explained his detachment. He certainly had no reason to be displeased about anything or anyone – and it was usually only when he was angry that he seemed to turn into a very different person from the warm, passionate man she had married.

Impulsively, she reached up and kissed his cheek.

"Happy New Year, my dearest!" she whispered. As Anthony

returned her kiss, she felt herself relaxing. Really, she was becoming quite ridiculously emotional these days, she chided herself. The least little thing seemed to reduce her to tears. One tiny cross word from Anthony or even a complaint from him about the food or a lost cufflink would cause her body to tense in a fashion out of all proportion to the issue. Not that she was in any doubt as to the reason for such emotionalism. Dr Petrie had told her it was perfectly normal in pregnancy and that she would soon begin to feel less nausea and become delightfully placid as her term progressed. She would probably put on weight, too!

It was high time she took her courage in both hands and told Anthony he was going to be a father before the coming year was out. The baby was due in the summer and it would not be long now before it would begin to show. She would tell Anthony tonight. In fact, it was stupid of her to have put off telling him for so long. Although he had maintained from the start of their marriage that he did not want a family for several years, once he knew the choice was no longer in his hands, he would quickly adapt to the idea.

She must tell him soon, for Guy had said that he had already filled in several dates for Anthony to go abroad in the new year, and Anthony would not want to be out of the country when his child was born. Because he spent such long hours at his office, it hadn't been difficult to conceal her early morning sickness from him. Nor had he noticed her inability to enjoy their love-making to the same degree. For the present, desire had left her and she had to simulate an eagerness she was far from feeling. How could she possibly have told Anthony that she preferred sleep to his caresses! It would be different once he knew the reason. Then he would understand and would not make the same demands upon her which once she had welcomed with such eagerness.

It was nearly two o'clock in the morning before she and Anthony were at last alone together in the big spare room in the tower where once, according to Aunt Willow, her poor crippled mother had spent her invalid childhood. As he came through from the adjoining dressing-room and climbed into the big, brass bedstead beside her, she moved trustingly into his outstretched arms. His cheeks were flushed, and by the way he drew her body against his own, she knew that he was anxious to make love to her. Easing herself a little way away, she reached out a hand to touch his face.

"Anthony, darling, can we talk? There's something I've been wanting to say to you and . . . well, this seems to me to be the right moment. I—"

"It doesn't seem the right moment to me!" Anthony broke in huskily. "I don't want to talk, Zandra. I want to make love to you." He reached out to draw her close again and felt her body stiffen.

"What's the matter?" he asked, his fingers toying with one of her nipples. "You like this, don't you? And this . . ." He kissed her hungrily, his mouth bruising her lips. "What's the matter?" he asked again. "You're not worried I've had too much of your uncle's excellent punch, are you? I can assure you I'll be careful!"

He turned to the bedside table and began searching for the protection he always used – or nearly always. There had been that one single occasion when he had returned from a week in the States and had been in too much urgency to bother. That was when she had conceived.

"Anthony, darling, there's no need!" she said quickly. "It won't make any difference now. You see, I'm already pregnant!"

Slowly, almost as if in slow motion, Anthony turned to face her.

"Did I hear you correctly? You're *pregnant*? My God, I hope not. I don't believe this. You aren't serious, are you? Is this your idea of a joke?"

Zandra caught hold of his hand and clung to it.

"Of course I wouldn't joke about such a thing. I'm going to have a baby, darling, and that's what I've been wanting to tell

113

you for ages. You don't mind, do you? I know we said we wouldn't have children for a while, but since it's happened anyway . . . Anthony, darling, say you are pleased."

He withdrew his hand and sat up stiffly.

"I'm damned if I will! Pleased! Good God, Zandra, that's the very last thing I am. I simply don't believe this. Are you sure? Do you know what you're talking about?"

Zandra bit her lip and clenched her hands to stop them from trembling. She had feared Anthony might not be exactly over-joyed – but she had not expected him to be so angry.

"Yes, I am sure; and yes, I know what I am talking about. Dr Petrie has confirmed it. The baby will be born in July, and I'm sorry if you don't want it, Anthony, but I do!"

Anthony stared down at her, his eyes once more that unfath-omable grey.

"So you've known for some time? Why didn't you tell me? Warn me? I dislike having bad news sprung on me like this."

Zandra felt her cheeks burning as anger replaced disappoint-ment.

"You may think it's 'bad news', Anthony, but I'm pleased, if you want the truth. I don't have nearly enough to occupy me and I can't for the life of me see why you should be affected. You're not going to be asked to take care of it!"

Anthony's mouth tightened into a thin line.

"If this is your way of getting back at me because I wouldn't allow you to have a job at Sky-Ways, then you have made a very big mistake, Zandra; one you will certainly regret."

Zandra's eyes flashed dangerously.

"Are you threatening me, Anthony? With what, may I ask? I'm going to have this baby and there's nothing you can do about it. As to my 'getting back at you', as you put it, if you stopped to think, you'd realize that it is *your* mistake, not mine. You were the one who was going to be responsible for protecting me against having a baby. As to my having a job, you may be able to control who Sky-Ways employs because you are the major shareholder, but you don't own everything, and you can't stop me working elsewhere however much you want to."

She broke off, realizing suddenly that her anger had tempted her to say far more than she had intended. Anthony knew nothing of Alternatives, the business she and Monica had been running so successfully these past two months. Already they had twelve society women only too pleased to find buyers for their unwanted model clothes; and twice as many wives with less affluent husbands only too willing to buy. Last week they had found a seamstress prepared to make any alterations that might be required – letting out a seam, putting up a hem, changing the trimmings so that a dress would not easily be recognized by its previous owner. One young woman had bought her entire spring wardrobe from their collection, changed every button, belt, bow and trimming so that even Monica had not recognized her own ballgown when she had met the buyer at a party! Neither Monica nor she herself had grown very rich yet on the profits, but Charles was wildly optimistic and was even talking about renting special premises so that he did not have to absent himself from home twice a week when the buyers called. The sellers sent theirs by post!

Anthony had by now climbed out of bed, put on his dressing-gown and was standing by the fire, his back towards her. When at last he spoke, it was to say in a flat tone: "I had intended taking you to Geneva with me in April, and then on to Germany. Your uncle said your brother, Jamie, was going to Munich on a family exchange visit when he leaves school next year. I said I would make enquiries about a suitable family when I was over there, and assuming I located one, you would have had the opportunity to meet them."

"But darling, I could still go!" Zandra cried, momentarily forgetting her earlier anger and dismay. "There's absolutely no reason why I couldn't travel with you. We aren't living in Victorian times any more when prospective mothers couldn't be seen in public! I'd love to go, and Jamie would be happy about

115

it, too, because he knows I know the kind of people he likes. It's a wonderful idea!"

"But no longer a practical one!" Anthony rejoined in a cold tone. "I have several important new business contacts in Germany and I was counting on you to ease the way; to assist me in establishing good relationships; to charm them. You are a very desirable woman, which is one of the reasons I married you, and you have the ability to make men eager to please you, though I don't think you are aware of it. In an unattractive, pregnant condition, they are hardly likely to find you quite so desirable."

Zandra was instantly and effectively silenced. She had not known that Anthony felt as he did about pregnant females; that he found them unappealing. She might have argued that when Jane had been carrying Giles, everyone had remarked upon the fact that she had never looked more beautiful! But pride would not allow her to dispute the point with Anthony. If that was the way *he* felt about her, then he could stay as far away from her as he chose. She would not be made to feel ashamed. Nor, when she came to consider the matter, was she particularly happy to learn that he was using her "desirability" to further his business interests. To be proud of her was one thing, but to flaunt her was quite another. She would infinitely prefer him to be jealous of other men's interest in her. Perhaps Anthony would not like it quite so much if she were to flirt openly with his clients! Maybe she should test his reactions by flirting with Guy! He was young, nice looking, charming – and she knew he liked her. But she suspected that he might be just the tiniest bit in love with her, and to encourage him for so trivial a reason would be most unfair.

Anthony was returning to the bedside. He stared down at her for a long minute and then said: "Well, Zandra, you have made your own bed so you'll just have to lie in it. I myself don't have the time, still less the inclination, to be a parent. I suggest you employ a capable nanny when the time comes who will keep it out of the way. We shall just have to be a lot more careful in future!"

It was *his* oversight, not hers! Zandra thought, near to tears. What right had he to hold her even partially responsible? And finally, knowing that nothing could be done to alter the situation, why, if he loved her, couldn't he see how utterly miserable his attitude was making her? Even if he didn't want the baby, he could at least have pretended he did, if only to put her mind at rest.

"I don't think you really love me at all!" she whispered, tiredness making her incautious. Anthony did not care for criticism. He took off his dressing-gown and flung it angrily on the foot of the bed.

"You are being ridiculous, Zandra. Whether I love you or not is hardly relevant. Now it's very late and I'm tired. I've no wish to continue this conversation and I suggest you, too, get some sleep." He climbed in beside her and switching off the bedside light, turned his back towards her.

He can't mean to leave things like this, Zandra told herself. Surely in a minute he would turn and take her in his arms; tell her he was sorry if he had upset her, and apologize for reacting to her news so badly? They couldn't possibly start the new year with this unpleasantness between them! It was not in her nature to prolong a quarrel; to let it simmer. She wanted them to make up and be friends, lovers again. Surely he knew how much she loved him and how important it was to her that he loved her in return? She could forgive him for those cruel things he'd said if only he told her he regretted them. People frequently said things in moments of anger or shock that afterwards they bitterly regretted. She had often in the past felt mortified when she had railed against Aunt Willow's discipline; or quarrelled with Jamie or with one of her friends. Once Anthony became accustomed to the idea, he would want this child as much as she did; be proud of his parenthood. He simply needed time to get used to the thought, and she had been tactless to blurt it out suddenly when he was tired after so long a day. With hindsight, it might have been better to tell him *after* they had made love!

For the next thirty minutes, Zandra lay wide awake waiting for some sign from Anthony that he, too, wished to make up their quarrel. His breathing sounded irregular and she was convinced he was, like herself, still awake. But his face remained rigidly turned away from her and when finally she put out a tentative hand to touch him, he ignored it.

Tears of disappointment mingling with fatigue rolled down her cheeks. This was no time to be miserable, she told herself furiously. Jane maintained that the reasons Giles was such a happy child was because she'd been so content all the time she had carried him. Well, she did not want a miserable, wailing baby. If Anthony didn't love it, she would just have to give it twice as much affection herself! Jamie, for one, would love it. She could imagine him being tickled to death to be an uncle – and he not yet seventeen! Oliver would love it as he did all children – Alexis, too. There would be plenty of replacements for her baby's father.

Comforted to some degree by her thoughts, Zandra was on the point of sleep when suddenly Anthony turned and, without a word, took her roughly in his arms. A minute later, he lay above her, and ripping her nightdress from her shoulders, he forced his tongue between her closed lips.

Frightened more by his roughness than the unexpectedness of his actions, for a moment Zandra resisted him. He caught hold of her wrists and pinioned her arms above her head. His mouth travelled down her body, seemingly devouring her. Then he forced one leg between hers and prised them apart.

He must know I don't want this! Zandra thought. He is out of control and he doesn't care! But even whilst mentally she hated what he was doing to her, as he thrust himself into her, she felt her body begin to respond. It was over a week since he had last approached her and surprisingly, she found herself becoming as aroused as Anthony. Without knowing she did so, she wrenched her hands free from his grasp and clutched at his back, drawing him closer into her. His skin felt burning hot and her own body was wet with perspiration as they rose and fell now in a wild frenzy of movement.

The thought struck her suddenly that they were coupling like two animals; that this wasn't loving! Then thought ceased and she was conscious only of her body's need for fulfilment and her hunger for it to be assuaged.

Only then did Anthony cry out. His voice was harsh, almost that of an antagonist as he gasped: "I want you, damn you! God, how I want you. You weaken me with this body of yours. Well, I'll show you who is master here! Say you want me. Beg me! You'll do anything I want, won't you, anything I want . . . this . . . this . . . this . . . !"

She wanted to tell him he was hurting her but she dared not do so lest he stopped what he was doing – and she was so close to that wonderful release she knew he could give her. At the same time, she sensed that this was wrong – that it had to be wrong for it to happen without affection, tenderness, love; but she was powerless to resist him. He was, after all, the master and she the slave.

Zandra was unaware of the tears pouring down her cheeks as she arched her body towards him and waited silently for release.

When she awoke next morning, Anthony's place beside her was empty. Her maid, Mollie, whom she always took with her to Rochford because of the shortage of servants there since they had been obliged to make economies, was drawing the curtains.

"Madam thought you'd like to have breakfast in bed this morning, Miss Zandra!" the maid said cheerfully. "It's a fine, sunny day and Mr Wisson and Lord Rochford have taken the children for a ride. Madam said she would be in to see you when you was woke up!"

As Zandra sat up, she became aware of her torn nightdress and the crumpled state of the bed. Hurriedly she pulled on her swansdown bedjacket and straightened the bedclothes whilst Mollie went back downstairs to fetch the breakfast tray. Memories of last night's events flooded her mind and her cheeks burned momentarily before they paled again as she recalled Anthony's horrifying attitude to the coming baby. She felt a sudden sense of desolation, for she knew instinctively that Anthony's violent love-making had not been born of love – any more than had her response, she reminded herself. They remained totally alienated and she could see no way in which their differences could be resolved.

When Willow came into the room, Zandra had not touched her breakfast. The coffee she had tried to drink made her feel sick, and she was close to tears . . . so close that she couldn't return her aunt's cheerful smile.

After one look at Zandra's white face and downcast expression, Willow sat down on the edge of the bed and, replacing the half-empty cup on the tray, took Zandra's hand in hers.

"I can see you're not feeling well, my darling. Can you tell me what's wrong?"

It was on the tip of Zandra's tongue to tell Willow of the dreadful quarrel she had had with Anthony, but before she could do so, her aunt added: "Would I be right in thinking you are going to have a baby, my dear?"

Zandra nodded, and was immediately enveloped in Willow's embrace.

"Both Jane and I guessed as much!" her aunt said. 'Anthony didn't give us a single hint this morning, but he was in excellent spirits so I imagine he is quite delighted."

The truth about Anthony's attitude, which Zandra was on the point of confessing, died on her lips. What was to be gained by making this loving affectionate aunt unhappy? And perhaps, after all, she herself was worrying unduly. Now that he'd had time for reflection, perhaps Anthony had come to terms with the thought of becoming a father. Hadn't Aunt Willow just said that he was "in excellent spirits"?

"You mustn't worry about feeling tearful and off colour at the moment," Willow was saying maternally. "Lots of mothers to be feel low at first, and some suffer horribly from early morning sickness." She smiled. "I see you couldn't face your breakfast, but you must try to eat, darling. You'll feel better if you do. You should have told me sooner, Zee-Zee. I would never have allowed you to stay up so late last night!"

For the first time, Zandra smiled.

"I enjoyed the party, Aunt Willow, and really, I'm perfectly well. I'm just a little worried – I mean, Anthony and I had made up our minds not to have children for a few years. I think he . . . he wanted me all to himself for a bit . . . to travel with him . . . that kind of thing."

Her aunt's smile broadened.

"I dare say your news came as a shock, darling, but now he's had time to become accustomed to the idea, I'm sure he'll be as pleased as Punch. Men always want a son and heir; and if they have a daughter instead, they dote on them. Believe me, Zee-Zee dear, if he isn't already so, it won't be long before your Anthony will be delighted, even if he does have to share you."

Despite her aunt's reassurances, Zandra awaited Anthony's return from his ride with nervous apprehension for she was well aware of the fact that her aunt hadn't heard any of the dreadful things Anthony had said to her, nor the vitriolic tone in which he had voiced them. It was something she could not easily forget. Nevertheless, when Anthony came into the morning-room where she was sitting by the blazing fire chatting to the other members of the family who had not gone out, he crossed the room at once and kissed her cheek. There was a faint smile on his face, and his tone was solicitous as he said: "Did you have a good rest, my dear? I tried not to disturb you!"

"Yes, thank you, Anthony!" she replied. "I was overtired, I think." For the fraction of a second, she hesitated before adding in as casual a tone as she could muster: "By the way, I have told Aunt Willow our news. I felt she ought to know in case she thought I was being disgracefully lazy; and needless to say, she has told everyone else!"

Within minutes, both Zandra and Anthony were surrounded

by the family eager to offer their congratulations. Watching her husband from the corner of her eye, Zandra saw that he was nodding and smiling like any man happy, in the same circumstances, to receive such felicitations.

"The news was a trifle unexpected, but of course, Zandra and I are delighted!" he was saying as Toby rang the bell for a servant to bring in some champagne. "I suppose since there's a fifty-fifty chance that it might be a boy, I shall have to think about putting him down for my old school – or perhaps it should be Eton. It's a Rochford tradition, isn't it, for the boys to go there?"

Only Pelham and Silvie were silent as everyone else started to talk at once. Catching one another's eye, each knew what the other was thinking – no wonder Anthony Wisson had suggested Eton, for his son might not be welcome in a school which he, himself, had so nearly been obliged to leave in disgrace.

Chapter 8

Guy removed his jacket and ran his fingers round the collar of his shirt. The July sun was stiflingly hot and the trees in Russell Square gave scant shade from the heat of its rays. There was not even a slight breeze to circulate the air. Although it was cooler inside the building, he had felt a desperate need to get out of Wisson's offices in Bedford Place; away from his desk and that odious buff file with its unsavoury contents.

Glancing at his watch, he saw that his lunch-hour was nearly over and knew that he could not delay much longer his return to work – and to the problem as to what he should do now with the documents he had inadvertently come across. Why, he asked himself, had his boss not destroyed them? Or if he had reason to keep them, then why had he not made certain that such confidential information was locked away in his safe? The safe was specifically for keeping the private documents that were not for office staff consumption.

When Guy had opened the file relating to the purchase of Havorhurst village and the Rochford land, it had been at the request of Lord Rochford who had wanted to check whether a particular stream lay on his side of the new boundary or upon

Mr Wisson's. Since Guy's employer was abroad, Guy had offered to make the check himself – a simple enough undertaking. Having established the facts, he was closing the relevant file when a small sheaf of papers clipped together had fallen to the floor. On top had been an invoice for services rendered by a private investigatory firm. It had been ink stamped as fully paid and Guy knew that such invoices should be in the hands of their accountant, whose office adjoined his own.

The accountant, a Mr Mackinson, was a grey-haired taciturn Scot, tight lipped and humourless. In the year that Guy had worked under him, he'd been constantly in Mackinson's bad books and consequently in fear of getting the sack! Mackinson had not only been critical of Guy's lack of accountancy qualifications, but he'd made it clear he resented Guy's background. He'd gone out of his way to ridicule Guy's speech, and constantly referred to him in heavily sarcastic tones as "our young *gentleman*, Mr Bristow!" The older man's dislike of him had been obvious to Anthony Wisson who had seemed amused by it. 'He resents the fact that you're such an obvious product of your class, Bristow, and that it is as much for this fact as for your brains that I am training you to become my personal assistant. You do not have to like him; just make it your business to get on with him as best you can. He's brilliant at his job and I don't intend to get rid of him!'

It would bring a string of invective down upon him if one of Mackinson's invoices went astray, Guy knew, and he had been on the verge of taking the invoice to him when he decided it might be prudent first to look through the papers attached to it, lest they belonged somewhere else. As far as was possible, he tried to avoid giving Mackinson a chance to criticize his efficiency. It was a decision he now desperately regretted, for the papers he had read with growing dismay were of the most confidential nature, and they related to the Rochford family.

By the date on the invoice, Guy realized that Wisson had requested the investigation to be made prior to his marriage.

Obviously he had decided to make sure that the family into which he was marrying had no hidden secrets that would rebound on him! It was in keeping, Guy knew only too well, with Wisson's *modus operandi*. His boss seldom took any action or made any decision without first checking thoroughly all the relevant facts – particularly the less obvious ones. It was a precaution which might explain in part why he was so successful in all his business undertakings. One of Guy's jobs was to make the more obvious researches on a future client's company affairs, his financial viability; his educational and career histories; his hobbies, sports, interests, insofar as they were known. Such information as he obtained was treated by Wisson as confidential and filed away in his safe where, as he had pointed out to Guy, it could do no harm to his potential client and might be useful for himself in his dealings with the individual.

Guy could see no harm in it, but this singularly confidential information about the Rochfords was somehow very different. Even Wisson must have thought so since he'd employed a private investigator, in preference to Guy, to make the searches into the past. Guy had already supplied a summary of Oliver Rochford's and Henry Barratt's flawless pasts, and Mackinson had verified the financial set-up of the airline, Sky-Ways, before Wisson had made his offer to buy it. This particular investigation could only, therefore, have related to his marriage to Zandra McGill.

Thoroughly dejected, Guy made his way back to his office. He was only too well aware that he could no longer delay dealing with the incriminating pages, and he was no nearer reaching a decision as to what action he should take. The one thing he did decide before postponing a decision by going out for a walk in the nearby square, was *not* to hand them with the invoice to Mackinson. That much at least he could do to protect the Rochfords. He had met nearly all Zandra's relations at her wedding and insofar as he'd had time to get to know them, he'd liked them very much.

Seated once more at his desk, Guy drew the offending papers

out of the top drawer where he'd temporarily placed them. Did every large dynastic family like the Rochfords have one or two such dark skeletons in their cupboards? he asked himself. As far as he knew, his own family – though untitled – had once been as affluent and respected as the Rochfords, but had no such colourful black sheep. If there were, neither of his parents had ever mentioned them, and it was reasonable to suppose that the Rochford family would equally have kept Zandra and all the younger generation in ignorance.

Guy had read only the first of the reports – but a half of the first page – before he'd put it down with a feeling of intense revulsion. The contents contained the kind of highly unsavoury details that, if ever they became known, would be bandied about by gutter-minded gossips – or worse still, would be food for blackmailers! Try as he might, he could not put out of his mind those first few incriminating facts. The page had been headed "The Honourable Sophia (Lucienne) Rochford" – a name that he had not at first recognized as being part of Zandra's family. On the first line was the date of birth of a female child followed by the date of her death a day later. This entry had been red-inked and a note by it referred to an exhumation of the infant's coffin in 1905, when it was found to be empty.

Intrigued by this extraordinary revelation Guy had been unable to put the page down. There followed an account which purported to be the true fate of the child at the hands of its great-grandmother.

14 March 1894: Infant removed at birth from mother, Lady Rochford (née Willow Tetford) by Lord Rowell Rochford's grandmother, Lady Clothilde, and placed by her with local wet-nurse until age of two.

1896: Sent secretly to a French convent – Couvent du Coeur Sanglant.

1905: When the child's convent fees ceased to be paid on death of Lady Clothilde, Sophia placed by nuns in service of French family.

1906: Now aged twelve, Sophia obtained new employment in a Parisian brothel – Le Ciel Rouge – where she remained for four years. She became known there by the name of "La Perle".

1910: At the age of sixteen, the girl returned to Rochford Manor and was renamed Lucienne by her father, Lord Rowell Rochford, and sent to The Norbury Establishment for Young Ladies to be re-educated as befitted her background. The scandal of her childhood was successfully concealed by the family.

1912: Lucienne (formerly Sophia) married to Count Alexis Zemski and successfully launched in Society. All documents relating to the above facts given into the custody of Count Zemski immediately after the wedding.

Note: It is unclear whether Téodora, the daughter born to Lucienne, Countess Zemski, six months after the marriage, was, in fact, Zemski's child; and this can be further investigated if you so wish. The girl subsequently died in a drowning accident in 1918 aged five.

At this point, Guy had ceased reading. Even now, he was finding it impossible to believe those cold, incriminating facts. Not only was Countess Zemski a stunningly beautiful woman, but she was the epitome of all that was to be admired and respected in someone of her social standing. She was one of London's most popular hostesses; had a beautiful home, two delightful children and was always much involved in raising money for charities, particularly those involving children, the poor and ex-servicemen. She was also on the management committee of a "Home for Fallen Women"! *That the countess herself had once been one of them was inconceivable.* The information contained in this report could be immensely damaging to her – and to her husband and children – if it got into the wrong hands.

Suddenly Guy's mind was made up. He would keep the report in the locked drawer of his desk until such time as Wisson next gave him the key to his safe; at which point he would slip it back where it belonged. There, hopefully, it would never again see the light of day. His employer must have been as shocked as himself when, having asked for a summary of the Rochford family's financial background, he had been given these kind of facts.

Perhaps, like himself, Wisson had put them down in disgust when he'd read them, Guy thought, and somehow forgotten that he had not locked them away. It was not often his employer was so careless for he was a meticulously tidy man – almost to the point of being pernickety. However, there were days when he was so busy that Guy was detailed to clear up the papers on his boss' desk, just as there were times when he'd been told to take over some of Wisson's personal tasks such as sending his wife flowers or buying her Christmas or birthday presents. Fortunately Zandra was always unaware that these tokens of love had been selected by him, Guy! He'd made sure that Wisson signed a number of cards in advance to go with such gifts.

One of these days, maybe, he would be able to understand his employer, Guy told himself as he settled down to writing the report Wisson had requested – a summary of the first six months' progress of the International Disarmament Conference in Geneva. When it had convened in February, sixty nations including the United States were represented and there had been high hopes that even if total disarmament was too high a goal, at least aggressive weapons such as heavy artillery, tanks, bombing aircraft and bacteriological weapons would be abolished. Wisson had spent several weeks over in Geneva and had returned with the conviction that in the end, nothing would be achieved.

"There will always be wars!" he'd stated categorically, "and we shall always need weapons to defend ourselves. To disarm now is to put the country once more at risk." The Germans, he further informed Guy, disarmed at the end of the Great War, were demanding the right to possess the same forces as other countries – and although France was against it, Britain along with the United States considered the request reasonable since the war had now been over for fourteen years!

When Guy had first learned about the forthcoming international conference, he'd found himself questioning his future to which he'd never really given much thought. The dire financial straits he and his mother had found themselves in after his father's death had led him to be grateful for any employment. What he would like to have done by choice was to go into the Diplomatic Corps like his father, but his lack of private means made this impossible.

Why Anthony Wisson should have given a second reading to the letter his, Guy's, godfather had written on his behalf was beyond his understanding at the time, but gradually he'd come to see the reason; he was perfectly at ease in places and company where a chap from a different background might not have been. He now realized that Wisson had had few social contacts prior to his marriage to Zandra; but after all the years he'd worked for him, he still knew nothing about Wisson's background other than that he'd sold his father's munitions factory when the war ended and become an arms dealer, bringing buyer and seller together with singular skill and always at a handsome profit.

At the time of his employment, Guy had not given much thought to the product in which his employer was dealing. Now that he was older, and a lot more worldly-wise than he'd been when he left school, he wished it were some other commodity rather than armaments. That they were necessary for defence was unquestionable, but they could also be used for aggression as was currently the case in the Far East where the Japanese had seized Manchuria and attacked Shanghai. As far as Guy knew,

Wisson had played no part in supplying arms to these countries, but the previous year he had been several times to the United States among other countries, and arms could easily be moved from one country to another. He was ignorant of the details of these various negotiations, and his employer had made it amply clear that it was not part of Guy's job to enquire into them. He therefore accepted that Wisson chose to play his cards very close to his chest, and that whether he, Guy, liked it or not, it was no concern of his how his employer made his money.

The ringing of the telephone interrupted Guy's reverie. He straightened himself abruptly as he heard Zandra's voice.

"Guy, it's me, Zandra Wisson!" she said. "I hope I'm not interrupting anything but . . . well, I need to get in touch with Anthony urgently. Do you happen to know when he's due back?"

"Tomorrow or the day after, I think!" Guy replied. "Can I do anything for you?"

There was a short pause before Zandra said hesitantly: "I'm afraid not – not this time, Guy. You usually can step into the breach, can't you? But not this time!"

There was a huskiness to her tone of voice which worried Guy. It occurred to him that she was on the point of tears. According to his mother, whom he'd told of Zandra's pregnancy, women in her condition were sometimes over-emotional; but recently when he'd had occasion to meet Zandra, she had seemed happy, confident, excited about the coming event; and had chatted cheerfully to him about the nursery she'd been decorating; the nanny she'd hired; and once, she had tried to involve him in choosing a name for the baby! She favoured "Rupert" after the dead uncle who had been decorated posthumously for bravery; but, she'd explained, her husband did not approve of the name; nor did he wish the infant, if it was a boy, to be named after his father. He had left it to Zandra to make all the decisions, Zandra had told Guy, and was far too busy to be involved with a child not yet born!

"At least tell me what the problem is, Mrs Wisson," Guy said now. "Maybe there is something I can do."

"Oh Guy, I wish there were – and please don't call me Mrs Wisson! I know Anthony has told you not to use my Christian name, but it really is silly to be so formal when we're friends."

Guy's heart leapt and he caught his breath as he struggled to keep his voice casual. So far he had managed very successfully to conceal his hopeless love for the girl on the other end of the telephone. Far too often, Wisson had obliged him to step into his shoes and cater to his wife's need of an escort. It was he, Guy, who had had to stand in for Wisson at a first-night performance of Robert Nichols' new play, *Wings Over Europe*; to drive her down to Eton to take her brother, Jamie, out for lunch; and, only last week, drive her to St George's in Hanover Square for the wedding of her friend Amy Johnson to the famous aviator Jim Mollison. Both she and Oliver had got to know the Yorkshire girl before her epic solo flight to Australia, and had invited her to spend a weekend at Rochford in the days when she was still struggling to get her licence! Standing beside Zandra in the church, hearing the bride and groom make their vows, Guy's sadness for his own ill-fated love had brought a lump to his throat, and he had been filled with a sense of hopelessness. He struggled now not to blurt out that he would do anything in the world for her rather than have her worried or unhappy. Almost with surprise, he heard himself asking in a calm, matter-of-fact voice: "Could I pass on any message for you? Your husband usually telephones me before I leave the office."

"Oh, would you? It's the baby, you see – I'm not sure but I think it may be on its way. I'm waiting for Dr Petrie to come, but—" She broke off to give a sharp gasp of pain, then tried to disguise it with a short laugh. "Actually, I don't think I need him to confirm it. Could you tell Anthony? I know he's fearfully busy but I expect he'll want to be here if he can."

"Most certainly he will, and I can do better than wait for your husband's call. I'll get a telegram off to him right away. And Zandra, don't worry! I'm sure everything is going to be just fine. Now is anyone with you? You aren't alone, are you?"

131

"No! Mollie, my maid, is with me; and I rang my cousin, Lucy, and she'll be round directly. It's just that . . . well, I do want Anthony to be here."

He already knew the name of the nursing home where she was to have her baby but he wrote it down again as she dictated it. As soon as he was off the line, he would have the florist send flowers and . . .

"I really am sorry to bother you like this, Guy. I'm sure you're frightfully busy—" Zandra was apologizing again.

"I'm not in the least busy!" Guy said reassuringly. He was far from happy about her being alone at such a time with only her maid for company, and he added quickly: "As a matter of fact, I'm rather bored and it's lovely to have someone to talk to. Do you feel up to chatting for a minute or two? I wanted to ask you if you'd heard from Mrs Rochford yet about your cousin Alice's wedding. It seems such a shame you had to miss it."

Since Guy hardly knew the Honourable Alice Rochford and had not seen her since she had gone to live with her French relatives in France, he was not in the least interested in her marriage but, as he had hoped, Zandra's mind was momentarily diverted from her present situation.

"Oliver and Jane got back from France yesterday – Aunt Willow and Uncle Toby are staying on for a week or two – and Oliver has some frightfully good snapshots. I'm going to make up an album which I'll show you. Alice looks really pretty. I can't say I awfully like the look of her husband but Jane says Alice absolutely adores him, which is all that matters. He—"

She broke off suddenly and Guy heard her say: "Oh Lucy, I'm so glad you're here. I was just talking to Guy . . . Guy, I'll have to go now. Thanks for keeping me company on the phone! I know you'll get hold of Anthony for me if you can."

"Good luck!" Guy said. "And here's a name for you to think about if it's a boy – Marmaduke!"

"You are an idiot, Guy!" He heard her short, husky laugh and then she was gone.

And that was the perfect description for him, he told himself. Nobody but a complete fool would fall in love with a woman who was crazy about her rich, successful, handsome husband and was about to give him his first child. The sooner he pulled himself together and stopped hankering over something that was utterly out of his reach, the better for everyone. Even his mother, wrapped up as she was in her own concerns regarding her indifferent health, had noticed his preoccupied, depressed moods and asked him what was wrong. Usually he succeeded at the weekends, by dogged cheerfulness and good humour, in jollying her out of her doldrums. It was becoming increasingly difficult to be kind to his parent who, he knew, enjoyed her sundry illnesses, the onset of which had begun with her widowhood. It was pity rather than love which kept his visits so regular – visits which he dreaded and could only avoid with a clear conscience on the rare occasions he was not in England.

Reminded suddenly of his employer's frequent trips abroad, Guy reached once more for the telephone. He must send a telegram without further delay. As far as he was aware, the baby was arriving ahead of schedule, else Wisson would not have been out of the country at such a time.

Having dictated the message to the operator, there was little more he could do until he knew on which Imperial Airways flight Wisson would return to England. In the meanwhile, he did not doubt that in these special circumstances, his employer would simply take the next available aeroplane seat home.

"Mrs Wisson, are you awake, dear?"

With an effort, Zandra opened her eyes. A nurse was bending over her, peering into her face. Her head was swimming and as the nurse spoke again, she wished the woman would be quiet and allow her to go back to sleep.

"Mrs Wisson, you have had your baby. It's a little boy . . ."

Suddenly, Zandra remembered – Lucy had rushed her into the nursing home in a taxi and the terrible pains had begun in earnest. She could not recall now how long they had continued – only a doctor's voice saying: "Your baby is coming now—"

She felt a surge of joy. "Can I see him, please?"

"Not just now, dear. You need to rest. You had quite a difficult time, you know. Here's a little drink – just a few sips, now. We don't want you being sick, do we? Then you can go back to sleep."

Too tired to insist, Zandra sipped the fluid and lay back against the pillows.

"Anthony? My husband – has he seen the baby?"

"Not yet, dear. Off you go to sleep now like a good girl!"

So the baby had been a boy – just as Guy had predicted. Marmaduke! As if anyone would call their child by such a silly name. There was a smile on Zandra's face as she drifted back into unconsciousness.

Staring down at the young, attractive face of her patient, the watchful nurse felt a moment of pity, knowing that when she awoke, the doctor would be obliged to tell Mrs Wisson that the baby she had birthed with such difficulty could not possibly live very long.

When Zandra opened her eyes again some two hours later, there was a different nurse at her bedside.

"Can I see my baby now?" she asked. She felt fully awake and filled with impatience to see her new son.

The nurse jumped to her feet and busied herself plumping up Zandra's pillows.

"Doctor will be round presently," the girl said evasively. She crossed the room to the table by the window on which stood a beautiful basket of white roses and love-in-the-mist interlaced with gypsophila. "Blue for a boy! Such a clever choice!" the nurse continued in her professionally cheerful voice. She brought the card over to Zandra: FROM ANTHONY WITH ALL MY LOVE.

Tears of happiness welled into Zandra's eyes. Despite his refusal ever to discuss their coming child these past six months, to look at the tiny clothes she had purchased or the nursery she had had decorated, or even to show any interest in the credentials of the nanny she had engaged, she had steadfastly believed that once the baby was born, Anthony would be as proud as any new father. Both Aunt Willow and Lucy had assured her that it was rare for husbands to develop a paternal instinct in the prenatal stages, and sometimes not until the child was beyond the infant stage. Now, not only the words on the card but the choice of flowers were a clear indication that he still loved her and perhaps regretted his recent coldness towards her.

"I'd like to see my husband," she said. "Did he say when he would be back? Do you know if he has seen the baby yet? Why can't you bring the baby to me now?"

"Goodness me, what a lot of questions!" the nurse prevaricated. "I'm afraid I can't answer them, Mrs Wisson. I've only just come on duty. Do you wish me to go and find out?"

"Yes, I do!" Zandra said firmly. "What time is it, Nurse?"

"Eight o'clock, Mrs Wisson. You should have had your breakfast by now but Doctor said you were to be allowed to sleep."

"Breakfast!" Zandra repeated. "You mean eight o'clock in the *morning*? What day is it?"

"Wednesday, my dear. Now don't fuss yourself. Doctor had to give you an anaesthetic, you see, and with all that gas and air beforehand, it's no wonder you've felt sleepy!"

As Zandra subsided back onto the pillow and the nurse disappeared, she tried to remember the sequence of events leading up to this moment. There had been the rush with Lucy to the nursing home, the increasing momentum of pain, the midwife saying the baby had changed its mind and was not going to hurry into the world after all. Then more pain. At some time that Monday night, Lucy had looked in to see her; told her that she was not to worry about anything as she had instructed one of London's leading obstetricians to take charge. She had also said that Guy had had a telephone call from Anthony and that he would be home as soon as it could be arranged. Then what had happened to Tuesday?

Between the terrible bouts of pain, Zandra remembered there had been doctors, nurses, the midwife in the room; a mask over her face. There had been stethoscopes, bright lights, the smell of antiseptic – and always, always the pain. Vaguely she could recall someone saying a forceps delivery would be necessary and a man's voice asking where her husband was as he was needed to sign a consent form for an operation. After that, she could remember nothing but a series of dreams – nightmares for the most part; waking once briefly in semi-darkness to find a nurse changing her nightgown and the pad between her legs, and urging her back to sleep. So that must have been Tuesday night, she told herself, and now it was Wednesday and she'd still not seen Anthony or her baby!

As her feeling of anxiety increased, the door of her room opened and Lucy came in, a tall grey-haired man in an immaculate pin-stripe suit following behind her. Lucy removed her white hat and gloves and dropping them on a chair, hurried across the room to Zandra's bedside.

"Darling, I came as soon as I could, and I've brought Mr Bingham with me. I don't know if you remember it, but he brought your baby into the world!"

Zandra returned Lucy's embrace and looked up at the doctor who was regarding her temperature chart at the foot of the bed.

"Glad to see it has gone down, Mrs Wisson!" he said, his voice sounding professionally calm. "You've had a rather trying time, I'm afraid . . ." He patted her hand, his eyes avoiding hers as he added: ". . . but I can assure you of this much – there's no reason why you cannot have another child in the future—" He broke off to give a professional smile. ". . . Not that I expect this to be your overriding concern at this moment! How are you feeling, Mrs Wisson?"

Zandra grimaced.

"A bit sore, to say the least."

"Yes, well, that's only to be expected, I'm afraid. You've had rather a lot of stitches – but as I said just now, no lasting damage."

He turned to the nurse who had accompanied him into the room. "You can leave us now, Sister. I'll ring if you're needed!"

Lucy sat down on the edge of Zandra's bed and took hold of one of her hands.

"Mr Bingham has something to tell you, Zee-Zee. It isn't the best of news, I fear, but—"

"We must never lose sight of the fact that every life is ultimately in God's hands, Lady Zemski," the specialist broke in promptly. "There is always hope, therefore, despite what we medical men may prognosticate."

He seated himself on the bedside chair and tried to calculate whether his patient's state of mind and body were strong enough to receive the bad news he must impart. According to Sister, Mrs Wisson had now demanded for the third time to see her baby, and it was proving impossible to withhold the truth any longer. Zandra solved the decision-making for him.

"Something is wrong with my baby, isn't it?" she said in a small controlled voice. "Tell me the truth, Mr Bingham. *What is wrong?*"

"I had hoped that . . . er, that your husband might have been here so that I could have explained matters to you both together. Lady Zemski tells me he should be back in this country very shortly and—"

"No!" Zandra said sharply. "I want you to tell me now, Mr Bingham. What's wrong with my baby? Why can't I see him?" Her voice rose as she demanded: "Are you trying to tell me he was stillborn? Or that he's deformed? Is that it?"

"Now, now, Mrs Wisson, you mustn't upset yourself."

"Zee-Zee, I've seen him!" Lucy said quickly. "He's a beautiful little boy. He's tiny – but quite perfect!"

Zandra let out her breath.

"Then why can't I see him, Mr Bingham?"

"Because, my dear, as Lady Zemski just said, he is very small – just over four pounds to be exact and I'm afraid his breathing is giving cause for concern. It was a stressful birth, you see – took longer than was desirable, although I do assure you everything possible was done in the . . . er, somewhat difficult circumstances. Your infant is in the Premature Babies Ward and is being very carefully monitored."

"Then why can't I see him?" Zandra said. "If he can't be brought to me, I shall go to him. I want to see him."

"Of course, darling, Mr Bingham understands that," Lucy broke in, "and just as soon as you're strong enough, they'll take you to see him. You've had a lot of stitches and—"

"It really isn't advisable for you to walk just yet, Mrs Wisson. Tomorrow, if your temperature stays down—"

"No, I want to go today, now!" Zandra interrupted fiercely. "I can walk . . . and if I can't, I'll go in a wheelchair. I'm going to see him."

She saw the swift glance that passed between the specialist and her cousin, and her fingers tightened around Lucy's hand.

"Something *is* wrong, isn't it? What did you mean by 'in God's hands', Mr Bingham? What are you both keeping from me?"

"Mrs Wisson, the baby is very weak and is not taking any nourishment. You might find it very distressing, and we do have to consider your condition. Your husband would not be too pleased if he returns to find we have not been taking proper care of you."

"You said he was 'very weak'? That he was not feeding? I'm not quite the fool you seem to take me for, Mr Bingham!" Zandra cried. "You're trying to keep the truth from me – you don't expect him to live, do you?"

"We're doing all we can, Mrs Wisson. Believe me, after thirty years in my profession, I have learned that miracles can and do happen. It is not to deceive you in any way that I have refrained from saying your child's condition is hopeless. The next few days will tell. Meanwhile, we can hope and pray."

"You can say that and still expect me not to see my baby?" Zandra said in a bitter accusing voice. "You're a mother, Lucy. Surely you understand even if this . . . this man does not? I've got to be with him . . . not tomorrow when it could be too late.

138

Now help me out of this bed or I swear I'll never forgive you for as long as I live!"

Lucy glanced once more at the specialist who, with a look of deep anxiety on his face, nodded his head.

"I'll get Sister to bring a wheelchair for Mrs Wisson!" he said.

As he left the room, he wished with even greater force that Mr Anthony Wisson had been there to protect and comfort his wife from the painful ordeal that was to come.

Chapter 9

July 1932

"Mr Bristow is downstairs, Zee-Zee. You said you wanted to see him!"

Lucy looked anxiously at Zandra's white, drawn face, her eyes full of pity. No one could have wished more fervently than she that Anthony had been here to comfort her young cousin. She had spoken to Sister before entering Zandra's room and was aware that the baby was not expected to live much longer. The tiny boy was just clinging to life, but there was no hope of his survival.

Zandra drew a long sigh and eased herself back against her pillows. Outside the window, she could see the topmost branches of the big plane tree moving slightly as the gentle southerly breeze rustled through the leaves. The hot July sun had moved to the west side of the hospital and the air in the room, though still stifling, had cooled a little and lost its sharp light.

"Yes, I do want to see Guy!" she said quietly. "I think he lied to you yesterday when he told you Anthony had telephoned to say he was on his way home. I'm going to make him tell me the truth. If Anthony had been in Geneva as Guy said, he'd be here by now."

Lucy's look of concern deepened. When Anthony's personal assistant had rung her, he had explained that his employer *was* in Geneva, and finding it impossible to extricate himself from various business commitments which were likely to detain him for at least another twenty-four hours. He would be back as soon as he could. Lucy had not passed on this last item of information to Zandra who had been so tense with expectation of her husband's imminent return that she had not felt able to disappoint her. Now, twenty-four hours later, Mr Bristow would have little alternative but to tell her the truth – that it was unlikely Anthony would be here before the following morning.

The previous night on her return from visiting Zandra, Lucy had told Alexis that Anthony's absence at such a heart-breaking time was, in her opinion, unforgivable. Alexis had expressed a more practical point of view. If all the nations were united in the proposed agreement to dispose of their armaments, he'd said, Anthony Wisson's entire financial empire could collapse. Even if only partial disarmament were to be agreed upon, he would virtually be out of business. Men like Anthony Wisson did not hoard their wealth in banks but invested it – as, for example, in Sky-Ways. He would quite likely have borrowed from the banks to expand the airline and buy all those modern aeroplanes Oliver was so pleased with! Interest had to be paid on borrowed money, and that would have to be found from income. If Anthony's income dried up, he would be obliged to sell some of his assets – and then, income from those investments could dry up. Consequently, if Wisson lost his money, Zandra would be the first to suffer and doubtless the fellow had this in mind when he decided upon his priorities! "It's not as if he could do anything to save the child's life if he were at the hospital," Alexis had concluded.

"But he could comfort poor darling Zee-Zee!" Lucy had protested and Alexis hadn't argued the point.

"Everyone is being very kind . . . about the baby!" Zandra said suddenly. "I can go down to see him whenever I want. Last night they woke me because they thought he would not last until morning. They called in the Chaplain to baptize him. I wouldn't let them do it before because I wanted Anthony to be there." Her voice faltered and sounded to Lucy very close to tears as she added: "I named him Rupert. I thought Aunt Willow would like that as she was so fond of Uncle Rupert." In her distress, she had momentarily forgotten that Anthony had objected to the name.

"I'm sure Mother will appreciate that, Zee-Zee," Lucy said gently. "She will be coming up to stay with me this afternoon and she asked me to tell you to expect her at tea-time."

Zandra nodded.

"Is Uncle Toby better then?" she asked, for Lucy had told her the previous day that her aunt was concerned about Uncle Toby's health. He had collapsed in church on Sunday and had been in bed ever since.

"The doctor says he can find nothing wrong with him – that it was probably just the heat which caused him to faint." Lucy smiled. "He told Uncle Toby he was too old at sixty-five to be playing cricket against the village team, especially when the temperature on Saturday was in the eighties!"

"I expect Aunt Willow will forbid him to be part of Oliver's team next year!" Zandra said, returning her cousin's smile.

Seeing that Zandra was looking a little less distraught, Lucy excused herself on the grounds that she had shopping to do, and said she would send Guy up to see her. He appeared five minutes later armed with two bunches of flowers.

"These are from your husband!" he said placing the large bouquet of red roses on the bed table. "And these are from me – a somewhat humbler offering, I fear!"

As he handed her the small bunch of Parma violets, Zandra buried her face in the sweet-smelling flowers to hide her tears.

"They are my favourite, Guy, thank you!" she said huskily. "How did you know?"

Guy sat down in the chair opposite her, grinning sheepishly.

"Oh, I heard you saying so once when we were down at Rochford Manor!" he muttered.

"That was thoughtful of you to remember. Guy, you know why I asked you to visit me, don't you? I want to know the truth. *Where is Anthony?*"

With a sigh of relief, Guy realized that at last there was no need for further prevarication.

"He's in Paris. Your Cousin Oliver has flown over to bring Mr Wisson back to Croydon. He should be with you early this evening."

"Oh, thank God!" Zandra burst out. "He may yet be in time. My baby's dying, Guy – you know that, don't you? They haven't actually said so, but I knew it when they insisted last night I must have him baptized."

Unable to bear the tortured look on Zandra's face, Guy bit his lip and stared down at his hands.

"I'm so very sorry, Zandra. To wait so long for the baby to be born and then . . . well, life can be very cruel sometimes, can't it?"

Zandra nodded, surprised that Guy should have put into words the thought that was uppermost in her mind at that moment.

"Mr Bingham – the obstetrician – came to see me this morning. At first he tried to convince me that there was still hope of a miracle, but in the end, he said: 'You're young and healthy, Mrs Wisson, and there is no reason why this time next year, you should not be carrying another child'!" She leant forward to look into Guy's face. "I know he meant to be kind!" she said brokenly, "but he simply doesn't understand how I feel. I wanted *this* baby, Guy – I wanted him very, very much, and when I sit beside his cot looking at his tiny little face, I can't bear the thought that I'm going to lose him. And there's nothing – nothing at all I can do to help him. I'll never go through this again – never, never, never!"

Worried by the note of hysteria in Zandra's voice and saddened beyond measure by her agonized cry, Guy took both her hands in his.

"Of course that's how you feel now," he said softly. "I don't think the doctor meant to imply that another baby would be a replacement for this one. He's a medical man and I dare say he simply wanted to reassure you that if ever you did decide to have another child, you could!"

Zandra withdrew her hands and reached for her handkerchief.

"You're a very kind person, Guy. You always try to take a charitable view of everybody, don't you? I suppose I just need to be angry with someone because I can't show God how angry I am with Him. I suppose I'm angry with Anthony, too. Why couldn't he have come sooner? I needed him so much. Do you realize he might even now be . . . be too late . . . to—"

"Zandra, don't torture yourself. I'm absolutely sure your husband would have dropped everything to be here if he understood how serious the baby's condition was. You must blame me. I told him the baby was very ill, of course, but that the doctors had said there was still hope. So you see, I'm the one you must be angry with."

It was a lie, for when he'd spoken to Wisson on the telephone, he had explained exactly how difficult the birth had been and the effect it had had on a baby of such a low birth-weight. He had reiterated several times how anxious his wife was for him to come home; told him that it was not only possible but probable that the baby would die very soon. Wisson could have been in no doubt as to the urgency of the situation, but all he had said was: "Make any excuse you can think of – say I'm on my way if you have to; but the fact is, I shan't be leaving for a couple of days at least – and even that's going to be damned awkward. My wife has got the best doctor and the most expensive nursing home in the country – there's nothing more I can do. As for the child – if it's sickly, it's probably just as well if it doesn't survive. Send some more flowers, Bristow. Make sure my wife has everything she needs and tell her I'll be home just as soon as I can possibly manage it."

Remembering his employer's words, Guy was finding it very hard indeed to be the "charitable" person Zandra thought him. If ever there was an occasion when a wife needed her husband, this was it; and no matter what deals, negotiations, worries Wisson might be concerned with in Geneva, they could not excuse his continued absence at such a time.

"Of course I'm not angry with you, Guy. You only told Anthony what the nurses and doctors keep saying – that there's hope," Zandra was saying. "I just wish . . . but he'll be home in a few hours' time, won't he? I so much want him to see his son . . . just once . . . before—"

She broke off, unable to voice the horror that was to come. She could not possibly explain to Guy – any more than she could to Lucy or Aunt Willow – how dreadfully important it was to her that Anthony should acknowledge their baby. Since that terrible night when she'd first told him of her pregnancy, he had refused ever to discuss it again. When the baby was baptized last night, she'd had no idea what Anthony might want her to call his son. She didn't even know if he'd be pleased to hear that it was a boy – someone to carry on his name.

As her pregnancy had progressed, Anthony had moved out of their bedroom and into his dressing-room, and he'd not made love to her since the night after the announcement that Britain had gone off the gold standard and she had hosted a dinner party for several of his banking friends and their wives! He had ceased then to be her lover, and though he had spoken to her perfectly civilly, even affectionately if they were in public, he had steadfastly behaved as if there were no baby on the way.

True to Dr Petrie's prediction, she had undergone a complete change of personality; turned, in fact, into a placid, contented, equable person who, once the early morning sickness had passed, delighted in every aspect of her condition and the baby's development. Even Anthony's absences abroad did not distress her as once they had, for she'd retired to bed earlier and busied herself in the daytime with preparations for the infant's arrival. She'd done little else but meet occasionally with Monica to discuss the ever-growing success of Alternatives; lunch with Lucy or spend the weekends at Rochford. She had not even bothered to go to Croydon and had abandoned any thought of flying.

Most important of all, Zandra had convinced herself that once Anthony saw the baby – and she was certain that it would be a boy – he would love it as she did. Now she truly believed that if he could only see his son for a few hours, he would share her grief. Perhaps with Anthony beside her, she could bear it better.

She turned now to look at her visitor whom she had momentarily forgotten. For some time now, Guy had become so much more than Anthony's efficient assistant. He was her friend. She had really enjoyed those days of her early pregnancy when Anthony had detailed Guy to drive her down to Rochford for a day or two. She and Jane, Guy and her nephew, Giles, had put on gumboots and taken Oliver's two Springer spaniels for walks through the trees surrounding the lakes. In the autumn, they had made bonfires of the piles of leaves that had fallen from the oaks, elms, chestnuts and limes. They had thrown bread to the hungry ducks and swans on the lake and one weekend, Oliver and Guy had repaired the rickety old tree house in the big lime tree which Uncle Pelham had built for Oliver when he'd been a small boy.

In the spring, when her bulk had made it more difficult to take long walks, she and Guy had strolled down to the farm with Lucy's daughter, Eve, to see the new lambs and piglets. They had watched her gathering primroses, wild daffodils and tiny bunches of the violets from the hedgerows to present to Aunt Willow. Later, she and Guy had joined the children for nursery tea, toasted crumpets in front of the gas fire and listened to *Children's Hour* on the wireless.

It was strange, Zandra thought, how on the verge of becoming a mother, how happily she had reverted to childhood; almost as strange as the easy way in which Guy had integrated with all the members of the family. Perhaps it was because he was younger than Anthony that he seemed to get along so well with Giles and Robin who were still shy with Anthony, treating him with the same respect as for their schoolmasters and always calling him "sir"! Or perhaps it was because, now that Guy knew the family so much better, he had revealed a wonderful sense of humour which, to the children's delight, often bordered on the ridiculous.

Aware suddenly that Guy was sitting silently by her bedside watching her, Zandra gave a self-conscious laugh.

"You must be thinking me terribly rude!" she said apologetically. "I seem to go into these day-dreams. It's probably those horrible pills they keep giving me which are supposed to make me feel better. To tell you the truth, I'm not quite sure if they're meant to ease the physical discomfort or prevent me getting hysterical about the baby." The smile left her face and it became taut once more. "Guy, can you press that bell by the bed? It's ages since the nurse came, and I want to know how he is – the baby, I mean."

Guy rose quickly to do as she asked, but before he could carry out the task, the door opened and Sister came into the room. She looked at Guy and then, with a professional eye, at Zandra.

"I'm sorry to interrupt you when you have a visitor, Mrs Wisson, but we thought you might wish to come down to the Baby Ward." As Zandra started to get out of bed, she hurried across to her and laid a restraining hand on her shoulder. "Now don't hurry, Mrs Wisson. We don't want you breaking any of those stitches, do we? Just stay there and I'll bring in the wheelchair."

Guy was already on his feet and as the nurse left the room, he said: "I'll see you on your way, Zandra, and then I'll be off."

Zandra's face was deathly pale. She reached out to grab hold of his arm.

"No, don't go, Guy. They wouldn't have called me if . . . they said I need not worry unless . . . then someone would come and tell me . . . Guy, please don't go. I suppose . . . would it be too much to ask you to . . . to come with me?"

"Of course I'll come!" Guy said quickly. "But wouldn't you prefer I should telephone Countess Zemski? She should have reached home by now."

Wordlessly, Zandra shook her head. Sister came back with a junior nurse pushing the wheelchair and they helped Zandra into it.

"Lucy had a little girl who died!" she said as if Guy had demanded an explanation as to why she did not want Lucy with her. "I don't want her reminded." She turned to the sister who was placing a pillow behind her back. "I'd like Mr Bristow to come down to the ward with me, Sister!"

The woman paused. There was a strict rule that only relatives were allowed into the Baby Ward for fear of infection – and then only with a doctor's permission. On the other hand, poor Mrs Wisson's husband had been held up somewhere abroad and it was never less than an ordeal for a mother watching her baby die.

"It is against the rules, Mrs Wisson – parents only, I'm afraid," she said hesitantly.

"Mr Bristow was going to be the baby's godfather," Zandra said quickly. "Please let him come with me, Sister!"

"Mrs Wisson needs someone with her!" Guy said firmly as he stepped forward. "I'll take responsibility, Sister, if anyone complains."

The nurse nodded. Hospital rules were made for a good purpose, as well she understood after eighteen years in her profession, but occasionally, they needed to be overlooked on humanitarian grounds, and the visitor seemed a sensible, level-headed young man.

As they made their way down in the lift, she gave a thoughtful sigh. It was a pity this particular infant had survived the actual birth. Now, the unfortunate mother had had time to become attached to it. After three days, it was going to be a very painful hour or two for her watching the baby die. It was its lungs, of course. There was nothing anyone could do. The breathing would just become more and more laboured until finally it ceased altogether.

She sighed again. The only help she herself could give poor Mrs Wisson was a good strong sedative when it was all over. Meanwhile, the ward sister would take over, and by the look of the young man accompanying her patient, he, too, would take care of her. The death would be easier for him, she told herself as she hurried away. He's not the father; nor the husband, either, though they'd have made a nice-looking couple – she so pretty and he the image of Gary Cooper!

As the baby ward sister placed the tiny bundle in Zandra's arms, Guy stood silently beside the woman he loved wondering how he could find the strength to endure the agonized look in her eyes.

When Zandra woke, it was to find Anthony sitting in the chair by her bed. He was reading the *Financial Times*, his head strained forward to see the small print in the dimmed light of the room. He seemed unaware that she was awake, and she wondered for a moment if she was dreaming. Then as full consciousness returned, she gave a little moan of anguish.

"Anthony!" she whispered. "Anthony, he's dead! Our baby has died!"

He put down his newspaper and took one of her hands.

"Yes, the nurse told me when I arrived!" he said. "I'm afraid I was too late—" He coughed uneasily and released her hand in order to reach for the handkerchief in his suit pocket. "Here, wipe your eyes, Zandra. You really must try not to cry. The nurse said I must keep you calm."

As the tears continued to pour down her cheeks unheeded, Zandra cried brokenly: "Oh, Anthony, it was awful . . . he couldn't breathe and . . . Anthony, have you seen him? They let you see him, didn't they?"

It seemed terribly important that he should have seen his son just once.

"They . . . er, suggested it, but . . . I really didn't . . . well, it didn't seem a good idea!" Anthony said awkwardly. "I mean, it must have been very distressing for you and I'm sorry, my dear, that you've had to go through this by yourself. I'm not sure if I could actually have been of much assistance to you. I . . . I'm not very good with illness, hospitals, that kind of thing. When I was quite young – ten or so, my mother was involved with a charity which provided comforts for convalescent soldiers who had returned from the Boer War. She took me with her one day and . . . well, it was not very pleasant, to say the least! Ever since then—" He broke off and crossed the room to stare out of the windows.

It was not only the sight of the amputated limbs and scarred faces of the war casualties he had objected to; it was his mother's sudden concern for someone other than himself.

"I am so sorry, my pumpkin, but we will have to postpone our visit to the canal this afternoon. I am needed at the hospital."

"But you promised! I want to watch the boats coming through the lock. You promised—"

It was the first time she had ever put his wishes second to anyone's other than his father's. She had never made friends in the neighbourhood in all the years she had lived there, devoting herself entirely to him, her only son. He was all the more precious to her, she'd often told him, because she'd had to wait until she was forty before he had arrived and would never have another child.

For once she had been immune to his tears or pleading. As he grew older, he'd come to realize that whilst his parents were prepared to indulge him whenever they could and deny themselves any of the luxuries of life in order to ensure he had a public school education and the best clothes, they were united in their conviction that they owed something to the less fortunate citizens of the country that had adopted them.

He was sixteen years old when his father first took him down to the factory which, after years of dogged hard work and unstinting devotion, his employer had finally agreed to sell to him.

"But how can you afford to buy it, Papa? Can you borrow the money?"

"I have saved it. Thanks to your dear mother, we have lived frugally and I was able to set aside something from my wage each week. Your mother, too, has made great sacrifices, for she was born and raised to a very different life from the one I have given her."

So all these years, his father had been saving to buy this big, bleak stone building – which looked anything but prosperous – when he could have afforded to buy a decent car, some well-tailored clothes, a respectable house where he, Antoni, could have invited one of his school associates home! When, had his father not been so penny-pinching, he could have given him, his only son, a far bigger allowance, seaside holidays!

"It is a profitable business, Antoni, and one day when I retire, it will be yours. Come now, I will show you inside. It will interest you, I think."

What interested him, however, was not the factory floor with its rows of machines turning out cartridges by the thousand to be boxed, labelled and despatched from the warehouse; it was the books – the big heavy account books with their scrupulously hand-written columns of figures. Whilst his father chatted to one of the foremen, Anthony leafed through them. The profits were indeed encouraging; but what caught his eye was an item in the close of year summary of those profits and the substantial deduction under the heading: WORKERS' BENEFIT FUND.

"What is that, Papa?"

"That, my boy, is what we set aside each year for our employees."

"A bonus if they do well, do you mean?"

"No, no, no, Antoni! It is in case they or their families are in trouble – there is illness, perhaps; or a funeral for which there is no money to spare; an injured child in need of a wheelchair. For the poor, there is always a disaster waiting round the corner."

"But it's not your responsibility to look after these people, Papa!"

"That is a matter of opinion. They work for me – sometimes all their lives. That puts me under an obligation to help them in their time of

need. It is the way this firm has always worked, Antoni, and will continue to do so."

"You are mollycoddling them, Papa. You pay them a fair wage, so it's up to them to support their wives and children. Does Mother know how much money you squander on them? And what about me? I could do with a far bigger allowance than you give me!"

How red his father's face now turned! How angrily the veins were pulsating on his forehead and shining bald pate!

"You would not consider the money 'squandered', Antoni, if it were your child in desperate need of an operation to save its life! As for your mother – she comes from a family where it was a matter of honour to ensure the well-being of their retainers. I know . . . I was their bailiff! I was one of them!"

"And you repaid this honourable family by eloping with the daughter of the house!"

How close his father came to striking him! Were he, Antoni, not a foot taller and forty-two years younger.

"You may think that the fine education you are receiving entitles you to make such an insulting remark to me. Well, understand me, Antoni! For some time now I have been worried about the kind of man you are becoming. You have brains, yes! Your reports are always excellent. You are, so your housemaster tells me, a credit to the school. For this I respect you – but I am no longer sure that I like you. Your mother can see no wrong in you and I would not want to disillusion her with my own misgivings as to your character. It takes more than brains to make a human being, Antoni. It requires also a heart. Remember that."

He paused briefly to draw breath, before continuing: "Without charity towards our fellow human beings, we are no better than animals. One day I shall hand all this over to you, but I can assure you, I shall not do so until – or unless – I consider you fit to step into my shoes! I will not have the name of Wisniowiecki dishonoured! Now get out before I lose my temper completely."

If there was one thing he wished even more than having any other surname but that of Wisniowiecki, it was that this fat, sanctimonious, bald-headed, shabby old man was not his father. As he walked home, he

152

resolved then and there that in five years' time when he came of age, he would disown both his parents. He had already discovered in a book in the Public Library how to change his name by Deed Poll.

He recalled, as clearly as if he could see the page, the figure relating to the sum of money set aside for the workers, and his face whitened in disgust.

Anthony's left hand gripped his wrist as, even after all these years, he remembered his feelings of anger and contempt for his father's declared intention to continue the wasteful Benefit Fund.

"I hadn't realized hospitals had this effect on you!" Zandra was saying. "I suppose I got used to them in the war. Rochford was a convalescent home for soldiers, and I more or less grew up in the wards; so hospitals don't horrify me."

Even as a young child of seven, she'd never once been frightened by the men's amputations; or dreaded her self-imposed task of keeping them amused. Conversely, Alice had cried each time she had seen one of the soldiers on crutches, and she had avoided the patients and doctors whenever she could. She was unable to overcome her antipathy; and Anthony, Zandra now realized, was the same. Nevertheless . . .

"Is there anything I can get you? Shall I ring for the nurse? They are looking after you all right here, aren't they?"

Anthony's voice sounded concerned, and for his sake Zandra attempted a smile.

"Everyone is very kind and the nurses are wonderful," she said. "But I want to go home now, Anthony. They won't let me out for another ten days – because of the stitches but" – her voice rose suddenly – "I can't stay here now. There's too much to remind me of . . . Anthony, I called him Rupert. I had to have him baptized, and it was the only name I could think of." Even in her distress, she sensed a change in his expression which made her uneasy. "You don't mind, do you? It was to please Aunt Willow!"

He would not meet her eyes as he said flatly: "Frankly, Zandra, it's not a name I would have chosen, as I think you already know; but it hardly matters now, does it? It's too late to change it. I think, my dear, it would be best if we try to put the past behind us, don't you agree? The future is what matters. There'll have to be a funeral, of course – you'll want it to be at Havorhurst, I suppose; but after that, I think you need a good long holiday. Some sea air would do you good, don't you think? We might take a cruise to America on the *Ile de France*. I heard a rumour that Lady Furness might be travelling over there next month. She's Gloria Vanderbilt's sister, you know, and a close . . . er, friend of the Prince of Wales. I'm told she's very jolly, so you might like her. It would cheer you up!"

I shouldn't be feeling like this, Zandra told herself as she tried to control her tears. Anthony is doing his utmost to be kind and thoughtful and yet I feel defeated. Perhaps he thinks it's bad for me to talk about the baby. Perhaps Sister or Mr Bingham has told him not to. Can't he see that I *need* to be able to share my sorrow with him? I know he didn't want the baby at first but . . . he must mind about it. It was part of him, too.

He was once more proffering his handkerchief as the tears dripped off the end of her nose.

"I think I should ring for the nurse, Zandra. You look very pale. It's late, too – nearly ten o'clock. I came straight here from Croydon and I really should go home and change out of these clothes."

"Yes, of course!" Zandra said, sniffing hard. "I'm sorry for being so thoughtless, Anthony. I'm afraid I tend to lose count of time in this place. I didn't realize it was so late. Did you have a good flight?"

Anthony stood up.

"First class! Oliver is an excellent pilot and we landed without a single bump! Now, my dear, I'll leave you in more capable hands. I'll be back to see you tomorrow."

"In the morning? As early as you can, Anthony. I can have visitors any time I want. Mr Bingham comes to see me between nine and ten and you'd probably like to have a word with him. He can explain why . . . what was wrong with . . . you ask him, darling. I can't bear to talk about it."

Or think about it, she told herself after Anthony had kissed her goodbye. She was grateful when her little night nurse appeared and chatted cheerfully about how distinguished Anthony looked and how lucky Zandra was to have such a good-looking husband.

"No wonder he isn't jealous of your friend, Mr Bristow!" the girl chattered on as she tidied Zandra's bed. "Who'd have eyes for anyone else with Mr Wisson for a husband. You make ever-so-romantic a couple, if you don't mind me saying!"

Zandra smiled.

"It's nice of you to say so!"

"I dare say it was love at first sight, wasn't it? There now, I'm going to fetch you a nice hot drink of Ovaltine – that'll help you to sleep; and Sister says you can have a sleeping pill if you have a bad night. Now you're not to get upset again. I promised that handsome husband of yours I'd not let you fall into the doldrums, though you couldn't be blamed for it if you did, poor dear. It upsets all of us when something like this happens. Now you settle down, Mrs Wisson. I won't be long."

The doldrums – is that what they call this black, bottomless pit of despair waiting for me to drop into it? Zandra asked herself. Momentarily, Anthony's presence had kept her away from the brink, as had the nurse with her silly chatter about Anthony being jealous of poor Guy! But sooner or later she was going to have to face up to the fact that nothing would ever bring her baby back. As long as she lived, she would never forget that last, shuddering breath as she had held the tiny body against her breast.

Guy had not believed her when she'd said she would never have another baby, but she'd meant it. It was not as if Anthony was anxious for her to provide him with a family – on the contrary, from the start he'd been averse to *this* baby's existence.

Well, her mind was made up – there'd be no more children. Monica had said there were ways now for a woman as well as a man to avoid pregnancy. She herself didn't want to have a baby because she was afraid of the pain of giving birth; but bad as Zandra knew it to be, it was not this she wished to avoid in future. It was the unbearable pain following the death of the child to whom she had longed for nine long months to give life.

Chapter 10

July – September 1933

"You're looking frightfully well, Jamie! I suppose it isn't possible but it seems to me you've grown a few more inches."

Zandra looked affectionately at her brother who lay stretched full length on the lawn, his arms propping his head as he smiled up at her. It was a shimmering hot July afternoon, and whilst her brother chose to soak up the sunshine, Zandra had set up her deck-chair in the shade of the big lime tree. Jamie had arrived home for the summer holidays the previous evening and this was the first time brother and sister had been alone together. It was six months since he had been packed off to Germany to learn the language, having, as was expected, failed to obtain his School Certificate.

"Our Jamie may not have brains but he certainly does have good looks!" Lucy had remarked at breakfast, and Zandra was surprised to see that far from blushing at the compliment, as would have been the case six months ago, he'd merely grinned. He had lost his adolescent spots as well as his self-conscious gawkiness, and seemed almost overnight to have changed from schoolboy to man.

"I stopped growing when I was sixteen!" Jamie was saying. "I

157

just look taller because I've put on weight – mostly muscle, I might add. It's the outdoor life I've been leading."

"I thought you were supposed to be going to Munich to learn German!" Zandra said with mock reproach. "Have you done any work at all? If so, you never mentioned it in your letters. As far as I can see, all you've done out there is ski, skate, hike, dance, sail and go camping with the daughter of the house!"

Jamie grinned.

"I can't begin to tell you what fun it is. Ingeborg is a really topping companion. Of course, she's a much better skier than I am and she skates really well, too, but I usually beat her at tennis. She's frightfully good at everything. She can play the accordion and she's a topping dancer, too! I can't wait for you to meet her, Zee-Zee. She's terribly easy to get on with and I know she's going to love Rochford although I've warned her it might seem pretty boring after the life she's used to over there."

"She can come up to London and stay with me! I'll take her to the theatre and the ballet, and show her the sights," Zandra said reassuringly. "It'll be good for you both to have a little intellectual stimulus after all that fresh air and exercise you seem to have concentrated on!"

Jamie sat up and hunching his knees, enclosed them with his arms.

He really has grown up, Zandra thought, and emerged as a very attractive young man. He had their mother's violet-blue eyes with dark lashes which might have seemed effeminate in a man except for the fact that his chin was square and firm, his mouth strong and, she noticed with amusement, he had managed to grow a moustache which made him look older than his years. It was hard to realize that her "little" brother would not even be nineteen until November.

"Your letters were very full of Ingeborg," she remarked. "Do I gather you have somewhat of a crush on her? You never mentioned any other girls."

Jamie laughed.

"There were lots of them around but not one to hold a candle to Inge. Did you get the snapshots I sent? Don't you think she's terribly pretty?"

Zandra recalled the tall athletic-looking girl with two long braids of fair hair falling either side of a round, almost doll-like face, the eyes unsmiling, staring directly into the camera. It was not what could fairly be called a "pretty" face, but it was certainly intelligent. Realizing that Jamie was obviously suffering from his first attack of calf-love, Zandra chose to nod rather than to dispute his opinion. Jamie was now in full flood.

"She's frightfully clever – especially at maths. Her parents wanted her to go to university but she wants a career that will let her be out of doors. When she has done her year here in England, she's probably going to get a job in the Youth Movement. That's one of the really good things about Germany, Zee-Zee. This National Socialist party Ingeborg belongs to is doing really marvellous things for young people – organizing camping holidays and things like that. It's a bit like the Scouts over here. Inge says it's going to be even better now that Herr Hitler has become Reichchancellor."

"Isn't he a Fascist?" Zandra asked doubtfully. "I seem to remember hearing Uncle Toby saying the Fascists were a lot of 'thugs'!"

"I expect he was talking about that Italian chap, Mussolini – the one everyone calls 'Il Duce'!" Jamie said vaguely. "This is the German Chancellor I'm talking about – actually, he's Austrian, but it comes to the same thing. Ingeborg says it was really terrible after the war – the poverty and unemployment and all that, and Adolf Hitler is putting the country back on its feet. He has abolished the Trade Unions and is redirecting the money they used to get to help the workers."

He paused briefly to draw breath before continuing: "Do you know, Zee-Zee, the workers are getting concessions to go to concerts and plays now, and they can have two weeks' holiday in the mountains or at the seaside and places like that, for practically nothing? Herr Hitler is having houses and roads built, too, and they've started on this amazing *Autobahn*. It's a huge road that's going to be over three thousand kilometres long when it's finished, and it takes two lanes of cars going in each direction with a grass division in the middle, so it'll be fantastically quick. Lots of the unemployed people are getting work because of it; and in the new factories. You know, Zee-Zee, there's an awful lot of rubbish talked over here about the Germans. I know they started the war, but they're just ordinary people like us, and I can't understand why Uncle Toby says silly things like "There's no such person as a good Hun!"

"You aren't old enough to remember what happened in the war, Jamie," Zandra said. "For one thing, the Germans used gas and for another, nearly all his friends were killed and his brother, Uncle Rupert. You can't wonder if Uncle Toby and his genera-tion feel the way they do."

"I suppose not!" Jamie said with a frown. "But that's all in the past now. Ingeborg's father was only saying last month that in Adolf Hitler's 'Peace Speech' to the Reichstag, he stated quite positively that he would agree to the disarmament proposals if the other countries agreed to Germany being treated as an equal. He said it was his earnest wish to help heal the wounds caused by the war. After all, Zee-Zee, it ended fifteen years ago, for goodness' sake!"

"Anthony was saying we should forget about it, too, at dinner the other night," Zandra admitted. "To be truthful, Jamie, I'm not much interested in politics although Anthony is always trying to educate me! I think he's afraid I'll make a bloomer at one of our boring dinner parties."

Jamie grinned.

"Are they boring? I thought Anthony knew heaps of impor-tant people!"

"Yes, he does – but they aren't really friends so much as people Anthony needs to cultivate for his business. The only person he invites to the house who I really like is Guy!"

"Gosh, yes! He's a jolly decent chap!" Jamie said grinning.

"Remember that time you both took me out from school? He took us on the river and gave us a slap-up meal at that super pub? And he tipped me a quid every time he came here when I was home for the hols."

Zandra smiled at these boyish memories, but her smile faded when her brother added: "Of course, Anthony's always very generous, too, but I don't seem able to get on with him the way I did with Mr Bristow. I always get the feeling I'm boring him, but then he's frightfully clever, isn't he?"

"I suppose he is," Zandra acknowledged, and anxious to change the subject, she said quickly: "Guy's a really good tennis player. We could ask him down one weekend whilst you're home to give you a few games."

She, herself, warmed to the spontaneous idea. Guy had become a good friend after those awful days in hospital. Their friendship had developed from being formal to informal after a chance telephone call he'd made not long after she'd returned home, to enquire how she was. Stupidly, she'd broken down in tears, and next thing, Guy turned up at the house and whisked her off to Regent's Park to the zoo, of all places! She'd tried to refuse the invitation which, in her state of depression, had struck her as ridiculous; but Guy had insisted that he'd always found the zoo the best possible place to cheer one up – and to her intense surprise, he proved to be right. They'd ended the day eating ice-cream cornets, and by the time he drove her home, she'd felt ten years younger.

It was mainly due to Guy's wonderful sense of humour, she had decided, that she so much enjoyed his company. There was no agreement not to do so, but neither of them mentioned their subsequent odd, irregular meetings to Anthony. In any case, he was usually abroad when they happened – presumably because these were the only times Guy was free to leave the office. They'd gone for long walks in Kensington Gardens; spent an afternoon watching the final at Wimbledon; taken a river boat trip to Greenwich; had a hilarious day in Hampton Court maze, and

161

another frightening each other in Madame Tussaud's Chamber of Horrors.

It was all harmless fun, and she had been strangely disappointed when without explanation from Guy, the invitations ceased and she saw him only on those occasions when he was in his working capacity for Anthony.

"I think Anthony keeps Guy fairly busy these days," she said now to Jamie. "I saw quite a lot of him after I came out of hospital, but . . . well, he hasn't been around much these past few months."

Jamie's cheerful face clouded.

"Are you still frightfully cut up about the baby, Zee-Zee?" he asked with genuine concern. "Aunt Willow wrote and said you never talked about it any more, so she thought you were – well, getting over it."

"Let's say I've accepted it!" Zandra said quietly. "It upsets Anthony when I talk about the baby, so we never do. It's best if you don't, either."

Jamie nodded.

"I dare say you'll have another one soon, old thing. Ingeborg is an only child but she says she's going to have dozens of children when she gets married. She's frightfully good with the young ones and wants to get a job working with children."

Zandra concealed a smile. Discussion on any subject, she realized, would find its way back to the girl who had clearly stolen Jamie's heart. It really didn't bother her that Ingeborg was German, for first loves rarely lasted very long and by this time next year, Jamie would probably be eulogizing about another girl. All that mattered now was that he was happy in Munich, and that the family Anthony had chosen for him was proving an undoubted success.

"I thought I might drive over to Ashdown Forest and give the dogs a long walk," Jamie said. "They always love going there. How about it, Zee-Zee? If we leave now, we'll miss tea but we'd be back in time for dinner."

Zandra rose to her feet.

"The exercise will do me good. I don't walk nearly enough in London!"

Jamie jumped up and linking his arm through hers, led her towards the courtyard where the cars were now garaged in the old stables. They now housed only two horses since the others had been requisitioned in the war, and the two ponies Oliver had bought for the boys once they had outgrown their Shetland pony. The remainder of the loose boxes now sheltered his Bentley, Toby's old Armstrong Siddeley, and the family Talbot which Aunt Willow and Lucy used for shopping or to get to the railway station. The groom, Jim Smithers, doubled as occasional chauffeur and kept the cars washed and polished. He was a self-taught, natural mechanic and Oliver was always threatening to steal him for Sky-Ways.

Delighted to be behind the wheel of a fast car, Jamie drove Zandra to Forest Row with the hood of the Talbot folded down in the hope that the rush of air in their faces would cool them. The noise was such that there was no further opportunity for conversation and he had time to reflect. He was deeply devoted to his sister although he found it difficult to show it. As children, Zandra had not only teased him unmercifully but had bossed him around with all the authority her extra five years gave her. But even in those days he had admired her, for she would not only stand up for herself – sometimes in the face of impossible odds! – but for him, too. Her easily aroused temper was offset by an equally ready sense of humour, and it was always fun being in her company.

Now, he thought uneasily, she was a very different person – much quieter and less ready to laugh and joke. Aunt Willow had written and told him Zee-Zee was finding it very difficult to get over the loss of her baby, but perhaps because he'd not seen her for six months, he was aware of something more than sadness in her manner, although he could not as yet put a finger on it. He'd not seen a great deal of his brother-in-law since the wedding, but he'd thought Anthony a very pleasant chap even if he had seemed a bit old for Zee-Zee. Apart from anything else, he was extremely generous with tips – especially at that time when Uncle Toby had had to reduce his tuck-box money! He was top-hole at choosing Christmas and birthday presents and a better tennis player even than Cousin Oliver.

As he crossed the main road from Tunbridge Wells and headed towards Hartfield, Jamie's thoughts returned to his sister. He knew she spent quite a lot of time at Rochford when Anthony was abroad. Maybe she was unhappy because they were separated so often, he told himself. After all, he had been secretly wondering how he would survive the eight long weeks of the holiday without seeing Ingeborg – and they were not even engaged! They were in love, though. On his last evening in Munich, he had plucked up the courage to kiss her on their way back from a boating outing on Tegenzee, and she had kissed him back. Moreover, she had promised to write to him every day.

She was such a splendid girl, Jamie told himself as he slowed to pass a large horse-drawn hay cart. He could hardly believe his luck. In his last term at school, he and his friends had talked a lot about getting to know girls and what was the best way to get them to like you. Not that you could actually go "the whole way" with that sort of girl, and there was a great deal of speculation as to who would be first to do "it" properly. No one that he knew had, although it was rumoured one of the prefects had done it with a cousin. He wished he didn't dream so much about doing "it" with Ingeborg! It sort of sullied her image; but there was no way you could control your dreams, and he tried very hard not to think about her figure which was about as feminine as it could be. She often wore a dirndl skirt with a low-cut white blouse, revealing the smooth, rounded curves of her not inconsiderable bosom; or, if they were dancing or skating together, she would lean against him so that he couldn't fail to be aware of it. He was quite hopelessly in love with her, of course, and maybe he'd tell Zee-Zee before he went back to Munich in September. Meanwhile, he really must try to put her out of his mind.

Zandra was equally deep in reflection. What had she done with

164

her life this past half-year whilst Jamie had been enjoying himself so well in Germany? Why, when nothing untoward had happened since she'd lost the baby, should she feel as if those months had been completely joyless? Dr Petrie had told her she was under-weight and that it was natural she should feel low. Keep busy! he had advised. The depression would soon go away. But it had not been easy to "keep busy". Her household was run with utmost efficiency by a retinue of servants; Monica and Charles were running Alternatives with huge enthusiasm and growing success. In February, at her friend Margaret Wigham's wedding, a surpris-ing number of the guests had selected outfits from Alternatives! There had been an even larger number who'd visited the shop unobtrusively when Winston Churchill's daughter, Diana, had been married at St Margaret's, Westminster in December. Uncle Pelham, who'd been imprisoned in South Africa with Mr Churchill in the Boer War and become a friend of his, had come over from France with Tante Silvie for that wedding, and their visit had helped to pass the days before Christmas.

In January, when she and Anthony had returned to London from Rochford after the festivities, there'd been a brief distrac-tion when thousands of the country's three million unemployed had made their hunger march to London to present a petition to Parliament. Anthony had insisted that the police should have been better organized to keep "the wretches" out; but Zandra shared Lucy's sympathy for the unfortunate men whose families were starving.

She had promptly enlisted Zandra's help to raise funds for the families of the poor and together, they had organized several charity balls, bridge drives, tea parties and jumble sales to which Alternatives had been able to contribute a large bundle of warm winter clothing. When Alexis had pointed out that a sable-lined, tweed coat might be of little use to a starving miner's wife, Lucy had swept the suggestion aside, saying that such a woman would be well able to cut up the coat for a child to wear, and the sable lining could keep several freezing children warm in bed!

Between them, she and Lucy had raised a very large sum of money, and they had only given up their good work at Easter when Alexis complained that Lucy was neglecting their children who were home for the holidays. Robin was attending a preparatory school and Eve was likewise at a boarding school in Bexhill. If Lucy continued to devote herself to the poor, Alexis had pointed out with his usual wry humour, they might not recognize their mama next time they came home from school!

If only Anthony were a little more like Alexis, Zandra thought, as Jamie parked the car in a lay-by and the two spaniels bounded off into the heather. Alexis was such a loving father, and so sweet with Lucy. He never seemed to object to her impulsive eccentricities. On the contrary, he'd once told Zandra: "It makes life quite exciting never knowing when I get home at night if the bathroom has been painted purple or the furniture moved or – and it has happened, I promise you – I discover that Lucy has given my brand new Hobbs brogues to a one-legged tramp. It's not even as if he could wear both of them!"

Recalling their laughter as she and Jamie followed the dogs on to the wide expanse of forest, Zandra appreciated what it was that marred her marriage to Anthony – *he lacked a sense of humour.* It seemed impossible, now this explanation occurred to her, that she had lived with him for three years and never realized it before. Anthony did laugh – always when one of his guests told an amusing anecdote; when he leafed through *Punch* and read a witty article; or when he watched an amusing Noel Coward play; but, she now recalled, never at himself.

"I think the dogs are on to a rabbit!" Jamie said beside her as the spaniels set up a chorus of excited barking. "Go to it, boys!"

Quickly, Zandra pushed to the back of her mind the rising feeling of dismay which her thoughts had evoked. She really was being stupid these days, allowing the silliest ideas to come into her head! Anthony was far too busy to have the time or inclination for frivolities. He worked tremendously long hours, and the amount of travelling he did was exhausting. No wonder he was tired when he was at home, not wanting to become involved in long conversations with her but preferring to listen to the news on the wireless; or read the papers. It did make it difficult sometimes for her to respond when without warning, he would suggest they go to bed as he wished to make love to her. Since she'd had the baby, she was seldom in the right mood to welcome Anthony's advances, and although she never denied him, she was afraid that he must sense her lack of enthusiasm. If he did so, he gave no indication of it, and seemed satisfied by these one-sided unions.

"Come on, Zee-Zee, race you to that fir tree. I'll give you twenty start!"

Jamie's boyish challenge swept Zandra back to her childhood, and she was smiling as, with the dogs at her heels, she raced her brother across the heather towards the tree.

"Out of consideration for your brother's feelings, I have waited until he returned to Rochford to take this matter up with you, Zandra. Sit down, please!"

Anthony was standing with his back to the drawing-room fireplace, one finger pointing towards the sofa in front of him. Zandra's chin lifted at his tone of voice. He was addressing her as if he were a schoolmaster and she a pupil on remand! she thought. Nevertheless, she sat down on the sofa and met his gaze. His eyes, she noted, were that familiar steely grey which presaged displeasure. His brows were drawn together in a frown and he was holding out a piece of paper which he proceeded to shake in front of her.

"Do you know what this is, Zandra? No? Well, allow me to tell you. It is a letter from my bank."

Zandra tried to search her memory for any especially extravagant purchase she might recently have made. Recalling none, she asked: "Have I been spending too much money, Anthony? I did give Cook a rise, but you knew that. What's this all about?"

Anthony's mouth tightened.

167

"That is exactly the question I am about to put to you. *What is this all about, Zandra?* I want an explanation."

Zandra felt her hands begin to shake as her temper rose.

"How can I possibly answer when I don't know what's in the letter?" she said coldly. "If you let me see it instead of waving it in front of me like that, perhaps I'll understand why you're speaking to me as if I was one of your employees!'

"Don't raise your voice to me, Zandra. Here, read it!"

He shoved the letter into her hand and she noticed with surprise that his was shaking. As she began to read, her heart sank for she understood now what had caused Anthony to be so angry. The bank manager had written:

Dear Mr Wisson,

It has been brought to my notice that there is a large sum of money in your wife's account which appears to be accumulating without any notable withdrawals. This sum now stands at five hundred pounds, and were it to be put into a deposit account, it could be earning interest.

I wrote to Mrs Wisson on 4 August regarding this matter, but having had no reply, it occurred to me that she might have overlooked it. As I am aware how meticulous yourself are with regard to your own affairs, I thought you might wish to draw your wife's attention to the financial advantages to her of my suggestion. I trust that by notifying you of the current situation, I am acting in accordance with your wishes.

I enclose a copy Statement of Mrs Wisson's account . . .

"It is *my* account. Mr Wilkinson had no right to involve you!" Zandra protested indignantly. "If I'd wanted your advice, Anthony, I would have asked for it."

Anthony's mouth tightened.

"You are my wife, Zandra, and as such you are my responsibility. Wilkinson did exactly the right thing."

Zandra's cheeks flushed a deep pink.

"No, he did not! It is my *private* account. If I'd needed your guidance, I would have asked for it."

Anthony leant down and snatched the letter from her. His face was now white with anger and he said furiously: "And what, may I ask, do *you* know about financial matters? You appear to have forgotten, very conveniently I might say, that you are my wife. I am the one in control of our finances – which brings me to the crux of the matter. Kindly explain the deposits in this statement." He waved it in front of her. "You will kindly tell me now just what has been going on behind my back."

For the first time, Zandra felt a qualm of bad conscience. From the very start she had said nothing to Anthony about Alternatives. Charles always paid her share of the profits directly into the account she had opened at the bank specifically for the purpose. It was the only secret she had ever kept from Anthony – but one that she believed to be justified. Her uneasiness gave way to a renewal of indignation.

"I may be your wife, Anthony, but you don't own me. It is entirely your own fault if I kept the shop a secret from you. You wouldn't allow me to have any money of my own. I wanted to work at Sky-Ways and you wouldn't let me do that – and for no better reason than because of what people might say if they knew your wife was earning money!"

She gave him a brief outline as to how the agency had evolved. "So you see, no one knows I'm involved in Alternatives – only Monica and Charles, and they've never told anyone. We're partners and all I do is tell friends where they can dispose of the clothes they don't want anymore; and, I might add, I prepare the books for Charles, so you see, I am perfectly capable of managing my own finances and those of the business. As to Mr Wilkinson's letter to me, I saw no need to reply to it since he merely made a suggestion I did not wish to take up. To have my money in a deposit account would mean that it would be tied up, and I have my own reasons for wishing to have it readily available. Does that answer your question?"

Anthony was now pacing the floor. His eyes were narrowed and his mouth was a thin line. Zandra had never seen him so furious, and for a moment, she was frightened. His voice was ominously quiet as he said: "Of all the many ways you could think of to irritate me, this must be the most obvious. Understand me once and for all, Zandra – *I will not have you working*. As it happens, I have already looked into Alternatives, and I am quite appalled to find that it's no better than a second-hand clothes shop! Are you quite out of your mind? I can see well enough how that pansy, Charles Boswell, could sink to such depths, not to mention that flighty wife of his. They are no better than all those other Bohemian types with their ideas about 'free love' and 'the equality of women' and that kind of tommy-rot! Isn't Monica Boswell that female who jumped into a swimming-pool in her underwear at a party recently? Frankly, I would prefer that you didn't associate with such people, and it surprises me that, with your upbringing, you don't have a better appreciation of the conventions."

"Monica is a good friend of mine and you've never objected to my inviting her and Charles to lunch," Zandra broke in as Anthony paused to draw breath. "I suppose this sudden objection to them is because of the shop. Well, you may choose to think me stupid, but you can't deny that Alternatives has been a great success." She pointed to the statement Anthony was still holding. "The figures speak for themselves – and it's *my* money just as it was *my* idea; and I don't intend to give it up."

"We'll see about that, my dear. I happen to know that Boswell is penniless. I also happen to know that Alternatives is registered in his name, not yours, and I very much doubt if Boswell will refuse my offer to buy you out. I might add that an offer has already been made to him . . . not in my name, of course."

"You can't do that . . . I won't let you!" Zandra cried, but even as the words left her lips, she knew that if Charles did agree to sell, there was no way she could prevent it. With a sinking heart, she realized that Anthony's offer must have been absurdly generous for him to be so sure of himself. Although the profits from Alternatives had proved more than ample for her and Monica's spending money, split as it was three ways, it was only a meagre sum for Charles who had a wife to support. He had come from a well-to-do family and was unaccustomed to economizing; and he made no secret of the fact that he and Monica continued to live a lifestyle very much in excess of their income, as a consequence of which they were hopelessly in debt. Anthony, with his usual efficiency, must have found this out, and it would be churlish of her to stand in the way of her friends' acceptance of his offer.

"There are times, Anthony, when I find myself wondering if I really know you – the real you, I mean. You're one of the most generous people I know, and yet . . . yet you can be quite cruel at times, cruel and ruthless. You said you loved me, but I don't think you really mind whether I am happy or not. I don't understand you. Why, for instance, does it matter so much to you that I should behave conventionally? What does it matter what other people think, anyway? Everyone knows you're rich and successful, and if I had a real job nobody would imagine it was because you couldn't afford to support me. It's not even as if *you* wanted my time. You once said you didn't want me to be tied to a job so that I'd be free for you to take me with you when you went abroad; but you never do any more. You've not once suggested it since you planned to take me to Germany to choose a family for Jamie. My being pregnant was the reason you gave for not doing so, but it's over a year since . . . since I had the baby. I simply don't understand you."

Whilst Zandra had been talking, Anthony had seated himself in an armchair and lit a cigarette. He seemed quite unperturbed by her outburst, and calmly blew a cloud of smoke into the air.

"It really is time that you ceased being quite so hysterical, Zandra," he said in a matter-of-fact tone of voice. "You appear – very conveniently, I might say – to have forgotten the tears, loss of weight and depression after you came out of hospital, which, Dr

Petrie told me, was only to be expected and must be tolerated. I think I was very patient under the circumstances – but you could not have expected me to find your company very enjoyable; so naturally I didn't take you abroad with me. You would hardly have been very invigorating company for my business contacts, would you? As for the death of the baby, other women have suffered similar experiences without using it as an excuse for going completely off their heads – and that is the kindest explanation I can give for this . . . this unsavoury enterprise of yours. I will not have you disgracing me, Zandra, do you understand? I had supposed when I asked you to marry me – mistakenly, I now realize – that as a member of Lord Rochford's family, your behaviour could be relied upon to be beyond reproach. Whether you like it or not, that is important to me in my business. You are my wife – and I expect you to behave as such."

These were not the words of a man head over heels in love, Zandra thought as she struggled to keep at bay the fear that followed his declaration. She had tried for some time now – usually in those long, wakeful hours at night – not to question Anthony's reaction to the baby's death. She had excused his delay in reaching the hospital – men did have vital business affairs that must be given priority. Not least, she had excused his total disinterest in the funeral arrangements, leaving them all to Guy, even to the wording attached to the tiny wreath. "Sort it out with Guy!" he'd said when she had asked for his choice of a farewell message. She'd even found excuses for his blank refusal ever to discuss the baby's few days of life that had been so tragically traumatic for her. She had convinced herself that his detachment was due to the fact that he felt guilty because he'd not been there to comfort and support her, or to see his baby alive.

Unwelcome as it was, the thought surfaced from the back of her mind, where, she realized, it had always been lurking – Anthony simply did not care about the baby, about her suffering, about her! The only time he'd ever shown love for her since their marriage was when he'd made love to her; and she could see now that this had always been one-sided; that his invasions of her body had been prompted by passion rather than love.

With no experience to guide her, she'd had no way of knowing whether other husbands behaved differently in bed. According to Monica, who was always astonishingly outspoken about such matters, Charles was exceptionally demanding. Some husbands, she'd related, only made love to their wives once a month, others once a week. Lots of women really enjoyed it, though others didn't; but men not only liked doing it, they – *needed* it because of the way they were made. That was always the best time to get round them, Monica had confided, because they were their most adoring when they wanted it!

Zandra had laughed at the time, knowing that nothing her scatty friend said should ever be taken too seriously; but now she could see that there could well be a great deal of truth in it – Anthony was *only* capable of showing love when he wanted her!

She felt a sudden urgent need to prove herself wrong; to prove that he loved her in the same way as she loved him; for without love, what kind of a marriage would theirs become? What did they have in common other than their home? When they were together, it was either at parties or at Rochford, and they were never alone. Perhaps, she thought, things might have been different if their tiny son, Rupert, had lived . . .

"Anthony, please don't let's quarrel about this!" she said softly. Kneeling down on the floor in front of him, she reached for his hand and leant her cheek against it. "I'm sorry if you're upset about Alternatives. Please try to understand! It's true I was terribly depressed after the baby and . . . well, running the shop with Monica and Charles does take things off my mind. We had great fun planning it and honestly, darling, no one does know I'm involved. If that stupid bank manager hadn't written to you, you wouldn't have known about it either. I couldn't see any harm in it – I don't now, and—"

"Be quiet, Zandra!" Anthony broke in sharply, pulling his hand away. "I have told you once and I don't intend to repeat myself – you will cease to be involved in the shop which I intend to close. Now get up at once. Suppose one of the servants were to come in and see you begging like one of those ghastly paupers Countess Zemski chooses to patronize!"

Slowly, Zandra rose to her feet. She was gripping her hands together to keep them from trembling.

"If I was begging, Anthony, it was not because I hoped to change your mind about Alternatives; it was for your understanding. I was trying to explain that I hoped for much more from my marriage than the material things you give me. I wanted a companion – a friend, if you like – so no, I won't 'be quiet'! You have stated your point of view, and I intend to give mine."

Her cheeks flushed, her head high, she stood with her back to the fireplace looking directly into her husband's face.

"Yes, I can find other things to do to fill in my time. As you have pointed out many times, when the weather is good, I can spend the day at Sky-Ways flying my aeroplane; I can help Lucy with her charities; I can go shopping, buy whatever I want. I can do as I please with the house. I dare say I could persuade you – as Dr Petrie has often suggested – to let me have another baby! But that's not what I want from you, Anthony – not any more. I want us to be together, laugh together, have fun, enjoy each other's company. Our marriage hasn't brought us closer, Anthony. We've been growing apart, and instead of waking up each morning looking forward to a new day, I dread it. I'm lonely . . . inside myself. Can't you understand?"

Anthony gave her a long, scrutinizing stare.

"Frankly, no! You've just had your brother staying here for two weeks; before that, you were at Rochford for a week. As I recall, you went to the Regatta, Wimbledon, and Goodwood; to several parties and weddings, not to mention your visits with your friends and cousins to theatre and cinema matinées. Your social diary—"

"Stop it, Anthony! You know that is not what I am talking about. It's us – you and me, and our marriage. I don't want it to go on as it is."

"So! What do you propose to do about it?"

The quietness of Anthony's voice misled Zandra. She said eagerly: "It's what *you* propose, Anthony. We're like strangers. We don't have a great deal of time together because you're so busy, but when you are at home, we don't really enjoy ourselves. Look at all those dreary dinner parties we have to give to people neither of us really likes. Couldn't we compromise – just have our friends from time to time; or go to a cinema on our own; or go to a dinner-dance? Or we could drive out of London somewhere and have a picnic – just the two of us; or go to the Lake District for a weekend and take long walks. Or if none of that appeals to you, we could go to Venice or Provence or Spain – just on our own."

"There are times when you really surprise me, Zandra. For someone whom I'd thought to be reasonably intelligent, you can be extraordinarily stupid. Don't you imagine I do quite enough travelling without having to go off to Spain or Italy or wherever? You suggest we 'compromise' – so perhaps I had better make it quite clear to you – I don't believe in compromise. I consider it a form of weakness to accede to someone else's wishes if they conflict with my own. I'm sorry if you are dissatisfied with your life, but I am perfectly content with mine. That's all there is to it."

It was at that moment that something deep inside Zandra died. She had been pleading for their marriage, but without love, it could only ever be barren.

"It isn't quite all there is to it, Anthony. I have as much right as you to enjoy my life. Since you can't see the necessity for this, then it seems to me we may as well put an end to our marriage."

Anthony stubbed out his cigarette and to her astonishment, he smiled.

"Don't be ridiculous, Zandra. I have no intention of terminating it."

"But I have!" Zandra said furiously. "We don't love each other any more, so what's the point in continuing with it?"

"The point is, my dear, that I do not intend to become a laughing-stock. You will not leave me now, or ever, unless I wish it."

"You can't force me to stay!" Zandra cried. "You can't lock me up like some insane Victorian husband! I shall go tonight."

Anthony gave a short, hard laugh.

"I doubt that very much. You see, Zandra, if you should choose to damage my reputation by walking out on me, I would be obliged to damage your reputation – or should I say that of your family? This may come as a surprise to you, but your attitude obliges me to enlighten you to a few salient facts. Your precious family have some very unpleasant skeletons in their cupboard. Did you know, for example, that your Uncle Francis was killed by a footman because he had raped the man's future wife? Or that your Uncle Rupert was a homosexual and had a German lover?"

For a moment, Zandra was shocked into silence, but something deep inside her told her that Anthony would not have made such scandalous accusations if they were untrue; and had she not often wondered why Uncle Toby and Aunt Willow always changed the conversation when she had asked about these two uncles? She couldn't imagine how Anthony had unearthed these family secrets, but she was not going to let him think that they gave him the upper hand. She returned his gaze squarely.

"Even if that is true – and I'm far from sure it is! – both Uncle Francis and Uncle Rupert are dead, so you can't damage them now!"

"Perhaps not, although I doubt if your Aunt Willow or your Uncle Toby would much appreciate such facts becoming a subject of gossip amongst their friends and acquaintances. However, I have so far only given you two examples. You also happen to have a living relative – Countess Zemski – whose background will most definitely not bear scrutiny, to say the very least."

"Lucy? Now I know you're making all this up, Anthony. Frankly, I'm finding this whole conversation thoroughly objectionable and – at best – utterly ridiculous!"

Anthony gave a short laugh.

"I do assure you, my dear, that I'm only giving you facts. I don't suppose you will believe this – I found it difficult myself, but it is true – Countess Zemski spent four years of her life in a French brothel where she was known as 'La Perle'. Now I really don't think you or your family would like *that* to become generally known, and it would, of course, ruin both your cousin and her husband socially as well as having a devastating effect upon her children were it to become common gossip."

"I don't believe you!" Zandra gasped. "Not Lucy! How can you say such things? You're out of your mind! You're just trying to frighten me – hurt me, because I said I didn't want to live with you any more. No, I don't believe any of this – *not a single word of it!*"

Anthony gave a curious little smile.

"Then it's time you did, my dear. I have documentary evidence to confirm everything I've told you. If you wish, I can show it to you."

Her stomach knotting in fear, Zandra whispered: "You can't seriously mean you would reveal these facts . . . if I left you?"

"Why not? An eye for an eye, my dear. You make a laughing-stock of me and believe me, you will regret it."

"But that's . . . that's blackmail!" Zandra whispered.

"Call it what you will. Think it over, by all means, but I'm sure you will come to your senses and agree with me that our marriage should continue as before."

No! Zandra thought as Anthony rose unhurriedly to his feet and without a backward glance, walked out of the room. No, in this instance, Anthony was mistaken. She might be obliged to submit to his threats and their marriage might have to continue, but never, ever as before.

Chapter 11

A week passed, during which Zandra exchanged no words with Anthony other than those necessary to maintain appearances when there were servants in the room. She told Mollie to move the Master's belongings into the dressing-room as she had not been sleeping well and was afraid her restlessness would disturb him.

Anthony made no comment and continued to go about his day-to-day affairs as usual – indeed, the normality of his behaviour was such that Zandra started to wonder if he failed to realize that as far as she was concerned, to all intents and purposes their marriage was over. For the present, she dared not leave him for fear that he might carry out his threat to disgrace her family; but for her, it had become a marriage in name only.

At the end of the week, as if there were nothing untoward between them, Anthony announced that he was going to Spain the following day and would be away for at least ten days.

"You can come with me if you wish, Zandra!" he said across the dinner table. "Spain is an interesting country and you look as if you could do with a holiday."

Bitterness filled Zandra's heart. Such a suggestion so short a while ago would have elicited a flood of excitement and

178

pleasure. Unable to keep the cynicism from her voice, she said quietly: "Why ask me, Anthony? I can't believe you have the slightest wish for me to accompany you."

He put down his knife and fork, and dabbed his mouth with his napkin.

"On the contrary, my dear. As it happens, I may have quite a bit of entertaining to do and you could be of considerable assistance. Like most of the hoi polloi, the Spanish like titles, and your connection with Lord Rochford could be useful. Your excellent French is another asset since not everyone speaks English."

Zandra's mouth tightened.

"I'm afraid I shan't be coming with you, Anthony. As you know, I haven't been feeling too well lately."

Anthony nodded. He did not seem surprised by her refusal and she wondered if he had expected it.

"I shall have to try and find time to take you on holiday when I return," he said calmly. "By the way, my dear, I lunched with Boswell today. He was somewhat surprised to learn that I was the prospective buyer of Alternatives. However, I explained that you no longer wished to be involved in the business. He quite understood and signed the necessary papers Mackinson had prepared. I saw Mr Wilkinson today and explained you would shortly be closing your account as there'd be no further payments into it. So we can now put this unfortunate episode behind us."

Zandra pushed back her chair and stood up, her face flushed with anger.

"How dare you do that! You had no right! I told you I didn't want to give up the shop. How dare you go ahead behind my back!"

Anthony's eyes narrowed and, unconsciously, he caught hold of his right wrist, and his fingers closed over the scars. Zandra's words had struck a chord of memory from the past . . . New Year's Eve 1916 . . . the second year of the war . . . and he was twenty-two years old.

"How dare you do that! You had no right! How dare you!"

His father's voice, cold, accusing. How old he looked, far older than his sixty-four years, as he sat slumped in the office chair, a copy of the accounts in front of him.

"We needed the money from the Workers' Benefit Fund for a more important requirement, Father!"

"More important? Listen to me, Antoni. I decide what is important and what is not. You are the financial manager, not the boss – not until I choose to hand the firm over to you, and after this outrageous action, that will not be for a long time yet. I will not have the Fund terminated, do you understand? You will reinstate it immediately. Where is the accumulated capital? Don't just stand there. Show me! I don't see any mention of it here."

"I opened a separate account . . . an emergency account . . . it doesn't show in last year's figures."

"I want to see the relevant papers – now, Antoni!"

Damnation! He had not expected his father to do more than cast a cursory glance at the end-of-year Profit and Loss figures. He must not appear disconcerted.

"Certainly you shall see them if you want, Father. I'll look them out when I get back from lunch. I have to rush off now. I'm late already and you know what a stickler Mr Finelli is about punctuality. I gather he has been busy negotiating a big order for us from the French."

"Mr Finelli can wait. I want every letter, every paper relating to this 'Emergency Fund' of yours here on my desk in five minutes. That's an order."

He'd known he was taking a big risk when he'd had the Workers' Fund capital transferred to a new account in his own name, but he'd gambled on the fact that after three years working at the factory, his father had ceased to supervise his activities, considering him to be responsible and trustworthy as well as ultra-efficient. Well, the time had come when in any event, he'd had enough of playing second fiddle to the old man. Since the outbreak of war, the factory had been working overtime, unable to keep up with the demands for ammunition from the Front. At sixty-four years of age, his father was too old, too set in his ways, to snatch this golden opportunity for expansion; besides which the silly old fool was convinced the war would be over soon. As if it could be quickly resolved with both sides bogged down in the mud in the trenches!

For a long time now, he, Antoni, had fretted at his father's stubborn refusal to consider the points he was making – namely that there was more than enough in the Workers' Fund to buy a second premises, put in machinery; and although there was an acute shortage of manpower, women were coming forward to operate the machines – and at a lower wage than their menfolk, too. The financial rewards of such a move could be enormous; but the old man had turned the idea down out of hand; and it was his own fault if he, Antoni, had decided to go ahead without his father's approval. It really didn't matter that he'd found this out now.

He fetched the papers from the safe in his office and took them to his father. The new premises had already been bought and the machinery was arriving next month, so he'd have had to own up to his unilateral action by February at the latest.

"I'm sorry if you're upset about this, Father! I would have discussed it with you weeks ago but Mother said I was to keep you as free from stress as I could. You know how worried she has been about your health. When you see the figures, I'm sure you'll agree that it really is a highly sensible move to be making, and that by this time next year, our profits should double. We could revive the Workers' Fund then if you're so concerned about it!"

Was the old man speechless from astonishment or anger? His face was scarlet and he seemed to be struggling for words. For over a year now, he had been under the doctor's orders because his blood pressure was too high.

"How dare you go ahead without my authority! How dare you!" The words were gasped rather than spoken. "You went behind my back – and that I will not tolerate. Well, I can do without your help, my boy. Banfield can come out of retirement and cope with the accounts. As for you, you can go and fight for your country alongside all the other young men. I should never have agreed to your claiming exemption on the grounds of it being essential war work you're doing here. I did so because of your mother who is blind to your faults. You're fired, Antoni, do you hear me? I don't want to see you in this building again!"

181

For a moment, he was not only angry but unnerved. As the adrenalin coursed through his veins, his brain doubled its working speed. Unconsciously, his left hand moved to grasp and conceal the scar on his wrist, and he said coolly: "I doubt if Mother will be grateful to you for firing me for so unjust a reason; and I dread to think of the tears she'll shed when she sees me leaving for the Front. The papers are saying the latest casualty lists are—"

"Don't blackmail me, boy! Your good looks and your charming manners don't blind me to your arrogance, your self-centredness, your guile. I disown you as my son. You'll never inherit—"

His father's clenched fist, raised threateningly in his face, dropped onto the desk top and gasping, he toppled back in his chair. His face was purple and his teeth were clenched in a grimace of agony as he reached falteringly towards the silver pillbox beside the inkwell.

So he was having the heart attack the doctor had been warning him about! He was trying to reach the pills that were to give him relief if the worst happened. The look in those red-veined staring eyes was one of desperate appeal – an appeal for help to which he, Antoni, was not going to respond. Perhaps if his father had not just fired him . . . perhaps if he hadn't been about to deny him the inheritance he had counted upon . . . No, he was not going to risk having to start all over again penniless. It was not as if his mother had money to give him. The old man had the money – and with it the power. What possible advantage could there be in handing over the precious little box of pills? None, that he could think of. There was froth coming now from the blue lips; the eyes were rolling. Almost certainly he was dying.

With a shrug, he turned away and, leaving the room, closed the door quietly behind him.

"It's my money; my account, Anthony," Zandra was saying. "You had no right to tell Mr Wilkinson I wanted to close it. I shall open another one at some other bank where you can't interfere!"

Anthony regarded her with raised eyebrows.

"Do sit down, Zandra, and stop behaving like a child. Open another account by all means but what do you intend to put in it now I've closed Alternatives – just as I would close any other business enterprise you opened. You seem to forget that I am the head of this household, and I have every right to do as I think fit. Fortunately I'm in a financial position to buy almost any business I choose to own, and believe me, every man – including Boswell – has his price! Money does bring power with it, you know."

Zandra remained standing.

"Is that why you don't want me to have any money of my own? So you can control everything I do? Well, you made a mistake, didn't you, when you gave me part of the Rochford estate" – her voice hardened as she added bitterly – "you remember, don't you, Anthony, those days when you were in love with me? If I want, I could sell some of it – and head of the household or not, you couldn't stop me! So I'm not going to be entirely penniless, am I?"

Anthony drew a long sigh.

"Please do sit down, Zandra, and lower your voice or the servants will hear you shouting. I wasn't intending to tell you this, but you oblige me to do so. No, you could not sell any part of the Rochford estate. Before our marriage, I had the deeds drawn up in my name but *I have not as yet transferred them to you*. You own nothing, and I am the only one who can sell them."

Zandra subsided into her chair, her face now white with disbelief.

"But you said . . . they were your wedding present to me you told everyone that . . . you can't mean this, Anthony!"

"Oh, but I do! And don't go running back to your family to complain that I've cheated you. I should simply explain that I have overlooked the matter and have every intention of transferring them when I can find the time to do so. Really, Zandra, I do wish you'd stop interfering in the way I run my affairs. You should know by now that you have nothing whatever to worry about – so long as our marriage continues, that is. That has always been the case. You really don't need money of your own

183

since you can, as always, charge what you like to my account. I am a relatively rich man and I see no reason why the sources of my income should dry up."

Zandra caught her breath.

"But why?" she asked in a small, hopeless voice. "Why do you want this marriage to go on? You don't love me. I don't think you ever did. Why don't you let me go? What hope of happiness is there for either of us now?"

Anthony's expression remained unchanged. He rose unhurriedly from the table and, taking Zandra's arm, conducted her to the drawing-room. For once, as he sat down in his usual armchair, he did not pick up the evening paper. He waited until Zandra was seated and then resumed the conversation as if there had been no interruption.

"Love is a word I consider to be greatly misused!" he said matter of factly. "Despite all the thousands of words written about it, I have yet to hear it clearly defined. If we're talking about romantic love, then I think it could justifiably – and far more correctly – be defined as lust. Nature has so formed men and women that they have strong physical needs which require expression and therefore a partner with whom it can be expressed. When a man is thus consumed by lust, he chooses to give it the more poetic name of 'love'. Similarly, nature provides women with a protective, nurturing instinct so that they can care for their young – a maternal instinct common to all animals, and that, too, is called love. If you examine the subject, you'll find, as I have done, that love is no more than a word the human race has devised to colour some of its basic emotions. As to our marriage, I have every possible reason for wishing it to continue. For one thing nature has given me the same physical needs as any other man and I have neither the time to look elsewhere to satisfy those needs, nor the wish to have a mistress."

He rose suddenly and went over to the sofa where he stood staring down at Zandra with a faint smile on his face. Then he reached down and, gripping her arm with one hand, he pulled her to her feet.

"It so happens, my dear, that from the day I first set eyes on you, I desired you," he said in a low, intense voice. "Your body has always been able to excite me. In addition, because of your background you have been able to open a great many doors for me socially. To give you but one example, your Uncle Toby and Oliver proposed me for the Carlton – a club I had previously failed to get into. Your taste is faultless; you have charm, youth and a disarming innocence which can be most useful when I am entertaining some of my worldly-wise business friends. All in all, my dear, I feel I have made an excellent choice in my wife. You have exceeded my expectations and therefore I do not have the slightest intention of letting you go."

So sickened was Zandra by all that she had just heard, she could no longer bear to remain with her husband a moment longer. With a brief "Excuse me!" she wrenched herself from his grasp and hurrying from the room, she ran upstairs. Try as she might, she could not reconcile the man she had married with this cold, calculating, callous individual who had assessed her – his own wife – much like a balance sheet. He had not chosen her from love but because of the advantages she could bring to him . . . and, now that she recalled his words, from lust; from the pleasure he seemed to derive from her body. Well, that much at least she could deny him! She had always treasured those intimate moments they had shared believing them to be the ultimate expression of the love they had for one another. Perhaps Anthony would not be quite so complacent about their marriage once he knew she would never allow him to make love to her again!

Zandra rang the bell for Mollie and telling the maid she was not feeling well, allowed the girl to undress her and put her to bed. Since returning home after her stay in hospital, she had slept alone in the big double bed, and Anthony in the adjoining dressing-room – an arrangement suggested by her as, from time to time, he was very late back from a business dinner; or had left the house before she was awake. It was to ensure she had the maximum amount of rest, she had maintained.

Once she had recovered her strength, however, he had returned to the marital bed whenever he wanted to make love to her. She had never yet denied him, but if he were to attempt to come into the room tonight, she would have no hesitation in telling him that from now on, he could find his pleasures elsewhere. She could see no way they could ever be reconciled now; that any further appeal for understanding was pointless; and she doubted if he had ever been in the least concerned with her happiness.

Not long ago, she had thought him the most generous man in the world – buying out Sky-Ways and giving Oliver and Henry such generous salaries; buying a large part of the Rochford estate for her. She understood now that he was merely buying power – power to fly where and when he wanted; power to bring her to heel as and when he might wish to do so. He'd admitted that he didn't want money for what it might buy, but for the power it gave him – and of course, he was right – it did! He'd been able to tempt Charles to sell him Alternatives; and hadn't Guy once told her that Anthony had given him a mortgage on his mother's house? That would have given Anthony a lasting hold over Guy should he ever want to leave his employ. It was perfectly clear to her now that Anthony manipulated people for his own advantage.

Zandra pulled the soft linen sheet up to her chin as if to protect herself from her thoughts, but nothing would keep them at bay as, randomly, they criss-crossed her mind. She had tried very hard to deny the fact that a little of the love she'd once had for her husband had died with her baby. Yet she could see no alternative for herself but to go on living under Anthony's roof! Her position was intolerable – unless she gambled on the chance that he had not – as he claimed – such damning evidence to back his threats to expose Lucy's past.

Wearily, Zandra accepted that it was a gamble she dared not take. Anthony was meticulous in everything he did, dotting every "i" and crossing every "t"! According to Guy, he researched thoroughly before entering into any new negotiations in his business so that, forewarned, he could never be taken by surprise or outwitted. No, she told herself, Anthony was not bluffing. Several times this past week, she had been on the point of going to see Lucy and asking her outright if there was any truth in Anthony's horrible allegations. In the end, her courage had failed her for deep down, she believed they might – anyway, in part – be true. No adult member of the family ever had talked or would talk about Lucy's childhood in France. Such curiosity from the younger generation was always neatly turned aside with the remark: "She was at a convent in France until she was sixteen!" The older members of the family, Zandra now realized, had closed ranks to protect Lucy.

It crossed Zandra's mind, as she tossed and turned restlessly in her bed, that she was like a squirrel in a cage, desperately seeking a way of escape. Perhaps, given a little time, Anthony himself would begin to realize that their marriage was a sham and that he should let her go. Not even he could be happy for long married to a woman he must now know hated him! Until he'd mentioned this evening the reasons he'd chosen to marry her, it hadn't occurred to her that her background could have been socially advantageous to him. As to his crude reference to "lusting" after her, there were a dozen unmarried girls prettier than herself and some with even better connections whom he could have married. Had he chosen her because he'd thought her more gullible than most? And did it matter now *why* he had opted to marry her?

Darkness had fallen and, overcome by her emotional turmoil, Zandra was on the brink of sleep when the communicating door to her room opened. She heard it close, and she reached out to turn on the bedside light. Anthony was approaching the bed, wearing his favourite Paisley silk dressing-gown. Without a word, he started to untie the cord. With a gasp, Zandra found her voice. It sounded high-pitched, unlike her own.

"No, Anthony! Please go away. I don't want you here."

Ignoring her request, Anthony removed his dressing-gown and tossed it onto the end of the bed. Climbing in beside her rigid body, he reached out an arm and switched off the bedside lamp. His voice sounded loud in the ensuing darkness.

"I've given you a week to come to terms with your situation, Zandra. I don't intend to extend that time."

He dragged back the bedclothes and before she could pull them up again, he straddled her body.

"Go away!" she cried fiercely pushing at him with both hands. "Go away, Anthony! Can't you understand? I don't want you near me. I don't want you ever to make love to me again." Feeling his hands searching for her breasts, her voice rose. "Get away from me. I hate you, do you hear me? You can't do this . . . you can't—"

Her voice broke off as his mouth came down on hers in a hard, painful kiss. She bit his lower lip but his gasp of pain ended in a laugh.

"You might as well stop fighting me, Zandra. I intend to have you sooner or later, so why don't you submit? It only excites me still more when you resist."

There was an ugly rasping noise as he wrenched the soft silk of her nightdress up above her thighs. With an effort, she raised one leg and tried to strike him with her knee. Both of them were now breathing deeply but Anthony was by far the stronger, and she could feel herself weakening as his determination to over-power her became more violent. The realization that he was about to rape her gave her renewed strength and she bit hard into his shoulder. With a cry of anger and pain, he momentarily released one handhold and struck her hard across the face. Although she had tried to avert her head, the blow caught her cheek and her eyes stung sharply with tears.

"Don't, please don't!" she whispered. "If you do this, I'll never forgive you."

There was no reply as roughly he twisted her onto her stomach and pulled her hips towards him. Ignoring her cry of pain, he thrust himself deeper and deeper into her. His breath on her neck was hot and redolent of cigar smoke which, she thought in an effort to block from her mind what he was doing, she would never be able to smell again without remembering this moment.

Finally he stopped and fell away from her. In contrast to her bruised, aching body, her mind was like a hard ball of steel. She was beyond tears; beyond words; beyond fear; beyond feeling anything other than an intense hatred for the man who had just violated her. She waited whilst he rose slowly from the bed, put on his dressing-gown and walked towards the door. There he paused and she heard his voice, quiet now and almost conversational in its tone.

'You would do well not to forget in future that you're still my wife and that when I have need of you, I shall expect you to comply with my wishes. Good night, my dear. I trust you will sleep well!'

Zandra did not know how long she lay immobile on the crumpled sheet too deeply shocked to move. Gradually she became aware once more of her body. Reaching up to feel her cheek, she realized that she was badly bruised. Even the gentlest of touches caused her to gasp in pain. Her arms and legs ached, too, but what really stirred her back to action was the warm, sticky dampness between her legs. Fighting back the onset of nausea, she sprang out of bed and, stumbling in the darkness against the furniture, felt her way to the bathroom. She was trembling violently as she ran the water into the bath and emptied an entire bottle of salts into it. Not waiting for it to fill, she plunged in and closed her eyes.

For several minutes, Zandra remained unmoving; then, as the bath water threatened to overflow, she sat up to turn off the taps. The warmth of the water had by now brought a return of feeling, and with sudden haste, she reached for the bar of soap and began to scrub herself until her skin was so sore she was obliged to stop. She sat for a minute, fearful that she might not have cleaned every last tiny vestige of Anthony from her. Then, as it crossed her mind that the water itself must be contaminated, she sprang out of the bath and wrapped herself in one of her large bath towels.

With it still around her, she stumbled back into her room and fell into the armchair. She could not bring herself to go near the bed where the crumpled sheets reminded her of her ordeal. If there was sleep to be had this night, it would have to be here in the chair for she dared not move to one of the spare rooms lest Anthony heard and followed her. Remembering that she had not yet done so, she got up quickly and with frantic haste, locked the communicating door as well as the door onto the landing. Then she subsided once more into the chair, drawing up her legs and curling herself into a foetal position.

She remained there shivering, tearless, for the remainder of the night, consumed by a paralysing fear that Anthony might try to break down the communicating door and rape her again.

Part 2

1936–1937

Chapter 12

September–October 1936

"I do so wish you could have been a godmother to at least one of my three babies!" Alice said with a sigh as Zandra returned the sleeping infant to her. "You're so good with them, Zee-Zee and they do adore you."

Zandra essayed a smile. Nothing must mar the day for Alice who was flushed with happiness at this, the christening of her third child. Understandably it had not crossed her cousin's somewhat simple mind that for her, Zandra, holding any tiny child in her arms invariably brought back the memory of her own baby. Nor could Alice understand why she did not want another. Now a Catholic convert, Alice believed strongly that it was a sin to practise birth control. She adored her two rather dull children and was clearly delighted to have produced yet another in the space of four years.

Tante Silvie had arranged for the party following the ceremony to be held here in her beautiful home, for Alice's house in Pau was too small to contain all her aunt's and uncle's many friends.

Alice's marriage to Claude Calonne was an undoubted success, Zandra thought, although when she had arrived for a month's holiday to coincide with the christening, Uncle Pelham had confessed to her that M. Calonne was not exactly his "cup of tea"! The couple lived a few miles away from the Casa Montijo in a small house with a tiny garden and were, by Tante Silvie's standards, extremely hard up. Clearly, Alice worshipped her husband who seemed to exert a mesmeric hold over her. It both amused and irritated Zandra, as well as her aunt, to see the way Alice, now a plump domesticated housewife, ran around like a flustered hen catering to her husband's and children's needs!

That Alice was entirely happy could be in no doubt. She had confided to Zandra that she was never homesick either for Rochford or for England, and had been only too willing to take French citizenship. After four years of marriage, she now spoke the language like a native and had adopted the customs and way of life of a Pau housewife. She was happy enough to see her relatives on the few occasions they came to France, but made no effort to make the long journey to England to see them.

"When the children are a little older, you really must take them home for a visit, Alice," Zandra said. "It will broaden their minds a little to see another country, and they can learn some English. By birth, if not by nationality, they *are* half British, and Aunt Willow would be so happy to have them at Rochford. It is, after all, their ancestral home! Aunt Willow did so much want to be here, Alice, but Uncle Toby has not been well, and you know what your mother is like – she won't leave him!"

Alice nodded.

"I do understand, Zee-Zee. After all, I wouldn't want to leave Claude! As to the children, I do try to speak English to Claudette, and she's quite interested in learning – when she's in the mood! She has quite a strong character – like Claude, I think. Brigitte is more like me. It's difficult to say who baby Henri takes after."

She continued to chatter on at length about her family and Zandra's attention wandered. The main salon in Tante Silvie's house was filled with a mixture of her friends and Alice's neighbours. Not surprisingly, they had formed two separate groups according to their respective classes. Only Claude had deserted

194

his bourgeois neighbours to mingle amongst the wealthy French and English, many of whom were his clients. One of the many things Zandra admired about her uncle and aunt was their support for Alice who had undoubtedly married considerably beneath her.

As Alice's attention was diverted by one of the guests, Zandra looked towards the group where her aunt was standing. As always, Silvie was quite beautifully dressed and looked every inch the chic Frenchwoman that she was. No wonder Uncle Pelham stood so proudly beside her, Zandra thought affectionately. Despite the fact that they were both now in their sixties, it was plain to see that they were still very much in love.

Their removal each winter to the south-west of France had proved a great success. Pelham particularly enjoyed the company of the very large number of British people who had chosen to live in Pau with its race course, golf clubs, local hunt, motor racing and casino. Silvie liked the elegant shops, concerts, the picturesque formal gardens and medieval castle, and the spectacular scenery. Many of the expatriates who had settled there were somewhat eccentric, but from among the medley, they had chosen some amusing, interesting friends.

Although her uncle and aunt entertained a great deal, Zandra had seen them equally content to be alone in one another's company. They were like Aunt Willow and Uncle Toby, she thought, unable to prevent the sharp pain of envy piercing her heart. She had no doubt that one day, Oliver and Jane would be just the same. Nor were these the only happy couples in the family. Jamie was besotted with his fiancée, Ingeborg, and despite the fact that he'd only just come of age, he was determined to marry her next summer. A sympathetic Oliver was employing him at Sky-Ways in order to provide him with an income; and Aunt Willow was allowing them to live at Rochford until they could afford to buy their own home. Then, not least among the happy couples, were her cousin Lucy and Alexis . . .

Zandra's thin face tautened and unconsciously her hands

clenched at her sides as always happened when she was in the company of these two relations, and sometimes when, as now, she was merely thinking about them. Several times she'd been on the point of asking Lucy outright if there really were any truth in those horrible accusations Anthony had made three years ago. She had thought, too, of asking Tante Silvie; but at the last moment, her courage had always failed, for if they were true and Tante Silvie was ignorant of the facts, then she, Zandra, would be revealing the very secret she had suffered these past three years to conceal. Sharing her life with a man she despised was a living hell. It was all she could do to remain in the same room with Anthony; and when he put on a façade of affection in public, involuntarily, her skin would prickle and her body tense.

Despite the warmth of the September afternoon, Zandra shivered. Perhaps, she thought, she could better endure the sham of her marriage to Anthony, if he could have shown her even a modicum of respect. In public, he did so, but in private . . .

Sickened by the thoughts she could never keep for long from flooding her mind, Zandra resorted to the antidote to which she had trained herself following that first night Anthony had forced himself on her. She imagined herself in her little Gipsy Moth high up in the blue sky. She conjured up the sight of the white cotton-wool clouds drifting past her; pictured the patchwork fields far below; felt the wind in her hair. By this method of escapism she had endured Anthony's subsequent invasions of her body. Immediately she heard him open the communicating door, she would shut her eyes, grit her teeth and cling tenaciously to her day-dream until he had left.

It was always a relief when he travelled abroad and she need no longer dread the nights. Now she herself was away from home for four weeks in surroundings where she could forget him entirely.

Tante Silvie came towards her, bearing a tray of canapés which she had taken from one of the uniformed maids.

"You are not eating, *chérie*! You must try these. I am determined, you see, that you should put on a little weight whilst you

196

are here. You are thin like a pencil! No wonder poor Willow is so worried about you!"

Zandra took one of the tiny salmon vol-au-vents to please her aunt. She'd not forgotten Tante Silvie's kindness to her when she had lived with her in Paris and enjoyed her secret flirtation with Léon! How very young and silly she'd been then! But her aunt had never doubted her innocence and had made light of her escapade to Aunt Willow. She had been immensely kind to Alice, too, who must be something of a burden to her socially. Both Tante Silvie and Uncle Pelham might so easily have taken a snobbish attitude to Claude. Not least she owed this holiday to Tante Silvie, for it was her telephone call to Anthony which had elicited his agreement to her being away from home for so long.

Zandra suspected there was another reason why Anthony had not raised any objections to her proposed absence. He was fully occupied flying to and from various countries in Europe. According to Guy, Anthony's foreign visits had to do with the sanctions on war materials which the League of Nations had imposed on Italy after they'd attacked Abyssinia; with the occupation of the demilitarized Rhineland by the Germans, and more recently with the outbreak of civil war in Spain.

No one could be less like Anthony than her Uncle Pelham, she told herself as her uncle crossed the room to put his arms affectionately around hers and Tante Silvie's shoulders – unless it was her cousin, Oliver. Their sense of fun sometimes bordered on the ridiculous, and they were always laughing. They appeared unwilling ever to take life seriously, although Zandra knew this was not always the case. Oliver remained dedicated to Sky-Ways and talked very knowledgeably about the huge advances in aviation.

"Tomorrow I shall take you on a little excursion into the mountains, Zee-Zee," her uncle announced. "Here in the south we can rely upon the weather, unlike England! A picnic, do you think, my love?" he asked, turning to Silvie.

She shook her head smiling. "Picnics are for the young!"

"And the young in heart, my darling!" Pelham replied, stooping to drop a light kiss on his wife's head. "It will be good for Zee-Zee. I don't think London life suits you, my dear. You are a country girl. Wisson should buy a house in the country for you."

Zandra managed a smile.

"He has to work very late sometimes, Uncle Pelham, and he needs to be close to his office."

"Yes, of course!" Pelham said. He was very fond of his niece whose high spirits and somewhat rebellious nature in childhood had appealed to him. He also admired her, for it was not every young girl who had the inclination – let alone the nerve – to fly aeroplanes. He, like Silvie, had been perturbed by the letter from Willow which had preceded Zandra. She had written:

> I don't think Zee-Zee has ever got over the death of her child, and we are all worried about her. She pretends she is perfectly happy but when she thinks no one is looking, her face is so drawn and sad! And, as you both will see for yourselves, she has lost a shocking amount of weight . . .

Both he and Silvie suspected that their niece's marriage was not proving to be a very happy one, although Zandra had vigorously denied it to her aunt who had questioned her soon after her arrival. Silvie now thought Zandra's uncharacteristic loss of *joie de vivre* might be due to the fact that she'd not so far been able to conceive another child.

"Zee-Zee denies quite adamantly that she wants one," Silvie had told her husband, "but I am far from sure that I believe her!"

They must do what they could to ensure she had a rewarding holiday, Pelham told himself as he moved away to talk to some other guests. There was no lack of entertainment to be had in Pau. He and Silvie were very happy with their new home, he often thought, although they were really content anywhere they were together. Despite the fact that both of them were fond of children, neither had ever felt the need for a family and were delighted to be uncle and aunt to their various nieces and nephews.

Watching Pelham walk away, still tall and upright despite his advancing years, both Zandra's and Silvie's eyes followed him with affection.

I must try to enjoy myself this holiday, Zandra thought, but it was not easy to be full of joy and laughter when the present was as barren as the future. It was hard to remember that she'd once been so wildly and passionately in love with Anthony, and he with her – or so she had imagined. She knew better now; knew that she had given her heart to someone who had never existed. It was difficult to understand how she could have been so blind to the truth; but then she'd been younger and far too inexperienced to recognize the difference between love and physical desire.

At least Hugh Conway had been sincere in his belief that he was in love with her and they'd remained good friends. She had been genuinely relieved of a feeling of guilt over his professed "broken heart" when three years after she'd married Anthony, Hugh had married the faithful Katherine Rose. She had even felt a moment of envy when last year they had produced twins. Zandra had been invited to be godmother to one of them and Aunt Willow to the other! The couple now lived happily with their two babies on Hugh's moderate income in a cottage in Havorhurst where he was the not-very-hard-worked solicitor.

Perhaps she would feel life was more meaningful despite her own unhappy marriage if her baby, Rupert, had lived, Zandra told herself. She still mourned him although there was a part of her now that questioned whether she could ever have given whole-hearted devotion to a son of Anthony's – more especially if the boy had grown to resemble him. Her women friends, Monica in particular, constantly alluded to Anthony's good looks – sometimes enviously. If anything, he was growing more handsome with the years; but when Zandra looked at her husband over a table or walking towards her across a room, she could see only the hard, calculating lines that made up his chiselled features; the coldness behind those grey eyes; the cruelty of his attractively curved mouth.

Forcing herself to abstain from so much speculation, Zandra set about enjoying the distractions her uncle and aunt were at such pains to provide. A week later she was on the verge of success when a telephone call came from Alexis in London saying that Toby's indisposition had worsened and he was now seriously ill.

"Alexis left me in no doubt that the situation is critical!" Pelham told Zandra and Silvie. "I think we should leave at once for England. If you girls can be packed and ready by tonight, we'll go first thing tomorrow morning. I'm sorry to spoil your holiday, Zee-Zee. Of course, you and your aunt could stay here if—"

"Oh, no!" Zandra broke in at once. "I must go back. Aunt Willow will need me there."

Her voice faltered and Silvie put a comforting arm around her shoulders.

"*Courage, ma petite!* It may not be as serious as your uncle fears."

But despite their hasty departure, the trio reached Rochford too late to pay their last respects to Toby Rochford. He died several hours before they had arrived to find Willow in a state of collapse. The doctor had given her a strong sedative so that she was not immediately aware of their presence in the house. Having said his last goodbyes to his brother, a solemn-faced Pelham joined the rest of the family in the drawing-room where Silvie, Jane and Zandra were discussing with Lucy how best to help Willow through the next few days.

"For Mother's sake, I think we should have a very quiet funeral!" Oliver said to his uncle.

White-faced, Zandra looked at Silvie.

"One of us must be with Aunt Willow when she wakes up – I think it should be you, Tante Silvie. I'll do the telephoning, shall I, Jane? You'll have enough to do with the house full."

200

Her voice broke, but she would not allow herself to cry as she made her way to the telephone in the recess beneath the big oak staircase in the hall. She decided to ring Anthony first – not because she wanted his support, still less his presence here at Rochford, but because he must be warned to keep his engagements to a minimum so that they would not be disrupted when she advised him of the day of the funeral.

It was not Anthony but Guy who answered her telephone call. He sounded surprised to hear her.

"I'm afraid your husband is in Germany. Is there anything I can do?" he asked.

"I'm in England, Guy!" Zandra said, suddenly immensely glad that it was he and not Anthony she was talking to. Her voice broke as she explained the reason for her unexpected home-coming.

"I'll get a call through to your husband at once. I'm most awfully sorry!" he said. "I only met your uncle a few times but he was always so very pleasant to me. To call him a charming man sounds dreadfully inadequate. I respected him enormously."

"I think everyone loved him!" Zandra said. "It's all so awful for my aunt. Uncle Pelham and Tante Silvie are here and that will help a little."

"Tell me what I can do to help!" Guy said trying to keep the eagerness from his voice. He was genuine in his liking for Mr Toby Rochford but the sound of Zandra's husky voice was undermining his determination to remain aloof. He'd known, after that terrible week when she had lost her baby, that the more often he saw her, the worse it would be for him. Nevertheless he'd invited her to go out with him, and they'd had some wonderful times together. Their friendship was entirely innocent, and only he knew that all the time his secret love for her was growing ever more intense. Afraid that he might soon betray his feelings, he had decided that he must stop seeing her – at least no more often than his work required. For the past year, therefore, he'd set out to do what he could to quash the love he felt for her.

That Zandra was for ever beyond his reach simply made no difference to the situation. Nor did distance help. He'd thought of her just as often when she was in France as when she'd been in London! Now he desperately wanted to see her even while he knew the sight of her would merely intensify his pain.

"Perhaps I could be of some help at Rochford Manor?" he suggested. "I could drive down this afternoon – deal with telephone calls – that sort of thing."

Zandra hesitated. It would be really nice to see Guy. Cool, calm, kind and efficient, he would be the perfect mainstay in a crisis. However, it was not necessary for him to make the journey.

"There's really no need for you to come down, Guy, but thanks all the same. But it does seem ages since I last saw you!" Zandra said. "Once . . . once things are back to normal, you must come down for a weekend. Oliver says you're the only tennis player who can beat him; oh, and Guy, there *is* something you could do for me. Could you possibly get through to Count Zemski's secretary and ask her to tell him Lucy says the Hallowe'en Ball invitations will have to be cancelled? She won't have time to do the cancellations herself."

"Tell Countess Zemski I'll do it at once!" Guy said. "I'll get a telegram off to your husband right away, of course. Are you sure there's nothing else I can do?"

"I'll ring again if there is. Thanks for everything, Guy," Zandra replied, her heart warming to the genuine sympathy in his voice. "Bye for now!"

As she replaced the receiver, Lucy, who had come to stand beside her, tucked an arm through Zandra's and they walked slowly across the hall towards the drawing-room.

"Such a nice young man!" Lucy said. "Your Anthony is lucky to have Mr Bristow on his staff. And he's not only nice but good looking, too! I'm surprised some young girl hasn't snapped him up by now. How old do you think he is, Zee-Zee? Thirty-ish? Do you think he might be engaged? We saw him at the theatre last week with a very pretty blonde girl who reminded me a little of Alice when she was younger. Now tell me about Alice! Is she as happy as ever? Tante Silvie says she's more French now than the French women! I can't imagine Alice hurrying off to Mass on Sundays. You know how she hated going to church as a child!"

With an effort, Zandra tried to bring her thoughts back to Alice, but as she made some suitable rejoinder, they remained with Lucy's previous remarks. Somehow the thought of Guy engaged disturbed her. In all the time she'd known him, it had never crossed her mind that he might one day marry. For one thing, he'd told her that he was obliged to spend most weekends and his holidays with his widowed mother; and had he not said that Anthony required him to be free to travel, to go anywhere, at a moment's notice? Anthony wouldn't like it if Guy had a wife who expected him to be with her at home.

No, that isn't the reason why I'm feeling disturbed! she thought as Lucy drew her back into the family circle. She didn't care in the very least if Anthony objected to Guy having personal ties. It was she herself who found the idea distasteful – and she could not for the life of her think why.

Chapter 13

November 1936

The Memorial Service for Toby Rochford was held in St Stephen's, Havorhurst village church, two months after the funeral. The little church was packed and Zandra, seated beside Anthony in one of the family pews, was unaware that Guy was standing with others in a group at the back. It was only as they were leaving that she caught sight of him.

Anthony had driven down from London for the occasion but left immediately after the service without Zandra who was staying behind to help Lucy and Jane to cope with the influx of relations.

It was a cold, wet, November day and as the crowd outside the church thinned quickly, Zandra noticed Guy about to slip quietly away. She hurried over to him.

"It was good of you to come, Guy!" she said. "I know your weekends are precious. Are you on your way to Eastbourne?"

Guy shook his head.

"No, I've no reason to go there any more. My mother died three months ago and I've sold the house!"

"Oh Guy, I *am* sorry. I never knew . . . Anthony didn't tell me!" Zandra said full of remorse. "I would have written! Why didn't you tell me?"

"You were in France at the time!" he said in his quiet voice. "Afterwards – well, you never met my mother and I could see no reason to add my concerns to yours."

"Yet you took the trouble to come to Uncle Toby's Memorial Service!" Zandra countered. Guy smiled.

"That's different! I liked your uncle very much." It was not the only reason, he thought. He'd come because he had desperately wanted to see Zandra. If he saw her, he'd told himself, it was just possible he would come to his senses and realize how absurd he was to imagine he was still in love with her. After today, he was unlikely to be involved with her any more, for he had made up his mind that he was going to leave Wisson's employ. There would, therefore, be no more occasions when he was detailed to drive Zandra to Rochford, fill in for her husband at a concert, choose birthday or Christmas presents for her.

"Are you going back to London, then?" Zandra was asking. She had removed her hat and, oblivious to the rain, was running her fingers through her glossy, brown hair. As she lifted her arm, the wide sleeve of her coat fell back and Guy noticed a livid purple bruise running from her elbow to her wrist. Without thinking, he reached out and touched it.

"That looks really painful!" he said with some concern. "Did you have a fall?"

To his surprise, Zandra grabbed at her sleeve and hastily pulled it down. Her cheeks were a deep pink and her eyes were downcast as she said quickly: "It's nothing! Yes, I fell! You haven't answered my question, Guy. Are you going back to London?"

She's lying, Guy told himself with a growing feeling of unease. He was quite convinced of it. Why else should she change the subject? Most people would have elaborated an accident which led to such an injury.

As Zandra turned to speak to some other departing friends who were anxious to make their farewells, he tried not to stare at her. She looked incredibly beautiful to him, the sombre black of

205

her overcoat and veiled hat giving her an air of fragility. Her vulnerability caught at his heart.

It's no use, he thought miserably, I shall always love her. And what *had* happened to Zandra's arm? If it was a simple fall, why hadn't she said so?

She turned back to him.

"Sorry about that! There are so many people who loved Uncle Toby! Guy, if you aren't in a hurry, I was going to look at my baby's grave. Would you come with me? You and I are the only two people who actually saw him those few days that he lived – other than the doctors and nurses, I mean. Can you spare the time?"

"But of course!" Guy murmured. He was unbearably moved by her request. Obviously Wisson hadn't thought it necessary to "spare the time" to see his only child's grave. His indifference must have hurt Zandra.

He linked his arm through hers and was immediately aware that she winced. It was not the bruised arm he was holding, but the other one. Frowning, Guy pretended that he'd not noticed. He relinquished his hold as he led her to where he knew the child was buried. The tiny oblong of grass, with its little white marble angel at the head, lay close beside an identical one. Both were brightened by a vase of cut flowers.

"Lucy and Alexis put those there early this morning," Zandra said following his gaze. She bent to straighten one of the blooms. "I'm glad we could lay my Rupert next to Lucy's little girl. I know it's silly, but I feel he won't be so lonely next to Teo."

The pathos of Zandra's words moved Guy so much that there was a lump in his throat. He knew the story of Countess Zemski's first daughter who had drowned in the Barratts' lake just before the end of the war when she was only five years old. Every family, he thought, had its past tragedies and perhaps the Rochford family more than most.

Zandra must have completed her silent prayer for she looked up at him now and said: "Do you *have* to go back to London now,

206

Guy? Couldn't you come back to the house? I'm sure you could do with some lunch."

Guy hesitated. Part of him longed to stay with her, but he was unsure if she was asking him from politeness or because she really wanted him there.

"Won't it be just . . . well, family?" he asked awkwardly. "I don't want to intrude!"

Zandra smiled, the gravity of her face giving way to a cheerfulness he had not seen for a long time.

"You're like one of the family, Guy . . . and the children will be pleased to see you. And I know Aunt Willow would be happy to see you, too."

And you? Guy thought. Do you want me there, Zandra?

As if reading his thoughts, the smile left Zandra's face and she said quietly: "And I'd be glad, too. You've been such a good friend to me, Guy, and at times like this . . . well, although Uncle Toby wouldn't want us to be miserable, it is a sad time. You can tell me all your news."

Oliver was waiting by the front door of the church.

"I was beginning to wonder if you'd got a lift home with one of the others, Zee-Zee!" he said, and held out a hand to Guy. "Nice of you to turn up, Bristow. Are you coming back with us for some lunch? They've laid on a cold buffet, I believe. Haven't seen you for ages!"

The two men shook hands and then Guy, explaining that he had come in his own car, said he would follow them back to Rochford. As he tailed Oliver's Bentley, he found himself wondering yet again how Zandra could have come by such nasty looking bruises. Surely, he thought, if she'd had an accident in a car or in her aeroplane, Wisson would have made some reference to it?

On second thoughts, Guy decided that Anthony would not have mentioned a minor accident for he very seldom spoke of personal matters. He sighed, wondering as he had many times this past year, how he could have remained in Wisson's employ for so long when he disliked the man so much. There'd been a time when he'd both admired and respected his employer. That respect had vanished when he'd found the private investigator's report on the Rochford family. His growing dislike of Wisson had accelerated when after the baby's death, he'd been detailed to write up a summary of his employer's conclusions regarding the disarmament talks, and he'd realized that Wisson had remained abroad from choice rather than necessity.

His overall feelings of distaste had crystallized into contempt when he had discovered that Wisson was completely devoid of ethics. He had been negotiating the sale of arms to both sides involved in the Spanish civil war, making a mockery of the declaration he'd made to Guy when he'd first offered him employment – namely that he believed the sale of arms to be entirely justified so long as the country or regime concerned intended to use them only for defensive purposes. A further discovery that Wisson was involved in the back-door sale of arms to Italy had increased his dislike. Since it was Il Duce, the Fascist, Benito Mussolini, who had attacked Abyssinia, there could be no justification for such illegal profit-making.

Guy's immediate inclination was to challenge Wisson, threaten to report him to the appropriate government department if he didn't change his ways. He was, however, loath to take such action. He knew that bringing Wisson into public disrepute must also affect Zandra.

At least his mind was made up on one point, Guy thought as he turned the car into the long gravel drive leading to the manor house – he was going to hand in his resignation on Monday. By a piece of extraordinary good luck, he had quite unexpectedly come into some money. Sorting through some old papers of his mother's following her death, he'd come upon a number of bonds, dog-eared and yellowed with time, and had decided to send them to a stockbroker friend to look at. A week later, he had received a letter telling him that a new vein had recently been discovered in the disused gold mine and that the bonds were worth what to Guy was a small fortune. His friend had written:

> "You're more than welcome to buy a partnership in the Pater's firm. We'd be glad to have you. The Pater says if you've been working for Wisson, you'll manage here standing on your head!"

He would have to tell Zandra he was leaving, he thought, as he parked his MG behind Oliver's car, and today would be as good a time as any.

The cold buffet laid out in the dining-room was an informal affair, and the fifteen or so members of the family helped themselves to food and sat in small groups talking quietly. Guy was eagerly pressed by Oliver's boy, Giles, and Robin Zemski to take the vacant chair between them. Robin was fair haired and blue eyed like his mother, Countess Zemski, Guy thought, wondering not for the first time whether that investigator's report could possibly be true. The countess was a beautiful, vivacious, gracious lady, and try as he might, he could not envisage her having such a dubious past!

Zandra's brother brought over his fiancée, Ingeborg, to be introduced. Jamie was obviously besotted by the athletic-looking German girl who seemed to Guy to have a simple, friendly personality which dovetailed very nicely with Jamie's uncomplicated nature. They were to be married the following year and, they both now insisted, Guy must come to their wedding.

"My father is the manager of the bank, yes?" Ingeborg said eagerly in her imperfect English. "Ve have many friends come to the vedding, and it is good for Jamie if the many family are for his side, too."

"Guy isn't family – just a friend, darling!" Jamie said laughing. "He works for my brother-in-law, Anthony."

"*Ach so,*" Ingeborg said. "You vill forgive the mistake, no? And you vill come to München for our vedding. In Germany ve make

209

velcome all the foreigners. You vill like München. Ve have very happy time there, Jamie and me, *nicht war, Liebchen?*"

"Absolutely spiffing!" Jamie agreed, looking adoringly into his fiancée's round blue eyes. "You really must come, Bristow. You'd enjoy it."

As Ingeborg moved away to speak to Lucy's sixteen-year-old daughter, Eve, Jamie said earnestly to Guy: "My cousin, Ollie, is a bit prejudiced against the Germans although he does try not to show it. I suppose because he was a prisoner in the last war, he still thinks of the Germans as enemies. Inge has been trying to explain to him that everything has changed now since Adolf Hitler took over the country. He's a really splendid chap and has done absolute wonders when you think what a ghastly state Germany was in after the war. I simply can't understand why Hugh seems to think he's some sort of threat. You know our neighbour, Hugh Conway, don't you? He's standing over there with his wife talking to my aunt."

Guy nodded.

"Perhaps Conway is like a lot of us who don't go along with the German Chancellor's creeds – all that anti-semitism and brutality towards decent people who don't care for his ideology. There are plenty of respectable, hard-working citizens who abhor what those brown-shirted, Nazi thugs are doing in Germany these days."

"Hey, that's a bit stiff, isn't it?" Jamie protested. "For heaven's sake, don't let Inge hear you! You've got to admit it, old chap – the Jewish influence in her country has to be dealt with, you know. She'll explain it to you better than I can. To tell you the truth, I'm not much up on politics – never was!"

He looked momentarily nonplussed, and then his face resumed its customary cheerfulness.

"Have you ever done any skiing, Bristow? It's a marvellous sport, though you do need to be fit! You'd love it. I'm going back with Inge after Christmas so we'll be able to go skiing again then. Oliver's letting me have a month off work. Jolly decent of him, don't you think?"

They were interrupted by Zandra who came across the room to stand beside them.

"The weather has cleared a bit and I thought I'd take the dogs for a walk. Do either of you want to come?"

Jamie shook his head.

"I promised to take Inge down to the village to see Upton, the builder. Oliver said she can convert part of the stables into a studio. She has taken up sculpture, you see, and she's frightfully good at it. Upton is going to have it ready by the time we get married. We said we'd take The Young down to the village with us. It's the Conway twins' birthday on Saturday and we're going to buy presents." He gave a brotherly wink at Zandra. "Bet you don't know Hugh Conway was once engaged to Zee-Zee!"

"As a matter of fact I do!" Guy said smiling. "It was six or seven years ago. Your sister had just broken off that engagement the day Mr Wisson came to see Lord Rochford about buying the airline."

"Good heavens!" Zandra said. "I'd forgotten you were there, Guy. What absolute ages ago that seems."

"I'd love a walk!" Guy said, eager for the chance to be alone with her. "I don't get nearly enough exercise in London."

"I'll find you some gumboots – and you can wear Uncle Toby's old mackintosh!" Zandra said. "See you at tea, Jamie!"

She led the way to the back cloakroom where gumboots, umbrellas, tennis rackets, fishing tackle and other such outdoor items were stored. Already Oliver's two Springer spaniels, sensing exercise, were scratching to get out into the garden. Guy went to help Zandra into one of the old raincoats. As she put her arms into the sleeves, she was unable to hide a wince of pain.

"Have you done anything about those bruises?" Guy asked, unguarded in his concern. "I mean, they looked pretty nasty to me."

As Zandra pushed open the door and the dogs rushed out ahead of them, she said with the parody of a smile: "It's nothing, really. You shouldn't be such a fusspot, Guy!"

"You mean, I shouldn't be such a nosey-parker!" he replied,

211

trying to match her tone. "Well, I know it is none of my business, but how *did* you come by them?"

"It was just a fall, Guy, I told you," Zandra said dismissively. By now they were half-way down the drive, the two dogs out of sight as they chased through the borders of rhododendron bushes. The November sky was overcast and rain, which had held off during lunch, was beginning to fall again. She pulled up the collar of her mac and jammed the rain hat further down over her head to hide the tears now coursing down her cheeks.

She had determined on the morning she'd left home for Rochford that she would be stoical; that she wouldn't give way to tears at the Memorial Service; that for Aunt Willow's sake she would pretend that all was well with her and that she was enjoying her life. But Guy – not a relation or even a close friend – had unfortunately seen the bruises, and his concern had started the tears she'd been determined not to shed.

"I'm afraid I may have offended you!" he said as the silence between them became more prolonged. "Please forgive me, Zandra. I really didn't mean to intrude. Now I've made you cry."

"It isn't that . . . you don't understand . . . oh, this is so silly!" Zandra protested as she tried ineffectually to stop crying.

Guy was shocked. It was raining quite hard now and he realized that in a few more minutes they would be drenched, yet he could not take her back to the house in the state she was in. Was it possible that the Memorial Service, moving as it had been, had affected her so deeply that it could have caused this breakdown?

Ahead of him, he saw the gates to the drive and the gatekeeper's lodge.

"Could we shelter there?" he asked. "You won't want to go back to the house just yet, will you?"

Zandra found her voice.

"There used to be a gardener and his wife living there, but not since the war. It's empty."

She shivered as the rain crept down behind the collar of her mac and dampened her shoulders. She felt empty now of any emotion other than that of helplessness. It didn't really matter to her what Guy wanted to do. He could make the decisions.

"The front door's locked. I'll try the back, and if that's locked, I'll break a window. I've got to get you out of this rain," he said firmly.

She stood silent and downcast as he disappeared round the side of the lodge. After a minute or two, the front door opened and Guy appeared. He took her gently by the hand and led her inside. The tiny hallway smelt musty and damp, and they were obliged to step over several large wooden crates in order to get into the living-room. Guy stared around him. There was no carpet on the bare boards, and stained dusty lace curtains hung lopsidedly across the small window. An empty wooden crate stood upturned in one corner and on top of it was a cracked china teapot without a lid.

Zandra was standing in the doorway motionless. She seemed oblivious to the tears still running quietly down her cheeks, and she was shivering violently. Guy gave her a quick glance and then turned and went over to the crate. Within minutes, he had broken it over his knees. Finding some old newspapers he laid a fire in the empty grate.

"That'll burn pretty quickly!" he said as he put a match to it. "I'll go and see if there is anything more substantial to burn upstairs. Sit here, Zandra. I'll be back in a jiffy!"

Leaving her huddled by the now crackling fire, he made his way upstairs where, in the second of the two bedrooms, he found two old kitchen chairs which broke apart at little more than a touch. He carried them downstairs.

"I hope the family won't think they have been burgled when they find these missing!" he said cheerfully. "Are you warmer now, Zandra? Let me take off that wet coat."

Once again, she winced with pain as he pulled the sodden garment over her arms. Gently, he drew her down beside him on the sofa and taking one of her hands, tried to rub some warmth into it.

213

"You're so cold!" he muttered. "I think I should take you back to the house after all and—"

"No, don't!" Zandra broke in sharply. "I can't face them, Guy . . . not like this! Let me stay here with you, please!"

"Oh, my dear girl, of course, for as long as you want!" Guy cried unguardedly. "I just wish I knew what to do, say, to comfort you. Is it your Uncle Toby? Do you miss him so much?"

He reached in his pocket and drew out a large, clean, white handkerchief. When she made no move to take it, he himself wiped the tears from her cheeks.

"Here, take it, Zandra. As my mother used to say, have a good blow!"

Now at last she smiled.

"You're such a kind person, Guy!" she said huskily. "I expect I would have been quite all right if you'd been nasty to me!"

"As if anyone could possibly be nasty to you!" Guy replied with a smile. He was totally unprepared for the look of utter desolation on her face. Something was very wrong and he could not let her go on suffering alone.

"Tell me what's making you so unhappy!" he urged. "You can trust me, Zandra. I'd like to think I'm more than just your husband's employee . . . that I'm a friend."

Zandra looked up into his eyes, her own anguished. The need to confide in someone was overwhelming. Why not Guy – the quiet, unassuming, thoughtful, sensitive Guy who had sat beside her during those long, painful hours as her baby gave up the fight for life? Yes, she wanted to tell him; she did trust him; but had she the right? He was, after all, her husband's employee and therefore owed loyalty to Anthony.

As had happened before, Guy's thoughts seemed to have mirrored her own, for he said now: "I think you should know that I'm quitting my job. My letter of resignation is already written and I'm handing it in after the weekend."

"Oh no!" Zandra cried involuntarily. "But why? What will you do? What has happened?"

Guy hesitated. Feeling as he did about Zandra, it was hardly ethical to run down her husband to her; yet he was certain she hadn't the slightest idea how Wisson was making his money.

"It's just that I don't agree with some of the decisions your husband makes!" he said vaguely. He gave what he hoped was a nonchalant shrug of his shoulders. "I've come to the conclusion I'm really not cut out to be in his line of business. I don't seem to be able to regard making money as the big priority in life – necessary, of course, but not if others have to suffer for your success."

Zandra's tears had dried, and watching Guy's face as he talked, she realized that he was being evasive.

"You're trying very hard not to say you think Anthony is ruthless, aren't you?" she said bluntly. "Well, you don't need to tell me, Guy. I've found that out for myself. But you're wrong about his priority being to make money. It's power Anthony wants – power over other people. I'm sure he won't want you to leave him, and he may well try to stop you. He can be remorseless when anyone opposes him."

Slowly Guy let out his breath. Zandra had made no effort to conceal the bitterness and contempt in her voice . . . and he had supposed that she loved her husband; was content in her marriage!

Zandra's declaration had come as a shock, so unexpected was it. For her sake, he was appalled, and yet at the same time, he was glad that she was not in love with Wisson.

"There's no way your husband can harm me!" he said. "When my mother was alive, he could have made things awkward, I suppose, because he held the deeds of Mother's house; but when she died, I redeemed the mortgage. I came into some money, and recently, I've been offered a junior partnership in a friend's stockbroking firm. So you see, I am independent of your husband. But you, Zandra – do you intend to leave him?"

Zandra's chin lifted, and for the first time that day, he saw colour come into her cheeks.

"If only I could!" she said in a low, bitter voice. "I hate him,

Guy. He is cruel, egotistical and as I said just now, utterly ruthless." Biting her lip, she slowly pulled up one sleeve of her dress. "I hadn't meant to tell you how I got these bruises, but you wanted to know, so I will. They were caused by Anthony's hands gripping my arms so that I couldn't get away from him." Hearing Guy's gasp, she said apologetically: "I really shouldn't be telling you the unsavoury facts of my marriage, should I? I don't imagine anyone as nice as you can believe a man can do such things to his wife. I couldn't believe it myself the first time it happened."

"*The first time!*" Guy repeated in a horrified voice. "You mean he has often done this to you? For God's sake, Zandra, why *don't* you leave him?"

Zandra put out a hand and covered one of his.

"I can bear it, Guy. I have to. He won't let me leave him."

"Damn him to hell!" Guy cried as he caught Zandra's other hand in his. "This can't go on. It's outrageous. You must divorce him, Zandra. You *must!* This is the 1930s, remember? You must tell Lord Rochford about those bruises. He'll get you a good lawyer. Wisson can't stop you leaving him. Divorce is not such a disgrace these days, and your family love you as much as I do – they'd understand." In his distress and anger, Guy was unaware that he had betrayed his feelings.

Zandra's voice was very gentle as she said: "I didn't know you felt the way you do, Guy. I ought not to have told you about Anthony, especially because there isn't anything you can do to help. I suppose it's wrong of me, but I'm glad you really do like me!"

"Good God, Zandra, I don't just *like* you, I love you!" Guy protested. "I've loved you for six long years! It's been hell at times trying to hide it – that's why I've done my best to avoid seeing so much of you this past year; but that's immaterial. For your own sake, *you must leave Wisson!*"

Abruptly, Zandra stood up, releasing her hands from Guy's warm grasp. With her back to him, she faced the fire, staring with unseeing eyes into the flames. Despite the heat, she was shivering once more.

"I can't, Guy, I *can't!*" she whispered. "He said if I tried to leave him, he could cripple my family financially – the Rochford estate . . . Sky-Ways . . . Havorhurst – but far worse than that, he can destroy the good name of everyone I hold dear. And the awful thing is, *he has the means to carry out his threat.*"

Had Zandra voiced that statement to anyone else, she might not have been believed. But Guy, remembering with chilling horror the incriminating documents he had locked in Wisson's private safe, knew only too well that it was true.

Chapter 14

November 1936

Alexis Zemski regarded his wife's uncle with a mixture of concern and affection. Pelham Rochford was only ten years his senior and although the two men saw little of each other nowadays, they got along extremely well. They had left the drawing-room and retired to the library where they were enjoying after-lunch cigars.

"A sad day for us all!" Pelham was saying as he stretched his legs out towards the big log fire. "Not that Toby would have wanted us to mourn him, poor old fellow. Can't help feeling sorry for Willow, though, eh? She seems quite lost without him."

Alexis nodded. At fifty-five, his hair was already streaked with silver and his moustache was white. Nevertheless he remained an upright manly figure who was not above turning a few feminine heads amongst Lucy's friends. He straightened his back, disliking intensely his reason for inviting Pelham to join him for a private talk in the library.

"With Toby gone, you're the senior member of the family now," he said. "So I thought you should be told about something that happened a few weeks ago." He paused as Pelham cast him a look of casual interest. "Lucy and I were burgled!" he said finally.

"Great Scott!" Pelham commented. "You kept that pretty quiet, old boy. Did the police catch the fellow?"

Alexis shook his head.

"I didn't report it. You see, whoever broke into the house knew exactly what they were looking for – and it wasn't the usual kind of thing a thief would steal."

Pelham now looked genuinely interested.

"What the blazes were they after then?"

Alexis drew in his breath.

"That's the problem, Pelham. They took Lucy's portrait."

Pelham grinned.

"Oh, that! You mean Dubois' one of her as a girl that hung in the dining-room? I never did like it much."

"Not *that* portrait, Pelham," Alexis said sharply. "I'm referring to the unframed one I kept in the drawer in my dressing-room . . ." Seeing Pelham's look of incomprehension, he added pointedly: "The one called 'La Perle'!" "Aaah!" Pelham's exclamation was indicative of his comprehension. Other than Willow, he and Silvie were the only two members of the family who knew that Alexis had kept the paintings of Lucy done by the French artist Maurice Dubois. The first had portrayed his niece as a bewildered, vulnerable child; the second a knowing, provocative, bewitching *cocotte* entitled "La Perle", unmistakably a harlot. No wonder Alexis had kept it locked away out of sight, for despite the passage of thirty years, the large expressive eyes, the wide generous mouth were undeniably Lucy's.

When Silvie had told Pelham all those years ago that Alexis was keeping the portraits, she'd explained to him that Alexis had wanted to prove to Lucy that he knew the events of her childhood had never been her fault; that she had been the victim rather than the wrong-doer; that her past did not detract from his love for her. Silvie believed Alexis' attitude had gone a long way to turning what had begun as a disastrously unhappy marriage into a marvellously happy one.

"But who on earth would want that painting?" he said now to

Alexis. "It isn't as if Maurice Dubois ever became famous. It can't be worth much, I imagine."

"That's the worrying question!" Alexis said quietly. "I ought not to have kept it. You see, it could be used – to blackmail me, I mean. In my line of work, I can't afford to be held to ransom. I'll have to tell my superiors if it isn't returned very soon. I'm giving the thief or thieves a month to offer it back to me, which I suspect is the idea. Whoever has stolen it must have some knowledge of Lucy's past and knows I couldn't let it become public."

"Great Scott, no!" Pelham said aghast. "Of course you must buy it back . . . I'll be only too glad to ante up if—"

"Thanks, but unless the price were really exorbitant, I don't think I'd have much difficulty meeting it. The trouble is, suppose I'm not asked to buy it back? Then I would never know when it might be used to blackmail me. That's why I'd have to tell my superiors."

Pelham looked uneasy as he digested this information. He could well understand that working as Alexis did in Whitehall, he could be particularly vulnerable.

"I've always assumed you were in some sort of secret service. Couldn't you use your chaps to find out who was responsible?" he asked.

Alexis avoided a direct reply.

"Naturally I am doing whatever possible to trace the culprit," he said, "but whoever it was, he managed somehow to slip quietly in and out of our house without any noticeable signs of a break-in; no damage; nothing disturbed. I am not even very sure *when* it happened. When your brother died, it occurred to me that we were all getting older and it was an appropriate time for me to have a fresh look at my Will. It was while I was searching for it that I realized the portrait was missing."

"I'm dashed sorry, old man!" Pelham said sympathetically. "Good of you to tell me, though no need, of course."

Alexis straightened his back. He was genuinely fond of

Pelham but there were times when he was not very quick in grasping the obvious.

"I thought you ought to know the facts because there could come a time in the course of duty when I might be obliged to call a blackmailer's bluff and if the fellow was not bluffing, then the whole story of Lucy's unfortunate childhood could become public knowledge. That would not only affect my family, but yours, Zandra's, Jamie's, possibly even Alice's, though I doubt that – not now she has buried herself in the South of France! It's a frightening thought!"

Pelham stubbed out his cigar butt and looked directly at Alexis.

"No point jumping fences before we get to them, eh?" he said. "Don't think I'll say anything to Silvie – you know what women are for worrying. As far as I'm concerned, I'll leave it up to you, old man . . . sure you'll manage things discreetly. Trust you absolutely, you see. We all do."

Fearing that the conversation was becoming too personal he changed the topic.

"Your boy is growing up by leaps and bounds, isn't he! Nice lad. Enjoying Eton? Talking of schools reminds me, did I ever tell you that I happened to know one of the housemasters at Wisson's old school? I mentioned Zee-Zee was marrying one of his old boys and he wrote back saying that Wisson's name in those days was Wisniowiecki – it seems he changed his name later by Deed Poll. I wrote to old Toby about it but forgot to ask him if he'd been able to find out more about Wisson's background. Too late now, of course. Bit embarrassing asking Wisson to his face; not that it really matters. Clever fellow, by the sound of it – started without a penny and lives like a millionaire now. Oliver was saying he's just invested in a new D H Dragon Rapide for the airline."

They were still discussing aviation when Lucy arrived to tell them to return to the drawing-room for tea.

"Zee-Zee and Guy are not back yet from their walk!" she said.

"They must be sheltering from the rain, poor things. The dogs returned an hour ago, soaked to the skin." Linking her arm through her husband's, she added: "It's a pity Anthony had to rush back to London! I do enjoy his company."

Alexis winked at Pelham.

"It's a good thing I am not a jealous man. My dear wife has succumbed to Wisson's charms."

Lucy laughed.

"Well, you must admit he's very good looking, darling; and so much more attentive than the average Englishman. Anthony talks to me about the things I'm interested in – music and my charities; and he has been quite incredibly generous with his donations."

"And he always sends you those enormous baskets of flowers each time he dines with us!" Alexis acknowledged with an exaggerated sigh. "Mind you, my love, I doubt if he bothers to send them himself. I expect he gets young Bristow to do it for him."

"I think you may be right about that!" Lucy agreed as they entered the drawing-room. "He seems to use Guy as a kind of alter ego – even to the point of getting Guy to escort Zee-Zee to theatres and things like that."

"If anyone is going to be jealous, I would have thought Wisson would think twice about allowing a decent, nice-looking chap like Bristow to squire his wife so often!" Alexis said drily.

Lucy laughed.

"Anthony knows he has no need to be jealous of anyone. Only the other day, Zee-Zee told me that her marriage was entirely stable and that she would never leave Anthony. I'd thought she might be lonely with him away so often, but she says she doesn't mind."

Seated side by side in front of the dwindling fire in the living-room of the gatehouse, Zandra was trying to come to terms with the fact that her friendship with Guy would have to come to an end. Now that he had declared his love for her, to keep him as a friend would not only be difficult, but quite unfair to him.

222

"When will you be starting your new job?" she asked, her heart sinking at the realization that he would no longer be in Anthony's office at the other end of the telephone, ready, anxious to help with whatever problem she had.

"I'm really going to miss you, Guy!" she said impulsively.

He turned to her eagerly.

"Are you? Then I do mean *something* to you?"

Zandra bit her lip.

"Yes, of course you do, Guy! I've always valued our friendship; but we can't go on with it. I'm married to Anthony and you have to forget about me."

Guy caught hold of her hand and pressed it between his own.

"What's to stop us remaining friends? Your husband has never objected in the past to my seeing you – on the contrary, he's made a point of throwing us together. Anyway, why in the name of God do you have to consider *him* after what he has done to you?" He touched her arm with his fingertips. "How *could* he, Zandra? How could he hurt you like that?"

"It was my own fault!" Zandra whispered. "He told me the very first time he ever forced himself on me that if I resisted him, he'd do the same again. I did understand the rules and he played them fairly – he never hurt me when I . . . when I submitted. But the other night . . . I was feeling sad about Uncle Toby, and . . . it was my own fault, Guy. I shouldn't have said no!"

Guy's mouth was a tight line of anger.

"There has to be a way for you to get free of him! You say he could destroy your family and has threatened to do so if you leave him! Well, maybe he wouldn't find it quite as easy as he thinks!"

It had crossed his mind that if, before leaving Wisson's employ, he could get hold of the key and open the safe, he could destroy those evil documents and with it, Wisson's hold over his wife.

"You don't understand, Guy! He has evidence – written evidence – which, if ever it were made public, could damage my family. I don't care about myself! But the others . . . the children, too—"

223

She broke off, close to tears once more.

"Zandra, I know where your husband keeps his private papers; and I think I can put my hands on the ones which could damage you and burn them. I'm leaving him anyway, so what would it matter if he found out I'd done it?"

Staring down at Zandra, seeing the look of hope dawning in her eyes, he felt a surge of excitement.

"I'll delay handing in my resignation until after I've done the job," he said, eagerly. "I wouldn't normally dream of doing such a thing, but betraying the trust of a man like Wisson wouldn't be on my conscience for two minutes. The way he operates is totally amoral. I blame myself for not seeing through him years ago!"

"Why should you have done, Guy? *I* didn't . . . and no one in the family has. They all like him. Oliver thinks the world of him. Aunt Willow, Jane, Lucy – they have all fallen under his spell. He can turn on the charm like a tap – I've watched him do it when he wants to impress someone; and he talks with such conviction, it never occurs to anyone not to believe him."

Guy had noted Wisson's way with women to whom he would appear to be giving his whole-hearted attention. When he left their company, they would suppose that they had captivated him, but far from being in their power, he would return to the office and instruct Guy to draw up a list of their idiosyncrasies – age, social status, food, wine and flower preferences; interests; degree of intelligence; social contacts of importance; family connections. It had seemed to Guy, at the time, a not unreasonable way to ensure that there was the right mix of guests at a dinner party; or as a reminder of the means to flatter the wife of a business contact. Now he could see a more sinister reason for those particular files – they gave Wisson power, power he used to manipulate people to his own ends.

"I'm going to help you get free of him!" he said. "You'll let me, won't you, Zandra? You do trust me?"

Zandra's face softened.

"You know I do! Oh Guy, I can't believe it might be possible after all. I didn't think there was any way out for me. It's been so hard – pretending to everyone that I'm perfectly happy. Now it seems *you* might be able to destroy the only means Anthony has to ruin my family. You are quite, quite sure he couldn't hurt you afterwards if he found out what you'd done?"

Guy smiled.

"Absolutely sure! I don't need his money and I don't need his patronage. He can't hurt me – and I'm not going to allow him to go on hurting you."

Zandra caught her breath.

"Dear Guy! You are really a very, very nice person as well as being resourceful and capable. I used to think I was, too, believe it or not! It isn't true, of course. I've made a terrible mess of my life and you're the one who's having to help me out of it!"

Guy gave a wry smile.

"Don't give me too much praise, Zandra!" he said quietly. "My motives for helping you may not be entirely unselfish. If you were free of Wisson, I'd have the right to try to make you fall in love with me! These past years have been a mixture of heaven and hell – heaven when I've been able to make you happy for an hour or two; hell when I've had to take you home to another man – and without even having the right to kiss you good night!"

"Oh Guy!" Zandra cried, her emotions stirred to something more than pity. "I never knew!"

"Why should you? Anyway, you never gave me any reason to suppose you were not in love with your husband." He gave a sudden smile. "Besides, I used to value my job and if your husband had suggested I was in love with you, I might have found myself demoted to office cleaner. Much as I wanted it, I have to admit that a grateful kiss from you would not make up for a lifetime spent wielding a brush and pan!"

For the first time that afternoon, Zandra gave way to laughter.

"You really are an idiot!" she said, and impulsively, because she was happy and at ease now in Guy's company, she leant forward and kissed him gently on the mouth. When she drew away, he cupped her face in his hands and there was no laughter in his face as he stared into her eyes. His own were luminous as he held her gaze. He saw her eyes widen with the first stirring of desire, and her breathing quickened. The moment lengthened while they continued to read the same message in each other's faces. Then, with a cry, Guy drew her fiercely into his arms and for the second time, their lips met.

In the brief moment before they drew apart, Zandra was conscious of only two things: the feeling of safety in Guy's arms; and the growing response of her body which had been so long starved of love. But as they separated, her mind began to whirl in confusion. Was she being unfair to Guy? She liked him far too much to hurt him. She must never allow him to kiss her again, she decided. Yet the thought was immediately followed by another – she *wanted* him to kiss her again. She wanted his arms round her, holding her against him. She wanted to stay in that warm, safe, loving embrace forever, and never have to return to the real world in which Anthony dominated her existence.

"We ought to go back to the house!" Guy said quietly. "The others will be wondering what has happened to us. I suppose I ought to feel guilty . . . but I don't. I love you so very much, Zandra."

She regarded him uneasily.

"I know!" she murmured. "And I'm glad; although I realize that's being selfish . . . to want you to love me, yet not being able to give anything in return. I really didn't mean this to happen, Guy. It isn't fair to you!"

Guy took her hands in his and unconsciously, she moved closer to him as he said: "Of course it's fair! You've been perfectly honest with me. I know you don't love me, but *you need me*, Zandra, and that makes me indescribably happy." He touched her arms gently with his fingertips. "No man has the right to hurt you the way your husband has. I hate the thought that you have to go back to him – but not for long, Zandra. I'll get those

226

papers as soon as I possibly can. Will you be all right for a week or two? I may not be able to get the key immediately."

Zandra attempted a smile.

"Of course I will. You really mustn't worry about me, Guy. Just knowing that it might be over soon gives me all the strength I need. Do you really think you'll be able to burn those papers? How will you know which ones they are?"

"I'll know all right!" Guy said forcefully. "Don't worry, Zandra, I know what I have to do."

Zandra shivered.

"I don't think Anthony is like other men. He's dangerous! He might hurt you, Guy."

"I told you, there is no way he can touch me!" Guy said confidently. "And even if there were, don't forget that *I* could damage *him* if I had to. For one thing, I'm pretty sure contravening sanctions is a criminal offence."

Zandra stood silently watching him as he raked out the embers of the fire. He was not quite as tall as Anthony and more stockily built, but nevertheless had an athlete's body. His head was nicely shaped, his face strong and open. It was a nice-looking face, particularly when he smiled. Then his mouth curved slightly upward at the corners and his brown eyes lit up with humour. It was, in a way, a boyish face, the expression straightforward, trusting and trustworthy in its directness. She felt a sudden longing to reach out her hand and touch the back of his head.

It would not be difficult to love this man, she told herself as Guy helped her back into her raincoat.

"Whenever I come into this room, I shall remember this afternoon!" she said. "Oliver is going to have the lodge modernized so it won't look like this any more, but this is how I shall remember it."

"Zandra!" Guy's voice was husky as he moved to stand in front of her. "If you can free yourself from Wisson, is there any hope for me? Is there a chance?"

She met his gaze, uncertainty in her eyes.

"I'd like to say there was, Guy, but I must be honest and the truth is I don't know what I am feeling at this moment. I do know I'm filled with gratitude for what you are trying to do for me; that I'm filled with hope now for my future, whereas when I came out of the church, I felt nothing but sadness, despair, hopelessness. I do know I like you enormously . . . I always have, but I can't tell you if it's more than that. I wish I could!"

To her surprise, Guy smiled.

"That's more than enough for me. At least you didn't rule me out of court. You might have said: 'Never! I could never love you!' Don't you see, Zandra, I, too, can hope now? And there's no hurry. I'll wait for as long as it takes for you to sort out your feelings. I give you my word I won't pressurize you. It's your happiness that is important to me, and if I can't be the one to make you happy, then I'll step out of the picture and settle for whoever can."

Touched by his declaration, Zandra reached up and kissed him gently on the lips. Guy did not try to take advantage of her gesture but deliberately resumed the mantle of friendship.

"Do you realize we've forgotten all about the dogs?" he said with a cheerful grin.

Grateful to him for re-establishing normality, Zandra returned his smile.

"Don't worry! They'll have gone back to the house. Look, Guy, it's stopped raining. And it's getting dark. You'll stay to tea, won't you?"

Guy hesitated as they began to walk back up the drive.

"I think perhaps I'd better not. One look at my face and your family will be asking what has happened to make me look so happy!"

He did not speak again until they approached the house where the driveway divided and part of it led to the courtyard where the cars were parked.

"You go in now, Zandra!" he said. "My car's over there. I'll telephone you the moment I have any news for you. Meanwhile, please do try to take care of yourself."

"I will!" Zandra replied. "You, too, Guy . . . and thank you for everything . . . most of all for being such a wonderful friend."

Guy was lost in thought as he drove back to London. He could not be sure if Zandra had intended her last remark to be a warning to him – that he could never be more than a friend. He understood that and appreciated her honesty; but it changed nothing. She liked him, trusted him, needed him – and from that foundation, it was but another step forward to love.

Chapter 15

December 1936

It was nearly ten days before Guy had the opportunity he'd been waiting for. Wisson had left the safe door open whilst he'd taken a telephone call from Germany in Guy's office, and Guy had had just enough time to retrieve the Rochford file. Unable to take it to his own desk where Wisson was seated, he slipped it beneath the seat cushion of the leather armchair used by visitors.

Now back once more at his own desk, he waited with growing impatience for the hands of the clock to move round. He had himself entered a dinner date in Wisson's desk diary and knew that he would be leaving the office early; but unlikely though it was, there was always the risk that Wisson might decide to relax in the visitor's chair and feel the bulky file hidden beneath him. When at last his employer put on his overcoat and Homburg and called good night to Guy as he left, Guy breathed a sigh of relief. He had now only to retrieve the file from its hiding place, put it in his own briefcase, take it back to his flat in Queensgate Terrace and burn it.

In the room adjoining his own, Mackinson, the accountant, was still working. So, too, was Miss Bird whose room also opened into Wisson's so that he could call her in to take a memo or a letter at an instant's notice. He would wait a little longer, Guy thought, until she and Mackinson had gone home.

A door banged and he recognized Miss Bird's voice talking to Mackinson. A few minutes later, still talking, they left by the front door. Glancing out of the window, Guy saw them standing together at the bus stop. Since all the other offices except Miss Bird's led into his own and had no direct access to Wisson's holy of holies, Guy knew he would not now be detected. He hurried into his employer's room. With a sigh of relief, he saw that the file was where he had left it. Picking it up, he took it back to his own room and stuffed it into his briefcase. He was on the point of turning out the light before locking his door, when he heard footsteps on the stairs.

Holding his breath, he stood motionless, waiting to see which member of the staff had returned. It was Wisson who opened the door. With a nod to Guy, he went into his own office and a moment later, returned. His face was expressionless as he said in a dangerously quiet voice: "I suspected it might be you, Bristow. Empty your briefcase, please!"

Slowly Guy did as he'd been asked. With quiet deliberation, Anthony reached out and took the file from him. Seating himself in Guy's chair, he laid it on the desk.

"Perhaps you'd care to explain yourself!" he said in a cold voice. "I find it hard to believe this is just prurient curiosity – although I must admit the contents make fascinating reading!" He leant back in the chair and gave an amused smile as he crossed one leg over the other. "You know, Bristow, when Miss Bird said she'd found the file hidden under the cushion in my office and that she thought you must have put it there, I didn't believe it. To be frank, I didn't think you had the nerve! However, the old trout seemed so certain, I decided to put it to the test – and here you are, caught red-handed!"

He uncrossed his legs and leant forward. The smile had left his face and his eyes had narrowed.

"I trust this has taught you a lesson, Bristow – never

underestimate the lengths a jealous woman will go to. Old Birdie has always believed she's in love with me and I really do believe she hates you almost as much as she hates my wife. Speaking of Zandra, I suppose I should have anticipated this." He tapped the file, his mouth curving into a humourless smile. "The brave knight dares all for the woman he loves! Very romantic and so very silly of you, Bristow, if I may say so!"

Guy's face flushed an angry red. "If you knew I was in love with your wife, why did you go out of your way to throw us together as often as you have? Or did you enjoy seeing how difficult it was for me to disguise my feelings?"

Anthony gave an indifferent shrug of his shoulders.

"I admit, it has given me quite a lot of amusement, particularly as I know my dear wife will never leave me. I have these, you see. They are my safe-guard. Now may I enquire what you intended to do with my property? Stealing is a serious offence, you know! Of course, I shall have to sack you now. What a pity you had to blot your copy-book, Bristow!"

"You don't seriously think I want to remain in your employment now, do you?" Guy said disgustedly. "I've been intending for some time to hand in my resignation but I was waiting until I had the chance to destroy those incriminating documents first. Frankly, when I first saw them, it was beyond my understanding why you should want to keep such . . . such information about your wife's family. Now I know it's for the purpose of blackmailing Zandra. As it happened, I didn't steal them then. I wish I had. They were attached to the back of an invoice I supposed at the time should have been given to Mackinson."

Anthony's expression remained unchanged.

"Yes, that was careless of me. You know, Bristow, when I had the Rochfords investigated before my marriage, it came as quite a surprise to discover so many beetles in the woodwork – not the least of them the scandal of the beautiful Countess Zemski's past! Intriguing, to say the least, don't you agree?"

Guy took a step forward, his face taut with anger.

"You disgust me, Wisson, and it's high time the Rochford family knew what kind of man Zandra married."

Anthony drew an exaggerated sigh.

"My dear fellow, do try not to be so naïve. Do you really think I shall let you keep this?" He pointed to the file, his voice now derisory. "The newspapers would have a field day if I chose to produce it, don't you think? So long as this remains in my possession, I hold the trump card. What a pity you won't be able to do the noble thing now and destroy it!"

As Guy reached out to grab the file, Anthony's hand moved more quickly and he caught hold of Guy's wrist.

"I shouldn't bother if I were you, Bristow. I can always obtain copies in exactly the same way these were obtained."

Guy's chin lifted.

"I don't believe that. I think you're bluffing! These reports are hand written!"

Anthony gave a prolonged yawn.

"Then it's time you learned a few facts of life, my boy. A competent burglar can break in anywhere, and a good Private investigator knows where to get hold of a good burglar. A country solicitor's office such as that of Bartholomew and Conway in Havorhurst is child's play for a skilled man. All my chap had to do was find the Rochford file and copy down any extracts of interest to me. He struck gold."

It was clear that Wisson was enjoying this revelation, Guy thought as he listened to him with growing dismay.

"Old Bartholomew, I gather, kept a kind of on-going log-book like his father before him – a diary, you might call it," Anthony continued. "Births, deaths, marriages and other such interesting data like the exhumation of the then Lady Willow Rochford's infant daughter were all meticulously recorded. Imagine how fascinated I was to learn that there'd been no body in the coffin! That's what set me on the track of Countess Zemski's childhood, although the baby was called Sophie, not Lucienne, at birth! However, this is wasting time. Let us return to you, Bristow. I shall not now require your resignation since of this moment, you are sacked – and you leave without a reference, of course. In fact, in the light of your disloyalty, I shall have to mention dishonesty as one of the reasons for your sacking. I have Miss Bird as a witness, so I don't think there would be any point in your denying it."

That Miss Bird was his betrayer was no surprise, but for a moment, Guy was frightened by the sheer evil of the man he was facing. Then his courage returned.

"You may think you hold all the cards, Wisson – but not quite all. I happen to know that you have contravened the recent sanctions regarding the sale of arms to Italy" – he noted the sudden frown on Anthony's face and added quickly – "and there are other similar dealings you wouldn't wish to become known. Moreover, if you were to accuse me of dishonesty, Wisson, I would certainly bring a countercharge of slander."

Anthony's eyes had narrowed as he regarded Guy speculatively.

"You are even more naïve than I had supposed, Bristow! Do you believe for one moment that I would leave documentary evidence of any 'illicit' transactions where you might find them? You have no proof whatever to back your accusations; and if it ever came to an investigation into my affairs, it would be your suspicions against my word. Mackinson – in his own considerable interest, I might add – would support everything I say."

I should have known that he would have covered his tracks, Guy thought, and that Mackinson, whom he'd never liked, would somehow be in Wisson's power.

"Nevertheless, I don't imagine you particularly wish your dealings to be investigated!" Guy said sharply. "And even if you managed to come out of an investigation with a clean bill, mud sticks!"

Anthony's mouth tightened.

"Indeed it does, Bristow! It would seem, therefore that we have reached an impasse. One word from you about my dealings and I swear to God I'll bring the Rochfords down with me. I can ruin them socially, and I can damage them financially. As you pointed out so succinctly – mud sticks."

He gave an amused smile. "Quite apart from the Zemskis, there is Oliver, for a start, who will lose his airline; and Zandra, the land which I – not she – owns. And I'll do just that and more if you ever lay a finger on my wife, Bristow. Let me make that clear. So it's up to you to decide whether to play your one and only card or keep your mouth shut."

Guy caught his breath. He knew Wisson too well to suppose he wouldn't carry out his threats – and if for no other reason, he dared not take the risk for Zandra's sake. The man was right – as long as he had the file, he held the trump card.

"It seems you leave me no alternative but to stay silent!" he said slowly. Then his voice deepened as he took a step forward and looked directly into Anthony's eyes. "But I am warning you, Wisson. I saw those bruises on Zandra's arms – and don't blame her for that since I discovered them accidentally. I forced her to tell me how she'd come by them; so I know exactly what you have been doing to her. If ever I find out you have hurt her again, the deal is off – even if the whole of the Rochford family suffers for it. I mean that!"

Just for a moment, Anthony's face whitened in anger, but he quickly hid it behind a veneer of impassivity.

"The love-sick swain protecting his beloved, eh?" he sneered. 'You'll never have her, Bristow – not as long as I live. She's far too useful to me. Ironic, isn't it, that with the Rochfords' past, their name is held in such high regard! They have been quite clever the way they've managed to conceal the rotten apples in their barrel! Quite apart from Countess Zemski's wanton childhood, two of my wife's uncles were bad hats. Rupert Rochford was a homosexual and had to leave the country following a scandal with the doctor's son! And Francis Rochford raped one of the household maids and was killed by the footman – the chap she was going to marry. Then there was Oliver's father, Rowell Rochford – not quite a bigamist but he did beget two children by his long-serving mistress. Of course, being who they are, the family had the money and the social éclat to get all these 'nasties' hushed up. Inherited money

235

and position equal power – and since I wasn't born with them, I've had to acquire them in other ways."

It was something Anthony was determined never to forget – how close he'd come to losing that essential start to achieving his goal. It was the summer of 1917. His father hadn't died that New Year's Day, but had suffered a small stroke from which he recovered briefly before, six months later, he had a heart attack and the end came. That was when Uncle Sigismund had come up from London for the funeral and dropped his bombshell.

"As soon as your father was strong enough after his stroke, Antoni, he came down to London to see me and he made a new Will. I have it here. It was drawn up by my solicitor and has been in my safe-keeping to date. I fear this may come as a bit of a shock to you, my boy, but he seemed to think it necessary to . . . er, disinherit you. He has left the factories to . . . er . . . to me, either to sell, or, if I so wish, to put in a manager to run the business for me. The only condition is that I . . . er . . . that I should not offer this position to you. There is, of course, a legacy to your mother for the purchase of an annuity which will provide for her needs during her lifetime. The house has also been left outright to her."

He took off his spectacles and polished them before replacing them on his nose. Clearing his throat, he continued in an obviously embarrassed tone: "I am extremely sorry that I am the one to be the bearer of this, er . . . of this distressing news, Antoni, but I was given to understand by your father that . . . er . . . you and he were not on the best of terms —"

"The lack of affection was entirely one-sided, Uncle Sigismund. I was devoted to my father and have put in a great deal of hard work at the factories – all of which has been to their significant benefit, I might say. I am at a loss for words! To say that I find this 'distressing' is to under-state my feelings. Frankly, I am deeply shocked, not to say deeply hurt. I would be more so were I not convinced that my father's state of mind has to be questioned, do you not agree, Uncle? He was far from well these past few years and could be quite irrational at times. I'm afraid he began to resent his dependence on me. It was very sad."

"Yes, well, old age is never very agreeable. However, he had been visited by my doctor the day before he made his Will and I understood at

the time that my doctor was prepared to vouch for the fact that his mental faculties were not in any way impaired. Therefore this Will is valid, my dear boy, and I shall be taking it this afternoon to your father's solicitor who, so I understand from your mother, has been indisposed recently which is why he was not with us at the funeral this morning."

"So Mr Talbot is as yet unaware that there is another Will?"

"Exactly! I have not mentioned this to your poor dear mother. I fear she may never get over this loss. You and your father were her whole world, as I'm sure you know. It will be up to you now, Antoni, to take great care of her."

"But of course! I was devoted to Papa and his passing is a great loss for me, too. I loved my father dearly and it upsets me more than I can tell you to think that after a lifetime of shared affection, he should have turned against me in this inexplicable fashion. As a matter of fact, Uncle, I think I can explain it. Soon after the war broke out, I changed my name by Deed Poll. That is to say, I altered it to Anthony Wisson. My father thought I was disclaiming our family name, Wisniowiecki, but of course, there was a valid reason for it. People . . . ignorant people, are suspicious of foreigners, as I'm sure you know. Even the royal family has just changed their name from Saxe-Coburg-Gotha to Windsor. Our family name was losing us a great deal of business, Uncle, so it seemed the obvious thing to do to change it. I don't think Father ever understood the necessity, and it would seem he never forgave me."

"But my dear boy, that explains everything. However, there is nothing we can do to change his Will. Now if there is any way at all I can be of assistance . . . I do have a few contacts here and there . . . a reference, perhaps, to help you into a new job? With your mathematical skills and the experience you have gained in your father's business, it should not be difficult. Or perhaps you will decide to join up? No doubt you have fretted that you could not do your bit for your country before now. Let me know which service you decide to volunteer for, my boy. We must keep in touch. Dear me, I nearly forgot. Your father asked me to give you this letter. Now I must say goodbye to your poor mother and be on my way. My train leaves at twenty-two minutes past the hour, I think."

"I'll come with you, Uncle Sigismund. The walk will do me good."

At twenty-one minutes past the hour, the sound of his uncle's train as it rumbled through the tunnel outside the station, alerted him to its approach. With a friendly gesture, he lifted his uncle's briefcase and took hold of his arm, at the same time moving nearer to the edge of the platform.

"It was good of you to come all this way, Uncle! I can't tell you what a comfort it has been to Mother and me to have you with us at this sad time."

"Think nothing of it, Antoni!" his uncle said, his words now drowned by the loud hiss of steam as the engine emerged from the tunnel. "God bless you, dear boy!"

"You, too, Uncle!" he replied as, with an indiscernible pressure of his shoulder, he toppled the old man under the oncoming wheels of the train.

It wasn't until later that evening after he had burnt the Will that he bothered to open his father's last letter to him. He had written:

Dear Antoni,

By the time you read this, you will know that I have disinherited you. You already know the reasons why. Before I go to my Maker I leave you with one last warning. Over three hundred years ago, a wise man wrote:

"Gold is the fool's curtain which hides all his defects from the world."

But not from the eyes of God, Antoni. I am leaving this world in the hope that you will come to realize that human beings are far more important than the enclosed . . .

In the bottom of the envelope, wrapped in a thin covering of tissue paper, was a single gold sovereign. With a look of fury on his face, he pocketed the coin and threw his father's letter into the fire.

For a moment, Guy thought Wisson had forgotten that he was there in the room with him. There was a scowl on his face and he seemed lost in thought.

"There are other things in life besides power," Guy said bitterly. "There is such a thing as decency – morality, if you like. You may force Zandra to remain with you, and you may have the means to stop me seeing her, but you won't get away with this for ever."

Anthony seemed to have recovered his composure.

"I can see no reason why I shouldn't, Bristow. Now I suggest you collect your private belongings and get out. If we run into each other in public, we will pretend I have accepted your resignation with good grace, and I shall expect you to behave towards me with the usual civility. Oh, and Bristow . . . one last word of advice – if you want to get on in this world, try not to make enemies. But for Miss Bird's vigilance, I might not have known the file was missing until I next needed it, and it would have caused me quite considerable inconvenience, not to say expense, to obtain all the information again."

He rose to his feet and felt in his inner pocket for the safe key.

"I'll lock this away myself!" he said. "You will hardly be surprised to know that I no longer trust you!" He paused as he walked towards the door of his office. "By the way," he added as an afterthought, "although I've known you were soft in the head about Zandra for several years, there seemed little point depriving myself of your services. You have been quite useful to me at times."

Guy stared back at the man disbelievingly.

"You were taking a hell of a chance, weren't you, asking *me* to be your wife's escort? I wouldn't have thought you were one for gambling, Wisson."

Anthony laughed.

"It was no gamble, Bristow. Zandra knows very well what would happen if she were ever unfaithful to me. Besides, it amused me to see you trying to hide your feelings as you danced attendance on her. Attractive woman, isn't she? I quite understand why you find her fascinating. She's damned good in bed, too – or used to be before she decided she didn't love me any more."

Guy took a step towards him, his face white with anger; but his raised arm dropped to his side as he said in a low, furious voice: "Damn you, Wisson – damn you to hell! You're the most evil

239

man I've ever met – and to think I once admired you! You make me sick."

Anthony laughed.

"Believe me, there are plenty of others like me. Now get out, Bristow. Take your moralizing and your noble gestures elsewhere because I've had quite enough of you for one day."

With a look of disgust, Guy picked up his briefcase and, turning on his heel, walked out of the office where he had worked for seven years. Not least of his emotions as he closed the door behind him was bitterness at the thought of all those years when he had done his utmost to help Wisson further his business.

Then the thought of Zandra and the hopelessness of any future for either of them swept away all other feeling. He would have to tell her now that he had failed after all to help her to get away from her husband. It might, retrospectively, have been better never to have given her hope in the first place.

As he made his way back to his flat in Queensgate Terrace, Guy tried to come to terms with the degree of Anthony's baseness. By his own declaration, the man was without scruples of any kind. How right Zandra had been when she'd called him "ruthless"!

He spent a sleepless night, turning over in his mind again and again his conversation with Wisson. He had not heard Miss Bird opening the communicating door and she must have seen him hiding the file! It didn't really matter. Wisson would have known soon enough that he, Guy, was the only person who could have removed it.

What he found equally hard to come to terms with was the amount of material Wisson appeared to have at his disposal to use against the Rochfords. Even if only half of the information he had was true, it was enough to damage the family very badly.

The following morning, he telephoned Zandra whom he knew would be back in London by then.

"Your husband isn't there, is he, Zandra?" Guy asked carefully.

"No, he left an hour ago. I'm alone. Guy, what's happened?

He told me last night that you'd resigned. He wouldn't say why – just that you wanted a change of job and he'd agreed to let you go. I thought you were staying on for a bit until—"

"Yes, I was, but that's impossible now," Guy broke in. "I need to talk to you, Zandra – but not on the telephone. Can we meet somewhere? It's very important that we aren't seen together, or I'd come to the house."

Zandra gave a breathless little laugh. She is worried, he thought, worried that what I have to tell her is not good news.

"Could I come to your flat? If you tell me where it is, I'll take a taxi."

Guy dictated the address and waited whilst she wrote it down.

"I'll be with you in fifteen minutes," she said. "It's bad news, isn't it, Guy? Don't worry, I promise I won't break down. I've been expecting it."

Yes, Guy thought, Zandra knew her husband better than he did – or had known about him a good deal longer than he had. He put down the telephone and busied himself preparing coffee and tidying up as best he could. Zandra arrived almost to the minute she had predicted. Looking out of the window as the taxi drew up, his heart missed a beat as he watched her climb out of the cab and pay the driver. She looked, as always, beautifully turned out. The brick-red suit and the jaunty little black hat were becoming; the gauntlet leather gloves and laced court shoes both fashionable and the essence of good taste. Yet in a way, he told himself ruefully, he'd found her just as beautiful in that old mackintosh and rain hat down by the gatehouse!

He opened the door at the top of the stairs. Smiling at him with total unselfconsciousness, Zandra reached up and kissed his cheek.

"It's good to see you, Guy!" she said as he led her into the sitting-room. She looked round her and her smile deepened. "Isn't it strange to think that I've never been here before, yet you have been in my house more times than we could possibly count." She sat down on the sofa and removed her hat and gloves.

241

Guy found his voice: "I thought you might like some coffee. It's in the kitchen percolating. I'll fetch it!"

As he left, Zandra stared round her. The room she was in was large and spacious with two big windows looking down over the street. The fireplace was Victorian, and Guy had obviously lit the fire some time ago for it was giving off a welcome warmth.

Nevertheless, Zandra shivered. She'd been able to tell by the sound of Guy's voice that he had not succeeded in freeing her from Anthony. In a minute, he would tell her so and the last vestige of hope would vanish. Poor Guy! He must be wishing so much that he had good news to impart.

She got to her feet quickly as Guy re-entered the room.

"Guy, what happened?" she asked nervously. "Anthony said you and Miss Bird had quarrelled and you thought it would be awkward if you stayed so you resigned."

Guy's eyes were cynical as he met Zandra's gaze.

"I suppose that's as good a reason to give out as any other, although as excuses go, it's a bit weak! Why didn't he simply sack Miss Bird? She's only the typist! It doesn't put much value on my contribution to the business."

Zandra frowned.

"It doesn't make sense, Guy. I know how Anthony valued your services. What really happened?"

Guy put down his coffee cup and sat down in the armchair opposite her.

"I might as well tell you everything," he said. "At least you'll hear the truth from me."

Slowly, without emphasis, he related his encounter with Wisson.

"I'm still finding it hard to believe all this myself!" he said. "All that charm, those perfect good manners, that bland affability, that generosity! Can it really be all a sham?"

With an effort, Zandra hid the despair in her heart. "We shouldn't let him get away with this, Guy."

Guy looked at her unhappily.

"We can't do anything, Zandra. He wasn't bluffing, you see. He has proof – and I don't! We simply have to go along with his terms."

"People say you should never, ever give way to a blackmailer!" Zandra whispered.

"You know, don't you, that if I was the one who'd be disgraced, I'd let him do his worst!" Guy said quietly.

Zandra nodded. 'I would too, Guy; but even to think of what it might do to Lucy, Alexis, the children, not to mention Aunt Willow—"

"We've no choice but to go along with him!" Guy repeated. "What concerns me is that it's so horrible for you – although I, too, have to pay a price. Now that I've left my job, I have no excuse for seeing you."

Zandra's face softened.

"Oh Guy, I wish for your sake you didn't feel the way you do but although it's selfish of me, I can't help being glad you do! It's hard to explain but it's very comforting to know you care. Even though you've left Anthony, we can be friends, can't we?"

Guy caught his breath.

"He knows I'm in love with you – and he doesn't trust me after yesterday. To be honest, I think he's quite right not to! Given half a chance, I'd whisk you off to some faraway country and never let him near you again! As it is, I don't intend to let him keep me away from you if I can help it. I just don't want to put you at risk and he's threatened to make trouble if I don't keep out of your life as well as his!"

Zandra sighed.

'I wish we were young again, Guy! I wish we could just go out together and have fun and laugh and do silly things and . . . and be happy! I do have fun when I'm with you. I've never forgotten that evening in Cannes on my honeymoon – sitting on the terrace with you drinking cocktails, and dancing afterwards; or all those concerts and theatres we both enjoyed so much; and the tennis parties with Oliver and Jane, Jamie and Hugh. I wonder if Anthony has ever realized quite how much time you and I have spent together?"

Guy's brows drew down in a sudden frown.

"I think he has always been very well aware of it and he has derived a certain amount of sadistic pleasure from it, knowing that I loved you and that he ran no risk of losing you."

Zandra's voice was bitter.

"Only of losing the love I once had for him; but he doesn't care about that. Truth to tell, Guy, I don't think he'd mind if I was in love with you. He knows that whatever I feel, he can still demand what *he* wants – and that I'm in no position to refuse him."

"I doubt if he would be so complacent if he thought you were being unfaithful to him!" Guy commented wryly.

Zandra's eyes were narrowed in thought.

"I wouldn't care what he thought. If I was sure he'd never know, if I wanted to, I'd be unfaithful. I owe him no more loyalty than you do, Guy. If I loved someone . . . if I needed to be loved—"

She broke off, realizing too late where her own thoughts had been leading her. A deep blush spread over her cheeks. She didn't know whether she could ever love Guy in the way he meant; but there was no doubt that she needed him. It was all too easy to imagine how lovely it would be to go to sleep with his arms around her, holding her, keeping at bay the bad dreams. She longed for tenderness; to be kissed as Guy had kissed her in the gatehouse. She knew instinctively that Guy would be a sensitive lover; and he had proved already how much he loved her . . . It would be so easy to love him! In a way, she did so already. Her body was certainly aware of his attraction for unconsciously she was leaning towards him, wanting him to put his arm round her; wanting to hear him say he would always be there to take care of her; to love her! Yes, she needed him, as a friend and as a lover who would help to erase the memory of her husband's cold, brutal advances. She wanted so much to feel like a woman again.

"Zandra, darling Zandra, don't look so unhappy! I can't bear it. I feel so damned useless."

Suddenly Zandra's mind became crystal clear. Guy loved her . . . wanted her, and she knew without doubt that if there were anything in the world he could do to make her happy, he would find a way to do it. Well, she could make *him* happy! She could let him make love to her. It would not be the kind of submission she was forced to make with Anthony – it would be because she wanted to give this man the same kind of happiness he desired for her.

She drew one hand gently from his and reaching up, touched his cheek.

"Find a way, Guy!" she whispered. "Find somewhere where we can spend a night alone together and where no one will know where we are or recognize us. If you can do that, I'll go away with you. I can't say if I love you, but I do know I need you and that I need to be loved, but I'll understand if you say it isn't enough."

Guy was staring at her with a look of disbelief mingled with joy on his face. He caught her hand and pressed his mouth against her palm.

"Enough?" he repeated huskily. "It's more than I ever dreamed of. I'll find a way that's safe – even from him. I love you, Zandra, I love you. You're going to get bored out of your mind hearing it!"

"Oh Guy!" Zandra whispered. "That's why I'm willing to go away with you for a few days, a night – but only if we can find somewhere safe."

He drew her to her feet and kissed her with an urgency she did not try to resist. There was only one thought in her mind – that now there would be something to look forward to, and the future was not quite so meaningless, after all.

245

Chapter 16

December 1936

"Good evening, sir!" Wilkes took possession of Alexis' hat, gloves and umbrella. "Madam will be pleased to see you home so early, sir. A bit upset by the news – we all are!"

Alexis regarded the man with affection. Wilkes had been with him since long before the war and was one of the best servants he'd ever had.

"It was inevitable, I'm afraid," he replied.

He crossed the hall to open the drawing-room door, the lines around his mouth and eyes betraying his concern.

As he entered the room, Lucy rose swiftly from her chair by the fireside and hurrying to him, flung herself into his arms. Her face was streaked with tears.

"You've heard the news of the Abdication, of course!" she wept. "It's so sad, Alexis. I simply can't stop crying!"

With a smile of tenderness, Alexis hugged his wife's slender body to him. Thirteen years her senior, he frequently forgot that she was not still a child in need of his love and protection. Her petite physique and large violet-blue eyes gave an illusion of youth and he was not alone in wondering how she could possibly be the mother of children of seventeen and fourteen! Already

246

their daughter Eve, the elder, was taller than Lucy, and Robin looked likely to match his own height.

"My darling, it's not the end of the world – or even the monarchy! We have a new king now and it is for him I, personally, feel sorry. He's quite unprepared for kingship!"

Lucy sniffed into her lace handkerchief.

"Yes, I know, Alexis, and I do feel sorry for the Duke of York! But Edward sounded so unhappy in his farewell speech. When he said that he couldn't discharge his duties as King without the woman he loved beside him, it nearly broke my heart."

"There have been a good many kings in the past who have managed it well enough," Alexis said wryly. "Baldwin was quite right to veto such a marriage. Imagine a twice-divorced American as Queen of England! If Mrs Simpson means so much to Edward, he should have handled the affair more discreetly and kept her as a mistress."

Dry-eyed now, Lucy sighed.

"But that wasn't what he wanted, was it?"

"It wasn't what Mrs Wallis Simpson wanted!" Alexis said drily. "The monarchy in this country is greater than its kings or its queens. It will survive very well without Edward. It's as well he was never crowned."

"You have always thought him weak," Lucy said, "but the people loved him and he obviously cared deeply about them."

Alexis sighed.

"Far be it from me to belittle his good points, but the fact remains, he didn't care deeply enough. Now, my love, I hope I am right in thinking we have no engagement this evening because I have something rather important to discuss with you – after dinner, I think."

The sombre tone of her husband's voice even more than the expression on his face caused Lucy to look at him anxiously. "Nothing is wrong with the children? With Mother? I do worry about her. She has not been really well since Uncle Toby died."

"Time will help!" Alexis said. "Come now, my darling, it's time we went upstairs to change. I believe you told me at breakfast we were having pheasant – my favourite, so I've no intention of being late!"

Momentarily diverted, Lucy's mood quickly disappeared and in her usual fashion, she kept Alexis amused with gossip throughout the meal. The indulgent smile on his face vanished as he followed his wife back to the drawing-room for coffee. All day he had been steeling himself for the coming conversation which he knew would shock Lucy quite dreadfully. It was close on twenty years since they had last discussed the past, and he had hoped that there would never be an occasion when he could not protect her from it. Even when the portrait of her had been stolen, he'd hoped that he might be able to buy it back from the thief and never have to mention its temporary loss to her. Now he had no choice but to bring the past back – and with it, uncomfortable fears for the future.

Replacing his empty coffee cup on the table, he took her hand in his and gently broke the news to her of the mysterious theft of her portrait.

'I am entirely to blame for not keeping it in a more secure place!" he ended. Aware that she was trembling, he added quickly: "It may have no significance whatever, Lucy. I have been waiting these past six weeks for the thief to write or telephone me with the suggestion that I might like to buy it back! Regrettably, that has not happened, although he might yet do so."

Lucy was gazing at him from horrified eyes.

"But what other purpose could a thief have for stealing it? You say nothing else was taken. It can only have been someone who knows . . . who knows who I was . . . what the portrait was. Alexis, I'm frightened. If the children ever found out . . . and what of you? Your career? Mother?"

"Try and keep calm, dearest," Alexis told her. "Naturally, we can't be complacent whilst we're ignorant of the thief's purpose, but we need not expect the worst. Nevertheless, I cannot be in a position where I am open to blackmail. As you know, my work is highly secret and I have access to a great deal of information that could be useful to a potential enemy. It is for this reason I have had to explain matters to my superior."

Lucy's face whitened.

"You've told someone – about my past?" she whispered.

"My dearest, he has always known – that is to say, from the time I announced that it was my intention to marry you."

"And he didn't object?"

"He was concerned – because of the possibility of blackmail; I had told him I would resign, you see, if I was not allowed to marry you."

"Oh Alexis!" Lucy said, tears springing to her eyes. "I didn't know!"

"You weren't meant to, my love!" Alexis said gently as he put an arm around her shoulders. "However, I know you'll understand that I have had to tell him about the theft. If that *should* happen, my department would be very anxious indeed to catch the man responsible – in case he is an 'enemy' agent. If he's just after money, they would not be so concerned."

"And if they don't catch him?" Lucy asked.

"Then I . . . we . . . have no alternative but to tell the blackmailer to go ahead and expose us if that is his intention. That's why I have told you, my darling – so that you can prepare yourself. Of course, if the picture were to be reproduced in the newspapers, it would undoubtedly cause a few raised eyebrows and set a few tongues wagging, but it is not in itself proof of your connection with Le Ciel Rouge. The only documents relating to those days are safely locked away in my desk, so unless you were recognized by someone who knew you in those long-ago days, we'd have no worse than a little unsavoury gossip to worry us."

Despite Alexis' attempt to reassure her, Lucy's dismay was so great that she looked at that moment far older than her years. She tried to keep her voice steady as she said to Alexis: "Suppose someone traced my movements from the time I left the wet nurse and was sent to the convent? The Mother Superior could have told them I went to work at that loathsome *maison de modes*. Monsieur Grimaud, the owner, knew that Blanche found me the job at Le Ciel Rouge. If someone was trying to link me with my past, he could have gone there to make enquiries. They all knew at Le Ciel Rouge that when I went back to Rochford, my name was changed from Sophia to Lucienne; and that I became your wife!"

Alexis, who had been listening attentively, now leant forward, his eyes narrowed thoughtfully.

"Yes, I agree the link *could* be made if someone set their mind to it. The point is, Lucy, who on earth would want to go to such lengths to discredit you – or me, I suppose?" He gave a long sigh and then added: "I'm sure we have nothing so drastic to worry about, my darling. Nevertheless, this discussion has given me an idea. We could ask your Uncle Pelham to make discreet enquiries; find out if anyone has been to Le Ciel Rouge asking questions about you. If not, we can assume we are dealing with a perfectly ordinary thief and rest much more easily. I can telephone your uncle now. It's not too late."

Lucy flung her arms round him.

"I love you so much, Alexis – so very much. Sometimes, in the middle of the night, I wake up and wonder what would have become of me if you hadn't found me, married me. I couldn't bear it if, after all this time, I were to be responsible for hurting you."

Alexis kissed her gently.

"I knew the risk when I married you, Lucy. Just think what my life would have been without you! And without each other, we would never have had Robin or Eve. Even if the very worst should happen, the children would stand by us. They adore you and they are old enough to understand that all those misfortunes occurred to you when you were only a child; that you had no one to protect you. Now I'll ring your uncle before it's too late."

When he returned from his study, he looked almost cheerful.

"It's all arranged," he told Lucy. "Pelham will go to Le Ciel

Rouge tomorrow and put a call through to us tomorrow evening. He asked me to give you a message of reassurance from your aunt. She said your mother went to unlimited lengths to ensure that the relics of the past were in safe keeping; and that only those who could be trusted ever held the keys."

Despite Alexis' attempts to cheer her, Lucy did not sleep well that night. Memories of the past disturbed her dreams and when she woke, she wondered how she could ever wait for the telephone call that evening.

Silvie and Pelham had an equally disturbed night, for deep into the early hours of the morning, they lay awake discussing the possible circumstances leading to Alexis' extraordinary request. Both of them were aware that Alexis' work was in some way connected with the secret service, for it was on some such mission that he'd been imprisoned by the Russians in the last war. That the enquiries Pelham had to make concerned Le Ciel Rouge and therefore Lucy's past, explained why Alexis had not used his own staff to discover whether anyone suspicious had recently been making enquiries to do with the events of eighteen years ago; that even after all this time, someone could have linked Lucy with the child, Sophia – and for no good purpose.

They discussed, also, the possible effect upon themselves. Pelham doubted very much if he and Silvie would be ostracized by Pau society where they had many French and British friends, if there was a family scandal. Nor was it likely to touch Alice who was now a French citizen and so much a part of the local *bourgeoisie* that she was unlikely to be connected with her London-based sister, Lucy, the chic Countess Zemski who was such a leading light in London society. Pelham's concern was mainly for Willow and the younger generation of Rochfords.

At breakfast next morning, Silvie announced that she had decided to undertake the enquiry herself, pointing out that a man asking questions at an establishment like Le Ciel Rouge could be a cause for suspicion. He could be taken for an official – a health inspector, she argued, or an income-tax inspector, or even a *gendarme* in plain clothes! Brothels such as Le Ciel Rouge were frequently monitored – or certainly had been in Madame Lou-Lou's day. Silvie wondered now if the old woman who had proved such a good friend to Lucy could still be alive.

Dressed unremarkably for her mission, Silvie made her way after breakfast to the Rue Steinkerque. With both courage and a considerable degree of curiosity, she rang the bell. The door of Le Ciel Rouge was opened by an elderly *concierge* who informed her that Madame Lou-Lou had "gone to her Maker" some thirteen years ago.

She eyed Silvie suspiciously. "You're not a friend of hers, are you?" she asked.

"I never met Madame!" Silvie said. "But I wanted to ask her about one of her girls who was here before the war. She has come into some money and I am trying to trace her present whereabouts."

At the mention of money, the *concierge's* face brightened.

"Maybe I can help you, Madame," she said, wiping her hands on her dingy serge skirt. "I was a maid here in those days, but I was brought up a good Catholic, Madame, and I'd have worked respectable if I could." She crossed herself, watching Silvie at the same time with small, beady black eyes as if to gauge the effect of this gesture of piety.

"I'm sure you would!" Silvie said encouragingly, delighted that she had so quickly found someone who might help her. "Doubtless you earn a better wage these days as a *concierge*. Nevertheless, a little extra help now and again doesn't go amiss, I dare say. Did I tell you there was a reward for anyone who can help me with my enquiries?"

The old crone looked eagerly at Silvie who was pointedly fingering her handbag.

"I may be long in the tooth but there's nothing wrong with my memory!" she said, emitting a shrill cackle. "Ask anything you want. Let's see now" – she scratched her straggly grey head – "there was Yvette – nice girl, she was, saving for her dowry.

Married her sweetheart, she did. She gave a party the day she left. We had champagne, too. I can remember—"

A remarkable amount, Silvie thought as she cut the old woman's reminiscences short.

"It's very cold standing here! Why don't we go and sit comfortably in that café across the road!" she suggested. "We could have an *anis* and talk over old times."

The woman looked at the clock on the wall behind her and said eagerly: "I'm allowed an hour off for my dinner, so I'll be free in ten minutes' time."

"Then I'll wait for you over the road," Silvie said. "Perhaps it would be as well not to tell anyone you are meeting me. We don't want to be interrupted, do we?"

"That we don't! *Au revoir* then, Madame. *A tout à l'heure!*"

The café was typical of its kind with marble-topped tables and a large bar serving drinks and coffee. Silvie ordered coffee for herself and sat down at a corner table to await the old woman.

She came hurrying in, her head covered in a shawl, prompt to the minute. She shuffled over to Silvie and grinned, showing several gaps in her teeth.

"Didn't introduce ourselves, did we?" she said. "I'm Jeanne Vincennes. Call myself 'Madame' though I weren't never married. Born ugly, I was, and no man ever fancied me. That was the reason Madame Lou-Lou never let me be one of them, you see – the girls, I mean."

She broke off to tell the hovering waiter that she would have an *anisette* – a drink she favoured but couldn't often afford, she explained to Silvie.

"Now where was I? Ah, yes, Yvette. She—"

Gently, Silvie interrupted her again.

"You must understand, Madame Vincennes, that I am not personally familiar with establishments such as the one where you work. Tell me, do these girls ever marry their clients? That is to say, do the men ever grow . . . well, attached to them?"

The *concierge* grinned as she took an overlarge sip of her drink.

"Have their favourites, the regulars!" she said. "Never heard of them marrying, though – not their sort. Might set one of the girls up somewhere . . . but marry them – no, not that I ever heard of."

"Yet I imagine there must be some bond between them if it is a long-standing customer," Silvie prompted. "Don't the men ever write to them? Send them presents? Ask after them?"

"Not that anyone's ever told me!" the old woman said sourly.

"So unless they marry like Yvette, they have no future?" Silvie pursued her line of questioning. "No fairy godmother to wave a wand and turn them from Cinderellas into princesses?"

Madame Vincennes choked on her *anisette* as she doubled up with laughter.

"Bless you, no! Though come to think of it, there were one – 'La Perle', Madame Lou-Lou called her. She used to tell us all stories about how she had rich, titled parents who'd one day come to find her and take her to live in a big house with servants and everything. *Enfin*, none of us believed her; but will you believe, an old man did come – an Englishman, and said it was all true and he'd come back for her later. She was heart-broken when he didn't return but then, after a while, off she went to England in search of him – and that was the last we saw of her." She paused to add drama to her next statement. "Or so we thought! But you'll not credit this . . . back she comes to see Madame Lou-Lou, dressed like she was royalty. Found her family, she had, *and* they were rich and titled like she'd always said."

Silvie hid her excitement and pretended to be surprised by this fairy-tale.

"That's a story for a romantic story-writer!" she said. "I dare say you've told it to others a thousand times or more."

The *concierge* shook her head.

"There hasn't ever been anyone as would have believed me before!" she said dubiously. She brightened up as Silvie ordered her another drink. "Though that isn't strictly true. Only a few months past there was a man – English, he was, too – who came asking about 'La Perle'. Said he had a painting of her and needed some background information because he wanted to sell it. He gave me a twenty-franc note – got me my winter coat out of the pawnshop and the medicine I needed for my chest."

Silvie reached for her handbag and drew out a fifty-franc note.

"It must be very difficult for you to manage without a husband to support you," she said. "I hope this will help."

"That it will, thank you, Madame. It certainly will!" the old woman cried, grabbing it quickly as if afraid Silvie would regret such generosity.

"This is all most interesting!" Silvie said. "Did the Englishman give you his name? Was he the portrait painter?"

"No, he wasn't no painter!" Madame Vincennes said instantly. "Get to know the types, we do, in this business. He wasn't no gentleman, neither. Could've been a salesman – something like that. Going bald, he were and he had bushy eyebrows and a black moustache."

"You've got a wonderful memory!" Silvie said flatteringly. "Fancy you recalling such detail."

"Well, it wasn't more nor a few weeks past I saw him. 8 December. It was the day after my sixtieth birthday, you see, which is why I recall it."

Silvie affected a little laugh.

"Perhaps he was an old admirer of 'La Perle'?"

Madame Vincennes snorted.

"That he wasn't. This fellow weren't old enough to have known about places like Le Ciel Rouge in her day. Now about 'La Perle'. She was here during the war with Yvette, Nicole and Fifi. Then there was Babette and I forget the others for the moment. One of them could tell you her married name. Just give me a minute or two and—"

"No, please don't trouble yourself now; tomorrow will do. I can call and see you again then, can't I?" Silvie interrupted. "Meanwhile, this is your lunch-hour and you haven't had anything to eat. Unfortunately I can't share a meal with you as I have to meet my husband and I'm late already."

Reluctant though the old woman was to see this unexpected benefactor depart, she believed that it wouldn't be long before Silvie returned, so she made no move to detain her. Silvie's curiosity did not surprise her but, as she tucked in to a generous helping of *ragoût* with considerable enthusiasm, she did wonder how anyone so shabbily dressed could part so casually with a fifty-franc note.

Silvie's face was drawn with worry as she recounted to Pelham the conversation she had had with Madame Vincennes.

"So someone *was* making enquiries, after all!" Pelham said frowning as he followed his wife into the dining-room. "Alexis thought it was unlikely."

"But that was two months ago!" Silvie pointed out. "Why hasn't Alexis been in touch with us before now?"

"Because Dubois' portrait of Lucy was only stolen recently," Pelham reminded her. "We can hope, therefore, that there's no connection between the man your *concierge* mentioned and the painting."

"Well, I hope you are right, *chéri!*" Silvie said. "For things to go wrong for Alexis and Lucy after all this time would be *vraiment intolérable.*" Although she had been speaking in English, in moments of stress she frequently slipped back into her native language and the last word was drawn out in its emphasis.

Pelham nodded. It would not just be intolerable but disastrous, he thought, and not only for the immediate family. Both Alexis and Wisson had prominent jobs and could not fail to be adversely affected by a family scandal.

As he attempted to turn his wife's thoughts back to her Christmas preparations, his mind continued to dwell on the dark cloud threatening them all. One could never be sure that the past was really dead and buried, he thought uneasily.

He turned to look at his wife who was now regaling him with details of her Christmas purchases. His face softened. The best thing he had ever done in his life was to marry Willow's French cousin. He loved her with a deep, steady devotion which he had no doubt whatever would endure until death separated them. They were in their sixties now, but God willing, they could hope for at least ten more years of happiness together.

Silvie looked up at him to enquire if one of her chosen presents was really suitable for its intended recipient. He smiled back at her as he nodded. He was suddenly eager to leave Paris – to get back to Pau. What with poor old Toby's death and now this worry about Alexis and Lucy, the past few weeks had been far from happy ones. In Pau where there were so many pleasant distractions, he told himself, he might more quickly forget the past and begin to enjoy life again.

Chapter 17

May 1937

Zandra stood at the window of her bedroom in the Bayerischer Hof looking down over the Promenadeplatz. The fashionable square in Munich was crowded with people. Somehow they looked happier, more purposeful than the usual crowds to be seen in London, she thought. Perhaps it was because Munich was filled with students, for whom this Bavarian city and its environs held so much to give them pleasure – the magnificent Staatsoper; the open-air skating rink; the theatres, festivals, concerts and everywhere, the *Bierkeller* where crowds of young and old gathered to enjoy the tall *Masskrüge* of Löwenbräu beer.

Yesterday, Inge and Jamie had taken her and Lucy on a tour of the city, the young couple as eager as each other to show them its sights and pleasures. In the evening, Inge's parents and the older Rochford wedding guests had joined them to watch an astonishing torchlight parade of Herr Hitler's brown-shirted troops goose-stepping down the wide avenues to the thunderous cries of the people, arms extended, shouting the name of their Chancellor. It was impossible not to be caught up in the heady excitement and enthusiasm of the display, although later, when they were alone once more in the hotel, Alexis, Anthony and

Oliver had reminded their wives that it was only three months since these same troops had marched into Austria and annexed the country!

"Not that the Austrians were unwilling to be 'reclaimed'," Anthony had pointed out. "You must have seen the welcome they gave the troops on our newsreels at home."

"Only because the Germans had been swamping them with National Socialist propaganda for ages and ages!" Oliver had protested.

"Well, at least there was no bloodshed!" Alexis had concluded the subject. "So long as Adolf Hitler remains true to his promise that he has no designs on other countries, he is welcome to his troops and his admirers!"

Zandra closed the window, for although the May days were warm and sunny, the evenings were still cool. In the adjoining room, Anthony was changing into formal evening wear. It was time she, too, changed her dress, Zandra thought as she crossed the room to open her wardrobe door. Tonight was Inge's and Jamie's *Polterabend* – a tradition that was carried out here in Germany in lieu of the English bridegroom's stag night. The Rochford family were to spend the evening at the home of the bride's parents in company with Jamie's and Inge's friends. According to Inge, the young people would gather at some point to watch the betrothed pair throw china at a wall. It was then the task of the couple to sweep up the broken pieces. If they were seen to complete this task in harmony, then, so tradition forecast, their marriage, too, would proceed without quarrels!

Uncertain which of her dresses would be most suitable for this unfamiliar occasion, Zandra's gaze went past the Paquin afternoon dress of Chantilly lace she would be wearing next day at the wedding, and stopped at a simple, black wool day dress. She caught her lower lip, frowning. She must have been quite mad, she thought, to have insisted Mollie pack this one amongst her smarter frocks. She had done so only because Guy had requested it.

"It will always mean something special to me because you were wearing it when I kissed you for the first time in the Gatehouse!" he'd said.

Zandra's frown deepened. It was too late now to have second thoughts. She had committed herself . . . agreed to Guy's suggestion that she meet him in Paris after Jamie's wedding. Anthony would be going straight back to London at the end of their five-day stay in Munich and, Guy had pointed out, it would be a simple matter for her to break the journey home on the pretext of returning with her aunt and uncle to spend a few days with them in Paris.

Five long months had passed since she'd told Guy that she would agree to their becoming lovers if he could find somewhere safe for them to meet. They had been afraid to do so before now because since Guy had left his job, Anthony had shown an unusual interest in all Zandra's movements, questioning her every night as to how she'd spent the day. Guy, too, suspected that he was being watched and agreed that they must take no risks. She and Guy had had to make do with telephone calls and one brief, public encounter in Harrods' banking hall! Guy was trying to be patient, he told her, but it was not proving easy.

It was not that she was having second thoughts about allowing her relationship with Guy to progress from friendship into an affair, Zandra told herself. Her mood of despair had changed to one of defiance as the weeks and months had passed, and she found it increasingly difficult to keep up the pretence of being happily married. In particular she despised the hypocritical way Anthony set about charming Lucy whenever they were in the same room. Watching her cousin succumb innocently to Anthony's façade of friendship, she knew he would not hesitate to destroy Lucy if it suited him.

Zandra's fears of the approaching rendezvous in Paris were not related to Guy but to Anthony, for soon after Uncle Toby's Memorial Service, he had admitted he was suspicious.

"I hope you aren't contemplating a small matter of adultery by way of revenge, Zandra? That would be a very big mistake, I do assure you."

Each time he'd left her bed, he said in the same cold, emotionless voice: "That will help you to remember you are my wife. Don't ever forget it, Zandra!"

It was a threat she could not ignore, and her pleasure at the thought of meeting Guy, even for one short weekend, was now soured by the fear that somehow Anthony would find out about it. Guy had booked them into a hotel in a quiet street off the Rue de Lille, under the assumed name of Mr and Mrs Kipling.

"I'd just been reading about Rudyard Kipling's burial in Westminster Abbey!" he'd told her on the telephone, "and Kipling was the first name which came into my mind, darling!"

Zandra's face softened. She always appreciated Guy's sense of humour which could materialize at the most unexpected moments. He had the wonderful ability to make her laugh when she least felt like it.

I do love him, she thought now. What had begun for her as a friendship had slowly, invisibly, grown into love.

Aware suddenly that she had been day-dreaming again, Zandra removed her navy-and-white linen coat and skirt, and sat down at the dressing-table. She'd wanted to look her best not only for Jamie's wedding but for Guy, and had had her hair cut and restyled before she left London. She was pleased now with her reflection. Her face had filled out a little since Christmas and so, too, had her body. There had been no more bruises, for she'd taught herself to shut her mind and submit without protest to any ordeal to which Anthony cared to subject her.

Later that evening, watching her young brother with the girl he would be marrying the following day, Zandra prayed that Jamie had made the right choice for himself. Inge was his first sweetheart and he'd never looked at another girl. She had all the self-confidence of a much-loved only child, and enjoyed being the centre of attention.

There were times during the six months Inge had lived at Rochford when Zandra had found herself resenting the girl's dogmatism. She would quote the National Socialist creed as if it were the Gospel! If Uncle Toby or Alexis ever referred to the war-like aspirations of "*Der Führer*" as stated in his book, *Mein Kampf,* Inge's voice would rise in Hitler's defence, and her big blue eyes flash angrily as she denied there was need for caution. Jamie, however, seemed to admire the girl's fanatical loyalty and was not the least bothered by it. He, too, admired the Führer and extolled the virtues of the Party. In any case, he argued, what did it matter what Germany was doing, since Inge was coming to live with him in England and would soon become indoctrinated with the British way of life?

Certainly Inge did not take after her mother, Zandra thought, as she seated herself beside Frau Zeller. Not only was the older woman short, dark-haired and painfully thin, but she was shy, retiring and very much dominated by her husband and daughter!

Inge's father, Herr Zeller, was conversing happily with Oliver, Jane and Tante Silvie. A tall, robust man from whom Inge had clearly inherited her thick, fair hair and blue eyes, he was describing with enthusiasm the various sights the visitors must be sure to see during their brief stay. Anthony, meanwhile, was engaged in conversation with a group of Herr Zeller's friends.

With an effort, Zandra tried to concentrate on making sense of her hostess' indifferent English. It was not easy, for Frau Zeller's head kept turning in the direction of Inge's uncle, Professor Walter Zeller, who was deep in discussion with Alexis. After a few minutes, the poor woman gave up the attempt to make casual conversation, and in a low confidential tone, said to Zandra: "The brother of my husband . . . he is Professor at *die Universität,* so alvays the long talk to *studenten* he makes. Now the same talk he make to ze English family of Jamie. *Das ist nicht gut!*"

Zandra gave her hostess a reassuring smile.

"I am sure Count Zemski is enjoying the Professor's conversation," she said.

"*Aber nein – nicht die Politik!*" Frau Zeller whispered in a distraught voice. "*Das macht meinen Mann sehr nervös* – how do you say in English?"

"I think you mean it makes your husband nervous if Professor Zeller discusses politics here at home?"

For a moment, Frau Zeller looked relieved; but her glance went once more to the two men and her expression of anxiety returned.

"I'll go and see if I can interrupt them, shall I?" Zandra asked kindly. As her hostess nodded vehemently in agreement with this suggestion, she rose and crossed the room to stand beside Alexis.

"I think Frau Zeller would like some of the others to have the chance to talk to the Professor!" she said. "I understand you are teaching at the university?" she added to the older man. He was gazing at her over the top of his steel-rimmed spectacles with a look of wry benevolence.

"My dear young lady – Frau Visson, is it not? – you are to be congratulated for your tact. I do not think, however, that my poor sister-in-law vishes for me to converse with *anyvone*. She is unhappy, you see, vith vat I have to say."

Alexis smiled.

"The Professor has been telling me that unlike Herr Zeller, he is not a member of the National Socialist Party, and he wishes as many people as possible to listen to the reasons why he holds such opposite views."

"And so Frau Zeller is afraid a family argument might take place!" Zandra said. "Well, don't worry about that, Professor. In our family, we frequently argue about all manner of things!"

The man nodded, his face now thoughtful.

"Indeed, Frau Visson, debate can be stimulating to the mind and it is particularly necessary here in this country. My students must understand that in most things in life, there are alvays two points of view, if not more!"

Alexis, too, was looking thoughtful. He said quietly: "The

Professor has been explaining to me that debate on any subject relating adversely to the National Socialist doctrine is now forbidden. It is very much to his credit that he feels morally obliged to continue to speak out against the Party, for he has been warned that if he does so, he will at the very least lose his job."

"But surely it's everyone's right to state their opinion?" Zandra said.

The Professor reached out and patted her hand as if she were a child.

"My dear young lady, in Germany now, no one but Party members must hold an opinion, far less state it if it is contrary to their creed or to the propaganda ve are being given. Here in this country ve have a dictatorship, not a democracy like your own. I fear for the future; and it is of immense relief to me that tomorrow my niece vill become the vife of your brother and thereby a citizen of your country. In England, she vill be safe."

"Safe!" Zandra repeated, shocked by the Professor's declaration. "But safe from what?"

"From further indoctrination, Frau Visson. At present, Inge can see no wrong in the Führer. It is not her fault that she is so blinded, for so she has been taught by the Party vat she must believe. In the Youth Associations ve call the *Hitler-jugend*, the children learn a prayer which, I think you will agree, is close to being blasphemous: 'He who serves Adolf Hitler, the *Führer*, serves Germany, and whoever serves Germany, serves God'."

He gave a deep sigh.

"Many such ideas are drummed into our children's brains from the age of ten. I've been trying since long before 1933, ven Hitler became Chancellor, to persuade my brother to send Inge to school in a foreign country – Switzerland, perhaps, or even England. But he refused to see vat vas happening to our German youth. Now, ven it is too late, he sees for himself the many crimes that are being committed – and permitted, for the so-called good of our nation."

Shocked by the Professor's admissions, Zandra forgot that

Frau Zeller had wanted her to stop him discussing politics with Alexis.

"Why is it too late, Professor? If you feel as you do, can't you leave Germany? Emigrate to another country?"

"If all of those of us who abhor the present government vere to leave Germany, who vould be left to try to counteract the harm that is being done?" the Professor said wryly. "Believe me, Frau Visson, there are a great many who feel and think as I do. I speak of ordinary men and vomen; people of my own generation who may have been your enemies in the last var, but who fought honourably for their country as you English did; decent-minded citizens who vish to live in peace vith their neighbours as vell as vith the rest of the vorld. They don't like vat is happening, but they are afraid to say so. If and ven they do, vays are found to make them suffer for it – the loss of their livelihood, places for their children in schools . . . I could go on enumerating such penalties and others even more severe; but I do not vish to distress you on this occasion. Ve are here to celebrate your brother's vedding, are ve not? He is a very charming young man and I am most happy for Inge."

As Zandra and Alexis moved away, Alexis said: "It never occurred to me that Ingeborg might have such an interesting relative. The Professor has an exceptional brain, although his outspokenness could have serious repercussions for Herr Zeller, and his wife knows it."

It seemed that Professor Zeller had also interested Anthony. When they returned to the hotel that evening, he was in a voluble mood and insisted that Zandra accompany him to the bar for a nightcap.

"Highly dangerous fellow!" he commented as the waiter brought to their table coffee for Zandra and a *Schnaps* for him. "When he heard I was in the munitions business, he was surprisingly conversant with the Geneva disarmament talks. He said Germany had determined from the start to rearm herself, and as far back as 1934 had already done so to a considerable degree.

The Professor was aware, of course, that since the breakdown of the talks, all the powers have been rearming."

"He was not suggesting that there'll be another war, was he?" Zandra asked uneasily. "Do you think it's possible, Anthony?"

Anthony shrugged.

"You saw those storm-troopers this afternoon. Wouldn't you say they looked a thoroughly military force?"

"Surely nobody wants another war!" Zandra cried. "Not even you, Anthony!" she added bitterly for she knew that he had begun to make his fortune when the last war ended by buying army surplus weapons for a pittance and selling them very profitably to poorer nations with limited defences.

"My dear Zandra, you cannot prevent a strong aggressor from attacking you if you are defenceless!" he said with an edge of scorn to his voice. "I am interested in Professor Zeller. A very erudite man! But a stupid one to speak out so publicly."

Ignoring his condescending tone, Zandra shrugged her shoulders.

"I like him! I prefer him to Inge's father. Oh, I do so hope Jamie is going to be happy."

Anthony ignored her comment.

"By the way, Zandra, the hall porter tells me there's an aeroplane leaving for England at five tomorrow evening. I have booked a seat on it, and it's my intention to leave the festivities in good time to catch it."

"I see no reason why you shouldn't slip away whenever you want, Anthony," Zandra said. "I imagine the wedding lunch will be over by then in any event."

Anthony finished his drink and gave an exaggerated sigh.

"Frankly, I find this all very tedious. Were it not for the necessity of keeping up appearances, I wouldn't have come."

"I wonder that 'keeping up appearances' is so important to you, Anthony!" Zandra said sharply. "I really can't see why my family's approval of you is of any consequence to you these days?

You have far more important friends and acquaintances than I do. Why do you still need me? Why won't you let me go?"

Her voice was low and urgent, but Anthony's expression remained unchanged. His voice was patronizing as he said: "You never seem capable of grasping the point, do you, Zandra? I will *not* have the whole world knowing that my wife has left me. What you want is immaterial to me. Outwardly we will remain a *devoted* couple for as long as I choose; and you will remain entirely faithful to me. I do hope you understand that, my dear."

Zandra felt a cold hand clutch at her heart. Was this a subtle warning that he knew she intended to be unfaithful to him? Had he found out somehow that she was meeting Guy in Paris?

"You have made your wishes perfectly clear, Anthony!" she said, forcing herself to look him squarely in the eyes. "If you mind so much about people's opinions, we could be divorced on the grounds that *you* had been unfaithful to *me*."

Even now Anthony showed no sign of emotion other than of impatience at her stupidity. He gave a disparaging smile as he replied: "I really do wonder sometimes how someone with the degree of intelligence I know you to possess can be quite so silly. A great many of our friends and all your family would align themselves on your side and ostracize me – and doubtless influence as many others as possible against me. And why should I put myself to the trouble and expense of divorcing you? I still find you an extremely desirable woman. In fact, it might surprise you to know that your indifference to me in bed gives me a certain satisfaction. My total mastery of you adds a further dimension to our love-making, although I will admit I enjoyed it even more when you used to resist me."

Zandra's face whitened.

"We do not 'make love'!" she whispered. "And your 'mastery' must surely be a hollow victory when you know the reason for it."

Anthony shrugged.

" 'Love-making' is no more than the satisfying of a sexual appetite common to animals as well as human beings. That is all sex is – a simple bodily appetite. It so happens that you stimulate my particular appetite very satisfactorily, and I don't intend to lose time or money finding an alternative."

"You are wrong, Anthony! People are not animals. They can love with their hearts and minds as well as their bodies. Have you never wanted to be loved – really loved – in the way I mean?"

His mouth tightened, his eyes narrowed and there was a harsh edge to his voice as he said: "I presume you are referring to the kind of blind devotion mothers bestow on their young – an unrealistic adoration that renders them totally vulnerable to life's unpleasant realities. No, my dear, it is money and the power it buys, not love, which protects the human race from life's vicissitudes."

For a brief moment, Zandra's feeling of revulsion gave way to one of pity.

"Then I'm sorry for you if you really believe that, Anthony." Her voice hardened. "Have you never heard the saying: *Gold is the fool's curtain which hides all his defects from the world*? What are you hiding, Anthony?"

She heard the sharp intake of his breath, saw his left hand reach out and grasp his right wrist and his knuckles whiten. His voice was razor sharp as he said bitingly: "I would remind you that you are in no position to preach to me. Your opinion is of no value whatever. You might reflect, however, on the fact that it is your *loving* devotion to your family which renders you power-less to thwart me. That fact might temper your view of love!"

"You disgust me!" Zandra said, rising to her feet. "I'm going to bed."

Anthony made a pretence of rising politely to his feet. He was smiling as he said: "Good night then, my dear. And don't worry that I shall require your services this evening. Sleep well!"

As Zandra hurried from the bar and took the lift up to her bedroom, her cheeks were flushed with anger and her eyes brilliant. If there had ever been any real doubt in her mind about meeting Guy, this conversation with Anthony had dispelled it utterly. In a strange way, his brutal exposition of his feelings had freed her, for she knew now that whilst it was true that she was his bodily slave, forced to be so, her spirit was as free as the wind. He had no power over her mind, her heart, her feelings. And Guy was there, in the shadows, waiting to help her. His voice, like a whisper on the wind, sounded in her mind.

"I love you, Zandra, I love you. Your happiness means more to me even than my life!"

Slowly Zandra unlocked the door of her room. Closing it behind her, she did not switch on the light but went to stand at the window where for a long time she remained, her face reposed and peaceful, staring out into the night.

Chapter 18

May 1937

Although the marriage service in the Protestant church was conducted in German, it was so similar to an English wedding that Zandra was able to follow it quite easily. She felt both pride and affection as she stared at her young brother. Jamie was now as tall as his uncles and looked very much the typical English gentleman in his black morning coat, black-and-grey striped trousers, grey waistcoat and silk cravat. Beside him, Inge was dressed in a beautiful white figured satin wedding gown with a long train held by two little fair-haired bridesmaids, daughters of one of her married friends.

Frau Zeller appeared to be in tears but her husband was gazing proudly at his only daughter. Beside him, the Professor stood upright, gazing for the most part at the high, stained-glass window beyond the altar.

It was not until they all turned to see the bride and groom walking back down the aisle that Zandra became aware of the two strange-looking figures standing stiffly as if to attention, by the door. Wearing dark overcoats and trilbys, they were clearly not wedding guests. Herr Zeller must have seen them at the same moment for, as he took Silvie's arm and started to follow

Pelham and Frau Zeller into the aisle, Zandra saw him turn his head sharply to look at the Professor. His florid face was white with fear and his agitation was unmistakable.

Oliver, too, must have noticed. Standing between Zandra and Jane, he whispered: "Don't like the look of this. I think those chaps back there are from the Gestapo and, if I'm not mistaken, they've got their eyes on the Professor."

Zandra glanced quickly at Anthony whose face was impassive. As they stepped out into the aisle she looked towards the Professor. He was adjusting his spectacles and moving along the opposite pew towards them. He took Zandra's arm as she murmured: "What are those men doing here in church?"

The Professor smiled down at her.

"They have been following me since ve left the house two hours ago. Don't vorry, my dear, they vill not try to arrest me until the vedding is over."

"Arrest you!" Zandra gasped. "But—"

"They vill have orders not to make a disturbance in front of foreigners," her companion broke in, smiling and nodding to acquaintances as they moved slowly down the aisle. "Please do not vorry. Your brother's vedding vill take place vithout incident."

It was not for Jamie and Inge that Zandra felt such concern. In the short while she had known him, she had come to like Inge's Onkel Walter, and by that look of fear on Herr Zeller's face, she was certain the Professor was in serious trouble. Only when they, together with Oliver and Jane, were in the back of the limousine taking them to the hotel, did she turn to her cousin and say: "Oliver, the Professor thinks those two men are going to arrest him – as soon as our family are not around to see them do so!"

Oliver looked at the older man sitting impassively beside him.

"Are you certain, sir?" he asked.

The Professor nodded.

"I have been expecting it, so I am not surprised. It surprises me only that they have vaited so long! These last few days, of

271

course, you and your family have been in Munich, so your presence has lent me protection."

"But what will they do to you, sir? They can't put you in prison just for speaking your mind, can they?"

The Professor gave an indulgent smile.

"Most certainly they can, Lord Rochford! A month ago, one of my colleagues at the university vas arrested – 'for questioning', they told his family. He has not been seen since."

"You mean he has been sent to a prison somewhere else?"

"Perhaps! Or to a labour camp. Like myself, he vould not be silenced and frankly, I doubt if his family vill see him again."

"But that is unbelievable – and intolerable!" Oliver protested. "We'll have to do something. We can't just sit back and allow these – these brown-shirts to browbeat you like this. Is there nowhere you could go, sir? Friends who would hide you in another part of the country?"

The Professor patted Oliver's knee like a kindly uncle.

"My dear young man, here in München ve are the least violent of our peoples. Ve are basically conservatively minded rather than revolutionary. For matters to have reached the stage they have here, you can be certain that they vill be far more serious elsevhere in Germany. If I vere to go into hiding, it vould be only a matter of time before I was exposed – and then there vould be retribution on the friends who harboured me. Now please do not allow my problems to spoil your enjoyment of the day. I vish my niece alvays to remember it as a happy one."

They had now reached the hotel where the Professor joined his brother and sister-in-law who were waiting to receive their guests. Zandra hurried in search of Anthony who had returned in another limousine with Lucy, Alexis, Pelham and Silvie.

"We simply can't allow this to happen!" she said to him when she was able to draw him to one side. In a low voice, she related the Professor's forecast of his possible future. "Isn't there anything we can do, Anthony? You have contacts in Germany. Is there no one with influence you could telephone and ask for their help?"

Anthony gave her an impatient stare.

"What kind of a fool do you take me for, Zandra?" he asked coldly. "No one in their right mind would be so silly as to try to interfere in the laws of a foreign country. If the Professor is being arrested, then he must certainly have contravened the law."

"But Anthony, all he has done is to speak out against the Party," Zandra protested.

"Which, for a clever man like the Professor, is an exceedingly stupid thing to do!" Anthony countered.

The further protest she had been about to make died on Zandra's lips as they were approached by some of Frau Zeller's friends. Aware that Anthony was watching her, she made pretence of talking to them, but as soon as he moved away, she excused herself and hurried over to Oliver.

"Anthony refuses to help the Professor!" she said in a low voice. "I'm sure he could if he wanted. But he won't get involved."

Oliver look doubtful.

"I can see his point, Zee-Zee. I suppose it really isn't our business." He frowned uneasily. "Tell you what, I'll have a word with Alexis and Uncle Pelham . . . see what they think."

It was not until after the long drawn-out lunch that he had a chance to rejoin Zandra. She had been sitting impatiently throughout the five-course meal being served to the wedding guests at four long tables. Her cousin had a conspiratorial grin on his face as he drew her to one side.

"Alexis said he's worried about Lucy. It could be dangerous to become involved, but Uncle Pelham thinks we might be able to get the Professor back to England," he announced. "He said you and Tante Silvie and he all have reservations on the night train to Paris and the Professor could travel in his place. He'll lend him his clothes, ticket and passport. There's only one border crossing and that'll be at night. As a rule, the steward collects all the passports from the couchettes and unless there's cause for suspicion, they don't wake people to check they match up with

273

their passport photographs – and even if they did, without his spectacles, the Professor isn't all that unlike him."

Oliver paused to draw breath before continuing his outline of the proposed plan. "Once across the border, the Professor would be in no danger and back in England, he would be treated as a refugee. Alexis says there are hundreds already who have been given asylum – Jews, mostly, who have been getting out whilst they still can before Herr Hitler carries out his threat to rid Germany of them."

"But what will happen to Uncle Pelham?" Zandra asked anxiously.

"He is quite sure that nothing will happen. He plans to report to the British Consul tomorrow that he missed the train, and that Tante Silvie went off without him, forgetting that she had his passport. Tante Silvie will be safely in Paris by then, so even if the German authorities discovered she had not travelled alone and suspected her of assisting the Professor, they couldn't arrest her once she was in France."

"And the Professor?" Zandra said. "Do you think he will agree with this plan? He could never come back to Germany, could he?"

"I doubt if he'd want to!" Oliver said drily. "Uncle Pelham is going to put the idea to him and Tante Silvie – then it's up to them if the plan is to go ahead. Meanwhile, behave as if you know nothing about all this – and not a word to Jane. She'd be scared to death if she knew what was up! It's a good thing Mother wasn't well enough to come with us. She'd have certainly put paid to the whole idea."

Zandra found it extremely difficult to keep her eyes from straying to the Professor who was moving easily amongst the guests as they drank their coffee. He was a brave man, she thought before her attention was diverted by her brother who came over to talk to her, Inge holding lovingly to his arm.

"We're going up to change in half a jiffy!" Jamie said. "Then we're off. It's been a top-hole do, don't you think? Inge's parents have done us proud!"

Zandra forced a smile.

"It's been a lovely wedding!" she said. "You look beautiful, Inge. Have a wonderful honeymoon, both of you. I'll try to come down to Rochford to welcome you home – in three weeks' time!"

Jamie grinned.

"Then back to work, I suppose. I'm sorry Aunt Willow wasn't well enough to be here. Will you telephone her and tell her all about it?"

"Ve vill have the many photographs to show your aunt and uncle, *Liebchen*," Inge said. "And I vill bring vith me the dress for her to see. Come, *Liebchen*, ve must say goodbye to my parents. Poor *Mutti* – she vill be crying again, I think!"

"I'm sure she will miss you, Inge," Zandra reminded her.

"*Ja, ja*, but it is *Papi* who is most minding, I think."

As they moved away, Zandra's attention was caught by the sight of Pelham who was standing now with a glass of wine in one hand, the other resting on the Professor's shoulder. Despite the hum of conversation, Zandra could hear her uncle's voice, raised far higher than was normal.

". . . really nothing to touch a good Havana, Herr Professor, take my word for it. Got some in the bar . . . had one last night. Come along, old chap . . . least I can do is treat you to a good cigar —"

For a moment, Zandra wondered whether her uncle had had too much of the German wine which had been flowing freely throughout the meal. Then, as the Professor rose to follow him out of the room, Pelham swaying on his feet, she realized that he was putting on a performance. Silvie appeared to be unaware of his departure. Zandra waited a few minutes and then, excusing herself on the pretext that she was going to powder her nose, she slipped quietly out to the bar. As she went through the foyer, her eye caught sight of the same two men she had noticed in the church. They were standing by the main door leading on to the street.

She walked unobtrusively into the bar. There was no sign of either her uncle or the Professor. She paid a hurried visit to the powder-room and returned to the private room where the wedding guests were still gathered. Her aunt came to stand beside her.

"You know what is happening, Zee-Zee, do you not?" she asked. "Your uncle is very excited. *Mon Dieu*, after all these years you would think he was too old for such crazy undertakings!"

Zandra smiled.

"But you have agreed to his plan, Tante Silvie."

Silvie shrugged her shoulders.

"Really, Zee-Zee, your uncle and I are too old for such cloak-and-dagger conspiracies! I know this, but he does not! By the way, is it true your Anthony is leaving in a minute?"

Zandra nodded.

"He is already packed and ready to go!" she said. "He has only to change his clothes."

There was a flurry of movement as word was passed that the bridal pair were about to depart. Wearing a gentian-blue coat and skirt and a beribboned Legroux hat of tan straw, Inge crossed the foyer to hug her parents. Jamie grinned happily at Zandra and waved his hand. With everyone calling out their good wishes and the younger men a few sallies, no one seemed to notice that neither the Professor nor Pelham had returned.

Zandra regarded her aunt with concern. She was slumped in one of the elegant Louis XIV chairs in her house in the Rue d'Artois, a small medicinal glass of cognac at her side.

Tante Silvie was no longer a young woman, Zandra thought, and yesterday's wedding nuptials had exhausted her even before the *dénouement* in Munich and the tension-ridden journey to Paris during which neither she nor the Professor had slept. The train journey had been particularly difficult for Silvie since she had been obliged to share her first-class sleeper with the stranger who had taken her husband's place. For once, she looked every bit her age which Zandra knew to be only five years short of seventy. The Professor had retired to one of her aunt's guest-rooms, but Tante Silvie would not move beyond a few yards from the telephone.

"Uncle Pelham is sure to be all right!" Zandra said reassuringly for the umpteenth time.

They knew already from a telephone call they had made to the hotel on their arrival in Paris, that he had been questioned by the German police about the mysterious disappearance of the Professor, as had all the other wedding guests and hotel staff. As planned, he had told the interrogators that he had delayed too long drinking in the station buffet with his nephew, Lord Oliver Rochford, had missed the train, and that his wife had departed without him. He forbore to say that although his questioners had not appeared suspicious, there was still a very real danger they would discover from the train steward that both bunks in the sleeper had been occupied and realize how the Professor had managed to get out of the country. He was, he informed his wife, obliged to wait in Munich until his "lost" passport was returned.

Silvie took a sip of the cognac and said thoughtfully: "Do you really believe those terrible things Professor Zeller has been telling us, Zee-Zee? It is too awful to accept!"

Pressed by Silvie, the Professor had told them during breakfast of the likely treatment he would have received if he'd been arrested. Intellectuals like himself who were known to be seditious were put into hospitals and their relatives informed that they'd had a nervous breakdown, he'd said. Visits were prohibited, and after a few days, the "patient" would be removed to a mental hospital for "treatment". Several months later, the relatives would be permitted a brief visit and would find the perfectly sane man whom they'd last seen was now a pathetic vegetable.

Although it was a considerable relief to have reached Paris safely with the Professor, where a sympathetic British Ambassador had taken over responsibility for him, Silvie's concern was now for the safety of her husband. Looking at her aunt's white, strained face, Zandra felt that she must not be left alone until her uncle was at least known to be safely on his way to Paris. Before leaving England, however, she had arranged to meet Guy at lunch-time at his hotel. She *must* let Guy know that she had been delayed.

"Tante Silvie," she said, hating the thought that she must lie to her aunt, "there is a telephone call I should make. It won't take long, but I'd made a date to visit a friend and as I'm going to be rather late, I need to postpone it."

Silvie sighed.

"But, of course, *chérie*, the telephone is there, but please, be as quick as you can. Your uncle may be trying to reach me."

"I will be quick – but . . . well, it's a private call, Tante Silvie," Zandra said haltingly. More than ever, she hated the thought of having to lie, but from the first moment when Guy had suggested the rendezvous in Paris, she had not felt justified in involving her aunt in her proposed clandestine affair.

Silvie now gave her niece a searching look.

"This 'friend' you are meeting . . . it is perhaps a man?" she asked, for she could think of no other reason why her niece did not wish to use the telephone in her presence.

Zandra nodded, annoyed to find that her cheeks were beginning to redden.

Silvie sat upright in her chair.

"I do not wish to pry, *chérie*," she smiled as she leant forward and patted Zandra's hand. "All the same, Zee-Zee, I care very much for you and I have to question whether you know what you are doing. This assignation – I take it that it is of a serious nature or you would have spoken of it before now? I am not seeking to stop you, *chérie* – only to warn you that I do not think your husband is a man to take a *petite affaire* lightly, eh?"

"I know that, Tante Silvie!" Zandra said. Suddenly, the longing to take her aunt into her confidence was overwhelming. "It's just that . . . I should never have married Anthony. We . . . we have nothing in common and . . . well, I don't love him any more – and I know now that he has never really loved me. Our marriage was a terrible mistake."

For a moment, Silvie did not speak. Then she said thought-fully: "This does not really surprise me, *chérie*. You do not have the appearance of a woman who is happy!" She sighed. "*Enfin*, there are many women like you who have found themselves in your position, and it is a dangerous one, for the empty heart will quickly find another to fill it." She paused before adding: "Are you sure it is right for you to take a lover?"

"No, Tante Silvie, I am *not* sure!" Zandra cried. "I just know I need Guy. I need to be with someone I care about and who loves me. And he really does love me. You know him, don't you – Anthony's former assistant – Guy Brisfow!"

"Aah!" Silvie let out the exclamation on a long-drawn breath. "Now I am beginning to understand! I have said to your uncle many times in the past that I thought Anthony was taking a very big risk in throwing you two young people together so frequently. Your husband was playing a dangerous game, I told your uncle, but he did not agree with me. 'Zee-Zee needs a strong, domi-nant man,' he said. 'Someone she can look up to and respect, and who better fills that role than her husband?' "

Her heart filled with bitterness, it was on the tip of Zandra's tongue to describe the methods Anthony used to dominate her, but at that moment the telephone rang.

"It could be my Pelham!" her aunt cried as with surprising agility for someone of her age, she sprang out of her chair and hurried across the room to pick up the receiver. Zandra saw the look of anxiety on her face turn to a smile of relief as she listened to her husband's voice.

"But that is splendid news, my darling!" she said at last. "Yes, of course, *chérie, je t'aime aussi!*"

A few minutes later she replaced the receiver. She looked twenty years younger as she turned to Zandra with shining eyes.

"Your uncle had just had a telephone call from the Consulate. They have a replacement passport waiting for him to collect so there is nothing to stop him leaving. He was questioned again by the Gestapo who seemed disinclined to believe he had lost his passport, but of course they could not disprove it, so they have no reason to detain him. He is hoping to take an aeroplane flight to Le Bourget at half-past four. There is no doubt that Alexis has pulled strings for all those silly formalities to have been completed so quickly."

Zandra rose from her chair and hugged her aunt.

"I'm so glad, Tante Silvie. The Professor will be pleased, too. He was so worried about the risks Uncle Pelham was taking, poor man. We must tell him as soon as he wakes up."

"And that is not all, *chérie!* Your uncle paid a visit this morning to the Zellers. It seems that the SS had been round questioning Herr Zeller, but as he was quite ignorant as to how his brother had disappeared or of where he might be, he could tell them nothing. Being a good Party member and well known to be in opposition to his brother's behaviour, he has been excluded from suspicion of having aided the Professor's escape. Herr and Frau Zeller think the poor man is hiding somewhere in Germany. They are worried for his safety, but pleased that they no longer have the dissident under their roof. Your uncle said they seemed eager to disown him!" She gave a quick, happy laugh. "Of course, your uncle was very discreet on the telephone – just in case someone was listening on the line!"

She paused to recollect her thoughts.

"Zee-Zee, we must think now of you. I am quite myself again now I know your uncle is safe, so there is no reason for you to remain here with me. But now it is *I* who am worried for *you*. If you are certain that you wish to attend this rendezvous with your young man, then it is most important that you are discreet. He is in a hotel? You are planning to join him there? To stay the night with him?"

Zandra nodded.

"Had you thought of the consequences if your husband telephoned this house and I, in my innocence, told him you were staying with an old school friend? Do you think he would have believed me?"

Zandra's eyes expressed her bitterness.

"No, I don't, Tante Silvie. I suppose I was counting on the fact that Anthony almost certainly won't ring me. He never does."

"I see! Nevertheless, if it should happen, *chérie*, I will say that you are asleep, or in the bath, or out shopping – whatever is appropriate, and that you will return his call later if the matter is urgent. You must leave me the telephone number of your hotel so that I know where to reach you if there is such an emergency. You must be very careful, Zee-Zee ... that is if you wish to preserve your marriage. Since you have not mentioned the possibility of divorce, I assume you do not intend to put an end to your marriage. The courts have little sympathy for a woman who commits adultery whatever her reasons for doing so!"

Zandra regarded her aunt with a mixture of surprise and gratitude.

"It's wonderful of you to be so understanding, Tante Silvie! I had supposed you would be very disapproving if you knew, yet here you are assisting me, and you are obviously more knowledgeable than I at managing an affair!"

Silvie smiled.

"I have never had to manage an affair as a married woman, *chérie*, since I have always remained deeply in love with your uncle. However, I have been called upon to protect quite a few of my married friends in the past. Does this shock you?"

"I am surprised rather than shocked!" Zandra said. "Surprised to know you have married friends who've had love affairs!"

"*Mais certainement, ma petite!*" Silvie said gently. "We all need love, do we not, at any age? Who was it said: *Morality was made for man, not man for morality*?" She sighed. "Only you can know in your heart if what you are doing is morally justified, Zee-Zee. Go now to your lover, *chérie*, but try to make sure that no one is hurt by this."

There were tears in Zandra's eyes as she hugged her aunt. Then she hurried over to the telephone and gave the operator the number of Guy's hotel. When finally her call was put through to him, his voice sounded anything but lover-like.

"Where on earth have you been, Zandra? You promised to ring the moment you arrived – *and that was over four hours ago!* I checked the trains so I know yours was on time. Why didn't you ring me before now? I've been worried out of my mind." He paused before adding in a quieter voice: "You're not having cold feet, are you?"

"No, it isn't that. I'll explain when I see you. I was just ringing to say I was on my way."

"Right, then I'll see you shortly," Guy said stiffly. "It's Room 205, by the way, and in case you've forgotten, you're Mrs Kipling."

"I hadn't forgotten!" Zandra said sharply, and replaced the receiver.

Her aunt was regarding her with raised eyebrows.

"That did not sound like a conversation between lovers!" she said gently.

"It certainly was not! He sounded really put out because I didn't phone him as soon as we arrived this morning! After that little *contretemps*, I'm beginning to wonder if I *am* doing the right thing!"

Silvie sighed.

"Only you can know the answer, *chérie*. Why not go and see how you feel when you are with the young man? You can always come home if you decide he is not worth the risks you are taking."

Risks which were far more serious than her aunt realized, Zandra thought as she put on her coat and hat, and went out to the street to find a taxi. Not for the first time, she asked herself if she was being cowardly not to gamble on the possibility that Anthony was bluffing; that he would not dare reveal Lucy's past because of the repercussions it would have on him as well as her family. He was related now by marriage to the very family to whom he would be bringing disgrace!

If it had been Anthony's word alone that Lucy had once worked in a French brothel, she would not have believed him;

but Guy had actually seen written proof of the facts. How could they not have a devastating effect upon poor Aunt Willow who was so frail these days? Lucy was her daughter, and people would surely blame her for not taking better care of her child. Questions would be asked. Why, when Aunt Willow had discovered that her daughter had left her French convent, had she not brought her home immediately? Whatever had happened all those years ago must remain a secret.

As the taxi driver took her to the rue de Poitiers, she knew she could not obtain her freedom at the risk of hurting the gentle, loving woman who had been such a wonderful mother to her. Nor must she burden her sympathetic French aunt by revealing the reason why she must stay married to Anthony. Tante Silvie would feel impelled to tell Uncle Pelham who would almost certainly wish to confront him. Decent, straightforward man that her uncle was, he would be no match for a man as ruthless and unscrupulous as her husband.

With a shock, Zandra realized that they had reached the hotel. She paid the taxi driver and hurried inside where she was greeted volubly by the elderly receptionist.

"Ah, Madame Kipling!" he exclaimed. "Your husband has been most anxious for you. You have arrived from Germany, no? I myself would not care to visit that country – not even if you paid me, Madame. It is too full of *les Boches, n'est-ce pas*?" He shrugged expressively and then quickly apologized. "But I am detaining you. The lift is there to your right, Madame. Your room is on the second *étage*. I hope you enjoy your stay."

He beckoned to a bell-boy to take Zandra's overnight bag and bowed her into the lift. As Zandra followed the boy down the corridor of the second floor, she was overcome by sudden nervousness. What was she doing here, in a strange hotel, masquerading as a Mrs Kipling without even being certain any more that she cared deeply enough for Guy to become his lover? Would he expect her to go straight to bed? Would she have to take off her clothes and . . .

The door opened to the bell-boy's knock and Guy stood there, his face expressionless. With a brief glance at her, he tipped the boy and took her suitcase, then closed the door behind her.

"It's a bit noisy, I'm afraid!" he said in a level tone. "The window looks down over the main street." He nodded towards a door beyond the big double bed. "The bathroom is in there – adequate, but the plumbing is pretty antiquated."

He put her suitcase down and turned to look at her, his eyes questioning. "I take it you *are* staying?"

"Yes, I said I would!" Zandra broke in quickly. "Guy, I am sorry I didn't telephone you the moment I arrived, but I'm sure you'll understand when I tell you about it. It all started two days ago in Munich when —"

"Since this is obviously going to be a long story," Guy broke in coldly, "I suggest you tell me over lunch. I've booked a table in a little bistro round the corner for one o'clock and it's half-past one now. Is that all right?"

"Yes, of course!" Zandra said quickly, surprise momentarily swamping her. Of all the meetings she had imagined during those three days in Munich, this was proving one she could never have envisaged. They had not even kissed! Nor was Guy's voice in the least loving.

Feeling both embarrassed and bitterly disappointed, she decided she would think up an excuse and go back to Tante Silvie's after lunch. Stiffly, Guy conducted her in silence along the corridor to the lift.

"The bistro is just round the next corner!" he said as they started to walk. "I expect you're hungry. It's a beautiful day, isn't it?"

No, thought Zandra, I'm not at all hungry and the day isn't in the least beautiful. This encounter she had been looking forward to for so long was turning out to be one of the most disconcerting and regrettable decisions she had ever made.

Chapter 19

May 1937

Claude Calonne broke off a chunk of bread and used it to wipe the last of the gravy from his plate, then he wiped his small, black moustache fastidiously with his napkin and untied it from around his neck.

"No cheese, Claude?" Alice asked anxiously. "I bought some *Brie* in the market this morning especially for you. You really don't eat enough, dearest."

Claude frowned as he turned to look at his wife's buxom figure in the chair opposite him. It was quite remarkable, he thought irritably, how anxious she was to "fatten him up". She, of course, ate far too much, and what had once been merely a plump, well-rounded figure had now, since the arrival of their three children, spread in all directions like an over-ripe *Camembert*. One would never imagine, to look at her in her voluminous, shapeless dresses, her hair pinned back in a bun, that she was related to Monsieur and Madame Rochford up at the Casa Montijo, or, even more unlikely, that she was the sister of Milord Rochford and that very beautiful lady, the Comtesse Zemski!

He was particularly irritated with Alice because she had flatly refused to accompany him to the wedding of her cousin, Jamie

McGill, to the German girl in Munich. He was not so much interested in visiting Germany as in being part of the Rochford family gathering where the Zellers would have assumed him to be from the same illustrious background as his in-laws. When the invitation to the wedding had arrived, he had instructed Alice to write at once and accept it. They would travel with Monsieur and Madame Rochford, he'd decided – with first-class tickets, of course, befitting his elevated status.

Alice refused to go. She did not care for these big social functions, she said. She felt dowdy, incapable of making conversation to strangers, let alone foreigners. She would not risk leaving the children with neighbours for so long a period of time. She wished to remain at home.

Anger, contempt, cajolery and finally threats could not make her change her mind. Nor, indeed, was Madame Rochford able to talk her niece round, and he had been obliged to face the fact that like many other rather stupid people, Alice could be as stubborn as a *mulet* when pushed to do something she disliked.

"You could accompany us on your own, Claude!" Madame Rochford had said doubtfully; but the truth was, he'd not felt able to cope in a foreign country without the social protection he believed his wife's presence afforded him.

He decided that this was now as good a time as any to make the announcement he was certain would cause Alice not a little anxiety.

"I am thinking of opening another *galerie* – in Toulouse!" he announced as the maid cleared away the dishes. He was gratified to see his wife's face flush as he dropped his bombshell.

"But, Claude, you are always so busy here in Pau. However would you manage another *galerie* in Toulouse?"

"I shall employ someone to run the new one. I can afford it, I am glad to say, thanks to the increased popularity these last few years of my *Galerie des Beaux-Arts* here in Pau."

It was a popularity he knew was due to the patronage of

286

Madame Rochford. She had gone out of her way to praise him to all her important friends, French and English alike.

Well, it was no more than his due, he told himself. When he had proposed to Alice, he had assumed (quite wrongly as it happened) that, being a Rochford, she would bring him a sizeable *dot*. How was he to know that the family fortunes had disappeared overnight in the Wall Street crash in America and that Alice was virtually penniless? As it turned out, it was nevertheless a good move to have made. His income had trebled and he was now a well respected member of the community. It was not beyond the realms of possibility that, given a few more years, he could become Mayor.

Against such benefits, however, there were distinct disadvantages. For one thing, he found it extremely difficult to meet Alice's matrimonial requirements. Like a lot of virgins who had come late to marriage, she was anxious to make up for lost time. Where in the first year he had found her quite reasonably desirable, her attraction for him had rapidly declined as with each pregnancy the number of folds of flesh had increased. Unfortunately her demands for his attentions had not decreased in proportion. It would be useful, therefore, to have a more than reasonable excuse to spend a few nights away from the marital bed each week in Toulouse.

As if she had also been thinking of his possible absences, Alice said anxiously: "But what shall I do when you are away, Claude? I shall be so lonely without you."

"You have the children, my dear. You are always telling me how important they are to your happiness."

Alice's face reddened once more with emotion.

"They are! Indeed they are, Claude!"

Her husband sighed.

"If this *galerie* in Toulouse does as well as I hope, we should be able to afford a bigger house!" he said, returning to the subject uppermost in his mind. "On the Boulevard des Pyrenees, perhaps. I have no wish to live outside the city in the country like your aunt and uncle do."

287

"Oh, but I like it here, Claude!" Alice cried, her face now creased with concern. "It's near the market and I don't have far to walk. I realize this house is too small for us now we have the children, but could we not remain in this district?"

"It is not the most desirable area, Alice!" Claude said with controlled patience. "Even you must realize that the people here – well, they are not the kind of people I wish the children to associate with."

Alice regarded him with dismay.

"But everyone is so friendly, Claude, and Claudette has her little friends next door and—"

"Exactly! Bonnier is a tradesman – a butcher, *nom de Dieu!* Do you wish our *petite* Claudette to grow up and marry one of their boys? There are times, my dear, when I question your intelligence."

Alice's expression was doleful.

"I know, dearest, I *am* silly at times. I was never very clever. I'm sure you know best, Claude, and I respect your opinion." Seeing that he was looking slightly mollified, she continued: "I always knew you were a very clever man, dearest. I told Tante Silvie so when I first met you and fell in love with you. Do you realize that was six years ago?"

She put out a hand and would have ruffled Claude's sleek black hair had she not learned by experience that he heartily disliked such gestures. She found it difficult at times to restrain herself, for she still thought him wildly attractive; but, he had told her, it was not the custom – in France anyway – for the woman to make advances; that was a man's prerogative.

Alice restrained a sigh. Loving Claude as much as she did made her long for the now rare moments of affection from him. Of course, she did understand his reluctance to make love to her. Being Roman Catholics, they were not allowed to prevent pregnancies and unfortunately, Claude had only to look at her, metaphorically speaking, for her to find herself a month later with child again. Three in five years! It could not go on, Claude said, and they must practise restraint, if not for financial reasons, then for her health.

As it happened, Alice told herself, her health was excellent. She never suffered from early morning sickness and she liked nothing better than to be proudly carrying Claude's child. There were times, when she stopped to think about it, that she could not get over how fortunate she was in finding Claude so late in life. There had been so many years before when she had thought she would never have a husband and children of her own and must be content simply to be an aunt to her nephews and niece.

"You won't be late home this evening, dearest, will you?" she asked. "I bought a rabbit in the market and Janine is going to cook your favourite *gibelotte*."

Claude's mood softened. One good thing about Alice was her quite obsessional interest in his likes and dislikes. She even acceded to his request that she give the children their lunch before he returned from work since he did not enjoy family meals. Much as she adored – and spoiled – the children, he always came first. That there was a price to pay was a relatively small aggravation – namely that he must from time to time inform her that he loved her dearly and, of course, demonstrate the fact in their big feather bed. For days afterwards, he would be irritable with Alice and the children, and more pointed in his rejection of her amorous advances.

Claude's dream of the second *galerie* had become more of a reality now that he'd told Alice in so many words that he was actually going to have it; and as a consequence, he felt more kindly disposed to her than usual. He stood up and kissed her plump cheeks.

"I will be home in good time, my dear!" he said. "I will bring a bottle of Bordeaux. It will go well with the rabbit."

Alice beamed. She was always happy when Claude was in a good mood. She hurried as fast as she could into the hall so that it was she, not Janine, who was ready to hand him his smart, mole-coloured bowler hat and spotless white gloves. Claude was always extremely fussy about his clothes and it was a point of honour with her that he always went to work looking as elegant as on the day she had first met him.

As the front door closed behind him, there was a patter of feet on the stairs, and the two eldest children came racing down to throw themselves on her. Of the two, Claudette bore a greater resemblance to her, but there was no mistaking who was their father. She adored them with only a slightly lesser passion than she adored Claude.

"Has *Papa* gone? Can we go to the *parc* this afternoon, *Maman*?"

"Can we go and visit Tante Silvie and Oncle Pelham?"

Their voices, interchanging with equal facility between French and English, were high-pitched and excited, as always when their father had left the house.

Alice smiled at their upturned faces.

"Tante Silvie and Oncle Pelham are in Paris, Brigitte, I told you yesterday they would not be home until next week. We will visit them then."

Although she did not really miss her family – there was so little time to do so – it was nice to have relations living so close, and she was particularly fond of Tante Silvie. But for her, she might never have met her darling Claude, and for that, she would be eternally grateful.

The silence between them was becoming more embarrassing with every minute, Zandra thought as she looked at Guy's impassive face across the table. The bistro was crowded and it had been some time before a waiter came to take their order. They had not even spoken during the short walk from the hotel to the restaurant.

As the waiter served their meal and hurried away to another table, Guy said stiffly: "I should have chosen somewhere quieter. I didn't realize they would be so busy here."

"I expect the food is good then," Zandra replied, wondering how she would ever manage to eat what she had ordered. Guy, too, seemed to be toying with his choice. Suddenly he put down his knife and fork, and for the first time since they had sat down, he looked directly at her.

"You said you would explain when we met why you took so long to telephone me. Now you seem reluctant to do so!"

His voice was accusing, and the look on his face was devoid of affection. If anything, he looked angry. Was he, too, regretting their assignation? Zandra asked herself. It had all been so different when they had planned this meeting in Paris. He'd been so anxious, so clearly desperately in love, and she so desperately in need of loving! They'd both known the risks and agreed to take them. Was he now, like herself, having second thoughts?

"Perhaps it hasn't occurred to you what these last few days have been like for me!" Guy continued in a cold, hard voice. "The waiting, I mean . . . watching the clock, telling myself: 'Only another two days, only two more nights' . . . and then, when I finally booked into the hotel yesterday evening, 'Only one more night and she will be here with me!'" His voice deepened as he continued: "Then it was hours, Zandra. I must have been awake half the night, counting the hours . . . 'Five, four, three, two, one . . . any moment now the phone will go and I shall hear her voice!'"

His eyes darkened as he regarded Zandra's white face.

"Then nothing . . . silence! So, I telephoned the station – '*Oui, Monsieur*, the train arrived on time!' So, where are you? What has happened? Have you had an accident? Did Wisson decided after all to accompany you to Paris? What has gone wrong? Another hour . . . and another . . . For God's sake, Zandra, what do you think I'm made of?"

His furious outburst, far from distressing Zandra, released the tensions which had been gripping her. Her voice was gentle as she leant forward to cover his hand with her own.

"Guy, I'm so sorry! I should have told you earlier what happened to me, but it's quite a long story and I thought—"

"Tell me now!" Guy interrupted, pushing his plate to one side. "I want to know. I want to understand."

It was several minutes before Zandra had finished relating the frightening sequence of events which might have cost Professor Zeller his freedom if not his life.

"So when we got to Paris, we had to go straight from the station to the British Embassy!" Zandra explained finally. "When eventually we got back to the house, poor Tante Silvie was exhausted but wouldn't rest until she'd spoken to Uncle Pelham. He wasn't in the hotel when she telephoned him, and so she left a message for him to ring her the moment he returned; so it didn't seem fair for me to occupy the telephone in case he was trying to reach her. I did think of going to find a kiosk outside, but I didn't dare to leave her alone in case there was bad news. Tante Silvie was afraid Uncle Pelham might have been arrested, you see. Please try to understand, Guy."

He had been holding his breath, and now he released it on a long sigh.

"You must think me a selfish, inconsiderate, insensitive brute!" he said. "I can only apologize. If I'd had the slightest idea . . . if I'd known the danger you were in . . . Zandra, forgive me. My only excuse is that I love you so damn much! I suppose at the back of my mind, I was certain you'd had second thoughts . . . about meeting me, I mean. I don't think I could have borne it if you'd called it all off. And I think you and Madame Rochford are incredibly brave to have helped that old man – a stranger at that!"

Zandra was smiling now.

"And Guy, I haven't told you this yet, Tante Silvie knows about us. I told her – and she has offered to help me. If Anthony telephones, she's going to make a plausible excuse why I'm not there. So we don't have to worry about him now."

"Thank God for that!" Guy said vehemently. "I *have* been worried, Zandra . . . for you, I mean. Your husband is a dangerous man and we'd be wrong to underestimate him."

Zandra nodded.

"I know, but let's not talk about him, Guy. I want what little time we have to be . . . well, happy, even if we have got off to the wrong start!"

Guy's face creased in a smile.

"A few moments ago I was about as wretched as you can get, but now I'm on top of the world. Darling . . . darling Zandra! I haven't told you yet how lovely you look!" He stared ruefully at her untouched plate of food. "It'll be stone cold. Mine, too. Let's order something else. The waiter will probably think we're mad, but who cares!"

The meal, which had begun in silence, now ended in a torrent of conversation. Guy wanted to know about the wedding; about Jamie's new relations; was Ingeborg still as pro her idol, Hitler, as when she had extolled his virtues at Rochford Manor?

Zandra, in her turn, wanted to know how Guy was enjoying being a stockbroker – a job he seemed to find lacking in excitement. He had joined the Territorials, however, to give his mundane life some variety.

It was after three o'clock before, arms entwined, they walked slowly back to the hotel.

"I wondered if you might like to go to the Casino de Paris tonight," Guy said. "I believe Mistinguett is performing there; or we could take a boat down the Seine – have dinner as we go; or if you'd prefer, we could go to a cinema, darling."

The endearment was spoken quite naturally but caught at Zandra's heart.

"We'll do whatever you like, Guy!" she said softly as they made their way upstairs in the lift. She felt totally relaxed now, and as Guy unlocked their bedroom door and followed her inside, she sat down on the bed and then lay back against the pillows and smiled up at him.

"I think I had too many glasses of wine at lunch," she said.

He sat down on the bed beside her and there was laughter in his eyes.

"That goes for me, too."

Zandra's heart melted with a sudden deep affection for this

293

man which caught her unaware. His sense of humour endeared him to her far more than any other of his qualities. She reached up her arms and entwined them round his neck.

"I think I'm in love with you!" she said. "I wasn't sure until now."

Guy cupped her face in his hands and stared down into her eyes.

"Are you sure, Zandra? I love you so much it's hard to bear sometimes – knowing I can never really have you; make you my own. I want you with me all the time. I want to go to sleep with you in my arms and wake up to find you still there beside me. I want to spend my whole life with you, have children with you, grow old with you."

Tears stung the back of Zandra's eyes. Guy spoke of children, his children, but they would remain unborn, no matter how much they would both like to have them. She thought of the child she had lost and for the first time, found herself almost relieved that he had not lived. The baby had been Anthony's – perhaps growing up to look like him; to behave like him; to be like him – and then she might not have been able to love him. At least she had been able to love the infant for the few days he had survived.

There were no words of hope for the future she could offer Guy but there were other ways to make him happy now.

"I want you to make love to me, Guy!" she murmured. "I need you to love me, very much!"

Her softly spoken request moved Guy to a fierce, compelling hunger which with an effort he controlled. He knew how violent her husband had been and he wanted above all to be gentle and tender with her. He wanted her to understand that for him, passion took second place to love. But as he started kissing her, her mouth, eyes, the hollow of her throat, it was Zandra who caught his hands and pressed them to her breasts. Now each became as impatient as the other. Still fully dressed, their bodies strained for greater closeness. Guy tore himself away and crossed

294

the room to draw the curtains. When he turned back to the bed, he saw that Zandra had already removed her frock. As she took off the last of her underclothes, he began quickly to undress.

Lying down beside her, his hands explored her body, his touch almost reverent.

"You're so beautiful!" he muttered. "No, don't move, my darling, I want to look at you, memorize your body. Do you mind?"

Zandra smiled.

"No, not really! But you make me self-conscious." She reached up one hand shyly to trace the strong, firm outlines of his body. "I think you're beautiful, too!" she whispered. "Guy, do you remember that time Oliver took us swimming in the lake? I came out of the water before you did, and I stood on the bank, watching you. As you came towards me, I . . . oh, I know you'll think this shameful, but I wanted you. I wanted you to make love to me, there, in the sunlight. It was the strangest feeling. It just happened and I knew it was wrong – me being married—"

"I don't think it's 'shameful', my darling," Guy said, kissing each of her palms in turn. "I'm only sorry I didn't know at the time how you felt, although perhaps it was as well!"

"Oh, Guy, how much time we've wasted! If only—" Zandra said.

"No!" he broke in, silencing her quickly with his mouth against hers. "The past doesn't matter – we're together now." He put his arms round her and drawing her closer against him, he kissed her passionately.

"I'll never forget the first time you kissed me!" Zandra murmured huskily. "Do you remember, Guy, in the Gatehouse? It will always have memories for me, and so will this room because it's the place where we are making love for the first time."

There was a boyish glint in Guy's eyes as he leant over her.

"For the first time, yes, my darling girl, but not, I promise you, for the last!"

Chapter 20

May–December 1937

If Anthony had even the slightest suspicion that Zandra had been unfaithful to him that all-too-brief weekend in Paris, he gave no indication of it. He seemed far more concerned by the risks she and Tante Silvie had taken in helping Professor Zeller to escape from Germany. Whilst welcoming this diversion of his attention from her personal activities in Paris, Zandra had been forced to listen to an hour-long lecture on the adverse effect it could have had upon Anthony's business negotiations with the Germans were the Professor's impersonation of Pelham Rochford to have been discovered.

Anthony's cold, scathing words no longer had the power to distress Zandra; only his physical demands upon her could do that. Now that she belonged body and soul to another man, she found it increasingly difficult to conceal her revulsion. Even the slight touch of his hand on her arm would cause her skin to prickle, and she avoided his company as often as was humanly possible.

Unfortunately, he seemed particularly anxious during the remaining months of the year to have her accompany him – first to several of the big parties held by prominent members of society to celebrate the coronation of King George and Queen Elizabeth; then to Czechoslovakia. In October, she was required to entertain his guests during the race meetings at Newmarket and Kempton Park, and when they were in London, give lavish dinner parties for his business associates.

In between such functions, Zandra was free to do as she pleased so long as she did not involve her husband; but although she enjoyed long sunny days spent at Rochford with the family, and magical hours flying her Gipsy Moth from Sky-Ways, all she really wanted was to be with Guy – and that was proving to be almost impossible.

In the first place, Guy was now convinced that his flat was being watched. Someone had moved into the house across the street, and Guy had several times seen binoculars trained on his window from the one opposite. Zandra herself was certain that the chauffeur whom Anthony had recently engaged was paid to spy on her, for Anthony insisted that this dour, silent employee drive her to her destinations in preference to using taxis.

It was only when Anthony himself required the services of the chauffeur that Zandra could go anywhere unobserved; and since Anthony never told her until the last minute that he would be needing the car, or when he would be returning home, she was unable to make any forward plans to meet Guy at some secret destination. Their only means of communication was the telephone.

"It's driving me mad!" she told him one Saturday afternoon. "I want to see you so much . . . so very much!"

"Darling, I know, but I can't allow you to take any risks. Something will come up soon. Perhaps your aunt in France will help us? Couldn't you pay another visit to her before Christmas? She'll be back from Pau at the end of the summer, won't she?"

"I'll write to her today. I can tell Anthony I want to do some shopping over there. I know he's planning to go to the States some time soon and that he wants me to go with him, so he'll expect me to buy some new, smart clothes."

"I hate you having to lie – on my account!" Guy said unhappily.

"On mine, too, darling. Oh, this is all so unfair on you, Guy. If it weren't for me, you could be enjoying yourself with some other woman instead of wasting your life hanging on in the hope that I can wangle a few days to be with you."

"Right now, I'd settle for a few hours. And don't start worrying about me, Zandra. Get this into your lovely head, my darling – I don't want any other woman, not even if she's as beautiful as Olivia de Havilland or as exciting as Greta Garbo!"

"Oh Guy, I do love you . . . so much! If I could only see you for a few minutes it would be something. Guy, do you remember my friend, Monica Boswell? Her husband's family are hosting a hunt ball next month. I could ask Charles to invite you to join his party. Anthony would never know we'd contrived it. You'd be expected to have a 'duty dance' with me – and at least we'd be in the same room. Does that sound crazy?"

"Absolutely, but I'll be there. Oh God, Zandra, there has to be a better way than this. I keep thinking about Countess Zemski, and asking myself whether if the truth about her past came out, it really would damage her as much as we fear. If it weren't for that—"

"Guy, don't go on. I've thought of little else, too. It isn't just Lucy – it's the whole family."

"Forgive me, darling," Guy said quickly. "I know you're right. It's just that sometimes I think about us having to live our whole lives apart when . . . when we could be so very, very happy together. I was being selfish."

"No, you weren't, and I know just how you feel because I have the same thoughts . . . and worse ones, Guy. I think about Anthony being killed in an accident or—"

"I wish I had the guts to kill him myself!" Guy broke in. "He deserves to die! But I don't fancy finishing my life on the end of a hangman's rope!"

"Guy, don't even joke about it!" Zandra pleaded. "We have to believe there is a future."

"That's what I keep telling myself. I'll never love anyone but you, my darling. I think of you all the time, and I live on memories of our days and nights together in Paris."

"There will be others, Guy, I promise. At least you know that I belong to you – in my heart."

At the end of November, Anthony departed to America without her. It was a welcome respite when he suddenly announced that he intended to travel alone, not least because his absence coincided with the hunt ball at the Boswells' house in Surrey, and now Zandra was able to meet Guy there without fear of Anthony's eyes on them during the evening. Nevertheless, they were obliged to limit the number of dances they had with each other and the closeness of their bodies as they danced lest any of the guests who were acquainted with Anthony were to gossip to him on some other occasion about the couple's intimacy. Only towards the end of the evening were they able to slip out onto the terrace and share a tantalizingly brief embrace before a downpour of rain forced them back indoors.

It was nearing four in the morning when breakfast was served to the exhausted party-goers, and a further three hours before the guests began to depart. Guy and Zandra were amongst the last to leave, she in the green Mercedes driven by the bleary-eyed, sullen chauffeur, McDillon; Guy in his MG.

"I'll ring you as soon as I get home!" Zandra promised, her own face as stricken as Guy's at the moment of parting.

Before she could do so, however, almost as soon as she entered the house, the telephone rang.

"That'll be Mr Young, I dare say!" Mollie commented as she took Zandra's fur coat from her. "He's rung twice already though I told him you'd like as not be home afore midday!"

Her heart, which had leapt at the thought that Guy might have been tempted to break their agreement and telephone her at home, now steadied its beat as she picked up the receiver. As Mollie had expected, it was Anthony's assistant.

"Ah, Mrs Wisson, I have been trying to reach you. I'm sorry to trouble you but I am really at my wits' end as to know what to do. I have received an urgent telephone call for Mr Wisson but I have had no reply to my cables."

"How can I help you?" Zandra asked, overcome suddenly by fatigue. Stifling a yawn, she added: "If you can't reach him, I certainly can't!"

"Yes, I realize that, Mrs Wisson, but I thought in the circumstances you might wish to stand in for your husband. I understand that an elderly lady he knows is dying, and has repeatedly asked to see him. There is not a great deal of time left, so I thought perhaps you might wish to go in Mr Wisson's place."

"An old lady?" Zandra asked. "Do you know who, Mr Young?"

"The matron of the nursing home said the old lady was a Mrs Wisniowiecki, a Polish lady. Our accountant told me that Mr Wisson has been meeting the bills for her residence in a Home for Retired Gentlefolk for many years. It seems the poor lady is now in a nursing home with only a few days to live, and she is most anxious to see your husband before she dies!"

"I don't know any Polish ladies, and I can't think of any reason why she might wish to see me!" Zandra said. "However, I can find that out, Mr Young. If you really can't reach my husband, then, of course, I'd be willing to go in the circumstances, if there is anything I can do. What is the address?"

"It's a long way away, Mrs Wisson – Cumbria. I have looked up trains and there is one leaving at ten-thirty should you decide to make the journey. Or McDillon could drive you which would take longer, of course, but be more comfortable for you."

Zandra's thoughts were racing. If the old lady was Polish, could this possibly be a relative of Anthony's? And if so, why had he never mentioned her? She must have some importance for him if he had been regularly paying her bills. Was it really necessary for her to travel all the way to Northumberland to visit a complete stranger? She was exhausted, and so, too, was McDillon.

The thought which now sprang into her mind caused her

heart to miss a beat . . . there was every reason to leave McDillon at home . . . to say she would hire another car and driver, and go up to Northumberland with Guy! If there were time, she and Guy could both snatch a few hours' sleep, leave after lunch and be half-way to Northumberland by evening. They could spend the night together *en route* and . . .

"Give me the telephone number of the nursing home, Mr Young," she said. "I'll speak to the matron, find out if this unfortunate woman really does want to see me."

She replaced the receiver and then lifted it again to give the operator the number of the nursing home. The matron answered it herself.

"It's most unfortunate that your husband should be abroad at such a time," she said in a cold voice when Zandra had identified herself. "I'm sure Mr Wisson would have felt it a duty to be here. Mrs Wisnowiecki talks of little else but seeing him again before she dies. He is her only relative, and—"

Zandra was in no doubt that the matron's tone of voice, though respectful, was nevertheless reproachful. And she could well understand why. Anthony had an elderly relative still living – and she, his wife, had never visited the old lady! Questions raced through her mind. What possible reason could he have had to hide the fact from her that he did have a relation – someone dependent upon him to pay her bills? It was extraordinary.

The matron was still speaking.

". . . are you there, Mrs Wisson? Mr Wisson's assistant, Mr Young, wouldn't give me your telephone number – and of course, Mr Wisson has always insisted that I should only contact him at his business address. I know it's a long way to come, but in the circumstances, I do hope you can make the journey. Your presence might be some comfort to the old lady. She's in a great deal of pain – a tumour, you see."

"Yes, yes, of course I'll come!" Zandra said quickly. "I'm sorry my husband can't be there. Please tell Mrs . . . Mrs—"

"Wisniowiecki, Mrs Wisson. I believe there was another

relative – her brother who lived in London, but that he died a long time ago, so there is no one else I can notify."

"I'll be driving up, Matron," Zandra said. "I won't be too late if I arrive at lunch-time tomorrow?"

"No, I think she'll last until then – especially if she knows you are coming, poor soul!"

Zandra replaced the receiver, then going to her room and dismissing Mollie, she rang Guy. He had just arrived home.

"I'm still finding it impossible to believe, Guy!" she told him. "Anthony said all his relations were dead other than those he'd lost touch with who lived in Poland!"

"I knew he supported an elderly woman in a Home for Retired Gentlefolk up north," Guy said. "The bills used to arrive monthly and I passed them on to Mackinson. But I had no idea Mrs Wisniowiecki was a relation! I assumed she was a retired employee or retainer, and I thought his support of someone like that was one of his better qualities. It must be all of three hundred miles to Carlisle. We'll be lucky to get half-way before dark, and the weather is pretty foul. Get a taxi to Harrods and I'll pick you up there at eleven-thirty."

"We'll be together, Guy, so I don't mind how long it takes. I just want to get there before the poor woman dies," Zandra said.

By six o'clock they had reached Doncaster and both she and Guy were exhausted when they booked into a hotel. Ever-conscious of the need to protect Zandra, Guy booked two rooms, one in her name and another in a fictitious name for himself.

"Don't worry, my love," he said as she met him downstairs in the dining-room, "I don't intend to use my room. Nothing in the whole wide world would prevent me holding you in my arms tonight."

Knowing that they still had a long day ahead of them on the morrow, they retired to bed as soon as they had finished their meal. Guy did not bother to go to his own room but slipped quietly into hers.

"I ruffled my sheets before I went down to dinner!" he said

with a grin as he undressed and climbed into bed beside her. 'In the morning, I shall get dressed and go down to breakfast suitably attired."

He took her in his arms and drew her to him with fierce longing.

"I'm trying not to be glad this has happened!" he said as he kissed her eyes, her lips, her throat. "I'm sorry this wretched woman is dying but I'll always be grateful that she chose to do so when Wisson was too far away to be told. Fate has been kind to us, darling."

Her fatigue forgotten, Zandra gave herself up to the passionate need that was now consuming them both. As in Paris, Guy proved himself a tender, sensitive, yet demanding lover, and Zandra's response was all and more than he could wish for. When at last she lay satiated and supine in his embrace, her head against his shoulder, her arms wrapped around his waist, she drifted into sleep knowing that whatever the world might say, God could not think it wrong for them to love one another. Her marriage to Anthony might be legal but *that* was the immoral union – not the merging of her body with the man she loved.

The morning dawned cold and foggy, and slowed their progress. As they drove northwards for mile after mile, Zandra said thoughtfully: 'Am I doing the wrong thing, Guy? Coming all this way to see a dying woman who doesn't even know me? The matron said it was Anthony who the poor old soul wanted to see. What can I say to her? Suppose she asks me why I haven't been to visit her with Anthony before now? I can't understand why he hasn't taken me with him when he visited her in the past!"

Guy steered the car carefully past a tarpaulin-covered lorry and said: "You'll just have to play it by ear, darling. I'm sure the old lady will be pleased to see anyone connected with your husband – and even if she isn't, at least this has given us a chance to be together. Will you tell Wisson you drove yourself?"

Zandra smiled.

"No, I shall say I hired a car and driver as McDillon wasn't fit

303

to drive, and that I paid you in cash. Otherwise he might ask to see your bill! He always checks what I spend."

"I can't think why! He's so well off these days he could afford to lose hundreds and not notice it, yet even in my day he watched the accounts like a hawk and was furious if he ever saw a penny wasted. Was he very poor when he was young?"

Zandra sighed.

"I don't know much about Anthony's childhood. His parents were poor – that much I do know; but he never liked talking about them. I don't think he and his father hit it off very well, but if ever I questioned him about his parents, he'd change the subject. I thought perhaps he was ashamed of them for some reason. He said he didn't have any photographs as they were lost when his home was burnt down not long after his father died."

"Perhaps the old lady will be able to throw some light on his past!" Guy said.

It was with no more than a natural curiosity that Zandra made her way alone to the nursing home. The journey had taken far longer than she had anticipated, and it was nearing tea-time.

"I hope I am not too late?" she enquired. "I'm afraid the weather was very bad."

The matron was regarding her with a speculative look in her sharp, grey eyes. Her voice was cool, unfriendly, as she said: "Mrs Wisniowiecki is very ill – but determined to cling to life long enough to meet you. I have to warn you that I doubt if she will last the night. The doctor has prescribed drugs for the pain, but knowing you were coming, she has insisted on a minimal dosage so that she will be fully conscious during your visit."

"Then perhaps I should waste no more time, Matron," Zandra said, and feeling the need to defend herself, she added: "I would have come before now had I known she was so ill."

"Your husband . . . Mr Wisson . . . he didn't tell you his mother was dying?"

Zandra barely concealed a gasp. Anthony's *mother*? The question hung on her lips but she managed not to voice it. What would this woman think if she knew Anthony had hidden such an important fact from his wife? She was beginning to understand the woman's antagonistic manner.

"My husband has been abroad – and I have been away in the country!" she said. "Now, I'd like to see the . . . Mrs Wisniowiecki, please," she added, as firmly as she could.

She was led in silence to a private room where the patient was lying in a high, hospital bed, her white hair neatly brushed back from her forehead, her hands folded over the spotless white sheet. She looked painfully thin, her grey eyes – so reminiscent of Anthony's – enormous in her skeletal face.

"Here's your daughter-in-law, Mrs Wisniowiecki," Matron said in high, falsely bright tones. "Now let me prop you up a little on your pillows. There! Now you can have a nice chat while I get Nurse to bring you both a cup of tea."

"How kind of you to make so long the journey – and with so horrible the weather!"

The old lady's voice was bird-like and so strongly accented, Zandra was only just able to interpret her words as she seated herself in the chair beside the bed.

"I would have come to see you sooner, Mrs Wisniowiecki, but Anthony has been abroad and I'm sorry to say, his office manager did not notify me until yesterday that you were ill. I am very sorry!"

"Ach, my dear, it is not your fault that the Good Lord has chosen so bad the moment to call me to the next life. I would so much wish to see my Antoni – but this I understand is not possible. But you, my dear, can tell me all about him. He is well, no?"

Zandra's heart was filled with pity as she saw the old lady's hands clench suddenly in pain.

"Anthony is in the very best of health!" she said quickly. "You are being well looked after here, Mrs Wisniowiecki? There is nothing I could get you?"

A brief, tired smile flitted across the old lady's face.

"There is nothing for which I have the need any more!" she

said. "I have been so worried about Antoni, and I am so happy to know that, after all these months, he has now become well again. I had waited so long for his visit, you see, and when he could not come because of the illness, it was much worry for me."

Zandra leant forward and, furious at Anthony's lies about his health, took one of the thin, white hands in hers.

"He is very well now, I promise you. He would have come to see you just as soon as he was better but . . . but he had to go away on business. He . . . he was coming to see you the moment he returned."

"Ach, yes, he would be so kind. He works so hard always, my poor Antoni! Always it is work, work and more work for him. So hard the struggle! But now he has a wife by his side to take care of him. I was so happy to hear he had found you, my dear. You are very beautiful!"

Zandra was trying to keep pace with the questions this dying woman's declarations posed. It was true Anthony worked hard – but his life could not be called a "struggle". Had the old lady misused the word?

"When he was only still the little boy, I would say to Antoni's father: 'See how clever he is, our son. One day he will make you very proud to be father to such a son.'" Her face clouded and her eyes held a look of distress. "So sad it was that my poor dear husband was not so clever as his boy. There was no money, you see, when he died – only the bills . . . so many bills; and it has taken all these years for Antoni to pay his father's debts – for honour of our name, you understand. I am a Krasinski and my family would wish for this. But I am sad that it put the big stone round the neck of my clever boy. Such a struggle for him! So little money for journeys in the train to visit his mother! No, I could not permit it. At least now there will be a little more for you, my dear, once I am gone. You must have wished the many times that Antoni did not have always the old mother to pay for all these years. So good he has been to me!"

Unable to meet the bright, trusting gaze of the dying woman,

Zandra turned away, sickened by the revelations of Anthony's lies. Too poor to pay for a train fare to visit his mother! Too ill to do so! What other lies had he told her?

"If you are not too tired, will you tell me about Anthony's childhood?" she asked. "You said he was exceptionally clever?"

The old lady's face lit up with pride.

"Ach, yes, indeed! I taught him myself until he was old enough to go to school – a good English school it was, just for boys. At school, too, he has always the good marks . . . but he was not so happy there. At home, sometimes he argue with his papa because even so young he sees that his father does not manage his factory so well. It is difficult, is it not, if the son is more clever than his father? Always there are the many quarrels! When my Antoni becomes twenty-one years of age, he changes his name for one that is more English, and this my husband cannot forgive."

Momentarily, tears filled the old lady's eyes.

"But I am Antoni's mother, and I understand how he feels!" she resumed her account of the past. "My son has been raised an English boy, so this is how he wishes to be; but his papa – he is proud of the name of Wisnowiecki and his heart is broken when Antoni refuses it. When my husband dies, he is still angry with Antoni, so he leaves the house to me and the factory to my brother; but Sigismund – he has the terrible accident when he falls before a train – and he has left everything to his wife's nephew whom I have never met. So sad was my Antoni when he must tell me that there are many bills his papa has left which we must pay. 'Mama,' he tells me, 'only if we sell our home and you go to live in the house for poor ladies like yourself can we manage!' This I do not want to do, but I am sad for my Antoni because it is his wish to go to London to find work to pay so many bills."

Her eyes filled once more with tears, and she allowed Zandra to give her a sip of water before her thin, wavering voice began again.

"Perhaps Antoni has told you what terrible thing is next to

307

happen. Our house has the big fire and we can no longer live there. But my Antoni is very brave. The money the insurance people give us will pay our bills, and he can go to London. He has found me first the nice place to live. He is sad to leave me but in London, always he is hoping with me that one day he will make his fortune and I can go to live with him; but it is right he should marry, and I know you have too small the little house for me to live with you. Now I have met you, I am happy that he has chosen so well his wife. One day you will give him children, no?"

There were tears pricking the back of Zandra's eyes as she leant over the exhausted woman and kissed her cheek. Now was a moment when she must play the part of a loving and devoted wife for the sake of this poor, misguided, dying old lady.

"We plan to have a family just as soon as we can afford it," she said softly. "If I may, Mrs Wisniowiecki, I should like to call my first little girl after you."

The old lady was smiling.

"I will ask the matron to give you my little gold brooch with the letters ANNA for your child. It was given to me by my mother, and I would like my first granddaughter to have it. The world has changed, has it not, since my poor husband and I were forced to run away together. My parents did not think he was a suitable husband for me, you see; but he was a good man – and I loved him. I never regretted it. You will understand this, for you, too, have married a good man who you love."

Zandra was saved a reply by the advent of the nurse with a tray of tea. She cast a professional eye at the patient and shook her head.

"You look a little tired, Mrs Wisniowiecki. Will you let me give you your injection now?"

The old lady smiled.

"In a few minutes, my dear. Let me hold my daughter-in-law's hand for the little moment longer. She has come so far to see me and it would be unkind for me to sleep whilst she is here."

"Just a little while then!" Zandra said, taking the old lady's hand in hers and bending to kiss the white cheek. "I am going to stay in a hotel nearby tonight, so I can come and see you again in the morning when you are rested."

But even as she made the suggestion, she knew from the expression on the nurse's face that it would be unlikely Mrs Wisniowiecki would awake from the longest sleep of all.

After she had said her goodbyes and was once more in the matron's office, she was unable to stem her tears as it struck her how inexpressibly sad it was for this frail, gentle old woman to have been needlessly denied the company of her beloved son.

The matron's manner was markedly more friendly as she recognized the genuineness of Zandra's grief.

"Your mother-in-law is such a sweet old lady!" she said. "There were so many times when your husband promised a visit and then, at the last minute, was unable to make the journey. I did wonder once or twice if the excuses were, well, just that! But his mother never doubted them. She lived in hope. He was all she had, you see."

"I wish I'd known earlier that Mrs Wisniowiecki was so ill," Zandra said. "No one told me!"

The matron could not conceal a look of surprise.

"Until you telephoned me yesterday, we were not aware that Mr Wisson was married," she said quietly. "When your mother-in-law arrived here a month ago from the Home for Retired Gentlefolk, we were told your husband was her only relative, and that we were to render our account to his office in London. According to Mrs Grieves who ran the Home, the accounts were always paid promptly although they were aware that Mr Wisson was hard put to meet the charges."

Zandra had no intention of satisfying the woman's obvious curiosity – a not unnatural one in the circumstances. "I'll come back first thing in the morning!" she said. "Now perhaps you could give me the name of a hotel not too far away?"

"Yes, well, there's the King's Head not four miles down the road. At this time of the year they're sure to have vacancies."

The coaching inn did indeed prove to be almost empty but for two dark-suited men whom Guy took to be travelling salesmen. The food was excellent and when they had finished their meal, Guy said: "You are beginning to look yourself again, darling. Was it really so awful? It's all impossible to believe. If Mrs Wisniowiecki is such a sweet old lady, why in heaven's name did Wisson bury her up in this outlandish place? Why did he tell you she was dead? At least he paid her bills, although I suppose if he'd simply abandoned her, she might have come looking for him, and then he would have been exposed for what he is – a cold-hearted, ruthless brute!"

Zandra shivered.

"When he gets home, I shall have to tell him I know about his mother. Perhaps he will explain things to me then."

Guy's face was thoughtful.

"It has just occurred to me, Zandra – whatever his reasons for hiding his mother – the fact of the matter is he didn't want you, or anyone else, to know of her existence. Suppose I threatened to publicize the facts? He's a prominent figure these days and I don't doubt some of the less savoury newspapers would make a meal of the story. How many people know his parents were Polish, for a start? He wouldn't have changed his name if he hadn't wanted to hide the fact. Then there's the matter of his father's debts . . . Don't you see, darling, we could threaten to expose him if he exposed Countess Zemski."

For a moment, Zandra's heart filled with hope, but then Guy shook his head.

"No, it wouldn't work. Wisson has always made a point of cultivating the press barons. His hospitality and lavish entertainment of them are legendary. He once got an injunction put on a newspaper whose editorial he took a dislike to. He'd probably do the same again with any story I gave them."

"But it would be the truth, Guy."

"It would still be risky, darling. Apart from that, whatever black marks there might be in the past against him or his family, he's had years to cover them up. As to hiding his mother away, he'd probably say she wasn't quite right in the head and couldn't have coped with London life; or simply didn't want that kind of existence."

"She loved him, Guy! All she ever wanted was to be with him."

"Something he could easily deny. No, my darling, I don't think my exposure of the existence of Mrs Wisniowiecki would prove much of a problem to your husband, still less so now you say she's unlikely to live much longer."

As had been expected, Mrs Wisniowiecki died that night and with her death, so, too, ended Guy's last hope of finding something about Wisson's past with which to counter his threats, for Mrs Wisniowiecki left no incriminating documents. The matron had passed on to Zandra only the old lady's birth and marriage certificates, a locket containing a picture of Wisson as a young child, and a Bible. She had not even left a Will.

"It seems that all her personal possessions were lost in the fire that destroyed the family home years ago, and she never again felt like keeping any mementoes," Zandra said sadly. "I told Matron to send her clothes to a charity and then I telephoned Mr Young. He's still had no word from Anthony and in the circumstances, Matron thought there was little point in delaying the funeral, so I said I'd arrange it. Will you help me, Guy?"

"I'll do anything I can, Zandra, you know that. And try not to be too sad, darling. At least we'll have a few more days together – a bonus we didn't expect."

After the funeral – at which she, Guy, the matron and the manageress of the Home for Retired Gentlefolk were the only mourners – they set off for London.

"You've been absolutely wonderful, Guy!" she told him as they neared London. "I don't know how I'd have got through this week without you."

He took one hand from the wheel and briefly held hers.

"You'd have managed, darling. And even if it wasn't in the happiest of circumstances, we have had some time to ourselves."

Both were silent, remembering the nights of loving they had shared. Dreading the coming parting, Zandra said: "Only six weeks more and we'll be together again in Paris. I've told Tante Silvie I'll go back to Paris with her and Uncle Pelham after their Christmas visit to Rochford and that you'll be joining me there. I love you, Guy . . . more every day, I think."

"More every day, I know!" Guy said with an attempt at jollity for he, too, was feeling wretched. "I suppose Wisson will be back soon?"

"At the end of the week, according to Mr Young," Zandra replied, her heart sinking. "But I'll ring you before then, darling."

Silent once more, they drove slowly back into the city each lost in thoughts that were deeply apprehensive and strangely identical . . . that if Anthony Wisson could mete out such callous behaviour towards his own mother, what possible hope could they have that he would one day withdraw his threats to expose Lucy, and set Zandra free? It was a hope neither one of them could any longer sustain.

Chapter 21

December 1937

It was five days before Anthony returned from America and Zandra was able to confront him with the question that had been burning in her mind, but first she must inform him that Mrs Wisniowiecki had died. No matter what his reasons for keeping his mother's existence a secret, news of her death could not fail to shock him, she reasoned.

Waiting until he was seated in the drawing-room with a whisky and soda in his hand, she broke the news to him. He put down his glass and fingered the scars on his wrist absent-mindedly. His expression was one of casual indifference.

"I am already aware of the fact, Zandra!" he said. "Mr Young cabled me to say that she was terminally ill!"

"Before she died?" Zandra said aghast. "Then you could have got home in time for the funeral and—"

"I really don't need you to tell me what I *could* have done!" Anthony broke in irritably. "The fact is, I did not chose to do so. Now shall we let the matter drop? I happen to be extremely tired after my journey."

For a moment, Zandra could not bring herself to speak. She

sat down heavily in one of the armchairs, her hands gripping the armrests as she tried to keep her voice calm.

"I think you owe me an explanation, Anthony. I accept that it's not my business that you chose to go abroad even though you knew your mother was ill. What I can't accept is that you never told me she was alive! How was I to explain to her . . . to the matron, that I knew nothing – nothing at all about her?"

Anthony's face remained impassive but his eyes narrowed, and his voice had a marked note of annoyance as he said sharply: "If I'd thought it desirable for you to meet my mother, I'd have arranged it years ago. Your visit was quite unnecessary; and had I been here, I would have told you so. I have, in fact, reprimanded Mr Young for exceeding his duties. One more such breach of confidentiality and he will be replaced. I am the one who will say what is necessary and what is not!"

Zandra's cheeks flushed a deep pink.

"My visit to your mother was not unnecessary! She was pathetically pleased to see me . . . and she was *dying*, Anthony! But it was *you* she really wanted to see. Doesn't that mean anything to you?"

Anthony's eyebrows lifted fractionally.

"Nothing at all, if you want the truth. Indeed, my mother's death comes as the proverbial 'happy release' for me. I have always found her devotion extremely tedious, to say the least. She was a stupid woman."

Zandra bit back the angry protest she would like to have made.

"I didn't find her so," she said stiffly, "and she adored you, Anthony. She even accepted those ridiculous excuses you gave for not visiting her – that you were too poor to afford the journey! That you were ill!"

A faint smile curved Anthony's lips.

"Which only goes to prove how stupid she was!"

Zandra let out her breath, a feeling of hopelessness welling up in her as she realized how totally inhumane her husband was. There was little point in continuing the discussion – and yet she could not let it lie there.

"So Wisniowiecki is your real name, and you shortened it to Wisson?"

"I didn't shorten it, Zandra. I changed it by Deed Poll. Wisson is my *real* name, and yours, too! You don't imagine I'd have got very far with a surname like Wisniowiecki, do you? Besides, I wished to distance myself from my background for obvious reasons."

At least Anthony was now being honest about his motives, Zandra told herself.

"And is that why you didn't have your mother to live with us? Why you never told me about her?"

"That – and other reasons!" Anthony said shortly, rising to pour himself another drink.

Reasons he certainly did not intend to give Zandra, he told himself; reasons he had been able to push to the back of his mind but which her silly questions had evoked. It was one of the few times he had been bested, and only his youth and inexperience had brought it about. He'd never since made a move without first seeing every eventuality.

Nor had he ever allowed himself to forget that day only a week after his father's death. He'd been summoned by the family solicitor, Mr Talbot, to come to his office for an urgent meeting with Uncle Sigismund's London solicitor. He'd known at once that something had gone wrong, and his uneasiness had deepened as he'd entered Mr Talbot's dingy little office.

This room is cold as well as shabby. Is Mr Talbot aware that his miserable little coal fire is smoking? The atmosphere is as chilly as the faces of the solicitors! The London fellow, Berkeley, hasn't responded to my smile or my handshake. He can't possibly have any suspicions, can he? The coroner was entirely happy at the inquest; the verdict was accidental death . . . Berkeley's expression is extremely hostile.

"I have here a copy of your late father's Will, Mr Wisson. Mr Talbot will verify the fact that it supersedes the one Mr Wisniowiecki made in 1910 leaving everything but the house to you."

Be careful! Don't say you know anything about it. Play for time. Why,

315

in the name of God, did I not realize there might be a copy when Uncle Sigismund produced it after the funeral . . . ?

"This comes as a great surprise to me, Mr Berkeley. I'm afraid I don't quite understand. Does it differ in any marked respect from the one we have? I think Mr Talbot has produced it for obtaining probate, have you not, sir?"

"Probate has not been granted as yet, Mr Wisson, and yes, it differs a very great deal. Perhaps you would care to read it?"

Read it slowly . . . look astonished, shocked, distressed . . .

"I simply cannot believe this! We were so close, Father and I . . . We'd made plans for . . . Mr Berkeley, are you perfectly sure my father was in his right mind when he made this Will? It simply doesn't make sense. Why on earth would he leave the factories to my uncle? Uncle Sigismund lived in London and, as far as I'm aware, knew nothing at all about . . . no, I really can't accept this."

"Mr Berkeley and I have spent over an hour discussing it, Mr Wisson. We are in no doubt whatever that this copy of the second Will is valid, although it has yet to be proven. We thought you should be aware of the fact before it is submitted. As for your late father's state of mind – Mr Berkeley also has a copy of a doctor's certificate which leaves no room for argument."

"I see! However, my uncle is no longer with us since he had that unfortunate accident. I take it that as his next of kin I will automatically inherit from him!"

It was a statement rather than a question.

"I'm afraid not, Mr Wisson. In your uncle's Will, which is also valid, his entire estate passes to his wife's nephew – Monsieur Digue – a Belgian. Perhaps you are acquainted with him?"

"No, I am not. Uncle Sigismund's wife died before I was born. My mother may have mentioned that she had a sister who was married to a Belgian, but I was unaware they'd had a son. As far as I recall, they lived in the Belgian Congo and the families were not in touch."

"I see! Well, Monsieur Digue now lives in Brussels. He will be coming to England once probate has been granted. He will no doubt wish to meet with you to discuss the hand-over of the factories."

Was there no way out of this intolerable situation? Why had Uncle Sigismund not told him of his intentions? At very least he could have told him he had a nephew even if it was only by marriage! Far more importantly, what had his father said to him that could have prompted Uncle Sigismund to leave such a windfall to a nephew he had, in all probability, never even met! And why, in the name of heaven, had he himself not realized that Uncle Sigismund's solicitor might keep a copy of his father's Will?

"This all seems very strange to me, Mr Berkeley. Perhaps you'd be good enough to explain why you didn't produce this second Will when my father died?"

"That is quite simply answered, Mr Wisson. For whatever the reason, Mr Wisniowiecki had not notified Mr Talbot here that he had made a second Will. I myself was unaware of your father's death until one of our clerk's read the notification. He recalled your father's somewhat unusual surname and brought the matter to my attention."

"Fortunately, before the matter of probate had gone very far!" Mr Talbot added.

Neither of those two smug-faced solicitors appeared in the least concerned that all his plans for the future had fallen apart; that he was now penniless – jobless. Not quite penniless, perhaps, because he'd saved most of the salary his father paid him and had invested it wisely; but he did not have the kind of capital he would need to go down to London and start his career as a financier. The sale of the factories was to have provided his start-up capital . . . No, he would not be so careless again! He would make it a golden rule to research every avenue before he committed himself.

It was not long after probate had been granted that the chance came to regain at least part of the start-up capital he needed. He was approached by a far-seeing property dealer who wanted to purchase his mother's house. The town had enlarged a great deal since the house had initially been bought, and the street was ripe for conversion for a shopping development. Anthony received an exceedingly tempting offer – one which fitted well with his own plans to remove to London.

The only snag was that the deeds were in his mother's name.

"This place is far too big for you now, Mother! It's expensive to run and we can't afford it. If you were to move into a smaller house, it would be better for you, and at the same time, I could do with the extra capital. It's economically absurd to have so much money tied up in a house you no longer need!"

There were the tears; the constant sentimental reminders of the memories of his father the house retained; the pathetic excuse that she was too old to start living in a new environment where she would be unfamiliar with the neighbours, the shops, the streets. If money was short, she would do without the maid; or he could sell some of her jewellery.

"You don't know what you are talking about. I can raise a thousand pounds for this house and you sit there suggesting a paltry saving on wages of a few shillings a week; a few pounds for those worthless baubles Father gave you! We may not get another offer like this one."

But neither pleas nor threats would move her. She had lost her husband and was not going to leave the home where they had spent nearly all their married life. It had so many happy memories! She loved the house – her home.

How he hated her – for her stubbornness, her sentimentality; her dogged refusal to accede to his needs.

At first, the hopeful buyer was prepared to wait until – as Anthony pointed out – he could get round his mother when her initial grief had lessened; but then another property in the same street was put up for sale and the man produced a deadline – the sale must go through in a month, or else the offer would be withdrawn. He had the necessary documents drawn up by his solicitor so that nothing more than Mrs Wisniowiecki's signature was required.

That signature was not forthcoming; and he, Anthony, was obliged to accept the fact that he was powerless to force his mother to make use of the pen he put in her hand. For a week after the sale had fallen through, he could not bring himself to speak to her. Each night when he returned from the factory, he sat at his desk, staring at the documents which could have meant such a necessary windfall.

It was then the idea occurred to him – he could still achieve his aims quite regardless of his mother's objections. If she were to die, as her beneficiary, the house would become his; then if it were to be burned down, he could not only claim the insurance money but he could sell the valuable site it stood on. Moreover, the two things could be accomplished simultaneously. It would have to be effected very carefully. Apart from his mother's demise, the penalties for arson with intention to defraud the insurance company would undoubtedly include a prison sentence. He decided, therefore, to make a last attempt to persuade his mother to sell. Although one buyer had called off the deal, there would surely be another, he told her. It was not too late for her to come to her senses and change her mind.

When she refused, he made his plans – a newspaper left too close to the fire by an absent-minded old woman who had gone to her bedroom for her customary after-lunch nap; a match to the paper and a dash back to his office to keep an appointment – five minutes would do it. By the time the room caught fire, he would have a cast-iron alibi.

It would have to be a Wednesday – the cook-general's half day off when she always visited her ailing sister. The fire must have time to take hold before his mother smelt smoke and called the fire brigade; a sleeping draught in her coffee would do the trick. Windows shut, curtains facing the street drawn, as was his mother's custom, to stop the sunlight fading the carpets and furnishings; and, in this instance, to prevent anyone in the street peering in and noticing the blaze. The house must be totally destroyed – beyond hope of repair; and his mother eliminated lest she revealed in her hysterical babble that he wanted to sell and she did not!

The plan seemed foolproof – but it was not. When the cook-general reached the station, she realized she had failed to put her money purse back into her handbag. With no alternative but to return to the house, she arrived in time to call the fire brigade. Although by then the damage done was extensive, his mother survived. For three days she was in hospital receiving treatment for smoke inhalation, but then . . . just when it seemed the police and insurance assessor were prepared to accept his explanation as to how the blaze had started, his worst fears were realized.

Would he ever forget her voice, rabbiting on?

"I should haf let my Antoni sell the house when he asked me . . . this *would neffer haf happened ... so silly I am and my boy is so cleffer ..."*

He needed every ounce of the brain she credited him with to answer the questions that followed from the increasingly hostile inquisitors. He was too clever to deny he'd wanted the sale to go through. Of course he had wanted it. Yes, he planned to go to London as soon as Monsieur Digue had found a new manager for the factories; and in his mother's state of health – and mind – she was incapable of running so large a place on her own. Didn't the accident prove it? The sale of the house would have been for her benefit, not his since the money from the sale would have been hers.

How could his interrogators know that he would have forced her to hand it over to him?

Nevertheless, the men were like terriers with a bone. Even though it was true that the sale of the property had fallen through, the insurance claim was none the less considerable, they pointed out. He, Anthony, was Mrs Wisniowiecki's only relative, was he not? In due course, he would inherit. And yes, they had checked his alibi but the distance between his home and his factory was such that he could have covered it after the fire had started. It was a warm day, so why were the windows shut? The curtains drawn? The police were called in.

In the end, they conceded that whilst he did indeed have a motive, not just for claiming the insurance, but for getting rid of his mother, they had no proof. For once he welcomed his mother's cloying adoration for she needed no prompting to declare on every occasion she was questioned that he was the most wonderful son any woman could hope to have! She had become hysterical when he'd told her – in front of his inquisitors, of course – that he was suspected of having started the fire himself in order to get rid of her! If they had hoped to use her as a witness for the prosecution in a case against him, those hopes were very quickly dashed.

There was only one moment when he felt any real fear, and that was when they raised the matter of his uncle's death. Accidental death, according to the coroner at the inquest; but they looked up the records and found that Anthony had been there on the platform with the old gentleman ... only a few feet away, one witness had said. The late Mr

Wisniowiecki had made his wife's brother his heir. Was there some reason why Mr Wisniowiecki had not mentioned his only son in his Will? What had caused him to change his mind?

They were near enough to the truth at that point for him to appreciate that they were not quite as stupid as he had first supposed. For the present, they were speculating, guessing. He decided not to give them cause to dislike him. He sympathized with their need in the circumstances to make such a very thorough investigation. It was their duty to do so and therefore he was willing to put up with the constant questioning. He regretted it only out of concern for the distress this inquisition was having on his poor mother. She had suffered a very severe shock on top of the shock of her husband's death, and to see her home in such a horrific state was adding to her distress. He would be grateful, therefore, if they would conclude their enquiries as quickly as possible for her sake, so that he could move her to new, permanent quarters where she might be able to settle down and make a fresh start. This was his only concern, and one he hoped very much they would appreciate.

Within the month, the insurance claim was paid in full both for the building and its damaged contents. He promptly booked his mother into a Home for Retired Gentlewomen as far away from London as he could find. She made no demur and left every decision to him, asking only that he came to visit her as often as he possibly could until he had made a home for himself in London where she could join him. She allowed him to persuade her to sign a power of attorney so that "he could more easily manage the financial complications resulting from the disastrous fire".

With the house duly demolished and the site satisfactorily sold to the same property prospector who had first approached him, he removed himself to London. Using his power of attorney he arranged for the annuity his father had left her to be paid direct to him. As it exceeded the monthly bills of the home she was in, it was only a minor irritation knowing that she must be supported until she died a natural death. A further "accident" would, he realized, be stretching his luck too far. By telling those he met in his new life that she was already dead, he had no reason to fear that the past would be revived. He had, he believed, put it behind him for ever.

It was unfortunate, he thought now, that after all these years Zandra had discovered his mother's existence; but from the sound of it, the old lady had said nothing untoward to arouse Zandra's suspicions. He would allay any lingering doubts once and for all.

"You really must not assume that all families are as close-knit as your own, my dear!" he said in a tone of gentle rebuke. "And do stop pacing the floor and sit down. I've no doubt you find this hard to understand, but parents can be extremely possessive," he continued. "You saw for yourself how . . . how my mother felt about me. If I had brought her here to live with us, we'd never have had a moment's peace. Before she became ill, she was a very demanding woman and she would have tried to rule your life as well as mine."

Zandra looked at her husband's impassive face and wondered whether, after all, she was justified in condemning him. It was true that she had not known Mrs Wisniowiecki before her illness. Anthony had never made any attempt to hide the fact that he was – and always had been – an ambitious man; that success was all important to him. She could understand in a way why he had not wanted a clinging, possessive, lonely old lady in the background of his life. But . . .

"Couldn't you just have visited her from time to time instead of telling her all those lies? She believed you couldn't afford the journey . . . and that's awful, Anthony. She didn't even know what a success you have made! Or that you had married! She could have come to our wedding!"

Anthony's eyes narrowed and his mouth tightened as he said: "I have had a long, exhausting journey on top of a very exacting business trip to the States, and I really do not wish to be harangued by my wife on my return. My mother is dead, Zandra, and beyond your care or, indeed, mine. Moreover, this is simply none of your business. Now I have a great deal of paperwork to catch up on, and I'd prefer that you do not mention my mother again. Is that understood?"

For several seconds, Zandra did not reply. Then she said coldly: "I heard what you said, Anthony, but if I live to be a hundred, I don't think I will ever understand how you could leave the country when you knew your own mother was dying; or without at least saying goodbye to her first."

When he did not reply, her hand went to her pocket and closed over Mrs Wisniowiecki's small gold brooch which she had intended to show him. Now, fearing that even his gaze might debase it, she knew that like so much else that mattered to her in her life, this keepsake could never be shared with him.

Part 3

1939–1944

Chapter 22

"I expect you could do with a drink before anything else, eh, Bristow?" Pelham remarked with a smile as he helped Zandra out of the front seat of his bottle-green Delage. He'd had the roof down during the four-kilometre drive from the railway station at Pau, and the June sun in this southern part of France was at its fiercest. Moreover, passing carts and wagons as well as the occasional car had thrown up clouds of dust which mingled with the heavy scent of the wild lavender growing by the roadside.

Two of the Casa Montijo servants emerged from the large whitewashed stone house to greet Guy and Zandra, and take their luggage from the car.

Silvie came out on to the terrace and hurried forward to envelop Zandra in her arms.

"I am so pleased you could come, *chérie!*" she said kissing her on both cheeks. "And you, too, Guy!" she added with genuine warmth in her voice. "I'm sure I do not have to tell you that my *grand garçon* here has been greatly looking forward to playing some golf with you!"

As they walked back into the house, she gave a mock sigh.

"I sometimes wonder if this husband of mine will ever come to

327

terms with the fact that he is in his late sixties and should expend less energy. A round of golf in this heat is not good for him, but he pays me no attention when I tell him."

"And you, my dearest, do not exactly set me a good example driving every day to Pau to entertain your grandchildren!"

As Silvie led the way into the *salon* where the shutters were closed against the June sunshine and the atmosphere was refreshingly cool, Zandra said anxiously: "How is Alice, Tante Silvie? Is she no better?"

Silvie's face clouded and her still-beautiful almond-shaped eyes narrowed as she replied: "I have now called in two different specialists to see her but it seems as if there is nothing they can do. They say it is a matter of time and will-power. She must accept that grief will not bring her child back and that life must continue – if not for her sake then for that of her husband and the other children."

There was a large glass jug of *jus de citron* on the table beside her which she now poured out.

"I rather think Bristow and I could do with something a little stronger, my dear!" Pelham said with a surreptitious wink at Guy. "We'll leave you to discuss Alice's problems and join you presently."

As he conducted Guy through to the library, Silvie drew a long sigh.

"Your uncle has been very patient, but I fear he doesn't fully understand the situation!" she said. "One should not, perhaps, expect it of a man, and to be honest, Zee-Zee, I am not sure if I altogether understand Alice myself. Other women have had babies prematurely who have died without succumbing to their grief. Your Aunt Willow told me you yourself were remarkably brave, *chérie*, when the same thing happened to you – and it is not as if Alice is without children. She has Claudette, Brigitte and Henri – yet she remains all day in her bed, day after day, refusing to eat more than a morsel, and all the time weeping. I have to say, I don't wonder that Claude is becoming impatient with her. It is six weeks now since it happened – and really, they cannot afford to go on employing the girl who takes care of *les petits*! Naturally, I pay the bills, but although Claude is well aware that the expense is nothing to me, he is a proud little man and dislikes being so obviously beholden!"

Zandra took a second long gulp of the ice-cool lemon juice, and with an edge of bitterness in her voice, said: "I have always suspected that Monsieur Calonne did not marry Alice for love but for her money! Or for the advantages that her relationship with you could bring to the marriage. Perhaps Alice has discovered that he doesn't love her, and for that reason rather than for the lost baby, she can't find the will to get better!"

"Whatever the reason, *chérie*, it cannot continue in this fashion. The children are becoming quite nervous. Little Henri is now wetting his bed at night, Brigitte bursts into tears at the slightest mishap, and Claudette, poor child, asks me every five minutes why her mother remains in bed and cries when she sees them. That is why I wrote and asked you to come. It is not so many years since you lost your baby, and I thought perhaps you could help Alice by your own example. Anthony made no difficulty about you coming?"

"No, Tante Silvie! I had expected that he might, since it is only eight months since I last visited you! There must have been so many times when your ears burned because every time Guy and I talk on the telephone, we say how grateful we are to you and Uncle Pelham for making these holidays possible. I don't know what we would have done these past two years if we'd not been able to spend these weeks with you. Guy is certain that Anthony is still having him watched, and although I think I might be weak enough to take the risk of meeting Guy somewhere in England, he is the strong one and won't allow it. He's such a wonderful person, Tante Silvie! What other man would deny himself the chance of a happy marriage and children for no more than a few weeks a year with a married woman who can never give him a home, a family? I feel so guilty sometimes!"

"Then you should not!" Silvie said firmly. "Guy knows very well that you are sacrificing your own happiness – even more than his – to protect your family. He is not tied to you except of his own free will. If he wanted another woman, then I'm sure you would never stand in his way. But that is not the case, is it? You are not afraid that Guy is growing tired of the *status quo*?"

"Oh no, Tante Silvie! At least, he has given no indication of it. I'm the one who wonders how long this can last. I lie in bed at night and turn over in my mind ways to get out of my marriage without harming Lucy, Alexis, Robin, Eve, Aunt Willow. I imagine going to the police, begging them for confidentiality if I name a blackmailer to them. Blackmail is a crime and they could imprison Anthony, and then Guy and I could . . . But it wouldn't work. There would have to be a trial and Anthony wouldn't hesitate to ensure all the horrid details became known. Last Christmas, I plucked up the courage to beg him yet again to let me go. He just laughed and told me his solicitor held a sealed letter he had written to the editor of one of the daily newspapers, and that if anything untoward happened, he had only to make a telephone call to his solicitor for it to be posted. He has anticipated my calling his bluff – except that it is not a bluff!"

Silvie frowned thoughtfully.

"Don't answer this if you would rather not, *chérie*, but does Anthony still insist upon sharing your bed?"

Zandra nodded.

"From time to time – though less frequently, thank heaven. I have taught myself to endure it. As for him – I think it means no more than the satisfaction of a momentary appetite; and of course, he gets pleasure from knowing that he has the power to do as he wishes with me. That's one of the reasons I never try now to resist him. At least he has no need to use physical force to obtain his objective!"

Silvie shuddered.

"That is no way for you to live, my poor child. You are very brave!"

Zandra attempted a smile.

"I'm not sure I could be so 'brave' were it not for the fact that I have Guy. We do talk often on the telephone, and we have these few precious weeks together – thanks to you and Uncle Pelham. In between our meetings, we live on our memories. We love each other so much, and Guy is wonderful to me. I tell myself I shouldn't complain because some women live their whole lives without ever knowing what real love is. Then I realize how fortunate I am!"

"*Chérie*, please let me tell Alexis, or you tell him. He has a great deal of influence. Perhaps he can do something—"

"No!" Zandra broke in. "It's no good, Tante Silvie. You don't know Anthony as I do. He's so devious."

There were tears in Silvie's eyes as she stood up to embrace her niece.

"I am far from certain if Lucy, or indeed Alexis, would agree to you protecting them in this way. However, that is a decision only you can make, *chérie*; and now we must stop wasting the precious time you have with your handsome Guy in talking of such things. You must go and find him. We shall not dine until nine o'clock, so you have time to be alone together. You are in your usual rooms."

With her customary thoughtfulness, Silvie had allocated them the two communicating guest bedrooms at the far end of the landing. As she accompanied Zandra and Guy upstairs, she slipped the key of the communicating door into Zandra's hand. It was kept locked as a precaution in the daytime in order to prevent the servants gossiping. Some of them returned to Paris when Pelham and she moved back to the capital for any length of time, and were well aware that Anthony, not Guy, was Zandra's husband.

As Silvie closed the door into the passage behind her and rejoined Pelham downstairs, Zandra hurried through into Guy's room to see if he had come upstairs. He was standing by his unpacked suitcases waiting for her.

Without a word, he opened his arms and she ran into them

and buried her face against his chest. He held her silently for several minutes before he led her to the big, beautifully carved, wooden bedstead and, drawing her down beside him, took her face in his hands and kissed her gently. Last night during the long train journey from Paris, he had made love to her in the cramped couchette with a furious passion to which she had become accustomed now as necessary to him after a long period of separation. Once the urgency of his need for her was satisfied, he was invariably gentle, adoring, considerate – wanting only her pleasure in their love-making. He had flown to Paris the day before Zandra, leaving word with the porter at the block of flats where he lived that he was off to Switzerland for a walking holiday in the mountains.

Although he wondered sometimes if such elaborate precautions to cover his movements were really necessary, from time to time he was convinced that Wisson was still having him watched. He knew through his associations with the City that Wisson was now an incredibly wealthy man and that the cost of a private investigator would be immaterial to him. As a result, he dared not take the risk that his trips abroad with Zandra were discovered. He hated this clandestine element of their affair and worried endlessly about the consequences for her and her family should they be exposed. For himself, he would willingly have allowed Wisson to do his worst, whatever that might be. It was doubtful if his partners would worry were he to be taken to court and sued by Wisson for alienating his wife's affections! But even if he lost his job, it would be a small price to pay for Zandra to obtain her divorce. He wished desperately that such an option was available to them.

Unfortunately, it was not he but the Rochford family who would pay the price of his indiscretions were they to become known to Wisson. He tried not to think about the life Zandra led as wife to another man – and such a man! When he thought of Wisson's physical abuse of her – something they never now discussed – he was aware that extreme though it sounded, he

332

would happily kill the man were he able to do so without repercussions for Zandra. In his heart, he knew that emotionally, she belonged utterly to him; that she loved him as deeply and enduringly as he loved her. Nevertheless, the thought of her stripped naked in Wisson's arms was torture to him and he was filled with a wild, primitive anger and hatred which he tried and, for the most part, succeeded in hiding from her.

At least he had been able to wangle an extra fortnight's holiday from his firm, and once again Madame Rochford and her husband had offered them sanctuary. He knew that Madame Rochford was deeply sympathetic to their situation and suspected that Zandra's uncle was similarly so; but in typically English fashion Mr Rochford avoided any reference to the subject and Wisson's name was never mentioned unless it were by Zandra. He, Guy, had grown to like the older man; to admire his good-humoured enthusiasm for life and his straightforward manner. Rochford was popular with his French and English friends and much respected by his servants. Guy knew him to be a good companion on the tennis court and golf course where they planned to spend the time whilst Zandra did what she could to help Alice out of her depression.

Guy had met Alice on his two previous visits to Pau and had found her both dull and somewhat unattractive. It had surprised him to find her three children so endearing, bearing in mind how unremarkable their parents were. Claude Calonne seemed devoid of a sense of humour and was irritatingly ingratiating. The children, however, were well-mannered and touchingly eager to be noticed.

On previous visits, he and Zandra had taken them off for outings, and it had astonished both him and Zandra how voluble and entertaining they were when not in the presence of their parents. Calonne ruled them with a rod of iron and Alice – ever dominated by her husband – upheld his many disciplinary rules and regulations, all required to quell their natural exuberance. Quite apart from the pleasure he, Guy, derived from Zandra's praise of his own management of them, he had enjoyed the expeditions they planned for them. Sitting at a café table with Zandra and the little ones, he could almost imagine that he and Zandra were like any normal married couple with children of their own.

Now, shafts of sunlight penetrated the half-closed shutters and striped Zandra's naked body with golden bands. Staring down at her in the aftermath of their love-making, Guy wondered if he would ever cease to be enraptured by her beauty. When they met on these all-too-rare occasions, it was as if he were discovering her for the first time, and his emotions were so extreme that he found difficulty giving them expression. Of one thing he was certain, he would never love another woman as he loved her; nor could he imagine ever wanting another woman. Sometimes as he made his way to work or glimpsed a pretty girl in a restaurant, he'd felt a fleeting basic instant of desire. Occasionally, he invited an attractive, available girl to a day at the races, a dance or the theatre. But he could not bring himself to pursue such relationships knowing that they could never ripen into love.

"I suppose we shall have to get dressed and go down to dinner soon!" Zandra murmured beside him. Her arm lay across his chest and she was idly twisting the sparse gold hairs as she spoke. "Are you hungry, darling?"

"Only for you!" Guy answered, turning to draw her body closer to him. He saw her eyes widen in a smile as she caught his meaning and reluctantly drew away from him.

"We can't, Guy. There isn't time!" she whispered. "You'll just have to wait until we go to bed."

Guy gave a mock sigh of protest.

"If I know your aunt, there will be at least five courses for dinner. I want you now . . . this very minute!"

He closed one hand over her breast and felt her nipple harden in response.

"Admit it! You want me, too, don't you?"

Zandra tore herself free and sprang off the bed, laughing.

"Yes, and you know it, you horrible man. If I didn't love you so much, I'd hate you!"

"And there's female logic for you!" Guy said as he lay back against the pillows, his arms now behind his head as he watched her cross the room towards the bathroom. "Do you realize I may not want you later?"

"Then I'll have to go without!" Zandra called back. "It would be a pity though because I shall certainly want you!"

Guy jumped off the bed and chased her into the bathroom. As she bent to turn on the taps, he leant over and pressed his body against her back. She straightened herself and turned to put her arms round him, drawing his face towards her and kissing him passionately on the mouth.

"I love you so much!" she murmured. "I still can't believe it, Guy – two whole weeks! I wish we could spend every minute together. I can't bear to waste a single one."

"Hopefully your time with Alice will not be wasted, darling," Guy said quickly. "And we both owe her something. But for her, you wouldn't have had the excuse to come down to your aunt's again so soon after the last visit."

"Oh God – the bath!" Zandra cried as she bent quickly to turn off the taps. "Another inch and Tante Silvie wouldn't invite us again."

"Don't even think about it!" Guy said, "and hurry up and get in before I beat you to it!"

They were like happy, carefree children as they raced one another into the water and fought to be first to find the soap.

Despite the thirty-odd years Pelham had lived in France, he still insisted on a cooked English breakfast, and although Zandra confined herself to the coffee and *croissants* Silvie enjoyed, Guy was happy to emulate his host. Throughout the meal, Pelham plied him with questions.

"Surely even Chamberlain can't still believe that the treaty with Hitler is worth the paper it was written on? Dash it all, Bristow, the painter fellow's gone back on his word already! He walks into Austria last year, occupies Czechoslovakia six months later, and is arming himself to the teeth whilst Chamberlain spouts: 'Peace in Our Time'!"

"I know, sir, but Parliament *has* agreed to conscription. It begins next month."

Pelham snorted as he chopped the top off his second boiled egg.

"Whilst the King and Queen go swanning off to Canada as if there were no crisis!" he expostulated.

"I heard from a friend in England that a lot of Jewish people are arriving there seeking refuge, with dreadful stories of the anti-Semitic demonstrations in Germany," Silvie said. "Do you think they can be true, Guy?"

"The general opinion seems to be that the stories are grossly exaggerated, Madame Rochford, but I suppose it's true that there's no smoke without fire. I'm afraid I'm not very politically informed. I've joined the Territorials so if war does come, I'll be ready to do my bit."

"Another war – so soon after the last!" Silvie murmured. "*Ce n'est pas possible!* You children are too young to remember . . . all those lives lost – and for what? So, you are a soldier, Guy?"

"Well, with my eyesight, I couldn't get into the Royal Air Force like Oliver and Jamie. With their flying experience, they walked in. Giles and Robin will be joining up next year."

"But they are still only schoolboys!" Silvie protested.

"Conscription is for everyone from eighteen to forty!" Guy said gently.

"How do you know all this?" Zandra's voice was unnaturally sharp. Guy looked across the table, his expression apologetic.

"Your cousin Oliver told me. I ran into him at the Eton 4 June cricket match."

"Why wasn't I told about Jamie?" Zandra demanded. "Why didn't you tell me, Guy?"

"Because you women always start imagining the worst, no doubt!" Pelham broke in. "Conscription is merely a precaution – and quite right, too. Frankly, I think we should have taken a firm stand against Adolf Hitler last year before he annexed Austria and we sold the wretched Czechs down the river."

Silvie reached for the big silver coffee pot, her hands trembling.

"What is the matter with the world?" she said. "They have only just stopped fighting in Spain!"

"Leaving that Fascist, Franco, firmly in control!" Pelham said succinctly. "Well, we shall just have to wait and see. At least that fellow Churchill seems to have got his wits about him even if Chamberlain still has his head in the sand."

"Finish your breakfast, *chérie*!" Silvie said, aware that Zandra was still shocked by the information Guy had imparted. "I promised the children we would arrive early this morning, so we mustn't be late."

"You can drop the two of us at the golf course, my dear!" Pelham said. "We can have a spot of lunch there and you can pick us up on your way home."

It was not until the two men had left the car and Silvie was alone with Zandra on their way to Alice's house, that she broached the subject of war again.

"I did not want to mention Anthony in front of Guy," she said, "but I wanted to ask you, Zee-Zee, surely your husband must know more than Guy or your uncle about such things? Arms are his business, are they not?"

Zandra drew a deep breath.

"He never discusses business with me, Tante Silvie – in fact, he is quite absurdly reticent about every aspect of it. Sometimes, I'm unaware which foreign potentate I have at my dinner table! Yes, he made me travel with him to Italy, and last year, to Czechoslovakia and Lithuania; but I don't speak the languages and when I meet any of Anthony's associates, they address me in English on subjects such as the weather in England, or if I like their food, or some other such inanity. I sometimes think Anthony must have

337

told them that I am mentally deficient in some way! No, I don't know what he does or why he does it or who he does it with. All I know is that he has been amassing a great deal of money. He no longer keeps a check on my housekeeping expenses and I am permitted to charge whatever I please to all the accounts he has opened for me. Ollie says he has poured money into Sky-Ways and the business is flourishing. As for me, Anthony now buys me jewellery that I imagine costs him a small fortune. He keeps it in a safe, to which he alone has the key, of course, and only produces it when I am going somewhere where I shall be noticed along with the jewellery. They are not gifts to me, Tante Silvie, but adornments to enhance one of his possessions."

At the bitter tone of Zandra's voice, Silvie reached out and took her hand.

"Then we will not talk more of that horrible man again!" she said. "We will speak of your charming *amour* with whom I might well fall in love myself were I your age! So handsome! So *gentil*!"

Zandra smiled.

"I think Guy's very well aware you like him, and that's why he flirts with you!" she said. "I could be jealous, Tante Silvie. You are still a very beautiful woman!"

"But, *chérie*, he has eyes only for you. I doubt if the Queen of Sheba could tempt him away from you, let alone an ancient old French lady like me!"

Their chauffeur – an olive-skinned Basque by the name of Pierre – drew up outside Alice's house where her three children were standing by the gate, waving excitedly. As the two women emerged from the car, the eldest child, Claudette, opened the gate and threw herself into her great-aunt's arms. The three children were dressed identically, even the little boy in a white pinafore. The girls' hair hung in plaits which had been tied with blue ribbons to match their floral summer dresses. They stood now suddenly shy as Zandra bent down to greet them.

"Claudette, how you've grown – and you, too, Henri! And you've lost a tooth, Brigitte! Let's see, how old are you now?"

The small boy hid behind his elder sister's skirt and it was she who replied to Zandra.

"I am six, Brigitte is five, and Henri is three!"

Her English, though accented, was faultless and – but for their French-styled pinafores – they would have passed unnoticed amongst a group of English children. Silvie told them that she would take them with their *bonne* to the local park to see the ducks and swans, an arrangement that would leave Zandra and Alice alone together.

As soon as the small party departed, Zandra made her way upstairs to Alice's bedroom. The shutters were closed and the room was swelteringly hot and in semi-darkness. Alice lay on her back against a mound of pillows and, as Zandra approached the bed, tears filled her eyes and rolled down her sallow cheeks.

Zandra wiped them away and took one of the inert hands in hers. She was shocked by Alice's loss of weight. When she had last seen her cousin the previous autumn, Alice had been grossly overweight and as a consequence, had looked nearer forty-five than thirty-five.

"Tante Silvie has been very worried about you, Alice," she said gently. "We all have, especially Aunt Willow. As your mother, she felt she should have been with you these past unhappy weeks, but she is really not well enough to travel; so I have come in her place."

Fresh tears welled from Alice's blue eyes but she made no reply.

"Believe me, dearest, I do understand how desolate you are feeling," Zandra continued, "but you are not going to get better shutting yourself away from everyone like this. I do know from my own experience that it helps if you can keep busy and active. You know, dearest, I don't think Aunt Willow will ever cease to mourn for Uncle Toby but even she, at her age, has realized that she has to go on living despite her ill health. And she has shown such courage. It is not as if she had children to distract her as you have. And they are such pretty, charming children, Alice! They are a real credit to you. Tante Silvie adores them – and Guy, who has come with me, can't wait to see them."

It was quite some time before Zandra felt that Alice was actually listening to her words, and she made no objection when Zandra pushed open the wooden shutters to allow some fresh air and sunlight into the room. Immediately it gave a less gloomy and depressing aspect. When Alice did speak, however, it was not about the lost baby.

"Claude does not understand!" she said in a small hopeless voice. "He says I am stupid" – she gulped and continued – "he says I should pull myself together. But I can't, Zee-Zee, I can't!"

She burst into a fresh storm of weeping.

Zandra gathered her into her arms and rocked her.

"It is not the same for a man!" she said gently. "Claude never knew that baby as you did. You carried it for six months and grew to love it; to look forward to the birth. You mustn't mind about Claude. You have Claudette and Brigitte and little Henri to comfort you." Despite herself, Zandra's voice held a wistful note as it crossed her mind that there would never be another child for her. "And you are still young enough to have another baby, if that is what you wanted, Alice. Please, dearest, try to come to terms with your loss. This grieving won't bring your baby back to life any more than my tears could bring little Rupert back to me. You must put the past behind you – or at least try to do so."

Zandra felt as if she might be reaching Alice through her curtain of tears which had momentarily dried, but as her cousin reached out to the bed table to take a drink of orange juice at Zandra's insistence, the glass tipped. As the orange liquid spread in a bright stain over the white quilt, Alice broke into a fresh storm of weeping; and when Silvie returned at lunch-time, Zandra was obliged to admit that the task of "reclaiming" Alice was not going to be a quick or easy one.

"I may have to stay longer, Guy," she said later when they were once more alone together at the Casa Montijo. "When I spoke to Alice's doctor this afternoon, he told me that he'd once had another patient with a similar extreme form of depression. He

340

has prescribed tonics and plenty of nourishing foods, but Alice barely touched her lunch tray."

"And Calonne . . . how is he bearing up?" Guy enquired. He gave a sudden grin as he added: "I don't think your Uncle Pelham is too keen on the fellow."

Zandra laughed.

"I don't think Uncle Pelham is keen on anyone who doesn't enjoy any sporting activities!" she said. "He does so remind me of Oliver! I think the most damaging thing he could find to say about anyone was that they were 'a rotten sport'!"

"Well, Alice seemed keen enough to marry an arty type!" Guy reminded her as he pulled on a clean white shirt and tied a navy-and-white cravat at his neck. He turned back to Zandra and in a sudden change of tone, said: "You look so beautiful, my darling. When this fortnight comes to an end, how am I ever going to leave you?"

She hurried towards him and wound her arms around his neck.

"Don't think about it! And anyway, I love you!" Her eyes clouded. "Guy, what you were saying at breakfast this morning – if there is going to be a war, will you be called up at once? Would you have to go away? Abroad?"

Guy's arms tightened around her.

"In the first place, there may never be a war but if there were – well, I suppose I would be wanted fairly quickly because of my Territorial training; but we'd be given embarkation leave if we were to be posted overseas, so you needn't worry that I'd just disappear without warning!"

For a moment, Zandra did not answer, then she said: "But you could be killed, Guy – like my two uncles and my cousin Philip and lots of our family servants and friends who were in the last war. Or you could be wounded. I can still remember some of those soldiers in the wards at Rochford when it was a convalescent home – seeing those poor men who'd been gassed or blinded – and the ones who'd had legs or arms amputated. One of them, a

Private Humphries, was my special friend and I was terribly upset when he died. Oh, Guy, I couldn't bear it if . . . if—"

Guy put his hand gently but firmly over her lips.

"Zandra, none of this may happen, and I'm not going to allow you to worry about an unlikely possibility. As Madame Rochford said, it is surely unlikely the King and Queen would go off to Canada if we were on the brink of war! Now I'm sure it's time we joined your aunt and uncle for tea. We don't want them imagining we spend every spare moment we have in bed, do we?"

"I don't know if that would bother me very much!" Zandra said as he kissed her before linking his arm through hers.

Nor me, Guy thought as he led her to the door; but his remark had served its purpose and brought a smile back to Zandra's face – a smile he knew would not be there if he'd confessed that, like Pelham, he believed it was only a matter of time before England would be at war.

Chapter 23

May–June 1940

"I have spoken to all the servants and they understand that there is to be no mention to Mother of poor Hugh Conway's death. She worries enough already, poor darling."

Jane nodded, glad that her sister-in-law, Lucy Zemski, had made the decision for her. Lucy was such a dependable person, and a tower of strength to the whole family. Even in the sombre green-grey uniform of the Women's Voluntary Service, she was a remarkably beautiful, very feminine-looking woman who seemed to be able to work miracles in these chaotic wartime conditions. She was on the Central Committee at the London headquarters, and with her social contacts and her indomitable spirit and energy, there seemed little she could not achieve when organization was needed.

Jane herself was in the local branch of the WVS where, Lucy had suggested, she could help the war effort and still be able to take care of Willow. Willow, though not yet in her seventies, was now a semi-invalid. She had never really recovered from the shock of Toby's death, and since the outbreak of war in September last year, she had retreated even further into spells of unreality. It was as if by doing so, she could ignore the dangers threatening so many members of her family now that the country had been plunged into another world war in her lifetime.

In a way, Jane could understand why her mother-in-law found relief in this manner. She herself lived in daily anxiety for her darling Oliver who, at the outbreak of hostilities, had immediately rejoined the Air Force. Every pilot in the country was needed to help support the British Expeditionary Force, and although he was ostensibly training younger men, she feared that as the German troops continued their uninterrupted drive towards the French coast and defeat for the Allied armies looked a strong possibility, he might soon be in action himself. There were simply not enough planes or pilots to cope with the situation, he had told her. The Germans, with their superior forces, had taken Norway and swept through Holland, Belgium and Luxemburg. The Allies could do little but retreat before the quick, determined advance of Hitler's élite panzer divisions. The *Luftwaffe*, with its Junkers, Messerschmitt 109s, Focke-Wulfs, Stukas and Heinkels had experienced pilots whereas most of the British pilots were perforce thrown into the mêlée after only a few weeks' training and had no experience at all of aerial combat. The Allies were losing far too many planes and pilots, Oliver had told her, and the factories, unprepared for war, could not produce replacement planes fast enough.

Not only did Jane have her husband to worry about but their only son, Giles, eighteen the previous month, had insisted upon following in his father's footsteps and was now in training.

It must be even worse for her elderly mother-in-law, Jane reflected. She had already lived through one war, only to be facing another with her two grandsons and her adored son at risk; and to make matters worse, although Zandra had returned safely from Pau, she was determined to join the newly formed Air Transport Auxiliary service. Formed at the outbreak of war, it consisted of a pool of civilian pilots who relieved the RAF by transporting dispatches, mail, news, medical supplies, civil authorities and ambulance cases by light aeroplane.

So far the pilots were mainly men with the exception of one or two women who were not allowed to fly overseas. Meanwhile, Zandra was helping to train as yet unqualified pilots at Sky-Ways, one of the many flying clubs now subsidized by the Government under the scheme called the Civil Air Guard. Willow had never ceased to consider it dangerous simply to be airborne; and Jane knew that she feared continuously for the safety of her favourite niece who nowadays seldom had time to stay at Rochford.

Jane's thoughts returned to Lucy's comment. Lucy was right to suggest that Hugh's death should be kept from her mother-in-law. Willow had grown fond of Hugh during his brief engagement to Zandra, and since his marriage to Katherine Rose, they had become frequent visitors to Rochford. Willow's English grandchildren were almost grown-up and the Conway twins made up for the fact that she never saw Alice's little ones. Willow would be devastated were she to know that Hugh had perished, along with all but thirty-eight of the crew of the destroyer HMS *Glowworm*, when it had been sunk by a German cruiser off the coast of Norway. Over two hundred and fifty men had died, Hugh amongst them. The thought of so many dead appalled Jane whose nature was such that she could not bring herself to kill even a wasp!

"I asked Alexis if he could find out what was happening in France to Guy's regiment," Lucy said. She walked over to the window to glance out across the lawn as if, by looking south-wards, she might see over the Channel to the French coast. "He says it's such a complete shambles out there with all our forces in retreat, that no one seems to know where anyone is! My poor, darling Zee-Zee. She hasn't seen Guy since his embarkation leave. Thank heaven Anthony was in the United States that week and she could spend every precious day with Guy. You know, Jane, I have never understood why she doesn't get a divorce. It's not as if it's such a scandal these days. Alexis told me not to inter-fere and has forbidden me to discuss the matter with Zee-Zee. He says she's probably trying to protect the family from a lot of unpleasant gossip; but I don't think Mother would be too upset by a divorce, and what do the rest of us care? It seems such a terrible waste of Zee-Zee's life – and Guy's. I've never seen two people more in love. He absolutely adores her."

"Perhaps she feels she owes it to Anthony to stay with him!" Jane suggested. "He *did* save Rochford for us – and Sky-Ways. I can't say I have ever really liked him much but he is very good to Zee-Zee . . . generous, I mean. She has everything in the world she wants."

"Except Guy! And children. I don't think Anthony wants children although Zee-Zee has never said as much."

"Well, he's been a wonderful 'boss' for Oliver, and look how good he is the way he's managing everything here at Rochford now Oliver isn't at home to see to the estate! Mother depends on Anthony a great deal – in fact, we all do."

Lucy turned back from the window with a sigh.

"I suppose we should be grateful to him for pulling strings to keep Inge out of that horrible internment camp. It's interesting, isn't it, how anti-German she has become since she married Jamie. I can remember when he first brought her back from Munich how she idolized Adolf Hitler!"

Jane smiled.

"That was a long time ago, Lucy, and she was very young! You must ask her to take you down to her studio to see some of the sculptures she has done. She's really very talented! And modest! No one is allowed on pain of death to see one of her models until it's finished and then she will only show it reluctantly; and we are not permitted to put them on display."

"Artistic temperament, I suppose!" Lucy said with an answering smile. "Anyway, Jamie still dotes on her; and from what I've seen of the two together – which isn't much, I'll grant – she seems devoted to him, even if she is a bit bossy!"

Jane sighed.

"It can't be easy being an 'alien' and I feel sorry for Inge. She's being cold-shouldered in the village by some of the shopkeepers;

and with Jamie in the RAF now, she really only has me as a companion – no one of her own age."

"I'll ask Eve to invite her up to London when she's next home on leave," Lucy said. "She rang me the other night and sent her love to you all. I gather she's thoroughly enjoying her life in the WAAF although she says there isn't much work for her to do. She can't tell us what she is doing because it's all very hush-hush and she even had to sign the Official Secrets Act! She shares a billet with some other girls down near Bath and says the country-side is beautiful."

"It would be lovely here if it wasn't for this horrible war!" Jane said wistfully. "The house seems so empty with everyone gone. I was wondering whether we shouldn't try and turn it back into a convalescent home, but Anthony thinks it would be too disturbing for Mother. It's a pity we couldn't take in those evacuees from London but I suppose the powers-that-be were right to consider we are too far from the village school for it to be practical."

Lucy nodded. She herself had helped to organize the evacuation of thousands of children from London at the outbreak of war. "The ones you were to have had have gone to the Barratts," she told Jane, "but if France is overrun, those poor children will have to be moved again since it's pretty obvious we shall be the next country to be invaded."

Jane shivered.

"It frightens me just to think about it. Oliver said we'll never give in. For one thing, Winston Churchill won't let us!"

"I was sitting in on a WVS conference last week about the chil-dren," Lucy said frowning. "With the war news so bad, we must get more of them out of London. One and a half million have gone so far but if, God forbid, we are pushed out of France, London will certainly be the next *Luftwaffe* target."

Jane shuddered.

"I don't know how you can speak so calmly about it, Lucy! You're so much braver than I am."

"Nonsense, Jane! You'll be surprised what you can do when you have to. I found that out when I nursed in a front-line hospital in France in the last war. Nothing could ever be as horrific as that. The only way to cope was to face each day as it came. Besides, my dear, it's easier for me to be calm now because I have Alexis home every night and he's always so reassuring, whereas you have the job of bolstering Mother's spirits the way Alexis does mine – and she is such a worrier!"

Jane smiled.

"That's for sure, Lucy. I don't think she slept a single night through after war was declared, worrying whether Zee-Zee would get home from Tante Silvie's. Then, when Zee-Zee did arrive, Mother started worrying about Uncle Pelham and Tante Silvie, and I don't know how many letters she wrote begging them to come back to England! Uncle Pelham won't consider it on the grounds that at their age, they would only be a liability. It's odd, really, but Mother never seems to worry about Alice. I don't think she ever loved her in quite the same way as she loves Oliver – or even Zee-Zee, who isn't her own daughter. One forgets she's only Mother's niece by marriage, and that there's no blood tie!"

"I suppose there's no need to worry about Alice any more now that she has fully recovered. Once she knew Claude wasn't fit for active service, she has been hoping to have another baby! You'd think three was quite enough, wouldn't you? Especially in wartime."

"It would probably be the best thing for her!" Jane said in her gentle way.

Lucy sighed.

"You're so much more charitable than I am, Jane. I get impatient with stupid people, and poor Alice was never very bright, was she?" She glanced at the small diamond watch on her wrist. "I really must be on my way. Mother should be awake by now so I'll pop up and say goodbye to her. My train goes at four-thirty and I want to be home before Alexis gets back. He promised he'd try to be early tonight. He's been so busy I'm often asleep before he comes home. I'll try to come down next week, Jane. Be sure to watch the post, won't you, and open any letter that you think might contain news of Hugh. And don't let Mother see the newspapers – or if she insists, censor them first. She may remember that Hugh was on the *Glowworm*."

As the taxi drove her away from the house, Lucy glanced back over her shoulder at Rochford Manor. It looked, as always, beautiful in the spring sunshine. Scarlet tulips lined the long gravel drive and the rhododendrons bordering it were breaking into flower. Poor Jane, she thought, alone with Mother in that great big mansion which had once been so full of life! Now she had only Inge, the dogs and the few remaining servants who had not yet been called up for company.

It was a slim hope that the war would be over soon, Lucy knew now. Although Alexis never spoke about his work in MI6, at her insistence he did discuss the progress of the war, and she knew that whilst the newspapers were encouraging the population to believe that the Allies were holding back the Germans, he was of the opinion that it was only a matter of time before France fell. He did not play down the threat of invasion and applauded the Government issue of gas masks for the civilian population and the compulsory erection of Anderson shelters for every household, in preparation for the expected air raids that would precede the arrival of sea-borne troops.

Alexis had not tried to prevent her joining the WVS although Lucy was well aware that he would have liked to send her to America or Canada where she would be out of harm's way. The discussion of such a possibility had been short-lived and ended with the mutual understanding that whatever happened, they would stay together, and that any alternative was unthinkable. If the King and Queen were prepared to remain in Buckingham Palace, Lucy had argued, the very least she could do was to stay and serve her country in the best way she could.

At the age of forty-six, Lucy was too old for the rigours of hospital nursing again, but her nursing experience and organizational abilities had been noted by the Dowager Marchioness of Reading, the founder of the new voluntary service, who had made her one of the first recruits. Lucy, in her turn, had encouraged many of her married friends to volunteer, giving as much time as they could. In the first few months of the war, Lucy had spent a lot of her time teaching First Aid to younger volunteers – married women with families, for the most part – who could not join one of the services.

They were urgently needed to assist the Air Raid Precaution services, man First Aid Posts, drive ambulances, and act as storekeepers, clerks or cooks for the Civil Defence services. Under-eighteen-year-olds volunteered to help in play centres set up for the children of mothers engaged in war work. In all, there were over thirty different types of work undertaken by these unpaid volunteers and Alexis did not discount their value and was proud of Lucy's dedication and organizational skills.

Three months after the outbreak of the war, Guy had left with his regiment to join the British Expeditionary Force who had been sent across the Channel to stop the German advance. Because of his time in the Territorial Army, he held the rank of captain but had had no experience of active service when he left. It was only a matter of time before the German army had pushed past the Maginot Line, and on all fronts, the British and French forces were in a state of chaos. With unprecedented speed, the Germans had invaded Belgium and by the end of May, Guy was on the Somme where supposedly the Allies were to halt their retreat and drive the Germans back across the river.

In the fighting that followed, with only half the regiment surviving after yet another crushing defeat, Guy found himself once more leading his men back towards the coast. With the French falling back on their flanks, the Messerschmitts and Stukas bombing them with little or no opposition from the RAF,

Guy was forced to face the fact that he and his men could soon become prisoners of war.

His spirits reached their lowest ebb as he watched his men trudging wearily ahead of him in straggling lines across the flat countryside. They, like himself, were utterly exhausted after the recent fighting and matters were made worse by the intense heat and the shortage of water. Some men tripped or toppled over from fatigue, others fainted, and Guy, together with a fellow officer, had to force himself to be ruthless with them, even kicking them if all else failed, in order to make them continue to what he only half hoped would be a place of safety. They covered only eight miles that day.

Often in a semi-stupor, Guy would find himself thinking of Zandra; imagining the two of them by the cool, shining water of the lake at Rochford; lying in bed at the Casa Montijo, watching the moonlight turning Zandra's beautiful body to silver; taking Alice's children on a lazy afternoon boat ride down the canal. Most of all his thoughts lingered on that unforgettable week's leave in Skye. He had received no mail from England since his embarkation, and in the total shambles of the retreating armies in France, he had no way of writing to Zandra.

Guy's fellow officer, a Kentish-born volunteer called Bill Robertson, had heard of the Rochford family although he had never met them. He was a good-natured, resourceful fellow who, until the outbreak of war, had been a broker on the Corn Exchange and was therefore an inexperienced soldier. Guy had come to rely on his second in command whose one concern was that they should never surrender to the *Boches*. His optimism was never failing, and although he now admitted that it seemed likely the BEF would be forced out of France, he had complete faith that the British navy would somehow get them safely home despite the fact that the Germans had already taken the all-important port of Calais.

When, at the end of that long, exhausting day, they reached Martainneville where the remnants of the battalion were reorganizing, Guy's spirits were only slightly revived. The other companies, like their own, were desperately depleted, and although a few stragglers joined them later, there seemed little chance of success for the planned counter-attack. Within hours, this inoperative plan was abandoned and yet again they were ordered to retreat.

The Germans were so close behind them that the men were becoming increasingly nervous. Once more they were dive-bombed and obliged continually to stop and take what shelter they could find. The BBC Radio communiqués did little to comfort them, admitting to the retreat of the troops further south. Despite the BBC reassurances that the RAF were covering their retreat, they did not see one British plane when they watched two hundred German bombers fly overhead.

By the fifth day, Guy learned that the Germans were in Rouen. The good news was that the Royal Navy were waiting at Le Havre to take them back to England.

Bill was grinning when Guy related the news.

"I told you the Navy would get us out!" he said, as he and Guy set about detailing the men to burn and destroy any equipment that was not essential for their evacuation. He seemed not to appreciate the enormous loss to the Allies the ensuing destruction meant – utter defeat of their two armies . . . and then what? Guy asked himself.

Bill seemed not to realize that England was obviously the next prize for Hitler's European empire. Bill had no wife nor even a serious girlfriend, and his parents had departed to Canada at the outbreak of war. He had no one, therefore, to worry about. He, Guy, on the other hand, could not look at the wretched French refugees trudging beside them with their carts and children along the dusty, bomb-cratered roads without imagining Zandra and her family likewise fleeing before the Germans and him not there to help them.

Halfway to Le Havre, they learned that the Germans had cut off their retreat, and they were ordered to make their way as fast and as best they could to a small fishing village south-west of Dieppe. Travelling at night, Guy had the added anxiety of not knowing where the enemy now was, and, to make matters worse, his convoy of men was frequently becoming split up. Parts of it were lost in the darkness since they had been forbidden to use lights. Even Bill's spirits were at a low ebb when eventually they arrived at their destination and were ordered to take up defensive positions outside the village. The sound of shelling and bombs falling on the little port behind them had finally undermined his confidence in their ultimate escape.

The following night, having destroyed all their personal possessions other than their rifles – which, as far as Guy was concerned, excluded his wallet containing his money and two snapshots of Zandra – they obeyed the order to enter the town. By the time they did so, it was to find it ablaze. Leaving Bill in command of the men, Guy went in search of Brigade or Divisional Headquarters, but, not unexpectedly, could find no such group. He returned and ordered his men down through the mass of wrecked and burned-out vehicles to the beach.

Bill swore vehemently under his breath as from the promenade he gazed out to sea. There was no sign of a ship.

"Not a single, solitary one!" he muttered as it started to drizzle with rain. Almost at once, Guy shouted the order to take cover as a steady stream of machine-gun fire opened up behind them to the west. The men took cover as best they could, and Guy set out once more in search of higher authority where he hoped to obtain some clarification of their situation. Wounded men lay everywhere, calling out for help, but there were so many hundreds of them that there was nothing he could do. His first duty in any event was to his own men, many of whom were also wounded.

A chance meeting with a senior officer proved of little help, for he was equally confused as to the Army's predicament. He agreed that Guy should take Bill and one of the men with him to the village a few miles north-east of them where he had spotted some warships lying close inshore. If evacuation was going to take place there, he suggested, Guy could return and collect his men.

They set off along the beach, the high cliffs affording them some protection from the Germans' cross-fire. As in the town, there were dead and wounded lying where they had been shot – some at the water's edge, some beneath the cliffs from which they had presumably fallen in an attempt to climb down to the shore. Both French and British lay together in their hundreds, those who were still conscious calling apathetically for water or for help.

As the two men reached their destination, the sun was once more high in the sky and the heat added to the plight of the wounded as well as to Guy's and Bill's discomfort. Moreover, they could now see that the decks of two warships – one of which had run aground – were already crowded with men. Both ships were under heavy fire, and the beached vessel clearly had no hope of escape until the tide came in.

As small fishing boats and dinghies took off from the beach, laden with men trying to reach the warships, they, too, were hit, the German gunners picking them off in horrifying numbers. The Germans were now firing from the east as well as the west and the two men, sheltering as best they could, saw that the newly arriving troops on the cliffs above the beach had even less hope than they did of escape. Soon after, tanks appeared on the cliff top and the grounded ship was hit. The sound of the screams of the men on board was the last thing Guy heard before he, too, was hit, and he fell unconscious onto the sand.

Anthony leant forward to switch off the wireless, and the big drawing-room of the house in Eaton Terrace was filled with an uncanny silence. Her face white with anxiety, Zandra stared across at her husband.

"What does this mean, Anthony?" she asked. "The Minister just said the Army was withdrawing from France and yet in the

354

next breath he was reminding us that in the last war, when we thought we were defeated, it was 'a prelude to victory'. Are we defeated or aren't we?"

Anthony's voice was little short of patronizing as he glanced at her over the top of his newspaper.

"My dear girl, *of course* we are defeated. Our chaps are in total disarray. They are making for the only bit of the French coast not already occupied by the Germans, in the desperate hope that the Navy will evacuate them."

"But surely they will, won't they?"

Anthony gave her an amused smile.

"Don't you have any idea how many men are involved? It's the entire British army – some three hundred and thirty thousand men – and that doesn't include the French soldiers who may also wish to avoid capture! As for the Navy, its ships are supposedly defending our shores or deployed in the Atlantic. Here, since you seem to doubt my word, have a look at this!"

He handed Zandra a copy of the *New York Herald Tribune* given to him by an American pilot who had flown over from the United States that day.

"That'll give you a better idea of what's going on. Our papers are censored."

Zandra's face paled. Anthony could have no idea why she was so desperate for news, or . . . her mind froze . . . was it possible he knew that Guy was with the BEF in France and was deliberately frightening her?

With a sense of foreboding, she took the American newspaper from him and with mounting horror, read the comments:

The British Expeditionary Force was all but given up for lost here tonight . . . In this epic tragedy the port of Dunkerque was the only hope of escape, and Dunkerque was under such brutal bombing by the numerically superior airmen of Germany that the prospect of removing the French-British force in the north was considered in London to be remote.

355

Thus the cream of the British army appeared, this sad and uncertain evening, to face extinction or surrender . . .

She looked up to see Anthony's grey eyes, their expression unfathomable, watching her.

"It was madness ever to take the Germans on," he said in a matter-of-fact tone. "They were getting ready for this years ago, and they have the best equipment in the world, whereas we – believe it or not – have to give our men broomsticks to train with because we don't have enough rifles; let alone tanks, aeroplanes or artillery. I've been telling them for years this would happen sooner or later and no one would listen to me. Well, now they've found out the hard way."

"Stop it, Anthony!" Zandra cried out. "You sound as if you're pleased you've been found to be right! How can we stop the Germans now – without an army?"

"The simple answer to that, my dear, is that we can't! If we don't call a halt, we'll be invaded and that'll be that, so we might just as well stop beating our heads against a brick wall and sue now for reasonable peace terms."

"You can't mean that, Anthony! I'd rather die than be under the thumb of those dreadful Nazis!"

"Well, you might entertain such noble sentiments, but the French almost certainly don't. From all accounts, they're on the point of surrender now, and since Germany has virtually occupied their country already, I can't say I blame them. You can't win a war without arms, my dear, as we found out in the last war when the Americans came in in the nick of time to bale us out. I can tell you this much, they don't intend to get involved this time. Roosevelt might be sympathetic towards us but the people won't allow it. I heard as much from one of the congressmen last week."

He stood up, yawning as he did so.

"I'm going to Ireland early tomorrow morning, so I'll get off to bed now."

As he walked towards the door, the telephone bell rang, and

he went out to the hall to answer it. A minute later, he called out to Zandra that Lucy was on the line wishing to speak to her. By the time Zandra picked up the receiver, he had disappeared upstairs.

"Zee-Zee, darling, it's me, Lucy!" She sounded breathless. "Are you busy tomorrow? If it's nothing urgent, I need your help!"

"I was going down to Rochford to see Aunt Willow," Zandra said, "but I can go another day. How can I help?"

"Well, don't pass this on, darling – it's for your ears only. I've just had Headquarters on the line and it seems as if a great many more soldiers than expected are getting back to Dover and the other south-east coastal ports. Hundreds of them are coming off the boats in a dreadful condition – wounded, some without clothes, all of them starving. They've been waiting on the beaches in France under fire, and even when they've managed to get on a boat, it's been shelled or bombed or something equally awful. There are huge casualties at sea, too. Anyway, darling, there are quite a few Frenchmen among our boys and as you speak the language you might be useful; so I managed to get permission to take you down with me. I thought you'd want to be there because of . . . well, you know who!"

Zandra's spirits – which had sunk to their lowest ebb following her conversation with Anthony – now soared. It wasn't, after all, a matter of *extinction or surrender*, as reported in the *Herald Tribune*. They were getting some of the men back to England – hundreds of them, according to Lucy, and Guy might be among them.

"Of course, I'll come, of course, of course!" she said breathlessly.

"I've got petrol for the Morris," Lucy said. "I thought we'd go to Rochford first and pick up Jane. She's done her First Aid training and you know how calm she is in a crisis. Inge can look after Mother. I want to get away early. Would six-thirty be too soon for you, Zee-Zee?"

"I'll go now, if you want!" Zandra cried.

She heard Lucy's soft laughter.

"No, darling, we'd only get lost in the black-out, and you know how difficult it is to find your way anywhere now they've taken down all the signposts. Go to bed and get some sleep – I have a feeling you'll need it."

But despite the undoubted wisdom of Lucy's advice, Zandra slept only fitfully until her alarm clock shrilled at five o'clock the following morning. It was not only the thought of the day ahead and what she, Lucy and Jane might find when they reached Dover; it was the thought that after months of tormenting silence, she might see Guy's face as he walked down the gangplank from one of the ships returning from France. The future was not important any more . . . nothing mattered other than that Guy could be alive, for in her heart of hearts, she had begun to fear that he might be dead.

"Dear God," she prayed as she had once prayed as a child in the belief that bargains could be struck successfully with the Almighty, "let Guy be alive and I'll never ask for anything again. Let him come back safely, even if I never see him again after tomorrow; even if he never holds me in his arms again; even if we can never love each other again; even if he is wounded. I just need to know that he is alive."

Chapter 24

May–June 1940

Silvie had used every argument she could think of to dissuade Pelham from returning to Paris to try to salvage what he could from their house in the Rue d'Artois. He was convinced that now the Germans were sweeping with such appalling rapidity through Belgium, it was only a matter of time before France, too, was overrun.

"You are nearly seventy years of age, *chéri!*" she reiterated. "You seem to think you are still a young man. *Nom de Dieu!* Am I married to an *imbécile?*"

Nothing she could say, however, could deter Pelham; and as the month of May drew to a close, he set off in their Delage with his chauffeur, Pierre. The situation that by now existed in the north of France succeeded where Silvie's arguments had failed. The French army was in retreat along the dusty roads south of the capital. It appeared to Pelham as he attempted to drive north, that the entire population of Paris had decided to evacuate the city, and the roads became steadily more and more congested by the tide of refugees. Not only were there struggling masses on foot but every conceivable type of wheeled conveyance, piled high with people and their household goods, was slowly building into a vast bottleneck.

Cars, taxis, fire engines, trucks, carts, refuse vehicles – even wheelbarrows and prams – had been pressed into service, and it quickly became clear to Pelham that it was unlikely he would ever be able to reach his destination. Moreover, he realized, judging by the items of news he was given by the occasional army officer he spoke to, even were he successful in reaching Paris, the city would be in the hands of the Germans by the time he got there!

He returned to Pau far more worried than he allowed Silvie to know. He brought with him two Dutch officers, Simon and Japp – refugees who had expressed the intention of getting a boat from Bordeaux or Biarritz to any country that would allow them to continue the fight against the enemy who now occupied northern France as well as their own country. Fed and supplied with fresh clothing by Silvie and money by Pelham, they were only at the Casa Montijo for two days, after which Pelham drove them to Biarritz. There they found the hotels and every other type of accommodation already filled with the more fortunate refugees from the north who, with money to pay their way, had made their escape before the general exodus.

Leaving the men in the care of a British couple who had a house in the town, Pelham returned once more to Pau where news had come through of the fate of the remnants of the defeated BEF. The exhausted men were, so it seemed, cornered, unprotected, on the Dunkirk and neighbouring beaches. The imminent fall of France was no longer in doubt.

"Britain will continue to fight, will she not?" Silvie said to Pelham as they sat down to dinner that evening. "Winston Churchill said on the wireless that it was their 'duty to defend the world'."

"I heard the broadcast in Biarritz," Pelham said gravely. "He also expressed his confidence in our power ultimately to defeat the enemy, but if the truth be told, my darling, I can't see how we can possibly do so alone!" He gave a deep sigh. "We can but hope that when the Americans realize our predicament, they may, after all, come to our aid. In one way, I wish I were back in England now; but as I wrote and told Willow, we would only be a liability. Already food is rationed – butter, sugar, bacon, ham, meat – and, of course, petrol. We're losing too many ships to the German submarines as it is, just in order to supply our basic imports. No, my dear, we can be more useful here. When I left Simon and Japp in Biarritz, it occurred to me that there must be many more brave men like them who will be trying to get out of France to continue the fight if France surrenders. We can at least help *them*."

Silvie looked at her husband's face with conflicting emotions. He had the eager, excited expression of a boy – yet he was an old man now.

"How could you help, *chéri*? If the Germans occupy France, they will most certainly put guards on all the borders and take over all the ports – Biarritz included!"

Pelham chuckled.

"Yes, indeed, my dear; but have you forgotten my fishing trips to that marvellous trout river over the Spanish border? What a splendid fellow and companion my guide, old Gaston, proved to be. He's still alive, you know – runs the tackle shop in Pau with his son, Jean-Paul."

Silvie motioned to the servant to clear the meal, and pushed back her chair.

"I still do not understand what Gaston has to do with the Dutchmen!" she said as Pelham slipped his arm through hers and led her to the salon where they were accustomed to drinking their after-dinner coffee. He sat down in his usual chair and packed a little tobacco into his pipe.

"Now I will explain," he said. "If Simon and Japp had been unable to embark at Biarritz, we could have taken them over the Pyrenees by that same route Gaston and I took to go fishing. Spain is a neutral country, so once over the border, the chaps could have got themselves to Gibraltar and found a boat there. Now do you see what I'm getting at?"

Silvie hid her smile of amusement at this imaginary scenario which sounded to her as if it could have come from one of Oliver's childhood Boy's Own adventure storybooks.

"Yes, *chéri*, I understand. But the last time you went fishing with Gaston, you were nearly ten years younger – and so was old Gaston. He must be in his late seventies now!"

"Of course, of course, I'm well aware of that, my darling, but" – Pelham paused dramatically – "but, my sweetheart, my beloved, my incomparable wife, Jean-Paul knows that route every bit as well as his father. As for me . . . well, maybe I could not walk so far these days, but I would not be needed. My task would be to do as I have done quite accidentally – find the chaps who are trying to get away, bring them back here and let Jean-Paul take them into Spain!"

Silvie could not bring herself to dampen his enthusiasm by voicing her own misgivings. There seemed little point in doing so since, as yet, France had not surrendered and the *Boches* might yet be forced to retreat. In her heart of hearts, she did not believe this could happen; but at least for the time being, they were perfectly safe down here in the south where life went on as usual except for the fact that many local families had sons and fathers in the forces. Alice, too, was in no danger, for, like herself, she was now a French citizen; and Pelham held a French as well as an English passport. She could understand his concern for the present predicament of his countrymen, and his frustration that his age prohibited him from doing his bit for the war effort. If the idea for this crazy scheme comforted her beloved, it did no harm to humour him!

"Do you think we should try to persuade Alice to go home to England if the Germans occupy us?" she asked. "I know she wouldn't want to leave Claude, but I am thinking of the children!"

Pelham shook his head.

"If England continues the fight – and I hope to God she will – Alice and the children will probably be a good deal safer here. If the British government wasn't anticipating invasion, they wouldn't have wired off and mined the beaches, or introduced those Anderson shelters, and taken all those other precautions. We must face the facts, my dear. Our air force is no match for the *Luftwaffe*, and we know from Poland, Norway and Holland what their bombing raids can do to civilian populations. London will be the next target, I fear."

Silvie shivered involuntarily.

"Zee-Zee is living in London – and Lucy and Alexis."

Pelham eased himself out of his chair and put a comforting arm around his wife's shoulders.

"They have Rochford to go to if the need arises."

He forbore from voicing his own doubts as to the safety of anyone living in a house as near to the south coast as Rochford Manor, for if there were to be a German invasion, it would certainly be directly across the English Channel.

"Let's see if we can pick up the BBC news," he said as he crossed the room to fiddle with the knobs of his new wireless. Reception was often far from good, but despite the fact that he knew the broadcasts were censored, at least they provided some idea of what was happening.

The news was only partially reassuring. It seemed that the Navy were managing successfully to evacuate a large proportion of the BEF. What Pelham did not yet know was that Belgium had capitulated the day before and the Germans were fast closing in on the thousands still helplessly stranded on the beaches surrounding Dunkirk.

When Alice arrived with the children next morning for their now regular weekly lunch with Silvie and Pelham, she seemed disinclined to talk about the war.

"It only frightens the children!" she said as she sat down beside Silvie in the garden whilst the little ones squabbled over the right to sit on their Great-Uncle Pelham's knees. Although hot and dusty after their walk up the hill to the Casa Montijo, the sight of the glass jug of cold *jus de citron* had revived their high spirits, and their shrill voices drowned the level, placid tones of their mother.

With pretended severity, Pelham quietened them, speaking – as he always did – in English. The children were bilingual and now appealed in French to their Great-Aunt to decide who should be favoured.

Silvie regarded them fondly. Henri, the youngest, at the age of four, was a handsome little boy and much spoilt by his adoring and indulgent parents. Brigitte was a quiet, placid child like her mother and unlike her volatile, independent elder sister, Claudette. Although only seven, Claudette was surprisingly mature for her age and tended to boss her younger siblings. Silvie suspected the child had formed the habit during Alice's prolonged illness, but Pelham insisted it was simply her nature. There were times, he said, when she reminded him of Zee-Zee, and he had a special fondness for her.

In his masculine way, Pelham had failed to understand Alice's depression. He'd vaguely resented the amount of time Silvie had been obliged to spend trying to raise Alice's spirits and supervising the care of the children before Zandra had arrived to take over the running of the Calonne household. He had no time at all for Claude Calonne with his bourgeois pretensions and snobbery. It was a continual surprise to him how the man had managed to produce three such delightful children, and in his declining years, Pelham was enjoying the novelty of his grandfatherly role. He enjoyed their uninhibited displays of affection as much as they enjoyed the stories he told them about England, about Rochford when he had lived there as a child; and he had identified their many English relatives.

He had promised to take them all home one day for a holiday to meet their grandmother, Willow, and their various aunts, uncles and cousins. That day now looked as if it must be postponed far into the future, he thought, as he hoisted Henri on to his shoulders, and conducted the children down to the croquet lawn where he was attempting to teach them the game.

"Is Claude very concerned about the war situation, Alice?" Silvie persisted as the group went out of earshot.

Alice, who had regained nearly all the weight she had lost when she was ill, shook her head.

"He thinks it is silly to continue fighting," she replied. "He thinks the sooner we surrender to the Germans, the better it will be for us."

"Then he cannot know much about the Nazi ideology!" Silvie said sharply. "If Claude thinks they would permit him to carry on his business as usual, he is in for quite a shock. In the countries they have so far occupied, they have stolen everything of value to send home and left the people close to starvation."

Seeing the look of distress on Alice's face, Silvie modified her tone. Whatever the facts might be, Alice would take her cue from Claude who was totally dominant in their relationship. How Alice could still imagine herself in love with the little Frenchman was beyond Silvie's understanding. He had been little short of intolerant towards his wife during her depression, and his children were patently afraid of him. They were quiet, obedient and totally subdued in his presence – quite unlike the boisterous, noisy trio who came to the Casa Montijo.

"I had a letter from Zandra last week," Silvie changed the topic of conversation. "She is still trying to join the ATA. The poor darling is desperately worried about Guy. She hasn't heard from him for weeks."

Alice frowned. She'd been too ill to take any notice of Zandra's lover when he had stayed last summer, but had met him at Tante Silvie's in previous years. Although no one had actually told her that Zandra and Guy were having an affair, she knew this was the case. Claude was also aware of it and had expressed quite violent disapproval. It was totally against his principles to condone adultery – a mortal sin in the eyes of the Church, he had declared. He could not understand how Tante Silvie and Uncle Pelham could do so by offering "the adulterers" a safe place for their "illicit rendezvous". It undermined his respect for her Rochford relations, he stated, and it was only "out of consideration for her, his wife", that he did not voice his feelings to her uncle and aunt. He had become extremely irritable when Alice – in a rare flash of cynicism – reminded him that the success he had enjoyed in his business was very largely due to her aunt's patronage, and his reticence might also be attributable to this consideration.

Being a good wife to Claude was not as easy as she had once supposed, Alice thought. She tried very hard to please him but more often than not, succeeded in irritating him. These afternoons when she walked up the hill to the Casa Montijo were a great pleasure as well as a relief, for here she could relax her guard knowing that however stupidly she might behave, neither her aunt nor uncle would criticize her or make her feel foolish, as Claude so often did. The children, too, were happier, less tense and quarrelsome in this homely atmosphere. Henri was the only one of the three who was not overtly afraid of his father; but then Claude, insofar as he ever showed affection for anyone, adored his only son. Unfortunately, Henri was too young as yet to take any interest in the *objects d'art* his father brought home to show him – a source of irritation as well as disappointment to Claude.

It did not occur to Alice as she discussed the older children's school progress with her aunt in the sunny garden, that she might no longer be in love with Claude. She realized that his treatment of her was far different from that of her uncle to his wife; of Alexis to Lucy, or Oliver towards Jane. Even more markedly was it different from Guy's towards Zandra; but this Alice discounted on the grounds that they were lovers. Claude, too, had been attentive and approving before their marriage. Claude, she comforted herself, was a Frenchman and she had been stupid not to anticipate that he would behave differently from the English husbands she knew.

Alice closed her mind to the fact that Zandra had told her that when she had lost her baby, Anthony had treated her in much the same way as Claude was behaving; that it was because her marriage was without love and affection that she had turned to Guy. It was better not to think too much about such things, Alice had long ago decided, but to be satisfied with the occasional crumbs of approval Claude threw her way – and the now very rare occasions he made love to her. He had stated quite categorically – a little cruelly, even – that it was her own fault that he avoided such intimacies. Since their religion did not permit him to prevent a subsequent pregnancy, he dared not risk her having another baby after her disruption of the entire household following the arrival of the last. He was of the firm opinion that had she tried, she could have "pulled herself together" – an option Alice knew in her heart had not been available to her. Those months of her depression were something she preferred not to remember, for there had been times when she'd seriously wished to die – even thought of ways of doing so! But for Tante Silvie's and Zandra's loving care and company.

She turned now to her aunt with a bright smile.

"I have started to make a patchwork quilt for Claudette's bed," she announced. "If you have any pieces of material I could use, perhaps I could take them home with me?"

"But of course, *chérie*!" Silvie said. "I have a white shantung skirt I no longer wear, and a red silk blouse – Claudette will like the bright colour. Come, my dear, we'll go up to my room and see what else I can find for you!"

As Alice followed her into the house, Silvie tried not to compare Alice's dull, colourless nature with Zandra's bright intelligence and humour. No wonder Pelham now preferred the company of the children to that of his niece! No wonder Guy was so passionately in love with Zee-Zee! On Sunday, she would

367

offer special prayers for Zandra and Guy – especially for Guy whom she knew to be part of the BEF and, in all probability, waiting for rescue in Dunkirk.

By the second day of the Navy's evacuation of the men awaiting rescue on the beaches in France, it had become obvious to Admiral Ramsay, the naval officer commanding operations at Dover, that the quantity of ships at his disposal were too few in number for his needs. Moreover, the larger vessels could not get into the only available harbour. It was small craft that were needed which could get close in to the beaches, he realized, and the task of finding them was put to the Ministry of Shipping.

The search for privately owned small boats began, and they were rounded up from rivers, estuaries and ports from the east coast to Cornwall. It was planned for these vessels to be manned by naval personnel, but in many cases when the owners were told in confidence why the boats were needed, they volunteered to take them to the muster points themselves. If the owner of a boat could not be found, then it was commandeered. When eventually it became clear that there were insufficient naval personnel to man the vast numbers of vessels made available for the emergency, the civilian crews were asked to volunteer for a month's duty in the Navy.

Few refused to assist in the evacuation despite the fact that their boats were unarmed, some had never been to sea, and they would be at the risk of bombs as well as shells when they neared the French coast. The boats were then stripped of everything but essentials, fuelled and prepared for the crossing. In addition to the Channel ferries already involved, the huge armada of small boats consisted of trawlers, skoots, yachts, tugs, barges, coasters, launches, cabin cruisers, RNLI lifeboats and smacks. No exact count was taken, but it was known that over eight hundred craft finally put to sea.

In Dunkirk, the situation was steadily worsening as further remnants of the BEF trudged exhausted past the town which had been bombed to rubble and was now a blazing inferno, and made their way as best they could down to the sand dunes. The stench of burning oil was everywhere as was the smell of the rotting carcasses of horses and the dead bodies of the thousand civilians who had been killed in the bombing raids on the city. On the beach, thousands of troops were already gathered and were attempting to find shelter of a kind in the dunes. Others stood in endlessly long queues awaiting their turn to climb into one of the waiting boats. A makeshift breakwater had been erected, consisting of lorries manhandled into the water. Planks were placed across the roofs of the lorries along which the men could file to board the bigger ships that could not come in closer to the shore.

Some of the men, despairing of reaching the end of the queues which stretched for as far as the eye could see along the width of the beach and into the water, tried to swim out to the waiting boats. Only a few reached safety, others drowning or being hit in one of the ceaseless machine-gun attacks from the Messerschmitts and Stukas strafing the beaches. Their bodies were washed in with the incoming tide, adding to the numbers of dead and wounded already lying unburied on the sand. In the scramble to escape, some of the boats became overloaded and capsized, and the rescuers were often obliged to beat off the desperate men with their oars.

Those who were resigned to waiting could do nothing for the wounded. The only water to be had was from the radiators of the vehicles which had been abandoned as their occupants arrived. Starving, thirsty, under fire, the men could do little else but pray that eventually their turn would come and that they would be rescued in the short time left before the Germans themselves arrived on the beaches. With the sound of gun-fire so close to where they were, they knew time was not on their side; that their chances of rescue were growing ever slimmer as ships and small boats alike were shelled and sunk.

Many of the privately owned boats had been laid up prior to

the emergency and were suffering mechanical problems. Those which could not be towed back to Ramsgate had to be abandoned, and they added to the congestion already in the water. Now, along with bodies, ropes and other wreckage, they were frequently fouling the rudders of the more seaworthy vessels.

Despite the setbacks, the bravery, endurance, ingenuity and determination of the Navy, Army and civilians was such that by the end of the fourth day of the evacuation, over seventy-two thousand men had been taken safely back to England.

Sitting beside Lucy as she drove competently down the steep hill into the outskirts of Dover, Zandra felt her hopes rising. From the cliff tops she had glimpsed the activity in the port as well as in the town. Ambulances, both army and civilian, were racing past them; a column of men – some bandaged, some in civilian clothing – trudged wearily from York Street into the Folkestone Road heading for the railway station. As if these exhausted, bedraggled survivors were victorious troops liberating their homeland, men, women and children were out on the pavements showering them with food, flowers, cups of tea. Some of the soldiers grinned and waved; others, with heads bent, were too tired to acknowledge the spontaneous adulation and sympathy offered them.

"They will be heading for their units!" Lucy said, adding grimly: "You might not think so, but those are the ones considered fit enough to travel! Lady Reading said that thousands more are expected today now they have found out that the Dunkirk harbour can be used after all for the evacuation. Communications have been hopelessly adrift and the Navy was told the harbour was blocked, so it had stopped sending in the warships. The local WVS have been coping magnificently, but Lady Reading thinks that as so many more men may now be evacuated, they can do with some extra help. I spoke to the Regional Administrator last night, and we're to go straight to the docks."

On the drive to Rochford to pick up Jane, Lucy had informed

Zandra that the men were arriving at many other ports along the south coast, so she was aware that if Guy were among the evacuees, she might not necessarily see him. Nevertheless, the bulk of the soldiers were being disembarked at Dover and she was filled with hopeful anticipation. She was unprepared for the sight which met her eyes as Lucy negotiated their way to the dockside, waving her way imperiously past the army and navy personnel who were maintaining some kind of order. The WVS had organized a canteen in the refreshment-room, and a never-ending stream of men – often too tired to do more than nod their thanks – were being supplied with mugs of tea. Rows of wounded men lay on stretchers on the quayside and Jane was at once detailed to take jugs of tea down to them. Zandra was detailed to interpret for the French survivors, obtaining what information she could, labelling them with their names and, as far as she could ascertain, their wounds, so that there would be less delay when they reached the overcrowded hospitals. Lucy's car was temporarily commandeered to take the less seriously wounded to hospital – and all the time, more and more men were being disembarked from the boats. Many of the vessels were damaged and had limped into the port. Those that were still seaworthy, having emptied their human cargoes, set out immediately again for the French coast.

In only a few minutes, Zandra realized that her dream of searching for Guy's face amongst an orderly column of men marching off the dock was little short of laughable. Despite the incredible, tireless efforts and determination of the Navy, Army and civilian organizations, the jetties were hopelessly congested, and the men had to be cleared as quickly as possible in order for room to be made for the next arrivals.

As Zandra made her way quietly and efficiently amongst the stretcher cases, she was touched by the look of relief on some of the *poilus'* faces when they realized that here was someone who could understand their language. To each she gave words of reassurance that they would be taken to hospital as soon as possible;

that she would do what she could to find out the fates of their friends, many of whom they had left behind on the beaches.

During a lull between the influx of men and the next arrivals, Lucy arrived with instructions for Zandra to accompany another member of the WVS to the town hall where some of the exhausted men had been taken. From there, the woman told her, Zandra was to go on to the cinema, the churches and the railway-station buffet and waiting-rooms where there were French soldiers amongst the British. These soldiers would ultimately be taken to a different destination from the British. In each of these hastily contrived reception areas, Zandra found members of the WVS supplying food, clothing, drinks and sandwiches to those still standing. Others had fallen asleep on the floor and were being rolled into lines, their boots removed, their feet washed and minor wounds bandaged. All were being supplied with postcards and telegram forms to send to their families announcing their safe arrival in England.

One of the young women handing out these postcards looked almost as exhausted as the survivors. She and her WVS colleagues had been working non-stop for the past four days, she told Zandra, only catching a few hours' sleep when they were unable to stay awake any longer. It was the same for all the volunteers, she said, but no one was complaining.

When later that afternoon Zandra returned once more to the docks, a fresh arrival of wounded lay in the place of those she had seen previously. Next to one of the Frenchmen lay a British soldier whose face Zandra recognized. At the end of Guy's embarkation leave, an army car had met him at the railway station, and Guy had introduced her to the driver – a middle-aged man from Kent who had once been chauffeur to the Barratts. They had exchanged a few words, and as Guy had climbed into the car and Zandra had been unable to conceal her agony at this parting, the man, Matthews, had said: "Don't you worry, miss. I'll see he don't come to no 'arm!"

He recognized Zandra at once, and despite the obvious pain

he was in from his bandaged head, he managed a smile. Her heart beating fiercely with sudden hope, Zandra knelt down beside him.

"I'm glad you got away, Matthews!" she said. "The ambulance will be here soon. They're terribly busy, I'm afraid."

"Pleased they are, miss!" the man replied. "Means more of us is getting 'ome. It weren't exactly a picnic on those beaches! Thought I'd never make it. Wouldn't have done but for this chap . . ." He nodded towards the Frenchman beside him. "Got me on my feet and helped me out to the boat. They're 'aving to leave the wounded as can't walk, you see. No room for stretcher cases."

Zandra's face paled.

"Captain Bristow . . . did you see him, Matthews? You were in his company, weren't you?"

Matthews frowned.

" 'E got to the beach, miss, but there weren't no more ships waiting to take us all off, so 'e and Lieutenant Robertson went off to recce further up the coast. Captain Bristow was coming back to get us if 'e found we'd a better chance there . . . but, well, 'e didn't come, back, miss, nor the Lieutenant neither. That's all I know, miss. One thing I am sure of is 'e wouldn't 'ave gone 'isself and left one of us be'ind. 'E were a right caring officer what did 'is best for us – wouldn't let us give up 'ope of getting back, you see. There was once I was that tired I didn't care if I was captured or even if I died – just wanted to sleep; but the Captain, miss, 'e wouldn't 'ave it. 'Ated him, I did then! But 'e were right, of course. I'm 'ere to prove it, ain't I!"

Seeing the stricken look on Zandra's face, he added quickly: "I reckon as 'ow 'e'll get back someways, miss. After 'e'd gone, we didn't think we 'ad a 'ope and then this Belgian trawler sailed in – like a ruddy miracle it were. 'E'll get back, miss, never you worry!"

But caught up in the miraculous rescue of so many more men than anyone had dared hope, Zandra had no time for further hope or worry as she went about her designated work. It was only when she, Jane and Lucy prepared to bed down for a few hours' sleep in one of the hotel rooms, that her deepest worries resurfaced.

"They're doing their best to keep lists of the names of survivors," Lucy said as they removed their shoes from their aching feet. "They let me see some of them, but I'm afraid Guy's name wasn't on them, Zee-Zee, darling. Maybe tomorrow, yes? I did manage to speak to a colonel from one of the Highland regiments who'd just got back from Dunkirk. He said the German tanks hadn't reached the port when he left. He seemed to think they might have halted to refuel or rearm or something, as by then there was virtually no Allied resistance to their advance. Whatever the reason, it meant the rescue could continue for a day longer than they had expected."

Zandra managed to nod her head which was throbbing with fatigue.

"I haven't given up hope, Lucy. Guy could have disembarked at Ramsgate or Margate or Deal – or one of the other ports. One of the WVS drivers who brought in a lorry-load of supplies said Headquarters were sending food and clothing all along the coast. They'd even had word that some of the smaller boats were losing their way or had been damaged and blown off course so were landing as far north as Sheerness!"

But despite Lucy's comforting words or, indeed, her own, she was filled with a terrible foreboding. If Guy were to have been killed, all meaning would have gone from her life. If it were possible, they were even more deeply in love when Guy had his embarkation leave than they had ever been.

Regardless of the danger of discovery, they had risked one whole week in a fishing lodge on the Isle of Skye where they had spent idyllic days and nights together, treasuring every second. Only once had they talked about Anthony. It was one of the few times Guy had ever expressed the extent of his dislike for her husband – a dislike not prompted by jealousy, he assured her, but because he knew him to be evil.

Zandra took care not to mention to him the extent of Anthony's ruthless sadism. From time to time, he still came to her bedroom and with that customary sneering smile on his face, forced himself on her. Always before he left, he would pull his dressing-gown over his white, naked body and stand at the foot of the bed, staring down at her.

"Admit that you really enjoyed that," he would insist. "Go on, you stubborn little bitch, admit you like being raped. All women like it. Go on, say it!"

She knew that her silence would only provoke further invective and fouler language, and that the quickest way to rid herself of his presence was to tell him what he wanted to know. She recognized that his verbal assaults were yet another form of his humiliation of her, and she took comfort from the fact that he seemed not to be aware of the heavy sarcasm of her tone of voice as she declared: "Yes, I enjoyed it, Anthony – and yes, I really wanted to be raped!" His lips would tighten and his eyes narrow as he gave a smile of satisfaction; but he was not yet ready to relinquish the pleasure his imagined victory gave him. She would wait silently for the inevitable epilogue that always followed her verbal capitulation.

"You don't deceive me lying there with your eyes shut pretending you aren't ready for it. Women like you Rochfords stick your noses in the air as if you were royalty and above such things as lust, sex; but when you get down to it, your kind are as keen as the rest." Now his voice would be edged with excitement. "Take your precious Countess Zemski – La Perle – that's what they called her in that French brothel. Well, let me tell you, my girl, that portrait of her shows what she's really like – a French tart. That's what she became before she was old enough to leave the schoolroom. Couldn't wait to grow up before she had to have it. Runs in the family, I dare say. Well, you had what you wanted tonight and that should keep you quiet for a bit. Good night, my dear, sleep well!"

She no longer cried when he left. Having washed all trace of him from her body, she would lie between the sheets and relive each moment she had shared with Guy until finally, happy once more, she would fall asleep. Guy was her refuge, the sole reason for her survival from her husband's sadistic bestiality. Guy renewed her faith, her trust, her respect for herself.

Once again, Zandra prayed. Lucy, for whose sake she endured and sacrificed so much, and Jane were already asleep, and remembering all too clearly Matthews' words, she could give way to tears. Guy had not returned to his men. He had gone off to look for another beach where there might be a boat, promising his men he *would* return, but *he had not gone back*. It could mean only one of two things – that he had not found another means of rescue or that he had been killed.

Chapter 25

June 1940

Although a total exceeding three hundred thousand Allied troops had been rescued from the beaches, there were still some tens of thousands who'd had no alternative but to surrender to the enemy when finally the Germans had reached the north coast. So many were the numbers that the Germans were hard put to find suitable prisoner-of-war camps to contain them. Dunkirk, the main evacuation beach, was in smouldering ruins; and the former occupants who had not been killed by shells or by the fierce bombardment had departed in desperate search of safety.

Some hundred and fifty kilometres to the south, Guy and Bill, despite their wounds, were being marshalled into long columns of men who were to be marched in a north-easterly direction.

Guy's head throbbed unmercifully from the bomb blast which had temporarily stunned him. Nevertheless he did what he could to assist his fellow officer who had sustained a debilitating wound to his left leg. Bill had made light of his injuries when, before leaving the beach, the Germans had separated the cases whom they were taking to hospital from those still able to walk. He was as determined as Guy not to remain a prisoner for the rest of the war, an inevitable consequence for the casualties. Sooner or later, he maintained on the day following their capture, they would find an opportunity to escape. Although he was barely able to complete the long marches between rests, opportunities were already presenting themselves since they had been allotted only a comparatively few German guards for such vast numbers of prisoners.

"You'd have a better chance of getting away without me, old chap!" he said to Guy as they straggled behind the column on the third day of their march. There was no guard behind them and it would be easy enough, he maintained, for Guy to dive behind a hedge or tree. Guy, however, refused to abandon his friend. Shortly before the Germans had arrived, they had made a pact to escape together and he was not prepared to go back on his word. For one thing, Bill spoke only schoolboy French and if, when his leg was better, he were to try to escape on his own, his chances of passing himself off as a French civilian were virtually nil. Guy, on the other hand, with his faultless command of the language, would be able to speak for both of them if they escaped together.

By the time they left their third staging camp, Bill's wound had started to fester. They had only their own medical orderlies to attend to the hundreds of exhausted soldiers, and with no medical supplies, little could be done for him. The fourth camp, however, was one of the main transit camps where over seven thousand other prisoners, mainly from Dunkirk and its environs, were already installed, and they were finally allowed the attention of three British medical officers who had arrived before them.

"I'm not reporting sick, Guy!" Bill said in a low voice. "I'd almost certainly be hospitalized and then what chance would there be of getting away? One of the MOs is a major and if he gave me a direct order . . . well, I'm just not going to give him the chance."

Guy surveyed the blood-encrusted bandage he had put on

Bill's leg that morning, with growing misgivings. The wound was yellow with pus and the area around it swollen and scarlet.

"Sorry, old chap, but I honestly don't think you have any alternative," he said. "You aren't going to get far even if we could get away from this place tonight – a possibility which I very much doubt; there are too many guards around. I don't imagine there's a chance of escaping until we're on the move again, and frankly, that leg of yours wouldn't stand up to it. It's getting worse every day."

Bill's eyes held an unmistakable look of appeal as he said quietly: "I could make it with your help, Guy. I heard one of the chaps say a guard had told him we'd only be staying here one more night. If we got away tomorrow . . . hid up somewhere . . . you might be able to find a French doctor to take a dekko at my leg. You said you spoke the lingo like a native; and you were the one who argued that not every Frenchman was as anxious to surrender as the ones we've seen on the way here. I'll bet there are some older ones who fought in the last war who'd help us." He paused momentarily and looked down at his hands. "Of course, you should really try and make it on your own . . . your duty to get home if you can . . . and all that—"

"Shut up and don't talk such rot!" Guy broke in. "We agreed to go together and that's all there is to it. I'm not bothered for myself, but for you. Have you considered that you could . . . well, looking at the worst side of it, you could lose your leg?"

Bill's mouth tightened.

"I think I'd almost prefer that to being shut up for the duration. God alone knows how long that will be – donkey's years, I imagine, now we've been kicked out of France. Just think about it, Guy. We're on our own now – unless someone can get the Americans to come in with us – and judging by what was going on on the beaches, I shouldn't think more than a third of our chaps got away, if that! How long is it going to take to get the Army going again – and a big enough one to get back over here and knock the Jerries out of France? No, I can't stand the thought of being shut up for years on end. I'm twenty-four years old and I want to enjoy my youth." He gave a sudden grin. "Have you thought what it would be like to go without a woman for the next five . . . ten years? At least I'd still be able to make love to a girl even if I did have only one leg!"

With only an occasional lump of stale brown bread and a spoonful or two of some indefinable stew to sustain them these past four days, Guy had been conscious of little else but his hunger, and the thought of making love had not entered his head; but Bill's words made him realize just how desperately he wanted to hold Zandra in his arms, feel the sweet-smelling warmth of her; hear her voice. To be parted from her for six months had been hard enough to bear, but if those weeks were to become years . . .

Besides which, he could never entirely erase from his mind the fear that she might be in danger from that bastard of a husband; that he, Guy, might be needed at a moment's notice to rush to her rescue! It was only with the greatest reluctance that he had settled for the *status quo* . . . of being merely Zandra's lover with never a hope of becoming her husband. He understood the risks to her family and her reasons for complying with Wisson's blackmail; and because it was what she wanted, he chose not to make things more difficult for her by voicing his own deep-seated conviction that they should go to the police and expose Wisson for what he was, whatever the risks to the Rochfords. At least Zandra's French aunt – the delightful Tante Silvie – was sympathetic to their relationship. She had even offered her beautiful home in the south-west of France for their clandestine holidays together. Had he not hated Wisson – and with such good reason – he might have felt more guilty about those secret assignations.

He gave a sudden shout.

"Great Scott, Bill, I've just thought of something!" he said. "Can't imagine how I never thought of it before. If we can get away and make our way down south, I know some people there who would help us. We know the Jerries will be swarming all over the Channel ports watching for stragglers trying to escape, but they won't be down in the south yet. We could rest up with these people, the Rochfords – he's English, she's French – and try to get a boat back to England from down there."

Bill's grin widened.

"That's it, then – I don't go to the medics! Give you my word, old boy, I'll do my best not to be a handicap. Be a good fellow and see if you can get some antiseptic or something from the MO . . . tell him it's just a minor gash not worth bothering about. God knows there are enough of us chaps for them to be dealing with, poor devils – and a right lot of scarecrows we look, too!"

Few of the soldiers had seen any water for days, and had had no opportunity to wash, far less shave. Their uniforms were in tatters and often barely recognizable as such. Many had appropriated civilian jackets, shirts, trousers – even female skirts left behind by their owners when they had fled from their homes before the advancing German forces. As no mugs, plates or cutlery had been provided in the camps, everyone had acquired a receptacle of some kind to contain their meagre ration of soup or water, and had food or cigarette tins attached to their waists. Some, like Guy and Bill, had managed to pick up blankets from kit that had been discarded by Allied troops on their way to the coast. Cigarettes were in desperately short supply and morale amongst some of the men was exceedingly low.

During the rigours of the retreat to the coast, the men had had at least some hope of rescue, but now they knew the long days' marches led only to confinement. Weakened by lack of food, weary to the point of inertia, often as not separated from their friends, many of the soldiers had for the time being lost their fighting spirit.

Fortunately the German guards were reasonably compassionate, and only once had Guy seen any sign of brutality – and that had not been towards the prisoners. A Prussian officer had driven past the long column of men and stopped his car in order

381

to apprehend the foremost German guard who had failed to get off his bicycle and salute! Not only did he shout abuse at the wretched fellow but actually hit him in full view of the prisoners. No one had spoken until the car was out of sight and then one of the British Tommies had walked over to the trembling, abject guard to offer him one of his precious remaining cigarettes.

Bill's leg wound worsened during the night but somehow he managed next day to hobble out of the camp with his hand on Guy's shoulder. There seemed to be no serious attempt by the guards to count the prisoners – perhaps because there were too many – and Bill's condition was not noticed except by the men around them whose bodies effectively concealed him. Before long, he and Guy were once again falling behind the straggling column. There were hedges on either side of the road, and seeing the effort Bill was making to conceal his pain, Guy said: "I think this is as good a chance as any we'll get, Bill. I've been looking at those ditches, and I reckon they are deep enough to conceal us. We can lie low until the column is out of sight; then I'll make my way to that farmhouse over there – see if I can get some help."

His face white with pain, Bill only nodded his agreement. As Guy stepped sideways off the road, pulling him down into the ditch beside him, he gave an involuntary groan.

"Damned leg hurts like hell!" he murmured apologetically. "Sorry to be such a nuisance!"

"Look here, old chap, we'd better get something straight right now. If the guard doesn't come back to check the rear of the column – and it doesn't look as if he's going to – then we've made it; we're free. Now I don't ever want to hear you say you're sorry again – never, do you understand? Not even if we're caught! I didn't have to agree to take you along, but I did; so stop being so bloody apologetic and let's think about our next move."

Although Bill's face was still deathly pale, he managed his familiar grin as Guy cast a final glance at the now empty road.

"Here, you'd better have this," he said, drawing a beret out of his trouser pocket and handing it to Guy. "I swapped it at the camp with a Frenchman in return for a Players . . . thought it would make a good souvenir when we got home. You'll look more like a Frenchman with that on.

Guy returned his smile, his spirits lifting. He still wore his khaki trousers but they were so ragged, muddy and dust covered that the colour was barely identifiable. They certainly did not look like the uniform kit of a British army officer. His shirt – a coarse striped cotton one he had taken off the washing-line outside an abandoned French cottage – was collarless and frayed at the cuffs, and was genuinely that of the French peasant he wished to appear.

"Reckon I'll get away with it if I happen to meet a Jerry!" he said. He paused before adding: "There's no one about so I see no point in waiting until this evening. If I go now, you'll be all right here meanwhile, won't you? I'll try not to be long."

Donning the beret, Guy eased himself out of the ditch and paused as he looked down at his companion. He wondered if Bill, too, had considered the possibility that he, Guy, might be caught and unable to return. In Bill's present state, there was no possible way that he could manage on his own.

"Look, if I'm not back by this afternoon, you'd better get yourself back onto the roadside and flag down a German car or something. Don't try and stick it out tonight. You'll need water for one thing. Not a damn cloud in the sky, so it'll be pretty hot again this afternoon."

"That's better than being cold!" Bill said firmly. "Now bugger off, Guy, before someone sees you and we're both caught!"

"I'll be back!" Guy said.

"Course you will, you idiot!" Bill grinned. "And bring a bottle of beer with you, I'm thirsty!"

Keeping to the hedgerows bordering the fields, Guy made his way cautiously towards the farmhouse. He could see smoke coming from one of the chimneys and, as he drew closer to the building, he saw a youth driving an empty hay cart towards him. After a moment's reflection, he decided that a bold approach was the best one and he strode forward purposefully to meet the boy.

As soon as he was within earshot, he hailed the lad whom he judged to be about thirteen years old. In faultless French, he called out a greeting. The boy drew the old cart-horse to a halt and stared down at him, curiosity overcoming his uneasiness. This man did not look like a German but his parents had told him to keep his distance from the soldiers.

"Your mother and father at home?" Guy asked. "Any Germans around?"

The boy looked nervously over his shoulder.

"They were here day before yesterday," he said. "Took all our chickens and two of our pigs. Said they'd be back, but they haven't come yet."

"Paid for them, I hope?" Guy said.

The boy scowled.

"Didn't give us a *sou*, m'sieur," he said. "My mother tried to make 'em but Father shut her up . . . told the officer we were pleased to be of help and all. We had a white sheet in the attic window saying we'd surrender and didn't want any trouble – but it didn't make any difference – they still stole the pigs, and my mother's chickens."

"So you don't think much of the Germans!" Guy prompted.

"Not if they take what's ours!" the boy said. "I've not seen you here before, m'sieur. Where're you from?"

"The south!" Guy said vaguely. "I came with a friend to look for some relatives in St Pol and got caught up in this miserable war. The Germans took our van and stuck a bayonet into my friend's leg when he objected. We were trying to find our way home on foot, but he can't walk any further so I'm trying to get help. Do you think your parents would let me bring him here to your farm to rest up until his leg gets better? I've plenty of money to pay them for their hospitality."

He took out his wallet from his trouser pocket and opened it to reveal the wad of French notes with which they had been issued on their arrival in France. For some inexplicable reason, their captors had not removed their few personal belongings when they'd disarmed them.

The boy looked eagerly at the notes.

"Dare say they would, m'sieur. Father said things weren't going to be easy now the *Boches* have overrun us. We're just poor farmers and it's hard enough to make a living without people stealing what's ours!"

It was to be hoped that the lad's parents would hold the same views, Guy thought, as he made his way to the farmhouse. The boy might have been deceived by his story, but he doubted if the farmer would be as gullible.

The woman regarded him nervously when she answered his knock on the door.

"My husband's out back in the barn!" she said quickly, wiping her hands on her apron. "You'd best speak to him." And she all but slammed the door in Guy's face. It was not the reception Guy had begun to hope for and he approached the farmer less assured of a welcome. The fact that the man had hung out a token of surrender was not a good sign in itself.

Once again, he told his story of becoming caught up with the advancing Germans. One hand leaning on his pitchfork, the man heard him out in silence. Then he said shrewdly: "Merchant or not, you'd have been called up for the Army, a young fellow of your age. You're one of those prisoners the *Boches* have been taking down the road these past two days, aren't you? I seen 'em, I have, when I was cutting the hay in the bottom meadow, hundreds of 'em, French and English all mixed up, and a right mess they looked, too. No wonder the Germans got the better of 'em. Supposed to keep the *Boches* out of France, they were; but from what I've heard, all you lot ever did was retreat—"

He broke off, as if aware that he had lost the thread of his conversation.

"You want my help, m'sieur, you'd best tell me the truth, eh?

But I'm warning you, I'll not do anything to risk my wife and son, or this farm! It weren't worth a *sou* when my father reclaimed it after the last war. Taken me twenty-five years to get it back to what it was. I'll not risk the Boches taking it from me now."

"I understand that!" Guy said quickly. "You are quite right, of course, we are prisoners of war – British, actually. I can't promise there'd be no risk, but if you can offer us a safe place to hide up for just a few days – that's all – until my friend gets better, then we'll go. We have friends down south and we're going to try to get down there. But I can promise I'll make it worth your while. See?" Once again, he brought out his wallet. The farmer wavered.

"Wait here," he said. "I'll speak to my wife. If she's against it, then you'll have to leave. Is that understood?"

He seemed to Guy to be gone a very long time. Glancing at his watch, he realized that it was in fact only ten minutes before the man returned.

"The wife says you can hide in the hay loft," the farmer said. "She won't have you in the house 'case the Boches come looking for you. She wants to know where your friend is. She doesn't want him found in any of our fields."

With a sigh of relief, Guy assured the farmer that Bill was not hidden in any of the farm fields. He did not, however, reveal where exactly Bill could be found for he was still not sure how far he could trust the man. It was not unimaginable that he might ride down to the nearest village on his bicycle and betray them to the Germans in the hope of obtaining a reward.

He was taken up to the loft above the barn which, he now saw, was partly filled with straw. Although it was stiflingly hot, it was an excellent hiding-place – and clean, too.

"I need water – and some bread and cheese, if you have it!" he said. He took out one of the notes and saw the farmer's eyes gleam as he stuffed it in his waistcoat pocket. Clearly hoping for more, he offered Guy a pair of navy-blue overalls hanging on a nail by the barn doors. As Guy struggled into them, he handed him a pitchfork and for the first time, he grinned.

"Look more like one of us now!" he said. "Is your friend badly wounded?"

Guy nodded.

"Then you can borrow the handcart. You speak good French, m'sieur," he added curiously.

"I spent most of my childhood speaking the language," Guy explained. "Thanks for your help – and please thank your wife. You're good patriots, my friend!"

Despite the assistance he had been given by the farmer, Guy still did not entirely trust him. He decided to go at once to collect Bill. On his way back across the fields, as he struggled to push the handcart across the stubble of newly cut grass, he realized how weak he was. The sun was still high in a cloudless sky and his face, neck and hands were wet with perspiration and burning hot. Halfway back to the ditch where he had left Bill, he halted in his tracks. He had heard the sound of vehicles far down the road.

Releasing the handles of the cart, he grabbed the pitchfork and made pretence of raking up some of the wisps of hay. From the corner of his eye, he could see a convoy of army trucks carrying soldiers. The vehicles were heading north with their black German insignias clearly visible on their sides. Although it seemed highly unlikely that so many troops were out searching for lost prisoners, he was nevertheless deeply anxious for Bill's safety – his own, too, for if Bill were found, they would surely come to the farm to ask questions.

The convoy passed by without stopping, however, and when he could no longer hear them, Guy completed his journey. Bill was lying flat on his back and seemed at first not to recognize him. Touching his friend's burning forehead, Guy realized that it was not just sunburn which was the cause but a high fever. The difficulty of lifting Bill into the cart was made worse by the fact that he himself was so weak. Every movement brought a moan of pain from Bill, as did the jolting of the cart as Guy dragged it step by step back across the fields. The distance seemed twice as long this time, and he was forced to halt again and again to catch his breath. From the adjoining field, the farmer's son glanced from time to time in his direction but made no move to come to his assistance.

When they reached the yard, a gander flew fiercely across from the duck pond and struck Guy viciously on the thigh, cackling so loudly that the farmer's wife appeared. Flapping her apron, she shooed the bird away and went over to look into the cart. Her expression, which previously had been hard and unfriendly, now softened in a look of compassion.

"Your friend's in a bad way!" she muttered. "I'll call Louis to give you a hand." Bending over Bill's inert form, she sniffed the air and shook her head as she added: "I'll bring you some water to clean his wound!" She walked over to the farm gate and cupping her hands, she hollered to her son.

Bill was barely conscious when Guy and the lad managed between them to pull him up the ladder and settle him in the loft on a soft bed of straw. The woman, who had introduced herself to Guy as Madame Dupont, returned with a bowl of water smelling of some strong disinfectant. She took out a pair of scissors from her apron pocket and knelt down to cut away the filthy, blood-caked bandage from Bill's leg. Surveying the suppurating wound, she said flatly: "He needs a doctor! There's one in the village but you can't go there – there's Germans all over the place." Her eyes narrowed and her mouth tightened. "Wouldn't be safe for the doctor to come here even if I sent Louis to fetch him. People 'ud talk." She glanced again at Bill's leg and, knowing full well that the Englishman might die if he wasn't attended to, she crossed herself. "Maybe Veterinary 'ud come," she said hesitantly. "He'd know what to do. We had a dog once . . . caught in a snare. Must've been there a week before he came home with a leg just like that. Right good sheepdog, he was, so Veterinary cut off the bad bit and he healed good as new. I could send Louis for him. He's an old man now but he's been helping out since young Veterinary was called up when the war started."

Guy was at first shocked by the thought of a vet treating Bill as if he were an animal; but try as he might, he could see no viable alternative. If Madame Dupont and her husband opposed the idea of a doctor being brought to the farm lest he cast suspicion on them, he and Bill could be ordered to leave. There was simply no way he could get Bill out of here in his condition and to a place of safety. On reflection, a vet was a doctor of sorts – an animal doctor! But would he come? And would he have the right medicaments for a human being? There were plenty of reasons why he might refuse to treat Bill.

Beside him and the silent Madame Dupont, Bill suddenly spoke in a clear, lucid voice.

"Frightfully sorry, old chap. Thought I'd be able to make it. Pretty groggy, I'm afraid—" his voice trailed away as he drifted back into unconsciousness.

"And you are going to make it!" Guy said, his mind made up. Something had to be done – and quickly. He looked at Madame Dupont's implacable face.

"Very well, madame! Your son . . . he'll be careful, won't he, not to give anything away, I mean?"

The woman's face creased into a grim smile.

"I'll make sure of that. We'll all be at risk if you two are found here. Louis can say the bullock's cut his leg and is took bad."

She turned to her son who was now standing in the barn below.

"Go and fetch Monsieur Marchette!" she told him. "Say nothing about the Englishmen to anyone – no one, you understand. If he's out, wait till he gets back. Hurry now!"

It was all of three hours before the boy returned. Behind him on a bicycle was a shabby, grey-haired man in his late fifties who looked white with exhaustion. Jean Dupont, the farmer, stood by his side as Guy peered down into the barn below. Clearly, the true situation had already been explained to the vet for he began to pull himself up the ladder without delay.

"It's kind of you to come, monsieur!" Guy said. "I realize you may be putting yourself in danger, but my friend is in great need of medical attention and Madame Dupont thought you could help."

Unlike the farmer, the vet appeared more than eager to help the British prisoners. A veteran of the last war, he was openly scornful of his compatriots in the village who had put up no opposition to the advancing Germans. Were he a younger man, he said, he would have fought to the death to keep them out!

He proceeded to do what he could for Bill – a limited amount in the light of the fact that he had been expecting to treat a bullock! He did, however, make a proposition which, after a moment's reflection, Guy decided to accept. Bill should be taken to Monsieur Marchette's own house that night in the hay cart. He was going to need very careful nursing, the old man explained, and medicines he himself could obtain without suspicion from the pharmacy – always supposing the Germans had not looted the lot! They'd looted all the village shops on their way to the coast. His house was a mile to the south of the village and was not likely to be visited other than by those who needed his services, so Bill would be as safe there as at the farm.

Guy could remain at the farm, the farmer said, and help with the hay-making when he'd had a day or two to pick up his strength. When his companion was better and able to travel, they could contemplate making their way to their friends in the south. Meanwhile, no one knew what the Germans had in mind. Monsieur Marchette himself believed that France would be occupied just as Belgium, Norway, Denmark, Holland and Luxemburg had been. Since the Lieutenant's condition obliged them to stay put for several weeks at least, he pointed out, they would have time to see what the invaders were planning and make their own plans accordingly.

"But my friend – he'll be all right?" Guy asked as the vet prepared to leave. "He won't . . . lose his leg . . . or anything?"

Monsieur Marchette refused to make any predictions. All he would say – and that accompanied by a shrug – was that he'd seen animals recover from worse injuries.

"The peasants around here are poor people," he said. "They don't call me in unless their own treatments have failed, and by then the wretched beasts have usually reached a pretty bad state; but I've saved a good many of them all the same. Have faith, *Capitaine*! We are all in the hands of God!"

At least neither he nor Bill were as yet back in the hands of the Germans, Guy told himself wryly as he went down to the barn to negotiate a price with the farmer for borrowing his hay cart. Bill had been given some sort of sedative, and was momentarily oblivious to any pain. As for himself, a big bowl of soup and a second hunk of bread and cheese supplied by Madame Dupont had served to revive his energy. He had but to deliver Bill safely to the vet's house without running into any Germans before he could do the one thing he wanted beyond any other – to lie down on the soft bed of straw and sleep.

Chapter 26

October 1940

"Captain Bristow is here and has asked to see you, sir!"

Alexis looked up wearily from the sheaf of papers on his desk.

"Who?" he asked, rubbing his eyes. He'd had little sleep these past few nights, for the bombing had been almost continuous as wave after wave of German planes had dropped their lethal loads on London. Approaching sixty, Alexis was no longer a young man, and the strain of long working days and sleepless nights was taking its toll. His hair was now completely white and his aristocratic features were drawn and etched with lines.

There was a smile on Wilkes' face. Alexis' longstanding servant had taken on the duties of butler after Parker left to join up, and he knew nearly all the family's visitors.

"Miss Zandra's friend, sir – Mr Bristow!"

"Good God!" Alexis exclaimed, his tiredness forgotten as he rose quickly to his feet. "For a moment, I didn't realize who you meant. Show him in, Wilkes – and bring up a bottle of Pol Roger. This calls for a celebration!"

Alexis had always liked Guy although he did not altogether approve of his relationship with Zandra. Lucy's insistence that Wisson neglected Zee-Zee did not strike him as sufficient excuse for adultery, although he did accept the fact that a divorce would cause great distress to his mother-in-law. Willow was so frail these days, besides which she was a great admirer of Wisson who, he himself had to admit, had taken much of the management of the estate off Oliver's hands. Nevertheless, he could not believe that, in these dreadful days of war, anyone had the time, energy or inclination to concern themselves with a society scandal.

Since France had finally surrendered at the end of June and the Germans were installed in Paris, it had been only a matter of weeks before the Blitzkrieg had started. As day after day and night after night the *Luftwaffe* formations crossed the Channel to drop their bombs, no one was in any doubt that it was Hitler's intention to demolish London and, if this did not bring about a surrender, to invade England. At such a time, who would even notice if the Wissons were divorced?

Privy as Alexis was to the true state of Britain's defences, he knew that with their present losses, it was only a matter of time before the brave efforts of the fighter pilots who were intercepting the enemy planes would be forced to come to a halt. There were simply insufficient numbers of planes coming off the production lines; and despite the hurried training of pilots, insufficient men. Those there were were on constant call, stretched almost beyond endurance as, heavily outnumbered, they did their courageous best to protect the helpless population who had no one else to defend them. The barrage balloons, the anti-aircraft fire were no real deterrent to the vast V-shaped formations of German bombers which were numerous enough to darken the sky as they flew overhead.

The door opened and Guy came in. Alexis rose stiffly to his feet and crossed the room to greet him. As he did so, the air-raid siren started up its mournful wail.

"Damnation!" Alexis said as he shook Guy's hand. "Want to go down to the basement, Bristow? Safer there, I suppose!"

"Whatever you think best, sir!" Guy answered. He'd arrived back in England the previous day and had spent the night in

Liverpool. As his train had brought him into London, he'd been appalled by the devastation he had seen around him – bomb craters, rubble, sometimes whole streets of houses demolished, fires still burning in places. He'd been astonished to see that people appeared to be going about their business as usual. Although during his stay at the Casa Montijo they had all listened in to the news and realized that things were very bad back home, they'd had no conception of quite how frighteningly awful it was. Perhaps the news had been heavily censored, he now thought, lest the Germans appreciated how successful their bombing raids were.

"I've given up going down to the basement now," Alexis was saying. "I reckon if the house got a direct hit, it wouldn't make much difference which room I was in! Besides, I'd never get any work done! If they get too close, I dive under the table."

Guy returned his smile.

"Then I'll try and be as fatalistic as you, sir!"

Alexis indicated one of the armchairs. "It's good to see you, Bristow. We'd heard of course that you and your friend had reached the Rochfords safely. We had no idea, though, when you'd get back to England."

Wilkes came in with the champagne and, seemingly impervious as the first crump of bombs sounded in the distance, he departed closing the door behind him. Alexis poured out the wine and frowning, handed a glass to Guy.

"I do worry about my wife when she isn't at home during an air raid," he said. "Silly, I suppose, as there might as easily be a direct hit on this house as on any other she might be in. The blighters even dropped one on Buckingham Palace the other day! Well now, Bristow, let's have your news."

"I have letters for you from Mr Rochford and Madame Rochford. Mr Rochford particularly wished me to hand his to you personally. I suppose you know already that he has turned the Casa Montijo into a kind of reception house for the chaps like me who managed to evade the Jerries? He's taking most of them by road to Marseilles, but it's quite a distance from Pau and if the weather is good, it's sometimes easier to get them over the mountains into Spain. That's the way I came. The whole of the Atlantic coast is now part of the occupied zone, as you know, and the demarcation line runs right down to the Spanish border. Fortunately when the armistice was signed, the Germans seemed much more interested in occupying the northern half of France and the border with Switzerland. They don't seem to have any idea, as yet, how many of us are getting away down south."

Alexis nodded.

"With Spain and Switzerland neutral, they probably reckon they have all the frontiers under control. But that won't last. Their Intelligence is extremely good. I'll want to know more about your route home later, Bristow, but first, how did you manage to get down to the unoccupied zone?"

"We were damned lucky, sir!" Guy said. "Believe it or not, it was a veterinary surgeon who fixed up Bill Robertson's leg – he's the young subaltern who escaped with me – and he hid him all those weeks whilst I was at the farm. It took a month before Bill was fit enough to walk; and by that time, Monsieur Marchette, the vet, had found out about a Frenchwoman called Simone who is one of a group of patriots who are resisting the Jerries in whatever way they can. Simone got false identity papers for us and a couple of bicycles, and we were sent to a farm near Tours. We had to hide up there for a while before another non-collaborator was found who helped us over the demarcation borderline to Loches."

Alexis was listening with great interest.

"Marshal Pétain had set up his Vichy government by then, I take it?"

Guy nodded.

"Believe it or not, it was almost as dangerous in the unoccupied zone as in the north. The place we went to was swarming with the *Milice* who, among other unpleasant activities for which they seem to have unlimited powers, were rounding up servicemen on the run. The population has been forbidden to offer food or lodging to 'Germany's enemies' and those caught doing so suffer terrible punishments. The *Milice* are also rounding up Frenchmen for forced labour in Germany – men to work in mines, factories or on farms; and they often catch British troops when searching for men trying to avoid transportation; or when they are on the hunt for the wretched Jews. According to our various 'hosts', the *gendarmes* often as not work with the *Milice*. It took us weeks to get to Pau – and we had some pretty narrow escapes. Bill couldn't speak a word of French so the fact that I'm bilingual helped, of course."

Alexis nodded.

"You got him safely home then?"

"Yes, he should be back by now – he lives up north."

Alexis refilled their glasses, his eyes thoughtful, before resuming the conversation.

"Tomorrow I'd like you to give me names and addresses of all those who helped you; your exact routes; what disguises you used; every detail you can remember."

Guy returned his gaze with a look of surprise.

"I wouldn't want to put any of those brave people who helped us at risk," he said. "My report . . . it would be confidential, wouldn't it?"

Alexis smiled.

"You can count on that. It's not idle curiosity, Bristow. We may be able to use some of those people to help others. We're losing a hell of a lot of planes over there, and even more important is the loss of pilots. Quite a few have managed to get back but we need every single one. These ghastly air raids we're having can only be a prelude to invasion, and every day that our boys are airborne trying to prevent the bombers getting to London, we lose more and more of our air force. I don't have to tell you, since you were part of it, that the evacuation of our troops wasn't exactly the 'victory' the papers chose to call it. We lost a third of our army and *all* our equipment. It's touch and go now, Bristow, although the people aren't being allowed to know how inadequate our defences are; not enough ships, planes, men; anti-aircraft guns; not even enough rifles to arm our Home Guard! Forgive me if I sound defeatist, but I thought you should know the truth. Now we'll talk of something else, shall we?"

For the first time, Guy had an opportunity to ask the question that had led to his visit.

"I wanted to ask you about Zandra, sir!" he said quietly. "Is she all right? I'll have to report to my unit tomorrow but I hoped I might be able to see her – let her know I'm OK. I had hoped Countess Zemski might be able to tell me where she is."

It was a moment or two before Alexis replied. Then, his mind made up, he decided this was no time to be moralizing. No one knew any more whether they would live to see the next day. It had become a question of pure chance as to whether or not the next bomb had one's name on it. The young man in front of him had survived some pretty awful pitfalls in order to get home – just as he himself had done in the last war when as a prisoner, he had escaped from the coal yards in the Baltic port of Memel, where he had been serving a sentence of three years' hard labour! Like himself, Bristow's first thought on reaching home was to see the woman he loved . . . and if in Bristow's case that happened to be someone else's wife, did it really count for much?

"Zandra's in the ATA now," he said quietly. "She's based at Hatfield but spends her time ferrying planes to whichever RAF station needs them most. She could be anywhere at this moment. With these dog fights going on all day long in the air, the demand for replacement planes is acute. As soon as Zandra delivers one, she has to get herself back to Headquarters to pick up another. She could be at an airfield, at Headquarters, or in some train or other trying to get back to base. She telephones my wife from time to time and she called in once on her way through London. One place I very much doubt she'll be is at Eaton Terrace."

"I telephoned there from the station," Guy said simply. A

WAAF standing near by had made the call for him because he'd once given Zandra his word he would never telephone her at home. "The maid said she was 'away on duty'. That's why I came here."

"Yes, well, maybe my wife can help when she gets back. She seems to have a great deal of influence one way and another. She could certainly telephone the ATA Hatfield HQ for you. Now, what are your immediate plans, Bristow?"

"I was going back to my flat tonight – if it's still standing!" Guy said. "If not, I'd thought of booking into a hotel."

"Well, you can't possibly go out on the streets in this barrage!" Alexis commented drily. "You wouldn't find a taxi for love or money, and if the air-raid wardens saw you, they'd bundle you into the nearest shelter. You'd better stay here. As a matter of fact, I'd be very glad if you did. You see, something has just occurred to me that I'd like to discuss with you – about your future!"

Guy looked at his host curiously.

"I'll be rejoining my regiment, sir. That's why I was determined to get home – so I could get back in action."

Alexis nodded.

"Yes, naturally, but your regiment has presumably been reformed without you in the past five months. Unless you rang them, they don't even know you are back in England, do they? Now, if you agree to the proposition I'm going to put to you, you might not be going back. There's something *far more useful* you could do for the war effort than mere soldiering."

In slow, measured tones, Alexis outlined the plan which had been forming in his mind – that Guy should be released from the Army for "special duties". He would be sent down to Beaulieu – a secret establishment where he would receive specialized training. If he passed the very rigorous tests, he would be parachuted back into France, there to help set up organized escape routes for the Allied servicemen known to be still over there.

It was estimated that there were a very large number of them in hiding, without knowing how to get home. It was also known that there were a large number of Frenchmen and women who, like the people who had helped Guy and his friend, were secretly disgusted by the surrender of their country and who were bitterly opposed to collaboration with the Germans. The task of some of the men handpicked for "special duties" was to liaise with such people; to organize safe routes, safe houses and get the service-men home. There were unlimited funds for radio sets and equipment to help them.

Guy leant forward eagerly as Alexis went on to outline the dangers facing Guy were he caught – questioning by the Gestapo and almost certain death. There would be no pressure put upon him to volunteer for such a dangerous operation, the older man stressed. If Guy did agree, he would be interviewed by the Department. If he were thought to be unsuitable for any reason, then the matter would be dropped, and Guy would return to his regiment as was his original intention.

They were still discussing the matter when during a brief lull in the air raid, Lucy arrived home. She greeted Guy warmly.

"It's so good to have you safely home," she said. "Zandra will be so thrilled. Have you seen her? Have you told her you're back?"

When Guy shook his head and recounted the reasons, she promised without hesitation to telephone Hatfield first thing in the morning. Tired though she was, she insisted on hearing all the latest news of Pelham, Silvie, Alice and the children before agreeing that bombs or no bombs, it was time they were all in bed.

"Alexis and I don't bother any more," she said, "but there are mattresses in the basement if you'd prefer to sleep there, Guy."

"I've learned to sleep absolutely anywhere – in a ditch, even a pig-sty once, Countess Zemski," Guy said as she rang the bell for Wilkes. "As for the air raid, the sooner I get used to them the better, I suppose."

"Well, just make sure you don't disturb the black-out curtains!" Lucy cautioned. "We don't want to make ourselves a target, although with so many fires raging all over town, I doubt if our little light would be seen! They seem to be going for the docks tonight, Alexis. It's terrible down there. I was lucky to get a taxi. The driver told me there'd been a direct hit on a house in Warwick Gardens, and there's been damage in Earl's Court, Pembroke Gardens and to St James's Church. If you've only just got back to England, Guy, I suppose this is all a bit of a shock for you. Never mind, we shall do as dear Mr Churchill said in his radio speech – 'fight on the beaches, in the fields, in the streets, in the hills and never surrender!' "

Alexis clapped his hands, his eyes gazing fondly at his wife.

"I'm beginning to think you should be in Parliament, my darling, making patriotic speeches of your own."

He put his arm around her shoulders and lightly kissed the top of her head. Watching them, Guy felt a pang of loneliness, his need for Zandra so intense that for a moment, tears stung the backs of his eyes. Later, as he lay alone in the Zemskis' luxurious guest-room listening to the violent crash of bombs far too close for comfort, he consoled himself with the thought that the tiny, irrepressible countess would ensure that he saw Zandra soon.

It was already dark when, sleep eluding her, Zandra tilted her head back against the hard upholstery of the train taking her to London, and allowed her thoughts to turn from aeroplanes to Guy. She had been woken by her alarm clock that morning and dressed herself wearily in her dark blue ATA uniform slacks and military tunic. Her forage cap under her arm, she had grabbed a cup of tea and a slice of bread and marmalade, and hurried to the airfield to begin the routine required before she could pilot the taxi-plane to the factory to collect yet another Spitfire. There was the password to be learned in case she was challenged by another aircraft; maps to be made ready, the positions of barrage balloons on her route to be noted, weather forecasts to obtain, her parachute to collect and flying kit to be donned. Finally, she had to get permission from Fighter Command to land at the aerodrome of her destination.

The flights were always taxing. Regulations meant she must fly below cloud level with its inherent dangers. She had no radio to guide her – only her maps, eyes and compass. Although officially she was not permitted to fly in heavy cloud or misty conditions, knowing how urgently her plane was needed, she frequently ignored the rule along with many other women, among them her famous fellow pilot Amy Johnson. She got on very well with Amy who, despite the notoriety her solo flight to Australia had won for her, was extremely modest and good fun.

Today's flight had been relatively trouble-free; but at Tangmere, where she had landed, the squadron was airborne, engaged in dog fights, and no one had had time to drive her to the nearest station. When she did finally reach the station, it was to find the trains to London cancelled because of damage to the railway lines which had not, as yet, been cleared. It was late in the day before at last a train arrived, by which time so many people were waiting that she counted herself lucky to get a seat. Her luck, however, did not hold. As so often happened, the train was shunted into a siding to allow a supply train to pass and then, as they neared London, it was halted altogether by a vicious air raid.

Now, from a crack in the side of the blacked-out train window, she could see the fires lighting up the sky over the city. The red glow in the sky, pierced here and there by the brilliant white shafts of searchlights, reminded her suddenly of one of the beautiful sunsets she and Guy had witnessed on a holiday in France. Arms entwined, they had stood in Tante Silvie's garden and watched as the great crimson globe had sunk slowly beneath the horizon, turning the tops of the mountains a deep fiery red. They had looked, momentarily, as if they were ablaze before the colour had faded to a delicate pink and then to pure gold.

Oh Guy, my dearest love! she thought. Are you there at the Casa Montijo now? Are you thinking of me? When will I see you? When?

It was over a month ago that Alexis had telephoned her to say he'd received a letter from Uncle Pelham with the wonderful news that Guy was safe with them. The letter had been delivered by a Frenchman who had arrived from Gibraltar with the intention of joining General de Gaulle's Free French forces in England. He had actually seen Guy, talked to him, and had told Alexis that Guy had stayed on when he'd left Pau because Guy's fellow officer, a Lieutenant Bill Robertson, was not yet fit enough to make the long walk over the mountains. The Lieutenant had been wounded in Normandy, and the wound had developed an ulcer which Uncle Pelham's doctor was treating. It was expected that both Guy and his friend would be returning to England very shortly.

It would be too late by the time this wretched train finally got to Victoria to telephone Alexis and Lucy and find out if there'd been further news about Guy. If the all-clear had not sounded, she decided, she would abandon the idea of trying to cross London in the hope of getting a train to Hatfield. Instead, she would book into the Grosvenor Hotel at Victoria, snatch some much needed sleep and travel to Headquarters on the first train out of London in the morning.

Wearily, Zandra closed her eyes, only to open them again as a sailor seated opposite her stood up to give his seat to a young ATS girl who had walked down the corridor and into their carriage. As the girl sat down, Zandra puzzled for a moment why her face looked familiar, for she was certain she had never met her. Then she understood the reason – the young woman looked remarkably like Inge, gold hair, forget-me-not-blue eyes and a pink, doll-like complexion.

Poor Inge! Zandra thought. It must be pretty miserable for her these days at Rochford, with Jamie stationed miles away in Wiltshire and seeing him only on brief, forty-eight-hour passes. She must worry about him constantly, as everyone knew what a dreadful toll the war was taking on fighter pilots. With only Jane, who was heavily involved in local WVS work, and dear Aunt Willow for company, Inge must hate the fact that she was an "alien" and couldn't therefore join one of the services. Eve, although she worked hard enough when she was on duty, had a wonderful time in the WAAF, and like Jamie, had wonderful food, too; whereas Inge had to try to provide reasonable meals on civilian rations which were painfully limited – only one egg, three ounces of cheese, eight of sugar and a mere shilling's worth of meat a week! Oranges, lemons and bananas were virtually unobtainable and the two-ounce ration of tea or coffee was perhaps the worst deprivation of all.

Nor were Inge's catering difficulties her only concern. An old school-friend of hers who had been in England when war was declared had been sent to an internment camp on the Isle of Man a month ago. Inge herself had had to attend a tribunal, and, like her friend, had been given an Alien's Registration Certificate putting her in Category C. As far as her friend was aware, only Categories A and B were being interned and Inge had been deeply shocked to learn that measures were being tightened up. She was due to report for a second time to the local tribunal which, fortunately, was chaired by the elderly but still sprightly Sir John Barratt, Aunt Willow's life-long friend. It was unthinkable that Inge, the wife of a serving RAF officer and related by marriage to the Rochfords, could face internment; but the Home Office had been unable to give the Rochfords any definite reassurance. Inge was convinced they had somehow discovered that she had once been a *Hitler-jugend* and an enthusiastic member of the Nazi Party, although that was over three years ago now, and she openly admitted that she should have listened to her Uncle Walter and realized how evil and dangerous Adolf Hitler really was.

The jolting of the train as it moved out of the siding and slowly resumed its journey stirred Zandra from her thoughts. Even if there were no further delays, it would be midnight before they reached London. Had it been on time, she would have made her way to Lucy's house, but at this late hour, both she and Alexis would almost certainly be asleep. Zandra smiled inwardly as it struck her how incredibly stalwart they both were, seemingly

403

impervious to the horrific bombardment which, at the first sound of the siren, sent most people scurrying into the shelters or down to the comparative safety of the Underground platforms.

Lucy was indefatigable, somehow managing to look immensely chic even in the somewhat drab colour of her WVS uniform. She succeeded in achieving miracles for the organization, obtaining supplies, concessions, agreement from the authorities, by her charming, if autocratic, assumption that no one would refuse her requests! That same charm had persuaded large numbers of women and girls to join the ranks of volunteers in one capacity or another. She travelled all over the country giving inspiring speeches which left her listeners – who had previously doubted their ability to be of help – fired with enthusiasm to enrol.

"My WVS work keeps me busy!" she had told Zandra, "and with Alexis working long days and most of the nights, what possible point would there be in my sitting at home? Besides, Zee-Zee, our organization is becoming quite indispensable. I can assure you, darling, that I am very proud and happy to be doing my little bit!"

It was by no means a "little bit", Zandra knew, thinking of the evacuation from the cities of all those children; the crèches set up to free mothers for war work; the teams who helped bombed-out victims, and at other such emergencies; and not least, their tireless help with the reception of the Dunkirk survivors. Considering how privileged a life Lucy had always led as the Countess Zemski, her contribution was all the more remarkable. But then everyone was having to adapt their lives to some degree or another. Even Anthony had been prepared to make concessions, reluctantly permitting her to join the ATA despite the fact that it meant he would be deprived of her presence more often than not.

Working as he now did for the Ministry of Supply, Anthony, like Alexis, was often home late; because of this and with the food shortages, the long, dull dinner parties for his business contacts were a thing of the past. Now, if he wished to entertain, he took his guests to the Dorchester Hotel or to the Savoy where it was still possible to get a tolerable meal. When she did go home, although Anthony was reasonably civil to her, she found his conversation immensely depressing. For one thing, he was in no doubt that the Germans would invade; but far worse, he ridiculed the idea that what was left of the Army, Navy and Air Force, together with the antiquated Home Guard, could possibly halt the expected invasion. He sneered at her accusations that he was being defeatist and that he was discounting the fighting spirit of the British people.

"You don't fight tanks with pitchforks and shotguns!" he said. "Britain will have to surrender just as the French have done; and if the Government has any sense of reality, they'd be seeking advantageous armistice terms right now before worse damage can be inflicted on the country."

As if irritated by her stupidity, he had pointed out that she could see for herself that London was slowly but surely being flattened; that she must know better than most how short of aeroplanes the RAF was. And had it escaped her mind that the Germans were no longer the only enemy? That Italy had become Germany's ally in June? Any fool could see that the odds against Britain were astronomical.

Like the proverbial ostrich, Zandra had decided to stick her head in the sand and not allow herself to become involved in future in such discussions. Instead, she did her best to steer the conversations round to Rochford Manor where, she had to admit, Anthony was coping very efficiently with matters concerning the estate – much to Oliver's and Aunt Willow's relief. They, of course, still believed that she and not Anthony owned the estate, for she had never been able to bring herself to tell them that her husband had not fulfilled his promise to make over the Deeds to her as a wedding present. They were still in Anthony's name, she thought bitterly, so he was only safeguarding his own investment!

As always, Zandra's reflections on her marriage ended with the renewed realization that much as she despised him, she could never leave him whilst so much was at risk. Her only hope was that Anthony would finally tire of their sterile relationship and find some other woman whose company he preferred. His sexual demands had diminished since the outbreak of war, but showed no sign of coming to an end. The fact that she was totally and utterly exhausted when she did go home for a few days' leave seemed only to increase his pleasure. The more aware he was that she objected to his attentions, the greater his apparent satisfaction when he bullied her into saying that she had welcomed them. As a consequence, she did her best to hide from him the fact that the only reason she wasn't flying was because she was dropping with fatigue and in desperate need of sleep.

Other than the passengers alighting at Victoria Station, there were few people on the platform. With an air raid in progress, most of the passengers started hurrying to the nearby shelter. Gripping her gas mask and the overnight bag she always carried with her, Zandra donned her tin hat and went across the concourse and along the station entrance to the Grosvenor Hotel. Two fire-watchers were standing by the blacked-out front doors and they waved a greeting as she went into the foyer.

"Best go down to the basement, miss!" one of them called out. "It's pretty bad out there. We just got word the blinking Jerries have flattened Bond Street."

The heavy crash of bombs landing in the close vicinity sent them all momentarily to the floor. The hotel shook and plaster dust fogged the air and fell on top of them in a white dusty cloud. As the dust settled, they could hear quite plainly the sound of the bombers receding into the distance. To Zandra's annoyance, she found that her legs were trembling as she got to her feet. It was not the first time that bombs had fallen close by, but this was the closest.

In those dreadful months when she'd believed that Guy must be dead, she had not really cared whether she was killed by a bomb or not. She had imagined then that she could never be happy again. It was different now. Since word had come through that he was not only alive but safe and well at Tante Silvie's house, she was convinced that God had answered her prayer and that they would be reunited.

For the past month, she'd minimized the risks she took when she ferried aeroplanes to the coast; was less casual when she studied maps and weather reports; ate as well as she could and looked after herself as best she could. Never once did she doubt that Guy would come home soon, but the strain of not knowing when added to the tensions of her job.

After snatching a few hours' sleep in one of the vacant bedrooms, Zandra left the hotel at first light. There was no sign of a taxi, and unwilling to go down to the fetid, overcrowded Underground where so many hundreds of people had sheltered during the night, she decided to walk at least part of the way across London.

As always after a bad air raid, the streets were a hive of frantic activity, the weary but determined populace trying as best they could to rescue the casualties and to repair the damage. Down one of the side-streets which had been the recipient of at least two bombs, Zandra could see firemen were still playing hoses on the smouldering ruins; others were digging in the rubble of collapsed buildings searching for buried victims. Ambulances were picking their way through the fallen masonry which air-raid wardens, civilians, servicemen and Civil Defence workers were attempting to clear. Members of the WVS were shepherding survivors and lost, crying children to reception centres; doctors and nurses were attending to the injured; people were searching frantically for missing relatives, friends. Policemen were trying to direct the traffic into areas where they could proceed to their destinations; cordoning off areas where an unexploded bomb was known or suspected to be. And in the midst of these rescue activities, the resolute citizens of London who had survived the night were making an early start to their places of work, not knowing even if their shops and offices still existed.

Anthony was wrong to discount the courageous, determined spirit of the British, Zandra told herself. One had only to look at the Londoners after a devastating raid to know that they were united in their refusal to admit defeat!

With a lift of her spirits, she made her way to Green Park where the early morning sun was glistening on the dewy grass. Unbelievably, birds were singing amongst the fresh green leaves of the trees, and she paused to listen. A woman passed her whistling to a dog which was racing after a pigeon. For a moment, it was possible to believe that this was peacetime. Then a lone Spitfire crossed the blue sky overhead and Zandra hurried on, reminded suddenly that she must get back to base and fly another of those Spitfires down to the coast.

When she reached King's Cross, it was to find she had half an hour to wait before the next train to Hatfield. Having tried without success to telephone Lucy from the Grosvenor, she decided to utilize the waiting time now by trying again. The situation was unchanged, the operator informed her; the lines were still down due to last night's raid. If it was urgent, Zandra might care to try again in a quarter of an hour.

"Thanks, but it's really not urgent!" Zandra said.

As she replaced the receiver, she was unaware that her call to Lucy would have revealed Guy's presence at Cadogan Gardens not five miles from where she stood, or that by missing this precious opportunity to see him, the chance to do so might not come again.

Chapter 27

October 1940

"Zee-Zee, darling, thank heavens you have come. Jane is in an awful state!"

Zandra removed her forage cap and sat down on the sofa beside Lucy who had arrived at Rochford earlier that morning. Zandra had hitched a lift to Havorhurst from Biggin Hill in a 15 cwt RAF pick-up, for the cross-country bus routes would have taken far too long. From there, the station taxi had taken her up to Rochford Manor. Lucy's telegram forwarded to her from the ATA Headquarters had left Zandra in no doubt that she was needed urgently at Rochford, and the Duty Pilot had agreed to get a replacement for her. As she was so near home, she could have forty-eight-hours' compassionate leave. She was overdue her leave allowance in any event.

"They won't let her see Giles!" Lucy was saying. "She's quite distraught!"

"But Jane is Giles' mother! Surely if it is a matter of life and death—" Zandra said hesitantly, but Lucy broke in: "They don't *want* her to see him – he's so terribly badly burned, you see. He crash-landed at Shoreham and his plane was already on fire, so by the time they got him out, oh, it doesn't bear thinking about!"

"Has Oliver been notified?" Zandra asked, her heart sinking at the thought of what Oliver must feel knowing his only son was not expected to survive. He was now commanding officer of an RAF Group somewhere in the Middle East and she doubted that he would get compassionate leave to fly home. A great many men serving overseas must have lost loved ones and they could not all be brought back to England.

'How awful for Jane having to face this without Ollie!" she murmured.

Lucy nodded. "Which is why I sent you that telegram. You and Jane have always been very close, so you'll be more comfort to her than I am. Besides, my darling, I have something else to tell you – good news this time, thank heaven! Alexis and I have been trying to get hold of you for the last two days. Guy is back in England. We left a message for you to telephone us but—"

"I did try to ring you!" Zandra said quickly. "I was in London last night but it was very late, and I thought you'd almost certainly be asleep. When I tried in the morning, your line was down. As soon as I got back to Hatfield, I was sent off again to get another Spit and bring it down here to Biggin Hill. Where is Guy, Lucy? Is he all right? Will I be able to see him? How long have you known he was back?"

As best she could, Lucy described her meeting with Guy and his longing to see Zandra.

'He had to go off with Alexis this morning to the War Office, but they'll be home later. Alexis is going to telephone me this afternoon to find out what's happening down here before Guy starts making plans to see you. We didn't know for sure whether Anthony might be here, you see; or when you'd arrive, darling. Guy could come down here tonight if you think it's safe for you both. Alexis said Guy was sure to get leave. How long have you got, Zee-Zee?"

"Forty-eight hours!" Zandra said. With Giles so horribly injured, it seemed wrong to be filled with such joy; but the thought of seeing Guy, talking to him in a few hours' time, momentarily put all other considerations from her mind.

"Where is Jane now?" she asked.

"She has gone to East Grinstead where she booked a room at some hotel or other – the Dorset Arms, I think it was, not too far from the hospital. Giles was taken to Brighton first but a visiting surgeon called Mackintosh – no, McIndoe – insisted on him being removed to a special burns unit he has opened at the Queen Victoria Hospital. Apparently he's using some kind of new techniques which are proving incredibly successful, and the doctor told Jane that if anyone can help Giles, McIndoe can. Jane wants to stay as close as possible to the hospital so she can see Giles the moment she's allowed to do so."

"And Aunt Willow? How is she taking the news?" Zandra asked anxiously.

Lucy sighed.

"We've only told her Giles had a crash-landing. She doesn't know yet about the burns. You know what Mother's like about the grand-children! I think she's even more doting about Oliver's son than mine! And Giles does so look like her darling Oliver. Poor Ollie – if he does know what's happened, it will be hell for him trying to fight a war with this on his mind – almost worse than for Jane."

"I'll ring the Dorset Arms and tell her I'll drive over at once. She ought not to be alone."

Lucy shook her head.

"No, darling, now you're here I'll go. We don't know what time Alexis will telephone, and you'll want to talk to Guy. Thank heavens I've plenty of petrol!"

Zandra nodded gratefully.

"I suppose I'd better phone home and leave a message for Anthony – about Giles, I mean."

"You don't think he'll try and come down to Rochford, do you?" Lucy asked anxiously.

"No, he's far too busy. Besides, there'd be no point in him coming. There's nothing he could do, is there? Where is Inge, by the way?"

"Sitting with Mother. She's really very good with her, you

know. I used to think Mother didn't much like her although she did her best not to show it; but these days – since the war started, I suppose, and Jane took on her WVS work – Inge has turned up trumps and Mother has got used to having her as a companion. She does so hate it when the house is empty."

"I'll go up and see them both. Then I think I'll lie down for a bit. We've been pretty much on the go one way and another, and I always seem short of sleep!"

More even than sleep, Zandra wanted to be by herself so that she could absorb the miraculous news that Guy was back in England, safe – and that in a few hours' time she would hear his voice, see him again.

Willow, however, was so thrilled to see her that Zandra did not have the heart to leave when her aunt begged her to stay.

"She talks about you many times each day!" Inge whispered. "Do please stay with her, Zandra – it means so much to her to have you here. Also it vould mean I could go for a little vile to my studio. Vith this so bad news of Giles, I have not had the chance to vork."

She bent and kissed the top of Willow's head and, with a cheerful smile at Zandra, left the turret room where the older woman now spent so much of her time. Willow seemed to take comfort in these surroundings, for the room had once been the laboratory of her beloved husband, Toby, and had long since been redecorated and refurnished as a sitting-room. The big drawing-room downstairs had been shut up last winter because of the shortage of fuel, so Willow's preference for the turret room was entirely satisfactory.

"You look tired, my darling!" Willow said as Zandra seated herself in Inge's chair. "It's this dreadful war, I suppose. Jane tells me there is nothing to worry about, but I sit here listening to those bombers going towards London and I cannot help worrying. And now this awful news about Giles! When he came to see me in his uniform – so proud of his wings! – I told Jane he was much too young . . . only just eighteen, Zee-Zee – a baby! They had no right to allow him into the RAF."

"Darling Aunt Willow, you know Jane and Oliver did everything they could to discourage him. Giles was an air cadet at school and it was inevitable he would join up the moment he was old enough. He'll be all right, you'll see!"

It was after six o'clock before one of the maids came upstairs to tell Zandra that Count Zemski was on the telephone and wished to speak to her. Her heart thudding, Zandra raced down the two flights to the hall and grabbed the telephone only to hear the operator inform her that the allotted three minutes were up.

"I'll ring you back!" Zandra shouted before the line went dead. By the time she had been put through to Alexis' number, it was to hear Guy's voice.

"Darling, is that you? Are you alone? Can I speak?"

"Yes, yes – and Guy, I love you!" Zandra said breathlessly. "Lucy said you might come down here? I can't wait to see you . . . oh Guy!"

She heard his low husky laugh and then his voice saying: "I'm on indefinite leave, darling. If it's all right your end, I'll be down on the first train I can get. Zandra, I love you! I can't tell you what it's been like waiting to tell you that. No one seemed to know where you were. Countess Zemski said you'd almost certainly stay at Rochford if you could get leave."

Zandra caught her breath.

"Yes, because of poor Giles – Jane needs me. Guy, I was in London last night. Lucy said you were at Cadogan Gardens, so we were only a few miles apart. Isn't that unbearable? If only I'd known! But there was a ghastly air raid on so I stayed at the Grosvenor!"

"Never mind, darling!" Guy said. "The important thing is I'll see you later today. With a bit of luck we'll be together in just a few hours. How much leave do you have?"

"Only a forty-eight!" Zandra said. "I've got to be back on Wednesday morning."

"That gives us twenty-four hours, then. Darling, Count Zemski showed me a photograph of you in your uniform and you look so beautiful!"

"What, in that get-up?" Zandra laughed. She felt deliriously happy. "Oh, I wish I was with you. I wish you were here, although it's a pretty grim time for everyone, waiting for news about Giles. Did Alexis tell you?"

"Yes, darling, and I'm terribly sorry. Try not to worry. I'm sure he'll pull through."

"Guy, now you're safely home, you won't have to go overseas again, will you? One of our girls has a husband in the regular army on General Wavell's staff and Anthony said General Wavell was in Egypt – though goodness knows how he knew that, unless it was from one of his Egyptian contacts. If your regiment is out there, would you have to join them?"

"Darling, I can't possibly answer that. Besides, I've been reading all those posters stuck up everywhere: CARELESS TALK COSTS LIVES! Even if Wisson does know any facts, he ought not to be telling you!"

"I suppose not! Guy, are you all right, darling? Lucy said you'd had a rough time in France."

"It wasn't that bad, sweetheart. It was tough on old Bill, though – the chap I had with me. He's OK now, but I don't think he'll ever be A1. He'll get a desk job probably, poor devil."

"Lucky devil, you mean!" Zandra said. "I wish you were going to have a desk job, Guy. At least I'd know you were safe!"

"What, in this country?" Guy said wryly. "I had my first taste of an air raid last night and I can tell you, darling, I was almost as scared as I was at Dunkirk. The Zemskis put me to shame, they were so calm."

"They're getting used to it!" Zandra said laughing. "Oh, Guy, I can't wait to see you."

"And I can't wait to hold you in my arms again. It's been far too long, darling."

"I'm sorry, caller, your three minutes are up!"

The operator's voice brought their conversation to an abrupt end. For a moment, Zandra stood in the hallway, her eyes closed as she tried to visualize Guy's face. Unconsciously, she was

414

straining her ears as if in the total silence, she could still hear his voice. Then the telephone bell rang and startled by the unexpected noise, she gave a little gasp.

Lucy was on the other end of the line.

"I'm with Jane at the Dorset Arms, Zee-Zee," she said, and gave the number of the hotel. "We're in a double room. Jane's up there now and I'm downstairs so I can speak freely. Things are pretty bad, darling. We went to the hospital but still weren't allowed to see Giles; but we did have a long talk with the matron. She said he was lucky to be under a surgeon called Mr Archibald McIndoe and if anyone could save his life, it would be he and his nursing staff. Apparently the nurses were all hand-picked by Mr McIndoe, and retrained to his way of doing things. He's bitterly opposed to the conventional treatment for burns casualties, and men like Giles are given saline baths to prevent loss of fluid which, I gather, is the biggest danger. Giles is heavily sedated so he isn't conscious of too much pain. The burns are on his face, hands and head, and he has fractures in both legs, and a lot of bruising. When Jane got over the shock of hearing all that, she begged Matron to tell her the truth – whether or not Giles was going to survive such terrible injuries."

As Lucy paused, Zandra called out impatiently: "Well, tell me, Lucy – what are his chances?"

"Matron wouldn't – or couldn't – tell us. All she did say was that Giles was young, healthy and had obviously been in excellent shape and that this would count for a lot. She's going to try to arrange for Jane to see Mr McIndoe tomorrow afternoon; but he's doing as many as seventeen operations a day and nearly all of them critical."

"So you'll stay on there for a while?" Zandra asked. "Guy's coming down later, by the way."

"Yes, I'll stay, although Jane is bearing up very well. She seems to have blocked her mind to everything else but the fact that Giles isn't dying. Oh, Zandra, I wish I could do the same! I saw too many badly burned cases in the last war, and those who did

415

live . . . well, they were grotesque. Of course I haven't said anything to Jane, but Giles is almost certain to be terribly disfigured. It doesn't bear thinking about!"

"I'm sure I read somewhere – *Reader's Digest*, I think – that nowadays they can graft on new skin with wonderful results. It may not be as bad as you fear, Lucy."

"Matron did say something about skin grafts, but I didn't really take it in, and I know Jane didn't. I'll find out more about it tomorrow. Give Guy my best wishes. I'll have to go now! I've told Jane she must come down to dinner because it's important she keeps up her strength. She's going to need it, poor dear!"

As Zandra put down the telephone, it occurred to her that she, too, should try and eat a proper meal. She had lost nearly half a stone since the outbreak of the war, and she had been slightly underweight even before that. The last thing she wanted was for Guy to think she looked ill, or to find her less attractive than he remembered. She would wash and set her hair first, and then see if she could find something pretty in Jane's wardrobe which she could wear. Events had happened so unexpectedly that when she'd left Hatfield that morning, she'd had no reason to suppose she would need anything more than her overnight case. Jane was a good deal plumper than herself, but she could tighten a dress with a belt; maybe find a precious pair of silk stockings – a rarity now that all the available silk was being used to make parachutes.

Feeling like a young girl again, Zandra took the stairs two at a time, but before she could go into Jane's room, she encountered Inge on the landing. When she explained her mission, Inge's round face broke into a smile.

"I vill lend you my Liberty dress," she said. "It is much more the better size for you than Jane's, I think. Now I am not longer invited to parties, I have not the occasion to vear it, so it is quite new. The fashion is still good, no?"

Zandra felt a sudden surge of guilt. Inge was her sister-in-law but she had never made any serious attempt to make a close friend of her. Now, because of her nationality, Inge had been quietly dropped by their neighbours and friends and, with Jamie away, her life must be terribly dull and uneventful. The girl was only in her mid-twenties, and were it not for the war, she would be having a wonderful time. Here at Rochford she did not even have her own family to support her. Nor had she had word from them since the war started although she had tried to contact them through the International Red Cross.

As if following Zandra's train of thought, Inge said wistfully: "You are fortunate, I think. You have both the husband at home and the lover!"

Both shocked and surprised to know that Inge was aware of her relationship with Guy, Zandra was lost for words. Her sister-in-law was smiling again.

"Do not fear I vill betray you, Zandra. No vone tells me this but ven Captain Bristow has visited here, I have seen the look he gives you and how you both try so much not to show how you feel! Also, I hear you just now on the telephone. He comes this evening to see you, no?"

"And you are not shocked?" Zandra asked.

"In my country, many girls have lovers. It is to make children, you see. If the girl is healthy and of pure birth, she is encouraged by the State to take a lover."

"You mean, if the girl is an Aryan she will help to build up Adolf Hitler's Master Race!" Zandra said, unable to hide the bitterness in her tone. "I suppose he needs to replace all those Jewish refugees!"

Inge's face was now expressionless as she said quietly:

"You must not think that I approve of vat Herr Hitler is doing. As children, ve vere taught by our parents and in school to believe he vas Germany's saviour and ve vere told about the many good things he vas doing to make our country important again. Now, since I am married to Jamie and live the many years in your country, I learn that there are many bad things he is also doing. But I am a good English vife to Jamie now, and I am very sad ven people in the village call after me the horrid names!"

Zandra stepped forward and put her arms around the younger girl.

"I am so sorry, Inge! It must be very upsetting for you; but I promise you, no one in the family blames you for what your country is doing. We are all immensely grateful to you for looking after Aunt Willow the way you do; and for making Jamie so happy. I know he adores you. It must be awful for you knowing each time he goes up in his plane that he's trying to shoot down someone you may have known; and that *they* are trying to kill *him!*"

"I do not allow myself to think about such things!" Inge said stoically. "I think only that soon the var vill be over and then Jamie vill come home. Then all vill be as before, no?"

Not wishing to undermine Inge's confidence, Zandra forbore to say that she could see no way the war could be won quickly – not unless the Germans invaded and the British were forced to surrender. If that happened, then nothing could ever be the same as before!

"Let's hope you are right, Inge, dear!" she said gently. Wishing to appear more sisterly, she added: "Will you take me to your studio tomorrow, Inge? I'd love to see some of your work."

Inge shook her head.

"Ach, no, Zandra, I do not allow no-vone – not even my Jamie – in my vork room. It is too easy for my models to become broken, yes? And many I have not yet finished. I have not the proper training, you see, and so I make many mistakes."

"I'm sure you are being far too modest!" Zandra protested. "Isn't that statue of the huntsman with his dog one that you did?"

Inge smiled.

"This I gave to Aunt Villow last Christmas. It is the only vone I think good enough for a present. So far, I have not another so good, but all the time, I am trying! Ven I succeed, I vill give to you, yes? Now ve try on the dress. The colour is good for you, I think!"

It fitted perfectly, and Zandra had no doubt that Guy would approve of it. The grey-blue, soft wool fabric cut on the bias moulded her figure and brought out the colour of her eyes. Her excitement at the thought of seeing him so soon had given them an extra luminosity and she could not help but be delighted with her reflection.

Her disappointment therefore was all the more intense when at nine o'clock, the telephone rang and Guy told her that he would not after all be coming down to Rochford.

"There's a helluva big raid on, darling, and I've had a job getting through to you. The Jerries have dropped some incendiaries somewhere near the station, and the roads have been cordoned off. I spoke to an ARP chap and he told me there were no trains coming in or leaving. Count Zemski has promised to fix me up with a car if things are no better in the morning."

It was a moment or two before Zandra could trust herself to speak. Then she said shakily: "Oh well, darling, I've waited nearly a year already so what's another few hours!"

"A few hours too many as far as I'm concerned!" Guy's voice was warm, loving. "Anyway, I'll be down as soon as I can. Do you—"

There was the sound of a distant explosion followed by a crackling on the wires before the line went dead. Knowing what London was like in an air raid, Zandra had little hope of it being reconnected. Slowly, she walked out of the house into the garden. There was no moon but the black sky on the northern horizon was lit up by a red glow. Once again, London was burning – reminding her of the nursery rhyme which was suddenly so appropriate. Above her, she could hear the steady drone of the enemy bombers as, guided by the fires raging, they headed for the capital. Even here at Rochford, over thirty miles away, she could discern the bright, pencil-thin lines of the searchlights criss-crossing the sky.

With a sigh of resignation, Zandra went back indoors. The fatigue which had threatened earlier now hit her with full force. She would go to bed, she decided. Not only did she badly need the sleep, but the time would pass more quickly if she was not aware of it. She would get up early, be dressed and ready waiting

419

when Guy arrived, for she knew he would come the very first moment he could.

She was awake at dawn, and with no desire to get back to sleep, she dressed and went down to the morning-room. With its door opening into the hall, she would be able to hear the telephone bell as soon as it rang. If the trains were running she was sure Guy would call her from London if he could so that she could be down at the station to meet him. If not, she could hear if a car drew up at the front door.

In Cadogan Gardens, Guy, too, had risen early, and was breakfasting with Alexis when Wilkes came into the dining-room to announce that Count Zemski was wanted on the telephone. When Alexis returned from his study, a moment or two elapsed before he said: "There's been a change of plan, Bristow – one that I'm afraid you won't be too happy about. I'll give it to you straight, old chap – your leave has been cancelled and you are to report for duty today. I'll give you the address in Baker Street where you are to report at 11 a.m."

Guy put down his knife and fork and looked across at his host in dismay.

"But they said I could have two weeks' leave, sir!" he protested. "As you know, I . . . I was going down to Rochford—" He broke off biting his lip. "Surely there's something you could do about this, sir? You obviously have a great deal of influence and . . . well, I've only been back from France a couple of days!"

"I really am sorry, Bristow. I did speak up on your behalf, but the fact of the matter is, they want you right away. Look, old chap, Zandra will understand! Not that you must give her any inkling of what's going on; but of course, you do know already how top secret this whole thing is, but it can't be emphasized enough. You were told, I suppose, that until your special training is finished, you're to refer to it as 'a refresher course'? Then, in the unlikely event of your not making the grade, you could rejoin your regiment without any awkward questions asked. If and when you do pass muster, we'll probably imply you've been posted to the Middle East, by which time you'd be back in France."

"Your colleague explained that yesterday, sir!" Guy said. "And that I would be given a completely new identity and have my appearance changed so that no one I happened to meet over there who knew me as Guy Bristow would recognize me."

Alexis nodded.

"With the exception of Mr and Mrs Rochford. As you already know theirs is one of the 'safe' houses; but they will be the only ones. Not even your contacts will know your real name. If, God forbid, the Gestapo got hold of you and found out you were a British army officer, you'd be shot on the spot as a spy. This will all be spelt out to you in due course, so I won't elaborate, except to say the obvious – no letters home, Bristow. If you feel you must keep in touch with . . . er . . . with Zandra, write a few before you leave and give them to me, post-dated, of course. Address them to me care of the Foreign Office and tell her it's a precaution in case Wisson were to get hold of them. Of course, you won't be able to say much – just personal comments, if you take my meaning."

For the first time, Guy wondered if he had done the right thing in agreeing to Alexis' cloak-and-dagger scheme for him to go back to France and try to establish a regular escape route with the help of the French resistance workers. He'd understood the dangers and the necessity – as well as his obvious fitness – for the job. What he was only just beginning to understand was that from the time he left England until possibly the end of the war, however long that might be, he would neither be able to see Zandra nor communicate with her.

"My leave, sir? Assuming I get through the course all right, I will get a chance to see Zandra before I go abroad again?"

"I would certainly think so, old chap!" Alexis said reassuringly. "I'm really sorry you're being rushed off like this so soon after you got back. You do realize this is a voluntary job, don't you? If you want to back down, no one will think the worse of you. It's just that you really are the ideal candidate, what with your recent experiences and your command of the lingo."

Guy's thoughts swung suddenly to the long columns of prisoners who had not escaped as he and Bill had done. They, too, were parted from the women they loved for the duration; no home leave for them! He had no right to complain, for at least he was free – or for as long as he could remain so. He'd have a better chance of survival on his next visit to France, Count Zemski had told him, for by the time he got back there, he would have learned a few of the techniques taught to those others who, it seemed, had already been sent into enemy territory for similar reasons. He'd go, of course. Getting back to "do his bit", was after all the main purpose that had motivated him and Bill to escape after their capture at Dunkirk.

"There'll be a travel warrant waiting for you at the station booking-office," Alexis was saying. "A car will meet you the other end, and you'll be provided with any kit you need when you get there. Just take your shaving gear – personal necessities. You can leave anything else you might have with me. Now, if you've finished your breakfast, Bristow, I suggest you get yourself ready. Your train goes at twelve noon – always supposing it gets away on time, which is unlikely these days!"

Guy stood up.

"Is it all right for me to ring Zandra now, sir? She's expecting me, you see, and—"

"Of course, old chap, but don't forget, as far as she's concerned, you're going on a refresher course; someone dropped out of the group due to start tomorrow, so the powers that be cancelled your leave and put your name down as a replacement – you know the kind of thing. And by the way, ask if there is any news of Giles, poor fellow, and perhaps someone could tell my wife I'll be home later tonight if she can get a call through. I'll try to phone her, of course."

Guy hurried through to the hall, praying that the lines to Kent were not down. They were indeed working, the operator told him, but were very busy and there could be an hour or more's delay. He went up to his room, and having made a neat pile of the few clothes he had purchased since he'd been back in England, he sat down at the desk the Zemskis had so thoughtfully provided for their guests, and started to write to Bill. The poor fellow was on indefinite convalescent leave up north but was hoping to be back with the regiment by Christmas at the very latest when he planned to meet up with Guy again. Bill would have to be told the same story about a refresher course, and then it would be up to Count Zemski and his cronies to think up a valid reason why he was not rejoining his regiment.

It was after ten o'clock before Guy was finally put through to Rochford Manor and heard Zandra's voice. She sounded happy, excited.

"Guy, darling, are you at Havorhurst? I can be at the halt in ten minutes. Oh, darling, I just can't wait to see you."

Biting his lip, Guy tried to keep his voice steady as he said: "I've been counting the hours, too, but darling . . . I'm afraid it's not good news. I'm not at the halt."

"Don't tell me the trains aren't running! Are you at Victoria?"

There was a brief pause before he said unhappily: "It's bad news, darling. I'm still at Cadogan Gardens. You see—"

"Not at the station? You mean they *have* cancelled all the trains—?"

"Zandra, listen to me, please. The trains are running . . . at least as far as I know. Darling, *I'm not going to be able to see you*. My leave has been cancelled. I've been posted and I'm leaving in half an hour. I'm so desperately sorry!"

For a moment, Zandra couldn't speak so great was her disappointment.

"I don't believe this!" she said at last. "What do you mean, posted? Where? I don't understand—" Her voice trailed away as tears threatened.

Quietly, Guy related the explanation he had been told to give

423

her, hoping that it sounded convincing. When Zandra spoke, she sounded lost, bewildered.

"I still don't understand. Why should you have to replace whoever it was who dropped out? What about your leave, Guy? It's not even a week since you got back to England. It isn't fair! Can't Alexis do something? You can't go, Guy, you can't!"

"Darling, you must know what it's like – orders are orders; and Count Zemski did try to get the posting quashed. Zandra, please, darling, don't be too upset. I know it's hellish, for me as well as you. You can't be more disappointed than I am. I don't think I slept a single minute last night for thinking about us being together today."

Zandra now sounded contrite.

"I'm sorry, darling – honestly I am. I know it's not your fault, but you'd think the powers that be would be just a little more compassionate. I suppose if you'd been a married man . . . no, I'm not going to think like that. Guy, I'm being silly. Forgive me! It's just that I do love you so much. How long will you be gone? Will you get leave when the course ends? If you tell me when, I'll make sure I'm off duty at the same time. We'll make up for this by having a whole week together. How long is the course? Two, three weeks?"

"I can't answer that, darling, because I just don't know. I was only given my marching orders an hour ago, so I'm almost as much in the dark as you are. Look, Zandra, I'm going to have to push off now or I'll miss the train. Just remember, I love you very much – far more than you know. I'll see you soon, sweetheart – the first moment I can."

"Promise?" Zandra asked childishly.

Guy, mercifully, was saved a reply as the operator intervened.

"I'm afraid your three minutes are up now, caller—"

"I love you . . . and I always will!" Guy said. And then the line went dead.

Chapter 28

March 1941–April 1942

Giles' life was no longer in danger, but the family were now aware that it would be years rather than months before he would be released from Mr Archibald McIndoe's care. The hundreds more skin grafts that would have to be made to restore his face to some kind of normality would require time, the surgeon had told Jane, since each graft from an unburned area of Giles' body required time to "take". Sometimes it did not do so and the whole operation had to be done again.

Jane was now growing accustomed to the appearances of the men in Mr McIndoe's Ward 3, and no longer found it so difficult to hide her pity and abhorrence at their grotesque disfigurements. Moreover, she was now able to relay to Oliver in her letters her implicit faith in the New Zealand surgeon's new, experimental techniques and her belief in his assurances that one day their son would be able to face the world again without attracting horrified stares.

"It's the most unconventional hospital ward I've ever seen!" Jane said to Zandra who had managed to call in at Rochford for a quick lunch after delivering another Hurricane to a nearby airfield. "The patients behave like a dormitory of rowdy schoolboys and the noise is beyond belief. You'd think they'd keep the ward quiet because some of the new arrivals are desperately ill, but Mr McIndoe thinks it's the best thing for a newcomer. It distracts them from the pain and the awfulness of their injuries."

"I think it's marvellous that the boys can be so jolly in the circumstances!" Zandra commented as Inge poured out the weak cups of tea that the household had taken to drinking since it had become so difficult to obtain coffee. No one could tolerate the bottled Camp coffee that was so often used as a substitute for the real thing, and the tea ration was carefully hoarded as an alternative.

It was now six months since Giles' crash-landing, and he was allowed out of the hospital for short spells between operations. He would go into the little town of East Grinstead with a group of his fellow patients – officers and men together since Mr McIndoe did not permit distinctions. A favourite haunt was the Whitehall Restaurant, where their often rowdy parties frequently went on until long after hours. The landlord, Bill Gardiner, disregarded the fact that his ordinary clientele might not care to drink in the company of men so horribly disfigured, and made the boys welcome. Those civilians who chose to follow his humane example were now as accustomed as Jane to the patients' appearances and joined in the revelry. Zandra had been to two such evenings and, despite the fact that she was so much older than most of the young men, had been subjected to a great deal of admiration and flirtatious banter. Her admiration for their courage was no less than Jane's.

She had welcomed such evenings for it took her mind off Guy from whom she had had only one postcard since he had finished his training. He had not, as he had expressed the hope in his earlier letter to her, been given leave at the end of the course, but had been posted "somewhere" – the usual euphemism employed in wartime in order not to chance any word of a regiment's location reaching the enemy.

426

Zandra supposed that Guy had returned to his former regiment, but she'd received an unexpected telephone call from his fellow officer, Bill Robertson, asking if she knew where Guy was because he wished to get in touch with him. To her disappointment, he was as ignorant of Guy's movements as herself.

Nor was Alexis able to cast any light on the mystery of Guy's disappearance other than to say that he'd probably been posted overseas and that mail from abroad was notoriously unreliable; Zandra mustn't worry! Fortunately, she had little time to worry. The battle in the skies was continuing with the fighters making valiant attempts to break up the massive formations of German bombers which, day and night, were slowly pulverizing London and other cities.

The factories were turning out ever-increasing numbers of aeroplanes which were desperately needed to alleviate the terrible RAF losses. Although there were more pilots now in the ATA, Zandra was rarely out of the air and only bad weather prevented the regular shuttles from factory to airfield.

Lucy, too, had only rare moments to spare. The day and night raids had left thousands of people homeless, and the WVS were stretched to their limits to cope with the ever-growing numbers of homeless. Urgent supplies had to be moved from one place to another where they were most needed; canteens and information bureaux must be manned, and the Home Guard assisted in whatever ways they could. People whose relatives had been killed or injured in the air raids had to be escorted to the mortuaries or hospitals where their loved ones had been taken. Yet never once had Zandra heard Lucy complain, or seen her energetic spirit flag.

"Do you know if Lucy and Alexis vill be coming down for lunch on Easter Day?" Inge asked. "Jane says Mr McIndoe is going to allow Giles home, and Eve and Robin are hoping to get leave. I have to know how many vill be here if I am to cater for so many. It is so difficult to get food now. I do not know how ve should manage vithout our chickens and rabbits, and the pheasants. I am afraid I do not have the sugar for the flapjacks Giles is so much liking."

Jane regarded the younger girl warmly.

"It's sweet of you to think of it, Inge dear, but Giles has to have an operation to his jaw before he can eat such things. Which reminds me, Matron was talking to me about the desperate shortage of space in the burns unit, and the urgent need for money to extend the facilities so that they can treat more patients. Every day, the number of casualties is increasing and they have room for so few! I have had a new batch of begging letters printed, and I wondered if you would do the envelopes and send them off for me, Inge?"

"But naturally I vill be pleased to do this!" Inge said with enthusiasm. She turned to address Zandra. "I have much sadness for these poor men vhich Jane tells me about . . . and every day more are needing this good attention Giles is having. It is very sad that so good a doctor can take only so few!"

"There's another new patient in the bed next to Giles – with burns far worse even than his," Jane commented. "They had to squeeze in an extra bed in the ward to accommodate the poor boy. Giles said his injuries are quite horrific. His outer clothing had been so badly burned, it fell off when he was fished out of the water. He'd somehow managed to land the plane on the sea and was clinging to the wreckage when the rescue launch reached him."

"If his injuries are so bad, do they think he'll survive?" Zandra asked. It had, after all, been touch and go for Giles.

Jane sighed.

"Giles thought he had a chance – something to do with Mr McIndoe's theory that salt water is the best first-aid treatment there is, hence the saline-bath practice he has instigated. They haven't yet found out who the pilot is, so no one has been able to inform his family. He's a bit of a mystery. Giles is keeping an eye on him, but although he mumbles occasionally, no one can understand him. There was a Czech squadron airborne not far away and three of their pilots were lost about the same time as two of ours were shot down, so they think he must be one of the Czechs, though the name on the identity disc didn't tally. Giles said there might well have been other squadrons airborne so he could be a Pole. It seems both they and the Czechs are a pretty wild bunch and although they aren't supposed to get involved, if they see the chance to go after a German, they'll join in the scrap irrespective of orders."

"You must be relieved to know Giles won't have to go through all that again, Jane," Zandra said. "At least he's safely out of it now for the rest of the war."

"It's my greatest comfort!" Jane agreed, "although certainly not Giles'. Like the rest of the boys in the ward, all they can talk about is getting fit again so they can get back in the air. Mr McIndoe encourages them to believe they will, because it helps their recovery, and he's fighting the regulation that says they have to be discharged from the RAF with a pension if they aren't fit in nine months. He says it's utterly absurd to think they can be put right in that time – that they should be thinking in years, not months. Given sufficient time, he maintains some *will* eventually be fit for active service again; and it isn't fair they should be turfed out because of an out-of-date regulation."

"No wonder he's so popular with the men," Zandra commented. "They're all young, aren't they, and it must be very frustrating for them being cooped up in a hospital for months on end with nothing to do but wait for the next operation."

Jane smiled.

"That reminds me of something I have to discuss with Matron tomorrow. Oliver wrote and asked me to make a sizeable donation to the hospital, and as you know, I've been doing what I can recently to raise funds. Well, Matron knew about our wish to help and when I asked her if there was anything else we could do, she told me about Dutton Homestall. Mr McIndoe is letting some of the patients go and stay with the owners between grafts, so it has become a convalescent home. I told Matron that

Rochford was a convalescent home in the last war, and she wondered if I might like to suggest to Mr McIndoe that we took in some of his patients."

She turned to glance round the room.

"It wouldn't affect you so much, Zee-Zee, but naturally you'd be involved, Inge. It might be good for Aunt Willow, too – you know how she hates this place being so empty. I'm sure Oliver would be in favour of it. Like me, he's so grateful for what they are doing for Giles. What do you think, Zee-Zee darling?"

"I think it's a wonderful idea," she said. "But on the practical side, we'd need money, wouldn't we? We'd need more bathrooms, for instance, special facilities, staff . . . that kind of thing. I'm sure Anthony would help – and Alexis, too, – but I'll have to ask Anthony before you tell Mr McIndoe we'll be happy to do it."

"But of course, darling, and we'll need him to help us get organized." Jane smiled. "When you speak to Anthony, tell him nothing may come of the idea. Dutton Homestall is only two miles from the hospital whereas we are quite some distance away. We couldn't take patients who needed daily treatments or anything like that . . . because of the petrol. It won't be easy to get local staff either, with so many of the villagers in the services now, or working in factories and so on."

"Ve could manage, Jane!" Inge said confidently. "It vould please me to help ven I have not so far been permitted. Then I, too, do my duty for the var effort, yes?"

Zandra felt a renewed pang of guilt. She had so seldom given any thought, still less time, to her sister-in-law. Since the Blitz had caused such death and destruction everywhere, the hatred of anything or anyone German had, quite naturally, intensified. Poor Inge had even received a death threat from an anonymous writer whose child had died as the result of a bombing raid; and she had received two threatening telephone calls which, so Jane had told her, had reduced the poor girl to tears. Jamie had been furious when he heard about it, but there was nothing anyone could do. She hoped now that the hospital governors would not raise objections to Jane's proposal simply because there was an "alien" living at Rochford Manor.

Anthony's reaction when Zandra told him of Jane's suggestion was initially more one of indifference than disapproval. In order to discuss the matter with him, she had deliberately opted to stay the night at Eaton Terrace – something she did now as rarely as possible. She'd waited until after they had finished the meal which she had ordered with particular care, hoping that his mood would be an amenable one.

"I should have thought Jane was busy enough with her WVS activities, and that Ingeborg had quite enough to do looking after your aunt and the house," he said disinterestedly as the servant cleared away the meal. He tossed his napkin onto the table and stood up; then preceded her into the drawing-room. Zandra waited until he had poured himself a brandy before she resumed the discussion.

"But Anthony, surely you can understand the need? Those men are in hospital for months on end. They need a breathing space . . . some sort of home life; a way of adjusting to people. They see each other's ruined faces and can't believe people won't look at them with equal horror; turn away; treat them as outcasts. Jane says the people in East Grinstead are being wonderful and many of them are offering hospitality in their homes. Why shouldn't we? And, as Jane pointed out, Giles will be coming home for good one day and it will be much easier for him if people in Havorhurst were used to seeing him the way he now is!"

Anthony looked at her flushed face dispassionately.

"You can't force people to accept something they find distasteful!" he said.

"No, but you can let them get accustomed to men like Giles. They are human beings, Anthony, and they don't want – still less deserve – to be treated like outcasts. We owe them so much, don't we? Their lives have been ruined fighting for us!"

"I really haven't time to debate such ethics with you, my dear, particularly as this whole issue is still hypothetical as I understand it."

431

"You don't really care about people, do you, Anthony?" Zandra said, quelled as always by his manner. "And sometimes I wonder whether you ever did! I don't understand you. Take your mother – didn't you ever love her? When you were a child, I mean?"

Anthony's mouth tightened and his eyes narrowed as, unconsciously, he played with the watchstrap on his wrist.

"And sometimes I wonder if you people who make use of this word 'love' so often could define it," he said coldly. "As far as my mother is concerned, I told you before that I had very little to do with her after I left home. Naturally, as a young child, I needed her. Naturally, as her son, I provided for her needs after my father died. Not everyone chooses to behave as your family does, my dear. Some people prefer to maintain their independence to being part of a cloying family circle!"

It was a long time since Zandra had allowed herself to become involved in an argument with Anthony but, tired and unhappy, she was stung to reply: "Yet you chose to become part of that circle when you married me!"

Anthony's mouth now relaxed in a supercilious smile.

"The advantages outweighed the disadvantages, my dear. I won't bother to enumerate them as you are doubtless well aware of them. One advantage, of course, was you! Quite apart from your family connections, you happened to be one of the few women I had ever found desirable. You may not be the most beautiful by any means, but there was something about you which appealed instantly to my baser instincts. In short, I wanted you . . . and it has been my policy in life to have what I want if there is a means of getting it."

Zandra's face paled.

"I know that now, Anthony. I know you never loved me. What I still can't understand is why you still want me. You know I don't love you. You know I want my freedom. We rarely talk, do anything together – even see each other now I'm away so much. You've achieved everything you wanted and you don't need me any more socially. Why don't you let me go?"

"Why should I? It doesn't matter to me in the very least whether you enjoy being my wife or not. You have your uses, my dear; and now that you have raised the subject, since you are at home for once, I might as well avail myself of the opportunity. It's a long time since I last enjoyed that very exciting body of yours, and as we seem to be blessed with a lull in the bombing tonight, we can make good use of that large double bed upstairs."

Unable to control her protest, Zandra cried out: "I don't want to, Anthony, you *know* I don't!"

Anthony gave a soft chuckle.

"But you always say that, my dear, just as you always admit afterwards that it was exactly what you did want!"

Zandra's resistance collapsed with the bitter acceptance of the fact that there was no way out of the trap Anthony had fashioned for her. Resistance brought only physical violence, but never stopped the act itself, only prolonged it. It gave him added pleasure and this much at least she could deny him.

As she walked wearily upstairs to her room, she tried very hard not to think of Guy; of how horrified he would be if he knew what was about to happen to her. Even to think of him was to involve him in the horrible event and he must remain in that other part of her mind which knew the meaning of love, and how beautiful the physical expression of it could be between a man and a woman. This was no time to give way to her worries as to where Guy might be; if he was in danger; why she had not heard from him; if he was even at this very moment thinking telepathically of her. She would think, instead, about Jane's plan to turn Rochford Manor back into a convalescent home, and comfort herself with the thought that no matter what she must presently endure, at least it had not occurred to Anthony that he could damage Jane's plan by withholding the money to finance it.

Six months later, Zandra went down to Rochford Manor to be part of the family circle waiting to welcome the first five of the burns patients to arrive. Giles, who had already been home for a weekend recently, was amongst them. They were all laughing and joking as they sat in the big drawing-room where a log fire had been lit as much for the cheerfulness of its blaze as for the need for warmth on this early autumn day. Willow and Zandra were striving hard not to show their pity and horror at the sight of the five mutilated young men. Jane was the only one accustomed to it after her many visits to Giles.

The conversation, after they had expressed their appreciation of their rooms and of this chance to be out of the hospital, centred mainly on their admiration for their surgeon. Giles, however, had something else on his mind which he had only so far expressed to his mother.

"It's about the chap who has the bed next to mine!" he told Zandra. "His name is Gustav Gebrauer; and when he was first brought in, they thought he was a Czech – in fact, we all did. Well, naturally, they kept him sedated for a bit and at that stage, they weren't even sure if he was going to pull through; so it was a couple of weeks before they brought in an interpreter. Next thing a chap from Air Defence Intelligence was down to interrogate him. That was when we found out the wretched fellow was a German!"

"You had a *German pilot* in the bed next to you!" Willow cried aghast. "Your mother never told me about this. How perfectly dreadful! Weren't you very worried, Giles?"

One of the other pilots, a young Scot with the inevitable nickname of Scottie, broke in gently: "If you'd seen the state the chap was in, you'd know there was nothing to worry about, Lady Rochford. He couldn't blink, poor devil, let alone lift a finger to hurt anyone. He's the worst case the Boss has had, which is one of the reasons he's so interested in him."

Giles leant forward on his free arm. The other was held aloft in a make-shift contraption that kept it close to his left cheek where a tube of healthy skin from his arm was attached to it.

"Believe me, Gran, Mr McIndoe isn't any keener on the Krauts than you are! In fact, Matron told me he'd turned away two Jerry

434

pilots . . . wouldn't have 'em in the place; but by the time they found out about Gustav, the Boss had got interested in him because he really was a challenge with so little undamaged skin for the grafts. Intelligence weren't interested in him because he obviously didn't present any danger to anyone, and was hardly going to try to escape in his condition! So it was up to the Boss as to whether or not he'd keep him. Typical of the Maestro, he said he'd send Gustav packing if we all voted against keeping the fellow. Some did of course, but most of us were for letting him stay, although it did mean he was taking the place one of our own chaps might have had. I know he's a Jerry and all that, but we knew there wasn't a prisoner-of-war hospital that could have coped with him. He's actually a jolly nice chap when you get to know him, isn't he, Scottie?"

"Much like one of us, really!" the Scot replied. "He told us his grandfather had refused to join the Nazi Party but his mother and father were both schoolteachers so they had been forced to in the end or they'd have lost their jobs and might even have been sent away somewhere to a "re-education centre" – whatever that might be! Gustav has a much younger brother and sister, and his parents were afraid what would happen to them if they refused to be party members."

"Surely your German pilot was a member, wasn't he?" Zandra asked.

"Yes, of course, although he admitted he didn't like a lot of what was going on – hounding the Jews – that sort of thing."

"Seeing the position he's in now, he's hardly likely to admit to being an admirer of Adolf Hitler, is he?" a quiet-spoken naval officer said dourly. He'd had several friends on HMS *Hood* which had been torpedoed in May; there had been only three survivors from a complement of nearly fifteen hundred men, and he was still very bitter about it. He himself was a survivor of a bombing raid on a naval base.

"But Gustav's an intelligent chap!" Giles said defensively. "He'd listened to his grandfather's point of view but there wasn't much he could do about it, and anyway, he and his school chums

435

had all been in the Hitler Youth Movement which had seemed pretty harmless – a bit like the Scouts in some ways. Music, wood-work and flying were his hobbies, and he didn't bother about much else until the war started. When he was called up last year, he was too busy flying to think about anything much but staying alive! He said dozens of his friends have been shot down by our lot. We were all in the same boat, really, except that fate put us on different sides."

"Lucky for him the Boss was too interested in his injuries to boot him out the moment they found out who he was!" the naval officer commented.

Jane stood up and handed round the large fruit cake for which Inge had somehow managed to conjure up the ingredients. When everyone had been served, she turned to Scottie.

"I know Giles has taken a liking to this German pilot, but what about you, Scottie? What do you feel, having a German in the ward?"

The young man's face contorted into a parody of a smile. He had new skin grafts on his forehead which would eventually provide him with a replacement for his eyebrows.

"I feel a bit sorry for him, actually, Lady Rochford. He doesn't have any of our privileges like going into town – that sort of thing; and he's the only one who's made to wear that ghastly blue hospital uniform. We can wear what we like!"

"And of course he doesn't get letters or parcels or visits," Giles added, "and let's face it, Scottie, one or two of the nurses do their duty but no more."

"What does 'no more' mean?" Zandra asked. There was a roar of laughter.

"Well, they're a wonderful lot . . . don't mind when we chat them up. They even go out with us to the cinema and let us take them to dances."

The remark came from a fair-haired, rather shy youth from Suffolk who went by the name of Tiny but happened to be well over six feet tall.

"Mr McIndoe hand-picks his staff, doesn't he?" Jane said smiling. She had been told by Matron that if any one of the volunteers who worked on Ward 3 showed the slightest sign of aversion or pity, she was speedily rejected by the Maestro. Jane knew only too well what it was like to be stared at by members of the public when she walked with Giles. Her son seemed able to take such rebuffs without resentment, but each time it had happened, she had felt like crying. The way the nurses flirted with these poor boys was clearly wonderful for their morale, and gave them hope that not every girl would turn away from them in horror.

"I'm organizing a petition to get permission for Gustav to come here!" Giles said. "I've even got Matron to sign it. Mother said *she* would, Gran, and I'd like you and Zee-Zee to sign it, too – the more the merrier. It isn't as if old Gustav could run away or anything – he can barely hobble! He couldn't possibly be a danger to anyone – and even if he did get away, he wouldn't get far with a face like his, would he? I doubt he'd get from one end of Havorhurst High Street to the other without the whole village knowing!"

"He's certainly got a good advocate in you, Giles!" Zandra commented.

"Well, I like him!" Giles said simply, holding out his cup for another cup of tea. "We're the same age and have the same birthday, so we're sort of twins in a way. Besides, suppose one of us had crashed in France instead of here. Wouldn't you like to think we were having a bit of a break in someone's home? That we were being treated decently?"

His comment brought a moment's silence, broken only when Inge came into the room. Giles had already informed his fellow ward members that his cousin had married a German girl, and that she lived at home with his mother and grandmother. They had not sounded particularly concerned or even interested until the project of Rochford Manor becoming a convalescent home was under way, and someone from the War Office dealing with prisoners of war had come down to vet Gustav. No decision had yet been given about his future, although the question of "parole" had been mooted. Once the young German pilot was allowed out of the ward, Giles had put it to the others, as Gustav's command of English was so limited, it would be practical as well as humane for him to have the chance to express himself in his own language with Inge.

John, the naval officer, looked curiously at Inge. He was surprised to see how young she was. She must still be in her twenties, he decided, whereas he had expected a plump German *hausfrau* in her forties! With her blond hair and very bright blue eyes, she was an attractive young woman. He stood up to shake her hand as Giles made the introduction. For a short moment, she was unable to hide her shock at the sight of his face, but almost immediately she had herself under control and gave him a friendly smile.

"You must tell me, please, if there is anything special that you and your friends like to eat. I arrange the food, you see, and vill do my best. It vill be more easy now ve have the extra ration books. Ven ve are alone here, ve do not buy the big joints or make the cakes and puddings. For many people together, it is more easy to manage."

Although Inge had not lost her accent, her English was now fluent, if not always correct, and she was soon engaged in telling the new arrivals about Sky-Ways and how Jamie had only become interested in flying after their marriage despite his family's interest in aviation. She spoke of the fun she and Jamie had had during his year in Germany; but tactfully avoided any mention of her involvement at that time with the Hitler Youth Movement. She did, however, mention her Uncle Walter and her sadness that he had died of a heart attack so soon after he had managed with the Rochfords' assistance to escape capture and possible imprisonment by the Gestapo.

Surprised to discover that he was actually liking Inge's society, John decided that perhaps, after all, Giles was right when he said that the ordinary German people were not so different from

438

themselves; that it was their Nazi leaders who had corrupted so many of them and pushed them into this appalling war. Not having met any Germans during the brief interlude between boarding school and the war, and not having travelled as Giles had done, John had had no previous contact with them, and had looked upon them simply as "the enemy". His attitude had been coloured by his father who'd been wounded in the last war and was forever stipulating that "there was no such thing as a decent Hun!" He was beginning to see now that his father may have been prejudiced and that perhaps they were not *all* bad!

Between them, Inge and Jane did what they could to arrange entertainments for their guests. Eve came on leave, bringing two of her WAAF friends with her; and each evening, they put on the gramophone, rolled back the Persian rugs and danced. On another occasion, Jane drove the men into Brighton to the theatre. Some ATS girls from a nearby Ack Ack site were invited to a cocktail party, and within a few weeks, visits to the Havorhurst Arms in the village had become so customary that if the young men missed a night, the locals wanted to know why.

Although Jane and Inge had said initially that they did not think they could cope with more than six patients at a time, it was Inge who now suggested that they could easily double, if not treble, the number. The sympathy the men had aroused in the village had prompted several of the wives of men serving overseas to offer their domestic services, and the Red Cross, who had taken on the responsibility of transforming Rochford into a convalescent home, was more than willing to broaden the facilities. Lucy and Zandra visited whenever they could spare the time, and Oliver, who had at last managed to get home leave, spent hours discussing the future he envisaged for post-war aviation, promising all the men that wherever possible, he would give them employment when he restarted Sky-Ways.

It was not until early in the spring of the following year that permission was finally given for the German pilot, Gustav Gebrauer, to fill one of the rare vacancies at Rochford. Although obviously delighted – and grateful – to be there, he seemed singularly ill at ease when he arrived. When Inge attempted to speak to him in German, he politely but firmly said that he felt it was discourteous to his English hosts to do so. He seemed more at ease with Willow who, for some inexplicable reason, took a liking to him, and emerged more and more often from her turret sanctuary to walk with him in the garden. It was she who, discovering that he'd been interested in woodwork, encouraged him to browse amongst the carpentry tools Oliver had used as a boy and had stored away in a garden shed.

Not only the German pilot's face but his hands, too, were grossly deformed. Although it was both difficult and painful for him to use his fingers, he was supposed to exercise them as much as possible, but no one had imagined he might still be able to engage in his former hobby. When one day he shyly produced a pair of pine book-ends for Willow, she was deeply touched and proudly exhibited them to the family.

As praise was lavished on him, the young German shook his head.

"Not good!" he said in his stilted English. "Before, I make . . . how do you say . . . the cuts?"

"You mean you carved them, old chap!" Giles said laughing.

"So! I have the many knifes – special, like the Maestro have for making the operation!"

"I'm sure we could get hold of some proper tools for you!" Jane said gently.

Gustav shook his head. Much of his scalp had been so severely burned, his dark brown, curly hair had only grown back in patches. He must once have been a nice-looking boy, Jane thought, for he had large, dark, expressive eyes which had not escaped Eve's notice. The surgeon was in the process of providing him with a new nose which must surely do something to improve his present appearance, they both hoped.

Gustav tried to flex his fingers and shook his head.

"No good now!" he said simply.

"Nonsense, boy!" Willow said sharply, surprising them all. "You won't know until you try! That's what my husband used to say to Oliver whenever he thought something too difficult for him. There's no such word as 'can't', Gustav."

"Honestly, Gran treats poor Gustav as if he were a child!" Eve protested to Jane when she was next on leave.

Jane smiled.

"I don't think he minds, darling. They talk to each other for hours, you know. They are good for each other."

Eve nodded.

"He's really awfully sweet with Gran, and it's quite remarkable how she seems to have come out of herself since he's been here. She was becoming such a recluse."

"And she's good for Gustav!" Jane replied. "He has put on weight and Matron says he'll soon be fit enough for his second rhinoplasty op. Now, tell me about you, Eve. How's that new boyfriend of yours?"

She should have known better than to ask such a question these days, she thought as she saw the look on her niece's face. The current love of Eve's life was an Australian bomber pilot, and everyone knew what their life expectancy was these days.

"Oh, he bought it on his last sortie!" Eve said in a deceptively casual voice. Like everyone else in her branch of the services, she had adopted an emotionless response when a pilot was missing or killed. Grief was always a private thing; a seeming indifference the only way of coping with the daily tally of losses.

With an effort, Jane bit back the expression of sympathy. She was very fond of Lucy's daughter who, quite unlike her mother, greatly resembled her grandmother. Tante Silvie had described a youthful Willow to her once, portraying her as a tall, slender girl with a beautiful figure, almost white-blond hair, dark, almond-shaped eyes and a gentle sensitive nature. Although Eve was a very modern girl, independent and capable, her sensitivity was very apparent. She was devoted to her brother, Robin, who was on Atlantic convoy duties, and Jane knew she worried a great deal about him for the U-boats were taking a terrible toll on Allied shipping.

"Zandra told me Anthony believes the Americans will come into the war soon," she said. "If that does happen, maybe we can hope for a speedier end to it. Then we can all get back to normal again. Won't that be marvellous, Eve?"

It was a moment or two before Eve replied. When she did so, her forehead was creased in thought.

"For most of us, perhaps!" she said softly. "But not for people like Giles, Scottie, Gustav and the others. Nothing will ever be 'normal' again for them!"

"Perhaps not!" Jane agreed. "But at least, darling, they are alive!"

Chapter 29

April 1944

Alice looked uneasily at the items of food lying on her kitchen table. The children would be back from school shortly and the less they saw, the less chance there was of them telling their schoolmates or teachers how well they were eating. When the Anglo-American forces established a foothold in North Africa, the Germans had promptly occupied the southern area of France where Marshal Pétain had set up the Vichy government following France's surrender. Since the occupation nearly a year and a half ago, life had changed dramatically – and one of those changes was the shortage of food. The Germans were appropriating most of it for themselves and nowadays everyone had to stand in long queues for the bare essentials. The small ration of meat was obtainable only on Mondays and Tuesdays; newspapers were censored; and there was a curfew which lasted until five in the morning. All the British nationals and servicemen who had not been able to escape before the Germans arrived had been arrested and interned.

At first, when the Germans came, it had been very frightening. Alice had been taken in for questioning as soon as they were informed of her nationality by the *Milice*. Fortunately, Claude

443

had been able to produce documents to establish that she was genuinely a French citizen now. There had been further questioning when Tante Silvie and Uncle Pelham had been under scrutiny; but they, too, were released, not only because they had French nationality but because, so Claude opined, they were deemed to be too old to constitute any danger to the enemy. They were, after all, in their seventies, and Uncle Pelham had, ingenuously, taken to hobbling everywhere on a stick whilst complaining vociferously about his imaginary arthritis.

The Calonne household, however, was not by any means suffering the same privation as most of the local population. Claude had seen to that by openly collaborating with the Germans, and by dealing on the flourishing black market. Nevertheless Alice was still extremely anxious, not only for her own safety but for that of the children. But her fear was nothing compared with that of Claude who, like herself, was only too well aware that Uncle Pelham had been housing escaped Allied prisoners ever since the war had started; and had been helping them either to Marseilles or over the mountains into Spain. With the occupation of Free France, his activities had become extremely dangerous, Claude expostulated, and her uncle was putting them all at risk. If he were discovered to be harbouring escapes, Alice, he and the children would be assumed to be accomplices and if not shot, they would of a certainty spend the rest of the war in prison!

As a safeguard, Claude had decided – and brooked no argument on the subject with Alice – to collaborate with the enemy in every way he could. He sold the German officers many of his valuable *objets d'art* at give-away prices. Soon, he was buying from the richer French families who were obliged to sell their heirlooms, antiques and jewellery to obtain the extortionate amount of money now needed to purchase food from the black-market. The price of butter had soared to 160 francs, coffee to 900 francs – when it could be obtained. The cost of half a kilo of sugar or five kilos of potatoes was now the equivalent of a clerk's daily salary. Knowing the pressing need of these people to sell what-ever they could, Claude paid low prices and passed these bargains on to the Germans as "a special favour", keeping enough back to ensure that he and his family did not go short.

When Alice had fallen in love and married Claude, she had not only adopted his nationality and religion, but had deliber-ately discarded her British upbringing in favour of her husband's. She had become a more devout French nationalist than the French themselves and, in many instances, a more dedicated Catholic. Only when she'd been ill had she ever missed a Mass on Sundays, Confession, or failed to observe Lent. Since the war, however, she had found herself strangely confused as to where her loyalties lay. It distressed her when, after the evacuation of the BEF, Claude and his associates had accused the British of abandoning the French to their fate by "running away". She had found herself repeating to Claude Uncle Pelham's arguments that the British had had no alternative; that to stay in France and fight when the battle was clearly lost would only have resulted in the decimation of the entire army, leaving the British no chance of continuing the fight from their own shores.

At first, when it seemed as if the German bombing of Britain was certain to win the war, Claude had convinced her that it was lost in any event; but as the months went by, the situation began to change. In the June of 1941, Hitler had invaded Russia and the threat of an invasion of England was removed. When the Japanese had attacked Pearl Harbor, the Americans had promptly joined in the war. American planes, ships and arms had poured across the Atlantic, and by the following year the tide had turned, and the Allies started making massive bombing raids on Germany. By then, Uncle Pelham was assisting in the escape of American pilots as well as the British.

Claude deplored the loss of French lives when the Allies began bombing German targets in France. He was obliged to admit it no longer seemed certain that the Germans would be the ultimate victors. Where before he had been reluctant to permit Alice to supply the Rochfords with the black-market food to which he had such ready access, he now did so more willingly, whilst pretending he was unaware that her uncle needed it to feed the men he was hiding.

Alice suspected her husband had decided that it would be advisable to keep a foot in both camps so that he could not be accused of collaboration if the war was won by the Allies. He would be able to excuse his open co-operation with the Germans, saying that it was simply in order to cover the assistance he was secretly providing for the Rochfords' underground activities. Alice herself was only too anxious to believe this was the case, and was happy to be able to pass on her belief to her aunt and uncle who, in sundry small ways, had expressed their concern as to Claude's reliability. Only a well-trusted collaborator, they had maintained, would be permitted to continue his business; to get petrol for his car. Nowadays everyone used *fiacres* or bicycles or walked! And those who had not the money to buy food from the black-market, and could not join their fellows in forays to the countryside to buy something edible from the farmers, simply starved to death. Yet Alice's larder was always full! It was a relief to her when her uncle and aunt not only apologized for misjudging Claude, but actively praised him for having played so convincing a role that any suspicions held by the Gestapo, the *Abwehr* or the *Milice* had been satisfactorily lulled.

For a long time, Alice had been tormented by indecision as to whether or not she should confess to her priest her involvement with Claude's black-market activities, and, even more potentially dangerous, her uncle's involvement with the Resistance. Claude had cautioned her many times about doing so, warning that in these dangerous times when no one could be sure where his neighbour's allegiance lay, or which secret organization he belonged to, not even a priest was to be trusted. Now, at last the Curé had let it be known amongst his flock that he was willing to turn a blind eye to the black-market on the grounds that without it there was little other way for them to exist!

Tante Silvie maintained that no clergyman could be anything other than anti-German when one considered the dreadful way they had rounded up and imprisoned the Jews; tortured those they suspected of spying; killed innocent people as a reprisal each time the Resistance took successful action against the enemy. Rumours abounded of the atrocities they had committed. Claude, however, maintained that they had no alternative but to take these measures now that they occupied such vast areas beyond their own national boundaries. Alice had thought better of repeating his opinion to her relations.

With a deep sigh, Alice began to pack some of the provisions Claude had brought home at lunch-time into the picnic basket she always took with her when she visited the Casa Montijo on a Saturday. It was a precaution lest she was stopped *en route* by a German or a member of the *Milice* who might demand to know what was inside. "A picnic for my children and me to enjoy in the mountains!" she would reply. If it was the *Milice*, Claude had instructed her, she was to add that he and two members of the *Abwehr* were joining them later; if a soldier, then she was to name two German officers with whom she was friendly. These particular "friends" owed him favours and would stand by him if there were any trouble. At least it would deter them from demanding to see what was in the basket and from wondering why she was taking large amounts of butter, flour and sugar on a picnic!

Claude, of course, had always been aware that Uncle Pelham did not wish to draw attention to himself by openly dealing in such large quantities of food, and could not see any reason why Alice or her husband should come under suspicion. Barely a day had passed when Claude did not bemoan the fact that his wife's relatives had not returned to England when they had the opportunity. But for them, he grumbled, he and Alice could sleep peacefully at night, whereas now they might at any moment be dragged from their beds and carted off to a Gestapo prison to endure heaven alone knew what tortures! They would, naturally, deny any knowledge of the Rochfords' activities – which in any case was limited – but he had never been confident that they would be believed.

Wringing his hands, Claude complained that it was not only the Rochfords who might make some dreadful slip. What about the Englishmen like Guy Bristow and his fellow officer? All those airmen? Suppose one of them had been caught at the Spanish frontier, tortured, obliged to confess who had assisted them? And any one of the many pilots who had parachuted from their aeroplanes and passed through the Rochfords' hands might even now be betraying them. Were it not for the need for Alice to maintain an appearance of normality by continuing her once-weekly visits to her family, Claude would have forbidden her to go near the Casa Montijo.

His ill-concealed fears for himself and his family's safety had aggravated Alice's concern for the children. She loved them devotedly – even more dearly, in fact, since she had started to doubt if she still loved her husband; although she chose not to think about this too much. She hated it when Claude brought Germans to the house and she was obliged to cook for them. She hated the way he fawned on them; applauded when they bragged about past victories; the ships their U-boats had sunk; the numbers of planes the *Luftwaffe* had shot down. She knew that Oliver, Giles and Robin were in the services, and she could not bear to think that any one of them might be one of the casualties. Only last week she'd had to bite her tongue in order not to throw back in their faces the recent surrender of the German army at Stalingrad and the Russian reclamation of Kiev; the victories of the British 8th Army in North Africa; the invasion of Italy! Although Claude would not permit her to listen to the broadcasts from London, Tante Silvie always passed on such news.

With yet another sigh, Alice put the now-filled basket at the back of the larder, and donning her coat – for even here in the south it could be cool on cloudy days in early April – she set off to meet the children from school. Claudette was quite a big girl now, quiet but intelligent, and although English was no longer taught and the language had been replaced by German, she insisted upon speaking English with her mother when Claude was not at home. The child had never forgotten Zandra's promise to take her to England and was determined, when she finally got there, that she would be able to converse with her cousins in their own language. With a child's persistence, she insisted that Zandra was the most beautiful, clever, interesting person she had ever met, and that when she grew up she wanted to be exactly like her. There was no game Zandra had played with her when she, Alice, had been ill, no story Zandra had read or told to her, no rhyme or song, that Claudette did not recall with total accuracy.

If Zandra was Claudette's ideal woman, then Guy was her ideal man. She would marry someone exactly like him, she vowed. She even conjured up likenesses to him in men she saw. Alice had been quite embarrassed on their last visit to the Casa Montijo when Claudette had suddenly rushed off and hugged one of Tante Silvie's gardeners! The child had been near to tears when she returned to inform them that she had mistaken him for her Uncle Guy. At close quarters, Claudette had seen that unlike Guy, the man had black hair and a moustache, and was unshaven. When Tante Silvie had laughed off the child's mistake and insisted that there was no such resemblance, Claudette had stuck out her lower lip and declared that even if the gardener's hair was different, he had eyes and a mouth and a body like Guy's!

As Alice joined the other parents at the school gate, Brigitte came running out, and with her usual impulsiveness, threw herself into Alice's arms. This child at least loved her mother more than anyone else. Although nine years old now, she still liked to sit on Alice's knee with her chubby little arms round her neck and be "the baby". She was jealous of little Henri who was still his father's favourite and somewhat spoilt because he was the youngest in the family. His devotion was centred on his Great-Uncle Pelham, and when they were at the Casa Montijo, Henri had no time for anyone else.

Claude disapproved of the way Uncle Pelham treated the boy. He thought Henri far too young to be taught how to handle a gun and aim at a target. Since there was no ammunition, Alice could see no harm in it; but Claude continued to object, if only to Alice. Uncle Pelham was also teaching him how to box. "Getting him into training!" Uncle Pelham would say with a laugh. "Ready for the day he's old enough to fight the *Boches*!" Alice had been obliged to bribe Henri with the promise of a mountaineer's penknife not to repeat the remark in front of his father. With a child's ability to take adult preferences for granted, Henri accepted the fact that his father spoke of the *Boches* as "friends", whereas his Great-Uncle spoke of them as enemies.

Walking home from school with the children, it was a relief to Alice that they now ignored the German soldiers who had become so familiar a sight in the streets that it would have been more surprising to see a Frenchman in uniform.

"What's for dinner, *Maman*?" Henri asked. He was always hungry and food was one of his priorities in life.

"I have some cold ham, Henri," his mother replied.

Henri's face brightened.

"And new bread?"

"Yes, I baked this morning. We needed bread for our picnic this afternoon!"

"Picnic!" Claudette echoed. "You say that every week, *Maman*, but always at the last minute you change your mind and we go instead to Tante Silvie!"

Alice frowned. Claudette was too sharp and one of these days would get them all into trouble with her passion for the truth.

"Uncle Pelham should have made my bow and arrow by now!" Henri said, his face pink with satisfaction.

"Whatever do you want that for?" Brigitte enquired.

Henri's expression was scornful.

"To kill the *Boches* of course, stupid!" he replied matter of factly.

450

"Hush, Henri!" Alice said quickly glancing nervously around her. "How often have I told you it is dangerous to say such things? You could be put in prison! I mean it, Henri – we all could."

The boy's mouth turned down and he kicked an empty Gauloise carton into the gutter.

"Well, that's what Uncle Pelham said!" he muttered truculently.

Her uncle should know better! Alice thought, her heart beating nervously. One would have thought that, involved as he was, he, of all people, would be afraid. Heaven alone knew how many men he was hiding! Not that she or the children ever saw anyone at the house; but there must be some if there was such a pressing need for her to take weekly supplies to them. It was best to know nothing, as Claude said, and then, if the worst happened and they were caught, she could answer truthfully that she knew nothing of her uncle's activities.

She was therefore ignorant of the fact that the man she had supposed to be Tante Silvie's gardener was indeed Zandra's friend Guy, who had recently returned from northern France with an American and two British airmen. Although there were now many well-established escape routes for those who were shot down, there were always a few who, for some reason or another, failed to meet up with their contacts – members of the resistance organizations who obtained false papers for them and passed them down the line to one of the Mediterranean ports.

After the occupation of Vichy France and the confiscation of even the fishing boats by the Germans, M19 had arranged for British submarines or destroyers to pick up the escapees at certain coastal places. Since it cost over ten thousand pounds to train a pilot, it was a matter of priority to get them back to England to man the planes now pouring off the production lines. Those men who either had no papers or who had not known where to go for help were rounded up by Guy and brought by him to the Casa Montijo.

It was Pelham's job to provide them with a safe house until they were fit enough to walk over the mountains with Gaston's son, Jean-Paul, as a guide, and into Spain where a British diplomat who went by the code name of "Monday" would take charge of them. Since the occupation, Jean-Paul had doubled his fee on the grounds that his job had become far more dangerous; and he only agreed to continue making these border crossings because the pay agreed by the British had recently been increased to forty pounds for an officer and twenty pounds for an enlisted man. Pelham did not enquire how Guy obtained this French currency, but he always brought large amounts of French francs with him, so Jean-Paul's fee presented no problem.

The Casa Montijo was ideally placed for their activities. Some three miles out of Pau, it was too far for passing traffic. The house lay at the end of a typical farm track lined by poplars, but it was still possible to see in advance if anyone turned off the road and headed towards them. The garden was at the back of the house and not visible from the front. The men, therefore, could come out from their quarters in the attics and take exercise whilst Pelham and Silvie kept watch. They now had only one servant, Monique, a cook who had been in their service since their days in Paris, and was absolutely to be trusted.

The only weak link was Alice! Pelham was fond of his niece and devoted to her children, especially Henri; but he had no illusions as to the weakness of his niece's character. Her miserable little husband, for whom he had never had any time, totally dominated her, and Pelham was by no means 100 per cent certain where Calonne's loyalties lay. In one way, it was to their advantage that he was fraternizing with the Germans. Alice was assumed by the German authorities and the *Milice* to share Claude's pro-German sympathies, and she could obtain through Claude the food he and Silvie so urgently required for their illicit guests!

The men were usually close to starving when they arrived, and if they were to make the long climb over the mountains, they needed feeding up; besides which, unlike Silvie and himself, they were young and had healthy appetites! They kept chickens, rabbits and a pig in the old farmyard; but at any time the Germans chose to do so, they drove up to the house and simply requisitioned what they wanted, including most of the fruit in the orchard. They sent soldiers to harvest the fruit, which was often highly inconvenient, for it meant the men had to remain in the attic for several days without exercise.

The Americans in particular fretted at the confinement and were impatient to get home. Unlike the British who had now been at war for four and a half years, they were unaccustomed to wartime restrictions and at their bases in England were provided with the best of everything – food, chocolate, cigarettes, which elsewhere were in desperately short supply; and even silk stockings to give their English girlfriends. They were totally uninhibited about the shortage of available women in their lives. Joe, one of their present three "lodgers", had only yesterday asked Pelham if he couldn't get hold of some loyal, trusted French girls, to keep them company! When this was related later to Silvie, she had excused the boy on the grounds that he was only twenty and, quite probably, had never had a girl!

These three would be leaving next week, Pelham reflected as he eased himself into one of the garden chairs on the terrace. Friday was market day and Jean-Paul could be on the road with a farm cart without arousing suspicion and could drive the men to the foothills under cover of some empty crates. The Germans patrolled the roads regularly and were accustomed to seeing the Frenchman. Only once had his wagon been searched.

Since those early days, he had not been stopped again although sometimes he did so of his own accord and gave the soldiers a bunch of "unsold" grapes, or a basket of strawberries, or a bottle of home-made wine. Guy was anxious to be off to the north again but never left until the last consignment of men were on their way, for if anything happened to Jean-Paul, he was the only one other than Pelham who knew the route over the mountains. The Allied bombers reached into the heart of Germany. Cities like Berlin, Munich, Nuremberg as well as munition factories were being heavily bombed day and night, and in the past year the numbers of airmen seeking escape routes had greatly increased. So, too, had the numbers of men and women in the various networks of the French Resistance who were being co-ordinated by the British, and their needs regularly supplied by Allied clandestine air drops.

Although Silvie was unaware of it, Pelham knew that a great many of these courageous underground activists had been caught by, or betrayed to, the German counter-espionage; and that each time Guy departed on one of his rescue operations, he was in great danger. Imprisonment, questioning under torture and death were the inevitable consequences of being caught, and it was something of a miracle that Guy had remained undetected for so long.

Pelham's liking and respect for the young man's courage and resourcefulness were now such that he worried about his safety as much as if Guy had been a member of his own family. Like Silvie, he hoped that once the war was over, Guy and Zandra would somehow be able to get together on a more permanent basis. The poor chap never failed to ask if there were any news of Zandra, and it was pretty obvious he was still very much in love with her. Known only by his code name, "Blaireau", he could not send word home to her that he was alive and thinking about her. He had once told Silvie that after all this time, Zandra probably thought he was dead, or that he had forgotten her.

As Silvie joined him in the garden, bringing with her the box of toys and books she always had ready for the children's visits with Alice, it occurred to Pelham suddenly that his wife looked pale and, though it had never occurred to him before, every bit her age. The constant strain they were under whenever they had "passengers" in the house was beginning to take its toll, he thought anxiously. If he had one regret about the work they were doing to help win the war, it was that Silvie must inevitably be involved. Although he knew she would not have it otherwise, he still loved her far too deeply to be able to sleep easily at night, knowing he had put her life at risk. Theirs had been an idyllic marriage and he could not envisage a life without her.

Silvie did not now sit down in the chair he drew up for her, but stood staring at him with an expression of anxiety.

"Do you realize it is nearly five o'clock, *chéri*?" she said in a low voice. "Alice should have been here an hour ago – you know how punctual she always is!"

Pelham glanced at his watch uneasily.

"Perhaps one of the children is ill . . . or Calonne wants her to do something for him. There are lots of reasons why she might not be on time!" he said reassuringly.

"Then why has she not telephoned me?" Silvie asked. "I tried to ring her but there was no reply. Pelham, I am worried!"

"Would you like me to take a look down the road? Perhaps one of the children has had a fall . . . sprained an ankle. I'll go and see, shall I?"

Silvie hesitated, her eyes thoughtful.

"No, *chéri*, it might not be safe. Suppose the Germans have stopped Alice on the road? You know we agreed that if that happened, she would say she was taking the children for a picnic. I don't want you to become involved. It's too dangerous."

"And if Alice is in danger? The children?"

"Claude can help them. You cannot put yourself at risk, *chéri* – not with Guy and the men here in the house."

"Then we'll give her another five minutes," Pelham suggested. "She may be here by then."

He would have been even more worried than Silvie had he known the reason for Alice's unpunctuality. Half an hour before she was due to leave for the Casa Montijo, Claude had arrived back from his shop with three Germans in plain clothes following behind him. Taking them into the salon, he had ordered Alice to bring in a tray of coffee, and in a low, harsh voice, forbidden her to leave the house.

"We are under suspicion!" he added in a hoarse whisper. "I am to be questioned."

455

Alice sent the children into the garden and, her hands trembling so much that the cups and saucers shook, she carried a tray of coffee into the salon. The three men barely glanced at her as she stammered a greeting. To her frightened mind, they looked unduly sinister; and her anxiety deepened as they remained silent whilst she was in the room.

Closing the door behind her, her instinct was to get as far away as possible; yet she found her feet glued to the floor.

". . . may be able to help you, *messieurs*!" Alice recognized her husband's voice, the tone ingratiating. "As a matter of fact, I was intending to report my suspicions about Monsieur and Madame Rochford, but—"

"But you did not! Why? It was your duty, was it not?"

Those were the guttural tones of one of the Germans, his accent marked despite the fluency of his French. His tone was threatening.

"I thought it better if I waited until I could produce some proof for my suspicions . . ." Claude's voice dropped so that Alice could no longer hear him. Her feet seemed rooted to the stone flags; her heart was beating suffocatingly and the palms of her hands were wet with perspiration. She must be mistaken, she thought desperately. Claude would not betray her uncle and aunt . . . he was too deeply involved himself in their activities . . . and what of the part she played? The children? Even if he did not care what happened to her, he *must* care about his children!

The voices rose again.

". . . collaborated well so far, Calonne. We have excellent reports of your co-operation. However, you are a devious lot, you French, and at the end of the day, we know you are married to an enemy of our nation. You have an English wife and English in-laws. You will tell us everything – everything, you understand. We do indeed wish to know about them."

There was a scuffle as if someone had overturned a chair, followed by a groan. Her husband's voice was now high-pitched as he cried out: "You can trust me, I swear it by the Virgin Mary.

Don't hit me again, I beg you. I'll tell you what you want to know. Believe me, it is not my fault that I am married to an Englishwoman . . . that is to say, I married her because she had connections, useful connections for my *Galerie*, you understand."

"Ah, the Rochfords! Degenerate British aristocracy! We know all about your wife's background, Calonne. We even know that two of her relations were active as spies in the last war! We know that your wife's uncle, Monsieur Pelham Rochford, was one of them. Calls himself a French national now. We shall search the house, of course, but it will be simpler if we know beforehand what we are looking for."

"I know nothing of such matters!" Claude's voice was cringing, frightened. "I was only a child in the last war, and—"

"But Monsieur Rochford was not! He may be an old man, now, but that does not mean he is to be trusted. We have reason to believe he is involved with the Resistance movement, and you can take it from me, Calonne, it is in your best interests to help us find out what he is up to."

There was another groan from Claude and a further cry.

"Can you not ask him? Question him? As you say, he is old and—"

"Idiot! If we alert him to our suspicions, his contacts would know immediately and halt their activities. We want them all, do you understand? We want to know how he is operating – if the Casa Montijo is one of their so-called "safe houses"; who brings the men to him; how he disposes of them; who his contacts are. Do you understand? We intend to find out – one way or another!"

No, he mustn't tell them – *he must not!* Alice thought wildly. They would shoot Uncle Pelham, Tante Silvie, too, without a second thought if they knew what had been going on all this time. And what guarantee was there that once they knew she herself was involved, they would not take her and Claude, too? Maybe shoot the children? It was rumoured in the town that sometimes the Germans took the young children after they had

457

shot the parents and sent them back to their own country for German couples to raise for future labour for "The Fatherland".

At last, Alice managed to drag herself away. She tiptoed over the cold flagstones into the kitchen where gasping, she leant against the draining board to steady herself. Despite her desire to believe that her own husband would never betray them all, she knew with horrible certainty that he would do so if it suited him; that he would never stand up to physical torture. Moreover, had he not said just now that he had not married her for love? Deep down, she had always known that Claude had never loved her; that he had resented as well as made use of the fact that her uncle and aunt were rich and part of a society denied him by the circumstances of his birth. At heart, Claude was a communist although that had not stopped him trying to make himself wealthy enough to buy the same privileges as the rich. No, he would not risk his own life to save hers!

Claudette burst in through the kitchen door, causing Alice to start violently.

"Why are we not leaving, *Maman*? We shall be late for tea!" she asked reproachfully.

Called back from the nightmare of her thoughts, Alice straightened her back and with an effort, kept her voice calm and low-pitched as she said: "Your father has guests, Claudette, German visitors, and he doesn't wish to be disturbed. We shall go to Uncle Pelham and Tante Silvie now but you must all be very quiet or Papa may try to stop us leaving."

"You look ill, *Maman*!" Claudette commented. "Are you sure you feel well enough to go?"

"Shh, dear, keep your voice down!" Alice said frantically. "Of course I am well enough. Now go and tell Brigitte and Henri to wait by the back gate. Tell them they *must* be quiet, very, very quiet . . . not even a whisper. Do you understand, Claudette? Your father will be very angry indeed if he hears a single sound! He will not permit us to go – because of the Germans."

Claudette looked at her mother curiously, instinct telling her that Alice's voice held a note of fear over and above the level of that which always accompanied her father's presence in the house. It must be because of the Germans, she decided. Despite her curiosity, she asked no further questions but nodded and went back into the garden to marshal her younger brother and sister. She knew it would not be easy to keep Henri quiet, for he alone was neither frightened of his father nor the *Boches*. She would pretend they were playing a game. Henri loved hide-and-seek. If she told him to hide by the gate, he would stay as quiet as a mouse.

Knowing that the heavy picnic hamper would slow her pace, Alice abandoned any idea of taking it with her. She pushed it further back beneath the larder shelf and pulled a sack of potatoes in front of it. Then she hurriedly scribbled a note for Claude on her shopping pad.

"*I thought it best to take the children for a walk so they do not disturb you,*" she wrote, and placed the paper on top of the scrubbed table top where Claude could not fail to see it. Without stopping for her own or the children's coats, she hurried out into the garden and joined them by the back gate.

"Why are we going this way?" Brigitte asked as Alice hurried them along the alley towards the footpath that led over the fields.

"Because we're pretending we're escaped prisoners of war, stupid!" Claudette said sharply. From the look on her mother's face as she had approached them, she was now no longer in doubt that Alice was terrified of something. But of what? *Were* the Germans who had come to the house with Papa the reason? Had Papa done something wrong?

"If I'm an Allied soldier, I want my gun!" Henri declared. "Then if the Germans catch us, I can shoot them dead."

"We're prisoners of war!" Claudette said, her own fear now causing her voice to be sharper than usual. "They don't have guns, stupid! Now hurry up, Henri. Brigitte, hold *Maman's* hand. *Maman* wants us to hurry!"

Too terrified to look back, Alice concentrated on climbing

the stile into the field. Her bulk was slowing her and she was already puffed. How long had she got, she wondered, before Claude realized that she had disobeyed him? Would he suspect that she was on her way to the Casa Montijo – perhaps to warn her uncle and aunt that he was probably even now betraying them? That they were under suspicion and in great danger? Brigitte and Henri were now running ahead. Only Claudette was slowing her pace to match that of her overweight mother.

"Uncle Pelham will know what to do, *Maman*!" she said. "Don't worry! We *are* going to the Casa Montijo, aren't we?"

Alice nodded, tears welling into her eyes. She felt so weak, and silly and helpless, her fear strangely more concentrated on what Claude would say when he discovered that she had warned her uncle and aunt, than of what the Germans might do. She must keep her mind on one thing only – to reach the Casa Montijo before the Germans did. Her legs felt like jelly and she was perspiring beneath her armpits and down her spine. Were it not for Claudette's calm, quiet presence, she might have given way to her rising hysteria and collapsed into a helpless bundle of tears.

"I'll run on and tell Henri we're going to Uncle Pelham's!" the child said now. "That'll make him hurry. He and Brigitte can go on by themselves, can they not, *Maman*?"

"Yes, yes, that's good idea!" Alice gasped. "But you'll come back, won't you, Claudette?"

"Of course, *Maman*!" Claudette said before running on ahead.

It was as if they had changed places, Alice thought stupidly. Claudette was the mother, she the child. It was a crazy notion, for what could a ten-year-old do if Claude or the Germans had heard their departure and were following them? Suppose they were doing so now, but keeping out of sight?

"Look behind, darling," she whispered when Claudette returned. "Can you see anything?"

Claudette shielded her eyes with her hand.

"Only a few cows; and I think that must be *Père* Augustin going down the path towards the church ... I think I can see his cassock. He's probably going to take Benediction! You can hear the church bells!"

I will pray, Alice told herself, reminded suddenly of the comfort her religion always was to her. The Blessed Virgin Mary would help her ... give her strength. She had not brought her rosary with her but she could still recite in her mind the Stations of the Cross.

Alice stumbled forwards, her hand on Claudette's shoulder. Lost as she was in prayer, she was startled by Claudette's sudden shout.

"There's Uncle Pelham, *Maman*! He's waiting at the end of the cart track with Brigitte and Henri! I think he's looking out for us. Yes, he has seen us, *Maman*, and he's waving."

"Thanks be to God!" Alice muttered devoutly. "Run on and tell him, Claudette ... tell him I think he's in danger – terrible danger. I'll have to stop a moment and rest. Quickly, darling, quickly!"

As she sank to the ground gasping for breath, Claudette took one brief look at her mother and then ran, her strong young legs carrying her quickly towards the waiting man. Pelham hurried forward to meet her. As she flung herself into his arms, she struggled for breath.

"*Maman* said to tell you – the Germans, they were at home with *Papa* and *Maman* thinks they're coming here. She says you're in danger!" Her breath caught in a strangled sob and her voice suddenly quietened as she added: "I think we all are, Uncle Pelham, and *Maman* needs your help."

Chapter 30

April 1944

Anthony sat in the back of the Flying Fortress which was taking him to England. He had been in Italy where the Allies, having taken Naples the previous autumn, were now fighting their way up north. The Italians had surrendered in September, but the Germans were putting up a determined resistance to the advancing troops who were now involved in a fierce battle for Cassino. It would not be long now, he thought, before they would be in Rome – and the fall of the capital could only be a prelude to their landing on French soil. There was little doubt now as to the outcome of the war. On the eastern front, the Russians also had the Germans in retreat, and now that the Allies had all but total mastery of the skies, the once mighty German Reich was fighting for survival.

He had backed the wrong horse, Anthony told himself bitterly. Convinced as he'd been at the outbreak of war that the Germans would quickly invade England and become total masters of Europe, he had decided to throw his lot in with them so that when the inevitable surrender came, he would be recognized as a collaborator and not robbed of everything he had spent his lifetime acquiring. As a precaution, he'd continued to do sterling work for England who, before American aid had arrived, were desperately short of weapons and ammunition. At the same time, he had passed word to the Germans, details of the equipment he knew the Allies to be manufacturing and later, that the Americans were shipping to England. It was perfectly possible to make contact in neutral countries with the *Abwehr*, and he'd had regular secret rendezvous with these gentlemen from the German Military Intelligence in Lisbon, Geneva, Casablanca and other such cities where he had legitimate reason to be.

Now, when he could see only too clearly which way the war winds were blowing, it was too late to back out of his involvement with the Nazis. They had, in their usual efficient manner, assimilated a dossier on him which, if it ever came to the notice of the British, would brand him not only as a Machiavellian arms dealer but a traitor. Many long years of imprisonment would await him, for he knew the Germans would have no interest in swapping him for one of their own men.

Their threats of exposure should he cease to help them were no longer couched in vague terms, he reflected uneasily. As they saw the possibility of defeat staring them in the face, they were becoming ever more ruthless, and their dwindling hopes were shored up only by the hope of defeating the Allies when they did make up their minds to land in France. They wanted details – of where the landing would be; of the numbers of troops; how it would be effected; who was to mastermind it; who would be in command – General Montgomery who had routed their own General, the hitherto invincible Rommel, in Africa? The American, Eisenhower? It was of vital importance to know this if they were to repel the invasion. Either he, Anthony, found out some of the answers or they would allow his dossier to reach the hands of the British!

Beside this unnerving threat hanging over him, his other worries paled into insignificance – one of these being the knowledge that Bristow was in England and, according to his, Anthony's, informant, was meeting Zandra again. What ate at the very core of his being was the thought that he was being cuckolded; that others must know of it but that he was no longer in a position to challenge her. This confounded war had made her far more independent, and he blamed himself for allowing her to join the ATA which meant that she was far less often under his roof. It had seemed a wise move at the time – to have a wife doing such valuable war work. The very last thing he wanted now was to draw attention to himself by renewing his threats to Zandra to expose the Countess Zemski's past. Alexis Zemski, he was well aware, worked ostensibly for the War Office, but he strongly suspected that Zemski might have revived his role of the last war and be once again involved in counter-espionage.

This was no time to threaten Zandra, he told himself uneasily. In any event, even if she confronted him with the fact that she intended to sue for a divorce so that she could marry Bristow, he was not even sure that he cared. If he survived his present predicament, it was probable that following an Allied victory he would be knighted for his services to his country; and with a knighthood under his belt, his position in society was sufficiently assured for a divorce to be no impediment. He could find himself another woman – a wealthy American, perhaps, who would be only too happy to add her fortune to his own in exchange for the title he would bestow on her. He'd always known that power was virtually unlimited if one were rich enough; but the fortune he'd amassed did not yet come into that category where a man could influence the world's money markets, a country's politics, or make or break a giant corporation. Meanwhile, he was obliged to turn a blind eye to Zandra's affair with Bristow.

In his pocket – coded, of course – was a list of names of contacts in England who were in direct communication with German Intelligence. The English had new sophisticated methods for detecting informants and radio operators, many of whom had been caught or who, under suspicion, had been obliged to escape back to Germany. There were still a number of "sleepers" – German nationals or sympathizers – who had been planted in influential positions or in innocuous environments awaiting the time when they would be needed; and these had recently been brought into service. It was up to him to find innocent ways to socialize with those living nearest to him, he'd been instructed, and pass on even the smallest piece of information he could obtain regarding the coming invasion. If there was one thing he could not tolerate, it was being given orders; but he knew himself powerless to object or refuse the German demands.

Anthony was frowning as one of the air crew – chewing on a piece of gum in that unpleasant habit of the Americans – put his head round the hatchway to announce that they would be landing in a quarter of an hour. Half an hour later, an obliging American officer drove him in his jeep from the United States airforce base into London and dropped him at his front door.

It occurred to Anthony, as he put his key in the lock, that he no longer had to wonder when he drove into London whether his house was still standing. The *Luftwaffe* had lost command of the skies and such aircraft as remained to them were needed to defend their armies and their cities, which were now the targets of massive saturation bombing by the Allies. The last German he had spoken to had assured him that Hitler had a secret weapon which would shortly have the most devastating effect upon the population of Britain; but whatever it was, Anthony could not see it having much success. The civilians had been able to withstand the dreadful air raids at the height of the *Blitzkrieg* and it seemed highly unlikely that anything the Germans had devised would now cause them to throw up their hands in surrender – and especially with news of the recent Allied victories in Europe to bolster their spirits.

Anthony ordered his manservant to bring him a drink, and sank wearily into an armchair. He was aware of a dark cloud of depression. For the first time in his life, it occurred to him that he was no longer a young man; that at the age of fifty-two, time was no longer on his side. Not since he had been a boy at school had he felt at such a disadvantage – and he had sworn then never to let himself be in that position again. Now he faced the fact that he was powerless to ignore the German threat. Any serious scrutiny by the British of his arms dealings these past fifteen years would be certain to condemn him; and once he was under suspicion, the British could be very thorough – more terrier than bulldog! he thought wryly as he envisaged them tracing his illegal and then traitorous activities.

"Shall I ask Mrs Beverly to cook something for your lunch, sir?" his manservant enquired. "Madam is lunching with the Count and Countess Zemski, and as we did not expect you home, sir, there is nothing prepared!"

So Zandra was on one of her forty-eight-hour passes, Anthony mused as he instructed his man to bring him whatever was available. She would be home later and he could do with some company – something to take his mind off his problems. He might hint that he suspected she was having an affair with Bristow; or suggest that the fellow had a mistress. That would wipe the smile off her face! Not that she often smiled at him. Alternatively he might suggest they employ some unusual variations to their "love-making" that he knew would be unacceptable to her. It had never yet failed to give him a thrill of satisfaction each time he overcame her resistance to him in bed. Unfortunately, she seldom gave him any cause to use force – something he found particularly sexually stimulating. He was in no mood to be thwarted tonight, and one word of dissent from her would be excuse enough to indulge himself. He would beat her with the kind of cane the prefects had used on him at school, and which he, in his last year, had enjoyed inflicting on the juniors.

"My name is WISNIOWIECKI – you blithering little fool. Wisniowiecki – I warned you yesterday that you'd get another beating if you got it wrong again!"

The miserable, skinny new boy was about to start blubbing again. The sooner young Jessup learned to control the habit now that he was at public school the better for him.

466

"Seems like I've no alternative but to teach you another lesson, Jessup – three, in fact. Lesson one: when I send you on an errand, you do it pronto – not after you've done your prep. Lesson two: fags should address their owners by their proper surnames. Lesson three: only snivelling little cowards blub. Now bend over!"

"I say, old chap, the little squit's only been here two days – give him a chance!"

"You mind your own business, Phillips. He's my fag, not yours. If you're so squeamish, push off to the common-room or somewhere."

Sharing a study with Phillips might not, after all, be the good idea he'd supposed at the beginning of this first term as a prefect. When he, Antoni, had thrashed Jessup yesterday, Phillips had interfered then, saying he should have warned the boy first, and that Wisniowiecki was a rather difficult name to master anyway. He'd have to warn Phillips to keep his nose out of his affairs, or else he'd make certain Phillips' investments came to a sticky end! Well, he'd gone now and there was only himself and the snivelling Jessup in his study.

He was looking forward to the next few minutes. The memory of the floggings he'd received as a new boy were still as fresh in his mind as if they had taken place last year rather than four years ago. Admittedly they'd stopped after his set-to with Elerson, but he could recall in detail the bitter, humiliating moments when he'd been made to bare his buttocks and the stinging swipes of the cane had brought tears to his eyes – and hatred to his heart. He'd had his revenge on Elerson – and Bellamy, too – but that had not stopped him waiting for the moment when he was in a position to inflict punishment on anyone thwarting him.

"Trousers off, Jessup! Bend over!"

"Please don't – please don't hit me too hard! Please, Wisnioeski!"

Stupid little idiot still couldn't get his name right. Now he would have to be taught a lesson!

He was unprepared for the strange sensations in his body as he brought the cane down in vicious swipes across the boy's childishly pink flesh. Pausing, he realized that he was actually getting an erection – something which had not happened to him yesterday when he'd administered punishment to his new fag. His cheeks were hot and his hands were

467

perspiring as he wondered whether to dole out a further six strokes of the cane. Better not, he thought as Jessup sobbed quietly in front of him. The way his body felt, he might make a mess of his underwear. He'd let Jessup go this time and satisfy himself in the usual way. There'd be other occasions when he would find out if the same thing happened again.

"Get out, squirt!" he ordered. He wanted the study to himself.

That was the first time it happened, but there'd been many others, he reflected now, although strangely, when he'd left school and had his first sexual experience with a woman, he'd forgotten about those early thrills until he discovered a place in Soho where he could pay for a woman to fulfil both needs. Illegal, of course, but a man could have his sex any way he wanted. If he paid the price, a woman was prepared to be chained, beaten, forced to beg for mercy the way Jessup had done. He did not go there often for fear he might be recognized, although it was easy enough to find similar establishments when he was abroad.

After his marriage to Zandra, whose body had succeeded in attracting him far more than that of any other woman he had met, he'd ceased going to the Soho establishment and confined himself to enjoying violent sex only when he was abroad. He'd come close to involving her once or twice – until he'd been frightened, by the obviousness of the bruises on her arms and shoulders. He'd realized then that her family might guess what he'd been doing and counteract what *he* could reveal about the Countess Zemski with a threat to expose his proclivities.

Tonight, however, he was in no mood to be shackled by the thought of the Rochfords. Unknowingly, the Germans had given him some additional, very useful information which he would not hesitate to use against his in-laws if they interfered with him. Meanwhile, knowing nothing of the German threats hanging over his head, Zandra was unaware that he would not dare now to expose the dubious past of the Countess Lucienne Zemski!

Cheered by the prospect of the night to come, Anthony picked up the *Financial Times* and settled himself more comfortably to catch up on the City news. The look of complacent anticipation was still on his face when, an hour later, he heard Zandra's front-door key turn in the lock.

Some seven hundred miles away from Eaton Terrace, in the fields bordering the Casa Montijo, Pelham looked down at Claudette's flushed, anxious face and glanced briefly at the distant crumpled form of her mother. Turning once more to the child, he said in a quiet, firm voice: "Take Brigitte and Henri to your Tante Silvie. Tell her I wish to speak to Blaireau immediately in my study – do you understand, Claudette? Monsieur Blaireau. Run now, as fast as you can!"

Waiting only to see if the girl was obeying his order, he hurried across the field to Alice. She was still gasping for breath when he pulled her to her feet, and was close to hysteria as she related the conversations she had overheard. Concealing his dismay at the seriousness of the situation, Pelham supported her weight as best he could and urged his niece back towards the house. By the time he reached it, Silvie was in the doorway waiting for him, her face white with apprehension.

"Claudette said the Germans might be coming here to question us!" she said as she took Alice's arm. "*Mon Dieu, chérie*, is this true?"

Too breathless to speak, Alice nodded.

"We may not have much time, my darling," Pelham said. "Take Alice with you and keep her and the children away from my study. I must make plans with Guy."

Only partially understanding the need for urgency, Silvie knew from the taut expression on her husband's face that the matter might indeed be one of life and death, so she asked no further questions.

"Guy's waiting for you. He has warned the airmen to be prepared to leave at once; and Monique is packaging some food in case it is needed."

Pelham gave her a grateful smile before hurrying away towards his study. Guy's face was grave as he hurried forward to meet him.

"There's just a chance Alice may have misinterpreted what

she overheard," Pelham said as he gave Guy a hurried résumé, of what had occurred in the Calonne household, "but I have to say I think the game is up, Bristow. We've always known we were taking a risk where Calonne was concerned. I gambled on the fact that if it came to the crunch, Alice and the children would be more important to him than saving his own skin. I suppose I should have realized he'd never face the kind of torture we all know they dole out to suspects."

"How long do you think we've got, sir?" Guy asked quietly.

"Not long, I'm afraid. If they've discovered Alice has left the house, they could be here at any minute."

"Then I'll get the men out right away!" Guy said. "Looked at from the Jerry point of view, Madame Calonne and the children have been coming here regularly. They'll never believe she wasn't involved – they know she's English for one thing. How long do you think she would stand up to questioning?"

"She's in pretty poor shape now!" Pelham said gravely. "Then there are the children . . ."

There was a moment's silence as both men reflected on the Gestapo's ruthless method of threatening children in order to extract the information they wanted from their parents.

"Best take them with us!" Guy said quietly. "What about you and Madame Rochford?"

Pelham cleared his throat.

"My wife . . . I don't have to tell you how much I'd like to get her away. But it's simply not on, I'm afraid. It's essential I stay on and try to bluff this out, and I'm afraid she wouldn't leave me; besides which, Bristow, neither of us is fit enough to get over those mountains. Nor could Alice make it."

"Then I'll take the children. Will they leave without their mother, do you think?" Guy asked anxiously.

"We won't give them the choice, Bristow. They're far too young to know what's best for them. Alice will have to stay with us – say the children have got lost and that she came here in a panic looking for them."

Guy nodded. "The chaps upstairs – I'll get Jean-Paul to take them over the border. He's half-expecting to have to make the trip shortly in any case; and I'll double his fee if he hesitates. If I could take your car to Saint Martin, sir? Hide it somewhere nearby."

"There's petrol in it," Pelham said, adding wryly: "Thanks to Calonne and the black-market! You'll just have to chance you won't be stopped by a patrol."

"If I can make contact with Jean-Paul, I'll get the men on their way at once. Our first priority has to be to get them back to base, and the children would slow them down and add to the dangers. I'll ask the Curé to find somewhere safe for me and the children to spend the night. You can get word to me via him if all this turns out to be a storm in a teacup. If I don't hear from you, I'll push on next day."

"Think you could get the children over the border by yourself, Bristow? Without a guide? You've done the trip before, so you know better than I that it's a helluva walk over those mountains. There'll be snow on top at this time of year. The children are very young. If we could think of another way—"

Guy returned the older man's gaze steadily.

"Whatever the risks for the children on the mountains, at least they'll have a chance, sir! Things could be very tough for them if they stay here."

Pelham nodded.

"If you can get them to England, they can go to my sister-in-law at Rochford. Jane will look after them; and there's that wife of Jamie's and Zandra. The children will be safe enough there. With a bit of luck, they can be reunited with their mother after the war – and that may not be too long now. It's up to you, old chap."

It was on the tip of Guy's tongue to express his concern for the safety of the elderly couple who had already done more than their fair share for their country; how could he possibly leave them here to the mercy of the Gestapo? Yet he knew he must stay silent, for Mr Rochford knew very well what might lie in store for them; and to voice it would only add to his distress. At least there was a modicum of hope that Alice Calonne might have misinterpreted what she'd overheard, and panicked.

"Don't worry, sir, I'll get the children home somehow," he said quietly.

Pelham reached out and put a hand on Guy's shoulder.

"Don't doubt it, old chap. Rather envy you spending a bit of time at the old homestead. Must be looking pretty nice at this time of year – some good fishing in the lake, I imagine." He drew himself up sharply. "Better get off right away, Bristow. I'll get the car ready . . . stick some rugs and things in the back . . . you'll need them when you get up to the snow line."

They most certainly would, Guy thought as he hurried out of the room. When he'd been at school in Switzerland, he'd been to many of the mountains in winter and he knew how bitterly cold it could be on the heights. The thought of struggling over the Pyrenees on foot with three small children was daunting, to say the very least. He had only made the trip once with Bill and Jean-Paul, and they had found it hard enough in mid-summer! He must hope that Mr Rochford could talk his way out of trouble. Then he'd have time to arrange an easier method of getting the children to safety, and he could slip back up north and continue his job.

As Guy disappeared, Pelham went through to the salon where Silvie was doing her best to comfort a weeping Alice. With a sensitivity beyond her years, Claudette was over by the window keeping the younger children amused whilst at the same time, watching from the casement to see if a car was approaching. She had cleverly made a game of it for her brother and sister – who would see the car first!

Pelham drew Silvie aside and put his arm around her as he outlined the plans Guy and he had made.

"So we shall stay, *chéri*!" she said softly. "You are quite right, of course – Alice could not endure the walk even as far as the foothills. And do not look so tragic, my darling. If the worst should

472

happen, I am quite willing to accept it so long as we are together. We have had a good, long life, have we not? And enjoyed so much happiness!"

Pelham could not trust himself to speak. He had always known of his wife's bravery but the courage she was now showing touched him to an even greater love and respect.

"*Dépêches-toi, mon amour!*" she said softly. "I will remain here with Alice and try to make her understand that when the Germans come, she is to say she is crying because she was out walking with the children and they became lost!"

Ten minutes later, Guy drove the three airmen and the three children away from the Casa Montijo in a southeasterly direction. Barely had he disappeared down the main road before a large black staff car bearing the German insignia came from the opposite direction of Pau and turned up the cart track leading to the house.

For a quarter of an hour, the relentless questioning by the three Germans was confined to the old servant, Monique. Then she was taken out into the garden and strung up by her feet to the eucalyptus tree. Pelham, Silvie and Alice were ordered onto the terrace to watch as the interrogators began systematically to beat her before their horrified eyes.

With stubborn courage, the old woman refused to admit that her employers had been harbouring Allied airmen. It was Alice who finally could no longer endure the sight. Throwing herself at the feet of the interrogators, she poured out between hysterical sobs, an admission that everything Claude had told them was true. Where was her husband? she pleaded. What had they done to him? Now that she had confessed, would they be merciful to her and to her uncle and aunt?

With a feeling of inevitability, Pelham resigned himself to the fact that there would be no mercy. The Germans had already searched the attics and found them empty, and now they wanted to know where the airmen were hiding. Alice could tell them nothing, since he, Pelham, had made sure she did not know what Guy and he had planned for the men or her children. Nor

473

was Alice aware of Jean-Paul's activities in the Resistance, or the route he took over the mountains into Spain. He would wait a few moments longer, Pelham decided, before he took the action he had hoped might never be necessary.

Only a minute passed before, with a shocking indifference to life he could not bear to witness, one of the interrogators shot both the servant and Alice. No longer in any doubt as to what must now happen to his wife and himself, Pelham reached for the gun he had hidden in his pocket. He was aware of Silvie's gaze fastened upon him and, his eyes never leaving hers, he smiled as he drew out the weapon and pulled the trigger, before turning the gun on himself.

Sitting in the back of the staff car, Claude Calonne crouched shivering, a terrified helpless jelly. Only at the sound of the first two shots, followed closely by two more, did he move. He forced himself to open the car door and, on trembling legs, crept round the side of the house. With a moan, he shut his eyes against the sight of the four figures lying motionless with the bright afternoon sunshine glinting on the ever-widening pools of their blood. He knew now that his betrayal of his wife and her family would not, after all, save him from torture, imprisonment or more probably, death. The Gestapo had not found the airmen, and since neither he nor Alice had ever known how the Rochfords got the escapees to safety, he would he unable to tell the Germans what they wanted to know.

He'd been a fool to trust them, he thought bitterly: to believe they would spare him and his family if he told them about the black-market supplies of food Alice took each week to the house; of the anti-German sentiments Mr Rochford had expressed to Henri; of the unguarded remarks Alice sometimes made about seeing trays of food prepared by Monique in the kitchen which could not possibly be for the household who had already eaten their luncheon; even of Brigitte's discovery of a cigar butt in the garden. She had used the gold band as a ring until he, Claude, had seen that it was an American brand.

Stupidly, he now realized, he had imagined that if he made mention only of his suspicions concerning the Rochfords' activities, they would believe him when he denied any actual knowledge of the fact that the Casa Montijo was a "safe house" – and had been so since the fall of France. Now they had shot Alice, her aunt and uncle, and even the servant; and with dreadful certainty, Claude knew that if he could not tell them what they wanted to know, they would kill him, too.

By the time Guy reached the outskirts of Saint Martin, the three children sitting on the laps of the airmen were already orphans – a fact they mercifully did not know. Only Brigitte was crying softly for her mother. Henri was engrossed by this unexpected encounter with real Allied pilots; and Claudette, better aware of the danger they were in, was pale and silent. Guy drove the car into a thicket where it would not easily be seen were a patrol to come searching for them, and left the occupants in it whilst he went to look first for Jean-Paul, and then the Curé. When he returned some two hours later with Jean-Paul, he was greeted with sighs of relief, for Claudette and the airmen had feared he might have encountered Germans or the *Milice* in the village.

Guy handed over the airmen to a grim-faced Jean-Paul. The guide had been reluctant to carry out his usual duties when he'd heard the reason for this sudden exodus. As Pelham had surmised, a doubling of his fee had outweighed his nervousness.

As he departed with the three "passengers", Guy gathered up the rugs and led the children on foot along the half-mile walk into the village. Following the usual procedure, he waited in the churchyard behind the curious Basque disc-shaped tombs until no one was in sight, and then hurried the youngsters into the comparative safety of the vestry. Before many minutes, the Curé appeared. His expression when he regarded the three small figures was dubious.

"They are so young, monsieur!" he said. "Far too young to go over the mountains!"

"They may be able to go by some other route, Père Benoit, if I am given time to arrange it," Guy replied in a low voice. "But I must be prepared for the mountains in case I do not receive word that there is time for an alternative." He explained briefly what had happened. The Curé's look of distress deepened.

"I would like to suggest that it would be possible for us to hide them here in the village for the duration," he said unhappily, "separate them, perhaps, and find people willing to take them into their families; but the danger is too great. From what you tell me, the Germans are already suspicious . . . and their searches are always very thorough. We could not be certain, either, that no one would reveal their presence."

The old man looked apologetic as he added: "*Hélas*, but I have to admit, monsieur, that I know there are collaborators amongst my flock. No one is to be trusted these days!" He drew a deep sigh and walked over to the children. "*Eh, bien, mes enfants*, I have brought you some food!" Patting their heads, he handed them two large round loaves filled with goat's cheese, and a bag of fruit and nuts which he had hidden under his surplice. Returning to Guy, he said matter of factly: "Their clothes . . . their shoes . . . I don't have to tell you these are unsuitable for mountain walking! And there will be snow up there! And the little one – he can be but seven or eight years old, *non*?"

"I know they are young, Monsieur le Curé, but these children have been well fed and they are healthy. If you can find them boots, warm clothes, we can travel slowly. We would need food, of course and" – he gave an apologetic smile – "if you could somehow get hold of a rifle for me—?"

With an unexpected smile, the old man nodded.

"Priests are not in the habit of keeping weapons, monsieur. However, I happen to know that one of my flock has a shotgun and a rifle hidden on his farm! Perhaps if you have a few francs to encourage him to be generous, monsieur? As you know, my people are very poor and the occupation has not made life easier for them, you understand."

As the old man ambled away to find what he could to assist Guy and with a promise to return before nightfall, Guy took Brigitte, tearful once more, onto his lap. It had occurred to him on the drive to Saint Martin that although he had no wish to frighten the children, it would be in the interests of their own safety to explain why they might have to make this journey over the mountains, and their ultimate destination. Only by doing so could he hope to quieten Henri's excited chatter and be sure that they obeyed his instructions without protest or argument. He was only too well aware that despite his assurances to Mr Rochford, at best the chances of them ever reaching the border, still less crossing it, were far from good. He was not even entirely certain if he could remember the route Jean-Paul had taken when the guide had led Bill and him to safety. It was, after all, over three years ago!

Could it really be that long since he'd last seen Zandra? he asked himself. Count Zemski must have run out of those post-cards he'd written to her a very long while ago, and he could hardly blame Zandra if she'd forgotten his existence, nor if she'd assumed he had forgotten her. It was true that the service-men he'd been responsible for rescuing had been asked to notify Count Zemski that "Blaireau" was alive and well! All he could hope now was that Zandra's kindly uncle had thought of some way to relay this fact to Zandra – a doubtful advantage since Zandra must wonder why, if he'd not died in action, he never wrote to her as other men serving overseas wrote to their wives and girlfriends.

Hastily, he put such thoughts aside and concentrated upon the task in hand. Brigitte dissolved once more into tears saying that she did not want to leave her mother! Fortunately Henri was diverted by the idea of going to England, perhaps on a boat or even an aeroplane. Claudette was silent and thoughtful. He drew her to one side.

"You are the eldest, Claudette, and nearly grown-up now," he said. "I am therefore relying on you to help me with your young sister and brother. You will have to be their mother for the next few weeks. I'm sure you must be feeling very frightened, and that is no disgrace. All of us have good reason to be afraid; but if you and I appear calm, then hopefully the little ones will take their cue from us. Do you understand what I am saying?"

Claudette nodded. Her voice trembled slightly as she said doubtfully: "I'm not really very grown-up, Uncle Guy. I shan't be eleven until June!"

"Of course, sweetheart, but I happen to know you are very sensible and very intelligent for your age."

"Did Aunt Zandra tell you that?" Claudette asked, her eyes brightening. "We shall see her when we get to England, won't we? Tante Silvie told me she was flying aeroplanes to help in the war! She's very brave, isn't she?"

"And so will you be, Claudette, and we shall tell her so when we see her!" Guy said encouragingly.

It was not long after the children had fallen asleep on the pews beside him in the gallery that word reached Guy that both the *Milice* and the *Abwehr* were out in force scouring the roads and countryside in the neighbourhood of the Casa Montijo; that the road to the house had been sealed off and the Rochfords' daily woman who went up each morning from the nearby farm to clean had been taken into Pau for questioning.

Any doubts that still lingered in Guy's mind as to the necessity for taking the children up the mountains were immediately quashed. He would do as the Curé now asked and leave at first light. He settled himself down as best he could on one of the narrow pews, but was too apprehensive to sleep.

He roused himself from a light, fitful doze long before daybreak. It was still dark outside by the time he had gathered up the provisions the Curé had brought them – a rifle and a leather pouch full of bullets amongst them – and woken the children. Somehow the priest had managed to obtain boots, socks, jerseys and coats for each of them, and a single rubber water-proofed cape. He tied the warm clothing into bundles for the children to carry on their backs, for he knew that once the sun came up, it would be warm long before they reached the foothills, and that the clothing would not be needed until nightfall.

To carry on his own back, he had a canvas rucksack – an old one of Jean-Paul's – containing several large round loaves of bread, some fruit, two bottles of water, a jar of ointment and some bandages for the expected blisters; matches, candles, and his own torch, maps and compass. With the rugs and shotgun strapped to the rucksack, and a coil of rope hanging from his waist, he was fully loaded.

When finally he set off with the children across the meadows, Guy was reassured by their high spirits. After a good night's sleep, they were now treating their escape as an exciting adventure, only Claudette looking behind her from time to time to see if they were being followed. They stopped briefly for a drink from a stream, and Guy allowed them to eat an apple and a small portion of bread. Henri scowled when he was told he could not have more, but Claudette quickly shushed him with the logical admonition that there'd be nothing for lunch if they ate all the food now. Brigitte suddenly declared that she wanted to go home; that she wasn't afraid of the Germans; some of them were quite nice and gave her *bon-bons*, she said truculently; and in any case, she wanted to see her mother.

This, before they were even a few kilometres on their way! Guy told himself with dismay. Fortunately, the sight of a rabbit scampering across the grass in front of them diverted the child's thoughts, and Claudette said: "Maybe when we get to England, *Grandmère* will let you have a rabbit of your own, Brigitte!" – something she knew her sister had always wanted but which their Papa would not permit. Thus it was Claudette who gave Guy the idea that he might take their minds off the long walk by telling them stories about Rochford Manor and the pleasures that lay in store for them there.

By lunch-time they had left the fields behind them and were climbing steadily up a rocky path much trodden by goats. The temperature was in the eighties and the children constantly demanded water. Seeing a small waterfall to the left of the track, Guy decided to stop and allow his charges to eat; and then to paddle in the ice-cold water trickling down from the mountains above them where the snow covering the peaks was melting. The thought of the snow on the summit was too unnerving for him to dwell on. He would take each hour of the day as it came, he decided. So far, he'd seen no sign of unusual activity below him in the valley, and the only human being he had so far glimpsed was a man herding some cows towards the village.

Whilst the children played, he took out his map and tried to gauge from the names of the mountain peaks the direction he needed to follow. As far as he could judge, he was travelling in a south-easterly direction. If he could continue this afternoon at the same pace as they had been climbing until now, they might reach the forest before nightfall. Although the track they had been following zigzagged between rocky outcrops, there'd been too many long periods when they'd been clearly visible to anyone with binoculars trained on the mountain side.

The children were enjoying their water play and were far from pleased when he forced them to lie down beside him and rest for half an hour. When he told them it was time to resume their climb, Henri was truculent, and was only persuaded to put on his back bundle when Guy told him they might find an animal in the woods which he would shoot so that they could eat it for supper!

As they resumed walking, Brigitte seemed for the time being to have forgotten her desire to be returned to her mother; but her constant stops to pick up a pretty stone or a snail's shell that took her fancy slowed them all down. So, too, did Henri's desire to climb every rocky out-jut they came across. Guy's promise that they would have far more difficult rocks to climb next day did little to curb the boy's sudden diversions from the goat trail they were following.

By five o'clock, it was obvious to Guy that they would have to stop where they were for the night. All three children were now

480

drooping with fatigue, their feet dragging, and only Brigitte's intermittent renewed demands for her mother broke the silence. Seeing some stunted bushes as they rounded a bend in the trail, Guy said cheerfully: "I think we might stop and make a camp here. The ground is too rocky to lie on, but we can break off some branches from those bushes and make comfortable beds for ourselves. We'll make one big bed, shall we, and share it? We'll keep warmer that way!"

For the next five minutes, the children worked with dwindling enthusiasm, after which Guy had to complete the job himself. The site he had chosen was sheltered, both from any sighting from the valley and from the breeze which was already cooling the stifling air. It would be a good deal colder when the sun went down, he reflected, as he untied the bundle of rolled-up rugs and instructed the children to lay the rubber cape over the make-shift bed and put on their jerseys.

He dared not light a fire to give them something hot to eat and drink, but by now they were too tired to notice. They chewed mouthfuls of bread already hardening from the day's heat, and by the time Henri was halfway through his meal, he was asleep.

"I think Brigitte's tired, too!" Claudette whispered to Guy. "Shall I put her to bed? She'll want a story after she has said her prayers, but we haven't got a book to read!"

"Then I'll tell her a story!" Guy said.

When finally Brigitte, too, was asleep, Claudette came to sit beside him. He felt her small hand slip into his and, sensing that she needed comfort, he put his arm round her.

"It's very lonely here all by ourselves, isn't it, Uncle Guy!" she commented. "Will we have to spend tomorrow night on the mountain, too?"

"I think that's almost a certainty!" Guy said. "But you mustn't worry, sweetheart – we'll get to England eventually, and then we'll be safe!"

"*Maman* said the Germans were dropping bombs on English people!"

"That's true, but they have safe places under ground to hide. At least there are no nasty Germans there."

Claudette bit her lip.

"Why do they want to kill us?" she asked. "Is it because *Maman* is English?"

"Partly, I suppose!" Guy said. "Also because they know your Mama has been helping the English, and the Americans, by making it possible for your Uncle Pelham to feed them. So you see, you must always remember her as being very brave."

"Will we really see *Maman* and *Papa* again, Uncle Guy – after the war is over?"

Guy's hesitation was only brief. He would not lie to her.

"I can't promise that, sweetheart. It depends on the Germans, you see."

He expected further questions but there was now a half-smile on Claudette's face.

"You keep calling me 'sweetheart'. Maman told me sweethearts were people who wanted to marry each other. When I grow up, will you marry me, Uncle Guy?"

"You might not want me to when you are older, Claudette. I'm a great deal older than you, and you will meet a nice young man of your own age and fall in love with him."

"What's it like – falling in love? Have you ever done it, Uncle Guy?"

Zandra – oh, Zandra, my love! Guy thought with a sudden ache of longing. Unable to speak, he nodded.

"You don't look very happy when you say that!" Claudette said. "In story books, princes and princesses always live happily ever after. Will you live happily ever after with Aunt Zandra when you get back to England? She's very pretty. I want to look like her when I grow up."

"And so you may!" Guy said quickly. "Now how about some sleep, sweetheart? We've a long day ahead again tomorrow."

Settling Claudette in the make-shift bed beside her brother and sister, Guy sat down on a nearby rock and watched the shadows lengthen as they spread across the valley. Lighting a cigarette, he tried to keep at bay his misgivings, for he had no doubt now that the Rochfords were almost certainly in prison if not actually dead. He felt a deep disgust for Claude Calonne who had betrayed them all – even his wife. Had he cared nothing for her – or for his children's – safety? Could he really have been so naïve as to imagine the Gestapo would take their youth into account?

Their safety was now in his hands, he reflected, and the old Curé had been right to suggest he might never succeed in getting the little ones to the border. The snow would be deep and their progress so slow that their food would run out long before they reached their destination. Worst of all was his growing conviction that he had lost the way.

Chapter 31

April 1944

The day was proving to be far more difficult than the last, Guy thought, as the following morning he urged the children up the steepening incline into the forest. With only the occasional shaft of sunlight piercing the trees, it was at least cooler, and Brigitte demanded to wear her jersey. They were walking now on a rocky path, the noise of their footsteps deadened by the carpet of needles fallen from the Scotch and mountain pines. There were tall silver firs, too, towering over their heads, and the occasional beech tree reminding Guy of home.

It was whilst the children were resting after their meagre lunch that he saw the ibex. A hundred and fifty yards away downwind, it had neither scented nor heard them. For the moment he had a clear view of it through the trees, and he prayed that it would not move on out of sight. As quietly as he could, he picked up the rifle and slipped off the safety-catch. He knew the noise of the exploding bullet would frighten the children, but with perhaps another two days' travelling to do, he reckoned that a supply of fresh meat was more important.

Only when he saw the beast lying on the ground did he stop to consider how they would eat it. To light a fire to cook one of the haunches must present a risk, although as yet they had seen no one else on the mountain. Although the flames would be hidden by the trees, the smoke would rise above them and would of a certainty reveal their exact location if someone was searching for them.

He tried to put himself into the minds of the enemy. It was not only possible but probable that the Germans would leave no stone unturned now they'd discovered there'd been "passengers" in the Casa Montijo; that they would suspect them of having made for the mountains as a way of escape and send out search parties into the hills. They would be looking for children, too, from whom they would hope to extract information. As he'd driven to Saint Martin in Mr Rochford's Delage, the driver of one of the cars they had passed might, if questioned, have mentioned seeing the Delage, and it could by now have been discovered in the spinney near Saint Martin where he'd hidden it. One of the less trustworthy villagers could have happened upon it and reported it to the *Milice*, in which case the Germans would guess they were somewhere on these mountains. On the other hand, was it not likely, he asked himself, that they would consider it madness for any individual, however desperate, to try to cover this kind of terrain with three such young children in tow? He, himself, thought it crazy – ever more so as the hours went by. Even if they reached the border without mishap, they had still to get by the border guards – and they would have been put on the alert.

I won't think about that now, he told himself sharply as, bidding the children to stay where they were, he walked through the trees to the dead animal and began gutting and dismembering it. He might risk a small fire after dark when they were deeper into the forest and the smoke would be less noticeable. There'd been a new moon last night and visibility had been limited.

When he returned to the children, Claudette was doing her best to quieten Brigitte's tears. He told the excited Henri how he would skin the haunches later, and wrapping them as best he could in his silk scarf, he pushed them into the bottom of the rucksack where they'd be least likely to attract the flies. Regretfully, he left the liver which he feared would leak too much blood into the remains of their dry food.

No more than a quarter of an hour after they had resumed their journey, long before he would have wished, Guy was obliged to stop once more. Henri was in tears, complaining bitterly that his blisters were too painful to continue. Of the boots the Curé had found for the children, his were the least well-fitting, and although Guy had stuffed dried grass in the toes, they had rubbed the child's heels almost raw.

Guy could see at a glance that if they were to proceed, he would have to carry the boy, but the haunches had made his rucksack very bulky and with the addition of the gun and the rugs, he saw no way he could give Henri a ride on his shoulders. At the same time, he knew the progress they were making was painfully slow and that the amount of food he carried would not last the journey.

As he bent down to put fresh ointment on Henri's feet, Brigitte tugged at his arm.

"What's that noise? Is it a bear?" she asked nervously, for she knew these animals, though few in number, lived in the mountains.

"Of course not, silly!" Claudette answered her uneasily. "That's a donkey braying!"

Guy caught his breath as he paused to listen. The sound came again and he knew he was not mistaken – that was the noise of a mule. It came from nearby, and he realized that there would be no time to hide the children. He grabbed his rifle and quickly inserted a new bullet. Almost immediately, a man emerged from his right leading a mule. The panniers on its sides were heavily loaded with wood. Guy slipped off the safety-catch and stepped forward to meet the woodcutter.

The man halted in his tracks and stared open-mouthed from Guy to the three children. It was impossible for his not-very-fertile imagination to conceive what they could possibly be doing up the mountains at this time of day. He knew that sometimes in the summer, foreign visitors would walk in the hills; that sometimes they came up the mountains to shoot or to fish; but not in this area – and never with young children! Nor, indeed, had there been any foreign visitors touring since the war.

He looked nervously at Guy's gun.

"You are from Saint Martin?" Guy asked after he had greeted him. Hearing Guy's cultured accent, the man touched his red beret and nodded.

"Then you'll know Père Benoît. He is a friend of mine!" Guy said quickly. He pointed to the mule. "I want to buy your animal!" he said. "I have money. I can pay you!"

Even more astonished, the man scratched his head.

"He's not for sale, sir!" he said in the Basque language. Seeing that Guy did not understand, he repeated the remark in the local French patois, adding: "He's my livelihood, you understand. But for him, I couldn't get the wood back home."

Guy smiled.

"I realize that, but I'll pay you well – well enough to buy another animal – a better one, perhaps."

"Ain't nothing wrong with him!" the man said, scowling. "Strong as they come, he is!"

"So I can see!" Guy said wryly. Unprepared as he'd been for this unexpected stroke of luck, he had so far been feeling his way with the owner of the beast; but now he decided that he had very little to lose by appealing to the man's patriotism. Basque or not, he could well be a collaborator; and when he returned to the village, tell the Germans he'd encountered a stranger with three children. Even if he had no love for the Germans, it would soon be common gossip in the village if he arrived home this evening without his animal or its load.

Nevertheless, it was a chance he'd have to take, Guy decided, for although the old Curé had provided thick socks and strong boots for the children, their legs were bare and they would be bitterly cold and wet once they reached the snow. They were finding the going difficult enough on hard, dry ground! With legs and feet sinking into deep snow, they might give up altogether. Even he would find it difficult.

Without mentioning the Rochfords, Guy informed the woodcutter that the children were being pursued by the Germans and that he was trying to get them safely over the border into Spain. He guessed that the man would suppose the children to be Jewish refugees, for it was common knowledge that when they were found in the homes of the sympathetic French people who had been hiding them, they would be thrown immediately into lorries or trains and transported to unknown destinations in Germany.

"That's why I need your mule!" he said simply. "Tell me what it's worth and I'll pay you . . . and for the wood, since you won't be able to carry it back to the village yourself!"

Once again, the man scratched his head. He had no love for the *Boches* whom he'd fought against in the last war; but the mule was his livelihood. Moreover, he was afraid if he helped these three unfortunate children and the man who was assisting them to escape, the Germans might punish him if they found out.

Sensing the man's fear, Guy said quickly: "The Curé will protect you; reward you, perhaps, for proving to be such a good Samaritan." He took out his wallet and extracted some large notes, blessing the crews of the Lysanders who dropped such vitally necessary sums of French money by parachute to the Resistance groups. Reluctant as he would be to do so, he knew that if the old peasant refused to sell, he would be obliged to shoot him – not to kill him, but to impede his ability to get back to the village quickly. Instinctively he tightened his grip on his rifle.

The woodcutter had noticed Guy's movement, and he shuffled uncomfortably as his eyes went back to the money. Perhaps this gentleman did not know the real value of a mule, or of the wood he was taking home! he reflected. If he were to ask twice their true worth . . .

One thing was for certain, the stranger would never get the children over the mountain without the animal. He must want the beast very badly! His eyes narrowed in a look of cunning as he named his figure.

Guy's hesitation was only brief.

"That's robbery, of course!" he said matter-of-factly.

"However, I do realize that you will be taking a risk. It would be best for us both if you tell everyone your mule fell into a crevasse, or met with some other such accident . . . although how you will account for all those francs I can't imagine!"

"What will I do with the wood, sir?" the man asked nervously as Guy began to unload the beast. "Someone will find it if I leave it here!"

Guy continued to throw the wood on to the ground.

"Say the load shifted and fell off before the animal bolted," he suggested. "Scatter it around a bit. Now give me a hand!"

When at last the mule was unloaded, he beckoned to the children.

"Up you go!" he said lifting Henri on to its back. "And you, Brigitte. Think you can cling on behind, Claudette?"

Thrilled by this chance of what Henri insisted was a donkey-ride, he and his two sisters wasted no time in settling themselves above the panniers. Guy hoisted his rucksack into one basket and the children's bundles into another, before turning back to the woodcutter who now stood silently watching him.

"You'll find the carcass of an ibex over there beyond that tall silver pine!" Guy said, pointing. "Your wife might forgive you the loss of the animal if you take home some meat!"

Taking up the rope now dangling from the mule's halter, he turned the animal around and urged it forward. The mule had been looking forward to getting back to the village, for it had not eaten since midday and was in no mood to go back the way it had come. Seeing that it intended to stand its ground with the stubborn determination inherent in its nature, Guy gave it a thwack over the rump, and reluctantly, it moved forward. He glanced back over his shoulder. To his relief, he saw that the woodcutter was already hurrying off in the direction of the carcass. For a moment or two, the children chattered excitedly amongst themselves, and then started plying him with questions. Did the animal have a name? Would they be able to keep it? Could they take it to England with them? What did it eat?

Guy's steps faltered and nearly came to a stop as he realized the implications of this last question. What could he give the animal to eat? There was no grass to graze and he had no grain to give it. The nosebag hanging from one of the panniers was empty but for a few wisps of hay indicating its earlier contents. How long could an animal like this go without food? he asked himself. Without water? It would be as well when they stopped for the night, for him to collect some firewood so that when they reached the snow line – hopefully some time tomorrow – he could at least melt some snow.

He had solved the problem of the children's transport, he realized, but in doing so had acquired further difficulties to overcome. At least he could be grateful that for the moment, his young charges were more than happy to be riding rather than walking, and that they were making far better progress. Some two hours later, the novelty was wearing off. They were stiff, they complained, and their bottoms were sore. Once more their spirits had sunk to a low ebb.

They were now deep into the forest and Guy decided it was time they stopped for the night. Within a few minutes, he had a small fire burning and the meat sizzling over the flames on a wooden skewer. The children were cheered by the bright flames and the delicious smell mingling with the pine-scented air. Although the fresh meat was tough when they ate it, they all felt better with full stomachs, and of their own accord after the meal, the children set about making the pine-branch bed on which to sleep.

Their faces, hands and knees were filthy – as was he, Guy realized; first thing in the morning he must try to find a mountain stream. He had tied the mule securely to a tree but, not surprisingly, without food or water, the wretched animal was restless, and he felt certain that it was in dire need of a drink. Their own water bottles were almost empty with barely enough liquid left to give the children when they woke in the morning. There was nothing, therefore, he could do to alleviate the mule's misery.

Once again, Claudette came to sit beside him after Henri and Brigitte were asleep.

"How much longer before we get there, Uncle Guy?" she asked, her tone not so much complaining as plaintive. "We are going to get there, aren't we? If we died here, we wouldn't go to Heaven!"

"Of course we aren't going to die here or anywhere, come to that!" Guy said firmly, "but whatever put that idea into your head? Of course you'd go to Heaven!"

"Papa said you have to have absolution before you die, but we don't have a priest here, do we?"

Guy caught his breath.

"You don't think anyone as good and kind as God would refuse to let you into Heaven when He knew it wasn't your fault you'd not been absolved, do you, sweetheart? Of course He would! I've no doubt about it. Anyway, I can assure you, we aren't going to die!"

"That's all right then," Claudette said, leaning her head against his shoulder. There was a moment's silence before she asked irrelevantly: "Why has your hair gone black, Uncle Guy? And you've got a black moustache. Brigitte said she'd seen you in Tante Silvie's garden, but Tante Silvie said of course it wasn't you!"

"She had to say that because she knew I was hiding from the Germans!" Guy explained. "It's what they call a white lie."

"It sounds like a black one to me . . ." Claudette murmured, but before Guy could explain the meaning, she had fallen asleep.

Alone now with his thoughts, Guy contemplated the problems that lay ahead. Tomorrow, he would have to stress yet again the danger of being caught by the Germans, for the children's initial enthusiasm for what they'd seen as an "adventure" was rapidly disappearing despite their acquisition of the mule! Brigitte dissolved into tears at the slightest provocation and at bedtime had cried for her mother until sleep overcame her. Henri was in some pain from his blistered feet, and clearly the stalwart Claudette was beginning to lose confidence in the successful outcome of this journey. So, too, was he, for he was even less certain now that he was following Jean-Paul's route. At one point during the day, the trail had divided in two directions, and he'd had to gamble on the right-hand fork with nothing more to guide him than the direction of his compass. With the zigzagging nature of the trail, they were constantly changing direction, and at times it was impossible to see the snow-capped summit of the mountain ahead.

The following morning, however, as the trees were beginning to thin out and the air to grow markedly cooler, there was a sudden sharp bend in the trail, and the dejected mule lifted its head and quickened its pace. In front of them was a narrow stream. It was gushing with bright, sparkling water pouring down from the melting snow above them.

Guy lifted the children to the ground and allowed the animal to drink its fill whilst he set about washing himself and them, despite their protests at the icy chill. Claudette borrowed his comb and tried to untangle her own hair and Brigitte's, and fasten it once more into pigtails as she had seen her mother do. Guy was glad to see all three of them in better heart when they resumed their journey. Fully refreshed, they demanded to be allowed to explore the route ahead on foot, but his own spirits did not lift until half an hour later. The acquisition of the mule had been their first piece of luck, he told himself, and the finding of the stream the second. Now the third lay in front of him in the form of a cigar butt! He dragged the mule to a halt and bent to pick it up.

"What is it?" the children asked in unison as they saw him smile in a mixture of delight and relief.

There was little doubt that this belonged to the American, Joe, and that judging by its condition, it had not lain here for long. To drop it was typical of Joe's lack of caution. As soon as the Resistance picked up an airman who had parachuted from a plane, the first

492

thing they did was tell him to rid himself of anything which could identify him. So well organized were these groups now that the "passengers" were quickly given French clothes, cigarettes, money and, as soon as they could be obtained, identification papers in false names. Joe, however, had refused to be parted from his cigars; and unbeknownst to his rescuers, had hidden them on his person. When he'd reached the comparative safety of the Casa Montijo, he had started to smoke them. Since all tobacco was in short supply, it was a dangerous thing to do, especially since the band around the cigar identified its origin; and both he, Guy, and Mr Rochford had forbidden him to smoke. Obviously he had yet again disobeyed the order to get rid of them.

Now, however, Guy could not have been better pleased with his find. It meant that he was unquestionably on Jean-Paul's route, and if they could make it through the snow and past the border guards, they had every hope of getting back to England.

For the first time, Guy allowed himself to think of the future. Undoubtedly, his cover must have been blown and he would not be able to operate secretly in France again. As a consequence, when he met up with Zandra, he could explain what had kept him silent for so long. Perhaps he would see her in a week or two's time – hold her in his arms again! At least he knew from Mr Rochford that she was safe and well, although he knew, too, that she was still married to Wisson. Was it possible, he wondered, that this long, awful war had changed Wisson's attitude, and that he might now consider a divorce? He, Guy, could survive these coming weeks happily if only he were certain that Zandra still loved him; still wanted him as much as he wanted her. It had been so long, he could not blame her if she'd forgotten him.

Pushing such doubts swiftly once more to the back of his mind, Guy lifted the children onto the mule's back and urged it on up the trail.

Zandra was paying one of her customary visits to Cadogan Gardens, only on this occasion she was there at Lucy's urgent request. She was radiant with happiness. Even now, half an hour after her arrival, she was still unable to believe that Guy was safely home. When Lucy had telephoned to tell her that she had some wonderful news for her and that Zandra must come round immediately, she'd dared not hope for more than a letter from Guy. It was over two years since she'd heard from him, and she had begun to despair that he'd been killed. Alexis had reiterated that the War Office would have heard if Guy had been killed or wounded; and he had done his best to offer comfort by assuring her that unless she heard from him to the contrary, she could assume Guy was still alive!

Those years had seemed agonizingly long, and now she was finding it impossible to keep her eyes from meeting Guy's; her heart from melting when he smiled at her. He and the children had arrived back in England an hour ago having been brought by a staff car from the RAF station where they'd landed. He was sitting on one of the Zemskis' large sofas, his arms around Alice's two little girls who were gazing shyly at the aunt and uncle they had never before met. He had shaved off the moustache he'd worn in France, and the black dye was growing out of his fair hair. His face was thinner and lightly tanned, but his eyes were unchanged, the expression in them all that she needed to see. The intensity of the love she felt was all but overwhelming, and it was only with an effort that she was able to concentrate on the story he was telling them.

Although the children were as yet unaware of it, she knew already from Alexis who had met her at the front door that her Uncle Pelham and Tante Silvie were dead, as well as poor Alice and the cook; but there had been such joy in her heart when Alexis told her Guy was waiting for her in the drawing-room, that there'd been no time for grief. From what Guy was now saying, it seemed that her Uncle Pelham had made the right decision when he'd heard from Alice that Claude Calonne had betrayed them all. According to Alexis who seemed to know the facts already, shortly after Guy's departure with the airmen and the children, the Germans had arrived at the Casa Montijo.

"I tried to make your uncle and aunt come with us," Guy said now, his face clouding at the memory, "but Mr Rochford was adamant. I think he was hoping he might talk himself out of trouble."

What Guy did not now say in front of the children – as he had to Alexis – was that he supposed their mother, who'd been hysterical, had put them all in danger; that he doubted if she would have been capable of standing up to the kind of rough questioning the Gestapo employed. Fortunately she'd known nothing of the route he'd taken which explained, perhaps, why they had not been followed.

"But for Claudette, I doubt if we would have survived!" he said with a warm glance at the child. "She was like a mother to her brother and sister, insisting they wash when we reached a stream; making them say their prayers before they slept; bandaging their feet when the blisters appeared. It was bitterly cold that night we had to spend near the summit, but she never once complained, did you, sweetheart?"

"You were very brave, darling!" Lucy said, smiling warmly at Claudette.

Henri had been standing quietly by Alexis' chair. Now he stepped forward.

"So was I!" he said indignantly. "I had a big stick and if the Germans had come, I would have hit them very hard and killed them. If I'd had a gun like Uncle Guy's, I'd have shot them all dead!"

"Yes, darling, I'm sure you would!" Lucy said.

"I was the quietest mouse of all when we crossed the border!" Brigitte declared. "And I didn't cry when the poor mule died – well, only a little bit. I only cried properly because I wanted *Maman*. When will we see her, Uncle Guy?"

Guy glanced briefly at Alexis, who shook his head. This was not the time to tell the children the truth about their parents. This distressing news could wait a little while until they had settled down at Rochford. Then the unfortunate fates of their parents and that of Pelham and Silvie would have to come out. It was a sad business, but at least Bristow and the children were safely back in England – a miracle, by the sound of it.

"The cold was the worst!" Guy said. 'In the daytime, the sun warmed us; but as you can imagine, the children needed many rests and our progress through the snow was desperately slow."

Brigitte's eyes filled with tears.

"The poor *mulet* died when we were on top of the mountain. Uncle Guy said it didn't have enough to eat, and if we gave it our food, *we* might die!"

"Uncle Guy buried it under the snow!" Henri declared cheerfully. "Claudette and Brigitte and me said a prayer. We wanted to sing a hymn but Uncle Guy said we had to get on or we'd freeze to death."

"Which, as you can see, did not happen!" Guy said, ruffling Henri's hair. He turned back to face Lucy and Zandra. "Once we reached Spain, I was able to bribe a farmer to take us to the next town in his wagon," he continued his story, "and after that, we took trains."

Henri's face brightened with remembered excitement.

"We heard the German border guards talking and we had to crawl on our tummies like Red Indians!" he announced. "Brigitte was frightened, weren't you, Brigitte, but I was brave like Uncle Guy!"

"Indeed you were, darling!" Lucy said. "Now you need never be frightened again. You are quite safe here in England. We don't have any nasty Germans here! Now why don't you three go down to the kitchen and see Cook? I asked her to make some toffee apples for you and they might be ready to eat."

At the doorway, Claudette paused to ask: "When will we be going to see *Grandmère* Willow? Uncle Guy said she would be able to tell us lots of stories about *Maman* when she was a little girl like me."

"Quite soon, I expect," Lucy said gently. "That's what we shall talk over now, darling."

As the door closed behind the children, Zandra went over to take Claudette's place beside Guy on the sofa. Guy took her hand quickly in his, and smiled down at her.

"It's wonderful to be back – and to see you again," he said softly. "You can have no idea how often I've thought of this moment. I have to admit that there were times during the journey home when I began to despair we would ever make it. If Mr Rochford hadn't been so certain that Calonne intended to save his own skin by putting the Germans on to our activities, I doubt if I would have contemplated crossing those mountains without Jean-Paul, let alone with three small children! I didn't enjoy frightening them by telling them what it was all about; but I had to when they were refusing to go any further. I even had to tell them some of the awful things the Germans could do to children; but it wasn't always easy to convince them. Some of the soldiers in Pau had tried to make friends with them – gave them sweets, that kind of thing. I suppose the poor devils were missing their own kids. They weren't all bad, you know – not the ordinary soldiers. It's the Nazis who are a law unto themselves, torturing and killing, using every sadistic method they can think up. Even their own kind are frightened of them!"

"You'll have to be debriefed in due course, Bristow," Alexis said, "but you've earned a few hours' respite before you report in. As soon as you telephoned me, I let the Department know you were back in England, and they said they needn't see you until tomorrow. I dare say they'll give you some leave after your debriefing – long overdue, I think!"

Guy did not try to conceal his questioning look at Zandra.

"I'll get leave when you do, Guy. We aren't nearly as busy as we used to be – and if they won't give me leave, I'll resign!" she added with a smile. "Perhaps you and I could take the children down to Rochford together and then go off somewhere?"

Guy nodded.

"I'd like to see the kids safely installed!" he said, adding: "The truth is, I've grown rather attached to those youngsters. We went through quite a bit together, and there's no doubt that it was doubly traumatic for them after the parting from their mother at such short notice. They weren't even certain at first that I was the man they'd known as Uncle Guy. I was sporting a moustache then, and this" – he touched his hair – "this was black, too; and the airmen were calling me by my alias, 'Blaireau' – French for 'badger' by the way!"

He smiled at Zandra.

"When we finally reached Madrid, the children clung like limpets and wouldn't even allow themselves to be put to bed in a separate room. It was the same on the train down to Lisbon. One of the diplomats' wives volunteered to look after them there, but they got anxious if I was away for more than a few hours at a time. We were held up for over a week while the embassy checked up on us and arranged the flight back. Henri enjoyed that, but I'm not too sure if the girls did! I'm afraid Brigitte, more than the other two, is really missing her mother."

"They'll settle down in time!" Lucy said reassuringly. "Children are very resilient. Look how all those evacuees adapted when they were whisked off to new homes! I'm told there are even some who kicked up a dreadful fuss when their parents wanted them back after the bombing stopped! Jane and Mother and Inge will take good care of the children – and they'll have that lovely garden to play in; all those old toys, too, up in the nursery."

"I suppose the 'guinea pigs' will come as a bit of a shock at first," Zandra said thoughtfully. Briefly, she told Guy about Giles and the burns patients who were now regular occupants of Rochford Manor, and had dubbed themselves "McIndoe's guinea pigs" because of the experimental work he performed rebuilding their faces. They had formed a club of that name with Mr McIndoe as President, she explained, and every patient was automatically a member. Later, she thought, she would tell Guy about the pilot, Gustav Gebrauer, who despite his nationality, had been allowed to join the club. He was still very much a recluse, spending a great deal of time in his own room trying to manipulate his woodwork tools. Curiously enough, it was only Eve who had managed to get him to talk about himself. They went for long walks together with the dogs and, Eve insisted, when there was no one else around, Gustav could be a very interesting companion. He was also an excellent dancer, and when the chaps rolled back the rugs, put on the gramophone and danced, Eve would drag him onto the floor and firmly ignore his obvious reluctance to join in the fun. There was no doubt that Eve was good for him and this past year, perhaps because of her interest in him, the other patients had started to treat the German pilot as one of themselves.

"We will have to warn the children not to stare at the patients!" Zandra said thoughtfully.

"I should think the men are accustomed to that by now!" Alexis commented.

"Children can be so brutally honest!" Lucy sighed. Aware suddenly that Zandra and Guy must be longing to have some time alone together, she glanced meaningfully at Alexis.

"Why don't we go into your study, my dear, and get on with that invitation list?" she suggested tactfully. She smiled at Guy. "We're giving a big party for Robin's twenty-first. Provided his ship gets back in time, he's been promised leave for it. You'll come, won't you, Guy? We'd like you to be here. We thought we would hold it at Rochford as it's so much easier to get food in the country."

It was Alexis who understood the reason for Guy's hesitation. He must know that whatever their private feelings about Zandra's husband, Wisson could not be left off the party list.

"There'll be no hiding the fact that it was you who brought the children home, Bristow!" he said quietly. "Obviously the family are all very grateful and will wish to include you as a family friend. We would look very unappreciative if we didn't invite you, don't you agree? You'll be something of a hero now in our family, old chap, whether you like it or not!"

"Then I'll certainly come to the party, sir, if you think it's in order."

As Alexis and Lucy left the room, Guy turned to Zandra.

"How do you feel about it, darling? What about your husband?"

"I think Alexis has answered that. Anyway, I don't care what Anthony thinks! Oh Guy, I'm still finding it hard to believe you're here – that I can actually see you, touch you!"

Guy's arms reached out for her and he drew her to him, murmuring: "If you knew how much I've been longing to do this ever since you walked into the room! I love you so very much! I don't think a single day has passed when you haven't been in my mind. Sometimes, when I was holed up somewhere, cold, hungry, utterly wretched, I would relive every moment we ever had together; and because I wanted you so desperately, it gave me the will to battle on."

"And I had begun to think you must have forgotten me!" Zandra said. "Did you get any of my letters, Guy? I wrote to you – hundreds of times, but you never answered!"

"Only because I couldn't. Half the time, no one knew where I was, and in any case Count Zemski couldn't send letters addressed to me to the Casa Montijo. Imagine if the Jerries had got hold of them! After Dunkirk, I was officially notified as 'Missing, Believed Killed' – at least, that was what was leaked to the Germans. No one in the regiment knew what had happened to me, apart from the CO . . . and even he didn't know the details, although I suppose he may have guessed something of the sort was afoot. I was parachuted back into France immediately after my special training, and I haven't been home since!"

"Four years, five months and three days!" Zandra murmured.

"It seems more like forty years to me." Guy was smiling as he lifted a tendril of hair back from her face. "At least I had snippets of news about you. Mr Rochford told me what a huge amount of flying you were doing and how conscientious you were! I tried to be pleased you were doing something you loved, but I kept thinking of all those RAF chaps you were meeting every day. I gathered from the army fellows we picked up that the RAF were something

500

by way of being heroes at home – knocking Jerry out of the skies and saving the country from invasion!"

"They were very brave!" Zandra said quietly. "The odds against them were pretty ghastly and . . . well, an awful lot of them were killed. Now it's the bomber pilots who are having a bad time."

Guy nodded.

"Yes, I know about the heavy raids – they've even bombed Berlin. It's only a matter of time now before we push them back where they came from. The war will be over before long and then . . ."

Zandra bit her lip.

"Don't let's think about that now, Guy! You're safe and we're together – and that's all I want to know."

Zandra was right – the future could wait, Guy thought, as his mouth sought hers. It was enough that they were both still alive and their love for one another had not changed.

"You are my girl, mine!" he said fiercely. "I shall always love you . . . always, always, always!" And he drowned her reply with further kisses, glorying in her quick, eager response.

Only a short distance away, in the study, Alexis, too, was holding the woman he loved in his arms. He was doing what he could to comfort her as for the first time she allowed herself to weep for Pelham, Silvie and Alice whom they would never see again.

501

Chapter 32

June 1944

"It's very nice. Thank you!"

The gratitude in Claudette's voice was tinged with reluctance. She replaced the small, upper tray neatly in the trinket box and closed the lid.

"I am happy that you like it. It is for the necklace and ribbons and hair holders, no?"

The hint of a smile touched the child's lips.

"You mean hair *slides*," she said, adding a moment later: "I expect Brigitte will want one now!"

"Then I make it for your sister!"

Silence fell between the man and the child. Claudette traced the carved letters of her name on the lid of the box absent-mindedly. Gustav Gebrauer waited, wondering if she would speak again. Until now, she had studiously avoided him since her arrival at Rochford nearly two months ago.

"It isn't my birthday!" she said. "You didn't have to give me a present."

"Yes, I know. I made the box because I like very much to make things."

"Like the fort you made for Henri, and *Grandmère's* bookends."

He nodded.

"*Grandmère* said it wasn't your fault, and that I should be sorry for you because of the way you look."

Gustav looked down at his scarred hands, not wishing her to see the pain in his eyes!

"I understand that a little girl like you does not vish to look at something vich is ugly; that you like to see only the pretty things."

"But I wasn't talking about your face or your hands!" Claudette's childish treble had the ring of honesty. She frowned. "It's all such a muddle. I wish I understood!"

"Perhaps if you told me about this muddle, I could help? It is not possible to be happy ven you are . . . how do you say it in English . . . infused?"

"I expect you mean *confused!*" Claudette replied matter-of-factly.

"Yes, that is it . . . *confused.* Since I am in the hospital, I, too, vas confused. I have to do very much thinking and then . . . then it becomes clear. I did not understand vy everyone is so kind to me . . . so anxious that I get vell and perhaps even make it possible for me to fly again one day, and to have the face that is not to make the people look another way!"

Claudette regarded him curiously.

"But Aunt Jane said that everyone is kind to Mr McIndoe's patients!"

"Ach, so! But I am not as the others, am I? I am their enemy!"

"Ooooh!" It was a long, drawn-out exclamation. "But that's exactly what I meant. You're German . . . and you killed my mother, and my Uncle Pelham and Tante Silvie, and maybe my papa, too. I don't want to like you. I want to hate you, but . . . well, it doesn't seem to work. I mean, I keep thinking you're just the same as everyone else – only kinder. I don't understand!"

Gustav's relief that the child had not been keeping her distance because she could not tolerate his disfigurement was replaced now by pity for her. How could children such as these three orphans understand about war? When it began, everything had seemed so simple – the Allies were "the enemy" and must be overthrown. They were a degenerate people who threatened his country; who had defeated them in the last war and ruthlessly brought Germany to its knees. The British were a cruel, evil nation who showed no mercy or humanity to their prisoners. Their soldiers killed women and children; their sailors left survivors from sinking ships to drown. Herr Goebbels' wireless broadcasts were full of such stories.

Gradually, in the hospital, he had come to realize that none of it was true; that it was propaganda put out to force the German people to believe that this war, started by Germany, was justified; that many of the accusations made against British servicemen could justifiably be made against the Germans. Had he not met and talked face to face with a naval rating who had been shot at in the water by a German submarine? Many of the man's shipmates had been killed, and he'd been fortunate to be rescued by a British destroyer.

It had been a long time before he'd come to terms with his conflicting loyalties and doubts. Then he had recognized the truth – the truth he would now try and explain to this little girl.

"Your grandmother tells me you three children are Catholics, yes? So you know, Claudette, there is good things and bad things in all people, and it is God who helps us to be good. It is the same for all the peoples in the vorld. In my country, too, some is good people, but also some is bad, and ve have the bad man who is the leader in Germany now."

"You mean Adolf Hitler?"

"Yes, the *Führer!* This is meaning the 'leader'! He has led the German people to make the var. To many he is become like God, and he vishes no vone listens to God no more, and listen only to him. This is vy he puts the priests in prison and closes all the churches, so there is no person to stop him doing the bad things. He has a very big army of his own who do as he tells them to do, and if any peoples disobeys him, they are put in prison or killed. These men in his army are called 'Nazis' because they belong to the *Führer's* National Socialist Party. It is their secret policemen who have killed your mama, Claudette, and your uncle and aunt. They are bad people, and it is my sadness that they are also German."

It was a long speech, but Claudette did not interrupt. When he stopped speaking, he saw that the frown had disappeared from her face.

"I'm glad you told me that. *Grandmère* said I mustn't speak to you about the war because you had suffered enough, and that I must be polite to you even though you were a German prisoner of war; and Aunt Jane doesn't like talking about the war because she doesn't like to think about what the Germans have done to *Maman*, and to my cousin, Giles. Perhaps someone in his squadron shot you down, Gustav? Or Uncle Jamie? Do you hate Giles?"

"Of course not, Claudette. He's a very nice young man. I am happy to think he is my friend. He has been very kind to me. So have all the peoples in your family."

"You like my cousin, Eve, best, don't you? I know she likes you because she told me so!"

Gustav cleared his throat.

"Your cousin is the very nice, pretty girl, and because she is kind, she vishes also to be my friend. Because I am a German prisoner of var, I do not have any friends, you see, and my family are a long vay avay."

Claudette nodded thoughtfully.

"I dare say you're lonely then," she said. "I'll be friends with you if you like. I get bored sometimes playing with Brigitte and Henri and it's quite nice talking to you. You don't treat me like a child the way the other grown-ups do. I'm nearly twelve now and that's almost grown-up, isn't it?"

"I expect you vill make many new friends ven you go to school," Gustav said. "Your grandmother tells me you begin in the autumn but she vishes for you to enjoy first the summer in this beautiful garden."

"There will be girls the same age as me!" Claudette acknowledged. "It's different for Henri and Brigitte – they've got the

Conways' twins to play with. Their father died at sea and their mother was killed by a bomb in London, you know, so they're orphans like us. Their grandmother's dead, too. That's why they've come to live here."

"Perhaps the var vill be over soon," Gustav said comfortingly. "Everyvone is saying it vill not be long now before the British and American armies invade France. Soon all your school-friends in Pau will be free again."

The promised invasion must surely be imminent, he thought. For days now long convoys of troops had been heading south towards the coast, thundering through the village day and night. According to old Mrs Rochford, she had had a job to cross the High Street to do her shopping; and Lady Jane Rochford had reported seeing a large tented encampment of troops in Borrowdale Woods bordering the south side of the Rochford estate. She had been walking the dogs and been halted by a sentry when she stumbled on the camp.

It was really quite remarkable, Gustav thought, what a difference these three young French children had made to the household. The Conway orphans had been quiet and subdued when they'd arrived three months ago following their mother's death. Now, with the arrival of the Calonne children, their high voices and laughter could be heard everywhere. After the first few days of intense curiosity, they'd treated the "guinea pigs" like perfectly normal people. Henri and Brigitte had suffered none of Claudette's qualms about his German nationality, and came frequently to his room to watch him at his woodwork, to play card games or simply to talk. Unlike the other adults, he had more time to amuse them and he loved their company, their uninhibited chatter. They seemed to have recovered very quickly from their frightening experience in France, and the new environment had obviously helped them to come to terms with the loss of their parents.

Most remarkable of all was the effect they were having on their elderly grandmother. Hitherto, Mrs Willow Rochford had been very much a recluse like himself, and, so the family had feared, was mentally as well as physically frail. Now she had taken on a new lease of life. She was, after all, not quite seventy, and the fact that the house was once more filled with children's voices had totally rejuvenated her. The little boy, Henri, was unquestionably her favourite with his quick, mischievous smile and affectionate hugs which he distributed to all and sundry, including him! There was a time when he, Gustav, had believed that no one ever again would be able to bear to hug someone so facially deformed as he was.

The child came running towards him now, Brigitte and the two younger children following behind. They were all shouting.

"*Taisez-vous!*" Claudette said maternally. "You know *Grandmère* likes to rest after lunch. You'll wake her up with that row!"

The irrepressible Henri ignored his elder sister.

"We've caught a spy – *a real one* . . . at least we think we have."

"Down by Aunt Inge's studio!" Peter, one of the Conway children, added breathlessly.

Gustav bit back a smile. Not surprisingly, the children's favourite pastime was playing war games. Today it was Spies and Counter-Spies. He had promised to build them this summer a wooden castle that was to be called "Colditz", the replica of the castle in Saxony where Allied prisoners of war were held. The children had heard about the extraordinary escape of some of the prisoners and were agog to play "escapes". Henri and Peter, of course, would be British prisoners, and it would fall to the girls, Claudette, Brigitte and Anthea Conway to take the part of the Germans. Gustav was supposed to be teaching them the German words for "Halt, who goes there!" and "Those accursed Englishmen have escaped again!"

"What have you done with your spy?" he asked the excited child.

"We haven't caught him yet, but we know he's there!" Henri gasped.

"He's got a radio set and he's sending out Morse to the

Germans!" Peter continued. He had set his heart on joining the Navy like his father – the naval officer who had perished in HMS *Glow-worm* – and he had been busy getting to grips with the Morse code.

"We heard him! We did, honestly. You come and listen, Gustav. He's in Aunt Inge's studio."

Gustav stood up and winked at Claudette.

"I think it is good we go now and look, if we are to have more peace, yes?" he asked.

Delighted to be addressed as someone old enough to patronize the little ones, Claudette slipped her hand in his misshapen one.

"They're just being silly as usual!" she volunteered as they walked slowly down towards the studio. The boys, with Anthea and Brigitte trailing in their wake, had run on ahead. They were crouching now beside one of the thick walls of the old stable which had been converted into a workroom for Inge when she and Jamie were first married.

With difficulty, Gustav knelt down beside them, and in imitation of the boy, pressed his ear against the cool rough stones. As he had expected, there was not a sound. Henri's face mirrored his belief in the reality of his make-believe game as he muttered: "He must have got away while we were looking for you, Gustav. Peter said the Morse wasn't English words so we thought you'd know if it was German. The spy really was transmitting. I promise, word of honour!" He grabbed Gustav's arm, scowling. "You don't believe me, do you? But it's true, isn't it, Peter?" His chin lifted and he crossed himself. "On the life of the Virgin Mary!" he said solemnly. "Now do you believe me?"

Claudette stepped forward.

"That's one of *Maman*'s rules – you can never fib on the life of the Virgin Mary. Henri must be telling the truth, Gustav."

Only now did it occur to Gustav that this might not, after all, be a game. But if it were true, surely it must implicate Mrs Jamie McGill? No one else but she ever went into the studio. It was her private workroom, and not even the servants were allowed in to clean.

This is absurd, he told himself sharply. He did not particularly take to his countrywoman and had quickly repulsed her earlier attempts to speak to him in their own language. It had struck him as ill-mannered to do so whilst he was a guest in an English household where no one understood German, although they all seemed fairly fluent in French. Since then, he had maintained a polite relationship of a superficial nature with her, and as a consequence, knew very little about her. He had met her husband, Jamie McGill, on several occasions and thought him a nice enough fellow, if lacking the personality and intelligence of his sister, Zandra; or the charm of Giles Rochford who had befriended him in hospital. He knew Ingeborg only as an integral part of the Rochford household – the efficient organizer of the domestic running of the house.

"Let's go inside and see what's in there!" Henri's urgent voice brought his thoughts back to the present.

"You can't go in, silly!" Claudette answered quickly. "Aunt Inge keeps it locked – and I don't blame her. You'd only break all the lovely things *Grandmère* says she makes!"

"No, I wouldn't! Anyway, we don't want to look at her silly old things. We want to see if there's a radio transmitter in there, so *you're* stupid, not me!"

Clearly a quarrel was brewing, Gustav realized. Was it possible Mrs McGill was still in the studio? Perhaps someone had broken in and was holding her at gun point whilst he made his transmission? But who? He'd heard no sound of voices.

This is utterly ridiculous! he told himself sharply. I'm getting as fanciful as these two little boys.

"We could get a ladder and climb onto the roof!" Henri was saying. "There's a skylight open up there."

Of course they were imagining the whole incident! Gustav thought. Nevertheless, he did not want them climbing onto the roof in order to satisfy themselves – and perhaps falling off onto the hard cobblestones of the courtyard.

"You cannot climb up there!" he said firmly. "It would be dangerous."

"Then I'm going to see if there's a door open," Henri declared and, with a seven-year-old's impatience, hurried off before Gustav could stop him, first to try the main door and then the tack-room door. Both were locked, he reported when he returned crestfallen.

Even more certain now that there was nothing whatever amiss, it crossed Gustav's mind that the simplest thing would be to send one of the children up to the house to ask Mrs McGill to come down to the studio with her keys and inspect it herself. But whatever would she think of such a request? She would have every justification for being very angry if the children were to disturb her on so absurd a pretext.

Yet still Gustav found himself hesitating. Suppose . . . just suppose, that the boys were right and someone had been transmitting – and that presupposed there really was a transmitter inside! It was unthinkable that, happily married to a Rochford, Mrs McGill could be a spy; and if not she, who else? Then again, if by some extraordinary chance, she had been transmitting, *who was he, a German like herself, to betray her activities?*

His thoughts really were becoming more absurd by the minute, he thought. Although he now accepted that the boys *believed* they were telling the truth, he was certain they must have been mistaken. The sooner they were convinced of that fact, the better. Then they could go off and find another game to play.

He glanced up at the wall of the studio and noticed that a window in what he assumed might have been a hayloft above the former stable-block had been boarded up . . . many years ago, by the look of it, for one of the boards was warped and rotting. It was too high for him to see in, but if he lifted Henri up, perhaps the boy could prise open a gap sufficiently large to peer inside.

"Perhaps there's a German spy hiding in the bushes watching us!" Claudette said nervously. "Do you think there could be, Gustav?"

"No!" he said firmly. "If there vas the spy, he vould be running away ven he sees us coming. But you can vatch for him if you like. I vill lift Henri up to that vindow. I think he can pull open one of those boards."

"Bags I!" shouted Peter, but Henri would have none of it.

"Gustav said me! Anyway, it's my aunt's studio."

"Well, I was the one what knew it was Morse!" Peter protested.

"Be silent you two!" Gustav broke in, his uneasiness sharpening his voice. At first his plan to end this charade had seemed a good one, but now he wondered how he could explain it to Mrs McGill if she were suddenly to decide to do some work; or to arrive here to call the children in for tea – both likely possibilities.

Gustav had not bargained for young Henri's enthusiasm. As the rotting board fell away leaving a sizeable gap, the boy wriggled out of his grasp and disappeared inside. For several long tense moments, he stood waiting; then Henri's face and shoulders appeared. Gustav grabbed hold of him and pulled. Henri fell with none too soft a bump onto the ground. He was scarlet in the face, and far too excited to be aware of any bruises.

"I saw it, I saw the Morse code lever!" he shouted. "It was in a suitcase with a wireless hidden under a green cloth near one of the naked lady statues. I saw it, Gustav, I really did! It's just like the one Peter's got, only bigger."

Gustav's thoughts whirled as he was forced now to face the fact that this really was no game; that what he'd thought to be the children's make-believe had become reality. What should he do now? Could Ingeborg McGill really be using the transmitter? And to whom was she sending messages – in broad daylight, too? That was madness! Could she be under some kind of duress? Was there someone else forcing her to betray the country she had adopted? And what a terrible irony that he, a German, should be the one to discover this horrible activity. He needed time to think . . . to make up his mind *whose* side he was on.

He stared down at the five upturned faces waiting expectantly for him to suggest the next move in this exciting game.

"If it is true someone makes the transmission . . . and ve do not know even if they make it to the enemy, do ve? Then ve must think of a good vay to catch him. Now ve tell no vone – ve make the secret between us, yes? After you have had your tea, you can come to my room and I vill have made the decision vat is best thing to do. Now, you tell no vone, not vone person. It is a very, very important var secret, do you understand?"

Round-eyed, they nodded.

"Even if they torture me, I won't tell!" Henri whispered hoarsely.

"Then you go now and have your tea. I see you all later!" Gustav instructed them.

"Aren't you coming?" Claudette asked.

"No, I have to think vat we do. If anyone is asking you, you tell them I have said I have the headache and vill go to my room."

As the five of them disappeared into the house, Gustav made his way back to the wrought-iron bench where – it seemed many hours ago – Claudette had come to sit beside him. He knew now what his biggest problem was – he did not want to believe that the guilty party must be Ingeborg McGill. What would happen to her if it was discovered that she had been transmitting to the Germans? Would she be shot? Imprisoned? Could she not have been innocently sending a message to an English friend?

Not in wartime! Gustav reminded himself sharply. He rose stiffly from the seat and walked towards the house. He could hear the clatter of plates and cups in the dining-room and, glancing in one of the windows, saw Mrs McGill sitting at a table with some of the airmen. The family, the nurses and their charges were all gathered at high tea – a practice the household had adopted during the air raids so that the non-residential staff could get home earlier. She was smiling as she chatted to the men and must have made some joke for they were all laughing, enjoying her company. It was this woman more than anyone else, Gustav reflected, who had raised the morale of these men; who was always ready to write letters for those who could not do so for themselves; who drove them to the cinema; helped them choose Christmas and birthday presents for their wives and children; partnered them when they were enjoying one of their impromptu dances. Then there was her obvious devotion to her husband, Jamie McGill. When he came on leave, they were like newly-weds. It was inconceivable that she would be supplying his enemies with information which might help to destroy him as well as his country.

Gustav stood silently, leaning against a wall of the manor house which had almost come to seem like home to him. It was cool here in the evening shadows and his head was aching as it so often did towards the end of a day. The Boss had told him it was to be expected after the recent operation he'd had to rebuild his nose. A nose of any kind would be an improvement, he told himself wryly; but he'd seen too many of the finished results to imagine that it could restore his face to normal.

If he was not careful, he would fall into one of his dark depressions which always occurred when he thought of the future and the utter hopelessness of his love for Eve Zemski. Quite apart from the fact that he was a German – and out of pity, no doubt, she never let her antipathy to members of his race show – with disfigurements like his, there was no prospect that she would ever be attracted to him. Fortunately he had been able to hide the way he felt about her when she was on leave; and to respond to her offer of friendship in a similar way, telling himself that he, a prisoner of war, was lucky to have even this much of her time and attention.

War was a cruel and terrible thing! he told himself. So many people were hurt by it – even little children like Claudette, Brigitte, Henri and the Conway orphans. Their resilience was their saving grace, for they could cheerfully re-enact in their games the terrible things their elders were perpetrating – only sometimes, for some of them, it was not a game.

Could Henri be confusing make-believe with reality? He and young Peter had *wanted* to "find a German spy"; and perhaps Henri had seen something resembling a radio set, a Morse keyboard, and convinced himself it was the genuine thing. If this was the case, then Ingeborg McGill was no more guilty of spying than he himself! Henri's mistake was possible – even probable. On the other hand, if the child had been right and he, Gustav, were to do nothing, how far-reaching might be the effects? Suppose Mrs McGill had information which could alter the course of the war? Affect the coming invasion? Would his silence make him indirectly responsible for the deaths of thousands more innocent people? Did he really want Germany to win this war and to see this kind, caring English family who had tried so hard to help him under the heel of the Nazis?

That he had come to feel almost a part of this family and to like the English people did not alter the fact that he had been born and raised a German; that he *was* a German. There was no doubt whatever where his duty lay – to protect his country-woman; to assist his country in every way at his disposal. However much he might despise the Nazi regime, Germany was his home-land; his parents, relatives and former friends were at terrible risk now the war was going against them. So, too, would his own future be at risk if Ingeborg McGill were to be found guilty. No one would believe that he had not been passing information to her – information he had managed to acquire in the ward, and in a house where five of its family members were in the forces. Mr McIndoe, whose anti-German sentiments were well known, would refuse to operate further on him and he would almost certainly be sent to a prisoner-of-war camp suspected, if not condemned, of also being a spy.

The noise of tyres on the gravel drive and the sound of a car engine alerted Gustav to the fact that Captain Guy Bristow had been expected to arrive in time for high tea. He was the Englishman who had managed to bring the Rochford children out of France across the Pyrenean mountains, and because of his extraordinary achievement, was now *persona grata* in the household. Not unnaturally, the children adored him and trusted him implicitly. He was a friend of Mrs Zandra Wisson who was also coming on leave, but according to Lady Rochford's announcement at breakfast, would not be home until very late. He, Gustav, could assume therefore that Captain Bristow would be on his own.

Gustav moved quickly from the shadows round the house to a position where he could see the drive. Captain Bristow had parked the car and was lifting his suitcase out of the boot. As he had guessed, there was no one with him.

The moment had come, Gustav realized, when he must make up his mind – should he step forward and reveal his suspicions, or remain here in the shadows and keep them to himself long enough for him to warn his countrywoman to get rid of the evidence Henri had found?

The meal had been cleared away and the patients were gathered round the wireless set in the morning-room listening to ITMA when Guy entered the house alone. With her usual efficiency, Ingeborg had already prepared a cold supper for him which she brought in from the kitchen as he joined Jane in the drawing-room.

"I go now to my studio to vork a little more. I am making the surprise for Aunt Villow's birthday," Inge announced as she placed the tray in front of him. "I shall see you later, yes?"

"The children are getting ready for bed!" Jane said as Inge left the room and Guy seated himself beside her. She laid down the patchwork blanket she was knitting and lowered her voice. "Zandra telephoned to say she'll be arriving at Havorhurst Halt at ten fifty-five. I told her you would meet her. I hope I did right, Guy dear. You're not too tired?"

Guy returned her smile.

"Most certainly not! Thank goodness she can make it. I've only got a forty-eight."

Jane sighed. "I suppose I shouldn't ask if it's embarkation leave, but everyone is talking about the possibility of an invasion soon.

There seems to be a bit of a flap on – masses of traffic, army trucks, tanks, that sort of thing, pouring through Havorhurst. However, least said about that the better, I imagine. By the way, Guy, you didn't see Gustav – the German patient – as you came in, did you? One of the children said he wasn't well and wouldn't be in for tea, but when I took a tray up to him, he wasn't in his room."

"As a matter of fact, I saw him in the drive. He'd been for a walk . . . had a bit of a headache, he said, and was going up to bed. I gather he had promised to read to the children later, but didn't feel up to it, so I said I would. Can't have them disturbing him, poor chap."

"Gustav is quite wonderful the way he copes with them all – better than a nanny, actually!" Jane said with her gentle smile. "Your three have settled down wonderfully well, Guy, seeing it's only two months since you brought them home. You're looking better, too – you've put on weight!"

"All that army stodge!" Guy said laughing. "I'm fighting fit again and jolly glad to be back with the regiment. How is your husband?"

"Oliver's fine although grumbling because he never gets to fly these days. He hates desk work, but someone has to do it. That reminds me, Guy, when I told him you and Zee-Zee would both be here tonight, he asked me to get up one of the bottles of vintage champagne he has been hoarding for the great day of victory! He said you had earned it, rescuing poor Alice's children the way you did!"

"That's jolly decent of him!" Guy said warmly. "You might imagine I would have managed to get hold of a bottle or two when I was in France, but the ruddy Germans had pinched the lot. Mind you, I think there are one or two Frenchmen who have buried a few bottles to dig up on the day they are liberated!"

"And who can blame them!" Jane said. "If you've finished eating, Guy, would you like to go down to the cellar and get yourself a bottle? There is ice in the kitchen, and if you go down now, the champagne will have time to chill before Zandra arrives."

"That's really good of you both!" Guy acknowledged. "I don't suppose I'll have the chance, so will you please thank your husband for me. I'll nip up and say good night to the children first, shall I? I dare say they heard the car and will be getting impatient!"

Although not surprisingly the Conway children held back, Claudette, Brigitte and Henri threw themselves into his arms with shrieks of delight as he went into their bedroom. It was some time before he could calm them, after which he tucked them up in their beds, read a story and drew the curtains. There were the usual demands for kisses and hugs; and when Guy finally managed to leave the room, he found himself strangely moved by their obvious affection.

That long journey had formed a bond between them all, he told himself as he went downstairs. He had become a kind of father-figure to them, and he was not far off feeling like a father now! Count Zemski had managed to discover that Claude Calonne had met the same fate as his wife and the Rochfords; that his act of betrayal had been for nothing since, despite the assurances the Gestapo had doubtless given him, they had shot him anyway. The children were orphans and would never go back to France now, Alexis had said. They would remain at Rochford, and hopefully after the war, one or other of the young married couples would adopt them. He thought Zandra the most likely, being roughly the same age as Alice and having no children of her own.

Somehow Guy doubted that Anthony Wisson would want to take on one, let alone three children who were not even directly related to him. It worried him, Guy, even to think about such a man becoming their adopted father. Wisson had been down to Rochford on several occasions since the children's arrival, and although Guy had obviously not been there at the same time, Zandra had told him that the youngsters tended to avoid him, preferring the company of their new friend, Gustav Gebrauer!

A deep frown furrowed Guy's forehead as he thought of the German pilot. It was still there when he made his way down to the cellar. He glanced at his watch. There were a further two hours to go before Zandra's train arrived . . . plenty of time for the champagne to cool! The fates were being kind to them, he told himself, for Wisson was not expected at Rochford until the weekend. He and Zandra would have at least forty of his precious forty-eight hours together.

The champagne bottles, stacked neatly on their sides, were covered in dust. Guy selected one and, turning off the light, made his way back along the servants' hallway to the kitchen. As he was about to open the kitchen door, he paused. Someone was in there talking on the telephone extension. Not wishing to interrupt what he assumed must be a private call (since whoever was making it had chosen to use the kitchen instrument rather than the one in the hall), Guy waited. A minute later, his suspicions were confirmed. It was Inge talking in German.

". . . Yes, I understand . . . Please, as soon as you can . . . No, Guy only arrived an hour ago . . . Yes, just the children, I think . . ." There was a long pause and then Inge said: "I'm sorry! I von't ring again. Good night!"

Guy backed into the cellar and waited until Inge left the kitchen and was walking past the door.

"Is that you, Jane?" he called out. "I'm not sure which of these bottles of champagne you meant. They all look alike to me!"

He heard Inge's footsteps halt. There was a moment's hesitation and then her face, perfectly composed, appeared at the door.

"Oh, it's you, Inge!" he said. "I thought it was Jane!"

Inge walked towards him.

"I vanted to get some vork done in the studio, but then I remembered I had not prepared a tray for Zandra. I vas just on my vay to the kitchen to make some sandviches for her, and then I think that she may already have had a meal."

"That was thoughtful of you, Inge; but if Zandra hasn't eaten, she can always rustle up something for herself," Guy said. "Ah, I think this is the right bottle! It'll be a lovely surprise for Zandra."

He picked it up for the second time and accompanied Inge upstairs. Zandra was not the only person who was going to be surprised tonight, he told himself, his face grim and determined. He would go down to meet her train early – and ring Alexis Zemski from the call-box there.

Chapter 33

June 1944

Guy replaced the telephone receiver and, leaving the call-box, walked out onto the station platform. It was deserted apart from a soldier with his girl whom he was holding in a tight embrace at the furthest end of the platform where the single, low-wattage bulb shed the least light.

"Evening, sir!" The elderly porter had emerged from darkness, his voice momentarily startling Guy. "Looks like the train's late again – it ain't been signalled yet!"

"Let's hope it has not been shunted into a siding somewhere!" Guy replied.

"Like as not, sir!" the man said, removing his cap to scratch his head. "Line's been that busy all day! Troop trains mostly! 'Asn't been this busy since they brought those poor army lads back from that there Dunkirk!"

Guy nodded.

"Well, it would seem they're heading in the right direction now!"

The porter grinned.

"That it does! 'Course, it could 'ave been one of them buzz bombs landed on the line. We 'ad one come down over

Bagton-way day afore yesterday – landed in the Smithers' bottom field – great big 'ole in 'is wheat, it made!"

"I suppose that's better than landing in the village . . . causing casualties."

"Aye, I don't disagree with that, sir." The man gave a derisive chuckle. "If them things is Adolf's secret weapon, can't say I think much to them, do you, sir? Ain't going to make no difference to the war, are they? Reckon we've all but got 'em beat at last, just like Mr Churchill said we would, God bless 'im!"

"Yes, it certainly looks like it! We'll be into Rome any moment now, by the sound of it; and the Russians have regained Sevastopol. It's all good news these days, isn't it?"

"Mr Churchill were right, weren't 'e, sir. 'E said we'd get the better of 'em sooner or later. The wife and me always reckoned 'e'd pull us through. Best Prime Minister we ever 'ad, I say!" He paused. "There's the bell, sir. Train'll be in any time now. You getting on, sir?"

"No, I'm meeting someone – one of the Rochford family actually."

"Oh, aye! Know 'em all, sir. Couldn't ask for better! Old Mrs Rochford, now – used to visit my wife that time she were ill with pneumony; sit there by her bed just like she were a n'ordinary neighbour. And Miss Jane – Lady Rochford, that is – kept my kiddies in clothes and toys when they was little 'uns, same as she did other folk when times was hard. Young Mr Oliver, now – 'e liked to come and watch them express trains come through. Thirty or more year ago, that must be! Seems like only the other day and now they's all in uniform. The wife and I were right sorry about Mr Giles . . . and them other ones up at Manor. Takes a bit of getting used to, their poor faces, like; but as the wife says . . . ah, there's the train, sir, if you'll excuse me."

As the porter hurried along the platform swinging his lantern, Guy forgot the war, forgot his telephone call to Alexis, forgot everything but the fact that any moment now, Zandra would step out of one of the carriages. His eyes searched eagerly for the sight of her slim figure, her face. He felt a touch on his shoulder and swung round to see her standing behind him, her eyes bright with laughter.

"I was in the front carriage," she said. "Hallo, darling!"

Regardless of the porter and the other passengers who had alighted, Guy swept her into his arms, releasing her only when the porter said apologetically: "I'll be going 'ome now, sir! If I could just 'ave the young lady's ticket . . . Evening, Miss Zandra!"

"Hallo, Bosworth! How are the rheumatics?"

The old man punched her ticket and handed her the return half.

"No so bad, miss, not now we're into summer."

"That's good. Well, give my regards to Mrs Bosworth."

He touched his cap and went off to find his bicycle. Guy took Zandra's arm in his and led her to the car.

"How are you, Guy? What's all the news? Who's at home?" she asked as she climbed into the passenger seat. "How are the children? Has that monkey, Henri, broken any more windows?"

Her last innocent question was like a blow in the solar plexus, bringing sharply back to Guy's mind Gebrauer's account of Henri's discoveries. He wanted desperately to be able to tell Zandra of the ominous developments at Rochford – but Alexis had forbidden it. No one, he'd said, *absolutely no one*, must be told. He, Guy, must say nothing and do nothing until the morning. Then, and then only, could he act.

"Nothing wrong, darling? You've gone silent on me!" Zandra said as he eased the car into gear and released the brake.

"Have I? I expect it's because I'm finding it hard to believe that you're really here, next to me, and knowing we've got two whole days together; that I'm not just imagining you!"

He heard her soft laughter and then felt her hand covering his on the steering-wheel. Once again, his mind emptied of every other thought as his body responded instantly to the warm pressure of her hand.

* * *

"Bang on – eggs *and* bacon!" Guy said jovially as he and Zandra sat down at the breakfast table. "Don't know how you do it, Inge!"

Alice's three children fought to be first to greet him.

"Aunt Jane wouldn't let us come into your room this morning!" Brigitte said reproachfully. She was clinging to his arm, her small red mouth turned down in a pout. "We've been awake for ages."

He kissed her and tousled Henri's head.

"Well, young man, I do believe you've grown!" he said.

"I'm going to boarding school next term, Uncle Guy!" the boy stated proudly. "I'm going to Uncle Giles' prep school and Uncle Jamie went there, too. I'm going to have a uniform and a cap with a school badge on."

"And how about you, Claudette?" Guy asked as Inge put a rack of fresh toast on the table.

"Brigitte and me are going to the Convent!" Claudette replied quietly. "Because we're Catholics, you see." She broke off as Jane came into the room and the airmen at the table rose politely to greet her. One of them held back a chair and she sat down.

"The porter said that the reason Zandra's train was late last night was because of all the troop trains passing through," Guy announced to the room in general. "They get priority, of course! He seemed to think it might be a prelude to the invasion."

There was an excited buzz of conversation as everyone discussed the possibility. Someone asked Guy if he was on embarkation leave.

"Well, I can't answer that – you know, old chap, careless talk and all that!"

There was a further outbreak of voices as everyone speculated as to where on the French coast the invasion might start.

"Of course it'll be Dover!" someone said. "Dover to Calais, the quickest route—"

"The Germans know that, Ginger, so it would be crazy to land there. They'd be ready and waiting . . . they aren't stupid.

Besides, they've already set up defences all along there. It would be murder!"

"It could be Folkestone–Boulogne—"

"Nonsense, that'll be defended, too. Bet you a quid it isn't Calais!"

Guy looked up at the men seated opposite him.

"Don't waste your money, old chap. Ginger's right! The Jerries won't expect us to land at Calais just because it's so well defended, so they'll be looking for us elsewhere. That's why we've chosen Calais. Of course, you RAF chaps will pulverize the defences first."

There was a sudden hush as everyone stared at Guy. His tone of voice had not been speculative. He had stated Calais as a matter of fact. Guy put down his knife and fork and touched his mouth with his napkin. When he spoke, he sounded apologetic.

". . . damned silly of me . . . shouldn't have . . . well, forget what I said . . . I mean, I was only guessing."

But he wasn't, Zandra thought, staring at him with a horrified gaze. If he was "in the know", how could he possibly be so irresponsible as to let slip what everyone knew must be the most vital secret of the war? *How could Guy, of all people, do such a thing?* He couldn't possibly be still tipsy after last night's champagne. Granted he had drunk most of it, for she'd only had one glass, but that surely couldn't still be affecting him. Besides, he'd been totally in control of himself when he'd made love to her.

"Any more toast, tea, anyvone?" Inge's voice broke the silence. "If not, I vill clear the table. You can get down, children. As Uncle Guy is here, ve von't do any vork this morning. Now off you go and tidy your rooms!"

As they disappeared, the telephone rang. Jane went to answer it and Inge turned back to Guy. "I am helping the children to make a collage for Aunt Villow's birthday next month. Ve add a little every day after breakfast before I go off to my studio to vork."

Jane came back into the dining-room. She looked flustered.

"There are three inspectors coming down from the Works

Department about the new extension – Rochford is going to be enlarged to accommodate ordinary convalescents, Guy. It was Anthony's idea, but I didn't know that it had been approved . . . or at least, only in principle. The man I spoke to just now said they were coming down to assess 'the potential', whatever that's supposed to mean! Anyway, I'd be grateful if everyone would tidy up a bit so we look a bit more professional."

There was general laughter, and the men left the room, promising Jane they would have their rooms fit for a CO's inspection. Guy turned to Zandra.

"I'm going to walk down to Havorhurst," he said. "I've a couple of letters I forgot to post last night. You stay and give Jane and Inge a hand, darling."

"I'd be grateful for your help, Zee-Zee!" Jane said. "You see, the men are coming down by train and I promised I'd be at the halt to meet them. However, if you're going in to the village, Guy, perhaps you could go in my car and save me the journey?"

"No trouble!" Guy said, adding in a low voice to Zandra: "See you later then, my darling!"

As Zandra pushed back her chair, she became aware of the German airman, Gustav, staring at her and Guy. He had not left the room with the other "guinea pigs". Had he heard Guy's endearment? she wondered. Was that why he was staring at them? No one other than the family knew of her relationship with Guy, and although everyone had been told of Guy's escape from France with the children and knew he was a friend of the family, the endearment must have sounded surprisingly over-intimate to the German prisoner.

Guy, too, had noticed Gustav staring at him.

"Shouldn't you be getting your room to rights, Gebrauer?" he asked sharply. "Lady Rochford has asked for your help, or didn't you hear her?"

What *was* the matter with Guy this morning? Zandra asked herself as she went upstairs to make her bed. On his last visit to the children, he could not have been nicer to all the "guinea pigs", and in particular to Gustav whose attentions to "his" children he'd greatly appreciated. Now she came to consider it, in retrospect Guy had not behaved entirely normally last night either. Usually, after they had made love, he would light a cigarette and with his arm tightly around her, they would talk, sometimes for an hour or more. It was a ritual of their lovemaking which she treasured because, as Guy said, once asleep he was no longer able to enjoy the fact that she was there, close beside him, her body touching his. They had so little time when they could be together that neither could bear to waste a moment of it apart. Yet Guy had just announced that he would go for a walk without her . . . and had not even bothered to ask if she wanted to go with him!

Having tidied her own and Guy's rooms, she went along the landing to pay a quick visit to Aunt Willow. The old lady always stayed in bed for breakfast but no longer remained in her room all day, now spending the best part of it downstairs. She seemed to Zandra to be in good health and in excellent spirits, and was delighted to learn that Rochford might once more become a fully fledged convalescent home.

Leaving her aunt to dress, Zandra made her way further along the landing to the nursery quarters. Only Claudette was there, sitting by the window, her shoulders drooping. Zandra hurried over to her. Horrified, she saw that the child was weeping.

"What's wrong, darling?" Zandra asked gently, kneeling down beside her.

For a moment, Claudette did not reply. Then she said: "I can't tell you . . . I'm not allowed . . . I promised—"

"Tell me what? Promised who?" Zandra prompted. The child's tears turned to sobs. Zandra produced a handkerchief and Claudette blew her nose.

"Whatever it is, darling, I'm sure it would be all right for you to tell me. Is it because Uncle Guy has gone off for a walk without you? He'll be back soon, you know, and you'll see lots of him. He's here for two whole days!"

"No, it isn't that . . . Aunt Zandra, if I tell you, will you promise not to tell anyone? Gustav might think I couldn't be trusted to keep a secret if he knew I'd told you."

"Gustav!" Despite herself, Zandra could not keep the surprise from her voice. She felt a shiver of apprehension. "Look, I think you'd better tell me what all this is about, Claudette. Perhaps I can sort it out for you and then you'd feel better, wouldn't you?"

Slowly, in fits and starts, Claudette related the events of the previous day. Finally, she ended with a rush: "Gustav said he would tell us after tea what we ought to do: and then he locked himself in his room and Aunt Jane said we mustn't disturb him because he had a headache. We were going to ask him this morning before breakfast but when I woke up, I had a horrible thought" – her voice broke – "he's a *Boche*, isn't he, Aunt Zandra? Like those horrible Nazis who killed *Maman* and *Papa*; and maybe Gustav *knew all the time* about the transmitter; and maybe Aunt Inge knows, too, because she's a German like him; and maybe they're planning something awful and I'm frightened. Maybe there's Germans hiding down in the woods and Gustav and Aunt Inge will tell them that Henri and Brigitte and me are here. And when we're all asleep, they'll come and kill us!"

"Hush, darling, hush!" Zandra said, her mind racing as she rocked the weeping child in her arms. "You've been letting your imagination run away with you. Do you know what I think? I think Henri has been playing too many 'pretend' games and got a bit confused between what's real and what's pretend. Do you understand what I am saying? What he saw just *looked* to him like a transmitter. After all, he is only eight years old and he doesn't know much about such things, does he?"

Claudette's tears ceased and she rubbed her eyes with her knuckles.

"Do you really think so? Henri does get sort of carried away sometimes. When he tells ghost stories, he gets too frightened to go to bed by himself and wants to get in with me! But, Aunt Zandra, suppose it was real – the transmitter, I mean? And why didn't Gustav tell us if he didn't believe it either? And why hasn't he told us what to do, the way he promised?"

"I don't know the answer to those questions, sweetheart, and don't worry any more about breaking your promise not to tell anyone. You were quite right to tell me, and Gustav was wrong to ask you not to do so; and I shall tell him so. As for the transmitter, how would it be if I go down to the studio now, this very minute, and ask Aunt Inge to show me some of her work? Then when I come back, I'm sure I'll be able to tell you that you've got yourself all upset about nothing! I expect Gustav thought the whole thing was a game and he's forgotten all about it!"

Although Claudette was reassured, Zandra was very far indeed from being so herself. If Gustav Gebrauer were involved in some form of espionage, what better "front" could he have put up here at Rochford than the one he had chosen – ingratiating himself with the children, spending time with Aunt Willow, pretending to be the grateful, self-effacing prisoner on parole? Everyone in the household liked and trusted him, and Eve, especially, had taken him under her wing. But Inge . . . her brother's wife! Had she, Zandra, not known very well how ardent a Nazi her sister-in-law was in those early days before her marriage, she would have instantly dismissed Claudette's suspicion that she could be involved. Now she recalled only too clearly how at one time, Adolf Hitler had been Inge's God. Even Jamie had admired him!

Making her way downstairs, Zandra recalled with a shock the incident at breakfast when Guy had so astonishingly – disgracefully, in fact – let slip such a vital piece of information. She might not have believed he was really "in the know" had he not subsequently looked so embarrassed and tried to cover the slip. If Gustav and Inge were involved, what a devastatingly important piece of news they had to give their countrymen! Perhaps this extraordinary story of Claudette's had not, as she'd first supposed, sprung from the disturbed mind of a child who, only a few months ago, had been living under the heel of the enemy

528

occupation. If there really was a transmitter, someone must be using it, and who else if not Inge, who spent hours alone in her studio and forbade entry by anyone but herself? And where was Inge? It was after half-past ten, and if she kept to her usual routine, she would almost certainly be down at her studio now.

Forcing herself to keep calm, Zandra crossed the hall and went out into the garden. The heat of the June sun penetrated the fabric of the thin, floral cotton frock she was wearing and, as she hurried towards the stable-block, small beads of perspiration broke out on her forehead. Opening the wooden door into the cobbled yard, she paused. Would Inge let her into the studio if she knocked? she asked herself. It was highly unlikely. Both the studio door and the door into the tack-room were always locked. To her knowledge, there were no duplicate keys. If she waited for Guy to come back from the village, he might know how to force a lock. It was the kind of thing he could have been taught when he had been specially trained for his underground work in France. But by the time he returned, it could be too late. If Inge *did* have a transmitter, she could already have passed on the information.

Zandra paused a moment longer. Despite the heat of the day, she was shivering – not from the cold, she realized, but from the knowledge that she was no longer questioning Claudette's fears, and had actually begun to believe in Inge's involvement.

She walked across to the main door and knocked.

"It's me, Zandra!" she called out. "Can I come in, Inge? I have to see you – it's urgent!"

"Can't it vait, Zandra? I am in the middle of something . . . the plaster vill dry out!"

"No, it's urgent . . . about Jamie!" Zandra added with sudden inspiration. Inge would surely open up if she thought there was ominous news about her husband.

There was a moment's silence, and then Inge opened the door, blocking the entrance with her body. She looked flushed and irritated.

"I can't talk to you out here, Inge!" Zandra said. "Please let me in!"

"No! I told you, I am busy . . . please say vat you must and go avay. I vill not have people in my vorkroom."

As Zandra took a step forward, Inge attempted to bar her way.

"I won't disturb anything, Inge. Now let me come in, please!" When Inge remained unmoving, Zandra said sharply: "What possible reason have you for keeping me out? You're not afraid of something, are you? Why all this secrecy?"

She saw the hesitation on the younger girl's face, and then suddenly Inge smiled.

"I am afraid only that you break something!" she said calmly, moving to one side. "You must think it silly that I do not like for people to see vat I am making before it is completed."

Wordlessly, Zandra stepped past her, her eyes quickly scanning the large room. At the furthest end, against the wall, was Inge's work table beneath which was a bucket of plaster. On the work bench was the half-finished model of a Spitfire, a large jug of water, a collection of tools and a bulky object covered haphazardly with a green cloth.

"I've always wondered how you worked, Inge!" she said in a friendly voice as she edged nearer to the table. "You make such marvellous things! Is that Spitfire a present for Jamie?"

By now, she had reached the table. Behind her, the door shut. As Zandra reached out to lift the green cloth, Inge spoke in a cold, hard voice.

"I think ve both know vy you are here, Zandra, so ve do not vaste more time. I was afraid one of those French children had been spying on me yesterday. I heard their voices, and ven I came here this morning, I saw that the vindow is broken. That is vy you are here, is it not? It is a pity they decided to tell you, Zandra. I vish it had not been you who has come spying on me."

"So you do have something to hide, Inge?" Zandra reached out towards the green cloth. From behind her, she heard the girl laugh – a harsh, contemptuous laugh.

530

"I see you are determined to search until you find my transmitter, so yes, I admit that I have vone. If you had come looking in half an hour's time, you vould not have found it for it vould have been destroyed. However, do not think you can stop me now, Zandra. In ten minutes, I vill make my usual transmission, only this time, thanks to your lover, I vill have something of great importance to tell my people. It vill be my finest achievement for the Fatherland!"

Zandra swung round as Inge stopped talking, her heart beating furiously as she confronted her sister-in-law. Drawing a deep breath, she said quietly: "But you won't have a chance to send that message, Inge. I won't let you!" Her hands trembling, she picked up one of the knives lying on the work bench.

Far from looking afraid, Inge gave another laugh. The sound of it sent a shiver down Zandra's spine.

"Oh, I think I vill, Zandra. You vill do exactly as I say," she said, drawing a small pistol from her overall pocket.

Now there was no smile on the girl's face – only a look of grim determination as she pointed the gun at Zandra.

"Over there, by the vall vere I can see you!" she said sharply. "And put that knife down, please." She took a step nearer Zandra. "I am sorry that you came, Zandra!" she repeated in a matter-of-fact tone. "I have alvays quite liked you, and you are Jamie's sister; but don't think I vill hesitate to use this if I have to. The Fatherland matters more to me than anything. You think you are vinning this var, don't you, but you vill see. The Führer vill never permit you to invade Germany. He knows that ve who believe in him are happy to lay down our lives for him. *Heil Hitler!*"

The protest that Zandra had been about to make died on her lips. She had only to look into her sister-in-law's face, now only feet away from her own, to see the fanaticism in her eyes. Inge was going to make that transmission even if it cost her her life – and any attempt to stop her would only result in the loss of her own. Any moment now, Inge's German counterpart would learn

531

where the invasion was going to take place . . . and there was nothing whatever she could do to prevent it.

Slowly, inexorably, she backed against the wall.

"Give me that gun, Inge!"

The man's voice startled them both. He must have come through the tack-room door for he was now standing in shadow at the far end of the room.

"Give me the gun!" he repeated.

With a cry of relief, Zandra recognized the voice.

"Thank God you've come, Anthony! She's going to transmit to Germany. She knows where the landing is going to be . . . the invasion. You've got to stop her. Thank God you're in time to stop her!"

Unhurriedly, Inge walked past her and to Zandra's astonishment, meekly surrendered her weapon to Anthony before returning purposefully to her work table. Anthony was still standing by the door into the tack-room. Aware that she could move now without danger, Zandra started to walk down the studio towards him. She did not have time to wonder what he was doing here. Her overriding thought was that he had arrived in time to stop Inge's transmission. She saw that he was smiling – a strange twisted smile . . . and then she saw the gun in his hand. He was not pointing it at Inge but at her!

For a moment, she wondered if she could be dreaming. Then as Anthony told her in a cold, hard voice to stay where she was, she knew that the nightmare was real. Anthony, as well as Inge, was a traitor. He knew what Inge had been doing. He had no intention of stopping the transmission, after which . . .

"You can't kill me!" she said quietly. "They'd find my body, and you or Inge would be arrested. Claudette knows why I'm here. You'll never get away with it, Anthony!"

Anthony's eyebrows rose, and his lips curled once more in the smile which was frighteningly familiar to her. She had seen it too many times in those moments when he knew he had her totally in his power. His voice, too, held the same, patronizing tone as he said: "You always have underestimated me, Zandra. You don't really think I'd be so silly as to shoot you here, do you? In a little while, when Inge has completed her task, we shall go for a drive, you and I. My car is outside in the yard – and what could be more natural than a husband taking his wife for a drive round the estate? Or that we should seek a little privacy in order to discuss the fact that your lover is visiting you here! There will be an accident, of course – and as a result of this unfortunate accident, I'm afraid you, my dear, will not be coming back!"

"This is Mr Saunders, the surveyor; Mr Hall, the builder, and Mr Soames, the Clerk of Works. I'll leave them in your care, Jane!"

Guy turned to the child who was tugging on his sleeve.

"All by yourself, Claudette?" he said as she drew him out through the front door into the garden. "Where are the other children?"

"They've gone down to the lake!" Claudette said. Guy looked at her white, tear-stained face and put a comforting hand around her shoulders.

"Didn't you want to play with them?" he asked gently. "It's a beautiful day and—"

"I was waiting for you, Uncle Guy! Aunt Zandra hasn't come back and I'm frightened, and I didn't dare go down there by myself and so I waited for you."

With a sudden feeling of apprehension, Guy caught his breath.

"Go where, Claudette? Where has Aunt Zandra gone?"

Claudette gulped and burst into tears.

"You must tell me, Claudette. It's terribly important. It wasn't Aunt Inge's studio, was it?"

The child nodded.

Involuntarily, Guy's grip on her arm tightened.

"Why? Why did she go there?" he demanded. He waited with growing impatience and then horror as, for the second time that morning, Claudette related the cause of her anxiety.

"But Aunt Zandra hasn't come back. I've been waiting and waiting!" she sobbed as she came to the end of her story. Guy let out an oath. Pushing the little girl to one side, he doubled off across the terrace in the direction of the studio. The sound of Claudette's screams followed him, but he did not stop. At the door into the walled yard, he paused, his hands clenching at his sides. Until this moment, he had followed his first impulse which was to prevent Zandra from coming to any harm; but now he found himself facing one of the worst decisions he had ever had to make – Zandra's safety, or the possible saving of hundreds of soldiers' lives.

During those long, dangerous years in France, Guy had been faced with other life-and-death decisions – whether he must kill a man – a woman even – or risk his own life and those of the men he was trying to assist. He had never hesitated. Now it was Zandra – the woman he loved more than anything in the whole world – whose life might be at risk. Inge *must* be allowed to make that transmission. It was for just such a purpose, Alexis had explained last night, that she had been allowed to continue operating. They had picked up her signals six weeks ago . . . monitored them. Guy's breakfast-time revelation would not be the first worthwhile bit of misinformation she had been able to give the Jerries. Alexis was convinced that the Germans would believe it was true. They now knew all about Guy, his years as a secret agent in France; that although he had rejoined his own regiment, he might easily have access to those who knew where the invasion would take place. It was perfectly reasonable for them to suppose that Guy might be off his guard amongst friends in a house where he was treated as one of the family. Provided his mention of Calais seemed a natural slip of the tongue, Inge would have no reason to doubt the misinformation.

If he barged in now, Guy told himself, Inge would never use that transmitter, and Alexis' plan would be aborted. It was three minutes to eleven – the time of day when Inge's contact listened in for her call sign. If he put his country first – and he knew he must – then he could do nothing to help Zandra for three more minutes.

Biting his lip, Guy stared round the courtyard, noticing suddenly that a large, black Bugatti was parked in one of the open-fronted byres. It was a big, expensive car, and there were not many in use nowadays because of the high consumption of petrol. It had a London number-plate, and for a moment Guy tried to place where he had seen such a car before. Then his eye caught the slight movement of an open door swinging gently on its hinges, and he forgot the car as he realized that he would have an easy entry by the tack-room into the studio.

He crossed the yard quickly and silently, and stood listening. There was no audible sound of a transmitter, but he could hear a man's voice – a voice he recognized. It was that of Anthony Wisson – and he realized then whose car he had seen. Drawing his army revolver from the holster beneath his left armpit, he edged himself into the tackroom. Now he could see through the door opposite into the studio. Sunlight was pouring through the big skylight, and beneath it stood Wisson. His arm was raised and he had a gun pointing at Zandra's head. His voice was low, but as Guy moved to the studio door, he heard all he needed to know. There was going to be a car accident from which Zandra would not be returning . . .

Instinctively, he took a step forward into the studio, his left arm raised to steady his revolver. The command to Wisson to drop his gun was never spoken, for Anthony had heard the movement behind him, and without the slightest hesitation, had turned and fired.

Oblivious to her own safety, Zandra ran forward as Guy's knees buckled and as if in slow motion, he fell backwards, his weight sending a statue of the German eagle crashing to the floor.

"You've killed him . . . you've killed him!" she whispered as she fell to her knees beside Guy's inert body. Blood was pouring from the wound in his head and was streaming down his face. As she tried to cradle his head in her arms, the blood poured down, dripping onto her hands and staining her skirt a crimson red.

"Oh, my God, you've killed him!" she said again, staring at Anthony in shocked horror. She saw Anthony shrug his shoulders indifferently, his expression impassive before he turned to watch Inge who had now begun to tap out her Morse message.

Suddenly, Zandra was consumed with anger – a fury so intense that she was conscious of one thought only – Anthony had killed Guy and so he must die, too. Guy's revolver, still loaded, had fallen from his hand. She picked it up, feeling the warm stickiness of his blood as she gripped the handle. She had no thought for the years of sadistic cruelty she had suffered at Anthony's hands; for the threats of blackmail; for the fact that he was a traitor. One thought overwhelmed all others as she aimed the gun at Anthony's back and fired – he was a murderer and had killed Guy without ever giving him a chance.

Inge had finished her transmission. She pushed back her chair and hurried to Anthony's side. Although Zandra had fired wildly with a trembling hand, the bullet had entered Anthony's back, and the upward trajectory had carried it forward and into his heart. Inge rolled him on to his back, realizing as she did so that she was alone now and could no longer expect help from the dead man lying at her feet. A trickle of blood was running down Anthony's chin from the corner of his mouth; and there was a look of surprise on his face. She turned to see Zandra bent once more over the body of her lover. Her soft keening was now the only sound to break the silence in the room.

Inge moved stealthily towards her, her mouth closed tight, her eyes narrowed in determination. Her heart was beating swiftly with excitement. She had made her transmission – and whatever happened now, her German contact had received the vital information. Moreover, she might yet save her life if she remained calm. Anthony Wisson's death left her unmoved. From the very first when she was told she might one day have an important role to play, she had been happy to make whatever

536

sacrifices were necessary – even to submitting to the operation before her marriage to remove her ovaries so that she could not have children. She had understood the need to be free of any emotional ties when her time came.

For seven long years, she had waited to be called on to make her contribution to the Führer's magnificent new Germany. She had prepared – just as she had been instructed – an environment and a daily routine which, when the time came, would allow her to operate a transmitter without causing suspicion. She had perfected her knowledge of the Morse code and silently, on a padded board, practised her speed of transmission. Suddenly, two months ago when she had almost given up hope of her services ever being employed, Anthony Wisson had come down to Rochford with a radio set, a code and instructions to make twice weekly transmissions of items she was able to glean from her relations in the services; from the "guinea pigs"; from careless talk in the village. Then, a month ago, she had been asked to try and ascertain where, as an invasion seemed imminent, the landing might be. Even the smallest pieces of information might be fitted in with those of other informants so that the whole would form a vital picture. The preconceived plan for her to have a private studio where she could indulge her hobby undisturbed and unobserved had finally proved its excellence. The transmitter would not be discovered accidentally; and her regular work schedule, during which she made her eleven o'clock transmissions, gave no cause for comment. There was always the danger of her radio signals being picked up, but Rochford Manor was in so isolated a position and the Rochfords themselves so beyond suspicion, that the risks were small enough for her to be told that during the present pre-invasion emergency, she could also transmit at four o'clock if required.

Until Alice Calonne's children and the two Conway orphans had arrived, few people ever went near the studio. It had come as a terrible shock when she'd heard the children's voices outside in the yard shouting that they had heard the Morse transmission. Later that evening, she had gone to check that nothing had been disturbed and was further shocked to find the boards of one of the studio windows had been tampered with. She had decided that the danger was such that it warranted a forbidden telephone call to Anthony Wisson to ask him what she should now do.

The obvious step was to get rid of the transmitting equipment; but she was loath to do so at such a crucial time in the war. She had, for instance, been able to relay the fact that this past week, there had been a vast movement of troops towards the coast – even an encampment of soldiers in the vicinity of the Rochford estate. When she'd spoken to Mr Wisson on the kitchen extension, warning him that someone might have got into the studio and discovered the transmitter, he'd replied that he would come down first thing in the morning and assess the degree of danger. He intended to find out if anyone in the family was taking notice of the children; if indeed they had discovered anything at all, which he was inclined to doubt. He would park his car down near the studio where it would provide an instant safe place for her to dispose of the equipment were it to prove necessary, he'd said reassuringly.

It was the most fortunate of decisions, Inge had realized when at breakfast that morning, Guy Bristow had made the unbelievable error of revealing the most important secret anyone could have imagined. He had realized his mistake almost immediately, of course, and tried to cover it up. Her excitement had been intense and difficult to conceal as she forced herself to carry on with her usual routine whilst waiting for eleven o'clock when she could transmit. She was buoyed up by the conviction that when Germany finally won the war and her part in it became known, the Führer himself might thank her!

Now, with this uppermost in her mind, she could see no reason to give a second thought to Anthony Wisson's death. She was grateful to him for coming to her aid in so timely a fashion; but it was his own fault that he had stupidly got himself killed in the process. After he'd shot Guy, he should not have left Zandra unguarded and within reach of Guy's revolver.

Inge was standing a few feet from Zandra now. She was still bent over Guy's body attempting to wipe the blood from his face – a pointless task, Inge thought scornfully, for it was still welling from his headwound! Her hand tightened over the hilt of the knife she had picked up from her work table. She knew exactly where she would strike . . . at the base of Zandra's neck. Then she could leave. There would be petrol in Anthony's car. She would drive as far as it lasted, and then take a train to Liverpool. From there, it would be easy enough to get to Ireland where there were innumerable safe houses – places where people were sympathetic to the Nazi cause if only because they were so violently opposed to the English!

Inge's arm rose, and there was a triumphant smile on her face which remained there after the bullet she could not have anticipated pierced her side and entered her heart. It killed her instantly so that she never even saw the face of the man who had fired the gun.

Epilogue

July 1944

"Well, who is going to tell me the truth, the whole truth and nothing but the truth?" Eve's tone was light-hearted, but the expression in her blue eyes, as they moved from one member of the family to another, was both expectant and determined. "Daddy wrote and told me the 'official' story, but he said I must wait until I came down here for my leave and then one of you would fill in the facts. All I know at the moment is that – according to Gustav – Inge had run out of some turps or something she'd needed for her work; that she had gone down to Havorhurst on her bicycle and been run over by an army truck in one of those convoys going through the village. And, of course, that a week later, Anthony's body was found in a bombed-out house in London. So which of you is going to tell me what really happened?"

Jane looked down at the pullover she was knitting and carefully picked up the stitch she'd just dropped. Because of the shortage of wool, she had adopted the wartime habit of unravelling a discarded garment and reusing the wool. This one had once been a sweater of Oliver's, and was exactly the right grey for Henri's new school uniform. With a sigh, she laid down her

540

needles. It was too hot to be knitting here on the terrace on this early July afternoon.

She looked questioningly at Zandra who was lying on her stomach on the lawn, her shoulder touching Guy's, her right hand clasped unashamedly in his. His head was no longer bandaged and now, a month after the "accident" – the official version of the shooting – the livid red scar looked almost like a parting.

Jane turned to look at her husband. Oliver, like Eve and Zandra, had been able to wangle a brief leave for his mother's seventieth birthday party. It pleased Jane to see him out of uniform. On this beautiful, sunny day, there was no sound of the hateful air-raid warning and not even the distant "crump" of doodle-bugs to remind them all of war. It was almost possible to believe this was a peacetime Sunday.

"I think Guy should be the one to answer Eve's questions!" Oliver said quietly. "As you know, I wasn't here at the time."

Releasing Zandra's hand, Guy sat up, hunching his knees and clasping his arms around them. Eve said impatiently: "I guessed at once that Daddy's version wasn't the real one. I do need to know the truth. It's important to me, Guy. I want to know if Gustav was involved in some way? I simply couldn't believe it when he joined us for Gran's birthday lunch party. I thought it was only supposed to be family; but none of the other chaps were invited. Why the special treatment?"

It was Zandra, not Guy, who answered her.

"Gustav saved my life, Eve . . . probably Guy's, too!"

Eve's head shot up and her eyes went to the lakeside where Gustav was remaking her Uncle Oliver's old tree house into a sentry post for the children. Their high-pitched voices, interspersed with shouts of laughter, filtered across the lawn.

"I'll start at the beginning!" Guy said quietly. "I expect your father told you that this is never to go beyond the family. If it ever got out, the repercussions would be disastrous for a great many people. You do understand that?"

Eve nodded, impressed by the seriousness of Guy's tone.

"I have signed the Official Secrets Act, so you don't have to worry! Daddy knows I can be trusted!"

"Then you must treat this as an Official Secret," Guy said quietly. He explained how exactly a month ago, the children's innocent game of "spies" had led to the discovery that Inge was in possession of a transmitter; that she had been using it to send information to the enemy. Ignoring the shocked expression on Eve's face, he continued: "MI5 knew about it, of course. Inge's signals had been picked up almost as soon as she started using the set, and her transmissions were monitored. They were going to pick her up eventually, of course, but they wanted to find out first who her contact in England was. Gustav Gebrauer might have been the obvious suspect; but seeing he was confined either to the hospital or to this house, it seemed unlikely that he could be the vital link they wanted."

"I simply can't believe that Inge was a German spy!" Eve said, her eyes wide with horror. "She was Jamie's wife . . . how could she . . . if she loved him—?"

"I don't suppose she ever did!" Guy broke in gently. "The Nazis were a lot more devious than we gave them credit for in those early days. They'd take a Hitler fanatic like Inge, train her in espionage and then plant her in a country under some innocent guise and simply wait until they needed to use her. I dare say it was quite a shock for her when she was told what she had to do and Wisson produced the transmitter and put her to work!"

"Uncle Anthony!" Eve gasped, her eyes turning involuntarily to Zandra. "You mean, *he was a spy, too?*"

"Very much so!" Guy said. "Your father told me that MI5 had their eye on him as well, but for different reasons. They knew he'd been double-dealing for a long time – selling arms illegally on a big scale. They knew he had German contacts among many others. What we shall probably never know is whether he was being paid by them or being blackmailed. They might have threatened to expose his illicit arms deals to the British authorities if he didn't collaborate with them."

Eve drew a long breath.

"I see now why Daddy wouldn't talk about it on the telephone, or put it in a letter!" she exclaimed. "Granny doesn't know all this, does she? She was saying at lunch how sad she was about Uncle Anthony's death. I think she always liked him."

"Granny only knows the 'official' version, darling," Jane said quickly. "We weren't going to tell you either, but well, Zandra and I thought that it wouldn't be fair to keep you in the dark – and your father agreed – seeing that you and Gustav . . . well, you've always been such good friends, haven't you?"

A faint blush spread over the young girl's cheeks.

"If you knew Gustav as well as I do, Aunt Jane, you'd understand why I . . . why I like him." Eve's voice was defiant. "I suppose you all think he's dull because he's so quiet, but he isn't at all dull. He's a very intelligent person and . . . sensitive . . . and—"

"Eve, it's because we understand how you feel, and because we know what a nice man he is, that we're telling you the truth about that awful day!" Zandra broke in. "Go on, Guy – tell Eve what Gustav did."

"After the children found out about Inge's studio, he had to make up his mind, poor chap – loyalty to his country, or loyalty to all of us – the family who had befriended him. He was proud of his country but he didn't want a Germany run by people like Hitler and his Nazis; and he'd already decided that when the war ended, he'd try to obtain naturalization papers so he could stay in England. Your father is going to use his influence to see that he gets them now – after what he did!"

"And what did he do?" Eve asked quietly.

"He knew he had to tell someone about Inge," Guy continued the story, "and that I was due to arrive that evening on a forty-eight-hour leave, so he decided to tell me. At first I thought he must have got it all wrong – his English isn't all that marvellous, is it? Then I heard Inge making a highly suspicious phone call – to Wisson, I realized later, though not at the time – and I took Gustav's story a lot more seriously. As soon as I could do so without arousing Inge's suspicions . . . when I went down to Havorhurst to meet Zandra's train . . . I telephoned your father from the call-box there to ask his advice. It was he who came up with the idea of my 'dropping' a vital piece of misinformation for Inge to pass on to the Jerries. At breakfast next morning, I pretended I knew where we were invading. It would have been such an appalling slip of the tongue, we were by no means certain Inge would believe it, but we thought it was worth a try. I think it helped that Zandra fell for it and nearly had a fit when I calmly announced we were going to land at Calais! Your father had forbidden me to tell anyone what we'd planned, so she knew nothing about Inge or the transmitter. It hadn't occurred to either of us that Claudette would tell Zandra about it, so I wasn't in the least worried that she might go down to the studio and interfere inadvertently with the transmission we wanted Inge to make."

"So, what went wrong?" Eve asked, enthralled now by Guy's story.

"Your father had decided that the time had come for Inge to be pulled in – but not until after the transmission, of course. Meanwhile, although I'd told Gustav to stall the children whom he'd sworn to secrecy, we knew there was no way we could keep them from talking about the transmitter indefinitely, at which point Inge, realizing she'd been rumbled, might try to get rid of the evidence; and Count Zemski wanted her caught red-handed. That's where the Works Department men came in – three of Count Zemski's chaps who could be around the house without arousing Inge's suspicions. The plan was for them to pick her up after the transmission and take her back to London for questioning. I don't think Count Zemski had decided at that time what was to become of her. As it happened, the decision was made by the events which followed."

"I was the one who nearly ruined everything!" Zandra said. "Guy went off to the village to collect the men, and it was whilst he was gone that Claudette broke down and told me about the

544

transmitter. I suddenly remembered Guy's mention of the invasion at breakfast and realized that if Claudette's story about the transmitter was true, Inge would be able to pass on information of crucial importance to the Germans – or so in my ignorance I believed! I panicked. You see, I didn't know anything about your father's plan or even that Guy knew about the transmitter; so instead of waiting for him to get back, I shot off down to the studio to confront Inge. At that point, I was still not entirely sure she was guilty, so it never crossed my mind that she might have a gun. Naturally, she wasn't going to let me stop her transmitting and, with a gun pointed at me, there was nothing I could do. Anyway, just as Inge was getting ready to operate, Anthony arrived. Obviously, it was him she had telephoned the night before to say she was in trouble, and he'd driven down to do what he could to help her. But when I saw him in the doorway of the studio, I naturally thought that, realizing the danger I was in, he would help me! Instead of which—"

"Let me tell Eve, darling!" Guy broke in, taking Zandra's hand once more in his own. He could feel her trembling. "Discovering that Wisson was involved was a very nasty shock for Zandra. She couldn't believe it when Inge gave him her gun and he stood there, in the middle of the room, pointing it at her while Inge got on with her transmission. I, meanwhile, had returned with the men and learned from an hysterical Claudette that Zandra had gone down to the studio. I was frantic for her safety – and also because I was afraid she might prevent Inge from sending out the false information your father had told me to give her."

He gave a wry smile.

"I had my revolver handy, so I thought I'd be able to deal with the situation. What I didn't bargain for was that Wisson was there. He shot me before I had a chance to disarm him. His bullet only shaved the side of my head but it knocked me out. I'd have probably come round in a few minutes, but when I fell, I hit my head pretty badly on the edge of a plinth and the MO said it was that blow rather than Wisson's bullet which caused my subsequent concussion."

Zandra shuddered.

"Guy's head and face were covered in blood – it was awful!" she said. "He was unconscious and I thought he was dead. It was all I could think about. It didn't cross my mind Anthony would almost certainly shoot me, too. I remember feeling angry – so angry that I didn't care about anything any more except that he'd killed Guy and so he deserved to die. I could see Guy's revolver by my hand and . . . it was like a kind of dream . . . I remember seeing my own hand picking up the gun, aiming, firing. I remember that the hand – it didn't seem to belong to me – was shaking so much I was afraid I might not aim straight."

"But . . . but you did?" Eve asked in a small, shocked voice.

"Fortunately, yes!" Guy said firmly. "You've got to understand, Eve, Anthony Wisson was even more dangerous than Inge. Yes, she was a spy, but he was a spy *and* a traitor. He would certainly have finished me off if he'd known I wasn't dead; and he'd already told Zandra that he intended to dispose of her! I imagine he knew by then that it was not just Inge's safety but his own life that was at stake. God knows how he hoped to get rid of our bodies – fake a suicide note for us both or something; or maybe he hadn't had time to consider it. You have to understand, Eve, the man was evil and Zandra had no option but to do what she did."

For the first time, Oliver spoke.

"It is important you *do* understand that, Eve!" he emphasized the point. "You can see now why your father arranged the cover-up; and we were damned lucky he was in a position to do so. It wouldn't have been fair to Zandra if she'd had to stand trial for her husband's murder. The repercussions on Mother – on all the members of the family – would have been appalling, and unjustified! Wisson was a very dangerous man in more ways than one and totally amoral – but we won't go into that since he can't do any more damage now.

"I think I do understand," Eve said. There was a brief pause

546

before she added, "Just now you said that Gustav had saved Zandra's life . . . but how, if he wasn't there? And who killed Inge?"

Guy resumed the story.

"Gustav *was* there! He had been keeping watch on the stable-block and had seen Zandra go down to the studio. Next thing he saw was me dashing in after her, and then he heard the shots. Knowing something terrible must have happened, he rushed across to the studio. The door was open and he saw me on the floor and Zandra kneeling beside me. He saw Wisson's body and then, to his horror, he saw Inge edging her way towards Zandra with a lethal-looking knife in her hand. It was one of the tools she used for her work."

He drew a deep breath and then continued:

"Of course, Gustav wasn't armed; but there was a gun lying within his reach – my gun, as it turned out – that Zandra had thrown aside after she'd shot Wisson. It was lying close to the door so Gustav grabbed it. He didn't mean to *kill* Inge – only to stop her from attacking Zandra; but she crouched down just as he pulled the trigger, and instead of the bullet hitting her in the legs, as he'd intended, it went into her heart and she died instantly."

"I suppose I should be sorry, but I'm not!" Eve cried. "She was Jamie's wife and he . . . we all trusted her. She betrayed us! She deserved to die!"

"Perhaps you're right, dear!" Jane said softly. "It would have been so very hard on Jamie knowing his wife . . . well, he never will know now, will he? I like to think that God took him when He did to spare him."

Zandra's voice was sharp with pain as she said sadly: "It seems such a cruel stroke of Fate for Jamie to be shot down just when we'd all started to hope that the promised invasion meant that the end of the war was finally in sight, and he would be out of danger." Tears filled her eyes, but she brushed them away. "In a way, I'm glad for him that it happened the way it did. At least he never knew Inge had died! He adored her, didn't he? He told me once he wished they had children but I suppose we should thank God they didn't now!"

Guy took her hand and for a moment no one spoke. Then he broke the silence.

"There's not much more to tell you, Eve. Gustav was about to go up to the house to get help when your father's men – the WD fellows – arrived on the scene and went into action. Two of them carried me up to the house where, as you know, everyone was told I'd been giving Zandra some shooting practice, and that there'd been 'an accident'. The other chap helped Gustav to clean up the mess in the studio and put Wisson's and Inge's bodies into the boot of Wisson's car. Fortunately, he'd come up the back drive and parked it out of sight in one of the byres, so no one had seen him arrive or knew he was here."

"By this time, your parents had arrived, Eve," Zandra broke in. "Your father had telephoned Jane to say he and your mother would be down to lunch. He'd wanted to be on the spot when Inge was arrested, you see, so of course, he took charge after the 'accident' and planned the cover-up."

"He was pretty quick-thinking!" Guy said approvingly. "Inge had been missed by then and your father got Gustav to say that he'd seen her earlier heading for the village on her bike. He'd already sent one of his men down to the stable-block with instructions to drive Wisson's car to Borrowdale Woods and hide it. When the fellow got back an hour later, Count Zemski told the three WD men that because of my accident and the need to make a search for the missing Inge, the rest of the survey could wait for another day. He insisted that he himself should drive them to the station."

"That's when I nearly messed everything up again!" Zandra said with a rueful smile. "I'd no idea that he was going to fake Inge's accident and I kept offering to drive the men to Havorhurst!"

"Not your fault, darling!" Guy intervened. "Anyway, by the time Count Zemski got back, he'd been able to deal with the local police and ensure there was no proper enquiry or *post mortem* or anything like that; and arrange for Inge's body to be put in a sealed coffin. What with the news next day of Jamie's death, it was a very quiet funeral and no one but ourselves were any the wiser. A week later, Wisson's body was found in a bombed-out house where it had been secretly dumped under a mass of rubble, and by then the invasion had started, so the newspapers barely gave his death more than a few lines."

"On the day it all happened, Eve, your mother took all the children to London for 'a holiday' – they returned last week, by which time we were all back to normal!" Zandra explained. "You see, Claudette was still going on about the transmitter, and the two boys weren't to be shut up, either. So, before they left, your father took them all down to the studio, which was perfectly in order by then, and showed them that the object they'd seen had simply been Inge's wireless set. He told them Gustav had known all along it wasn't a real one, so he'd treated their discovery as part of the game and forgotten all about it! The children were terribly disappointed; but they accepted the explanation. They had to be told about Inge's death, of course, so that gave them something else to think about. Lucy said it didn't actually seem to bother them very much! They were far too excited about going to see Buckingham Palace and to the zoo. Needless to say, Henri's favourite expedition was the visit to the Chamber of Horrors!"

Eve turned now to look at her Uncle Oliver.

"Do you really believe that no one will ever find out the truth?" she asked. "Weren't there inquests? Interrogations?"

Oliver smiled.

"You'd be surprised what powers people like your father have behind the scenes," he said. "Especially in wartime, my dear! You must remember that two days after the débâcle here, the whole country was focused on the landings in Normandy. No, there's no reason I can see for the true facts ever to come out. Other than the five of us, and your mother, of course, there is no one else to reveal them. Your father and his cronies most certainly will not. Apart from the need to protect the family good name, they were only too happy to have unrestricted access to all Wisson's clandestine activities, and the leads they are getting to his associates. Both Zandra and Guy have been able to help them quite a bit. As to Gebrauer letting any cats out of the bag, it certainly wouldn't do a prisoner of war any good for it to become known he had shot and killed a woman, would it? Even if she was a German! Besides, it was he who tipped off Guy about the transmitter in the first place, which is a clear enough indication of where his first loyalties lie."

Zandra said mischievously: "I hope you don't mind, Eve, but I told Alexis I had a feeling that Gustav might even be joining the family one of these days."

As the four smiling faces turned to look at Eve, she jumped to her feet, her cheeks colouring a deep pink.

"How can you say such a thing?" she protested. "I never said . . . you've no reason whatever . . . I mean, just because I said I *liked* Gustav . . . oh, you're impossible, all of you! I'm going in to fetch Granny. You all seem to have forgotten it's her birthday!"

"Methinks she doth protest too much!" Oliver said laughing as Eve escaped through the garden door into the house. "Mind you, if the two of them did decide to get married, there'd be quite a few hurdles to be crossed before they could do so. I'm far from sure if an English girl would be allowed to marry a German POW."

"Perhaps not until after the war!" Zandra suggested. She looked shyly at the man beside her. "Guy and I have decided to wait until then," she said. "We haven't told you yet, but Guy got a letter this morning saying he'd passed his last medical, and that he can go back to being a soldier at the end of the week. His regiment is right in the thick of it and he can't wait to join them, can you, darling?"

Guy's face mirrored his confusion.

"Yes and no . . . I mean, obviously I want to get out there and put my oar in, but naturally I shall hate not seeing you for a while."

"Don't tease him, Zandra!" Jane said reproachfully.

"Well, if you don't get there soon, old chap, the war will be over!" Oliver put in laughing. "We really do seem to have made a damn fine start, don't we, what with a well-established beach-head over sixty miles long; and, I gather, we've encircled the Jerries and got one hell of a lot of them retreating up the Cherbourg peninsula! With the Russians breaking through the Mannerheim Line and fighting now to take Minsk, our good friend Adolf must be shivering in his shoes. The Americans—" He broke off as he caught sight of his mother coming out onto the terrace, and rose to his feet.

"I must go and get the cake," Jane announced, setting aside her knitting. "Will one of you two tell Gustav and the children it's teatime? He really is so good with them, isn't he? Claudette told me the other night that she likes him better than she liked her father! Mother and I thought you and Guy might adopt Alice's three after you're married, Zandra. Your uncle and I are a bit old to cope with more than Peter and Anthea! Or if Eve and Gustav were to get married, you could share them all between you!"

Willow stood for a minute in the doorway as Jane walked past her. She was listening to the distant sound of the children's laughter. It was strange, she thought, how therapeutic it could be. This morning in church, she had felt a chill of melancholy steal over her when the vicar had said prayers for those soldiers, sailors and airmen overseas who, he reminded them, were still in peril. For all the wonderful news they were receiving now and the general belief that the war would soon be over, he had declared, the continuing loss of life even in victory, must not be discounted.

As she had joined in the prayers for the dead and wounded, Willow's thoughts had turned inevitably to the death in action of her nephew Jamie, three weeks previously. It had upset her very badly. There was only Zee-Zee left now to remind her of her sister-in-law, Dodie McGill, the little crippled child whom she had befriended when, little more than a child herself, she had come to England to marry her first husband, Rowell Rochford.

His death had been as much a release for her as Anthony Wisson's death was for Zee-Zee. Lucy had told her what a cold, sadistic man Anthony had been beneath that veneer of courtesy he'd always assumed. She, Willow, grieved for Jamie, therefore; and for her brother-in-law, Pelham and her dearest friend, Silvie, both of whom she prayed were in heaven now with her beloved Toby. It comforted her to think that Inge was with Jamie – poor Inge, who had died so tragically only a day before him.

The Lord giveth and the Lord taketh away, she thought now, and the good Lord had been wonderfully generous in His giving to her. There was her beloved son, Oliver, coming towards her now, as caring and devoted as ever! God had spared him, and kept Zee-Zee safe, so for these blessings alone, she had cause to rejoice; and even if Oliver's boy, her grandson Giles, had suffered so terribly, he, too, had been spared and would have been here today were he not back in hospital having yet another operation on his poor face. If anyone was doing God's work, it was Mr McIndoe, performing such miracles!

And there, of course, was her dear, sweet Jane who had always proved such a wonderful daughter-in-law, propping up the whole family in her quiet, efficient manner. She, Willow, should have guessed that Jane would find a way to provide a birthday cake for her. She was holding it aloft now, the icing aglow with tiny wax candles.

"I couldn't get seventy on, Mother!" Jane said, "so I've put one for each decade."

"Happy birthday, Mother!"

"Happy birthday, Aunt Willow!"

"Happy birthday, Granny!"

"Happy birthday, *Grandmère!*"

Willow sat down in the chair Oliver was holding out for her and stared round the group of smiling faces . . . Eve's – so pretty! Zee-Zee's – so loving! Jane's – so reassuring! Gustav's – so gentle! Guy's – so very handsome! And the children . . . Claudette, Brigitte and that mischievous Henri – so excited! It was a pity little Peter and Anthea Conway were away, staying with their elderly Conway grandparents – but at least almost all her own precious family were here.

"Cut it, *Grandmère!* You must cut the cake and wish."

Willow smiled back at Brigitte.

"I do not need to wish, my darling," she said, "for I have everything in the world I need to be happy."

"Can I have your wish then, *Grandmère?*"

"No, you can't, Henri! It's *Grandmère's* birthday." That was Claudette, of course, who had not yet abandoned her maternal role. "You *must* make a wish, Grandmère, and don't tell us what it is or it won't come true."

Behind Claudette's head, Willow could see Guy and Zandra, arms and hands entwined, looking into one another's eyes. They are sharing the kind of love Toby and I shared – all those years ago! she thought. My darling Zee-Zee will be happy now! Very soon that poor young man will be back in the front line and for Zee-Zee's sake, I shall pray for him.

"Have you forgotten, Grandmère? You've got to blow out the candles and wish!" Henri said, pulling impatiently on her sleeve.

Willow looked down once more at her youngest grandchild.

"I *am* making a wish, Henri – but it is not for me. It is for your Aunt Zandra," she said, for she knew that the happiness of her favourite niece would never be assured unless Guy came safely home.

"Tell me, *Grandmère.* Just tell *me!* Whisper it!"

"No, Henri!" Willow said, tears of happiness in her eyes. "I shall never tell anyone because it's very, very, *very* important that my wish comes true."

Do you love historical fiction?

Want the chance to hear news about your favourite authors (and the chance to win free books)?

Mary Balogh

Charlotte Betts

Jessica Blair

Frances Brody

Gaelen Foley

Elizabeth Hoyt

Lisa Kleypas

Stephanie Laurens

Claire Lorrimer

Amanda Quick

Julia Quinn

Then visit the Piatkus website and blog

www.piatkus.co.uk | www.piatkusbooks.net

And follow us on Facebook and Twitter

www.facebook.com/piatkusfiction | www.twitter.com/piatkusbooks

piatkus